VIENNA PRELUDE

Vienna Prelude

BODIE THOENE

MONARCH
Tunbridge Wells

First published in the USA by
Bethany House Publishers, Minneapolis, Minnesota

First British edition 1992

Front cover illustration by Dan Thornberg

With the exception of recognised historical figures, the characters in this
novel are fictional, and any resemblance to actual persons, living or dead, is
purely coincidental.

ISBN 1 85424 156 7

Printed in Great Britain for
MONARCH PUBLICATIONS LTD
Owl Lodge, Langton Road, Speldhurst, Tunbridge Wells, Kent TN3 0NP by
Clays Ltd, St Ives plc
Reproduced from the original text by arrangement with
Bethany House Publishers

This story is for Rachel, the firstborn of our love. If God had not given her to us as a daughter, she is the kind of person we would still have searched for as a friend.

Contents

Prologue

It was a tiny shop, tucked discreetly in among the other shops along London's Oxford Street. The first morning, even with the address written precisely on the slip of paper in her hand, Ernestine had almost walked right past it. That was a common mistake, they had told her later. Generations of musicians had been marching right past the door of Holt and Sons and then back again. Eventually, it seemed, all the finest string players found the entrance, just as the finest string instruments in the world somehow managed to turn up here. Names like *Stradivarius*, *Amati*, and *Guarnerius* were matched with hopeful violinists whose names were much less well known than the names of the instruments they hoped to play and purchase here.

"It is our goal," the elder Holt had said with a slight, dignified bow, "to match the finest string instruments in the world with musicians who might do them honor for yet another lifetime of their existence."

Unfortunately for Ernestine, such cherished instruments were far beyond her financial means. She was a student now at the Mozarteum in Salzburg. The cost of her schooling alone had required sacrifice for her family in New York. Her talent was exceptional, no one could deny that, but mere talent alone was not enough to match her with one of those cherished instruments now tucked away in the vaults of the shop. She had not dared to hope for that. She had not dared to even ask to see the creations from the great violin makers. There was no use deliberately tormenting herself with something she could never possess. She had traveled here with a goal in mind: to trade her old violin for something that was smaller and more suited to her hands. Quite simply (her teacher had told her a dozen times), her violin was too large for her.

So she had written to Holt's of London and had come here to the shop with money she could hardly afford. Now, three days later, she sat forlornly in Holt's tiny, walnut-paneled practice room, ringed by a half dozen instruments. They fit her hands; they fit her meager budget; but each violin was mediocre in tone and quality and would remain so no matter who played them. Of course the Holt family knew this as well. The finest instruments could find a hundred voices in the hands of a master musician. That could not be said for the violins that Ernestine had played hour after hour from the opening of the shop until its closing. The disappointment in her eyes had begun to show in the eyes of the Holt family as well. It was obvious that she was capable of more—deserving of more. . . .

It was nearly three-thirty in the afternoon when Ernestine replaced the last of the available violins in its case. There were no more instruments within this price range for her to try. Her trip to London had been a waste of time and money. She wrestled down her unhappiness and sat back in her chair for the first time in hours. Her neck and shoulders ached. She had not noticed the pain until now—now that she was finished.

A soft knock sounded on the door. The youngest of the sons poked his head into the room. His brow was wrinkled with concern and sympathy. He knew before she told him.

"Not quite right, eh?" he asked apologetically.

She smiled slightly and shook her head, spreading her empty hands toward the violins on the table beside her. "They are all very nice," she began, "but . . ."

"You must not be too terribly disappointed." He glanced toward the instruments. "Violins come and go every day around here, you know. Every day. Sometimes it takes months, Ernestine. Violinists have been known to take months making such an important decision. You have been here only three days, after all." He was trying so hard to be cheerful and encouraging, but it was obvious that he knew how she felt. He had been the first to read her letter from Salzburg. He knew her financial limitations, and for three days the family had heard the intensity of her music. It was rare that a young musician with such talent came along, even more rare than the appearance of the finest instruments. What this beautiful young woman needed in her hands was far beyond her reach—for now, at any rate.

She lifted her chin slightly. "Yes. Maybe another time." She clenched and unclenched her hands. "You have all been terrific," she said in her American twang. "Really great."

"It has been our pleasure, believe me." The young man pushed his wire-rimmed glasses onto his nose. He bowed slightly, and Ernestine thought how much like his father he seemed in mannerisms and looks. "We have had the pleasure . . . the very great pleasure of hearing you play these last few days, and someday perhaps you will be back and . . ."

He turned as his father entered the cubicle. The elder Mr. Holt stood half concealed by the door. His face showed none of the disappointment of his son. "No luck, Ernestine?" His face was slightly flushed as he glanced toward the unwanted instruments. "Well, I thought we might have a bit of a problem when I first heard you play. Quite a gift you have, and I quite expect to hear you playing on the BBC one day soon."

His compliments did little to cheer her up, but she stood and extended her hand. "Thanks. Thanks . . . You have been so helpful and I . . ."

"Not helpful enough, I'm afraid." He nodded toward the violins. "I had thought we might have a bit of a problem. . . ." he said again.

"Will you write me?" She bit her lip and frowned as the realization that she was going back empty-handed sank in. "If something comes in? You have my address at the Mozarteum."

The elder gentleman clucked his tongue sadly. "I doubt that we will ever find just what you are looking for, Ernestine. Something that sounds like a Stradivarius with a price like these . . ."

She felt apologetic. Had she been too particular? "Oh! I mean . . . if something turns up . . . like . . ." She could not think what might turn up that she could afford. She flushed with embarrassment. She had come expecting the impossible.

The elder Holt tugged at his vest and stepped around his son. He carried a battered violin case in his hand. "Perhaps like this?" He finished the sentence for her, then placed the case on her chair and opened it. Inside was a delicate instrument with an almost golden color.

His son crossed his arms and nodded approvingly. "Yes. Here is one you might try, Ernestine. Good idea, Father."

Ernestine frowned and stared at the instrument for a moment. Her head was throbbing now, and she was certain that trying this one last violin would make no difference. They had as much as said that she could never find what she wanted for what she could afford.

Sensing her reluctance, the elder man bowed slightly and took the instrument from the case. "One last try, Ernestine," he urged gently.

She took the violin from him with a weary smile. After all, they were trying so hard to help her. "One more then."

This time they did not leave her alone in the practice room as she raised her bow to the strings and began to play. Warm and rich, the music of Mozart filled the room and flowed into the hallway, drawing others from the shop toward the cubicle. Here was the voice she had been hoping for, notes so clear and full . . . After a few moments, tears filled her eyes. She stopped and lowered the bow. This was no ordinary violin they had brought to her. She started to look into the instrument to see the maker's label.

"No." Mr. Holt put his hand out. "There is no need for you to know until we've finished talking."

She was filled with frustration. Why had they done this to her? Why had they allowed her to play what could never be her own? The agony must have been evident in her eyes as she stood in the center of the room and cradled the violin in her hands. "This is not . . . like the others," she whispered in an almost inaudible voice. "You know I can't—"

"Sit down," Mr. Holt instructed. "You are quite right," he said. "I had not realized how extraordinary it was until you played it."

His son had said nothing until now. "We have had it two weeks. But we were uncertain . . ." he began to explain, then looked at his father for help.

"You see, it has no history. It is a very unusual instrument. Someone found it just last year tucked away in an attic in an old house in . . . well, in Eastern Europe."

"Eastern Europe?" Ernestine asked. Occasionally, she knew, fine instruments found their way out of Communist countries. But it was a rare occurrence and extremely dangerous for whoever carried them into the West.

"Such instruments have a way of finding their way to shops such as our own on occasion. Many are forgeries, of course. Copies of Strads or perhaps . . ." The young man looked at his father. "Perhaps copies of the work of someone like Andrea Guarnerius." He shrugged.

Ernestine looked down at the golden-hued violin in her hands. *Guarnerius?* The master had created his violins with the skill of Stradivarius in the late 1600s. Some violinists preferred his instruments above any others . . . Had she just played a Guarnerius violin? What kind of cruel joke were they playing? She blinked up at the two men. "This is not a copy," she said simply.

The two nodded in unison. "That is our opinion," said the elder man. "But its history is a complete mystery. It has no provenance. We can find no proof, no records. It was discovered in an attic by a young chap who brought it over the wall with him. Oh yes, the label says quite clearly *Andrea Guarnerius Cremona 1674 . . .*"

She resisted the urge to peer into the F-hole to see the label. She did not dare look at the violin. It *was* the work of the master! It had survived three hundred years, and now she held it after so many others! She had caused it to sing as three centuries of musicians had done before her! "Why have you let me play it?" she asked, feeling that she did not want to let go of it. "You know there is no way that I can—"

The elder Holt interrupted her. "It is our goal," he said solemnly, "to match the finest string instruments in the world with musicians who might do them honor for yet another lifetime of their existence." He bowed and smiled. "Apart from the voice it has in your hands, we have no proof that it is anything more than a mere copy. It is simply a mystery to us . . . and must be priced accordingly."

1

Night Music

1936

Streams of iridescent twilight streaked the sky above Gothic towers. Soft pink and blue melted into a deep, star-flecked purple in the east. The spires of Prague's Hradcany Castle blended into the darkness, and lights in the castle windows shone like evening stars not yet risen to their places in the heavens. The tall bell tower of Hradcany and the greenish cupola of some lesser-known spire held the broad canopy of evening suspended just above the hundred towers of the city.

Elisa Linder and Leah Goldblatt slowly crossed the ancient Old Town Square as others hurried home from work. Set in the cobbles, flat stone crosses marked the places where the noblemen of King Wenceslas had died as martyrs for the sake of a cause almost forgotten. Elisa's father had told her all about it; when she had come to Prague with him as a child, she had stepped around the crosses as though the blood of the martyrs were still wet and fresh on the ground. She was nearly twenty-three now, and still she watched the cobblestones carefully. In the half light, she felt the presence of a million vanished souls, four hundred years of history crowded into this one moment.

"You know," Leah said wearily, "we're the only two left in the orchestra still trying to see the sights." She flipped through the small red Baedeker's guidebook. "Everyone else wore out after Paris."

"And think what they missed."

"Sore feet." Leah looked up at the sky. "After this, tonight's performance will be a relief. At least we'll get to sit down. Are you ready to quit for the day?" It was getting colder, and a wind had sprung up almost as soon as the sun disappeared.

"One more thing." Elisa took Leah's arm and pulled her toward the window of a dark shop. *W. Hainz—Clockmaker* was stenciled in a faded gold arch across the glass. Inside was a large clock surrounded by gold cherubs, each pointing to the time in London, Paris, New York, and St. Petersburg. St. Petersburg was now Leningrad in Bolshevik Russia, but the old clock had obviously paid no attention to the politics of passing time. "You see," Elisa said with the same awe she had felt as a girl, "with a clock like that you could get up whenever you wanted. In New York there are people who haven't even had breakfast yet."

Leah was manifestly uninterested. "Look," she replied with a stern poke to Elisa's ribs, "the only thing I care about now is a few minutes' rest, five minutes to change, and a minute and a half to make it to the concert hall!"

Elisa stood for a moment more, still seeing the reflection of a six-year-old girl with thick blond braids standing beside her father. She turned to Leah and said quietly, "At home we have a clock that was made here one hundred years ago. You see? Some places don't change at all. Prague will always be Prague. . . ."

"Fine." Leah sounded rushed. "Well, someone better tell the old clockmaker that it's 1936. St. Petersburg isn't St. Petersburg anymore, and Germany is now the Third Reich. Everything changes, Elisa. Except the time the concert begins. So, do you mind terribly? It might be breakfast in New York, but in Prague all the barons and baronesses are already in their satin."

————

Elisa and Leah made their way upstream through the throngs of concertgoers who moved toward the wide doors of the theater in Prague. Elisa clutched her violin case and looked back over her shoulder as little Leah struggled to heft her cello against the tide of silks and furs and top hats. For a moment, Leah's determined young face was almost lost from view; then up came the top of the cello case like a shield before her, parting the waves.

"Excuse me. Pardon me. Excuse me, please!" Leah's soft Viennese accent rose up above the hum of the crowd. Elisa laughed, thankful that her instrument was no larger than a baby and much easier to carry than Leah's unwieldy cello. In restaurants and on trains, Leah was forever asking for another seat for her "mummy."

"Leah?" Elisa called, unable to conceal her amusement that the principal cellist had to battle the audience to get backstage. "Are you all right?"

"Excuse me, bitte. Pardon . . ." Leah's voice took on an edge of irritation.

"Maybe we should go in the front entrance with them." Elisa stood on tiptoe. She was a full head taller than Leah and still could only see the cello case.

Suddenly Leah's soft voice turned harsh. "If you wish to hear the concert tonight, you will let me pass, please!"

In an instant top hats doffed and mumbled replies of apology were heard and then the human sea parted for Leah and her cello. Her face was flushed from the effort, but with the utmost dignity she dropped the case to her side and walked deliberately to where Elisa waited near the corner of the huge stone building.

Elisa nodded regally. "Well done, your Highness."

"They could have killed me—or worse, broken Vitorio to pieces." She patted the cello case affectionately. "Cattle." She straightened her coat and ran her fingers through her bobbed hair. "I hope they don't overrun the stage tonight."

"We should have just gone in the front entrance with them." Elisa picked a few tufts of fur off Leah's shoulder, compliments from a patron's coat.

"They wouldn't have let us in," Leah grimaced. "We don't have tickets." She surveyed her appearance. "I look as if I have been in a cat fight." She brushed her coat, then sized Elisa up and down in mock disdain. "And look at you!" she sniffed. "Perfect. *Perfect.* I tell you, it's disgusting. Didn't we just walk through the same crowd?"

Elisa tossed her long blond hair and blinked innocently at Leah. "It would be easier to walk, Leah, if you played a nice little fiddle instead of strumming a mummy. I told you that in Salzburg four years ago." She took Leah's arm and they walked together down the darkened alley to the stage door.

"By then it was too late, anyway. You should have told my mother when I was four." She shifted the weight of the cello, leaning slightly to the left in her awkward, familiar stance. "My father was hoping I would be a boy and grow up to be a bellman. This is as close as I could get. Shlepping a cello case all over Europe."

Elisa laughed at Leah and nudged her slightly as Rudy Dorbransky ran toward the stage door and scrambled up the steps as though he were being pursued. He did not notice either of the young women in the alleyway.

"What's wrong with him?" The door opened and a wave of sound escaped as musicians warmed up backstage. With a soft click the door shut as Rudy slipped inside.

"He probably got into another card game." Leah rolled her eyes. Rudy was famous for his ability to find a card game in a strange city.

"Well, if he's just now here, we must be late. You know he's always late."

"Unless someone is chasing him." Leah pulled her coat tighter around her.

"You aren't late until the houselights go down." Elisa stepped aside, giving Leah room to lug the cello up the steps. "Besides," she giggled conspiratorially, "did you see the conductor last night?" She opened the heavy steel door and they were immediately assaulted by a deafening cacophony of instruments hooting and wailing. "Five minutes before the performance, he wasn't even dressed!"

Leah waved a hand in disinterest. "I keep expecting him to come out on stage without his pants some night." She tapped her temple lightly and crossed her eyes. "Yes?"

Elisa nodded broadly in agreement. The roar of practicing musicians made conversation in a normal tone of voice impossible. Members of the orchestra were everywhere, each playing particularly difficult passages of the symphony. Unwinding their scarves and flinging their coats onto a long wooden bench stacked with other coats, Leah and Elisa uncased their instruments and joined the noisy ritual. In twelve days they had traveled to a dozen cities in Europe, playing the same program in each place. Tonight's appearance at the German Theatre in Prague marked the end of the exhausting tour and, appropriately, they were playing Mozart's *Prague Symphony* in the city where it had first been introduced. It was sure to please the crowds of isolated Germans who lived in Czechoslovakia and clamored for tickets to every performance. Elisa knew that the local German newspaper reported every musical event in faraway Vienna, while it totally ignored the opening of a new play in the Czech National Theatre. The Czechs and the Germans maintained separate theaters, churches, and universities. Tonight, the Vienna Symphony Orchestra belonged to the German-speaking residents of Prague. This possessive sense of ownership by the audience would make them wild with joy and appreciation even if the musicians themselves were bored with the program they were about to play.

After the concert, while the rest of the orchestra climbed wearily onboard the train back to Vienna, Elisa would catch the train north to her home in Berlin for the Christmas holidays. The thought of seeing her family again so soon filled Elisa with a sense of excitement. Tonight she played for her mother and father, even though they were in Berlin.

As though reading Elisa's mind, Leah nudged her. "Did you have any trouble getting your ticket?"

Elisa shook her head. "No. I'm the only person who wants to go *into* Germany," she laughed. "Everyone else wants out!"

With a nod of agreement, Leah hefted her cello and scurried off to find a place to warm up.

"Full house!" Shimon Feldstein boomed over the din. As the percussionist, Shimon had little to do until they were actually onstage where he could stand beside his great "kettles of thunder." Always before a performance he released his excess energy by prowling through the halls backstage and announcing the condition of the evening's audience—who was there and whether they were subdued or excited, sober or drunk.

Elisa did not need Shimon to know the condition of tonight's audience. She had played in this theater half a dozen times; the orchestra had always been received more warmly here than anywhere else in Europe, it seemed—including their home base at the Musikverein in Vienna. She had come to love the ancient city with its hundred church spires, the Old Town Hall, the mysterious streets and delicious food. Mozart had loved Prague, and in the beginning that had been enough for Elisa. She never had enough of exploring forgotten corners of the city. Today she and Leah had enjoyed a picnic out on Charles Bridge and eaten a pleasant lunch as the murky Moldau River swirled below their perch. Leah had taken her into the dark interior of the Old-New Synagogue and the old Jewish cemetery where headstones leaned on one another for centuries of musty companionship. Elisa had then spirited Leah away to the church of Jan Hus, who had been martyred as a heretic for his part in the Reformation. Every corner of the city was a history lesson.

Even though Elisa was from Berlin, her father had arranged for her to carry the passport of a Czech citizen, of German Aryan background. Not even her closest friends realized that she was the daughter of Theo Lindheim, the well-known Jewish department store owner in Berlin. Her mother actually was Aryan, but to be half-Jewish in Germany was more than enough. And so her stage name was Elisa Linder, a slight deception that made it possible for her to play professionally in Germany, though Jewish musicians had been banned from performing in public for over a year. Only now, as a private citizen, would she return to Germany. For two weeks she would be Elisa Lindheim again. Her violin would return to Vienna under Leah's watchful eye.

Twice, Elisa had nearly told Leah about the passport and the fact that her real name was different from the one Leah knew her by. Often she had suggested that the little cellist take an Aryan stage name just in case the Austrians imitated the actions of their powerful German neighbor. Already in Vienna there was talk—quiet murmurs that Austria would be better off joining Hitler's Reich. Leah would simply not hear of it. She was Jewish, and she was Austrian. Everyone in Vienna knew that. Vienna was her hometown, and never would Austria be subject to what happened in Germany! So the issue had been settled. In spite of the fact that Leah Goldblatt was the most talented cellist in Austria, Hungary, and Poland, she had to remain home whenever the orchestra toured Germany. Her only comment was "Their ears are not worthy, anyway!"

Elisa's crisp Berliner accent was immediately recognized by any who heard her speak, but she simply explained that she had moved from Berlin at an early age. She had been quite young, after all, when she had gone to Austria to study at the Mozarteum. Hitler had not even been in power then, and her Berlin home had been an exciting, open place to live where little thought was given to a man's heritage.

But now, when the tour scheduled concerts in Berlin, she gracefully bowed out. In Berlin, she was Elisa Lindheim. A hundred friends would recognize her instantly. Over the course of the last two years, her father had managed to send her considerable sums of money, nearly all of which was safely tucked away in a Swiss account. And Elisa, to the amazement of her struggling musician friends, lived quite well in her little flat two blocks from the concert hall in Vienna. Life was good; even now she did not feel the shadow of Hitler's growing power in Germany.

"Five minutes!" called Shimon loudly as he passed Elisa. With more intensity she played a difficult bar in the second movement. *Perhaps*, she thought wistfully, *someday I will be Elisa Lindheim again and play this in Berlin*. In spite of the noise around her, she heard only the sound of her own instrument. She stopped and began again, letting her fingers fly over the fingerboard. She felt a soft tap on her shoulder.

Elisa opened her eyes to the handsome, worried face of Rudy Dorbransky. His thick, dark hair tumbled down over his forehead; frightened eyes gazed down at Elisa. He was undoubtedly the most handsome of the single men in the orchestra, and had talent as a violinist to match his good looks. There had been a moment two years ago when his strong hand on her shoulder might have caused her heart to skip a beat. But other women in the first violin section had warned her about him, and she had listened. Now she looked at his bloodshot eyes with disapproval, and she continued to practice.

"Rudy," she said almost maternally, "go look in the mirror. Comb your hair and straighten your tie. Did you shave today?"

He ignored her comments. "Elisa—" He mopped his brow and attempted a charming smile. "I ran into a bit of difficulty today, dearest—"

She held her bow poised for an instant. "Another ordinary day for you, eh, Rudy?"

"There was a gentlemen's card game at the hotel, and—"

Elisa knew what was coming. A dozen times Rudy had hocked his magnificent instrument to pay gambling debts. He did not need to explain what had happened. It was obvious on his face. "Where is your Guarnerius?" she asked coolly. He had the finest instrument in the orchestra—a gift from a middle-aged woman admirer. Elisa had never gotten over the feeling of anger when he used the violin as collateral for a debt. Twice she had loaned him money when no one else would, for the sake of the Guarnerius violin. Rudy's charm had worn away entirely by now.

"I'll pay you back!" All pretense dropped away as he pointed to where his instrument gleamed softly in its case.

"You said that last time."

He held up his hand in solemn oath. "I promise."

"I don't have a shilling, Rudy," she told him flatly. "You are wasting your time."

"They are going to break my hands!" he pleaded, holding up his long, strong fingers before her face.

"A gentlemen's card game, eh?" She tossed her golden mane, disregarding his misery. "Well, Rudy, if they break your hands, you won't be able to hold the cards, will you?" She smiled, resumed practicing, then blinked innocently at his indignant expression.

Defeated, Rudy shrugged unhappily and walked to the next of his hardhearted companions. Each, in turn, looked alternately embarrassed, angry, or indifferent to his pleas. They shook their heads and made their way past him onto the stage of the great gilded concert hall. Only Shimon, adept at judging the human condition, patted Rudy on the back and engulfed the hand of the violinist in his own huge hand. Unfortunately, pity was all the gentle percussionist had to offer. Everyone knew that Shimon used coffee grounds three times to save money. But perhaps Shimon's massive size would keep anyone from breaking Rudy's hands if all else failed.

Elisa, third chair among the first violins, could clearly see Leah's position on the opposite side of the conductor's stand. They took their places and Leah looked up at her and grinned impishly at the thought of the maestro coming on stage without his pants. Elisa felt the color rise in her cheeks, and she was suddenly seized with an urge to giggle. She determined that she would not look toward Leah during the rest of the evening for fear of the thoughts that might pass between them. Nothing could be worse than for a principal cellist and a violinist to burst out laughing in the middle of a performance. Elisa cleared her throat and tried to fix the appropriate expression of intensity on her face as the concertmaster rose and raised his bow for the orchestra to find its note by his.

A hush fell over the audience, and the houselights dimmed on the audience, a flower garden of silks and jewels waiting expectantly for the maestro to enter. Elisa adjusted the music stand slightly and exhaled as a thunderous burst of applause announced the entrance of the conductor behind her. He bowed and waved slightly to the audience as he passed her chair. Shaking hands with the concertmaster, he stopped a few feet from her. Elisa still did not look toward Leah. She would not. But yes, the maestro had made it on stage in Prague with his pants on.

––––––––

Stephan Günther passed the ornate building of the German concert hall just as the first notes of Mozart's *Prague Symphony* rose up. He heard the sound fill the gilded cavern and then escape in muffled melody out onto the damp and deserted streets of the city. For a moment, Günther paused at the bottom of the white stone stairway that led into the hall. He searched the sidewalk in the vain hope that someone had dropped a ticket. It was a foolish thought; tickets to the event had been sold out for weeks. There was no hope at all that a common clerk could acquire entry to such a place. He glanced up to where the doorman was eyeing him with some suspicion. The doorman in his bright uniform and spit-polished shoes was better dressed than Günther. It did not matter. One day Günther would be dressed as an officer. He would walk up these steps, and women would watch him. Men would nod in respect. Günther closed his eyes as the music swelled, tenderly caressing the hundred spires of Prague, then drifting gently down the Moldau like autumn leaves swirling on the water.

He barely noticed the clack of the doorman's heels against the steps. "Bitte," said the doorman, his gold braid shining, "you will have to move along. No Czechs are allowed here, you see."

Günther opened his eyes angrily. "I am German," he answered curtly. "As German as any within the hall."

"Still, you do not have a ticket."

Günther did not answer. He turned and began to walk away. The second movement of the piece had begun, and now it pursued him, mocking his ragged shoes and overcoat. The doorman chuckled and Günther spun around. "Yes. I am German," he spat fiercely, then raised his hand in a casual salute. "Heil Hitler," he said under his breath, and the smile on the doorman's face vanished.

Günther put his hand to his head, astonished at his own behavior. Tonight, did he not plan to betray the very cause that he had just saluted? Of course, it was only a small betrayal—just enough to buy him a new pair of shoes and a good overcoat. Still, within a few hours he would become the Judas that his comrades in Czechoslovakia raved against in their secret Nazi meetings. He plunged his hand deep into the pocket of his coat and fingered the small paper-wrapped packet. *Perhaps I will use the money to purchase a ticket to the next concert as well,* he thought, imagining the doorman's reaction to his arrival. A brief smile flickered over his tortured young face.

He rounded the corner and made his way toward the Old Town where his companions waited in the dark bowels of a beer house. Tonight they would sing and raise their steins in salute to the Fatherland, and Günther would join them. After all, his was only a small betrayal, he mused again. The cause would not suffer over a few passports, more or less.

2

Birth in the Darkness

The jingle of sleigh bells echoed from the steep, snow-covered slopes of the Tyrolean Alps. It was already dark, but the little mare pulling Franz Wattenbarger's sleigh knew her way home. Franz held the lines loosely as the horse leaned into her burden without faltering. Far below, the lights of the village of Kitzbühel glistened like a cluster of jewels against the mountain. Franz looked over his shoulder and could almost feel the warmth of glowing fires and smell the hot dumplings simmering in their neighbors' kitchens.

In the distance Franz heard the shrill, lonely whistle of a train. That cry had lured many of his friends from the mountains, but for Franz, such a sound seemed feeble compared to the shriek of the eagles who soared above the craggy peaks of his home. After living twenty-four years in the shadow of these mountains, Franz had decided that, unlike his brother Otto, he would never leave. The seasons sang to him—ageless hymns with whisperings he could feel, but not fully understand.

Tonight the scent of woodsmoke mingled with the clean aroma of the fir trees that bordered the pastures of their farm. Ahead he could see the shimmering glow of the lantern in the barn where Otto and Papa waited with a young heifer about to give birth. The night seemed wrapped in an eternal magic, and the mountains sang of life and home and things that remained forever unchanged.

In his pocket Franz carried a letter from Vienna sent on behalf of a family looking for an out-of-the-way place to spend their holiday in the Alps. This sort of inquiry was sent through the priest of the village and then relayed to some farm family willing to share their chalet with guests from the city. For three years in a row *Feriengäste* had come to stay at the Wattenbarger home. The rent they paid had been a gift from heaven to see their farm through hard times. Franz patted his pocket and the crackle of paper reassured him. He and Otto would have to move to the small hut at the far end of the farm, but there would be money enough to see them through again this year.

Otto resented the presence of strangers in the house, but then Otto seemed to resent much about their life nowadays. Only a year ago Otto's wife had died, and he had left to find work in an automobile factory in Stuttgart. He had returned to the farm barely six months later. Thin, haggard and bitter, he said little about his time in Germany. Their little sister Gretchen had teased him that perhaps his heart had been broken by some pretty Stuttgart woman, and he had glared at her as though he might strike her. Then he had stalked off to bed without a word.

Twice Franz had tried to speak with him. Otto had told him in no uncertain terms that he should mind his own business. Tonight when the heifer had gone into labor, Papa had sent Franz off to Kitzbühel for the supplies. Franz guessed that Papa wanted to have a word with Otto. Mama simply looked grieved. She spoke sternly to him, and then gently. She tried to joke with him, and even wept once when he stormed out of the house. A loaf of warm, home-baked Roggenbrot heaped with butter did nothing to draw the heart of Otto back to them. The cry of the train whistle had snared his heart, and he was always looking away, always looking toward the horizon as though he could see some terrible storm brewing beyond the peak of the Kitzbüheler Alpen.

As the sound of his sleigh bells reached the farmhouse, Franz saw the door open and his mother gazing out into the darkness. She was plump and pleasant at forty-five. There was still color in her cheeks and only a trace of gray streaked her hair at the temples. Marta Wattenbarger managed her home and children with a discipline and care that showed in the gleaming floors of the farmhouse and the bright embroidery on the boys' jäger jackets and little Gretchen's dirndls.

Franz leaned forward a bit and squinted at the sight of her. Tonight her easy smile, usually so evident on her face, was gone. She wrung her hands and frowned toward the sound of the bells, at last calling out in German, "Franz! Is that you? Hurry, Franz! Papa and Otto are in terrible need of your help!"

Franz slapped the lines down hard on the back of his mare, jogging her into a lope up the road. She stopped at the door and Marta grasped the bridle.

"What is it?"

"The heifer!" she replied. "The calf is turned. Neither Papa nor Otto can get a grip. Papa's hands are too big, and Otto's arm too short."

As if on cue, Papa stepped out of the barn. "Well, what are you waiting for?" He seemed angry. "We've probably lost the calf, and we'll lose the heifer too!"

Franz was already peeling off his jacket as he sprinted toward the stable. Gone was the feeling of peace that had ridden up the slopes with him. Inside the stable, two dozen milk cows were tethered to their stalls. Liquid brown eyes gazed at Franz expectantly. Otto, covered from head to foot with manure and bits of straw, groveled on the floor behind a large heifer in obvious distress. At the sound of Franz's voice, she rolled her eyes and bellowed mournfully. Her sides were heaving and she was covered with sweat.

Franz tossed his jacket and shirt onto the hay. "You wouldn't think she would have trouble."

"She's big enough. But the first calf, you know," said Karl, brushing sweat from his brow. "Otto and I just aren't built for this sort of fishing."

Otto's arm was extended up to the shoulder as he grimaced and attempted to reach the calf's hoof with the loop of a rope. "Well, I can't do it!" Otto spat. His dark red beard was caked with filth. He withdrew his arm and rolled to one side, then rose stiffly as Franz washed his arm and soaped it slick.

The heifer looked at him, then laid her head on the straw with a groan as another useless contraction struck.

"Poor dear." Marta knelt to stroke her cheek. Franz had been unaware that his mother watched the drama. "Poor Hilda." The heifer lifted her head slightly, then let it fall again as Franz dropped down and worked his hand and arm into the birth canal.

His arm was longer than Otto's, but it was also bigger and more muscled. He stretched out on the cold floor and gently probed inward in search of a tiny hoof.

"Well?" snapped Otto. "It was there. Just beyond my reach. You should—"

The heifer moaned again and a fresh contraction began, the muscles constricting Franz's arm.

"There now," soothed Marta. "It will be over soon." Then she whispered a prayer just barely audible.

"Yes." Otto sounded bitter as he washed the sticky mess from his arm. "We've lost the calf, and we're going to lose the heifer, too."

"You don't know that yet," said Marta, defensively. Franz knew how his mother held a special affection for this heifer. "Besides, she doesn't need to hear it."

Otto slipped on his shirt, then stood scowling over Franz as he strained to reach the calf. "I told you, Papa, we should have killed the heifer and at least taken the calf. Mother would have raised it. Now we're going to lose them both."

"Shut up," Franz warned, his fingertips brushing a hoof. "I can—I can feel it."

"So could I. But you won't reach it." Otto looked toward Karl. "This heifer should be put down. See how she suffers." Turning as if to go, he asked, "Do you need me for anything else?" It was obvious that everything was over as far as he was concerned.

"Yes," Karl said coolly, ashamed of his eldest son's attitude. "We'll need your strength when we pull the calf."

Otto shrugged and sat down, brushing his trousers off and attempting to remove the manure from his beard.

Franz laid his cheek against the heifer's hip and scrambled for a firmer foothold on the cobbled floor of the stall. Only a fraction nearer and he could close his fingers around the hoof. The heifer groaned as yet another contraction racked her body. Franz grimaced with the force that tightened around his arm. "A fraction—" he breathed. "Come on. Just a bit . . ."

Marta comforted the little heifer as her eyes rolled back in agony and exhaustion.

"Over soon, little girl," Marta caressed the muzzle. "First is always the hardest."

"This time the first is the last," Otto mumbled. He was uninterested, cold and hungry, and unhappy with his father for some reason.

But now was not the time for Franz to wonder about the conversation between his father and Otto. The contraction built to a bone-breaking intensity and then lessened. Franz could barely feel his own fingertips. He wiggled his fingers slightly, surprised that a hard, wet bone rested beneath his hand. For a moment he did not speak; then his fingers closed around the twisted leg of the calf. "Front leg," he grunted. "The other one . . . here's the problem—" He tugged gently, mindful that he could tear open the heifer's uterus. "The other leg. Turned back at the knee."

"Can you bring it forward?" Karl knelt beside his son.

Franz did not answer. He closed his eyes and gritted his teeth as he maneuvered his fingers inside the vise-like grip of yet another contraction. He held tightly to the knee of the calf, and as the muscles released he could feel the nose of the baby tucked beneath the right front leg. Carefully, Franz rotated his own position so that he lay on his back with his hand cupped beneath the muzzle of the calf. Flexing his fingers forward, he began to move the head around the tangle of the leg until it was straight in line with the birth canal.

"Yes," Franz said breathlessly. "Now the loop. We'll have to pull it."

Karl handed Franz the soft cotton rope and again Franz reached inward to loop the end of the rope around the calf's front legs. He secured it, but was unsure whether it would hold the force of their pull. At least the heifer seemed more comfortable now that the position of the head had been righted. She looked up at Marta as though to ask if the ordeal would soon come to an end.

With the next strong contraction, Otto joined Franz and Karl at the rope. Franz still lay behind the heifer with his arm inside to guide the gangly legs of the baby.

"She's moving!" Franz said breathlessly as the legs and head inched forward.

The heifer bellowed piteously, and Marta continued to soothe her with gentle words.

Franz held tightly to the hoof of the calf, almost certain that the little beast would emerge in pieces. Still, the muscles pushed downward until at last a muzzle and two spindly legs emerged.

"Come on, little girl," Marta urged the heifer. "One more good push and pull!"

As though Hilda understood Marta's words, the heifer pushed hard with the next contraction, and as the men gave one final tug, the calf slipped out onto the straw. The newborn lay there silent and still for half a second before Franz pulled the birth sack from over its nose and began to rub the calf vigorously with straw. It gasped and shuddered. Shortly after, the heifer expelled the afterbirth and rose up slightly to examine the tiny heaving creature behind her—a mottled brown color with a white face and long, spindly legs. It bleated and coughed as its mother ran a rough warm tongue over the offspring's face again and again. Franz continued to work on the calf as Karl and Marta cleaned up the mess and replaced the soiled bedding with fresh straw. No one spoke, but Franz saw his mother brush away a tear and raise her eyes in gratitude toward heaven.

After a few minutes, Otto slung his coat over his arm. "I'm going to wash up. I have a meeting in the village. You don't need me any longer." It was not a question. He had simply had enough.

Karl shook his head slowly as Otto left the barn. "Perhaps he should have stayed in Stuttgart," he said softly. "For three hundred years we have farmed this land and milked our cows; given birth and seen death . . ." There was amazement in Karl's voice that his eldest son could not find even small pleasure in an event like tonight. "Where has he gone, Mama?" asked Karl softly. "Where has he gone?"

"He buried his heart beside Katrine. That is all, Papa. Everything here reminds him of her. Even us. Three years he was married to that girl, and it is as though that is all the life he ever had." Marta shook her head as she stroked the bull calf gently.

Karl lifted his chin and leaned against a post. "He is young. Our first-born." He looked at the calf. "He will survive." Then he forked more straw into the stall. "No one ever claimed it was easy."

Franz rinsed his arms quickly in the cold bucket of water. He did not want to be included in his parents' conclusions about Otto's grief for Katrine. There was a darker reason for Otto's strange behavior. He had begun to withdraw from them even before his wife's death. Now Katrine's face, her smile, and the shine of her eyes haunted Franz. Her love for his brother had been the one thing that had almost driven Franz from his beloved mountains. For three years he had tried not to notice when she brushed her fingers across Otto's forehead, or followed him with her eyes when he walked by. Katrine had loved Otto. And all the time, Franz had loved her with a desperate, silent ache that taunted him in the dark of night when he heard her laughter through the wall of the bedroom.

When Katrine had died and Otto had gone away, Franz had found some measure of peace again. Nights in the big chalet were quiet, his longing silenced. Katrine was out of reach and out of his sight, but even with that came some satisfaction that she did not lie in the arms of another man. She was no longer Otto's, either.

"What do you think, Franz?" asked Karl, gazing at his son. "Maybe if you would find a bride, Otto could also find another woman to comfort him . . . to give us grandchildren."

"No, Papa." Franz could not say more. He could not tell all the things he felt. Katrine was only one woman, but she had been the only love of two men. Two brothers. Neither would love again, of that Franz was certain. And Otto had long ago found other things to occupy him—things that had in the end pulled even him away from Katrine.

"There are so many girls in the mountains," Karl tried again, leaning heavily on the pitchfork handle. "My sons are blind?"

"Not blind," said Marta firmly. "Just careful." The lantern light shone on her face and her eyes searched Franz's for some answer. For an instant he thought she must know what his secret was, what it had been like to watch Otto and Katrine together.

"Yes, Mama. Careful," he mumbled, busying himself with the other stock. But he knew his brother was not careful about friends and ideas. Sometimes Franz was certain that Otto hated the farm—hated Austria now.

"Katrine was herself a widow. She knew about love, Papa. Such a girl as Katrine will be hard to find. But the lakes are full of fish, ja?" Her voice sounded more resigned than hopeful. Franz knew that his mother had not entirely approved of Katrine at first. Yes, Marta was also careful for her sons. "Otto will come back to himself. Back to us."

Karl did not reply, and his silence expressed his doubt. "Perhaps it is best if he leaves again. Maybe there is too much of *her* here."

Otto's silent bitterness did make life difficult for all of them. But Franz had seen his mother's grief when Otto was gone. It was better to suffer with him here than to suffer without him.

"He wanted to be a priest before he met her," Marta said almost wistfully. "Do you remember that, Karl?"

"Remember? It scared me to death. There is something strange about the thought of calling your own son *Father!*"

Franz laughed. "Otto has always acted like my father!"

Marta rose from the straw and raised her nose in regal disapproval of their jokes. "He would have been happier than he is now."

"No doubt!" exclaimed Karl, nudging Franz. "Just think how happy you would be sitting in the confessional all day and hearing about everyone else's sins! Not quite as fun as doing something to confess about, but—"

Marta gave him a hard clout on the head. "You are hopeless!" she snapped. "I'll go and make tea."

As the stable door slammed shut behind her, Franz and his father roared with laughter. There was something remarkably absurd about the image of Otto in the cloak of the church. "What your brother needs now, my dear Franz, is a lovely heifer who will give him a brace of sons to call *him* Father!"

There was much more to it than that, Franz knew, but somehow his parents saw life in the most simplistic terms: love, children, the church. The world around them trembled in the sinister shadow of Hitler's plans for Germany, and yet Karl and Marta Wattenbarger could see no further than the borders of their farm. They did not suspect that Otto had brought the shadow of darkness to their very doorstep.

3

The Exchange

Piles of orchestra luggage were stacked on the loading platform of Prague's vast railway terminal. Musicians sprawled here and there on the long mahogany benches. Saints gazed down from high niches in the stone walls, and every footstep and whisper echoed like sounds in a cathedral.

Leah and Elisa sat off by themselves and giggled at the postures of various members of the company who dozed without dignity. Shimon Feldstein slept in a sitting position on a trunk beside his tympani. His head nodded slowly forward to his chest; then suddenly it jerked back and his mouth fell open, closing briefly only to fall open again. Leah covered her mouth with her hand in an attempt to muffle peals of laughter. Even after weeks on the road together, Leah never quite got bored with the sleeping positions of her friends. The bulletin board in the hall in Vienna was always filled with candid photographs of exhausted musicians curled up on benches or dozing among the baggage. On this trip, however, someone had secretly taken Leah's camera into custody early on, so she had to content herself with simple observation.

"Look," she nudged Elisa. "All we need is a few flies to turn loose, and he would inhale them all!" More laughter as Shimon began to lean precariously to the side. "Look, look! He's going over!"

Elisa watched the somnambulant balancing act for a moment, then scanned the place for some sign of Rudy. "I thought Shimon was going to protect Rudy from his card-playing gentlemen friends." She sounded slightly worried, and Leah eyed her with amusement.

"Since when are you worried about Rudy?"

"Actually I'm worried about the Guarnerius," she replied flippantly. "Although if Rudy would ever settle down—he is a great violinist, you know."

"The world is full of great violinists. Almost any one of them has more sense than darling Rudy. Did you hear the latest?" She leaned close and whispered, "He's seeing the wife of a formerly prominent politician in Vienna."

"Yes?" Elisa was not surprised. Rudy was always in the middle of something unsavory.

"Yes. And this politician has very definite connections with Germany, they say. He is now in prison." She rolled her eyes in exasperation. "Imagine. A Jewish violinist and the wife of a pro-Nazi! Ridiculous, if you ask me. Rudy has rocks in his kopf!"

"The same woman who gave him the violin?" Elisa asked in amazement.

Leah nodded and shrugged. "He says they are only friends. I should have such friends." Leah patted her cello case. "It took my parents six years to pay for my cello. And it is only a Pedrinelli."

"A sweet fiddle," Elisa nodded approvingly.

Leah lifted her nose in the imitation of the wealthy concertgoers. "Can you imagine how much his Guarnerius cost? Have you seen the label? Made in 1674, I think. Rudy told me all about it once when he was trying to get a loan from me."

"I have thought of it," Elisa said enviously. "It makes me angry every time I think of it. Hocking a Guarnerius—"

"He had to pay the rent. Three months' rent."

"Did you help him?"

"Never."

"Did he lose his apartment?"

"No. The Nazi's wife paid his rent. She is a big patron of the arts." The sarcasm in Leah's tone was not lost on Elisa.

Elisa nodded and searched the enormous waiting room for sign of Rudy. He still was nowhere to be seen when the first announcement for boarding boomed out over the public address system. "Too bad his friend isn't here now," she muttered, slightly worried about the irresponsible young virtuoso.

"All boarding. Track three for Vienna!"

Leah gathered up her things and embraced Elisa quickly. "Well, don't worry about your little friend here." She patted Elisa's violin. "I'll look after your fiddle and feed the cat. Just go and have a good time. Berlin and *where*?"

"The Tyrol. Skiing. A few days to shop in Berlin, and then my father and I meet Mother and my brothers in the Tyrol."

Leah squeezed Elisa's hands. "Well, don't break anything."

As though waiting for the announcement, musicians stirred from their various corners and shuffled onto the waiting train. Elisa hugged and kissed friends goodbye as though they were members of her own family. Indeed, she had come to think of them as relations. Shimon gave her an all-engulfing bear hug and then helped Leah juggle cello, violin, and baggage onto the train. Still there was no sign of Rudy.

"I don't think Rudy made it," Leah lifted the window and called down to Elisa. Now she sounded worried.

Shimon poked his head out and grinned broadly as he pointed to the entrance to the ladies' room. Clutching his violin, Rudy sneaked out the door and charged across the lobby toward the platform.

"Leave it to Rudy!" Shimon roared. "Hiding behind skirts again!" Members of the orchestra cheered his run, encouraging him as the locomotive hissed impatiently.

"Rudy! Rudy! Rudy!" they shouted.

Without stopping, he ran directly to where Elisa stood below the window. He thrust his violin case into her arms. "A *loan*, Elisa!" He was sweating, almost panicky. "Just enough to get me through the holiday!"

The wheels of the train began to move. "Rudy! Hurry up! Come on!"

"Rudy, I can't!" Elisa attempted to give him back the instrument.

"You're the only hope I have!" he pleaded. "I'll pay you back! There! You see! Keep my Guarnerius, darling! You see how I trust you?"

Against her better judgment, Elisa rummaged quickly through her handbag and pulled out enough cash to last a normal man two months in Vienna. Rudy would spend it in no time, then borrow from one of his lady friends to pay Elisa back and redeem the Guarnerius. She handed him the cash, and he kissed her hands in gratitude, then leaped aboard the slowly moving train.

"That's the last you'll see of that!" Leah called playfully.

Elisa shook her head in disagreement and held up the violin case. "You're all witnesses!" she answered. "He pays me back or I keep the Guarnerius!"

The orchestra members gave a collective cheer and wished her good holidays. No sooner had the train left the station than Elisa missed each one of them, including Rudy. Holding his precious instrument in her arms, she watched until the last glimmer of the caboose light vanished in the fog that had descended on Prague. It was an hour until her train was due to leave for Berlin. The station now seemed vacant and lonely. She sat down on a long, empty bench beside the one small suitcase she had chosen to take to Berlin. It was wise to travel light in Germany these days since everything was subject to search. She had sent everything else back to Vienna with Leah, and if she needed anything, she would simply make a trip to Lindheim's Berlin store.

Suddenly, she felt very drowsy, the weeks of travel and work settled on her and she closed her eyes and leaned her cheek against the violin case to doze until the train for Berlin arrived at midnight.

———

No music brushed the towers of Prague now.

In the midnight silence of the mist, it seemed to Günther that the very streets of Prague were alive. The cobblestones were simply the scales of some giant, slumbering serpent who would awaken at the touch of the man's shoes upon its back and turn to devour him with a roar. Dark houses, their carved portals gaping down at his guilt, leaned and mocked him as he tried to walk more softly. Above the gables and rooftops, the hundred spires of Prague's great churches receded into the fog. He wiped the sweat from his brow and looked up, hoping for a glimpse of the tower of Tyn Church, or beyond, St. Nicolas Church or the Hradcany Castle. They had vanished. *Vanished!*

The musty scent of damp earth surrounded him. His footsteps echoed loudly as if someone were following. Mist assaulted his eyes, causing him to blink rapidly as he strained to find his way through the crooked streets of the Old Town. From some unseen corner the shrill laugh of a woman sounded, and a man's voice joined hers. Günther sighed in a moment of relief that he was not the only human invading the domain of the night. And then the laughter sounded again. Louder. Was it laughter meant for him?

He gasped and stopped, leaning against the cold wet stone for a moment to clear his mind. Sweat and mist trickled together and ran down his face. He did not bother to wipe it off. He wished he had not lingered so long in the beer hall beneath the arcade. He leaned his head back, and the serpent earth began to move. He felt sick. Drunk. He listened as the laughter of the man and woman drifted away. Their voices teased and toyed with one another, and their footsteps grew faint.

Beyond them Günther could hear the rush of the Moldau River as it foamed angrily against the piers of Charles Bridge. *Yes! Charles Bridge!* It was there. There just beyond his vision. Günther fumbled in the deep pocket of his tattered overcoat. He felt the reassuring smoothness of the paper on the small bundle. Opening his eyes, he stepped out onto the scales again and walked more steadily toward the sound of the river. He prayed that the old woman was still there.

He crossed Mala Strana square and walked toward where he knew the bridge was. Grayness swirled up from the river, stinging his nostrils and clinging to his eyelashes. Statues of saints, blackened with age, lined each side of Charles Bridge. They, too, seemed alive tonight, and he was suddenly seized with the desire to run through the gauntlet of their silent vigil. Ahead he could just make out the soft glimmer of votive candles. Their lights danced in shadows on the faces of Günther's unearthly companions. *Have mercy on me! Mary, Mother of God! Have mercy!*

Where was the old woman? Had she gone? Günther staggered forward, his fingers unconsciously clutching the package. Was he too late? Now the Moldau roared beneath the bridge. He stopped in confusion beneath the outstretched arms of Christ on a cross that proclaimed, *Holy, Holy, Holy God!* Günther cursed and strained to see through the fog.

Near the center of the bridge was the statue of St. John Nepomuk. Five stars graced his crown. His blackened sandstone features smiled gently into the light of the votive candles flickering beneath him. *Tacui—"I was silent!"* The saint had died for his silence. Günther wondered how he had agreed to this scheme, wondered now if it was too late for him to turn around and go back to his little government office in the ministry of passports. *Tacui!* Only the silent saint had witnessed him here. The old woman was gone. She had not waited for him to come.

He fingered the package in his pocket and pulled it out. One flip of his wrist, and the evidence would be lost forever in the dark waters of the Moldau River. He held his hand poised as he debated the ending of this ill-fated adventure. *But the money!* They had promised him so much! Already he had been through the worst of it. All that was left was the exchange. But the old woman was not here!

He cursed quietly again, and then crossed himself and asked forgiveness of the stone figures surrounding him. The Moldau stirred louder, and the bridge seemed to sway and rumble.

"Hello?" Günther called. "Is anyone here?"

The sharp click of boots sounded behind him. Günther whirled around to see the grinning face of Sporer emerge from the bridge tower, a small pistol in his right hand. "Yes, Günther. We are here."

From the other end of the bridge, two more men appeared from the mist beyond Nepomuk. Their expressions were twisted with the anger of his betrayal. They moved slowly toward him, their boots louder than the rumbling river. Günther flipped his wrist and the packet sailed over the stone railing, spinning end over end into the blackness.

"Sporer, I was just—"

"That will do you no good." Sporer's voice carried the desolation of judgment in it. "You are either with us or against us, Günther."

"I am with you!" Günther backed closer to the rail. "It was nothing!"

"I suppose we will not know that now, will we, Günther?" Sporer sneered; the light of the votive candles glared on the lenses of his glasses, and the fire in his soul concealed his humanity.

"Please, Sporer! It was the money! They promised me money!"

Sporer reached out a gloved hand. Günther flinched as though he was about to be struck. Sporer laughed. "Just the money?" He patted Günther on his shoulder and Günther grinned in nervous relief.

"I was going to toss it away. You saw. I was not going to go through with it."

"Why?"

"I . . . I just was not going to."

Sporer patted him again and smiled. There were no eyes in his face. Only the fire. The fire. "So, maybe you should have gone through with it and split the money, eh, Günther?"

Günther's face reflected confusion and fear. The thrust of the gun into his belly caused him to gasp. He had met the serpent at last.

The shot rang out loudly, and Günther's twitching body flipped backward over the rail and fell with a splash into the swift current of the Moldau. The quick slap of boots against the stone signaled the retreat of the patriots who claimed Prague and all of Czechoslovakia for the Fatherland.

And St. John Nepomuk kept his vow of silence as the old woman shuffled out onto the bridge to wait.

———

Elisa slept soundly as the train finally crossed the frontier and arrived at the border of Germany. The shriek of brakes and the jarring of the sudden halt awakened her. She opened her eyes and brushed a strand of hair back, then gazed around the compartment in drowsy confusion. Where were Leah, Shimon, Rudy, and the rest? For a moment she tried to remember where the orchestra was playing next, and then the details came back to her. By now, Leah was tucked into her own soft bed in Vienna.

The train was instantly invaded by uniformed men in jackboots who shouted orders and roused every sleepy passenger out onto the loading platform of the depot in Weimar.

"Schnell! Schnell! We do not have all day! Bring your baggage! Everything bring with you! Schnell! Hurry!"

The gray sky suited Elisa's mood. Everything in Germany seemed gray: uniforms, towns. And since Hitler had come to power, rudeness was in vogue.

Elisa clutched Rudy's violin in one hand and her small suitcase in the other. Orders were shouted for the men to form one line into the building and the women another. Elisa shivered with the cold. They were to be strip-searched, a common practice on the German side of the frontier. She hoped the rooms were heated. Slowly they shuffled forward. No one grumbled. Few dared to speak for fear of drawing the attention of the snarling, shouting young soldiers. Elisa envied the members of the orchestra and imagined how they had simply stepped off the train in Vienna and taken shared cabs to their flats.

A tall, stoop-shouldered man stood just inside the doorway. He wore a heavy coat with a fur collar that gave him the appearance of a vulture as he scanned the passports and directed passengers to the appropriate table.

Elisa's grip on the violin case caught his attention. He smiled slightly and then glanced briefly at the small red mark along Elisa's jawline that identified her as a violinist. She held out her passport, and he waved her through without looking at it.

"We shall have to look through your baggage, of course, Fraülein." He sounded apologetic.

"Of course," Elisa agreed, silently wondering how the man would behave if he had looked at the passport of Elisa Lindheim, Jewess.

"A cold morning, ja?"

"Quite."

"A glance through your baggage will be enough." He nodded toward a screen with heaps of baggage piled around it. "Heinz!" he called, and a short, harried-looking young soldier emerged. "Take these things for the Fraülein." He gently, even politely, took Elisa's bag and the violin case from her and handed them to the man. Then he smiled again and said to Elisa, "Just wait here. Only a moment and you may board again."

Other passengers cast angry, fearful looks in her direction. They would assume now that she was some important member of the Reich—or at least related to someone in authority.

Moments later, the young man came out from behind the screen again and handed the bag and the violin case back to Elisa. "Quite in order." He gave a slight bow and then raised his hand in salute, "Heil Hitler!" He said it as though he were wishing her a good morning.

She raised her hand slightly and replied, "Good day." Then she looked at the tall vulture-like man beside her. "Am I finished?"

"More than enough, Fraülein. You may resume your place on the train." He tipped his hat and Elisa nodded, then left the others shivering on the platform. She had not experienced such politeness in Germany since 1933. She did not question her luck, even when three other passengers were arrested on first examination of their passports. Life in the Reich had become a strange paradox of brutality and obliging charm.

Elisa sat quietly in the empty train and placed the precious violin across her lap. She opened the case and lifted the lid, gazing for a long time at the soft golden patina of the Guarnerius. This morning she had happened to meet with a man who appreciated music and recognized her as a musician. Tomorrow, or next week, she could just as easily be searched by some ignorant Brownshirt who would smash the priceless instrument to pieces for the joy of his own power to do so. Elisa suddenly wished that Rudy had not left the instrument with her. She wished that she had loaned him the money and not taken the responsibility for carrying something so unique and irreplaceable right into the heart of Nazi Germany.

As the first of the passengers came glaring past her, she closed the case. She felt like apologizing, but she did not know how to explain such behavior. Within a matter of hours she had crossed a frontier and stepped through the looking glass into a bizarre world where the Red Queen wore a swastika on her arm and danced as she shouted, *"Off with their heads!"*

As the train jerked into motion at last, Elisa closed her eyes and determined that she would not think about it anymore until she had to. Somewhere in the back of her mind remained the vague hope that she would not cross the border into Germany again until the looking-glass world became right once more.

4

Guests

The bull calf was five days old and confidently butting his patient mother as he demanded his warm, creamy supper. Franz dumped a measure of grain into the manger, then stood and watched as the baby slurped happily. He had been an early calf, and his arrival was really a surprise. When Franz and his father had purchased the heifer last spring, they had known she was pregnant, but had not expected the birth until early March. As it turned out, the new calf and fresh supply of milk were a godsend. Two other cows had gone dry the week before, so the Wattenbarger supplies of salable milk and butter were short. Even after the calf had his share, the new cow produced nearly as much milk as the other two milk cows.

Franz liked her. She had a sweet disposition and probably would happily nurse two more orphan calves. He stroked her soft muzzle and considered purchasing an extra calf or two at the sale in March. "You are a lifesaver, you are," he said. "You bring us a few extra shillings for butter, and I'll bring you more children." The cow blinked solemnly. "Two, maybe three more to take care of, eh?" he added.

At the sound of his own words, Franz paled and slapped his forehead with his palm. "Dummkopf!" he shouted to himself as he fumbled in the pocket of his coat and pulled out the crumpled envelope he had received from the priest five days earlier. "*The guests! People to care for!*" He hurried from the cow barn into his mother's kitchen. She stood over a steaming kettle of venison stew. Her hair was pulled back beneath a white cap, and her apron bore traces of the day's chore of bread-making.

"Franz?" she asked, startled by his pale appearance as he waved the unopened letter beneath her nose. "What? Franz?"

"Mama, I'm sorry. I forgot. The priest—" She took the letter and tore it open.

Gasping, she groped for a chair as she read the words, ". . . *Arriving December 8!* Franz! That is *today*!"

"Mama, I forgot!"

"You *forgot*? I will beat you with a good stout stick!" She jumped up and shook her flour-covered fist beneath his nose.

"I'm too big to beat! I'm . . . I . . . it was the calf! I just forgot!"

"You mean you had this since *then*? Himmel!" Her face was red, eyes blazing. "You are not too big! Six foot three you may be, and as brawny as an ox, but I'll always be bigger than you! Big enough to beat a boy who needs it!"

Franz looked down at his little mother. He knew she was serious and backed up almost to the counter where loaves of fresh bread were piled high. "*When* are they coming today?" He tried to pull her attention from himself.

She glanced down at the letter again and gasped louder. "Get the sleigh! Hitch the team! Mein Gott! You . . . *you*! Franz, get to the Bahnhof! The mother and her two sons are arriving *now*!"

Franz gazed meekly around the kitchen, a disaster of dirty dishes and flour-covered counters. "Maybe we should make them wait, Mama?" he asked timidly.

Frau Wattenbarger roared loudly, chasing him back out into the stable. With her hands waving in the air and her apron billowing, she shouted, "Just *go* and get them! At least only the three are coming tonight. Two others coming in a few days! They can take your room." She raised her nose slightly. "And you will sleep in the barn tonight!"

Franz could hear the shrill whistle of the train rounding the Kitzbüheler Horn as he urged the little mare into a lope. Mercifully, the train was late. The holiday guests would not suspect that they had not even been expected until a mere hour before their arrival.

It was dark when Franz passed through the village. Lights shone down from frost-covered windows, making yellow pools on the snow. Heavy timbered houses looked as they had for over three hundred years. He drove past the Golden Griffin Hostel and smelled the rich aroma of chops and sauerkraut. His stomach rumbled. Mama had said he would have to give up his portion of the evening meal until after the guests were fed. He wished the train were an hour later so he could gulp down a stein of beer and half a dozen chops before picking up the arrivals.

He tied the little Haflinger mare to the hitching post in front of the station just as the train clanked and squealed to a stop. The Kitzbühel stop lasted only long enough for passengers to disembark, and only a handful stepped off the train tonight. His passengers were easy to spot. A tall blond woman of about forty and her two sons wrestled their luggage and skis onto the platform as the train chugged away. One of the boys

was about seventeen—tall and thin, but still without the muscle of manhood. The other boy appeared to be about fourteen. His black hair and
serious dark eyes were a sharp contrast to his fair skin. As a matter of
fact, all three of them looked as though they had not been in the sun for
a very long time. Their faces seemed tense and worried. Franz bounded
up the steps and smiled broadly as he called, "Frau Linder?"

The woman hesitated a moment, then smiled tentatively. "We are to
meet a driver?" She studied Franz with a gaze that seemed adept at sizing
up people.

He was suddenly conscious of the cow manure on his boots and the
work clothes he wore. He brushed a lock of his curly brown hair back
beneath his cap and bowed politely. "Allow me to introduce myself. Franz
Wattenbarger." He did not offer to shake hands. He had not washed since
his chores in the barn. "My family works to make your stay at the chalet
most comfortable." He stepped back as the boys appraised his disheveled
appearance. "My work was only just finished when my mother sent me to
fetch you."

As though sensing his discomfort, Anna Linder smiled slightly and
nodded her head. "I am Frau Anna Linder. And these are my sons Wilhelm"—she touched the oldest boy on the arm—"and Dieter."

The two teenagers nodded curtly and Franz noticed the way their eyes
glanced nervously around the station. They seemed almost fearful, certainly too serious for boys who had just come to the Tyrol for a vacation.

Wilhelm held the skis and Dieter managed the ski poles. Forgetting
his soiled hands, Franz clapped Wilhelm on the back. "Ready for a good
time, I see?" His bright blue eyes gazed steadily until he caught Wilhelm's
glance and held it. Only then did the serious young man dare to smile.
"You fellows have been too long in school, I think." He hefted the luggage
and led the way to the sleigh.

"School?" began Dieter, "Oh no, we—" A hard nudge from his brother
silenced him.

Franz pretended not to notice. He did, however, detect that while Mrs.
Linder's accent was unmistakably Viennese, both boys had the bold, hard
accent of Berliners. "The weather in Vienna has been rainy, I hear," he
said to Wilhelm, who looked uneasy.

"It always rains this time of year in Vienna," Anna Linder replied confidently as she stepped between Franz and the boys. "But not so bad as
in Salzburg." Her words were cheerful, but her eyes seemed to look past
Franz as though she carried some dark secret.

He nodded and loaded the baggage and tied up the skis. Tyrol was
full of people with haunted, frightened expressions these days. Their letter
may have come from Vienna, but the cut of their clothes, the pallor of
their skin, the weariness of their eyes all spoke of Germany. Franz decided
that he would not pry. He would not make them have to lie. It was quite
obvious that they were people of affluence. If they had not wanted to

remain secluded, they would have chosen to stay somewhere other than the chalet of a poor Austrian farm family. He glanced at Frau Linder's long, delicate fingers—strong hands, but unaccustomed to physical labor. He could not help but think about the calloused hands of his own mother—how she scrambled around the house, shouting orders and changing bedding while everyone tried to stay out of her path.

Franz caught Wilhelm's eye again. "You like to ski?"

The young man nodded, but did not smile again. Life was serious. Too serious for such conversation.

Franz decided that if there was to be conversation on the trip up the mountain, he would be the only one talking. "I have two younger brothers. About your age, I would guess. They will show you where the best slopes are for skiing." He tried to maintain the feeling of holiday, although their behavior told another story. "There is the best skiing in the world here."

"Last season we went to Bavaria—" began Dieter, but he was again nudged to silence.

Bavaria. In Germany. Franz saw Wilhelm's eyes glance around again to see who might be listening. "Bavaria!" exclaimed Franz, as though he did not notice. "Well, you are from Vienna. Austrians. You know there is no skiing in Germany like there is in the Tyrol."

"Actually we are from Prague," corrected Frau Linder. "Our passports are Czechoslovakian."

Franz had no doubt that the passports were indeed Czechoslovakian, but he also knew the difference in accent. "Your letter came from Vienna," he said.

"Yes," Frau Linder was quick to reply as they climbed into the sleigh. "Our daughter is a musician there. She made the arrangements for us."

"And she is coming?"

"Yes. In a few days. With her father. He has some . . . business, and they are coming in a few days."

As Franz clucked the horse into motion, he sensed that even the simplest of questions seemed almost too much for his passengers to handle. He lapsed into silence as they glided into the night. The guests talked quietly in guarded tones to one another, commenting on the moonlight on the snow, the lights of the village—matters that usually went totally unnoticed by most boys their ages. Yes, the Tyrol was full of cautious conversation these days—German accents explaining Czech passports or visas to France. It did not take a genius detective or a Gestapo agent to figure out that the Linders, if that was their real name, had not come for a holiday. They had rented the chalet as a way station until they found someplace to go. Franz could only guess that this woman's husband and daughter must still be in Germany. And so she had brought her visions of the Gestapo and arrest along with her.

"My mother is quite a good cook," Franz remarked, startled at his ability to be mundane. "Are you hungry?"

John Murphy sipped his Coke and stared down at the traffic inching along Berlin's Unter den Linden. From his corner room on the third floor of the Adlon Hotel, he had a perfect view of the somber British Embassy on Wilhelmstrasse and the expansive German Interior Ministry on the other corner. A block away he could just make out the glaring spotlights that illuminated the Bronze horses atop Brandenburg Gate.

Murphy was the envy of every foreign correspondent in Berlin. Americans always got the best rooms, it seemed. Most assumed it was Hitler's attempt to placate the Yankee journalists who were the quickest to report unpleasant incidents among the German population in the young Nazi regime. Whatever the reason, Murphy was treated well by Goebbels, the propaganda minister in Hitler's Cabinet. Often, he was given first crack at some new turn in the maze of Nazi policies. Last month, for instance, Goebbels had arranged for a private interview with Herr Ribbentrop after the Germans had signed a pact with the Japanese to protect the Western world against the Russian Communists.

Murphy grinned now at the memory. Ribbentrop had paced back and forth as he explained the alliance against bolshevism. The "master race" of Aryans was now allied with the Japanese "master race," and together they would save Western civilization. That was the way Hitler wanted the story reported in the American press.

Murphy had asked incredulously, "The *Japanese* are going to protect the Western world?"

Ribbentrop had nodded seriously in reply. "Exactly."

"Would you repeat that?" Murphy had asked.

Ribbentrop had no sense of humor. Of course, neither did Goebbels or Hitler, for that matter. Maybe Murphy was the only one struck by the ridiculousness of the pact. He had written it just as they told him: *JAPANESE AND NAZIS SWORN TO PROTECT FREE WESTERN NATIONS*. The story made it through the Nazi censors, and then the staff in New York had rewritten it from a little different point of view. No one had thrown Murphy out of the Adlon Hotel yet, and Herr Hitler was still hoping to persuade the Americans and British to remain uninvolved with Germany's "private affairs."

Tonight, a dozen morose reporters gathered in Murphy's room. They drank gin and tonic and smoked in silence as they waited for the BBC to begin its broadcast of King Edward's final speech as king.

The British Embassy seemed even more quiet and melancholy than usual. The lights in the upper floors were out, and Murphy guessed that the diplomatic staff was gathered in the large parlor to hear the news. Two British reporters seemed a bit more "in their cups" tonight than usual. Murphy half expected a funeral dirge to erupt from the embassy.

Amanda Taylor from the London *Times* came up quietly behind him and stared down at her government's Berlin outpost.

"Pretty quiet down there, huh?" said Murphy, glancing at the tall, slim brunette with appreciation.

Amanda pursed her lips and raised her eyebrows, a sure sign that she was about to make a pronouncement. "They're all daft, if you ask me. Why all the glooooom?" She pronounced the last word loud and long, her red lips properly enunciating every vowel. "One would think he had died instead of fallen in love!"

Someone on the sofa called a little drunkenly. "Yeah. A fella falls in love, he might as well die, Amanda. Same thing."

She rolled her wide brown eyes and clicked her tongue in response. "Well, I think all of England should throw them a party. Instead they are—"

"Kicking them out?" Murphy said with a wry smile.

"Mrs. Simpson doesn't need any more wedding parties," added Johnson. "'She's already been married a couple of times, ain't she?"

"Well, so what?" Amanda flipped the curtain. "I think it is positively the most romantic thing . . . the most . . ." She gestured broadly as she searched for the appropriate word. "For a man to give up his *crown* and his *kingdom*—"

"For a broad?" squeaked Timmon's tipsy voice. "The guy is nuts."

Amanda whirled around and faced the all-male group with the fury of a woman defending chivalry and knights of old. "Romance!" she hissed. "Haven't you baboons ever heard of the word?"

"Yeah!" quipped Murphy. "You can buy it right down on Mittelstrasse at the cabaret. It's real cheap, too. About *half a crown*, Amanda!" A delighted roar of approval rose up from the male ranks. Murphy took a little bow, and Amanda thumped him across the head. She was always a bit too much of an educated Amazon for his taste. He decided not to argue further about the matter and shrugged as he turned back to his watch post.

"Come on, Amanda," the guys razzed. "You got no sense of humor?"

Her lips turned down in an unbecoming pout. "You louts! You simply have no sense of what is noble and—"

"Yeah. What do we know?"

"Reporters." Each man mimicked a line she had said.

"In Berlin, no less."

"Dreary Berlin at Christmastime."

"Stuck here while the love story of the century is happening in England. Blast! A king gives up his throne to marry a divorced commoner!"

"And here we are in old Herr Hitler's city with nuthin' to write home about!"

Murphy laughed but did not join in. He continued to look down at the sidewalk and the jammed streets. Horns blared, and a drizzle caused people to struggle with umbrellas, or turn up their collars and run for cover. The guys were right. Berlin at Christmas was a dismal place—at least since Hitler had come to power. People had still been smiling and unafraid when Murphy had first come in 1933. Now, three and a half years later, there was just the constant drizzle of the Reich's propaganda.

Amanda bantered on furiously with the unrelenting company of hopeless skeptics. Murphy searched the faces of the pedestrians in the cold avenues below for some hint of their thoughts. He stepped forward, almost pressing his forehead on the glass as he caught sight of a young Fraülein raising her arm to a passing taxi. The young woman's shoulder-length blond hair clung in damp wisps to her finely chiseled face. She was tall and slender, aristocratic looking. Murphy found himself wishing that he was out in the rain, or maybe driving the cab. This was not the type of girl he could meet at a cabaret, however. She was more the opera or symphony hall type. He squinted as the taxi splashed to a halt and a smile of grateful relief spread across her face. *A dancer? She probably came out of the Academy of Arts on the Pariser Platz*.

"Hey, Murphy!" called Timmons, clanking the gin bottle. "How can a guy get some lime around here?"

"Call room service," Murphy replied distractedly as the woman brushed her hair back with a graceful sweep of her hand and spoke to the taxi driver through the window. "And put it on your own tab! I don't run a restaurant!" She opened the door of the automobile and slid in, revealing a nicely shaped leg. Then the door closed and she was gone. Murphy shrugged and looked back toward the British Embassy as the woman's taxi drove away, leaving behind a wake of rainwater.

"Let us know when they bring up the hearse to haul King Edward's portrait out, will you, Murph?" Timmons stirred his drink. "That's as close as we're going to get to this story, I'm afraid."

Murphy turned around just in time to see Amanda's back as she stalked out of the room and slammed the door angrily behind her.

"She's got no sense of humor!" grumbled Timmons.

"Yeah!" replied Johnson with a nervous laugh. "That's why she got this assignment."

"Yeah?" Timmons slurped his drink loudly. "So why are all the rest of us here?"

Johnson shrugged thoughtfully and stretched out on the floor. "Exile," he answered gloomily. "Somebody up there just don't like us no more!"

5

Coming Home

The taxi driver grimaced and pounded his fist against the horn in irritation. The sound simply blended with the impatient blasts of a thousand other horns in the commercial district of Berlin.

Elisa Lindheim glanced at her watch, then looked out the rain-streaked window of the cab. It was not yet five o'clock, but it was already dark. The bright marquees of Berlin's great department stores reflected on the hoods and windshields of the automobiles that inched down the slick streets. On the sidewalks, Christmas shoppers awkwardly clutched packages and umbrellas and vied for places on the crowded trolley cars. No one seemed to notice the Christmas decorations in the glittering shop windows. In spite of the season, the face of Berlin was grim and cold. Elisa looked up beyond the lights to where the great red banners of the Reich clung to the dripping facades of every building. The black mark of the swastika caused her to shudder involuntarily.

Elisa had shuddered when she saw the banners the day she arrived. Berlin had changed, and her few days at home had shown her that the swastika was casting its dark shadow everywhere.

The cab lurched forward a few yards, halting inches from the bumper of a large black Mercedes. The driver beat out a rhythm on his horn again.

"It seems I might travel faster on foot," said Elisa.

"My apologies, Fräulein," the driver shrugged helplessly. "It is another of Chancellor Hitler's building projects, you know. Down with the old Berlin, up with the new. The streets are torn up everywhere. It could be years before traffic is free again."

"Years?" Elisa looked out at the drizzle. "I don't have that long, I'm afraid." She opened her handbag. "It is only two blocks to Lindheim's; I can walk."

The cab driver frowned and appraised Elisa's finely tailored clothes and the perfect blond curls that framed her face. "Walk if you like, Fräulein," his voice carried a warning. "But I would not walk to *that* store for Christmas shopping."

Her blue eyes glinted angrily at his words. "Why?" she asked him, even though she already knew what his answer would be.

He shrugged. "You have been gone from Berlin a long time if you do not remember that this is a *Jewish* store. Only Jews and very foolish people shop there now." His voice carried the tone of a man putting forth a perfectly logical argument.

Elisa did not reply. All of Germany was filled with such logic these days. She checked the meter and counted out the exact fare. No tip, not even a *thank you* for the information. Elisa was sure that when the cabbie counted out the change and discovered she had not tipped him, he would curse beneath his breath and remark that she, too, must be a Jew. On that point he would be right, despite the fact that Elisa had inherited her mother's "Aryan" good looks.

"I will walk," she said curtly, opening the door to a blast of cold, wet air. She slammed the door behind her and scurried between stalled vehicles to the crowded sidewalk. Opening her umbrella, she joined the jostling shoppers. For a moment, she closed her eyes and breathed deeply. Voices and Christmas music mingled with the cacophony of automobile horns in the city symphony so familiar to Elisa. For a moment it was almost as if nothing at all had changed while she had been in Vienna. Berlin was still her home, the city of her childhood dreams and happiest hours. Beneath her umbrella, the crooked cross of Hitler's flag seemed simply another thundercloud that would pass, taking its storm with it. She would pretend that it was Christmas in Berlin as it always had been and as it always would be. . . .

She made her way through the throng, feeling a sense of relief as she pushed open the great glass doors of Lindheim's Department Store. Shaking the raindrops from her umbrella, she stood to the side and gazed over the crowded aisles with satisfaction. It *was* Christmas—at least in Lindheim's. Men and women strolled along the counters. Clerks smiled and offered help. Small booths were set up to provide the famous gift wrapping service that made even the smallest gift seem extraordinary. The sweet aroma of perfume drifted through the store, and a string quartet played the music of Mozart from a red carpeted platform beside a giant glittering Christmas tree. Marble pillars were wrapped with broad swaths of red cloth, giving them the appearance of giant candy canes.

Elisa felt a surge of pride for her father. *Ironic,* she thought, *that Christmas should seem most real here, in a Jewish store.* She smiled at the thought. Her family was devoutly Lutheran, even though her father clung proudly to his Jewish heritage. Her mother was Aryan, with a lineage pure enough to please Hitler himself. *Why then,* she wondered, *is the issue of being Jewish so all-consuming these days?*

In spite of everything, Theo Lindheim had managed to carry off the image of the most carefree of all holidays for the "Master Race." There were no Nazi flags flapping from the roof of his building. The only swastikas to be seen were worn on the armbands of the soldiers who crowded the aisles of Lindheim's with everyone else.

Three years ago, the sight of such soldiers would have been unthinkable. After the Great War, her father had told her that Germany had been stripped of great tracts of land and denied the right to ever rebuild its army. Elisa shook her head at the uselessness of such decrees. Only twelve years later, Adolf Hitler and the National Socialist party had burst on the scene. They had taken over the government of the Weimar Republic with only a thirty-three percent vote. Rearming had begun immediately, as had construction of the concentration camps for those who opposed the Nazis. The Versailles Treaty was merely a slip of paper since France and Britain had refused to enforce it.

Decrees against the Jews of Germany had gone hand in hand with the rearming. Theo Lindheim had been spared much of the persecution others were now enduring, simply because he had been a great hero for the Fatherland during the "war to end all wars." His trophy case contained two Iron Crosses, and he walked with a limp from a wound received as a fighter pilot in the last battle above the Argonne. Elisa was proud of him—proud that the guests around their dinner table had been among the great men of Germany. They came less and less often lately, but still, no one denied that Theo Lindheim was a great German patriot, even if he was a Jew.

Elisa passed unnoticed through the shoppers and climbed the familiar stairs to the mezzanine. She could have greeted every clerk in the store, but they were all busy, and she was too preoccupied to make small talk. They would want to know about school in Vienna and what her plans were. Some would have even asked her about her romance with Thomas von Kleistmann, and that was one topic she could not face—not now. Christmas was supposed to be a happy time, full of love and laughter and friends. Her relationship with Thomas was one thing her father's status as war hero had not been able to save. There was a law now in Germany that the blood of a pure Aryan could not co-mingle with that of the defiled Jew. It was not a matter of religion, they had explained to Thomas. It did not matter that the Lindheim family were baptized Lutherans. A little water could not wash away their Jewishness. As an adjutant on the staff of Admiral Canaris, Thomas could not continue to see Elisa. He had been told this in a very polite and logical tone; there had even been some sympathy in the voice of the officer. But the law was on the books, and violation was punishable by severe prison sentences.

Elisa shook her head slightly to brush away the thought. She had denied herself the luxury of self-pity while she had studied and practiced in Vienna. The solitude of the practice cubicle had been filled with the passion of her music alone. In Austria, no one ever stopped to question her heritage. She was beautiful and talented, a violinist of great potential, according to Professor Ryburg at the Academy. She had lost herself in a world of music and hard work. Letters from Thomas von Kleistmann had been burned unopened rather than returned to him at the risk of Gestapo interception. In Vienna she had not had the time to miss him. Now, at this instant, in the familiarity of Berlin, she found herself searching the faces of the young officers in the store and hoping against her own will for a glimpse of Thomas. She almost regretted that she had come home to Berlin for a few days of shopping before the family took their December holiday in the Alps of the Austrian Tyrol. Certainly there were no terrible edicts against love in Austria. Those laws had only come with the dank rain of the swastika's thundercloud. Elisa drew herself up. Perhaps she would not come home again until all this had passed away as her father and Thomas von Kleistmann believed it would. She would stay across the border and fall in love with whomever she wished. She would play the music that was now forbidden for Jewish musicians in Hitler's Germany. The sound of Mozart followed her up the stairs—it was a reminder that, as a racial Jew, it was against the law for her to play "German" music in public. Even in her own father's store.

A tall, strong-jawed Wehrmacht soldier smiled and touched his hand to the brim of his cap as he passed Elisa. She lifted her chin and looked the other way, unwilling to give him the satisfaction of even a glance. *The taxi driver was wrong*, Elisa thought. *More than Jews still shop at Lindheim's. But a great many fools come here.*

Elisa was well aware, of course, that legally, *technically*, Lindheim's was no longer a Jewish store. Theo Lindheim had the foresight to pass the control of the store on paper to a select group of his German business friends. His office still remained where it had always been on the second floor, and decisions were still relayed to him; but the names of five Aryan board members kept the store on good terms with the Nazi government. Even though it was illegal to export "Jewish capital," Elisa had overheard her father and mother discussing the bank account in Switzerland . . . *just in case*.

"*In case of what?*" Elisa had asked. Didn't her father's war record protect them all? Didn't their baptism into the Lutheran church mean anything? —

When the signs began appearing in shop windows *Juden unerwünscht—Jews unwanted,* Elisa had ignored them. With her blond hair and fine-boned features, she was often the object of frank stares and longing looks by the same Nazi youths in S.A. uniforms who lay in wait for the Jews outside the synagogues. And she hated them—not as a Jew, but as a German; she hated what they had done to her homeland.

Others who also hated them were systematically disappearing in midnight raids by Himmler's Gestapo. Names like Dachau and Oranienburg were whispered in hushed tones.

Admiral Canaris, who was the head of the Abwehr, feuded frequently with Himmler over the lawless policies of the Gestapo. The result was simply that Canaris had fallen out of favor with Hitler. Perhaps it made no difference to the career of Thomas von Kleistmann that he had turned his back on her. There could be no future for him if Canaris ended up in forced retirement in Dachau, like so many other fallen leaders.

The thought gave her no pleasure. A young couple kissed on the landing, and suddenly Elisa felt angry at Thomas all over again. He had only to cross the border into Austria where she still played the bright music of Mozart on her violin! He had only to come to her there, and she would be his, no questions asked! How she had loved him once! And now what a terrible tangle her feelings of love and hatred had become!

At the top of the stairs to the right was a small, crowded lunch counter. Beyond that was the office of Theo Lindheim. Elisa debated going first to her father's office, or picking up the ski clothes she had left with the tailor for alterations the day before. Putting a hand to her hot cheek, Elisa decided it would be better to see her father after she had calmed down. There had never been a time in her life that he had not been able to read a mood in her eyes. She was certain that they would now be a very pale blue, and she was not up to having him ask her what was troubling her. A session with Grynspan the tailor and a new winter wardrobe would no doubt brighten her outlook.

She turned left and wound through the bright bolts of Christmas fabric. Lindheim's fabric department had always been famous in Berlin. Satin and velvet lined the aisles as women wandered through the maze of bright yardage. At the back of the department, a small sign announced *Alterations*, and behind a blue brocade curtain, the soft ticking sound of an old sewing machine could be heard.

Elisa pulled back the curtain and stepped into the tiny, cluttered world of Grynspan the tailor. Patterns and material covered nearly every available inch of space. Suits dotted with chalk marks hung from a large rack beside the sewing machine. Three Luftwaffe uniforms were finished and hung just inside the door. German Air Force officers, it seemed, had not forgotten the exploits of Theo Lindheim.

The tailor sat hunched over the sewing machine, guiding the fabric and pumping frantically on the foot pedal. Assorted pins hung from his tight lips. He looked as he had since Elisa was a little girl. There was only one change in his appearance; he had stopped wearing his yarmulke, which had marked him as a Jew and easy prey to the Brownshirts.

His sixteen-year-old son Herschel sat in the back corner of the workshop and labored over the buttons on a man's pinstriped suit. Neither of them looked up from their work, and Elisa waited silently in the doorway and listened to the news on the radio that sat on the shelf just above young Herschel.

London: December 10, 1936, will be a day long remembered. The blue-and-white flag of the Duchy of Cornwall fluttered slowly to the foot of its mast at 10 o'clock this morning on the high turret over Fort Belvedere. It was a signal that made history, for at that moment King Edward was renouncing the greatest throne on earth so that he could marry the woman he loves . . .

Elisa blinked hard and exclaimed, "Well now, there is one fellow on earth willing to face a little criticism for love!"

Herr Grynspan and Herschel both looked up, startled to see her standing in the midst of their workroom. "Fraülein Lindheim!" The tailor sputtered around a mouthful of pins. "How long have you—"

Elisa raised her hand for silence as the broadcast droned on in the tone of a funeral dirge:

Mrs. Wallace Warfield Simpson, tears streaming down her face, heard the words announcing that the King Emperor of whom so much had been expected had laid down his crown and scepter so as to be free to marry her and live the life of an ordinary mortal.

"Well, what do you know!" Elisa said loudly.

"We should all be so lucky, yes?" said the tailor, pivoting on his little round stool to face her. "What we Jews wouldn't give to live the lives of ordinary mortals, eh?"

"Papa!" Herschel exclaimed, looking frightened by the old man's comment. "You must not say such things!"

The old man jerked a thumb at the boy. "You see. If I were an ordinary mortal I could open my mouth and not be afraid someone was listening." He patted his round bald pate. "I gave up my crown too, Herschel. The Brownshirts don't like little hats on Jewish heads."

"Papa!" protested the boy again. He flushed deep red when he looked up to see that Elisa was smiling conspiratorially at him.

"Perhaps the uniforms have been wired for sound," Elisa winked, and the darkly handsome young man flushed deeper.

"I would not be surprised," Herschel said bitterly. "Papa, you must be careful."

The old tailor waved a hand in disregard. "I am the best tailor in Berlin. The German Luftwaffe officers would sooner go naked as not have me to sew their pretty uniforms as long as no one tells Göring!" He spoke bravely, but the words were far from convincing.

"And I would rather go naked on the ski slopes than not have you sew my clothes, Herr Grynspan," Elisa said impetuously. She was immediately embarrassed by her own words. "I mean . . ."

Herschel raised his eye brows slightly, then looked down at the buttons on the suit. His ears seemed to be on fire.

"There, you see, Herschel," said the old tailor, confidently accepting the compliment. "There you have it from the mouth of the owner's daughter. So what are you worried about?"

"First staying alive. Then going to the university!" Herschel said too loudly.

"In the meantime, Herr Lindheim is paying you a wage. The Nazis would have something else in mind if it weren't for him. Not the university, I think."

Herschel ignored his father's comment and looked directly at Elisa. He had always had a terrible crush on her, even when they were small children. When he was ten and she was a mature seventeen, he had confessed his adoration for her and she had told him it was hopeless. Since then, he had always acted aloof and somewhat distant to her. "And how is Vienna? Do they treat even Jewish girls well there?"

"Only if they dress well and talk nicely to their elders," she replied evenly.

"And of course it is important that they have lots of money," he said sarcastically.

"Herschel!" his father half rose.

"Never mind, Herr Grynspan." Elisa was amused. "Just sew his lips together while he is sleeping tonight."

Herschel smiled broadly at her words. "It will do no good, Elisa. I can still write you angry letters, even with my lips sewed tight."

"Then why don't you?" she met his smile. "I would love to hear from an ordinary mortal."

The old tailor sighed and shuffled to the stack of packages. "Since you are this high, you children have been arguing. I never know about what. I stopped worrying about whether I would lose my job over it years ago. Now I am only hoping that your father, God bless him, and I both survive this scourge, this plague of locusts, eh?"

"Maybe I will sew *your* lips together Papa," Herschel said beneath his breath.

"First you have to learn how to thread a needle," the old tailor retorted. He leveled his gaze at Elisa. "Your father sent you to Vienna. If things get worse, Herschel is going to stay with an uncle in Paris. Maybe he can go to the university there, eh?"

She glanced at Herschel, who labored over the buttons as though all his hopes and dreams were not contained in his father's words. "Don't wait to send him," Elisa's voice grew gentle. "Yes, the Sorbonne for Herschel. He will be a great scientist someday, I am sure of it."

"Or maybe I will marry a rich young Jewish girl?" Herschel smiled briefly at her. "Then I will not have to think about school or Nazis."

She gathered her packages. "As long as she is also an American, Herschel." She winked at him and slipped out into the bright lights of the fabric department once again. She could hear Herschel laughing as his father scolded him for his impertinence.

"Marry a rich girl indeed!"

"You would not like Elisa Lindheim as a daughter-in-law? Then we

would not have to worry about the Gestapo."

"They are no safer than we are. Not much, anyway...."

Elisa's smile faded. The old tailor was probably right. She held her packages tightly and looked at the familiar store as though she were seeing it for the last time. Suddenly, she wanted very much to see her father, tall and sternly handsome with his gray hair and deep blue eyes. She hurried toward his office, longing to feel the security that she had felt as a child playing beside his huge mahogany desk. All that had been so invulnerable and dear now seemed no more solid than reflections on the water. One stone tossed into the pool could cause it all to ripple and vanish forever.

6

Abdication

Thomas von Kleistmann placed his cap on the seat of the empty chair beside him. It had become the arrogant custom of the men in uniform to leave their hats on indoors, but tonight Thomas felt small and embarrassed by such new customs.

Theo Lindheim pressed his fingertips together and leaned across the broad desktop. His eyes were intense, probing. *Just like Elisa's eyes,* Thomas thought.

"And why do you come here to tell me this?" Theo demanded. "Certainly you risk your . . . career. Not only do you know of such events, but now you have shared this information with a Jew." His words were not harsh. In the light of what was happening now in Germany, Lindheim's question was valid.

"Herr Lindheim, you were a great hero for the Fatherland—"

"I am certain this is an embarrassment to the government, eh? A Jewish war hero."

Thomas nodded and looked down at his hands. "To some men in the government, yes. But there are others, Herr Lindheim. Men who have not forgotten." he lowered his voice. "They have not forgotten what Germany was—"

"Then they had better keep their memories to themselves, Thomas. Such things might interfere with what the Führer plans for the future." He glanced at the crisp, white envelope that Thomas had placed on the desk. "The future does not include Jews, eh, Thomas? Not even heroes of the Argonne?"

Thomas did not meet Theo Lindheim's gaze. He pursed his lips in unhappy response. "There are lists, Herr Lindheim. Endless lists—"

"Germany has become a nation of lists, has it not?"

"It is nothing your friends can stop. Himmler and his S.S., his Gestapo . . ." He searched for words to describe what Lindheim already knew. "They are beyond the control of—" he stopped. He wanted to say that the Gestapo was beyond the control of law and decent humanity, but humanity was a word that was also being used less and less these days.

"Canaris is an old friend," Theo said sadly. "Does he know that you have come?"

Thomas simply blinked at him in response; then he looked at the envelope again. "He was aware that Elisa and I—" He faltered and began again. "When this came across his desk, he passed it along to me. For filing."

Lindheim tapped his pen on the S.S. insignia on the envelope as though he were crushing a spider. "This is from Himmler's office. How has it come to Canaris?"

"Himmler's Gestapo watches Canaris, and Canaris watches Himmler."

"And Herr Hitler watches them both." Lindheim opened the envelope and pulled out the neatly typed memo. He frowned as he skimmed the contents:

T. Lindheim—Jew hiding behind association with Protestant Pastor Jacobi of Gedachtniskirche. Claims conversion. Jacobi has been advised about proper denunciation of racially impure from his pulpit. Jacobi refuses cooperation. Suspected of anti-Nazi sentiment.

"So." Lindheim's voice contained an edge of controlled anger. "Now they will hound Carl Jacobi because I am a member of his church?"

"This is one small matter they have against Pastor Jacobi. Believe me, you are not the issue. Not the only issue."

"They have put me on a list, then?"

"They are searching for a case against Jacobi," Thomas shrugged helplessly. "They are building cases against every churchman who does not conform to the party line."

Lindheim tossed the memo onto the blotter with disgust. "I see. Yes. The case against me is already established by my Jewish birth certificate. And my children? Half Aryan? Born and raised in the church?" He smiled bitterly. "Yes. I almost forgot. That issue was settled by your superiors. It is not a question of religion, but of racial purity. And half a Jew is still a Jew."

"You can see, Herr Lindheim, it is not even a question of the church. Not even the churchmen are safe anymore." He shook his head and ran his fingers through his thick black hair. "There are lists, you see."

Lindheim studied the grief-stricken face of the young man before him. Theo never ceased to be amazed at the ironic contrast between Thomas and his Elisa. Thomas, whose pure Aryan blood was unquestioned by the S.S., nevertheless had dark hair and swarthy skin—in these times, enough evidence to make the authorities suspect a Jewish background. Theo's own daughter, who was half Jewish, easily passed for Aryan, with her blond hair, fair skin, and blue eyes. Tall and handsome, at twenty-six years of age, Thomas von Kleistmann looked much as his father Wilhelm von Kleistmann had looked when Lindheim had served in his squadron in 1918. He had been the eldest son of an old Prussian family, commanding his men with the correctness and discipline of a true soldier. Wilhelm had died in a plane crash, and Lindheim had first seen little Thomas in the faded image of a photograph taken from his father's blood-soaked jacket. "Thomas," Theo said gently, "you do not remember your father."

Thomas looked up sharply, not wanting to hear the words of Theo Lindheim. "I have brought you this—correctly, I think."

"Why do you serve them?" Again, the probing eyes tore at the young man's soul. Thomas ignored the question and pressed on.

"You should have your passports in order, just in case. Perhaps it would be wise to warn Pastor Jacobi."

"Pastor Jacobi has already warned *me*, Thomas. Last week when they came to the church. He told me they had approached him about our excommunication from the Lutheran church. The Führer spoke publicly on Martin Luther's hatred of the Jews that afternoon."

"Then I needn't have come."

"Yes. It was important for you to come. Important for your own soul, and for my friends as well." Theo shook his head. "Why? *Why*, Thomas? Why do you serve them?"

"I am a German."

"So am I."

Thomas looked away. "I am a German like my father was."

"You mean Aryan? As Pastor Jacobi is. And he is on the lists."

"I do not wish to also be on their lists, then," he blurted.

Lindheim sat back in the deep leather chair. "If you are not on their lists, then the list becomes *your* list as well as theirs, I think." He added quietly, "Your father would not have been one of them."

"And if everyone who disagrees leaves? Who will be left?"

A sharp knock sounded on the door of the office. Thomas placed his cap on his head and stood as Elisa's voice called, "Papa?"

"One moment Elisa," Theo called. Then he lowered his voice and directed Thomas to the back door. "You came in that way." He extended his hand. "It is not likely that we will meet again soon, Thomas."

"May I not see her?" Thomas looked pained and eager.

Lindheim shook his head slowly from side to side. "For what purpose? She is over you now. So, goodbye, Thomas von Kleistmann." His firm handshake guided the young man to the door that led out through the storage room and down a narrow flight of stairs into an alley.

Theo Lindheim's cheerfulness was forced as Elisa entered the office.

She could sense his uneasiness, and perhaps he was aware of hers.

"Who was here, Papa?" she asked, glancing toward the back door.

"No one. An errand boy." He brushed aside her question at the same moment he slipped the long white envelope into the pocket of his overcoat. "We should hurry now, Elisa. Our train leaves in three hours. We have to close up the house."

"There is not so much to do." Elisa was puzzled by his brusqueness. He seemed too eager to escape the store; always before he had left reluctantly. Perhaps the words of the tailor had been right. Perhaps there was no safety left even for Theo Lindheim in Berlin. She did not dare repeat old Grynspan's words to her father, but a knot of unexplained fear gripped her stomach. She suddenly felt the urge to lock the door behind her. "Papa?" She questioned his preoccupied stare at a family portrait that hung on the wall behind his desk. In the photograph Elisa and her two younger brothers sat beside their mother as Theo stood with his hands on his wife's delicate shoulders.

Theo turned to his daughter after a moment. "When you walked in tonight," he said almost wistfully, "I thought how very much you look like your mother."

Tall and slender, his wife Anna carried herself with the aristocratic bearing of her vocation. She had been a young and promising concert pianist when Theo had first met her. Elisa had grown up hearing the story of how Theo Lindheim had waited at the stage door of the concert hall for Anna Koenig after her performance as soloist for Schumann's Concerto in A minor. He had been a young pilot in the Kaiser's army on leave for a week in Vienna. While the other men in his squadron had spent their time in the cabarets and brothels of the city, he had returned each night to listen to Anna perform. And he had fallen hopelessly in love.

Now, he reached up impulsively and took their family portrait from the wall. He held it for a moment as though trying to capture the carefree emotions of those days. Then he frowned and looked at Elisa. He could not conceal the desperate worry in his eyes.

"We cannot miss our train," he said slowly. "Anna and the boys will be waiting for us in Austria, yes?" He slipped the photograph into his briefcase; with that gesture, Elisa knew that he was indeed saying goodbye to Berlin and everything he had worked for. She stared hard at him.

"Please, Papa." Her voice was hoarse and seemed far away. "Please, we should hurry." Did he feel the same ominous sense of desperation that she now felt?

He clutched her arm and guided her quickly out the back door and through the storeroom. Crates and boxes towered over them, and Elisa felt the same unreasonable fear that had come to her as a child when she played hide-and-seek in this same dark room. Her breath came quickly and her mouth felt dry. Still, his footsteps were deliberate and firm. She wanted to run down the rickety wooden steps to where her father's cherished old BMW waited. He set the pace, and once the cold night air washed over them, he began to talk in calm and everyday conversation.

"And does the professor say that you will be with the symphony soon?" He smiled at her and held tightly to her arm as they descended the steep stairway.

"I . . . he is encouraging." This conversation was for the ears of someone else. Someone listening from the deep shadows of the alleyway. Elisa cleared her throat. "Of course, at my age, Mother was already performing onstage in Berlin and Vienna." She hoped that her words sounded casual.

"Your time will soon come," Theo said. Then he raised his chin slightly as though he was sniffing the wind for an unseen enemy.

Elisa felt herself blanch. Stage fright. The audience was indeed there, watching their performance from the discarded packing crates behind Lindheim's department store. "By spring . . ." Her voice faltered. Theo squeezed her arm in encouragement. "By spring the professor hopes I will be ready for an audition."

"Good. *Good!*" They stepped onto the cobbles of the alley. A few yards and they would be in the car. "Have you decided yet what you will play?"

"I need to talk to Mother about it." Elisa focused on the shiny hood of the car. Raindrops had beaded up and reflected the lights from the main street behind them. Car horns still sounded frantically from all around.

"Mozart, perhaps?"

"So common in Vienna now days. Perhaps something by Schumann. Or Grieg." She felt teardrops hot behind her eyelids. Her throat constricted, and she hoped her father would ask her no more questions until they were on the Austrian side of the border.

Theo's hands did not tremble as he unlocked the door and tossed Elisa's packages into the backseat. He was so brave, so confident. Was she imagining the threat she now felt? He patted her on the back and she slipped into the cold interior of the BMW. The smell of pipe tobacco and leather mingled together and somehow comforted her. Theo slipped in behind the wheel and started the engine. His profile was tense and his jaw firm as he pulled slowly away from the back of the store. Elisa looked only at him, even though she wanted to search the shadows for some sign of the men she sensed were surely watching their every move. Her heart thumped loudly in her ears until even the blaring traffic seemed distant.

A strange smile was fixed on her father's face as he pulled onto the street. He looked repeatedly into the rearview mirror, and only after they had traveled two blocks did he finally speak to her.

"Well done," he said softly.

"Papa, *who* . . . ?" All pretense of the charade vanished.

"We are Jewish," he answered simply, and his reply defined the *who* of her question, even though it could not answer the *why*.

"Was it them? In the office before I came in? Gestapo?"

"Don't worry." He turned onto a dark sidestreet. Elisa turned around to see if they were being followed. The road behind them was empty. "We should have had you meet us in Austria," he said under his breath.

"No," Elisa responded, feeling a little more brave. "It is better this way. Better that they know I have come home for the holidays as usual. Mama and the boys have gone ahead to the Tyrol. The Gestapo thinks I am a student in Austria. It will be less likely that they will suspect if you cross the frontier with me, Papa. You needed me here this week. You needed me to help you get away."

He looked at her in amazement. No word of this plan had ever come from him, and yet she understood perfectly. The unexpected visit from Thomas von Kleistmann had only been confirmation that time was running out for him here in Berlin. "We have three hours. Three terrible long hours until our train leaves." He seemed grateful for her quick comprehension of the situation. "It will not be safe for us to wait at the train station. The Gestapo swarm on every corner there. I am certain that the house is being watched. Are you strong enough to go home and act as though this is simply a night like any other? Get out your skis for the trip, and—"

"Yes. Yes, Papa. We will open the window a bit, and I will play some Mozart for you . . . and for them as well."

Theo smiled at his daughter. "Yes. You are like Anna," he said proudly. "Like your mother." They passed the towering edifice of Pastor Jacobi's church. Sadness, anger, then resignation passed over Theo's face. "It is best," he said quietly. "Best if we leave. Pastor Jacobi has slipped his head in a noose for us."

"Oh, Papa . . ." Elisa searched the great shadowed building. So many times she and her mother had performed there. So many Christmas concerts had been played within those walls. "Can we ever come home again?"

He did not answer. Gone were the words of comfort that he had offered only last summer when the Olympic games had been held in Germany. The signs had all come down then. Hitler had not wanted the world to know that the main plank of the Nazi platform was that of hatred. For a few short weeks they had all hoped—hoped that the terrible campaign against the Jews of Germany was at an end.

But that, too, had only been a charade. When the flags and banners had been taken down, the signs had reappeared in the shop windows and on the park benches of Berlin. Only a week after the games had ended, Thomas had received his warning. Only three weeks later, Elisa caught a glimpse of him as her train pulled away from the station in Berlin. That image she carried with her for all the lonely months she had spent in Vienna. In the darkest nights when she lay alone in the tiny bedroom of her flat, that image had returned to her—his face anguished with longing, his hand half-raised in a distant, unspoken farewell. She had turned her eyes away from him, as though she had not seen.

The hand he had raised in farewell to her was the same hand he now raised in salute to Hitler. It all seemed so hopeless. Was it possible that the voice that once spoke of love to her now shouted the same terrible slogans she heard over the radio? Could the arms that had held her so gently now grasp others against their will? Again, her mind rebelled at the thought.

"I am glad we are leaving, Papa." she said suddenly angry. "I'm glad to be leaving a place that lets this happen." Then, as the church slipped out of view, she murmured, "What will happen to Pastor Jacobi?"

"He will not leave of his own free will," Theo answered solemnly. "He is a good man. A good son of Germany. There are many, Elisa. We must hope and pray that perhaps—" He did not finish the thought. Everything had gone too far now even for hope to live in Germany. "There are many good men who will not leave."

Elisa put her hand on her father's arm. "And many more who *must* leave, Papa!"

He nodded curtly, and they rode the rest of the way home in silence.

———

The BBC radio broadcast began a sad and stirring rendition of *God Save the King* as King Edward ended his abdication speech. Murphy could imagine that there was not a dry eye in all of Britain. Even his cynical newspaper companions in the Berlin Hotel room sat quietly now. Johnson reached over and snapped off the radio.

"Well," said Timmons. "All for a dame. What do you know!"

"He's taking a lot of people down with him." Johnson sounded angry. "This is more than some guy quitting a job as haberdasher in Macy's, you know. He's turned in a crown, not a top hat."

Murphy nodded, and for the first time since the broadcast began, he turned from the window to face the group. "He's right. This stupid, stupid thing—it's going to mean the end of Winston Churchill's career. They're already looking for a place to string him up."

"Why?" Timmons leaned forward. He was the youngest of the men there and had originally come to Germany to cover the summer Olympic games. Politics were mostly lost on him. "Churchill? You mean the little fat guy that looks like a bulldog? What did he do? Introduce the king to this dame, or something?"

Someone nursing a bottle of Glenlivet swore quietly at the question.

"Don't you read the papers?" Johnson howled and thumped Timmons on the shoulder. "Winston Churchill was the one guy who stood up for ol' Edward. They're great pals, I guess. He'll probably be maid of honor."

A renewed hooting filled the room, releasing some of the tension.

Timmons gave a half smile, still not clear on any of it. "Yeah. I don't get it."

Murphy opened another Coke and sat down beside the confused young reporter. "Let's put it this way, kid," he instructed. "Winston Churchill was the only guy in England who believed the king would come to his senses if he was left alone. Everyone else kept pushing. You don't push a guy when he thinks he's in love, right? So Churchill went against massive public opinion. Unfortunately for all of us, the guy is going to get the axe."

"The axe? So what has that got to do with us?"

The men in the room, most of them drunk by now, exchanged glances, unspoken comments on Timmon's ignorance.

"Timmons"—Murphy's tone was patronizing now—"you never heard of *Arms and the Covenant?*"

Johnson joined in. "Probably the one organization with any backbone left in England. Everyone else is pacifist. Isolationist. *Leave Hitler to his business as long as he doesn't bother us*. You heard of that, Timmons? Meanwhile, the Germans have broken every part of the Versailles Treaty—"

"Like when they rearmed." Murphy said, trying to jog political memories that just weren't there for the kid. "See, after the big war in 1918, the Germans signed an agreement that they wouldn't rearm. They were also supposed to stay out of the Rhineland bordering France."

Timmons nodded vaguely. "Yeah. Yeah."

"So Hitler rearmed. Is still rearming. And, in March, *last* March, Timmons—you remember last March, don't you? German soldiers marched into the Rhineland. The League of Nations did nothing. France and Britain did nothing. Hitler broke the treaty, and nobody did anything. You get it, Timmons?"

Timmons took another drink. "I wasn't here last March," he answered defensively. "I didn't know what was going on."

"Neither did anyone else," Johnson had reached the limit of his patience. "That's the point." He snatched his hat off the table and stalked out of the room, slamming the door behind him.

"What's with him?" Timmons looked hurt.

"Churchill is about the only person in England with his eye on Hitler." Murphy sat back, a wave of depression settling over him. "He was just starting to get a little attention, too. And now this. The House of Commons wants to lynch him. His own people have drifted away. The Arms and the Covenant movement to rearm Britain is up in smoke," he finished wearily.

"All because of a dame." Timmons shook his head slowly from side to side.

A strange little smile fixed on Murphy's face. "Yeah. I'll bet Herr Hitler and his goons are just loving this. Churchill was the one guy who has been begging England to show a little backbone. Now he might as well curl up and die." He held his finger to his temple and pulled an imaginary trigger. "That's all, folks." He looked at Timmons, who was staring back with confused intensity. Several others had drifted off to sleep and were snoring loudly from different parts of the suite. "You understand now, kid?"

"Sort of."

"Okay." Murphy patted him on the back and then got up to look out the window again. The huge red banners flapped like waiting shrouds for Berlin and for the people of Germany—for all of Europe. "Sort of. That's all any of us understand about this place and this people and what's happening here. God, it scares me." His voice had dropped to a whisper. His breath formed a faint mist on the windowpane. Car lights reflected the red of the Nazi flag until the streets and sidewalks seemed wet with fresh blood. Murphy shuddered involuntarily. "Why don't they listen over there? Why don't they believe it?"

"Nobody likes a Jeremiah," Timmons responded with an innocence that displayed more than a glimmer of wisdom. "As long as it don't affect them. Sure. They'll lynch this Churchill guy and make up to Hitler—"

"Not bad for a sports writer," droned someone from the floor behind the sofa.

Murphy let his breath out slowly, not wanting to respond to Timmons. Maybe the kid was right, but Murphy was hoping for another synopsis to the story. He glanced at his watch. "Okay, you lugs. Get out. Get out of here, will you? I've got a train to catch, and you're in my way." He roused them and shoved them out the door like a sheep dog running his flock out of the pen. He had two hours, but those were hours he wanted to spend alone.

The reek of stale cigar and cigarette smoke was almost suffocating. He opened the window and breathed in the fresh cold air. Closing his eyes for a minute, he leaned his head against the window frame and hoped that he was wrong about what he told the kid. Tonight he hoped he had been playing Jeremiah, and that every fear he felt was imagined.

7

Departure

The appearance of the large, dignified Lindheim home on Wilhelm-strasse seemed almost startling to Elisa. The three-story stone house with wide balconies and broad gardens, hedges and lawns trimmed with care—what would become of it when they had gone? Why had it remained the same when everything else in Germany had been so irrevocably altered?

They did not speak as they climbed the front steps. Until the moment her father turned the switch to the lights of the foyer, Elisa had not realized how beautiful her home was. Until then, it had not entered her mind that they were finally and truly leaving the place where she had spent her entire young life. The broad marble stairway that led to the bedrooms glistened in the light. The eight-foot-tall grandfather clock ticked steadily as it had for a hundred years among the Lindheim family. Its silver face shone down on them.

"Did I ever tell you?" Theo Lindheim asked quietly. "My great-grandfather traded a matched pair of horses for the old clock. It was made by the Jewish clockmaker in Prague. Remember? My father always said it would last longer than any of us . . ." His voice trailed off. He tossed his hat onto the walnut sideboard and looked up into the lights of the crystal chandelier like a small child. He looked for words and tried to speak. Elisa pretended not to notice the tears in his eyes. Leah had been right. Everything, *everything* was different now.

"Gather your things," he said at last, as he turned to walk to his study. "Take only what you will need—what you can carry easily."

The inside of his study was lined with the finest volumes, many first edition classics. Over a thousand books towered from floor to ceiling. Of all her father's possessions, he had been most proud of his library. What, of all these precious friends, could he carry into exile with him tonight?

She stood back from the doorway, unwilling to intrude on what must surely be a painful parting from well-loved possessions. He flicked on the small brass reading lamp beside his comfortable red leather chair. For a moment he stood searching the dark oak shelves, skimming the titles. Then he reached up to touch the spines; sliding his fingers along until they hesitated, he stopped on the slim red leather-bound volume of Goethe's *Faust*. Elisa shuddered at her father's grim choice, just as she had trembled when he had read the terrible story of the man who had sold his soul to the devil in exchange for great power.

Theo stroked the cover, then slipped the book into his pocket. Elisa turned and hurried to cover the beautiful furniture in her mother's music room. She did not let herself touch the white ivory keys of Anna Lindheim's grand piano. Her mother had played her farewell of Schumman's piano concerto only two nights before. Elisa had not understood the tears that had trickled down Anna's cheeks that night. Now it was all clear. Too clear. She would carry the sound of her mother's music away with her, and hope that somehow the walls of this great and happy house would remember only songs and laughter of their family. No doubt, when the Nazis learned that they were not coming back, everything would be taken away, just as it had been with other Jewish families. No hands would ever again caress the ivory keys as Anna Lindheim's had done.

Elisa did not turn on the lamp in her bedroom. Soft light from the hall filtered in and reflected on the tiny rosebuds of her wallpaper and the deep, rich, patina of the hand-carved bed and inlaid chest. The furniture had once belonged to her mother when she was a child. Elisa had often lain awake at night and traced the swirl of the walnut burls with her eyes as she imagined young Anna Koenig must have done. She found it comforting that her mother had said her bedtime prayers and dreamed sweet dreams within the safety of these same four corners. *Down quilts, a kiss on the forehead, and a wish for pleasant dreams . . .*

A row of porcelain dolls gazed wide-eyed at Elisa from the shelf above the chest. Dressed in lace and silk, they represented many pleasant hours of her childhood. She would take one—only one, just as her father had chosen one book from his thousand. She would leave the rest. She sat slowly on the edge of the bed and stared back at the dolls. *Who would imagine it could be so hard to choose? I am a grown woman. I have long since stopped playing with dolls. A silly thing to agonize over. To pity the playthings that I will leave behind. They are only things. This is only a place. It is not me, really, or Mama or Papa or the boys.* And yet, it seemed that bits and pieces of her soul remained here within these walls and precious possessions.

Each doll had a name, and Elisa spoke each name in farewell. Perfect curls and unblinking eyes; velvet caps and tiny shoes; lips that still smiled as they had when she was seven years old, scolding her little coterie for some imagined offense. How could Elisa choose one over the other? In the end, she could not. She left them all behind.

Lifting the edge of her white lace curtains, she looked down on the wide street below the house. A block away, two men stood beside a black Mercedes, clearly watching the Lindheim house. Elisa was relieved that she had not turned on the light. A cold wave of fear rushed over her and suddenly, she was no longer filled with regrets for what they must leave behind.

"Papa?" she called softly as she heard Theo's footsteps on the stairs.

He joined her at the window and looked out. "They have been watching us for weeks," Theo said in a hoarse whisper. "That is why we can take nothing with us. Nothing but skis and clothing for a holiday. He let the curtain fall. "We must not even let them see a tear. Not a hint of regret. We are going to Austria to ski. Do you understand?"

Elisa bit her lip and swallowed hard. She nodded, privately embarrassed that she had wasted even a moment of sadness over furniture and playthings from her childhood. "Yes, Papa."

"Go on then. Gather your things. I will watch a moment more."

A moment more, thought Elisa, turning the irony of his words over and over again in her mind. Since 1933, her father had watched and waited. He had watched as the Ten German Commandments became the laws of Nuremburg: *Thou shalt keep thy blood pure. Consider it a crime to soil the noble Aryan blood of the people by mingling it with the Jewish breed. For thou must know that Jewish blood is everlasting, putting the Jewish stamp on body and soul to the farthest generations. . . .*

He had watched as his rights as a citizen were stripped: *Only those who are our fellow Germans shall be citizens of our state. Only those who are of German blood can be regarded as our fellow Germans, regardless of creed. Hence no Jew. . . .*

Only once, in the long recitation of new racial laws, had Elisa seen her father smile. In September of 1935, a swastika flag had been ripped off the SS *Bremen* in New York harbor. Hitler had used the incident to prohibit Jews in Germany from displaying the Nazi flag. On hearing of the prohibition, Theo had laughed out loud and raised his glass in a toast. "To Deutschland," he had said. "Heil Deutschland!" The Nazi flag had never flown at Lindheim's, and now he was certain it never would.

These days a man could claim no other kingdom, creed, or brotherhood, except the doctrine of the Nazi party. Catholics, Protestants and even Freemasons, were denied their German citizenship unless they pledged allegiance to the Nazi party above their personal convictions. Fear and brutality had become the staff by which Germany was ruled. Now, there was nothing left to wait for except the dreaded sound of hobnailed boots on the stairway. And even those who vowed loyalty and remained behind as citizens and members of the party were ultimately denied all rights of citizenship. Somehow in this bargain with the devil, they lost everything, just as Faust had sold his soul.

Elisa finished covering the furniture and returned to the upstairs bed-room where her father sat quietly on the edge of the bed.

"Papa," she said quietly, "everything is ready. I am ready now."

He nodded and turned to her. His face looked almost haunted with grief. He looked down to where the violin case sat beside the door. "One more thing, child," he said. "We should leave our home with music, yes?"

Elisa unlocked the case and pulled the blue silk scarf from the instru-ment. The wood of the Guarnerius glowed in the soft light from the stairs. "What, Papa?" she lifted the instrument to her chin.

"Something happy, I think." He lifted his head. "Mozart. No one plays the first concerto like you can."

"Mozart?" she faltered, lowering the bow.

He had already opened the window slightly for the benefit of the watch-ers. "Yes, Elisa. It has been so long since you have played Mozart in this house."

It was a final, defiant gesture—one which Elisa could not fully un-derstand, and yet she obeyed. She closed her eyes and began to play. The strong voice of Rudy's precious violin reached every corner of the old house and floated out through the open window to where the men waited for some transgression of new German law. She swayed with the sweet, clear melody, playing for her father and the old house, and—for the last time—for Berlin.

Her eyes still closed, she felt a wash of cold air on her face as Theo opened the window even wider. She was no longer afraid. Somehow the music had carried her fears away. When she finished and opened her eyes, her father was smiling. He stood with his back to the window. "Do you think they even imagine what they are losing, dear Elisa?"

She returned his smile and replaced the violin in the case. "Musicians. Doctors. Professors. No, Papa. They will only search us and make certain we carry away nothing in our pockets."

He closed the window. "You may still play Mozart openly in Austria. They will not be able to take that away from us."

Suddenly she wanted to cry. Reaching out her arms to her father, she held tightly to him like a little girl afraid of the dark. "No, Papa," she whispered. "We take our souls with us. They cannot have our souls."

————

Theo paid all the household accounts for a full two months in advance. It would give them time, he reasoned, before the Gestapo figured out that they were not coming back.

Elisa talked excitedly about snow conditions and the coming holiday as they loaded the car. It was as though the two men were not across the street watching every move. The truth was that Elisa would have wept openly when the key turned in the door the final time had it not been for the presence of the Gestapo.

The drive to the train station was only a matter of minutes, but the obvious glare of headlights behind them made it seem much longer. *Why were they being followed if we are not also going to be arrested?* Elisa wondered. Was it simply that the hounds had been sent to nip at their heels and make certain that Lindheim the Jew was really leaving? Every law that had been passed over the last two years had driven Jews by the thousands into exile, forcing them to leave their life savings and businesses behind. They were luckier than the thousands who now languished in the concentration camps for "political" crimes. Release of loved ones from the camp was often a matter of paying ransom in the form of fines to officials of the S.S. and Gestapo, and arrests were often repeated within a matter of days.

When men like Pastor Jacobi and Pastor Niemöller spoke out against such practices, they too were detained and harassed and threatened. The Nazi Reich had declared war against the church in Germany. Those churchmen who were stripped of their rights as clergymen were slowly being replaced by those who preached what the government commanded. A man like Jacobi would never abandon his flock of his own free will, Elisa knew, and it was simply a matter of time before he would also be absorbed into the slowly grinding wheels of the concentration camps.

Carting luggage and skis, Theo Lindheim and his daughter made their way through the great arched portals of the Berlin train depot. Huge engines hissed and thrummed impatiently at the loading platforms. Theo had been right: at every pillar stood an official of the S.S. or the Gestapo. The two men who had followed them from the house were simply immersed in the tide of uniformed men who flooded the station. It seemed to Elisa that there were more officials than passengers in the cavernous waiting room. She fixed a smile on her lips, although inside she was cold with apprehension.

"Come on." Theo led her to a bench and placed luggage and skis beside a marble pillar. He glanced at his watch. "A few minutes until boarding."

Elisa wished they had waited until the last minute before they had arrived. This moment seemed worse than all the rest. Worse than the store. Worse than the house. But she nodded, still smiling and sat down. Theo remained beside the luggage.

Within a few seconds, a small man walked toward them. He seemed almost lost beneath the flapping of a heavy coat. Elisa did not look directly at him as he stood to one side of her and cleared his throat. Was he one of the men who had followed them from the house?

"Bitte," he said quietly.

Elisa glanced at him absently as if to ask, *Me?*

He smiled a quick, too-polite smile and extended his hand. "Your passport, Fraülein?"

Theo had already stepped between them. He towered over the unctuous little man. "Your reason for demanding my daughter's passport?" He was smiling and courteous, but firm.

"She is your daughter, is she not, Herr Lindheim?" he asked, undaunted by Theo's size. Yes, he was the man from the house.

"So what?"

"A Jewess, yes?"

Theo's eyes narrowed. "A German."

The little man shrugged. "A matter of interpretation these days, Herr Lindheim." He had obviously talked with Theo before. He jerked his thumb toward a small sign that was on the end of the bench. *No Jews Allowed.* "The law." He smiled more broadly.

Elisa stood up as though she had been burned. Her face flushed red. In all her time in Austria she had not seen these odious signs on public benches. In the few days she had been in Berlin, she had ignored them. No one had asked. But people were being arrested for smaller offenses than this. "I have been abroad," she said in explanation.

"One can be arrested for such ignorance," the man said. "The law is the law and we must enforce infractions. As an example, you see?"

Theo simply stared down at him as though he could not believe the words.

Elisa licked her lips and swallowed hard. She looked up at her father, then stepped farther away from the bench.

"She looks quite Aryan, Herr Lindheim." The little man leered at her. "Are you certain she is your daughter? Perhaps the milkman stopped in while you were away? A little visit with your wife from an Aryan milkman and here is the result—"

Theo did not reply. The color was deep on his cheeks. Elisa felt tears of fear and shame sting her eyes. She prayed her father would not respond to this brutal sport. She put her hand on her father's clenched fist. "Papa!" she whispered, knowing that if Theo struck the Gestapo agent, it would mean the end. It was the law. A Jew striking an Aryan meant execution.

The little man showed his teeth again. "Ah well, even if she is not your daughter, she is still *half*-Jewish. It is still against the law for her to sit on public benches."

Theo did not bother to correct the little man concerning his daughter's racial heritage. Elisa also kept quiet, and the agent pulled out a small leather notebook. He flipped open the pages and frowned, as though he was searching an official record. "And she has done so several times in the last few days, I'm afraid. Here. Yes. On the seventh near Tiergarten. And tonight she rode in a taxi—"

Elisa felt as though she would faint. The world spun around her and she looked at the passengers who hurried past. They all looked embarrassed by the inquisition; they all looked afraid. "I did not think . . . the law was not in effect when I left."

Theo put his hand up to silence her. "What do you want?" His voice

was weary. "Why have you confronted us here tonight? You know where
we are going, and why." He pulled out his passport and the special permission papers that had been granted to him as a Jew so that he could
leave Germany for two weeks.

"Perhaps you should realize, Herr Lindheim . . ." The ratty little man
enjoyed his work, and Elisa hated him for his power. "There are a few
men like you protected by your war record and by the memory of President
von Hindenburg. Out of respect to him, the Führer overlooks the fact that
you are Jews, yes? But von Hindenburg has been dead for two years, Herr
Lindheim. And the law is still the law." He turned his eyes on Elisa. "Maybe
it would not be so bad for you to stay with us a few weeks. To guarantee
your father's return. Perhaps you would learn to respect your betters." He
spoke in a sweet and patronizing tone that sickened Elisa.

She longed to sit down on the forbidden bench. "Am I under arrest?"
She stepped nearer to him and matched his looks with fierce eyes.

The agent shrugged again. His grin faltered just a bit, and Theo saw
his motive. He was acting on his own initiative in this matter; he wanted
money, not Elisa.

"There is a fine, I believe," Theo said in a hushed tone. His anger and
disdain was undisguised.

The smile returned. Lindheim had gotten the message. "A thousand
reichsmarks."

"I don't have that much. It is against the law to take so much out of
the country as a Jew. Have you forgotten?"

"Everyone knows you always take more than that."

"Only if one is leaving permanently." Theo sounded impatient as the
loudspeakers blared out the boarding call for their train.

"You can leave tomorrow, then," said the little man. "One day, more
or less—"

"Perhaps five hundred? And a bank draft for the rest when I come
back? I am certain you will still be on the corner of Wilhelmstrasse."

Elisa had the distinct impression that this exchange had taken place
more than once between her father and this little man—perhaps many
times, over many trivial issues.

"It would be wise if I were to search your luggage" came the reply.

"You know I am a man of my word, Herr Müller."

Elisa was surprised that her father used the man's name. Müller
nudged Elisa's suitcase with the toe of his shoe.

"Open," he said to Elisa. Then he gave the violin case a kick that sent
it toppling from the heap.

She resisted the urge to cry out, even though the instrument was valued
at many times more than they were permitted to take from the borders of
Germany. Obediently, she knelt and opened her bag. Herr Müller reached
down and in one motion held up the case and dumped out its contents.
Ski clothes, sweaters, bras, and panties that had been packed so neatly

fell in a jumbled mess onto the tiled floor. Elisa looked away as Müller held up a bra and laughed. It was then that she noticed another man: tall and lanky with dark brown hair and a distinct expression of anger on his young face. He grimaced slightly and looked down as she caught his frank and open stare. He sighed and shook his head thoughtfully for a moment as he took out a note pad and strode to where Müller pawed through Elisa's clothes.

Another Gestapo man? Elisa stayed beside her bag. She was humiliated but defiant as Müller commented on every article of clothing. Her father could do nothing.

The newcomer cleared his throat when Müller remarked on the lace of Elisa's bra. "Typical of a Jewess. German women wear plain wool and cotton. Decadent. Ridiculous extravagance."

"Arresting these people for underwear violations?" asked the tall young man. "A new Reichstag law? Something about what women should wear?" He had an American accent and a slight smile curved his lips when Müller looked up, startled at his interruption. A dozen other people hurried by as though nothing were happening.

"Gestapo business!" Müller snapped. Then he added with disdain, "Not the business of foreigners. Englishman."

"American," corrected the young intruder. "And you're wrong. It *is* my business. I am a news reporter. You want to see my press card?" He extended his wallet. Müller had turned his attention on him now, but did not even bother to inspect his credentials.

"So? What has this to do with you? Or your newspaper?"

"We're always interested in new laws in Germany. I mean, suppose some American couple came here to honeymoon and the wife got arrested on violation of lace statutes?" He shrugged as though he were perfectly serious. "That is the material for international incidents."

"Get out of here before I arrest you also!" Müller hissed.

The newsman had already extended his hand to Elisa. "John Murphy." He introduced himself as though he were meeting her at the theater. "*The New York Times*."

She nodded. "Elisa Lindheim. And my father, Theo Lindheim."

John shook his hand. "*The* Theo Lindheim, I presume?"

Theo looked embarrassed, uneasy. "Simply Theo Lindheim."

Murphy began to jot notes. He asked Müller for his name. Müller raised his chin angrily. "Also none of your business. They have violated an ordinance," he added defensively. "Now, if you will leave me to it."

Murphy frowned thoughtfully. "Violation of ordinance." He wrote each word down. "Which one?" He pointed to the clothes. "Something, uh . . ." He searched for words. "You see," he said, changing the subject, "I have been asked to write a little piece on everyday life in Germany. I've seen an unusual number of arrests lately. This is as good as any. Beautiful young woman, wife of Theo Lindheim, arrested. You see? It makes good copy. She's Aryan and he's Jewish?"

Elisa did not correct him. She began to gather her things with the hope that Müller would somehow be distracted by this brash American journalist. She did not care if he thought she was Theo's wife. She would only be happy if they could catch their waiting train.

"She is his *daughter*," Müller spat. "And no more in Germany will you see Jewish industrialists with beautiful German women!" He narrowed his eyes as though he were pronouncing the end of all such terrible relationships.

"Yes. I forgot." Murphy stuck out his lower lip. "Another law." He turned to Theo. "So what are you in trouble for?"

"My daughter sat on a bench," Theo said. He raised an eyebrow and a flicker of understanding passed between the two men.

Murphy scribbled in his notebook: *Sat on bench*.

Müller stepped between them. "If you interfere, you will also be arrested."

Murphy held up his hands innocently. "Don't let me stop you. I'm just out for a story, see?" He stepped back and stood with his pencil poised. "It is all yours," he said. "Spell your name for me."

Müller stood blinking at him. He had missed his opportunity for the five-hundred-mark bribe. He could not take a single mark while this American observed. But Lindheim would be back, and they would settle the issue of violations then. "Herr Lindheim," he said politely, "please accept this warning. The law is the law. There is little we can do but enforce it. This time since your daughter"—he looked at Elisa—"has been abroad, we will be lenient."

Murphy smiled benignly and nodded as he wrote the word *lenient* and underlined it. "Yes. Very good."

"You must, however, respect the law of National Socialist Germany if you are to be welcome here as our guest." Müller's face showed that he feared he had gone too far with those words. "Germany is fair with everyone who obeys her laws and statutes . . ."

The announcement sounded again on the loudspeaker. "May we go, Herr Müller?" asked Theo.

"*Müller*," scribbled Murphy. "Good show, Herr Müller. You make a good impression for the Fatherland."

Müller smiled in relief. He nodded abruptly. "Remember what I have said, Herr Lindheim. Yes, you must catch your train."

Murphy took over the conversation as Elisa and Theo scrambled to repack her scattered possessions. Müller did not even seem to notice as they struggled off with their arms loaded with gear. She heard Müller proclaim "Heil Hitler!" at the end of the interview.

Murphy responded with, "Twenty-three skidoo!"

Elisa's heart was still pounding as they rushed toward their compartment. The door seemed very far away at the end of a distant tunnel. Voices and faces were a jumbled blur of noise and light. Now she was not sorry to leave Berlin, even if it was forever. Only after the train was hours from the station did she think again of the brash young American who had certainly rescued them.

8

The Dragon's Prey

Within a few short days, Wilhelm and Dieter Linder had learned to laugh all over again. From early morning until the last stubborn rays of sunlight disappeared, they skied on the slopes of the Kitzbühel with the two youngest Wattenbarger brothers. Wilhelm had grown quite fond of seventeen-year-old Gretchen Wattenbarger, and cast longing looks in her direction over meals with the family. Herr Wattenbarger had taught them the finer points of milking cows and churning butter, and they had made themselves useful wading through muck in their tall Wellington boots. What the Wattenbarger children considered drudgery, Wilhelm and Dieter attacked with an enthusiasm born of too many long months cooped up indoors in hostile Berlin. Mucking out stalls was a delight to them. Herr Wattenbarger used their work as an example to hold up to Friedrich and Helmut, the youngest of his four sons.

Franz joined in the fun each evening, teaching the boys to play the card game of Watten. Otto, however, simply ate his meal in silence and then retreated to the privacy of the small farm hut across the pasture. Even the Linder boys frowned when they looked at Otto. There was something serious and unhappy about Otto's manner; his entrance into a room would cause their laughter to fall silent.

Anna Linder was still polite and correct in her conversation, but unlike her sons, the worry had not left her face or her voice when she spoke. Wilhelm and Dieter had stopped being so careful, but she remained cautious and veiled in her conversations. She laughed at the antics of the children and, Franz thought, there was a genuine happiness that her sons were enjoying themselves after what must have been a difficult time. But her laughter often stopped before anyone else's. She looked away, and Franz could almost read her thoughts. *Yes. She is wondering about her husband, her daughter.*

One morning in the kitchen Franz had asked his mother if she noticed anything different about the Linders. Frau Wattenbarger had nodded and answered in a whisper, "Frau Linder is worried, Franz. That much is plain." Later, in the barn she had said, "Unless this fellow Hitler is stopped, there will be a million more wives and mothers who carry secrets and hide their fears from strangers. Yes, we may see many more faces like Anna Linder's. Beautiful, and very, very sad."

Frau Anna Linder was indeed very beautiful, Franz thought, observing the elegance with which she moved. And somehow her sadness made her seem even more attractive. She carried the grace of Vienna with her. Franz noticed that his father was rigidly proper and polite with her, as though he were addressing a baroness. Perhaps the woman truly was of the aristocracy. Many of the nobles had been driven from Germany by the regime of the obnoxious little paperhanger in the Chancellery.

Franz enjoyed letting his imagination play on the mysterious circumstances of their guests. And lately, he had found himself almost obsessed with wondering about Elisa Linder, the daughter of whom Frau Linder spoke so often.

"A musician in Vienna . . . she plays the violin with the symphony . . . Is she beautiful? Why yes, yes. She is quite beautiful I think. . . ."

"And she knows everything!" Wilhelm had added. *"Make her sleep in the barn, Frau Wattenbarger!"*

Only this morning, Frau Linder had shown Franz a snapshot of Elisa. *"Taken three years ago beside the Spree River . . . "* she had said. Immediately she caught herself, but she saw in his eyes that he knew the picture had been taken in Berlin! Before she had said it, he *knew!* As though caught in a terrible secret, she quickly put away the photograph.

"Yes, she is a pretty girl," Franz had said, and Frau Linder had scurried off to air the bedding or straighten the bedroom. Elisa Linder was pretty, Franz thought, but not really so remarkable. In the photograph she had squinted into the sun and seemed almost gangly in her appearance. The daughter was not nearly so beautiful as the mother.

Tonight, as Franz hitched up the mare for the ride into the village, he felt a sense of excitement. Frau Anna would ride with him, and together they would pick up her daughter and Herr Theo Linder. Franz was interested to see what kind of a man had so totally captured the heart of a woman like Frau Anna.

He pulled the sleigh around to the front door and held the mare steady as Anna emerged from the warmth of the farmhouse. For the first time since she had come here, there was a lightness, an excitement about her that made her seem no more than thirty. The lines of worry around her eyes were gone. She stepped out and inhaled deeply, as though savoring the clear air and anticipating her reunion with the man she loved.

Franz stared hard at her, and in spite of himself, he felt stirring. *Yes, she is beautiful. Beautiful and young.* "You are happy, Frau Anna?" He looked away and pretended to adjust the bridle.

"Yes, Franz. It has been difficult to be here in such a beautiful place and have no one to share it with."

He looked hard at her, afraid that she would see the thought that played in his mind. "Yes," he responded as her smile faded. "I know what you mean."

She looked thoughtful, standing with her hand on the seat of the sleigh. "Very soon"—she seemed amused by his frank stare and now spoke to him as if he were a small boy—"*quite* soon, my husband and I will have our twenty-fifth anniversary. One gets accustomed to sharing beautiful things with someone after twenty-five years."

Franz blushed in spite of himself. He leaned down absently as though he were checking the bit. "You must have married quite young," he said. She *had* read his thoughts.

"Twenty." She stepped into the sleigh with dignity.

He cleared his throat, now doubly embarrassed as he calculated her age. "I would have thought you married at nine or ten," he laughed, and she laughed with him. "Your husband is lucky to have a wife so beautiful." The compliment was sincere, and he wondered again about what sort of man could win such a prize.

Suddenly she sounded quite young as well. "You think so, Franz?" she asked eagerly. "I want to look as fresh as the mountains tonight."

This was the first moment that Frau Anna had shown her heart in any way. Gone was the veil of secrecy. Franz could see that there was something in the love this woman had for her husband that somehow enhanced her beauty. "Good wine ages well," Franz said quietly, and she laughed again as the sleigh started into motion with a jerk.

———

John Murphy did not sleep as the train clattered slowly across the dark countryside of Germany. Endless searches and unexplained delays had put the schedule back by several hours. Now he doubted that they would cross the border into Austria before daybreak.

At every whistle stop along the way, men in uniform and officials in gray trench coats and high boots had gotten on and off the train. Murphy had watched each platform in dread that he might see Theo Lindheim and his daughter being led away in handcuffs. Somehow, his intervention in Berlin had given him a sense of responsibility. He was angry with himself that he couldn't simply leave it alone now that they were on the train. This small, unreasonable anxiety for the welfare of total strangers was costing him a night's sleep.

He reached up and switched off the light, then pulled his hat low over his eyes in an attempt to rest. Moments later he tossed his hat angrily onto the empty seat beside him and stared out the window into the darkness once again. Tiny villages and silent farmhouses slid by until at last the train slowed and rattled into Munich.

The inevitable Gestapo agents stood waiting on the platform just as they had on every platform in every village in the country. *Don't these guys sleep?* Murphy wondered, rubbing a hand over his unshaven face.

The train had not come to a complete stop before the officials had swung up into a car. Murphy could hear them banging against the doors of compartments, shouting orders, and searching weary passengers.

"We have word there are smugglers on board," a harried voice called to a conductor. "Open by order of—"

Murphy rolled his eyes and jammed his hat down on his head as someone pounded on his door.

"Keep your shirt on," he mumbled, pulling the door open and reaching for his papers with one practiced move.

He was met by a small man, remarkably like Herr Müller who had harassed the Lindheims at the Berlin station.

"Your papers, bitte." The man held out his hand in an almost effeminate manner.

"Does the Nazi government have some kind of factory or something? Turns out little Gestapo agents? You all look alike." He spoke in English as he gave his papers to the man.

"I do not speak English, Herr Murphy." The man scanned the forms. "American, I see. A reporter." He exhaled loudly. "Your destination?"

"Berchtesgaden."

The agent's eyebrows went up slightly. "Oh? Official business?"

"You might say that. An appointment with Herr von Ribbentrop. Possibly a conversation with the Führer." He could not resist the temptation to name drop.

The man's hands began to tremble. "Ja? The Führer?" He handed Murphy back his papers without further questions.

"Right. I was supposed to be there hours ago, but the train keeps getting delayed." He frowned angrily at the sound of luggage being tossed out into the hall. "I'll have a word with Herr Hitler about German trains, you can count on it."

"We have orders to—" The man looked genuinely frightened.

"Ja. I know all about it. I have heard it all night." More fists crashed against doors as he spoke. "You know, in Italy Mussolini has made all the trains run on time. Your Reich could take a lesson." Murphy scowled and leaned close to the agent's face. "So. What is your name?"

The Gestapo agent turned on his heel and stomped down the corridor, shouting at his comrades, "We have an important official on board! Finish up!"

Murphy stepped out into the corridor and stood against the doorjamb to watch the retreat. A tall officer bearing the jagged insignia of an S.S. officer hurried past, then stopped to stare back at Murphy. "And who do you think you are? Why are you watching?"

"I am the important American official," Murphy said evenly. "I have an appointment with the Führer."

The soldier's eyes grew wide with astonishment; then he scurried away after the little Gestapo man. He stepped over a pile of clothes that had been dumped out of a suitcase into the corridor; with one final glance back at Murphy, he vanished into the next car. A moment later the train lurched once and rattled out of the vast Munich train station. Murphy could hear the sound of muffled sobs from the compartment across from his. He wondered if the voice was that of Elisa Lindheim. Without thinking, he raised his hand and knocked gently on the door. A fat, bald man of about fifty answered. He stared angrily up at Murphy. "Ja?" he demanded, pulling his bathrobe tight around his bulging middle. A gray-haired woman with sagging cheeks and red swollen eyes sobbed behind him. She did not seem to notice Murphy.

He blushed and stepped back. "Wrong . . . pardon me. Bitte!" He doffed his hat and struck off down the corridor, stopping only when he reached the clothes strewn in front of compartment 7A. *Delicate stuff. Lace underwear.* He had seen it all before. *My God, did they take her off the train?* He snatched his hat from his head and stood staring dumbly at the belongings of Elisa Lindheim. He knelt impulsively as though to gather them up, his sense of failure and responsibility heavy on his mind. *While I was playing the wise guy, they got her off the train.* Shaking his head, he picked up a handful of clothing. Just then, the door to 7A opened and he was suddenly eye level with a gorgeous set of legs that curved gracefully upward into a blue satin dressing gown.

"Oh—it's you again!" Elisa exclaimed, and for an instant Murphy thought she would slam the door on his face.

"I recognized your stuff." He thrust the clothes into her arms and stepped back, feeling guilty somehow.

"Every Gestapo agent in Germany recognizes my things." She was angry, but not at him. "They seem to be drawn to women's lingerie." She stooped to gather her belongings, and he bent to help her. "*No!* Please!" Now she was the one embarrassed. "I can do this myself." Her voice cracked slightly as though she might cry.

"Not great representatives of the male race, are they?" He tried to sound sympathetic, but instead stammered in his clumsy effort to comfort. "I . . . uh . . . hope you are all right, Miss Lindheim."

She did not reply or even look up at him. Her soft golden hair tumbled down over her shoulders and hid her face from him as she piled her clothes back into the open suitcase behind her.

"Where is your father?" he asked after a painful silence.

She continued to work mutely.

"Miss Lindheim?" His question was more gentle, probing her for a reply. A sense of dread filled him once again. "Where is Herr Lindheim?"

At that, her shoulders sagged and she ran a hand through her hair.

She remained motionless on the floor until at last she looked up with a tear-stained face. "They took him." The words were barely audible.

"Took him?" He knelt beside her. "Why? What did they say? Why?"

"Questions." She wiped her eyes with a nightgown. "That's all they said. *Questions!*"

It was nearly two A.M. For an hour Murphy sat across from Elisa and listened as she recited the events that had led to her father's arrest.

Murphy felt guilty. Guilty for not paying better attention during the last inspection, and equally guilty because in spite of himself he could not help noticing the slim, delicate beauty of the woman who seemed to trust him so completely. He could not help but wonder if he would have been so eager to reach across and touch her hand if she had been homely and ragged.

"They said . . ." She paused and groped for words. "They told him they had to ask him about some contributions he had made to a Zionist organization."

"He is a Zionist?"

Elisa shook her head. "I don't know." She spread her hands helplessly. "I *don't* know! In these times . . . lately . . . there have been so many people who have come to him for help. Mother said the stream was endless."

"Why didn't he leave sooner?"

Elisa leveled her gaze at him as though the question was insulting. "He is a loyal German, Herr Murphy."

He looked away. "Of course. I wasn't questioning that. He's just the sort of man the Nazis hate most. Last week I read a policy release from the S.S. They are more favorably inclined toward Zionists than toward assimilated Jews. Himmler suggests that Jews be allowed to emigrate to Palestine because then all the trouble will be in one spot." He looked at her for a reaction. Her face was set and no emotion showed in her eyes. "He says that the Germans will be sure to catch up with the Zionists in Palestine."

"My father is not particularly political, Herr Murphy. He simply remained silent and helped as best he could."

Murphy found himself staring at the graceful curve of her neck and the red mark on her jawline. She raised her hand self-consciously to touch it. "That is all I know. I have been in Vienna—in Austria—for nearly three years. I am only home on holidays, and each time I come back it is worse. Much worse. It is not Germany anymore."

"And Austria?"

"When Hitler sent his Nazi gangsters to murder Chancellor Dollfuss in Vienna, I was near enough to hear the shots. That was two years ago, Herr Murphy. Surely you know that the Austrian government of Chancellor

Schuschnigg is anti-Nazi. Austria and Italy have a treaty against German aggression. We have nothing to fear in Austria."

"There are plenty of Nazis in Austria, Fraülein."

"Yes. In prison with the assassins of Dollfuss."

"There are still plenty of anti-Semites running around. Nazi or no." The woman was obviously a political infant. She had no idea of the undercurrents rippling just beneath the surface in Austria. As for the pact with Italy, Murphy did not explain to her the purpose of his visit to Hitler's mountain retreat in Berchtesgaden. The reporter had little doubt that Mussolini was soon to strike some bargain with Hitler that would pose a grave threat to Italy's treaty with Austria. And hundreds of Nazis in Vienna had been given amnesty after Hitler had guaranteed that Germany would not interfere with Austrian government. This agreement between Hitler and Schuschnigg was already being violated.

"My heritage is not known in Austria, Herr Murphy," she said quietly. "And I do not intend to ever cross the border into Germany again."

False identification papers are expensive, Murphy thought, *but with enough cash they are available. No doubt Theo Lindheim took care of this small detail for his family.* Murphy only hoped that the man had not done it too late to help himself. "Your passports are Austrian, then?" He frowned. "Why did you use your German papers tonight? They are plainly marked that you are Jewish and aliens at that."

"Herr Murphy"—her tone was patronizing—"surely you must know the penalty for use of false identification papers in the Reich. We have been watched for months. Watched all the way from the train station in Berlin, I am certain. Even after you helped us. The Gestapo knows who I am even now. I can use only my German identification while I am on this side of the border or I will suddenly wake up in a concentration camp."

He nodded, still concerned about the Austrian papers. It was only a matter of time before the Nazi foothold in Vienna became a broad highway to power. "Why did your father choose Austrian papers?" he asked again.

She sighed and brushed her hair back. "My papers are not Austrian," she said. "We are not so naive as that. Since the murder of Chancellor Dollfuss in 1934, we have all had documents from . . . a safer place than Austria. A place where the Nazis will never have power."

She had not given him the details, but he was relieved for her all the same. "I don't believe the Gestapo will hold your father long." Murphy reached across and took her hand in his.

Her eyes searched his face, almost pleading. "No one knows what I have just told you, Herr Murphy. I did not know for certain until tonight that my father was planning on leaving Germany permanently. Mama and the boys left a few days ago. Papa thought it would be safer if we left at different times. He wanted to make certain that they were safely across the border, you see."

"And what about you?"

"I am registered as a student in Vienna. That has been the case for several years. The Nazis do not trouble themselves with me—not usually. Papa thought it would seem more natural if he traveled with me. But they were watching anyway; they knew where Theo Lindheim was all along." Her face was filled with grief and worry. "What will they do with him, Herr Murphy? Why have they followed him so far and then—" Her voice broke, and she covered her face with her hands. "I wanted to go with him. When they took him away, I asked to go, but he would not allow it. Please, Herr Murphy, you are American. Can you do something? Will you make inquiries after him?"

"Sure." He grimaced as she began to weep softly. "Sure, I can ask around if he isn't released in a few days." He knew in reality that there was little he could do. When it came to matters of arrest and detention, the Nazis were clear that they resented any sort of interference. He had already brought himself to their attention and would undoubtedly hear about it. "If this is only a matter of paying a fine—"

"Ransom," she corrected bitterly.

"If they don't suspect that he is leaving the country permanently—"

"If they hold him longer than two weeks, my mother and brothers will have to return to Berlin. The *Ausweis* is valid for only two weeks."

Outside in the corridor, the porter called, *"Next stop Berchtesgaden!"*

"My stop," he said, his voice betraying the concern he felt for her safety. This was the final stop before the train crossed the border into Austria. Would the Gestapo also arrest Elisa between Berchtesgaden and Salzburg?

"Yes. Your stop." She brushed away a tear and raised her chin as if to say she could manage. Outside in the station, the platform was cluttered with uniformed S.S. soldiers. Nearly all of them wore the insignia of the special Adolf Hitler Corps.

Murphy looked first at the soldiers and then at Elisa, then back to the loading platform again. He made no move to return to his compartment to gather his luggage. "Good grief," he muttered. "Don't these guys sleep?"

His remark was in English, which Elisa understood readily. She answered with a slight British accent. "No, Mister Murphy. The devil never sleeps."

Somehow her answer in English convinced him that he must not leave her to cross the border alone. "You speak English." He sounded surprised and pleased.

"A bit. Father thought it might be useful. It is a language not unlike German." She glanced toward a group of officers standing together beside the door into the tiny station. "Unfortunately, the similarities between two peoples stop there. One of the reasons Hitler hates the Jewish people so desperately, you know."

Murphy looked puzzled.

"Berchtesgaden! All off for Berchtesgaden!" The porter called.

"Yes. Herr Hitler dislikes it that we can live anywhere. People without a home. At home in any nation." She smiled sadly, then lapsed into her native tongue. "You should go now." She looked pained. "Danke." She extended her hand; he took it, but remained seated.

"I'm going to cross the frontier with you," he shrugged. "I can catch the next train back from Salzburg."

Elisa did not take her hand away. She bit her lip and nodded hesitantly, not attempting to dissuade him. "Danke."

————

Murphy had always been fascinated by the fact that Hitler had chosen Berchtesgaden as his private mountain retreat. The tiny mountain village was located on a spur of German land that jutted into Austria and over-looked the Austrian city of Salzburg far below. It was common knowledge that Himmler had assigned a special S.S. corps to construct a fortress in the mountains for the Führer, which would be hewn from solid stone and accessible only through a shaft that rose to the peak.

Eagle's Nest, the Nazis called the place, but privately men whispered the words *Dragon's Lair*. And so it seemed to Murphy. The Dragon watched among the crags overlooking little Austria. Below him in the towns and villages, the Austrians felt his presence. Among them were those who were committed to the swastika flag flying over their land as well as Germany. Hitler's Berchtesgaden retreat had become a symbol of the po-litical drama quietly taking place from Vienna to the mountains of the Tyrol.

When Murphy stepped off the train in Salzburg, he could not help but notice the difference between the people of Austria and their aggressive neighbors. In Salzburg, men wore the traditional waist-length coats and knee breeches of their ancestors. There were a few business suits among the crowd, but those were mostly foreigners.

Most obvious was the absence of military uniforms. Yet nearly every Austrian wore the red-and-white striped armband indicating loyalty to the government of Chancellor Schuschnigg's Catholic party.

Elisa held tightly to Rudy's violin as a porter managed the rest of her luggage. The train from Berlin would travel on to Vienna, and she would make the short connection into the Tyrol from Salzburg. Murphy watched her when she was unaware. Without the presence of her father, she seemed very much like a lost child. Again and again she lifted her eyes up toward the mountains. To Germany. Toward the *Dragon's Lair*. Murphy could only imagine what she felt after the ordeal of the night's passage and the arrest of Theo Lindheim.

She sat quietly on an oak bench inside the quaint Salzburg depot. Against a pillar, her father's skis were propped beside hers. Murphy bought her coffee and sat beside her until the call for Innsbruck and the Tyrol was made.

"Well," she said shyly, "I don't know how to thank you. I cannot imagine what I would have done if you hadn't come along."

"I'll ask about your father," he said again. Suddenly he did not want to let her go—or he wanted to go with her. "How can I get in touch with you again?"

"*All aboard!*" shouted the conductor, and they moved forward, wrestling the skis onto the train.

"If you are ever in Vienna"—she lifted her violin case slightly—"go to the Musikverein. My name in Austria is Linder."

He tipped his hat and stepped back as the wheels of the engine turned slowly over. "Vienna. The Musikverein," he repeated. She smiled a melancholy smile and looked up again toward the mountains, and then she was gone.

Murphy stood beside the empty tracks for a long time staring after the small red lamp on the last car. In the far distance a whistle wailed and echoed back from the towering peaks above the sleeping city. Instinctively Murphy looked toward Berchtesgaden and the tiny lights that beamed from the slopes just across the border. In the blackness of the early morning, it was easy to imagine that the eyes of the Dragon himself were turned this way, watching John Murphy with interest.

9

Arrival

Three trains had already passed through Kitzbühel since Frau Anna and Franz arrived at the Bahnhof. The smile had long since disappeared from her face, and the fine lines of strain and worry returned to her features.

"Frau Anna—" Franz glanced at the clock on the wall of the waiting room. "The next train does not come until four in the morning. That is two more hours."

For a moment she did not reply as the last train chugged away without anyone having disembarked. "They will be on that one, then." She looked at him and smiled with a superficial confidence. "Four A.M., you say?"

"We can wait at the Golden Griffin, if you like. Heinz, the old desk clerk there, will brew us tea. He is up all night like an owl anyway. There will be a warm fire in the fireplace and it will be more comfortable for you—unless . . ." He tried the words carefully, hoping she would listen to reason. "Maybe it would be best if you went home to bed now. I am used to being up late. What with the cows and horses, something always keeps me until dawn. I will come back and wait for your husband and daughter, and when you wake up they will be there."

She patted his hand, then looked away into the darkness as though she could will the hours to pass more quickly and any moment Theo and Elisa would step off the train. "I have spent more than half my life sitting up with children. Like you sit up with your cows, Franz. If there was a contest for sitting up and worrying and praying, I am afraid you would lose and I would win."

"Well, then—"

"But a cup of tea sounds nice." She stood and smoothed her coat, still unable to take her eyes from the silent, empty track.

There was a small office at the Bahnhof where tickets were purchased and telegrams were sent and received. A gray-haired woman in a dirndl and heavy wool cape sat at the desk behind the wire grid. A small stove warmed the space, but still she looked cold and tired in her vigil. As Franz and Frau Anna passed, the telegraph key began to click rapidly like chattering teeth. She sprang to life and began to scribble the message at the same time she called for Franz.

"Franz! Franz Wattenbarger! A message from Salzburg for you!"

"Salzburg!" He brightened and took Anna's arm. "There, you see? They are delayed, Frau Anna, but they are across the border and into Austria now. No need to worry."

She pressed a hand to her temple and sighed loudly with relief. Then she realized that Franz somehow understood the reason for her worry. All the talk about Vienna and passports from Czechoslovakia now seemed foolish. "Has it been that obvious?" She asked.

"No. Not obvious, Frau Anna. But quite common nowadays in Austria. We are quite different from our big neighbors on the other side of the frontier, you know. We tend to notice people instead of what their travel documents say." He shrugged. "Anyway, they are safe across our border now. Most certainly."

The telegraph operator slipped the message beneath the grid. "From Salzburg. If you are Frau Anna Linder, this is for you." The woman did not smile, and she looked away quickly as Anna scanned the message and the brief light of hope faded. She read it once and then again, at last letting her hands fall limp at her sides.

"Only Elisa is coming." She said flatly. "My husband is detained . . . by business," she added as the telegraph operator looked up as though to judge her reaction. Anna raised her head and smiled bravely, conscious that the act must continue—in public, at any rate. In spite of what Franz said, there were many in Austria who did not think that this side of the border should be any different from Germany. "So. My daughter will be here on the early morning train, young Franz. A cup of tea will be nice while we wait."

Franz would have recognized Elisa Linder even if he had never seen her photograph. She looked so much like a young version of Frau Anna that Franz found himself staring as the two women embraced. The stunning beauty of Anna Linder was echoed in her daughter. The photograph of Elisa by the Spree River had been inadequate, to say the least.

The girl clung tightly to her mother, laying her cheek against her shoulder. Clear blue eyes of limitless depth reflected sadness and fear and worry, but only briefly. A whispered word from her mother, and Elisa regained her composure in an instant, just as Franz had seen Frau Anna pull herself together a dozen different times.

The telegraph operator watched them with open curiosity. One quick glance in the direction of the office, and Elisa was ready to perform.

"The fresh air has done you a world of good, Mother."

"A day or two and you will feel better as well. You should see your brothers! A shame your father could not set business aside for once. Ah, well, a few days and he will join us. So much to do before Christmas . . ."

Franz gathered the luggage, including the extra pair of skis left by Theo Linder. The baggage was light. Elisa carried the violin case, and did not look at Franz with any more interest than if he were a porter.

"May I carry that for you?" he tried to take the violin and load it onto the sleigh with the rest of the baggage.

With the air of a woman talking to a servant, she dismissed his attempt to be helpful. "No. This is far too valuable to be loaded with the baggage."

Frau Anna noticed the indignant look on Franz's face. He frowned slightly, uncertain that he liked this young woman. She certainly lacked the grace of her mother. *But then again*, he reasoned, *she has probably endured a terrible night*.

Frau Anna caught his arm. "Franz." The word was spoken with affection, and Elisa looked startled by the tone. "Elisa, this is Franz Wattenbarger. He has been more help than I can say. He stayed here at the station all night . . ."

She managed a smile of gratitude. "Forgive me. I have been thoughtless." She turned the full effect of her eyes on him, her expression a mix of sadness and gratitude and the same worry Franz had seen in Frau Anna over the days. "I thought you were just—"

He nodded and bowed slightly. "Just driving the sleigh," he finished for her. "It has been my privilege to accompany your mother through the night."

"Through the long night." Anna watched as the train chugged away from the station. It seemed she still could not believe that Theo had not gotten off. "I am most grateful for the company, Franz. And perhaps soon you will also meet our Theo."

Elisa's expression clouded as her mother spoke, and she looked as if she would cry any moment. Franz simply nodded and tried not to look at her face as he helped them into the sleigh. There was nothing to say. Frau Anna smiled wearily and slipped her arm around Elisa's shoulder.

The ride back to the farmhouse passed in almost absolute silence. No doubt there would be tears and explanations in the privacy of their room, but neither Frau Anna nor Elisa wanted to show such depth of feeling to Franz. He admired their control, but somehow felt that everything had already been expressed by the look in Elisa's eyes.

The story was plain to read. The extra pair of skis and fine leather luggage monogrammed with the initials *T.L.* shouted the obvious fact that somewhere between Berlin and the border of Austria, the husband of Frau Linder had been forcibly taken from the train. Business had indeed detained him, but it was not his own business.

Yes, there would be tears later, but Franz did not need to see them fall in order to guess what his passengers were feeling. They could not see the stars that stretched from mountaintop to mountaintop; their vision was turned inward as they imagined the face of the man they called Father and Husband, and wondered where he was now. They could not hear the jingle of sleigh bells echoing from the slopes; their ears heard words shouted in false accusation, fists slamming against the flesh and bone of Theo Linder's face. Such things were common nowadays. Such terror and uncertainty made hearts blind and deaf to things that were beautiful in the world.

Franz slapped the lines down hard on the back of Edelweiss, the little mare. As though sensing his urgency, she pulled harder up the incline toward home. "You ladies will need to sleep a while after tonight," he said, breaking the silence. "Mama will already be up for the milking. Perhaps you would like to eat before—"

There was no answer. Franz glanced back to see Elisa with her head against her mother's shoulder. Her eyes were closed, and he thought she was asleep. Then she raised her hand to brush away a silent tear. Perhaps she had not heard his voice, either.

———

The wonderful aroma of pastries fresh from the oven pulled Elisa from a restless sleep. Her mother, worn out from the previous night's ordeal, slept beside her on the massive bed. Elisa gazed up at the huge bedposts, carved into grapevines and tiny flowers. The wood was smooth and mellow with age, in contrast to the rough-hewn beams of the walls. For a moment, Elisa was disoriented. Was it morning? Had she slept the clock around and awakened to this cozy, unfamiliar room? Or perhaps she was not awake at all. Maybe the terrible events of last night never happened. She was dreaming even now while she slept in the Hall of the Mountain King.

She ran her fingers through her hair and stared into the dark rafters of the ceiling. The weight of her worry pressed down on her. None of it was a dream. The man Murphy. The Gestapo agents shoving her father off the train. Jackboots and shouts. Her clothes scattered all over. No. It had happened, and now some gentle hand had lifted her up in her blind exhaustion and dropped her into this strange place.

She heard the distinct laughter of her brothers downstairs and the friendly chiding voice of the farmwife as she scolded them for stealing Christmas cookies. And there was another voice, playful and untroubled. *What was his name?* Elisa closed her eyes and thought of the husky young peasant with hands big like Shimon, who beat out thunder on the tympani. How far away that all seemed now! Vienna; her friends in the orchestra: Leah, Shimon, Rudy—it had not even been ten days, yet their laughter seemed a distant lifetime from her. Then she had only been going home for the holidays. But her trip had been a descent into the darkest hell of Faust.

Elisa sat up. Had it only been last night that her father had plucked the slim volume from the bookshelf? She slipped from beneath the quilt and tiptoed to the rich leather suitcase. Careful not to awaken her mother, she opened it and sat for a moment as the aroma of his bay rum aftershave and pipe tobacco filled her senses. *Papa.* It was like having him come into the room. With a cry, Anna woke up.

"Theo?" she gasped. "Theo? Is that you?"

"No, Mama." Elisa was instantly sorry she had opened the bag in search of the copy of *Faust*. "Papa put a little book in his suitcase. I was just looking—"

"Oh." The syllable was racked with disappointment. "Oh," she said again.

Elisa sat cross-legged on the floor and gazed at her mother's agonized expression. She seemed suddenly so old. Elisa had never seen her look so worn. "Go back to sleep."

Anna shook her head and sat up, her legs dangling from the edge of the bed. "What time is it?"

"Suppertime soon," Elisa replied quietly. She found the little red volume tucked beneath a neatly folded shirt. "Here it is, Mama." She held it out, and Anna took it almost reverently.

"*Faust*," she whispered. "Of course. Germany." She uttered the name heavily, as though she spoke of a dead loved one. "Faust."

"What should we do, Mother?"

"Do? What can we do? Nothing. Not now. Hope and pray they release him. We must not tell your brothers. If the Gestapo does not let Theo go, we will have to go back." She bit her lip. "Unless we can find some way to stay across the border after our *Ausweis* expires. They cannot punish him if we have some legal reason to stay."

She contemplated the smooth red leather of the book. "Like Faust, we need time. But time runs short, and the Dragon is . . ." She faltered, then looked up at Elisa with a half-embarrassed smile. "I am talking nonsense."

"You are right about the boys. They shouldn't have to worry. They could let it all tumble out. And—I assume no one knows any of this."

Anna nodded. "Young Franz knows *something*."

"Franz. Yes. The one who drove us home last night. How much does he know? Is he to be trusted?"

"He knows nothing, really, Elisa." Anna seemed almost too weary to care anymore. "But he *guesses*. At least, I think he does." She seemed puzzled by him. "Sometimes he looks like he is drawing a picture of me with his mind. A good young man, I think. No Nazi."

"Still it is not wise to tell anyone anything of our business."

"You are right. The only secret kept is the one we do not tell. Whatever Franz thinks he sees in me cannot be proven. He would not try to hurt us. But his brother—" She lowered her voice to a whisper. "His name is Otto. And to him we must not reveal anything at all. He is strange; even his mother looks puzzled by him."

Elisa had only seen Otto at a distance when they arrived at sunrise this morning. He gave them a cursory glance as he walked by and entered the cow barn. Elisa had felt instantly ill at ease, and after her time in Berlin she did not like such looks. He seemed to resent their arrival. "Perhaps he is—"

"One of them? No. I don't think so. No. This family is all Austrian. His mother told me he lost his young wife last year and since then he has been troubled."

Elisa felt foolish. She was seeing a Nazi behind every bush when in fact Otto was just a grieving husband. "Poor man." She looked at the feather bed and wondered if it had belonged to him and his wife. "No wonder."

"All the same"—Anna was not so quickly moved—"it is better to say nothing at all to anyone. We must just keep smiling. As far as anyone knows, your father is delayed by business. And we will hope and pray that it is true. Maybe they will let him go. It must be just some silly mistake. Theo Lindheim was a great hero of the Fatherland. The memory of old von Hindenburg. It will not let this foul little Hitler harm a great hero like Theo." She was talking very quietly as though the words were meant to comfort herself.

"Of course, Mother." Elisa joined in the optimism. "After all, they said they wanted only to talk to him about contributions or some such nonsense. Something about a donation for the Zionists."

Anna sat very still and silent, frowning down at the floor. "I did it," she said at last. "For young Herschel Grynspan. Yes. I gave him a little money for the meetings. A small thing. How do they know such small things, Elisa?" She shuddered.

"We must be very careful, Mother. Papa would want us to be careful!"

───────

It was not a discussion of German policies toward Austria that drew nearly fifty newsmen to the village of Berchtesgaden but rather the events unfolding in Spain. Since July of 1936, a civil war had been raging between the leftist Republicans and the right-wing Nationalists led by the Fascist Franco.

Earlier, Mussolini had pledged Italy's support of Franco in return for concessions in the Western Mediterranean. Now Russia had moved in to aid the left. This move opened the door for Hitler to forge a union with Italy. Today Hitler and Mussolini were together in Berchtesgaden.

The press gathered together in a small restaurant two blocks from the train depot. Murphy sat quietly in the smoke-filled room and listened to the speculation in a babble of a dozen languages. It was common knowledge that Mussolini distrusted Hitler and had been open in his disapproval. Italy had signed a pact with Austria against German aggression and had guaranteed to step in in the event that German troops ever threatened the little nation that separated Italy from Germany. Yet for nearly two days Mussolini and Hitler had been locked in deep discussion about Russian intervention in Spain.

When at last Hitler and Mussolini made their appearance before flashing cameras and shoving reporters, it did not take a genius to imagine the results of their conference. The Reich would follow the lead of Italy and increase military aid to Franco's forces in Spain. Together Italy and Germany would stand firm against the aggression of the Communists in Western Europe. When all other nations stepped back to do nothing, *Il Duce* and *der Führer* would link arms and form a mighty wall.

Murphy shuddered involuntarily as he watched the two leaders smiling and chatting before the whirring news cameras. A French reporter raised his hand and shouted the question, "How will this union affect Italy's treaty with Austria?"

Mussolini inclined his head slightly, glanced at Hitler and replied loudly, "Not at all. The matter was not discussed."

"How will Germany aid the forces of Franco?" shouted another reporter.

Hitler leaned close to his interpreter, who repeated the question. "The Reich has recently recognized General Franco," Hitler said. "Now we have put lightning in his hand."

Blitzkrieg! The word had been bandied about in Nazi circles for months. Murphy had heard it a dozen times from Göring, who was eager to try out the new armaments and aircraft of the German war machine. Spain would now provide the perfect proving ground for the German war toys. Hitler looked pleased with himself. He posed for more photographs at the side of Mussolini. The friendship of these two would undoubtedly please Franco, who was at a standstill in his siege against the forces in Madrid. But the sight of Mussolini grasping the hand of Hitler was certain to strike dread in the hearts of the Austrians just across the border.

Murphy felt angry at the entire charade. He was relieved when the show ended and the two leaders drove off through the cheering crowds recruited for the occasion by the German Propaganda Ministry. The ability of Hitler's Minister of Propaganda to rustle up so many people for such occasions always amazed Murphy. The swarming multitudes seemed capable of making more noise than a mob watching a football game back home. But he always had the distinct impression that many among them were literally cheering for their lives.

In all the clamor, the whereabouts of Theo Lindheim and his detention receded far in the background. There was no opportunity to discuss what he had seen two nights earlier, and, much to his disappointment, no one was willing to listen. *"An official matter,"* he was told. *"Not your business."*

Murphy finished his notes and pocketed his notebook with the helpless feeling of a non-swimmer watching another man drown. The smile on Mussolini's face somehow seemed even more ominous and unsettling than the tears of Elisa Lindheim. While Britain and France pledged "noninterference" in Spain, the two Fascist powers of Germany and Italy were using events in Madrid as an excuse to flex their muscles. At this moment, Murphy could only wonder if everyone in England was sleeping, or crazy, or maybe both.

Two British reporters had watched the same spectacle today; both were convinced that their stories would be lost amid the drama of King Edward's abdication and Mrs. Simpson's new wardrobe.

"It's much more pleasant to read a fairy-tale love story than a union of two trolls plotting to carve up Europe between themselves," said James Ward of the London *Times*. "It will take six months for the House of Commons and the British public to remember that there *is* a Hitler. And Spain? You know what the English think of the events in Madrid! It's a long way to Tipperary, Murphy boy. And the New York papers aren't any more interested in this Italian-German courtship than London is!"

Reluctantly, Murphy had to agree with him. That night as he hastily scribbled the story on the train back to Berlin, he realized that *blitzkrieg* would not strike fear in the hearts of his readers; it was nothing more than a foreign word that would probably be cut by his American editor.

10

Family Divided

Frau Marta and Herr Karl were kind people. Sometimes while the boys roared over a game of Watten, Elisa would catch Frau Marta casting a concerned glance toward Anna. The eyes of the farmwife always seemed to hold the gentle assurance that she knew much more than she would say. Yet never did she pry for even the slightest bit of information. Elisa appreciated the privacy they were given to grieve without intrusion. Somehow the illusion that everything was fine seemed important to her mother as the days passed.

"Theo will love this place," Anna often said. And though it became more obvious each day that Theo was not coming, Frau Marta always joined in the terrible playacting with enthusiasm.

"When your husband Theo comes we shall have a celebration! I will make him a cake! What kind of cake does Herr Theo like best?" The questions never probed deeper than what sort of food Theo liked and whether he enjoyed skiing.

Franz looked at Elisa with the same sad eyes as his mother, but whenever Elisa glanced toward him, he quickly turned away. She wondered what he was feeling. He hardly spoke a word to her and walked the opposite direction if he saw her coming across the farmyard. And yet, he held her in his eyes. She had seen it, and it confused her.

Herr Karl had taken her down to the basement workshop and showed her Franz's delicate wood carvings. Purest innocence was captured in the face of the Madonna—innocence and deep sadness. And the figure of Joseph did not look at the tiny infant Jesus, but gazed with love and tenderness at Mary as she held the child.

Elisa had never seen such beauty cut from hard, unfeeling wood. And when she spoke to Franz of her response, he had shrugged and turned away, as though he could not accept her judgment of his work. He was a strange man. Boisterous and rough with the boys, he wrestled and skied and hiked for miles through the snow with them each day. But he had barely uttered a word to Elisa since he had driven her home from the train station the first early morning of her arrival.

Otto, the oldest of the sons, was hardly around at all. Except for meals, he worked in the barn and slept in the cabin across the pasture. Most nights he left for Kitzbühel early after supper and did not return until late.

But tonight, the wind roared fiercely from the north and a stark white veil of snow powdered the ground. Everyone stayed in the Stube, the living room of the main house. Hot, spiced cider and plates of cookies disappeared as the boys played Watten, betting pocket knives and compasses. Gretchen watched Wilhelm with wide, doe-like eyes, as Anna and Frau Marta washed the dishes. Otto read for a while and then retreated into the basement workshop as though he could not tolerate the noise any longer.

Elisa wrapped a blanket around herself and sat beside the fire pretending to read. Franz was clearly winning the card game when Frau Marta emerged from the tiny kitchen and clapped her hands for attention. Anna stood at her right shoulder, smiling at Elisa as though she had a secret.

"Attention! *Attention,* everyone!" called Frau Marta. "Franz and Karl! You stop cheating those poor boys!" Everyone laughed. Elisa noticed how sad her mother's smile seemed. *She is thinking of Papa. Of our house in Berlin at Christmas. Parties and laughter. Music. Gone. All gone.*

"What is it, Mama?" asked Herr Karl, gathering the cards.

"Tonight, we are going to have a Christmas concert! Ja! Our Elisa is going to play for us! Play the *violin*! And, Papa, you can get your accordion too if you like, ja?"

Everyone applauded and whooped. Elisa did not feel like playing, but she bowed to the wishes of the company. *We will do our best to carry on. Even without you, Papa, we will do our best.* She was certain that Anna had suggested the performance entirely for that purpose. *Keep up the show. Everything is fine. All will turn out well.* But Elisa had stopped believing it.

Elisa had not opened the case of the Guarnerius since the night she had played the last time for her father in Berlin. She removed the silk scarf that covered the instrument and felt her heart swell with the ache of missing him, missing home the way it used to be. Here, she could play whatever she wished. She would play the same delicate melody she had played for Theo. She would play for him, wherever he was, and hope that somehow he heard her.

The firelight glowed on the faces of her little audience. Young Gretchen's hair shone like copper, and Elisa noticed that it matched the highlights of Franz's beard. All the Wattenbarger children had warm brown eyes that looked at her expectantly as she tuned the strings, as if she was about to give them a fine and cherished gift. Elisa covered the chin rest of the instrument with a soft handkerchief and raised it to her shoulder as though she stood before a royal audience in Vienna. Then she smiled, a curious smile at Franz, and he blushed and looked quickly away.

She lifted the bow and began to play the bright, happy melody that Mozart had written as a young man in Salzburg. The violin came alive in her hands. She closed her eyes, letting the music flow from her soul into the sighing wood, then up and out like leaves swirling in an autumn wind—swirling, dancing, singing, as the trees swayed in the last rays of sunlight. Elisa herself swayed as the music took her far away from lonely thoughts and fears that had pursued her through each day. Had heaven opened now and soothed her heart with a song from the throne of God? All the things she felt but could not say came tumbling out, note on note in a voice that reached up like a prayer and a hope.

This is me, God! Elisa. I once saw you in all the world. But the world is dark now, Lord. Full. Full of darkness. Close your eyes for a moment, God, and let me sing to you. Let me remember that you are here. Here in the notes. Smiling down as I play for you. Just this moment, God, let me sing to you. And maybe in the song, I will forget whether I am singing to you, or you are singing to me ..."

When the last note swirled and echoed in the rafters, Elisa opened her eyes to the spellbound faces of her little audience. The music hung in the air after she lowered the bow, and then Herr Karl clapped his large hands together and stomped his feet on the stone floor in unbridled approval.

"More! More!" he shouted, and the others joined in. She bowed slightly and laughed with genuine delight for the first time since she had arrived.

Only Franz did not look at her. He sat very quietly staring at his boots. His lack of interest hurt her for only a moment; then she shrugged slightly and raised the violin again to play the sonatas of Mozart and Beethoven—music that had not even been written when the Guarnerius was carved three hundred years earlier. Again she closed her eyes and let the melodies carry her away. Only this time when she finished and opened them again, Franz had slipped quietly out of the room.

"Refugees, most certainly from Germany. Do you hear the accent of the boys?" said Otto as Franz sank down onto the cot in the tiny little hut. "The Linders are not Communist. Too rich, I think. German Bolsheviks are dirty, ragged creatures, always wanting to divide up what everyone owns and distribute it—"

"That sounds more like the Nazis, if you ask me." Franz did not like his brother's accusing tone. He was tired and not ready for an analysis of the Linders. "But from what I hear the Nazis don't divide what they steal."

"The Nazi party says it takes only from the enemies of the state ...

from the Jewish industrialists who have grown rich at the expense and suffering of the German people."

Franz stared at him. Often since Otto had returned from Germany he had discussed the National Socialist rhetoric as though he might believe it. Franz sighed. "It is cold in here," he said quietly. "Throw another log on the fire, will you?"

Otto laughed a short, bitter laugh. He wanted to talk, wanted to argue about the real matters of the world, and Franz would have none of it. Otto stirred the coals of the fire and tossed a small chunk of wood onto the grate. Then he tried again to stir Franz, only this time he used a different poker. "The girl . . . what is her name?"

"Elisa."

"Ja. Beautiful, don't you think?"

"All right, I suppose," Franz rolled over and faced the wall as the flames flared up. The heat warmed his back. The echoes of her music warmed his soul, building a fire that he resisted. He could not think of her—not now.

"Not a Bolshevik!"

"You said that."

"Probably elitists. Maybe her father is a rich Jew." He laughed. "You can tell by the cut of their clothes. The way they carry themselves. Better than everyone, they think. Better than a poor Austrian family." He jabbed the wood a little harder. "She would not look twice at the likes of us. Farmers. Dairymen."

"Fine. I haven't looked at her either." Franz sounded bored, but he felt his insides churn as Otto spoke. It was not the words themselves that provoked him, but the way Otto seemed determined to argue. And the truth was that he had thought of little else but her.

"Ha!" Otto tossed another log onto the grate, and a shower of sparks rose up the chimney. "I *saw* you look at her! Yes. You noticed. You were looking at her the way you size up a fine heifer . . ." He paused and pronounced each word with a caustic clip. "The way you used to look at Katrine."

Franz sat up and whirled to face Otto's eyes blazing triumphantly. "Katrine was the only good thing about you, Otto." His anger matched that of his brother now. "And she is gone."

"Why don't you admit that you are glad she's dead!" Otto shouted, all pretense of control vanished.

"You are a crazy man!"

"I saw! I saw all of it. The way she teased you. She touched my face, then looked at you to see how you reacted." Otto was sweating now. The little room was bright with the flames in the fireplace and stifling with the fierce heat. He clenched and unclenched his fists. "And I *hated* you for it. *Hated you!* Now this new woman comes, and you are watching again. Like you watched Katrine. You think I don't see?"

"Life here has been terrible since you came back!" Franz did not address Otto's accusation. "Rages and moods! Why don't you leave? Leave us in peace! Hire someone to write Mama a letter once a month to say you are well even if you are dead! I don't care!" He lay back down and turned away from Otto. There was no winning in an argument with him. The only safety was in silence.

"I did not like the life of a refugee," Otto said dully. "I do not like this. Now." He glanced around the room. "Living in this hut with *you* because my bed is taken up by refugees."

"So go stay in Kitzbühel!" Franz snapped as he closed his eyes. "Or maybe I will."

"Then who would shovel the manure?" Otto's voice was taunting again. "And who would keep these new women satisfied? The way you satisfied Katrine when I was not around, eh?"

Franz swore loudly and jumped up, hurtling himself at Otto. With a cry, the two brothers toppled back over a chair and fell onto the hard plank floor. Franz struck with his right fist, smashing Otto's nose with the first blow. Blood spurted, drenching his hands as he slammed Otto's head back on the planks again and again. Only seconds passed until he noticed that Otto was limp, accepting the brutal punishment without resisting. Otto's face was covered with his own blood, but Franz could see his expression was still triumphant as Franz let him go and drew back. Otto had pushed him to this violence, and in that was some sort of perverse victory.

"You are a fool!" Franz hissed. "I never touched Katrine. And she only saw *you*, Otto. Never me. If I killed you now, it would be for her honor. She was in your bed. Not mine. And yet you say such a thing—" He stood up. His bloody fist was still clenched. Otto stared up at him, still certain that he had spoken some terrible truth. A slight smile played on Otto's lips. "You should be the one in the churchyard, not her!" Franz shouted again. "And if you had accused her of . . . of any unfaithfulness while she lived, I *would* have killed you for the sake of her honor!"

Otto laughed at him and ran the back of his hand across his bloody nose. "An interesting response from a man who claims he never loved her!"

Franz narrowed his eyes as though trying to remember the man that Otto had once been. *Was this my brother?* "I never said I didn't love her. But she was yours, Otto. I would have killed any man in the village who said otherwise. And if you speak her name again in such disgrace, I will kill you as well." Franz glared down at him for a moment as if to be certain that Otto believed him. Then he grabbed his hat and coat and left the cabin, slamming the door and leaving the madness of the accusation behind him.

Franz did not know where to go once he had stepped out of the cabin. It was cold, and the clouds of the storm still hovered over the black peaks to the north. His hands were sticky with Otto's blood. He did not dare go into the house and risk being seen by his mother.

Frustrated, he stood for a moment in front of the cabin. Maybe it had been worth a beating for Otto to get him out of the hut for the night.

He sighed, angry at himself for taking the bait, angry at Otto for the madness that had come over him. Then he tramped across the snow-covered field toward the dark barn. He had spent many nights sleeping in the warm straw. He would do it again tonight.

When he entered the barn, Franz was met by the glow of a lantern hanging from a post. He mentally chastised young Helmut, who had no doubt left it burning after the evening feeding. The soft bellow of a cow greeted him as he stepped into the warmth. Then as the door swung shut, he saw a startled Elisa Linder perching on the rails above the stall of the new calf.

"Well!" he said, sounding as though he had caught a thief.

"Good evening," she replied, then looked back toward the calf. "He is a pretty little thing. Wilhelm told me I should come look."

The lantern light caught the shine of her hair and the glow of her skin until she seemed almost golden. *Like the angels over the manger*, thought Franz, and he determined that he would remember her expression when he worked on the carved angels for his mother's creche. He had forgotten his own bloody, disheveled appearance and when she looked back toward him, her expression changed to one of concern. "Are you hurt?" she asked in alarm.

"This?" He looked at his sticky hand, suddenly embarrassed. "No. A bloody nose is all. Nothing." He went to the water barrel and drew a bucket of ice cold water to wash. He hoped that she would not notice that it was not his own nose that was bloody. He splashed water on his face, startled when dark red liquid clouded the water. He had hit Otto harder than he intended, but not harder than Otto deserved.

Franz wondered what Otto would say if he knew he was in the barn with one of the women who had been a part of the argument. Franz was ashamed that Elisa's name had been mentioned in such a way. Katrine was past hurting, but here was someone very much alive and with a vulnerability that had stirred his protectiveness from the moment he had seen her. He looked up as he dried his hands on clean straw. She was staring at him with undisguised concern. Her deep blue eyes glistened in the light, completing the image of some beautiful, spiritual being that had come to bless the tiny calf sleeping in the hay beside its mother. The memory of her music made him breathless.

"Did you fall?" she asked, breaking the spell.

"Yes," he answered curtly as the memory of Otto's accusation assaulted him again. "It's dark out here. You need to be careful on your way back to the house." He hoped his warning would send her on her way. He wanted to brood all by himself. And he could not risk the inward longing he knew her nearness might stir in him.

"I brought the lantern. Helmut lit it for me. I . . . am I keeping you from your work? I just came out to be alone a bit. The boys are all so full of nonsense and noise, and I . . ."

Franz picked up the pitchfork and scooped hay into the troughs even though he knew the cattle had been fed hours ago. They did not seem to notice the extra portions, but stood quietly chewing their cuds. "No bother, Fraülein," he said.

"My mother says you have been most kind and . . . *sensitive*." There was so much expression in that last word that Franz plunged the pitchfork into the hay and stood still to wonder about it.

"Austria is full of refugees on holiday, Fraülein."

"Then you know."

"I have guessed enough." He decided not to pretend ignorance any longer. "Enough to know that you should be careful." His voice took an edge of bitterness. "Even households are divided these days. One might find Nazi sympathizers sitting at the supper table and never know."

Anna's words to Elisa raced through her mind. *Otto, the other brother* . . . "And at your own table, in the *Herrgottseck* of your home? The place you call *The Corner of the Lord?*" she asked quietly, "Are we safe there?"

"My mother would tell you yes," he paused, feeling almost as if his words were a betrayal of his family. Yet not even his mother knew of the dark thoughts that filled Otto these days. "She would say, '*In the corner of the Lord* all are welcome and safe in our home.' But above the Herrgottseck, Elisa, there is a crucifix. We eat our meals in its shadow, and I remember that Christ was betrayed by the kiss of a friend." He hoped she would not ask more. Then he added. "If you are no friend of the Nazis, then even here you must be careful."

"I see." She looked away as though trying to comprehend all that he had just told her. *Families divided* . . . Then she looked back to him and slipped off the rails of the stall. "Thank you for your honesty."

He nodded curtly, indicating he would not say more.

She continued to stare at him. "Should my mother and brothers leave your farm?"

"No. It is no different anywhere. At least here you *know* . . ." *Know what? What does she know? That my brother is a Judas who believes whatever madness he wants?* "We are isolated here. Austria is not the Reich, no matter how much Herr Hitler wishes it. There are many more of us for the Church and the government of Chancellor Schuschnigg than those who favor Anschluss with Germany." Then he added with a glance toward the cabin lights shining through the barn window, "Perhaps those who favor such madness will leave us and go back to Germany."

She turned away from him, and reached over the rail to stroke the side of the cow. "The blood you washed away," she said, "was it your blood?"

"My blood and my brother's is the same," he answered. "It simply flows through different hearts." He stepped up beside her, suddenly relieved that he could talk to someone. He had not dared to share Otto's Nazi leanings with his family. For months he had remained silent about it, just as he had remained silent about many other things. "There are places in the Alps I can show you, where two snowflakes fall from the same cloud and land a fraction of an inch from one another. Through the winter they sleep side by side in the peace of this place. When summer comes, the sun shines on them and they begin to melt. And though they came from the same womb and have shared the same bed, when the heat comes, one snowflake melts and flows down toward the Rhone River and the warmth of vineyards and farmland to the south. And the other? It flows downward into the cold waters of the great Rhine River of Germany." He looked at her, surprised to see tears brimming in her eyes. "Two . . . *snowflakes*, you see . . . and in the end they finish their journey in two opposite oceans. That is the way it is in these mountains. There are places I can show you . . ."

For a long time, Elisa did not answer him. She rested her cheek on her hand and continued to stroke the brown flank of the cow. The silence was not uncomfortable for either of them, and somehow Franz felt as though he had known her for a long time. Everything Otto had said about her was untrue. There was nothing in her manner that made him feel small. "Thank you," she said at last. Her voice was hoarse.

"For what?"

"For months I have been wondering—" She frowned and looked over the back of the cow as though she were seeing someone else. "I . . . I . . ." She groped for words. "There was someone I loved—" Elisa turned her eyes on Franz and in one look displayed her soul. She did not need to tell him that she was hurt and confused. She did not need to say that she, too, had been betrayed by one she loved. It was all there—a book, open for him to read.

Franz lifted a hand to touch her cheek. His hand was rough and calloused, but he held her face gently. She blinked up at him, surprised by his touch, and yet, somehow, *grateful*. For an instant they remained motionless; then he leaned down slowly and kissed her lips tenderly as though trying to kiss away the hurt. He held her close and wondered about the stream that had carried her lover away into the heart of the Reich. *What a fool the man must be. What a fool!*

"Tell me," she whispered, "why did you leave when I played the violin?"

For a long time he did not answer. "It was your soul, Elisa. I could see your soul, beautiful and clear, and I could not bear the beauty of it . . ."

11

The Innsbruck
Connection

It was well past midnight when Elisa slipped into the bed beside her mother. The house was dark and silent.

"Mother—" She nudged Anna awake. "Wake up, please. We need to talk."

"Where were you?" Anna asked in a sleepy voice.

"Shhhh." Elisa put a finger to her lips. "I've been in the cow barn. With Franz."

Anna sat up and fumbled to light the lamp beside the bed. As the flame sputtered, she turned to Elisa with an alarmed look. "What time is it?"

"Nearly one."

"What have you been—"

Elisa looked amused by her mother's concern. After all, she had been on her own for several years. "Talking."

"Talking? All this time?" Anna brushed straw from Elisa's sweater.

Elisa smiled and nodded at her mother.

"Hmmm." Anna pulled her robe around her shoulders.

"But listen, Mama, you were right. Right about Otto. Franz says we must be careful. *Very* careful around Otto."

Now Anna looked terribly concerned. She would rather worry about a few kisses than the politics of their hosts. "Only him?"

Elisa nodded, then continued with a rush. "Yes. Everyone else is very . . . *Austrian*. Not even Frau Marta or Herr Karl suspect that Otto is pro—"

"Why did Franz tell you all this? If it is such a secret—"

"Oh, Mama, he is so wonderful. So . . . kind."

"But, Elisa, you have only just met him!"

"We talked a long time. I told him about Thomas, and he told me about . . . someone." She waved her hand in front of her face as though turning the page of a book. "But mostly he told me that there are lots of ways that people from Germany can get an extension of their travel papers. Maybe you and the boys won't have to go back if Papa doesn't come."

Anna seemed almost indignant. "He is coming! I *know* he will come. They can't keep him."

"But it may take longer than the two weeks allowed on your permit. Franz told me about a family from Munich who—"

"Elisa, if your father does not come soon I must go back. The boys can stay here—stay with you. But, Elisa, I must . . ." For the first time Elisa saw tears welling up in her mother's eyes.

She reached out and embraced her, then took her by the shoulders and looked her square in the eye. "You must not rush into anything, Mother! Don't you see that's what the Nazis are after? More hostages. More Jews for ransom."

Anna drew her breath in sharply. "You *didn't* tell Franz that your father is Jewish? That in the eyes of Germany we are all Jews?" She was shocked and fearful.

"No. It wouldn't matter to him, I'm sure; but listen, he has a plan! If Papa doesn't come in a few days, there are ways for us to stay without arousing the suspicion of the German authorities . . ."

Anna cleared her throat and tossed her head as if to indicate that she was entirely awake and ready to consider anything that might forestall their forced return to Germany. "Franz is . . . impertinent," she said almost haughtily. "But trustworthy, I think. We have nowhere else to turn. Today I almost went to the village priest, but—"

"There are better ways. More organized." Eagerly, Elisa pulled a carefully penned list from her pocket and laid it on the quilt in front of her mother. "We'll have to go to Innsbruck—"

"Innsbruck? An hour and a half by train."

"Mama, that's the point. Our German papers are made out to *Lindheim*. We cannot hope to have them changed here where we are known as *Linder*."

"You told Franz our identity?"

"No. And he didn't ask. He doesn't want to know. But he knows enough to figure out that our real name cannot be Linder. The point is, Kitzbühel is a small place. People talk and ask questions, and they want to know everything about everyone now days."

The memory of the telegraph operator flashed through Anna's eyes. "Yes. Your father will not write to us here. You are right. If we go to Innsbruck . . . yes. It is a big city. Strangers pass through all the time. For one day we can be Lindheim. Fix our passes, mail a letter to Theo—" The last thought caused her to cloud up with emotion.

"Right. Anything that comes into Germany—a wire or a letter—will be read by the Gestapo. We must give them information, stories of our family's vacation. Tell how we miss Papa and hope he comes soon. You see?"

"Will it do any good at all, Elisa?" Anna was close to despair. She seemed almost afraid to hope.

"Mother—" Elisa put her hand on Anna's arm. "Letters to Papa from Innsbruck will be read by the men who keep him. Innsbruck is only across the pass from Germany." She frowned. "If Papa should get away somehow, by some miracle, the Gestapo will not look for him to come to Kitzbühel, but to Innsbruck, you see?"

Anna nodded, certain that she would not sleep again all night. "We should make some tea," she said absently as she studied the list.

"We can leave for Innsbruck tomorrow, if you like. If we tell Frau Marta that we want to go Christmas shopping, I am certain the boys can stay here without us." For a moment there was excitement and hope in her voice; then she shuddered at the thought of all that was against them.

Anna turned her sad eyes on her daughter. "I am afraid, Elisa. Afraid that there are no miracles left for anyone in Germany anymore." She looked at the volume of *Faust* lying on the bedside table. "What miracles can there be when Germany has sold her soul?"

For the first time in all the days of worry, Anna cried. She buried her face in her hands and let small sobs shake her shoulders. Elisa patted her helplessly on the back. "Where is all the world that this can happen and everyone looks the other way? Where is England? Where was France when Hitler took the Rhineland and broke the Treaty of Versailles? They could have stopped him then, Elisa. He has shown himself to be some sort of demonic genius to the German people. He takes what he wants and claims it is for the good of the people. He has taken everything your father worked for. A lifetime of work. And now he would take Theo's life as well. How can this happen? *How?*"

Elisa did not answer. She could not. Often she had heard men speak of Adolf Hitler as the bully on the block. Day after day he proved just how much power a bully could obtain if others simply stepped back and allowed it. First he had proved the power of intimidation in Germany. The laws of humanity and the Weimar Republic had been twisted for his own use. Now he was conducting international policy in the same way. The fate of Theo Lindheim would not stir more than a passing comment in some London club. And yet Elisa could not help feeling that the terrible things happening to her father and thousands of other innocent people in Germany were somehow setting the stage for the future. Perhaps her mother was right. Maybe in all the world there were no miracles left. "They say that England is too far away to help, and God is too high up to hear—"

"God is not too high, Elisa." Anna drew herself up and wiped her eyes. "He is where He has always been. Either in the heart of a man or not. We have watched the laws die, your father and I, and it is like Pastor Jacobi said, *They crucify the Messiah again when they crucify true justice*."

Elisa blanched at the strength of such words and the certain fate of such a statement against the new laws of the Reich. "He said that?"

"Yes. And they arrested him, warned him to excommunicate all Jewish believers in his congregation or he would be arrested again. They released him, and he warned your father. We knew we had to get out then."

"They will kill Pastor Jacobi for that."

"Yes." Anna sighed and leaned back on the pillows. "He told your father he was content with his fate—that men had also killed Jesus for speaking the truth." Anna took Elisa's hand. "There are no miracles, Elisa, but it is not because God is too high up. No, He is still being crucified with men like Jacobi and ten thousand others in those terrible camps. Maybe even your father. We have to admit that possibility, I suppose. The Nazis and their torchlight marches, the flag, the pagan symbols. They will crucify men to satisfy their need for a sacrifice to this god of theirs."

She leaned her head back wearily. "It has gone too far. People let it go too far. And now it has taken over because no one spoke loud enough against it. The few who have are already dead, or rotting in some prison. Your father has been lucky up until now. The people admired him. Now I suppose Hitler will find some way to make him an enemy of Germany; he has done it with so many others. Everything that is good—" She shook her head as she stared at Theo's skis propped in the corner. The two women sat silently for a long time, and downstairs they could hear the call of the cuckoo clock hanging in the Stube.

"It is two in the morning, Mother," Elisa said gently. "Do you still want a cup of tea?"

"No." Anna raised her eyebrows slightly in resignation. "No. It is too late. We should sleep, and perhaps there will be one more miracle when we wake up."

———

Drawing on some hidden, inner reserve of strength, Anna Lindheim descended the steps into the low-ceilinged Stube with a smile on her lips. Frau Marta greeted her like an old friend and bustled about preparing a hearty breakfast of sausage and eggs as Anna explained their plans for the trip to Innsbruck.

"Certainly!" Frau Marta exclaimed. "Go and have a good time! Your fellows will be fine here with Friedrich and Helmut. No doubt we will see them only at mealtime." She babbled on happily as her seventeen-year-old daughter Gretchen served them fresh bread and butter churned just that morning in the pre-dawn hours.

Gretchen was as silent as her mother was verbose. Her thick red hair was braided and carefully pinned up. She smiled shyly as she poured tall glasses of frothy milk, and blushed when Wilhelm openly stared into her gentle brown eyes. Elisa suspected that Wilhelm's obvious interest in the girl was one reason he did not want to ask the Wattenbargers' opinion about Jews.

"You will stay out of trouble, boys?" Anna asked her sons.

They both nodded in unison and their faces reflected the innocence of angels. "Of course, Mother."

Frau Marta ladled eggs onto their already heaping plates. "And if they do not behave . . ." She waved the spoon threateningly in the air. "I have four sons of my own, don't forget."

Dieter laughed nervously, and Wilhelm continued to gaze at Gretchen with undisguised interest. At seventeen, Wilhelm was already nearly six feet tall and had the same ruggedly handsome features of his father. Elisa was convinced that shy little Gretchen was as interested in him as he was in her. "You may need something a little stouter than a spoon to beat my brothers with, Frau Marta," she said.

Wilhelm shot her a sullen look, then returned his gaze to Gretchen. "Because she is twenty-three she knows everything," he grumbled, and Gretchen giggled approval of his remark.

Their looks were not lost on the sturdy farmwife. "They'll be out in the snow today," she murmured. "That will cool them a bit, I think."

"Can Franz take us to the station?" Anna asked.

"No. Otto and Franz are helping their father at the barn this morning. We have a mare in foal. Franz has been sleeping in the barn. A fine little mare, and this is her first. Friedrich will take you." She disappeared into the kitchen, and the matter was settled.

———————

Three hours later, Anna and Elisa stepped off the train in Innsbruck. The sky, a clear blue, seemed suspended on the jagged white peaks of the mountains that reared up from the valley slopes in every direction.

There was a telegraph office in the Bahnhof, but Anna walked past it and out of the station onto Rudolfstrasse.

"The place is thick with German tourists," she whispered to Elisa. It was easy to distinguish the Germans from the native Austrians.

Tourists from Berlin and Munich often sported the comical little moustache inspired by Hitler, while the Tyroleans had long, drooping moustaches and wore the red and white colors of Austria on their armbands. The Chancellor of Austria was from the Tyrol, and in this part of the country the people made their politics quite clear to visitors from across the border. They made their statements without uttering a word to the German tourists.

Porters, guides, and carriage drivers accepted German marks, but they did not accept the strange notions of their guests. Even those who spoke with soft Viennese accents were looked upon with some suspicion. Coffeehouses frequented by native Tyroleans were often rocked with laughter about the flatlanders and their curious ways. Publicly, however, the Austrians were polite and correct in their relations with the Germans, ready to remind them that the Tyrol had been part of Austria for five hundred years, but only briefly was it linked to Prussia. Hitler's claims that Austria should be unified with Germany were scoffed at in the face of history.

Nearly all of these pleasant Tyroleans could name ancestors who had lost their lives in a battle against the Germans in 1866. Most of them believed that their independence from the grasping tentacles of the Nazi Reich would be safeguarded by the League of Nations and an alliance with Rome and Hungary. It was certain that Italy did not want the Germans at their back door, and only Austria stood between the nations of Germany and Italy. Innsbruck itself was the crossroad, the buffer that separated the two giants. If Hitler moved against Austria, the government of Vienna had the promise of Rome that Italian forces would come to the aid of little Austria.

The street was lined with horse-drawn carriages. Anna called up to a driver. "We are in need of a good hotel. Tyroler Haus we hear is close to the Bahnhof, bitte." Her accent betrayed her Viennese upbringing. He smiled and tipped his cap. The smile was genuine. She was obviously an Austrian.

"The Tyroler Haus is just there. On Bahnstrasse. Have you any luggage?" he asked, climbing down from the carriage.

"No," Anna answered hurriedly. "We need a room for a friend. Danke!" She took Elisa's arm and walked quickly toward the hotel, which was directly across from the Post and a branch of the telegraph office.

Elisa recognized the place from Franz's description as they entered the lobby of the typically Tyrolean hotel. The building had probably been built two hundred years earlier. Heavy beams and low ceilings were dark with the patina of age. "A hotel room?" she asked as her mother stepped up to the desk.

Anna did not respond to her; instead, she addressed the gray-haired old man in leather breeches who slipped mail into the slots of the boxes behind the counter. "Have you a room, mein Herr?"

He turned slowly, appraising her over the top of his spectacles. "It is high season, Fraülein," he explained. "Nothing at all, I'm afraid. No. Nothing." On his sleeve the colors of Austria were tied.

Anna looked disappointed. She frowned, then stared hard at his armband. He noticed her gaze and smiled slightly. "When will you have a room available?" she asked, lowering her voice.

"Perhaps a day or two. Is there some way I might help you?"

Anna looked into his face, then back at the armband as though she was making a decision. "Yes. I think you might." She hesitated and looked at Elisa. "We need to rent a room."

"I have no rooms today."

"Then for tomorrow."

He checked the registry. "Of course. Yes. Tomorrow. And for how long will you need the room?"

"Until Christmas Day. Perhaps longer, but at least until then." She smiled her most charming smile, and he slid the registry across the counter to her.

"You have just come in on the train? You have luggage?"

"No luggage. The room is for a friend." She signed her name.

"Also from Vienna?" He seemed pleased that he had recognized her accent.

"No. From Berlin."

A veil of reserve immediately dropped over his face. "From Berlin." There was a coolness in his voice.

Anna leaned closer. "We are *hoping* he will come." There was an urgency in her tone that made the old clerk meet her gaze.

"Yes. I see." He looked troubled as he studied the name written on the registry. "He is coming alone?"

"There may be others who ask about him. Or they may ask about me. How long I have been registered, things like that. They may ask about my two sons." Anna gestured toward Elisa. "And my daughter."

"Yes," he nodded. "And do your children like Innsbruck? They enjoy skiing?" He studied the name again, then added, "Frau Lindheim?"

"Very much." She was certain that the old Austrian understood some of what was happening. "And they hope to see their father before Christmas."

"Indeed. Innsbruck is such a fine place for the holidays. Much more pleasant than Berlin. Berlin is so gray and dreary now days I hear." He winked knowingly. "The Tyroler Haus shall eagerly await the arrival of your husband, Frau Lindheim. He will not have far to go from the station . . ."

"There may be a message sent to me here."

"It will be in your box when you return."

"And now, I am in need of a good physician." She touched his red and white armband. "One who perceives distress as clearly as you do."

"I hope you are not ill!" The old man seemed alarmed.

"My oldest son, Wilhelm, has injured himself on the slopes."

"Wilhelm." He repeated the name as though filing it away in his memory. "Ski injuries are quite common in Innsbruck." He wrote down the name of a doctor and slid the paper to her. "Doctor Wertmann. A good fellow." He lowered his voice. "Jewish. Also from Berlin recently. He is quite discreet, Frau Lindheim."

"I recognize the name." She folded the paper and put it in her coat pocket, then opened her purse to pay. "How much do I owe you for the room, Herr—"

"Schroder." He held up a hand in protest. "You owe me nothing, Frau Lindheim, until the guest arrives, ja? And we will hope for your sake that he comes. At that time I will happily accept payment for lodging. You will need a room number and a key." He turned to scan the boxes, then pulled a key out of number seven. "A French couple has the room until tomorrow.

I will hold it open for Herr Lindheim after they check out."

———————

Elisa was astonished at the ease with which they had made a much-needed connection in Innsbruck. They had, in fact, told the old clerk nothing incriminating, and yet, she had given him all the information needed in the likelihood that the Gestapo should check their lodgings in Austria. When asked, he could tell them that Frau Theo Lindheim was staying at the hotel with her three children, and that the oldest boy was injured in a skiing accident.

Then Anna spoke with Dr. Wertmann, and he agreed that Wilhelm should remain immobile for at least a month. Certainly they would not be able to return to Berlin until the boy had recovered somewhat. An extension of their *Ausweis*, the German travel permit, was easily arranged through the Fremde Intelligence Office near the hotel on Rudolfstrasse.

Armed with all this information, Anna and Elisa sat down for lunch at the Cafe Maximillian, and spent the next two hours writing a series of letters to Theo in Berlin. Each letter was dated in sequence through Christmas and reported the progress of Wilhelm's recuperation after the accident, as well as the details of their holiday in Innsbruck. Each expressed the desire to see him soon and the hope that the government mix-up would soon be straightened out.

Stamped and sealed, the letters were then left with Herr Schroder at the hotel. One letter would be posted each day until the arrival of Theo Lindheim.

A final stop at the telegraph office relayed the urgent message that Wilhelm had been badly injured while skiing near Innsbruck. The return address was listed as Tyroler Haus, Room 7, Bahnstrasse, Innsbruck, Austria.

12

The Bait

Theo Lindheim had not shaved in three days. He sat in the red leather chair in his library and stared up at the shining volumes on the shelves. As daylight streamed through the window, he reached up and turned off the reading lamp on the table beside him.

He ran a hand wearily over his face and pressed his fingertips against his throbbing temples. The outcome of his arrest in Munich had been a simple matter of answering a few questions, and then he was escorted back to Berlin on the morning train. An official car had driven him to his own doorstep, and he had been dropped off with the Gestapo assurance that additional "routine questioning" would take place within a week or two. His travel permit had been revoked.

He had not been asked the whereabouts of Anna and the children. The Gestapo had no interest in where they were now. With Theo Lindheim back in Berlin, his wife and children would return.

Theo now understood everything quite clearly. He had offered a sizable amount of cash to the officer who had brought him home.

"Herr Lindheim, you are a Jew, and therefore an alien. Everything in your possession now, down to the last reichsmark, is already owned by the state. You cannot offer us anything *here*!" The man had laughed at the absurdity of Theo's naive offer.

"Then, why am I being held?" he questioned with dignity.

"We suspect that a man of your former financial stature would not have attempted to leave Germany unless you also have considerable assets banked outside the country."

"I have stayed within the law."

"No doubt. We have checked everything. There was a time when it was not against the law for a Jew to have accounts outside Germany. No doubt your wife will arrange for some of that capital to come back into this country in exchange for visas—for the sake of the Reich." He looked amused. "Of course, she will have to return here as well. We shall hope she arranges to finance her own *Ausweis* and those of your children as well."

So Theo had become the bait that would draw his family back into the clutches of the Reich—but not until they had arranged for a ransom to be paid from outside of the country. Now he knew that the sequence of events had been quite deliberately staged from the beginning. Travel permits had been granted, but no matter how or when the family tried to leave the country, at least one of them was destined to stay behind as hostage. Had it not been for the intervention of the American newsman at the station, Elisa would have been arrested and detained until Theo returned with Anna and the boys and appropriate payment from a Swiss account had been arranged. Theo had heard horror stories of young Jewish women left to the mercies of the Gestapo. He was thankful that he had been taken from the train instead of Elisa. To have watched her being led away would have been more than he could have endured.

Cradling his head in his hands, he tried to think what he could do next. How could he keep Anna and the children from returning to Germany and playing into the hands of Himmler's Blackshirts? Even if a ransom were paid, there was no guarantee that the entire terrible cycle would not begin all over again. Next time, perhaps, it would be Anna taken to the police station. He could not bear the thought.

"Anna," he whispered. "My beautiful Anna." He stood stiffly and moved toward the towering bookshelf. For a long time he surveyed the titles, at last resting his eyes on a row near the ceiling containing the works of William Shakespeare. The set was a rare edition published in the early eighteenth century. No doubt when the S.S. tore through the house, the volumes would be destroyed or confiscated.

Theo shook his head in disbelief at the certainty of the event. "Ominous. Yes, Anna," he said as though she were at his side. "Ominous that they burn such works."

He rolled the walnut library ladder to the front of the shelves and climbed toward *Hamlet*, *King Lear* and *MacBeth*. "Perhaps such a world is not worth living in, Anna. If this is indeed to be the way of things." He stretched out his hand and chose a copy of *Romeo and Juliet*. "We were so young when we saw this at the English Theatre in Vienna. I remember how you gripped my hand and wept when Juliet held up the dagger. Later you said you would not live without me, Anna. But you must, dearest. You must live and be safe for the children. You must not come for me."

Theo stroked the cover of the book lovingly, caressing its satiny surface as if he were touching Anna herself. He flipped the pages slowly, then lifted the open volume to his face and inhaled deeply the rich scent of antique leather, paper, and ink. With a sigh he set *Romeo and Juliet* aside, pulled out several more volumes of Shakespeare's tragedies, and drew a revolver from its hiding place behind the books on the shelf. "You must not come back to Berlin, Anna." He pocketed the small, ivory-handled weapon and climbed down, clutching the copy of *Romeo and Juliet* in his left hand.

———

Admiral Canaris towered over Thomas von Kleistmann's cluttered desk. His face was angry as he flipped a copy of Anna's telegram toward Thomas.

"I thought perhaps you should know, since you have some special interest in this case," Canaris said as though he was testing the depth of Thomas's concern.

"Innsbruck," Thomas repeated as he read the wire. "Is this confirmed?" He was hoping, of course, that the information was wrong. He measured his response so that he appeared disinterested.

"The Gestapo agent in Innsbruck has verified their presence there." Canaris almost smiled. "Of course, the Gestapo was formed only for police work inside Germany. They lack our resources. They are idiots and gangsters, for the most part." He hesitated. "Our informant in Innsbruck reports that the two women were in the city for only one day. They are obviously staying elsewhere."

Thomas felt sweat bead up on his forehead. He wondered why Canaris was telling him about a case he had nothing to do with. Had his visit to Theo Lindheim's office been reported? Was Canaris testing his loyalty and his truthfulness now? "Yes, I assumed they would—that is, they are probably staying in a smaller village, away from prying eyes, if your suspicions are correct."

Canaris studied him for a minute of silence until Thomas cleared his throat uncomfortably. "And what do you think, young von Kleistmann? Do you believe my suspicions? Will Theo Lindheim attempt to escape?"

Thomas stared hard at the telegram. "Frau Lindheim will not leave him here in Germany to his own fate, if that is what you are asking. Wherever she is, she will not leave him here alone, not as long as he is free. If Himmler has him thrown into Oranienburg, that is another matter. Then there will be nothing for her to do. But if he is still free, at home, in Berlin, able to move about—"

"But not cross the border."

"As you say."

"Theo Lindheim is a man I once admired. This is not my doing."

Thomas did not reply. He did not tell Canaris that he believed Theo Lindheim would never allow his wife and children to reenter Nazi Germany. Thomas was certain that he would stop them some way. "Certainly he knows he is being watched."

"Night and day by Himmler's Gestapo. Technically, this will not become a matter for us to contend with in the Abwehr unless Lindheim somehow escapes from the state police and crosses the border. An impossibility, I am told."

Thomas frowned. There was a hint of disappointment in Canaris' voice. Was he disappointed that the Abwehr was not involved, or that Theo could not escape the surveillance of Himmler's men and cross the border?

"If he is arrested"—Thomas groped for some word that might help Theo remain momentarily free—"then Anna Lindheim will not return. It is that simple. The Reich will not ever recover the funds that have been taken out of the country."

"Yes. Our conclusion exactly. And that of the Führer. He insists that Himmler continue the game of cat and mouse." There was an edge of anger and disapproval to Canaris's declaration, but Thomas did not dare question it.

"And what do you say?"

"I say, you know him well."

Thomas flushed and looked down uncomfortably. "Yes. He and my father—"

"We know all about that." Canaris snatched the wire from him. "But this is the Third Reich now. We are all expected to do our duty. Loyalty, you know."

"I wish no duty in this matter." Thomas leaned forward, almost pleading with Canaris.

"You know him well." Canaris brushed the protest aside. "Himmler has a half-dozen gangsters watching him. We have let the telegram go through to him. I need one good man to watch his movements, von Kleistmann."

"I ask that you choose someone else."

"I have already chosen."

———

Nearly thirty minutes passed as Theo sat behind his desk and contemplated the small pistol on the blotter. Again and again he mentally rehearsed his options. A roster of names and familiar faces of old friends rose up and then faded away one by one. Yes, there were men from among his old squadron who now served as officers in the Wehrmacht. Most had been serving Germany when upstarts like Hermann Göring were still carrying school books. Those noble few remained in their positions in the hope that they might still be able to reverse Germany's downward spiral toward war. Months ago these men had expressed their loyalty to the old order and their friendship to Lindheim, but that very declaration had been a way of saying goodbye. They could not hope to have the slightest influence in the government if they continued their twenty-year association with Theo and the Lindheim family. In August, the S.S. had written a concise definition of the Nazi party line against stiff-necked churchmen, Freemasons, and all Jews: *The Jew as a person is an enemy of National*

Socialism, as proven by the difference in his race. . . ." The logic was that anyone having friendship with a Jew must also be an enemy of Germany.

Elisa had already returned to Vienna when this edict was issued. She did not have to see the silent stony faces of dear friends as they passed on the street. Yes, of course, they still came to the big store. Old Grynspan altered their uniforms as though nothing at all was wrong. But these were small and ineffective acts of defiance.

There was no one to help Theo now. The phones were undoubtedly tapped. Watchers stood on every corner along Wilhelmstrasse. For Theo to attempt to approach those men who had been his friends would mean their certain destruction. He knew he could not chance that, not if there were to remain any good men at all among the military hierarchy. This was something he must face alone, with the dignity of a soldier.

He pulled out a clean sheet of stationery and groped for some word of explanation and comfort for Anna and the children. They must not, under any circumstances, return to Germany, and the only way to prevent that was by his death. He had studied the issue in every light, and now that he saw the inevitability of it, a sense of resignation settled on him. There was also some slight satisfaction that Hitler's diabolical forces would lose their hostage and the ransom in the bargain. Twenty years before, Theo had fought for Germany. Now, he reasoned, he was about to fight his last battle for the nation he loved.

The letter was short and to the point. Theo addressed the issue of his own death with the same directness with which he had conducted his life and his work.

> *Beloved Anna and children. Do not grieve for me, but for Germany. The Nazis take all, but not our souls, and thus they have lost the battle before it began. What I do now must be done. Know that I love you each one. Your loving husband and father.*

Theo sealed the envelope, then climbed the stairs to shower and shave and dress as though he were going to work. His leg ached. The jagged scar left by bullets from a French machine gun throbbed the warning that it would rain today in Berlin. Theo had often joked about his built-in barometer. Now, he rubbed it, vaguely astonished that soon he would feel no more pain at all.

Dressed in a dark double-breasted suit, an overcoat, and a black slouch hat, he looked as though he were going to work, like any other day. He pocketed the gun and the letter, confident that if he was detained he would put the weapon to good use before his tormentors could stop him. As for the letter to Anna, he knew he could not risk sending it to her through the mail. No doubt it would be intercepted. But there were ways around such things; as he conceived his plan he had remembered John Murphy, the American news reporter. Most of the foreign correspondents stayed at the Adlon Hotel only a few blocks away, and if he could find

Murphy, he might find the help he needed.

For a moment more, Theo stood in the foyer of his home. He was past sentiment, beyond regrets or sadness. His mind was firm and he moved without emotion. He stared blankly at himself in the mirror as though he were seeing the photograph of a man long dead.

As he turned to leave, the doorbell buzzed insistently. Theo slipped his hand in his pocket and let his fingers curl around the grip of the gun as he opened the door.

"Telegram for Herr Lindheim!" snapped a stern-looking boy of about twelve. On his sleeve he wore a swastika armband. He appraised Theo coolly and with disdain.

Theo uttered a few words of acknowledgment in a voice that sounded very far away. He resented the intrusion. He wanted nothing to distract him, to pull his mind from its deadly purpose at this moment.

"Three Reichsmarks," said the boy.

Theo paid him without speaking, and then shut the door on the boy's "Heil Hitler!" He was tempted to throw the message away, assuming that it was some additional warning or instructions from his captors. Then he skimmed the envelope and the point of origin . . . *Innsbruck!* Instantly his heart beat faster. His hands trembled at the realization that he held a precious word from Anna. *Do not weaken me, Anna. Do not come to me now when I am so certain of my course!* Theo caught a glimpse of himself in the mirror again. The icy reserve and determination had vanished. In its place stood the image of a man filled with longing for his family and his life; the face was pale and filled with anguish.

"Do not call me back to you, Anna!" he said aloud. "I cannot! The choice is made!"

At that, he shoved the unopened telegram deep into his pocket and stepped out into the drizzling rain.

13

Lindheim's Resolve

Murphy sat on the windowsill of his cluttered hotel room. His long legs stretched to the top of his desk, and he thought how easy it would be to simply kick his typewriter onto the floor and smash it to pieces among the wads of discarded paper that overflowed his waste basket. He was in a lousy mood, homesick for New York City and the sight of an American woman. Homesick for anyplace besides the Adlon Hotel and Berlin in a rainstorm.

It was pouring out on Wilhelmstrasse. Pedestrians splashed through puddles on the sidewalk, while inattentive taxis drove by, cutting wakes through the water on the street. Murphy grimaced at the German women in their black rubber overshoes and ankle-length raincoats. Except for the fact that their dripping hair was a bit longer, it was difficult to tell some scowling women's faces from the men's. Of course, there was Elisa Lindheim. But then, maybe she didn't count, since she was no longer in Berlin.

The thought of her filled him with a strange restlessness that bordered on anger. Most of the guys had steered clear of him since his return from Berchtesgaden. They had all assumed that the current diplomatic dance between Hitler and Mussolini had upset him. Actually, it was the haunting image of Elisa that returned again and again to his mind. Her wide, help-less eyes gazed pleadingly at him as she asked what he could do to help Theo Lindheim. The answer was *nothing!*

Inquiries at the American Embassy had only yielded embarrassed shrugs. A word placed here and there brought Murphy the information that Theo's *Ausweis* had been canceled. Lindheim was back in Berlin until further notice.

Murphy's work had suffered through the days, and so had his con-science. The whole Lindheim matter was really none of his concern, and Murphy had come to the conclusion that his own motives for interest had been rotten. Elisa was a good-looker, all right, and had that kind of "helpless-little-fawn" quality that always stopped him in his tracks. He could imagine how she might repay him if, in fact, he could really help her father out of a jam. The realization that his interest was based on Fraülein Lindheim's shapely beauty filled Murphy with an enormous amount of self-reproach. He figured he had every right to be angry at himself.

He scowled at the typewriter, at the empty sheet of paper staring back at him. He closed his eyes in a moment of frustration. When Elisa's imploring face materialized before him once more, Murphy opened his eyes and frowned down at the German women sloshing down Wilhelmstrasse. The whole world was falling apart, and he was thinking about a girl he would probably never see again.

"The Musikverein in Vienna . . . the name is Linder. . . ."

Murphy ran his fingers through his hair, wishing that he could forget the name and the address. *Vienna . . . Musikverein . . . Linder.* The information made his stomach ache. If it had been written down, he would have torn it up and thrown it away. Unfortunately, the name and address burned indelibly into his memory, along with the image of Elisa's golden hair tumbling over her shoulders as she stooped beside her suitcase. Murphy inhaled, somehow imagining that he could catch the scent of her perfume. Instead, the smell of stale cigar smoke filled his head and made him cough.

"Stinks in here," he muttered, opening the window slightly. The roar of traffic and rain brought him back to the reality of Wilhelmstrasse. He looked out onto the grayness of the day and shook his head slowly. "Nobody wants to be here, Murphy," he said to himself. "Nobody is in Berlin by choice."

At that, he lifted his eyes toward the British Embassy. A lone figure of a man walked quickly by the gloomy building. The man walked with a limp, his face hidden beneath an umbrella, but it seemed to Murphy that there was something familiar about him. Behind the man, two plainclothes Gestapo agents followed at a discreet distance. It was easy to spot the agents. They did not have umbrellas, yet they tried to look relaxed and nonchalant in the middle of the worst downpour of the season.

Murphy watched the man a moment more; then his eyes widened and he almost choked. "It's Lindheim!" he cried. "Theo Lindheim!" A slight movement of the umbrella had revealed Lindheim's grim and determined face. He dodged traffic clumsily as he limped across Wilhelmstrasse toward the Adlon Hotel. His two pursuers stayed close behind, oblivious to the torrential rain. Lightning flashed and thunder boomed like antiaircraft fire above their heads.

To Murphy's amazement, Theo walked directly beneath his window and then made a dash for the canvas awning and the front entrance of the hotel. The Gestapo men quickened their pace and also entered the building. Murphy noticed two more plainclothesmen watching from across the street, and another pair waiting beside the British Embassy.

For an instant, Murphy thought what a coincidence it was that he would see Theo Lindheim just as he was thinking about Elisa. But he promptly dismissed that notion as nonsense; after all, he had not thought about much of anything else but Elisa for days.

Murphy was just about to head for the lobby when a sharp knock startled him. Before he opened the door, somehow he knew that Theo Lindheim stood on the other side.

In one move, Murphy pulled Theo into the room and shut the door behind him. He slid the bolt closed with a click, then turned to Theo, who looked more startled than Murphy.

"How did you know—" Theo began.

"I saw you out the window. Did they follow you up here?"

"I took the elevator to the fifth floor and then walked down two flights. One of your reporter friends showed me to your room. I think the men who followed me are looking on the floors above." Theo stopped and wiped the raindrops from his face. "It does not matter," he said with resignation. "Soon enough they will find me again." He looked wearily around the room as though he longed for a place to sit down.

"I thought you were at Gestapo headquarters." Murphy pulled him toward a chair, then closed the heavy draperies. The room was dark, but Murphy did not turn on the light.

"Why should they keep me there?" Theo smiled bitterly. "They want Anna and the children to come back. They will not close the vise any tighter until there are more hostages within their clutches."

Murphy nodded and Elisa's clear eyes became vivid in his mind again. "Your daughter reached Austria safely." He tried to console the desperate man before him.

"Yes. So I assumed. A wire came for me this morning. From Innsbruck. I haven't read it. I suppose the S.S. and the Gestapo read it first since I am under suspicion." He pulled a white envelope from his pocket. "They must not come here. It is a trap. I am the bait."

Murphy stared at the envelope. It was unmarked in any way. "What is it?"

"A letter. A farewell to my family, Herr Murphy." Theo's voice was steady and without self-pity. "I cannot address it. The Gestapo will then know they are not in Innsbruck. I cannot mail it; it would never reach them." He leveled his gaze on Murphy. "If perhaps you will be across the border of Germany, perhaps in Austria—"

Murphy did not reply for a long time. He stared at Lindheim's trembling hand. The determined face was almost as white as the envelope. "A farewell?" Murphy asked. But it was not a question. The meaning of Theo's words were clear.

"They must not return to Germany," Theo said again.

Murphy leaned away from the outstretched message. "I can't take that to your family," he said, ashamed all over again that he had not done more to help.

Theo withdrew his hand and looked away. After a slight hesitation, he stood up. "Yes. I should not have involved you. Goodbye, Herr Murphy." He turned to go, but Murphy caught him by the arm.

"Wait a minute!" he cried. "What I mean is . . . there has to be something else. I mean, if you are thinking about—Herr Lindheim, I don't want to be part of your—"

"My death?" Theo sounded amused. "Herr Murphy, you are an American. Perhaps you do not know how very insignificant my death will be to the Third Reich. I simply wish to save the lives of my family. A reasonable desire. And all I ask of you is that you mail this when it is convenient. The act will already have been accomplished, and I assure you that you will have no part in my death . . . only my goodbye."

"Can't you find another way out?"

"They have canceled my *Ausweis*."

"No. I mean, can't you get across the border another way?" Murphy was desperate, grasping at straws. Theo Lindheim seemed suddenly more than the object of Elisa's concern. Here was a noble and honest man locked in a hopeless situation. He had chosen his own death as the safest way out for his family, and the reality of the situation suddenly overwhelmed Murphy with the need to *do* something.

Again, Theo smiled at the suggestion. "I have thought of it myself. But perhaps you did not notice the Gestapo regiment following me." He laid a hand on Murphy's arm. "We are strangers, you and I. This is not your concern or responsibility. I simply ask that you see that the letter is delivered."

Murphy nodded mutely. He was watching a man drown and did not have a single line of hope to toss to him. "I . . . yes. Certainly."

Theo passed him the letter. "The address is to my daughter. Not difficult to remember—"

Murphy said it before Theo had a chance. "Musikverein. Vienna. The name is Linder." His words sounded hollow as he stared at the blank envelope.

"She told you this?" Theo was surprised.

"I crossed the border into Austria with her. After they took you."

"Thank you. The kindness of a stranger—much greater than my own countrymen." He stepped closer. "If you see them . . ." He paused, searching for words. Was there more that Murphy could say? Something more than Theo's own brief note? "Never mind." He extended his hand. "Danke, Herr Murphy." He turned to leave, limping slowly toward the door.

Murphy watched him for a few seconds, feeling as though he had somehow gotten himself caught up in the plot of some tragic movie. "Herr Lindheim!" he said suddenly. "Colonel Lindheim. Stay a while." Murphy surprised himself. For the last five minutes he had not thought of Elisa as more than the recipient of this terrible letter.

"I cannot," Theo muttered.

"Just hold on, will you? Stay and . . . dry out at least."

Theo looked apologetic, then threatened by Murphy's eagerness to keep him. "There is nothing to change what must be done, Herr Murphy."

Murphy looked around wildly for some purpose to delay; he needed time to think. The typewriter and the crumpled paper caught his attention. "No. Yes. I mean, if this is the way it has to be, Herr Lindheim, at least help me out. Maybe help others, too. I would like to talk to you. Get a story about all this for the American press."

Theo smiled doubtfully. "There are a hundred Jewish deaths that go unheeded every morning. This is a small thing. Small."

"Just—" Murphy felt him slipping away. "Just a few minutes. This is not anything American readers could believe, see? But you are a pretty big man in Germany. A war ace in France and—"

"And a Jew. Racially impure to the present government. There is little else to say."

"So that's it? I'm taking your letter. You owe me a few minutes. A few words."

Theo stood with his hand on the doorknob. He looked first at Murphy and then at the typewriter. Murphy was, in effect, blackmailing him into talking. After all, the newspaperman had the letter. Theo nodded reluctantly, then limped past Murphy to sit down on the sofa again. His right hand was thrust deep into the pocket of his overcoat and his fingers tightly clutched the pistol grip as though by its touch he could hold firmly to his resolution.

Brandenburg Gate behind his car, Thomas von Kleistmann pulled to the curb of Unter den Linden just across from the Adlon Hotel. Plainclothes members of the state police were evident everywhere, even in the rainstorm. Thomas set the hand brake and opened the windows a crack, then settled back to wait. Theo Lindheim had limped into the hotel ten minutes earlier.

Thomas was here only as a matter of obedience to Canaris, certain that his presence as a member of the Military Police was only a gesture on the part of his superior. If Theo were to be arrested again, there was no doubt that the Gestapo had first call on the prisoner. Thomas had been sent as an observer, and the chore made him resentful. Why had he been chosen for such a duty when Canaris most certainly knew about his former relationship with the Lindheim family? He would have married Elisa in a minute if she had accepted him three years ago, before the Nuremburg laws passed. It had been her decision to wait, not his. If he had thought it would have made any difference, he might have crossed the border into Austria himself; but once she had seen him in the uniform of an Abwehr officer, she had become cold and angry toward him. He did not write her anymore. At first he had hoped she would answer him; when he was certain of the fact that he was also being watched, he had not dared address any piece of mail to Elisa Linder in Vienna. The connection was too obvious. It was only a matter of time, everyone said, until Austria was also a part of the Reich. He feared for Elisa if that happened.

The windshield of his car began to fog and he opened the side windows wider. Outside, rain washed the air clean of exhaust fumes from the traffic. He rubbed a small round circle on the window and looked out at the hotel. Then he laid his chin on the top of the steering wheel and watched as two more Gestapo agents walked slowly up the street and stopped outside the front entrance of the hotel.

Surely Theo is smart enough to know he cannot escape, thought Thomas, amused by the fact that Theo was inside the building, warm and dry, while a dozen of Himmler's henchmen stood soaked in the cold street. The government was undoubtedly afraid that it would lose a fortune if it lost Theo Lindheim. Thomas had even heard it said that fat little Göring had once paid a call on Theo, on the pretext of one former fighter pilot visiting another. The result of the visit was that Göring had come away awed by the fine art and furnishings of the Lindheim home. From that moment, it was assumed by men in the know that Göring had to figure a legal way to appropriate the property and possessions of Theo.

This sort of action was common among Hitler's closest advisors. Without fail, they always got what they lusted after. Thomas was glad that Elisa had been out of the country—no doubt she would have been regarded as a prize for some S.S. officer. While the law against intercourse between a Jew and a German was in effect, it still did not stop the commonplace act of rape by Nazi soldiers against Jewish women. These acts were never prosecuted—they were, in fact, looked upon with some amusement by the authorities.

For all these reasons, Thomas had urged the Lindheims to obtain foreign passports and be ready to leave at a moment's notice. Now Thomas thought ironically, *I should have advised them to leave without any notice at all.*

He had told Theo that even Austria must be only a temporary stopping place. Hitler had, of course, signed the pact with the Austrian Chancellor Schuschnigg that Germany would respect the right of the Austrians to choose their own destiny. Schuschnigg had the assurance that no move would be made by the Nazi party to stir up trouble in Vienna if amnesty were offered to the Nazis imprisoned there. Schuschnigg had taken Hitler at his word, and thousands had been pardoned for their part in the rebellion of 1934 and the assassination of Dollfuss.

"Schuschnigg is a fool," Thomas said aloud. He had seen the secret documents that had been sent to Vienna and the leaders of the Nazi party there. They were to arrange an incident, something to cast blame on the

Jews. Hitler was devious in his dealings, and always created a reason to strike, even if there were none. Exactly what the incident would be, Thomas did not know. Members of the army looked on such political subterfuge with disapproval. Most of the old Weimar generals who remained in power talked fearfully that Hitler was pushing the country toward war.

Thomas shook his head. He did not believe Hitler wanted war. He was certain that the generals did not. No, Hitler was motivated by a bottomless lust for power—just as Göring lusted after rare art and beautiful women, no matter whose they were. This pursuit of Theo was not borne out of hatred for him as a man or a Jew. All of that was just an excuse—an excuse for lawless men to take what belonged to others. It seemed strange that those who served the Hitlers and the Himmlers and the Görings believed the constant lies. *"The Jew is our misfortune."* It was those little men in the service of greed who were the most violent, the most dedicated to the brutality of the racial policies. They murdered and terrorized for one reason only: because they could. They were the law of lawlessness; the power of evil was their creed and their joy and their god!

With a shudder, Thomas stared at the men who stood waiting for Theo. Why did he not come out? If a ransom was required, he could pay it, and perhaps they would let him go. But even as the thought ran through his mind, Thomas dismissed it. Those shivering creatures waiting in the rain enjoyed their game. A cat with a full belly will not let a mouse go unharmed; they would not sell their right to intimidate Theo Lindheim. That was the way of Germany now, and Thomas was sent simply to witness the inevitable.

14

Decoy

The alterations shop of Lindheim's Department Store was in more disarray than usual. The racks were crammed with suits and dresses and uniforms left for last-minute alterations. Grynspan the tailor and young Herschel worked feverishly on hems and buttons and sleeves. They stopped for a few minutes to wolf down their lunch, then returned to their tasks.

Old Grynspan hardly noticed the tall lean man in the dark overcoat who entered the room. Herschel looked up from a row of buttons and immediately froze with apprehension. The stranger's face was in shadow, but he still wore his hat. *Gestapo!* Herschel's heart raced, although he knew he had no reason to be afraid.

"Papa," Herschel said quietly, and the urgency in his voice caused the old man to look up from his work to see the man near the doorway.

"Can I help you?" the old tailor asked almost absently.

"I have come to pick up a uniform, if you are Herr Grynspan."

"I am Herr Grynspan, and if I have what you need—" He stood but did not move until the man stepped out into the light.

The stranger's face was gaunt and worried. Herschel noticed that he spoke with a trace of British accent. "Good," said the man. "It is a Luftwaffe uniform . . ."

"Belonging to?"

"A former officer of the Luftwaffe. Retired."

"His name?"

The intruder continued. "You made the uniform three years ago. For a special event honoring the war dead."

"Three years ago!" Herr Grynspan scoffed. "I have nothing of such . . ." His voice faltered and a flicker of suspicion crossed his face.

"Don't give him anything, Papa," Herschel whispered.

The man moved toward them. He seemed almost angry. "You know what I'm talking about."

"I don't know *you*." Herr Grynspan shrugged and smiled in mock ignorance.

"It doesn't matter who I am."

"Indeed it does, in these precarious times. I cannot give away suits of clothing without some identification."

"Then please accept this." The man extended a crisp hundred-mark bill.

"I was paid already for the work in question." Herr Grynspan did not look at the money. If this was indeed a Gestapo trap, he would not sell his life for a mere hundred-mark note.

"Yes, the officer told me you were paid even though the political events in Germany prevented him from ever wearing the uniform." The man raised his eyes to the tall walnut cabinet in the back of the room. "It is in there, I believe."

The tailor hesitated. Herschel leaned closer and hissed in desperation, "He could be Gestapo! You can't give away a Luftwaffe uniform . . ."

"If you refuse, I will simply take it."

"Then perhaps I will call the authorities." Grynspan's eyebrows went up, and the man laughed at the threat.

"You want to be a witness for the Gestapo, eh, Herr Grynspan?" The man walked toward the cabinet. "It would be better for you if you continue to act ignorant about this, I think. The officer insisted that you not become involved any more than is necessary." He opened the cabinet himself and stood looking blankly at the row of Luftwaffe uniforms. "I'm going to take one of these, old man. Your clients will not like it if I take the wrong one."

Angrily, the old tailor tore through the uniforms until he pulled a colonel's Luftwaffe uniform from the back. "Here it is. But if anything happens—any investigation—I know nothing."

"That's fair." The man placed the hundred-mark bill on the cutting table and, obviously pleased with himself, demanded a box for the uniform. "It is raining. And there are curious people on every corner who would wonder what I am doing with this."

Herschel quickly wrapped it. Then, his heart still pounding with fear, he returned to work on the row of buttons, even though he could hardly hold the needle.

———

The cadre of Gestapo agents watching the Adlon Hotel had grown weary since Theo had entered the building three hours earlier. From his window, Murphy counted an even dozen dripping, miserable men out on Unter den Linden and Wilhelmstrasse. They were concerned, no doubt, by Theo's disappearance inside the building, but as of that moment the order for a full-scale search had not been issued. After all, everyone in

Berlin knew that the entire foreign press corps was staying at the Adlon, and the last thing the Nazi government wanted was a reported arrest of a Jewish war hero showing up in all the international newspapers.

The Gestapo agents had every exit of the large hotel covered; from the side entrance to the kitchen, Nazi police were watching for the distinctive limp of Herr Theo Lindheim. There was no way he could leave the Adlon without being seen, followed, and arrested for questioning. His extended time inside the hotel would undoubtedly arouse the wrath and suspicion of the Nazi Ministry of Justice. Even so, they would not arrest him until he was well clear of the meddling eyes of the foreign press. The Führer had given express orders that only positive impressions should be made on outsiders. The detention of Theo Lindheim would hardly be considered a good image of Nazi public relations.

Murphy had his story now, but had not yet written the ending.

"How many of them?" asked Theo from across the room.

"Twelve. Probably more."

"They will spot my limp."

"That's what we are counting on." Murphy glanced at his watch. "A couple minutes more," he said quietly. He looked up into the stormy sky. "Pray to God it keeps on raining, Herr Lindheim," he muttered.

As if in answer to his words, a gust of rain blew against the windowpane with a fierce rattle. The Gestapo men ducked their heads and shoved their hands deeper into overcoat pockets. At that exact moment, protected by an umbrella, dark overcoat, and hat with the brim pulled low, a man limped from the Wilhelmstrasse exit of the hotel. His features were hidden, and he tucked his face under the collar of his coat as he scurried toward Unter den Linden and hailed a taxi.

Gestapo agents stiffened at the sight of him and immediately exchanged hasty words. Two men ran out onto the street and hailed another taxi to follow after the first. Murphy clapped his hands in delight at the sight. "Nice show, Johnson," he said. Then he turned to Theo. "They're following Johnson."

"How many?"

"Four. Four down. Eight to go." He glanced at his watch again. "There goes Timmons." His voice was excited as he related the exit of Timmons from the Linden Street door. "He's got the limp! Perfect! Keep the umbrella low, Timmons, boy! You can't see his face; he's got the hat brim down low. Dressed all in dark clothes. They're buzzing about him across the street. Yes! There go four more. Timmons is walking . . . limping. Hailing a taxi!"

At two minute intervals, four more imitation Theo Lindheims recruited from the press corps exited the Adlon Hotel. Gestapo agents dispersed to follow their limping quarry as Murphy clutched Theo's arm and led him down three flights of stairs to the main lobby of the hotel. Dressed in the striking uniform of a Luftwaffe officer, Theo simply blended in with a hundred other uniformed men who moved confidently across the marbled foyer. He, too, wore the bill of his cap pulled low on his forehead. A pale gray overcoat was slung over his arm and he and Murphy talked animately about the force of the French Air Corps and that of the Reich. They walked slowly toward the revolving doors. Murphy's hands were wet with perspiration. It was only a matter of minutes before the decoys would be stopped and released and the Gestapo agents would flock back to the Adlon.

Theo inhaled deeply and continued to talk as Murphy flagged a taxi. Neither of them looked up to see if the watchers were still on the street corner. Theo strode forward, aware of the fact that his uneven gait must be obvious. Rain hammered down on his cap as Murphy nudged him into the cab, then slipped in behind him and slammed the door. Only then did they dare look out onto the street. One, lone, unhappy officer stood beside a streetlamp, his bleary eyes fixed on the revolving door and anyone who dared come out. At that moment, Timmons exited a taxi at the Linden entrance and limped hurriedly back into the Adlon. A car full of Gestapo men pulled up behind him, and the four occupants leaped out. One ran into the hotel while the others resumed their positions.

It was all Murphy could do to keep from laughing out loud.

As the taxi pulled out into the flooded street, Theo reached into the pocket of the gray overcoat and pulled out the rumpled telegram. He had hope; he could read it now. He skimmed the words on the thin paper, folded it, and pushed it back into his pocket.

Murphy caught Theo's glance and raised an eyebrow. Theo nodded silently, and turned toward the front seat as the cabbie spoke.

"Where to?" he asked impatiently.

"Tempelhof." Theo's voice bore the confidence of command.

"Bitte, Colonel," smiled the driver. "Yes. Tempelhof Airfield. I should have known. I recognize the uniform of a Luftwaffe officer. I gave Herr Göring a ride when his car broke down. I told him and I will tell you, it is my dream to be a Luftwaffe pilot." Young eyes glinted with admiration as he looked at Theo in the rearview mirror.

"And what is your name, bitte?" Theo played the role to the hilt.

"Johann Schmidt," said the driver.

"Germany will need good pilots, Johann. Let us see how well you navigate through a rainstorm, eh?"

———

Men had been scurrying out into the rain from the Adlon all afternoon. Now, as the clouds above Berlin grew even blacker, suddenly every man who emerged from the towering building had a limp.

Thomas von Kleistmann laughed in spite of the seriousness of his assignment as he watched Gestapo agents gesturing to one another in confusion. *"There he is! Limping, you see! There is Theo Lindheim. No, there!"*

Even Thomas had been uncertain of the six men in their trench coats, their faces concealed behind hats and umbrellas. Any one of them could have been Theo. In fact, Thomas knew they had to be foreign newsmen. No doubt their newspapers would hear of their involvement in this deception. Probably nothing much would happen. Nothing could be proved, after all. One of them would say he was limping because he had a pebble in his shoe, while another claimed that he always limped when the weather was damp.

Thomas found himself inwardly cheering as the last limping impostor came out of the Adlon to get into a taxi. And then Thomas suddenly went cold inside. At the instant one taxi returned, he saw the unmistakable form of Theo Lindheim dressed in the uniform of a Luftwaffe officer. Thomas swallowed hard, unable to tear his eyes away from the familiar figure. How many times had he seen Theo dressed in his uniform as they traveled to the cemetery together to pay respects to Wilhelm von Kleistmann. Theo had even named his oldest son after Thomas's father, and had often said to young Wilhelm, *"You are named for a great man. A true patriot of the Fatherland, and more than that, my truest friend. Hold your head high, young Wilhelm. Yes. You are named for greatness."*

No one else was watching the uniformed officer and his companion as they stepped into the blue cab. Only Thomas recognized the man who had been his only link with his own father. *"Wilhelm would have been proud of you, Thomas. Sometimes I feel him looking down on us and smiling, you know? I can think of nothing greater than the house of Lindheim and the house of von Kleistmann joined."*

Theo's cab pulled slowly from the curb as half a dozen Gestapo agents swarmed around an indignant young man who pointed to his shoe and proclaimed that he had nothing to do with any plots. Thomas looked at the angry agents and considered what it would mean if the Abwehr were to stop Theo from escaping. Himmler would certainly find less favor in the eyes of Hitler. Thomas von Kleistmann would be the hero of the department.

Thomas smiled and turned the key in the ignition. His car roared to a start and he pulled into traffic just as a deafening crash of thunder boomed over the Adlon. He smiled slightly and shook his head. "Don't worry," he said, rolling his eyes upward toward the thunder. "I am only going home." Then, as Theo's cab turned onto Wilhelmstrasse, Thomas lifted his hand in brief farewell and turned the opposite direction on Behrenstrasse.

Theo was dressed in his Luftwaffe uniform. The taxi was not moving toward the train station, but directly toward Tempelhof Airfield. A series of lightning bolts flashed down to the ground and Thomas frowned at what was almost certainly Theo Lindheim's last hope. Perhaps it was no hope at all, but somehow it seemed better than the web that waited for him here if he stayed.

Flights to Frankfurt, Munich, and Paris had been canceled one after another. As darkness gathered above Tempelhof Airfield, disappointed passengers grumbled and filed out to find taxis back into the city. It would be morning at least before the next plane left Berlin, and even then, ticket holders were advised to call before they made the trip back to Tempelhof. Theo and Murphy filed through a crowd of angry officers and diplomatic couriers, who grumbled among themselves about the unreliability of air travel. Most would take the night trains that departed Berlin every half hour.

Theo turned to Murphy. A bolt of lightning caused the lamps of the waiting room to dim and flicker a moment. "This is where we say goodbye, my friend." Theo extended his hand.

"You sure you don't want to try the train?" Murphy replied as yet another flash cracked the sky above Tempelhof.

A slight smile played on Theo's lips. He shook his head almost imperceptibly. "I have flown in worse."

"When?" Murphy frowned, genuinely worried as the torrential downpour increased.

"Those are stories to tell my grandchildren, Herr Murphy." He turned slightly and looked toward the door that led out to the runway. There was no one standing guard. Out on the front sidewalk, porters blew whistles, and disgruntled men crammed into cabs. One young man labored over the piles of tickets behind the counter. He purposely avoided making eye contact with the unhappy people who crowded in the line before him.

"You're certain?" Murphy lowered his voice.

With a curt nod, Theo turned away from him and walked unnoticed toward the glass doors that led to the tarmac. Murphy was the only one who watched him, the only one interested. A dozen small planes waited outside in the pouring rain. Lightning cut a jagged hole in the sky, making the aircraft and Theo Lindheim seem even smaller and more vulnerable.

Murphy stared openly. Men passed him, unseeing in their own unhappiness. The overcoat still over his arm, Theo strolled along the line of small planes like a man searching for his automobile in a parking lot. Twice he stopped to peer into the cockpits; then, he moved on to the next plane.

Murphy's heart hung in his throat as he watched the selection. For a moment he was filled with the fear that Theo would not find a plane suitable to fly. When he stopped at the side of an ancient biplane and put on his overcoat, Murphy was afraid that he had simply found another way to kill himself.

As if responding to Murphy's thoughts, Theo looked up through the window into the waiting room. *What does he want?* Murphy looked around. Theo was still unnoticed. "Okay," Murphy mumbled, walking toward the door. The wind blew fiercely against the door as Murphy shoved it open. Theo's overcoat flapped wildly. Murphy sprinted toward him; inside the lighted building, the passengers looked only toward the front entrance, where porters wrestled baggage into overcrowded vehicles.

"You can't fly this!" Murphy protested, yelling above the wind.

The WW I vintage plane rocked and groaned in the gale. "I will need help!" Theo unstrapped a tarp from the propeller, letting the wind take it.

Theo grasped Murphy by the arm and fixed him with an intent gaze. "The telegram!" he shouted. "From Anna, an address in Innsbruck—the Tyroler Haus. It may be a decoy, a cover for me."

Murphy nodded, water streaming from his face. "I got it!" he yelled back. "But you can't fly in this kind of storm!" Murphy held tightly to his drenched hat.

"I will need help starting the engine!" Theo called above the howl. "Remove the blocks from the wheels! We'll have to push her out onto the runway!"

"Herr Lindheim! You won't get her off the ground."

Theo turned and scowled at him in a sudden, angry resistance to his words. "Tonight this storm is sent for me!" He shouted, gesturing toward the backs of the preoccupied passengers. "One way or another it will take me far from Germany, Herr Murphy!" Rain trickled from the bill of his cap, stinging his eyes. "Now help me push, or leave me to my own fate!"

Murphy stared at him in frustration. Here was a man who planned to shoot himself a few hours before. A fragile biplane and a tempest that had grounded every flight in Germany looked better than the alternative. Murphy kicked away the wheel blocks and grasped the wing struts as Theo leaned his back into guiding the aircraft onto the dark runway. Murphy prayed that there would be no sudden burst of lightning to illuminate their actions. "Can you find your way into Austria?" he asked as Theo climbed into the cockpit.

"I am heading directly to Prague." Theo settled in the cramped, open seat behind the controls. "If I am delayed"—his voice was matter-of-fact—"you still have my letter! Tell Anna and the children what has happened!"

As the reporter looked up at the pilot, suddenly he was struck with the courage and nobility of this man Germany had declared an enemy of the state. "I'll try Vienna first," Murphy promised. "The Musikverein. Then if I don't find her—" Murphy stopped, overcome by the feeling that he was watching the execution of a great man. Yes, Murphy would find Elisa. He would tell her of the brave and impossible attempt of her father to join them. Perhaps Theo felt that this was better than a bullet—more suitable, somehow. Murphy nodded in silent agreement. "I'll tell them!" He bellowed against the unrelenting wind.

"Tell the men, the reporters, I give my thanks, ja? Grüss Gott, Herr Murphy!" He saluted. "You will need to crank the propeller on three!"

Murphy nodded again and backed away, grasping the antique wooden propeller and heaving it downward with all his weight behind the push. To his surprise, the motor coughed and turned over with a deafening roar that blended into the sound of the wind. Water sprayed Murphy, soaking through his overcoat. He dodged a wingtip as the biplane spun into the wind and then, like a small bird lifted on a breeze, the aircraft lifted off the ground. It hovered in the dark sky over the field for an instant, and then, as lightning split the black clouds all around, it disappeared behind a curtain of rain. For a long time, Murphy stood alone on the wet cement and stared off where he had last seen the aircraft bucking and rocking on the air currents. He expected to see the bright burst of an explosion as the conclusion for his news dispatch. Instead, a more distant bolt of lightning arched toward the ground, and for an instant, Murphy thought he spotted the tiny aircraft as it cut a wake through the tempest.

15

A Matter of Conscience

Admiral Canaris, chief of the Abwehr of the Third Reich, tossed the file across the desk to Thomas von Kleistmann. "It was foolish of you to go to Lindheim's office, Thomas. Foolish."

"The Lindheims have been friends of my family since—" Thomas attempted a weak defense.

"All the more damning for you." The older man's ice-blue eyes searched Thomas' face. "Could you possibly imagine that Himmler was not having Theo Lindheim watched? You thought that the Gestapo would not open a file on you as well?" He drummed his fingers impatiently on the folder. "They have made copies in triplicate, no doubt. One for themselves and Himmler, one for Hitler, and one for me, of course. Quite embarrassing that a member of my staff is caught sneaking down the back steps of a Jew's office. And then his former lover emerges ten minutes later."

"I did not even see Elisa!" Thomas snapped. "I did not know she was there."

"That is not in the report, as you may well imagine."

"They may say what they like in the report."

"They will. And they have."

"Certainly the Reich cannot condemn an innocent visit."

Canaris leaned closer and smiled bitterly. "That is where we have all made our mistake. Or have you forgotten so early? The Reich may tell you whom you may love and whom you must hate. Oh yes, Thomas, the Reich can dictate the inward life of every man."

"Not the inward life." Thomas looked up sharply. "Only the outward show."

"Are the two not the same?" Canaris leaned back. "Ah well, a philosophical question. One we should have thought of in 1933 before it was too late." He smiled slightly as though hoping for some signal from Thomas in reply.

Thomas sat impassively. "So. I have broken some law. Oh yes. I have forgotten it is a law now. I spoke with the man who was a friend to my father, and to me since I was a child."

"You cannot cover your act by sarcasm. There is too much at stake here. If *you* advised him to leave the country—"

"Then Hitler will simply nationalize all of his property and possessions and Germany will be richer for it."

"They would have done that anyway, sooner or later."

"Then one less prisoner to feed at Dachau . . . or one less bullet for a Jewish industrialist."

Canaris slammed his fist on the desk. "Enough! Don't you realize that S.S. bullets are looking for places to lodge? If not the brain of a Jew, then perhaps the head of a young officer in the Abwehr!"

"Yes. That has occurred to me. And Germany would lose a loyal son."

"Loyal to what? To whom?" The face of Canaris was intense. "To the laws? The laws change every day. If we are told that day is night and night day, then it must be so or we will perish with those who are too proud to be liars."

"I am a liar," Thomas said. "Black is white." There was a sense of weary desperation in his voice that matched the pain in once-honorable Canaris.

Canaris ran a hand through his silver hair. "No. Only men of truth admit to such a thing. There are many now among us who play at being liars. But it is only a game." His eyes held those of Thomas. "Do you know why they gave me this report? This report of your meeting with Lindheim and his daughter?"

"I can guess."

"Yes. They test my loyalty to them now. I am supposed to turn you over to them."

"I supposed as much."

"I have decided to give you another chance to prove your loyalty to the Fatherland, Thomas von Kleistmann. We are in need of good liars now, or I fear we will fall to the Father of Lies."

Thomas looked down at his hands and then back at the folder. He was afraid to hear the words of Canaris—afraid that he was to become one more sacrifice in the long line of Nazi sacrificial victims. "What more can I do to prove my loyalty? A hundred times I have denied my conscience—"

"Yes. Your conscience. Yourself." Canaris was not directing his words to Thomas any longer, but had suddenly turned inward. He frowned and stared for an uncomfortably long time at the young man's face. At last he spoke. "Perhaps it is time to find it again. A delicate balance. The truth. A lie. A man's conscience." He waved a hand distractedly in the air. "So.

We must find a post for you. For Thomas von Kleistmann. Perhaps in Paris? Among the French? Do you speak French? Or perhaps in England? Do you fancy a trip across the Channel, Thomas?"

"It doesn't matter. One place is as good as another," he said quietly.

"Yes. The climate of Berlin cannot be healthful for you now, I am certain of that." He dipped his pen in the brass inkwell on his desk and took out a sheet of stationery with his name on the letterhead. "The signature of Admiral Canaris is still worth something, although Himmler and the Gestapo would scratch it out if possible." He paused mid-stroke and looked hard at Thomas. "This may yet be your death warrant." His voice was almost sorrowful. "But if you stay it is a certainty that—"

"You have not yet said what is required of me."

"I am not yet certain what is required of you. But when I know, you must swear by your duty—"

"Duty to what? To whom?"

"Your conscience. Only that."

———

Herschel Grynspan had fallen asleep with his head on the makeshift desk in his tiny garret bedroom. The pen had fallen from his hand, smearing the clean, white sheet of stationery beneath it. Beside his chair a dozen scraps of wadded paper spoke of his effort to write the letter he had carried inside for so many days.

Dear Elisa, I am writing in the hope that you have gone away from this place and found. . . . Dearest Elisa, How often I have thought about your kind words for me about the university, and. . . . Dear Elisa . . .

He dreamed of her now, as he had every night since he had seen her last. She was smiling, looking at him with the love and respect a woman has for her man. Together they stood on a corner of the Kudamm as endless parades of Nazi soldiers passed by. Boots crashed against the pavement as the men marched in perfect unity toward a wall of flame that reached to the sky. Row on row they disappeared into the fires as Elisa held Herschel's hand in hers and smiled softly at the spectacle.

It was not the crash of boots that woke Herschel from his sleep but the shouting of angry voices outside on the street.

"Open! In the name of the Reich!" A short burst of automatic machine-gun fire accompanied the voices, followed by the sounds of splintering wood and hobnails crashing up the stairs. "Grynspan!" they cried, and Herschel knew at once who they were and why they had come.

He gathered his scraps of paper and lit the corner of one sheet with the flame of the candle. Fire devoured his thoughts and words, and his dreams were consumed in the bewildered cries of his father and the weeping of his mother.

"Where are they, Jew?"

"I do not know! I cannot—"

"Shut up! Jewish pig! Come with us! If we cannot have it from you easily, then we shall get it from you hard!"

"But please! I only worked for the man. I am only small. A small man! Herr Lindheim would not open his mind to me!"

"Then we will open your mind. With an axe!" A loud thump followed and then another scream from Herschel's mother. They did not come up the garret stairs to search for him. Why?

Herschel blew out the flame and rolled under his bed, trembling with terror. He pressed his ear against the floorboards and listened to every blow and every moan in the room below his.

"Please," his mother pleaded. "He is no one. You cannot find what you want here! Please!"

Hot tears rolled from Herschel's eyes and he wiped them away, afraid that they would drip through the boards and onto his father's unfeeling tormentors. Minutes passed. The blows subsided.

"If he knew he would talk. So he worked for the Jew Lindheim. Maybe he doesn't know."

"Come on. We're wasting time." A final thump sounded as a boot gave one last blow to the unconscious tailor. Herschel winced as though he had taken the force of it himself. Why did they not come for him? *Why?* He hardly dared to breathe as their footsteps retreated down the dark stairway.

His mother began to cry out, "Lazer! Lazer, my dearest! My husband! What have they done? Oh, what have they done to you?"

The words of the Jewish physician fell heavily on the Grynspan household. "Lazer, you will certainly lose your left eye. Two ribs are fractured. You are lucky to be alive."

From his bed, Lazer Grynspan said weakly, "Is any man lucky to be alive in these days? Better we should not have been born, I think. Better."

Herschel stood at the foot of the bed, gripping the footboard until his knuckles turned white. His mother sat weeping beside her husband and whispering the same word over and over again. *"Why? Why?"*

"Because they are animals, Mama. Not men. They are like the Golem. Made of clay. Mindless to the bidding of their master."

"My dearest Lazer—so kind. Why would they do this?"

The doctor gently bandaged the tailor's head and left a small bottle of pills. "There is nothing else to do. Normally, of course, he would be at the hospital. But there is no opening for Jews, as you know." He smiled bitterly, his face reflecting his own anger in the flickering light of the candle. "No place for Jewish doctors, either."

"Herschel—" The old tailor held out his hand to his son. "No place for tailors. Or sons of tailors . . ."

The young man knelt at his father's side and clasped his hand gently.

The knuckles were swollen from the sole of a Gestapo boot. "Yes, Papa, I am here."

"Then you must not be here!" The tailor's voice took on a new strength. "You must go now . . . to Paris. Go. Stay with your Uncle Israel. He has a little shop . . ." He faltered. "The university. Remember . . ."

"You should be still now, Herr Grynspan," the doctor said gruffly.

"But, Herschel . . . he is our son. Our only son. He must leave."

"Papa, I will not leave you." Herschel felt suddenly ashamed that he had not come to the aid of his father, that he had not run to fight the men who had beaten the old man so savagely. "I am here."

"Then you must *not* be here!" Lazer cried again. "To Paris! They must not harm you . . ." He groped for Herschel's face and brushed his fingers lightly on the boy's tears. "For your mother and me. Herschel, you *must*."

"Yes, Papa. Yes. Only rest now. Please," Herschel begged. "Please get well."

————

Wood shavings, like tiny curled ribbons, fell onto Franz's gray leather knickers and drifted onto the stone floor of the workshop. The delicate creche was complete, but this morning Franz worked to finish one more angel. This was the angel Franz had seen smiling down at the newborn calf. The miracle of birth, the promise of new life, *hope*—these shone in the face of the small wooden carving. Franz was uncertain now if he had seen all of that in Elisa's smile that night in the barn. Maybe he had heard it as she played her violin. Over the days and nights of watching her, his heart had gathered a composite picture of her soul, and now he recreated the image in wood. *Perhaps*, he thought, *I will give it to her when we open small gifts before the mass on the eve of Weinachten*. He brushed a shaving from the perfect little face and sat staring at it for a long time. *Maybe it would be better if I keep this for myself. Elisa is leaving the day after Weinachten. Back to Vienna. I will carve something else for her and keep the angel for myself*. He set the angel carefully on the shelf above his table, then turned on his stool as Frau Anna carefully descended the steep steps of the basement.

Anna seemed even paler today than she had the day before. Each day, she quietly bore the agony of silence with her head high. But Elisa had told Franz that Anna was not sleeping well, and now the tension and worry were showing on her face.

"Yes, Frau Anna?"

She clung tightly to the banister as she spoke. "Your mother says . . . she says—" Anna touched her forehead and swayed a bit on the step.

Franz jumped from his seat and bounded toward her, his arms extended to catch her fall. He was just below her when her knees buckled and she tumbled toward him. In one motion, he gathered her up and climbed the steps into the Stube.

"Mama!" he shouted. Not stopping, he took the main stairs two at a time. "Mama, come quick!"

————

Tucked beneath the quilts in the big feather bed, Anna looked like a little girl. Elisa stood at the foot of the bed while Frau Marta sat beside Anna, stroking her hair and speaking quietly to her.

"You must not bear all this alone, Anna," she gently chided. "For days you pretend that nothing is wrong. And we pretend like we do not know. Dear Anna, you are very valiant, but you must not bear your heartache alone."

Tears streamed from Anna's eyes, dampening her hair and the pillow. Elisa fought to control her own emotions. Never had she seen her mother so broken; never. It tore her heart; at the same time she almost choked with rage against the powers who caused so much needless misery.

"Oh, Marta," Anna sighed, grateful for the farmwife's comfort. "I just cannot think what to do. I cannot *think* what I must—"

"Shhh." Marta took her hand. "Your Theo would not like to see you sad or ill from grief. You must rest now and stay well for when he comes."

"But is he . . . coming? Who can know? Marta, you don't know what it has been like for us."

Elisa saw a flash of anger in Marta's eyes. No, she could not know, but she could imagine. "We will pray together for Theo, Anna. God sees when we do not see, ja?"

Anna nodded. A frown furrowed her brow, and she said in a small, helpless voice, "I do not want to go on without Theo. I can't . . ."

"Hush now with that kind of talk, Anna." Marta was firm, and Elisa was grateful for the woman's strength. Elisa had no words to comfort her mother, and to see the facade of strength crumble so completely was frightening. "You *will* go on, Anna. Not because you want to, but because you *must*. For your children. Theo's children."

Anna squeezed her eyes shut. She shook her head in denial that she could go on living and breathing without Theo. And then, with a moan, she began to weep openly, stretching out her arms and clinging to Marta. "How? How can I live? I have never been without him! What if he doesn't come? What if they don't let him come? Oh, why isn't he here, Marta? Theo. *Theo!*"

Elisa turned her face away and bowed her head to brush away her own tears. Anna's questions rang in her ears, and inwardly she shouted them back into the face of heaven. *If you are God, why is this happening? Why? Why must we be torn apart? If you are God, then you are wicked and terrible and full of lies!* The face of Thomas von Kleistmann rose up in her mind. *He loved me. I know he did. How has this happened? There are no more dreams left for us. What will Mama do if Papa doesn't come? And who will I love without Thomas? How can I ever love again?*

Marta did not try to answer Anna's questions. Instead, she crossed herself and prayed quietly—for Theo, wherever he was, and for the ache in Anna's heart to ease. Elisa thought how empty the prayers sounded. The words rattled around in the ancient rafters and then returned to them like dead leaves falling from the trees. No life. No shade of hope. Only a cold wind that blew into their very souls.

For an instant, Elisa was angry at Marta, too. *Why waste the effort of talking to a God who will not hear anyway?* Then she turned and saw the grateful eyes of Anna gazing up at Marta.

"Thank you," Anna whispered. "Thank you. Yes. God can see Theo. And if He has taken him away, then—"

Elisa covered her ears, unable to bear the thought. *If Papa is dead, then what?*

"You must not stop hoping, Anna, until you know for certain what is the truth. But there is only one safe place to put our hope. False hope will make you weak and ill. Father Ulrich says we must look only to the Lord. There is our only safety."

As Marta spoke, Elisa wondered how much she knew about Otto's secret life. Did Marta suspect that her own son had Nazi leanings? Would she still speak so confidently if she knew what kind of meetings he went to each night?

Marta's soft, guttural voice spoke with such tenderness that the words seemed almost like a tranquilizer. "Doesn't the Heilege Schrift say, 'Though a mother might forsake her children, God will not forsake us'? Yes, we love our children, and God loves us even more than that. Find your comfort there. Life is so hard . . ." Her voice trailed off as though she were remembering some crushing moment when hope seemed far away. Then she tucked the quilt tighter around Anna. "Yes. I know how hard. No answers. Nothing to do. Nothing to do but wait and pray and give our hope back to God, ja?"

Anna nodded weakly. "I am so tired."

"Of course you are. You have not slept in all the time you have been here." She blew out the lamp. "So sleep now. Rest. It is God's good medicine."

Elisa stood over her mother for a moment more as Marta moved toward the door. Anna did not open her eyes, but the corner of her mouth turned up slightly in a half smile. She had surrendered something as Marta had spoken. There was nothing else to do now but pray for a miracle or for the strength to bear God's silence.

16

Evening at the Embassy

Timmons and Johnson each scanned through the pages of the Berlin daily newspapers in search of some mention of Theo Lindheim's escape from the Adlon.

"Not a word. Nuthin'," said Timmons, tossing the newspaper onto Murphy's cluttered floor.

"What'd you think?" Johnson did not sound surprised. "You think the Gestapo is going to announce that some guy got out of here right under their noses and flew out of Tempelhof during the worst storm in ten years in a biplane? Fat chance. They don't want anyone to know. Not until they've got him again."

"They don't know about the biplane." Murphy, stretched out on the sofa, had come to the same conclusion when nothing had showed up in print after a week.

"Maybe he didn't make it." Timmons frowned and leaned back against the wall. "If that little plane made it over the mountains in that kind of storm, the Luftwaffe ought to let bygones be bygones and make him a Field Marshal!"

"Yeah." Johnson looked downcast. Every day the coterie of "Murphy's Men," including Amanda, had been hoping for a happy ending to their adventure. Tonight, Christmas Eve, would have been the perfect night to read the end of the story. "If he crashed up there, nobody's gonna find his bones for a hundred years. The Alps and a biplane are not a good combination, if you know what I mean."

Murphy did not want to think about it anymore. He still had Theo Lindheim's farewell letter to his family. He had hoped that there would be some indication that Theo had successfully run the gauntlet of storm troopers and lightning on the same night. "You know," Murphy said in a sleepy voice, "Old Goebbels sure would have made use of the propaganda if Lindheim died in a plane wreck. Maybe no news is good news, in this case."

Timmons bit his lip and stared at the front page containing a transcript of Hitler's holiday greetings to the people of the Reich. "I don't think they know," he looked up. "You know? I think we skunked 'em good, us limping around the block and going off in all directions. For all they know, Theo Lindheim might still be in here in the Adlon writing the news for American newspapers." He crossed his arms as though the thought gave him a great deal of pleasure.

"You're right," Johnson said. "But if the guy didn't make it over the border—"

Murphy frowned and looked over at his leather briefcase on the table by the window. Theo's letter was safely tucked inside a false bottom. It seemed to shout at Murphy: *If Theo didn't make it, his wife and kids will be heading back this way soon. You gotta tell them, Murphy. Vienna. Musikverein. Elisa Linder. Violin. They'll have no way of knowing that he tried to escape unless you get word to them. If he's not there by now, pal, he ain't coming.*

"Oh, well," Timmons said, as though he had been discussing the outcome of a World Series game, "Amanda told me that she and a bunch from the London *Times* have been invited to the British Embassy for a little reception. That new Ambassador Henderson has arrived, you know. Are you guys up for a little Christmas tea?"

"And cookies," Johnson added dourly. "Preferably American cookies, though." He stroked the air in an hour-glass shape, making it clear what he wanted in his Christmas stocking. "I'm sick of these German dames and sick of these British dames."

"Amanda's okay. Nice-lookin' dame," said Timmons, halfheartedly. Everyone was homesick for a little companionship, and all the American women in Berlin these days were either married to diplomats or well beyond the age of being interesting.

"Amanda's got no sense of humor," Murphy droned, although his mind was racing as he decided what he must do about Theo's letter.

"Nobody's got a sense of humor in Berlin," replied Johnson. He sniffed as if he was bored with the entire idea of a Christmas reception at the British Embassy. "They say this new British ambassador, Henderson, is definitely pro . . . real chummy with Göring."

"Yeah. Amanda says Göring is supposed to be at the party too. Some sort of official welcome to the new British ambassador."

"I'll bet he's coming dressed as Santa Claus, huh?"

"He's fat enough," Timmons laughed. "Yeah. Göring as Santa Claus. He'll come in and steal the candy from all the little kiddies' stockin's!"

Murphy sat up and stretched, suddenly intrigued by the thought of seeing Göring. "Let's go." he said, as though it was settled. "A little talk with Santa Claus might be real enlightening."

"Yeah?" Timmons was confused. Hardly anything was more boring than a British press reception. On Christmas Eve in Berlin the only thing that really seemed worthwhile was a quart of schnapps to drown a really heavy depression.

"Yeah." Murphy put on his overcoat for the short walk to the embassy. "You can get drunk later, Timmons. Göring flew in the Luftwaffe with Theo Lindheim in 1918. Rumor has it that Göring has had his eye on Lindheim's house. And his car. And his paintings. You get the idea? If anybody is going to be real interested in the whereabouts and political nonstatus of Lindheim, it will be Göring."

"You gonna pump a German Reich officer for information at a reception?" Timmons sounded amazed.

"You bet," Murphy said as he walked toward the door. "Lock up if you're coming too. And if you're not, put the room service tab on your own room, will you?"

———

Timmons and Johnson trailing behind him, Murphy dashed across the street to the British Embassy. Göring's long black staff car was parked in the front. Little swastika flags posed stiffly on the fenders. The car, Murphy had heard, had belonged to a rich steel magnate who had supported the Nazis because they had smashed all labor unions in Germany. The industrialist had grown disillusioned, however, when Hitler had insisted that only Nazi party members could supervise the steel mills. A few months later, Hitler began siphoning off the steel magnate's profits until every cent he had gained by the ruin of the unions was now piling up in the National Socialist coffers.

Murphy thumped the hood as they passed. Now the industrialist was a refugee in France, Hitler had the steel mills, and Göring had the limousine. *Serves the joker right,* thought Murphy as he showed his press pass to the doorman.

The inside of the British Embassy was very—English, to say the least. The portrait of King Edward had been replaced by a portrait of his brother George, and George didn't look any too happy about the arrangement. From the expression on his face, he had not planned to spend the rest of his life as ruler of the empire. No doubt he thought that Edward had gotten the better deal—a life with Mrs. Simpson with none of this foreign policy nonsense to worry about.

Murphy searched the faces in the crowd for the new British ambassador, Nevile Henderson. Tall and stoop-shouldered, Henderson wore a neatly trimmed moustache and had the almost cadaverous look of a country schoolmaster who had never done anything more significant than deal with the squabbles of ten-year-old boys. The man stood facing Field Marshal Göring, whose vast collection of medals and ribbons took up nearly every inch of space on his military tunic. Henderson actually appeared to be impressed by such a garish display. He had a ridiculous, awe-struck sort of smile on his face as Göring told of his latest hunt.

Murphy could not help but mutter, "Where did they dig this guy up?"

Timmons overheard and laughed out loud. "Reminds me of a Latin teacher I once had."

Johnson nudged Murphy hard in the ribs. "Has the British foreign office gone nuts? They sent *him* to deal with Hitler!" Johnson swore under his breath and stomped off to find the buffet table. Amanda charged out of the reception room a moment later looking for Murphy. She had the same look of disgust on her face when she caught sight of Göring's great hulk, preening for the frail skeleton Henderson.

"Really!" she snapped at the sight of the two of them. She grabbed Murphy by the arm and pulled him through a group of drinking, gossiping reporters toward the library. Then she slid the doors of the room shut and spun around to face him. "Everyone at Whitehall has gone mad! This ridiculous little man! Ridiculous! Murphy, do you see what they've sent to *deal* with the situation over here?" She was red-faced and sputtering with anger.

"Obviously they don't want to deal with it!" Murphy was quiet, already resigned to the inevitable. "Hitler has been saying he'd rather have an alliance with Great Britain than Italy. So, London has sent someone innocuous to—"

"Innocuous!" Amanda's face grew more red. "He's not innocuous; he's barely alive!" She swore and gasped out, "*Henderson?* He's been in Argentina for the last century. Göring with his medals and his nonsense— he's already got Henderson spellbound! *What, what, what* can they be thinking over there?"

"They aren't thinking. That's obvious. They stopped thinking when Hitler marched armed troops into the Rhineland's demilitarized zone and nobody did anything."

"This is the end! Do you know what Henderson said to Göring?"

Murphy could only imagine what could come from the mouth of a man so totally bamboozled by a large belly decked out with ribbons. Couldn't Henderson see that Göring wore *rouge* on his cheeks, for goodness' sakes? Nobody liked Göring except Hitler and Göring! "Okay," Murphy said in a monotone, "should I sit down to hear this or what?"

"First!" Amanda's voice cracked and her eyes bugged out a bit. Murphy thought she looked better when she wasn't upset. "Ha! Yes! Ha! *First!*"

"*First* calm down, Amanda." Murphy tried not to look either amused or worried, even though he half expected her to fall on the floor and kick and scream or turn blue.

She took a deep breath and began again. "I heard him say it, plain as anything." She raised her hand as if to swear.

"What?"

"In this strange little awe-struck voice, Henderson said, 'I'm not the

least bit anti-Semitic, Herr Göring, but I certainly do not like Jews!' "
Amanda repeated the statement with such a sickeningly aristocratic accent
that Murphy knew this was nothing she could possibly dream up.

"That ought to endear him to Göring."

Amanda buried her face in her hands. "I am so ashamed," she said,
nearly in tears. "To think one of my own countrymen—the ambassador
of my government . . ."

"Cheer up, Amanda, it could be worse." Murphy did not know how
Nevile Henderson could be worse, but he could not think of anything else
to say.

"Oh, but it *is* worse, Johnny!" she cried. "He has already told Göring"—she closed her eyes and gulped as though repeating the words was
painful—"that as far as he was concerned, Nazi Germany could *have*
Austria. It didn't make any difference to the British government!" She
finished the dreadful pronouncement of Henderson's mission of appeasement to Berlin, and then she groped for a place to sit down.

Murphy remained rooted to the floor. "How do you know he said that?"
He could not make himself believe such madness. "How?"

"I heard it from the Austrian ambassador, poor fellow. He is staggering
around out there."

"Some press reception," Murphy said hollowly. "What are we supposed
to do? Snap pictures of Göring with his arm around Henderson? Something
for the family album?" He was getting more angry with every passing
second.

"When I walked by"—Amanda sounded pitiful—"I heard Göring ask
the little weasel to come hunting at his lodge. Like a couple of Boy Scouts
playing camp. London has sent over just the sort of fellow Hitler likes to
squash. There is nothing to respect. Nothing that remotely resembles the
greatest empire on the face of the earth. Europe is overflowing with Jewish
refugees from Germany, and London sends a man who doesn't like Jews
either. What next? What, Murphy? Will they stop emigration to Palestine
next to show their mutual dislike of Jews?" Now she wept in earnest—
angry, frustrated tears. Murphy knew that Amanda had covered Hitler's
war against the Jews and the church since he had come to power. Last
week, a young pastor who had been supplying her with information had
been arrested and sent to Oranienburg. Her conclusion had to be that if
anyone in the British government was reading her stuff, nobody really
cared as long as Hitler left Britain alone.

Murphy stared at her for a long time. He could not even think of what
he could say to comfort her. "Yeah," he said at last. "Rotten. Just lousy
rotten."

Beyond the dark, paneled doors, Murphy heard the patter of polite
applause. He slid the doors back to reveal Nevile Henderson and Göring
standing before a cluster of photographers with their glasses raised. Timmons and Johnson stood together with dark scowls on their faces as they
scribbled their notes.

"A toast to Field Marshal Hermann Göring. A fine chap. A man I consider my friend as well as our ally!" Henderson sipped his wine, and flash bulbs popped as Göring joined him.

"And here is to the great hope that both our nations may also continue in their bond of friendship."

Murphy almost groaned at the words. There was nothing honorable here tonight. Nothing honorable in this sort of display. It turned his stomach. He had seen Theo Lindheim disowned by his own country! He had watched a man of true honor being stripped of everything he owned and threatened like a criminal until he was forced to run. Murphy was certain that Göring was behind much of the final intimidation. Göring was, after all, the glutton of the Reich. What he saw, his appetite demanded. He had not admired the honor of Theo Lindheim, but he had coveted the respect Lindheim's honor seemed to bring him. The contrast between the two men was an impassable gulf. *Göring in his pompous uniform, clinking and clanking from the weight of the medals. An overstuffed boar pretending to be a lion for Germany! I would love to see him bust out the seat of his pants right now!*

One thing was certain, someone like Hermann Göring would never fill the shoes of Theo Lindheim. Göring would try—at least, he would try Theo's shoes on. Then he would strip the house bare of everything of beauty and value and declare Theo either dead or a criminal.

Göring threw his head back in contrived laughter at Henderson's attempt at wit. No one else even smiled, but it did not matter to Henderson; he had won the approval of *Göring*!

Murphy watched the circus with the sensation that he would throw up all over the polished wood floors if he didn't escape soon. He had already determined that he would not mention Theo Lindheim tonight, after all. Why give Hermann Göring an opportunity to justify or explain away the racial policies of the Third Reich? Was he not standing in an embassy where the ambassador of a great power had confessed that he didn't much like Jews either?

Murphy felt his lip curl a bit in revulsion. "I'm leaving, Amanda," he said quietly. She did not answer for a while. Her tortured eyes remained fixed on Henderson and Göring. "They're going to do a song and dance routine soon—tea for two, or something. And I can't take it anymore."

She nodded bleakly, understanding exactly what he was feeling. "Where can we find you after?"

"Vienna."

"Vienna? But . . ."

"I'll be back next week."

"You got a scoop?"

"No. I just got a snoot full, if you know what I mean." Murphy grabbed his hat and bowed slightly to her. She was really a pretty on-the-level dame. And nice legs, too.

"Well, Merry Christmas, then, Murphy," she shrugged. "This may be our last."

17

Silent Night

Murphy caught the last plane to Vienna. The silver Ford tri-motor was occupied by five other passengers, all of whom seemed as intent and introspective as Murphy. He did not want to talk with anyone right now, and was grateful when no one sat beside him. Murphy dumped his hat and briefcase on the empty seat beside him as a warning to any strangers who might have been hoping for a little conversation. He reserved the empty place for himself tonight and shared it with his own thoughts and concerns as the little plane roared over the Alps.

Looking down on the snow-covered ridges, he half-expected to see the shattered remains of Theo Lindheim's little biplane—perhaps a frozen body lying stiff on the ice. But there was only the last glimmer of sunlight playing red and pink against the darkening sky until the snowy slopes and the patches of trees melted into the darkness. *The guys are right*, he thought grimly. *If Theo is down there, no one will find him for a hundred years.*

When the plane passed over Vienna, the bright lights of Christmas celebration winked up like a miniature fairyland. Murphy could distinctly see the five tall spires of the government Rathaus where Chancellor Dollfuss had been assassinated by Nazis two years before. Tonight, the Gothic facade of the building was dusted lightly with snow and bathed in light. It seemed more like a castle made of glistening sugar cubes than the place where Chancellor Schuschnigg now trembled at the thought of what Hitler was plotting next for Austria.

There seemed to be no traffic moving down the broad, elegant Ringstrasse. Trolley cars were nowhere in sight, and only a few tiny human figures trudged along, leaving footprints in the snow as they crossed the street without even looking up.

The plane landed without fanfare and Murphy noticed that there were no other passengers in the terminal. Vienna had closed up for the night. It had shut its doors to strangers, and Murphy found himself feeling suddenly foolish and alone as he stood on the sidewalk and hailed the last taxi in the city.

"Where do you wish to go?" The driver was a rough-looking Hungarian who smelled of schnapps and slurred his words. But there were no other taxis, nor could Murphy hope that one might happen along.

"The Musikverein," Murphy said gruffly as though he knew what he was doing.

"There is nothing happening there tonight." The driver laid his arm on the back of the seat and peered at Murphy. "What do you want to go there for?"

"I have a friend—" He stopped, suddenly irritated that the driver expected an explanation. "Just take me by there, will you?"

The driver shrugged a resigned reply and shook his head slightly as an indication that he had picked up a crazy man. Murphy stared glumly out the frosty windows as they passed slowly through the empty city. He wished now that he had stayed in Berlin with Timmons and Johnson and Amanda and the rest of the gang. Then he would have ended the night full of schnapps, drowning his sorrows among familiar faces, at any rate. The feeling of loneliness became almost overwhelming as the wheels of the car rolled to a stop in front of the totally dark building of the Musikverein. Murphy sat silently and stared up at the large front doors. The driver cleared his throat impatiently and the meter clicked loudly.

"You are getting out here?" the cabbie asked.

"No." Murphy heard the embarrassment in his own voice. "I, uh . . . my plane was late. I was supposed to meet someone here, but—take me to the Sacher Hotel." He felt some relief in the lie. The cabbie warmed up to him after that and seemed pleased that his passenger was not such a fool after all.

"Ah yes! Sacher's is a very fine hotel. You have stayed there?"

"Yes." Murphy did not want to talk. He could not shake the gut-wrenching emptiness that had settled over him. What had he expected to find here on Christmas Eve? Elisa Lindheim with her arms open and waiting?

"You can get a good Christmas meal there. You know the Viennese; at noon on Christmas Eve, the ladies disappear from the streets and banish their husbands from the houses, yes?" He warmed to the subject and rattled on. Every word was a reminder of how alone Murphy felt tonight. "All day they cook, and then at dusk the men come home. You won't find anyone out now but a few Jews and Socialists on their way to a meeting. All of Vienna is inside eating stuffed blue carp!" He laughed loudly and slapped the steering wheel as though he had told a joke.

"Why aren't you home?" Murphy asked dully, still looking out the window as they passed the large domed structure of the State Opera House.

"My wife worked late. I work late. But I will have my carp! Yes. My wife's mother is coming, God help me. And her brother, too. I wish it could be just the two of us. And a little schnapps, if you know what I mean." He laughed again and Murphy did not respond. He did not like the taxi driver and was relieved when the cab arrived at the stately Sacher Hotel, not far from the Opera House. Without comment, Murphy checked the meter and paid the driver, then stepped out of the car without waiting to be wished a Merry Christmas. Murphy was not in the mood to hear the greeting that was not so totally beyond possibility for him. *Rotten Christmas! Miserable holidays! Bah, humbug! Scrooge had the right idea,* he thought as he tramped disconsolately across the red floral carpet of the deserted hotel lobby.

A very Jewish-looking hotel clerk registered him, and Murphy could not help but speculate that this was an employee of Sacher's that was probably kept well out of sight during normal daylight hours of operation. Anti-Semitism was not unheard of these days in Vienna, either.

The soft clink of silverware against china told Murphy that at least Sacher's famed restaurant was open for business tonight. He shoved his room key into his pocket and left his suitcase at the coat rack, then approached a polite but reserved headwaiter.

"Dining alone, sir?" There was an edge of pity, even disapproval, to the man's voice.

Murphy nodded and followed the white starched shirt to the white starched linen-covered table. Crystal and silver glistened. A small string quartet played Christmas melodies in the corner. Sacher's was the most homelike of all the great Viennese hotels. Maybe that is why Murphy had thought of it, but tonight he did not feel at home.

Attentive, proper waiters hurried through the dining room, serving foreign dignitaries and visitors who must certainly not be from Vienna, or they would not have been out on such a night. Black coats. Black ties. Shining black shoes. Music. The musicians were playing "Silent Night"; the hymn was almost an Austrian national anthem. Murphy followed the words of the melody and still found no comfort. "Silent night! Holy night! All is calm, all is bright. . . ."

He thought about his mother and father in faraway Pennsylvania; then, almost unable to bear the ache, he stared at the musicians. They were all men. Murphy wondered if any of them knew Elisa. He wondered if he should ask them. All through salmon cake with roe, consommé, and turbot with shrimp sauce, he imagined finding her alone at her apartment, taking her into his arms and telling her . . . "Telling her?" he muttered at last. *Tell her what? Your father is dead, I think. Probably cracked up in the Alps. Here was his final letter. By the way, Merry Christmas. You want to go out for a drink?*

The absurdity of his flight to Vienna on Christmas Eve suddenly became even more painfully clear. The quartet played the bright chorus of

Good King Wenceslas as Murphy raised his hand to summon a passing waiter.

"Ready for a Sachertorte now, sir?"

"Right. I'll take it to my room."

The waiter looked concerned. "Was everything to your liking?"

"Fine." Murphy did not admit that he had not tasted much of the meal.

"No coffee?" The waiter seemed astonished that a patron could leave the table without sampling the Viennese coffee.

"In my room."

"Anything else?" The waiter looked hurt.

"Ja," Murphy nodded in resignation. "A quart of brandy if you've got it."

"In your room also?"

"Ja," Murphy replied solemnly. He would not ask the musicians if they knew Elisa. Now, he was almost afraid they would say yes.

"It is a shame to be alone on Christmas, sir," the waiter offered sympathetically.

"Yeah," he replied in English. "Me and Scrooge, huh? Me and the Ghost of Christmas Past."

The waiter smiled at him in a puzzled way, then bowed slightly and hurried off to the kitchen.

Murphy wiped his mouth, then tossed the napkin onto the table in a gesture of disgust. He leaned back in his chair and gazed around at the cozy opulence of Sacher's dining room and thought about the reception at the British Embassy. Apparently someone in England was already playing Scrooge to Austria's Tiny Tim. *Bah, humbug to Austria. Is that it? Then it's the Ghost of Christmas Future I should worry about tonight.* He was sure that Austria's future was most certainly the depressing topic of conversation at the press party in Berlin. Glancing down at the briefcase containing Theo's farewell, Murphy decided that he would make it his personal business that Elisa's future would be safe. He would warn her. Regardless of what happened, she and her family would have to leave Vienna. Tonight he was surrounded by Jewish musicians, Jewish desk clerks, probably even Jewish waiters. He could not warn them what the future might hold for Austria. Did they know already? Did they suspect?

Tonight the Ghost of Christmas Yet to Come marched in a goose-step and raised a hand to salute *"Heil Hitler!"* Tonight the ghost wore a swastika on his armband instead of the simple red and white colors of Austria. And yet, on this silent night, the horrible specter seemed all but invisible in Vienna. Murphy could only wonder if he was the sole person at Sacher's who could hear the anthem of Hitler's hordes echoing distantly from beyond the mountains.

————

On this Christmas Eve in Kitzbühel, it was easy to see how the song had been written in the Alps of Austria: "Silent night! Holy night! All is calm, all is bright. . . ."

Snow clung precariously to fragile tree branches. A whisper would send white clumps tumbling to the ground. But there were no whispers—only silence. A spray of stars lit the sky from one jagged Alpine peak to the other, glistening and holy in their radiance like the host of angels who sang good news to the shepherds outside of Bethlehem.

But the shepherds had been afraid, Elisa knew. They had fallen to the ground and trembled in fear. And the lyrics of "Stille Nacht" failed her tonight. She could find no calm within her soul. There was no peace in the beauty, no hope in the brightness of the stars.

Elisa glanced at the face of her mother and knew that she felt the same ache. Silent days had passed. Together they had traveled twice to the Tyroler Haus in Innsbruck and inquired if any word had come from Theo in Berlin. The narrow mail slot was empty, and now, tonight, hope of some miraculous reunion had died.

Anna's hands trembled as she opened the door to the bedroom. She fixed a smile on her face and shoved her hands deep into the pockets of her overcoat. She would not let the boys see her unhappiness. *Your father is not feeling well,* she had told them. *He is not up to the journey.* The deception was somehow merciful. Elisa knew that her mother was not able to face the grief and worry of Wilhelm and Dieter. At this moment it was all she could do to force herself to lift her chin and descend the narrow steps into the Stube.

"Merry Christmas! Merry Christmas!" The words held a thousand memories of other times when indeed there seemed to be an unshakable calmness over the world on this night.

Eager smiles, shining eyes, and blazing hearth surrounded them with distant echoes. *Music and laughter. Snow falling softly onto the gentle earth. A whispered secret and knowing glances. Scents of cakes and pastries filling the great Lindheim house on Wilhelmstrasse. The midnight chiming of the tall old clock. "Your great-grandfather traded a matched team of horses for the old clock. . . . I wish I could carry it away in my pocket. Wish I could carry away your mother's piano too. . . . Glad you play the violin, Elisa dear. It is small enough to carry out of Germany. . . ."*

But the house on Wilhelmstrasse—the blazing lights, the clock, the sound of the piano filling every corner of the parlor . . . none of that mattered anymore. There was only one thing missing on this silent night. . . .

"When do you think Papa can come?" Dieter asked, disappointment thick in his voice. "Herr Karl has taught me some carving, and I made a camel for Papa."

"Not bad," teased Wilhelm, holding up the lopsided beast. "Like something I saw once at the zoo in Berlin. They call it a giraffe."

Dieter did not laugh. He took the carving from his brother and tucked it into his pocket without comment.

Franz glared at Wilhelm and thumped Dieter on the back. "You have the makings of an artist, Dieter. Mother still has my first camels. You see?" He pointed toward a rudely carved creche that was given a place of honor beneath the Christmas tree. "Yours is better than mine." Franz reached into Dieter's pocket and lifted out the camel; then he carefully placed it in the center of the little wooden scene.

"What? Four camels for the wise men?" Dieter asked.

"They brought an extra. In case one went lame," Herr Karl said. "That is why they were wise!"

"They must have been German," Otto added somewhat gruffly. "Sensible wise men."

Everyone laughed as they donned their coats and scarves, and Otto grinned—one of the few smiles Elisa had seen from Otto in all the time they had been in Kitzbühel. It softened his features and made him seem handsome.

Anna walked slightly ahead of the group as they arrived at the little church in the village. Elisa could not help but think how small and alone her mother seemed without Theo. He had towered over her, but at the same time he had seemed a shadow of strength and protection for her.

Tonight, Franz walked at Elisa's side. He did not hold her hand, but Elisa could feel the gentle brown eyes that moved from her to Anna and then to the boys with concern. Somehow he knew the strength they needed just to face the recital of the old familiar story without the presence of Theo. *Was there anything more important to the people of these mountains?* Maybe there was nothing so important anywhere on the earth. In his carving, Franz had captured the love that Joseph had for Mary. Elisa had been reminded of it when Frau Marta had unwrapped the new Christmas creche. *The eyes of Joseph, seeing only Mary. Loving her. Wanting to protect her. Yes. Franz knows about love.*

Now Franz looked at Elisa the same way. He held her with his eyes, caressing her face with a glance the way Elisa once dreamed Thomas might do. But Franz was not Thomas. Just as there could be no one else for Anna but Theo, tonight Elisa felt the despair of being loved, yet being unable to return that love. Even with Franz beside her, Elisa was alone. Even the kisses of this strong and gentle man had not erased the memory of other lips on hers.

Theo remained in Germany by force. Thomas remained by choice. Elisa could not think which was the greater pain. Her private anguish was compounded by the fact that the man she loved was now part of the terrible force that kept her father from his family. She hated Thomas for that, and yet still loved him for what they had once been together. Had he ever looked at her the way Joseph looked at Mary? The way Franz looked at her now as they knelt together on the red velvet cushions?

She closed her eyes and murmured the words of the liturgy. Still she felt Franz's eyes holding her face in the flickering candlelight; he was so hopeful, so filled with compassion for their unhappy silent night. *Why can't I love someone like him, God? Must Thomas always stand between me and a really kind and simple man? Does it have to be so complicated to love? Look at him, kneeling there. He is praying for Papa. Praying for me. Has my heart died in me? Am I made of wood, more unfeeling than the carved figures in the creche?* Elisa tucked her chin and prayed harder— prayed for Theo to come to them, prayed that someday she might love a man as her mother loved her father. But the night was silent. Hope was still and lifeless within her. There was no face that came to her but the face of the man who served their enemies. *Thomas! Thomas! Thomas!* If only he could somehow help her father escape! If only Theo and Thomas would come into the crowded little church and kneel beside them now! Her prayers ascended in *hopes, wishes,* and *dreams* that had no bearing on reality. She knew that when the service ended, Anna would rise up alone and walk out alone to face the terrible silence of this most holy night. No word from the man she loved. No hope of help from the one man Elisa dreamed would make their world right again. There were no miracles expected this Christmas in Kitzbühel. Theo was not coming. Thomas would not help.

All of Vienna was asleep now, dreaming in silent wonder of the holy birth of a Jewish child two thousand years before. The midnight mass at St. Stephan's had long since ended. Fresh snow covered the footprints that scattered in a thousand directions from the steps of the great cathedral.

Sporer watched two lovers from the shadows of these steps as the two walked quickly toward the Judenplatz. The tall handsome man held his arm protectively around the woman's shoulders.

Sporer's hand moved instinctively to the hard steel of the revolver tucked into his belt. It would be so simple to kill the couple now, and yet, his orders were to wait until enough evidence had been gathered to make the deaths of these two worthwhile to the plans of the Reich.

As if sensing the presence of something in the shadows, the tall man paused beneath the streetlight and looked back toward the entrance of St. Stephan's.

"What is it, darling?" the woman's soft voice carried easily across the square.

"Nothing," her companion said as he continued to gaze toward the shadows. "Really—nothing . . ." He frowned, then looked down at her. He kissed her lightly on the forehead.

The gesture seemed to Sporer a desecration. The woman was beautiful. Red hair and fair skin seemed to glow beneath the streetlamp. Sporer would enjoy smashing the skull of this traitor when the time came. He would look forward to the moment when Berlin sent him word that they had lived long enough. They had already lived too long in his opinion.

"It's Christmas, love." The woman laid her head against the man's chest. "And we can be happy, can't we?"

"I am worried for your safety, Irmgard." The strong voice trembled. "If you are linked to this . . . They will make him talk before they kill him. They will . . ."

"No." She put a finger to his lips. "Think about the children, darling! Think about the little packages! Of all fellows, you will make an unlikely St. Nicholas!" She laughed and then tugged his arm, pulling him down the narrow lane into the shadows of the Judenplatz.

Sporer did not bother to follow. He had seen enough tonight and it was Christmas, after all.

18

Christmas in Austria

Murphy had fallen asleep in his clothes. Now as he lay across the bed, his feet dangling over the side, he was unpleasantly aware of the dull ache in his knees and the leaden weight of his shoes on his feet.

Outside in the dim light of an icy cold Christmas morning, the bells of the city's cathedrals chimed happily as though the sky was clear and bright. They rang in seemingly endless celebration, their clanging chorus vibrating icicles and rattling Murphy's windows. He groaned softly and rolled over, drawing his knees up stiffly as he kicked his shoes off. The bottle of brandy stood as a half-empty reminder of the reason for Murphy's headache. He was miserable. Every pore in his body felt the noise of Vienna's bright bells. He squeezed his eyes shut and gently laid a pillow over his face to shut out the sound. Even the ticking of the alarm clock seemed too loud. The cathedral bells were almost unbearable. He groped to loosen his stubborn necktie.

There was only one consolation he could find in such a hangover—no doubt he would have been experiencing the same misery if he had stayed in Berlin and consumed this much booze with his comrades. Only in Berlin he was certain that the Christmas bells would be somehow more reserved and careful in their ringing. Hitler's birthday received more celebration in recent years than did Christ's.

The thoughts of Berlin did not ease his discomfort. He clumsily unbuttoned his shirt and pulled it off, leaving his necktie in place around his bare neck. His eyes burned in their sockets; his temples throbbed, and in all of it the foolishness of his Christmas journey mocked him. Who did he think he was, Sir Galahad, rescuing some damsel in distress? He should have waited a couple more days—at least until Christmas was over. There was nothing happening at the Musikverein. The cab driver had told him that, yet still he had insisted that she would be there. What did he think? That Elisa Lindheim—Linder, whatever . . . *lived* at the Musikverein? That she was sitting there waiting for John Murphy to walk in?

He groaned again. His mouth was worse than dry. His tongue felt as if it were wound in gauze after oral surgery, and he opened one eye to scout for the bathroom in the event that he might throw up. *Merry Christmas, Murphy. And welcome to Vienna.*

Eyeing the booze on the night table, he cursed quietly. He hadn't been drunk in almost two years. Not since the night Susan had left him standing in the snow for two hours outside Radio City Music Hall in New York. That had been a night to forget. So why was he thinking about it now? He had picked up a tall blond Rockette after the show and had proceeded to show her a night on the town. Of course she hadn't really been a Rockette, and after a few drinks she had stolen his wallet and disappeared out the back door of Minsky's forever. So much for his luck with women. Now here he was deserting his post in Berlin to become the bearer of terrible news for a girl he had met only briefly.

She's forever going to associate you with bad news, Murphy, he reminded himself. *Just do your reporting and disappear. Don't expect anything from this girl. She's a lady. And you're a reporter. A reporter with a hangover.*

Still he had not been able to shake the haunting sadness of her eyes, or the soft sheen of her hair as it tumbled down over her slender shoulders that night on the train. The thought of her made him ache all the more. He sat up too suddenly and shuffled to the bathroom to splash cold water over his face. Bleary eyes stared back from the mirror, and he could feel each individual tile beneath the soles of his feet. He brushed his teeth and smiled grimly with the foamy toothpaste still in his mouth.

"No doubt about it, Murphy," he mumbled aloud. "You got it bad for this girl. Mad-dog Murphy. Foaming at the mouth." He spit and splashed cold water over his face again, then worked to remove the knotted necktie that dangled in the sink. With a sigh, he gave up and flipped it over his shoulder.

Outside, the chorus of Christmas bells continued to chime. Murphy leaned heavily on the doorjamb and looked toward the window. If Elisa was in Vienna, she could hear the bells now as he could. Somehow that awareness made him feel tender all over again. Protective. Worried for the Ghost of Christmas Future. *Elisa!* The familiar ache returned, more painful than his throbbing head. He would wait here in Vienna until the Musikverein opened, and he would find her. He would stay as long as she needed him, do whatever he could do to help. Then maybe she would look at him with those ocean-deep eyes of hers and see John Murphy looking back at her . . .

He shook his head slowly at the foolishness of his thought. "One night on the train, and look at you!" he muttered. "*Look* at you!" After one night on a train, he was certain he could not be in love, but it felt bad enough, whatever it was.

He tugged on the tie in one final, futile effort to loosen it; then he padded back to the bed and lay down carefully. One thing was evident to Murphy: he was no knight in shining armor, but the lady was in distress whether she knew it or not. So Murphy would sleep this off and then do his best, *whatever* that meant. It was pure fact that his motives were mostly rotten—at least he *suspected* that they were not totally pure. Maybe he *would* still be in Vienna if the bewildered girl on the train had been homely and dull. But one thing was certain: he wouldn't be feeling this way about the whole mess. He wouldn't be lying here Christmas morning with a hangover and aching like a schoolboy with his first crush.

He wanted to see her again—welcomed the excuse, as terrible as the errand was that brought him here. And that made him angry at himself while at the same time it compelled him to stay and search for her. Life had been all right before he had met her. He had not felt particularly empty or lacking in anything. He could buy what he needed to keep himself satisfied. Now suddenly he was alone, empty and miserable. He was miserable even before the brandy and the hangover.

Christmas in Vienna, and all he wanted under the tree—under any tree—was Elisa Linder.

The portrait of Emperor Franz Josef hung on the red silk-covered walls of Sacher's restaurant and stared down at Murphy. Although Murphy would not admit it to the waiter, he was not impressed with the taste of the Sachertorte and ordered apple strudel instead.

"The Musikverein?" The young waiter frowned. "There is not a concert there until New Year's Eve, Herr Murphy. Each year there is an all-Strauss concert. And then again on New Year's Day. But probably both are sold out. There are many other musical events in the season, however . . ."

"No. I was interested in the first thing at the Musikverein."

"It is the Vienna Philharmonic that plays there. And of course on Sundays there is the concert. But you will never get a seat now. Those are subscription tickets. Held by the same families for a hundred years, and—"

"New Year's Eve?" Murphy interrupted, mentally calculating a week-long stay in Vienna.

"Must it be the Musikverein? You can see, today the street musicians are out in force again already." He sensed Murphy's concern and felt somehow personally responsible to see to it that a customer got satisfaction in Vienna. This concern, known as *Gemütlichkeit*, permeated the city; it was part of the atmosphere that made Austria so charming.

"My friend is a violinist with the orchestra, you see, and I want to hear her play."

"Which orchestra, mein Herr? There are several in Vienna. The Symphony, the Philharmonic, a dozen chamber orchestras—all of them playing some time or other at the Musikverein." He frowned. "No doubt she will be playing for the season now. They all are. She gave you this address and nothing more?"

Murphy felt more foolish than ever. It was obvious that Elisa had some reason why she would not give more specific information than the building on Bösendorferstrasse. Perhaps she had intended that he write her there first. Such a general address would certainly add to her protection. She had not mentioned which orchestra she performed with, and it might take Murphy weeks to check with every one of them.

"Musikverein. That's all she told me."

"Ja. Maybe you should go there. Someone might know where she lives, Herr Murphy." The waiter could tell that Murphy had not come to Vienna for the sake of musical appreciation. "You might also go to the State Opera House, ja? Just around the corner. If she is well known and perhaps plays with the Vienna Philharmonic . . . and at the Konzerthaus is the Vienna Symphony."

"How far?" Murphy looked out as a trolley car trundled past the window.

"Not far. Lothringerstrasse." The waiter looked amused. "This violinist?" He smiled. "She must be very pretty, ja?"

"Hmmm," Murphy nodded distractedly. "Big. A couple hundred pounds. Really big."

"Ah yes!" The waiter grinned broadly. "My Gretl is also big. More to love, I say!" He winked, and Murphy nodded enthusiastically. "She is young and soft?" He asked.

"Soft, anyway," Murphy said seriously. "But mature. Maybe fifty."

The waiter became serious. "Ja. I see. Then very rich, I suppose."

"Loaded." Murphy used the American term, and the waiter puzzled over it for a moment before he poured Murphy's coffee cup full.

"You will find her, Herr Murphy. There cannot be too many rich, round women playing the violin in an orchestra, I think. As long as you know her name."

Murphy did not admit that he was not even certain that Elisa had given him the correct identification. Today he would walk back to the Musikverein and ask around—if there was anyone there to ask. *Who knows?* he thought. *Maybe a janitor or stage hand will know her. Somebody will recognize her. There can't be that many beautiful blond violinists around, can there?* He had thought this was going to be easy, and maybe he was making it more complicated than it really was. There had to be some reason why she gave this address, after all. Hadn't Theo given the same address? There was one Musikverein in Vienna, and one Elisa. He would find her. If her mail went there, he would hang around until she picked it up. For a week or so he would disappear, and nobody in New York would mind—he hoped. After all, Timmons and Johnson and that new guy Murrow were still in Berlin. He frowned down at the strudel. Maybe to be on the safe side, he would cable New York and indicate that he was hot on a story in Vienna. It might, in fact, be the truth.

Murphy tipped the waiter a bit more than was customary, wrapped the strudel in his napkin, and slipped it into a folded newspaper. He might need it if he had to wait at the Musikverein long. He wired New York and gave the Sacher Hotel as his residence before he trudged through the park toward the place of Elisa's address. The snow on the front steps remained undisturbed, and two sets of footprints led to the stage door of the Musikverein concert hall. Murphy followed them, feeling a little like Sherlock Holmes tracking his quarry.

The stage door was unlocked, and Murphy entered the building without knocking. He called loudly, startled at the way his voice expanded in the vacant hall. Row on row of plush velvet seats waited silent and empty. Murphy looked out, imagining what Elisa must have seen with each performance. He felt suddenly very close to her. This was her place, familiar ground to her.

The sound of footsteps approached behind him, and Murphy turned to face a bent and weathered little man dressed warmly in a heavy coat and cap.

"Ja?" He asked, somewhat aloof and stern. This was obviously *his* place too, and he did not welcome the tall foreign stranger who had entered uninvited.

"Guten Morgen." Murphy tipped his hat. "I am looking for someone."

"There is no one here but me!" the old man snapped. "So unless you are looking for me, you should go away, thank you."

Murphy did not let the man's reply stop him. "Her name is Elisa Linder. She gave me this address."

"She does not live here. Why should she give you this address?" He was scowling. Suspicious.

"It was a mailing address, but I—"

"Ja. The young musicians give this as the address for mail because they move so often. So why don't you write her a letter, then? Goodbye." He turned his back on Murphy and started to walk away.

"Wait a minute!" Murphy stepped in front of him, at the same time dropping a bill onto the floor. He stooped to pick it up and waved it like a flag beneath the old man's nose. "Did you drop this?" It was a ten-shilling note, and the old man stopped in his tracks and stared at the money.

He took the bill after a moment. "I cannot tell you what I do not know," he shrugged.

"What *do* you know?"

"What I told you. She comes here to pick up her mail. As do many young musicians. She has gone since the holidays, I think. I have not seen her."

"When will she—"

"I do not know that."

"Does she come quite regularly? A special time of day?"

"Around four o'clock every day or two."

"You do not have an address?"

The old man hesitated, hoping for another bribe. Murphy complied, slipping a five-shilling note into his hand. "Not an address for her. No. But she has a friend, Leah Goldblatt. A cellist. A very excellent cellist at that. Perhaps the most excellent—"

"Her address?"

"You must not tell Leah Goldblatt that you gave me money. I could lose my job, and then where would I be? Out on the street with the rest of the beggars. Perhaps I should not chance it—" He frowned, and Murphy pressed yet another bill into his palm.

"That's the last," Murphy lied. "Where is this Leah Goldblatt?"

The old man turned and shuffled off toward a dark office. He flicked on the light and flipped through the telephone book, sliding his finger down the page. "Ah!" he said at last. "The telephone she shares with four others. But here is her own address. There is nothing for Elisa Linder in the book. Probably because she is quite beautiful, and young men would be likely to call on her even if she did not want them to." He smiled broadly, revealing an uneven row of teeth stained by years of drinking the dark Viennese coffee.

Murphy groaned. He had paid twenty shillings for an address out of a phone book! He scribbled down the number and address and left. He could hear the uproarious laughter of the old man as he hurried out the stage door. *Yep, Murphy, you are one fantastic investigative reporter.* He patted the slip of paper in his pocket and tucked his chin against the blast of cold air that blew small flakes of snow along the sidewalk. A new storm had gathered, and the street musicians who had been playing so happily an hour before were now packing up their instruments and scurrying for cover.

———

Murphy followed two stout women in fur caps and galoshes into Demel's Konditorei, a pastry shop laden with tortes and cream puffs of every size and description. Not surprisingly, the counter was three deep with customers who flocked in for last-minute treats for friends or relatives. A few solitary souls sat in the rococo dining room, where marble floors and gilded stucco were surpassed in elegance only by the desserts on display. Demel's was almost the only pastry shop open for the holiday, and the long lines jostling for the last dozen bonbons or chocolate *confiseries* spoke of the Viennese passion for sweets. The aroma of chocolate, freshly baked pastries, and cakes was almost more than a mortal could bear.

No doubt Murphy would have been affected like everyone else if it hadn't been for the fact that he was still lugging a hangover with him. He stood in the center of the crowd and searched for a telephone. A gilded phone booth was tucked discreetly in the far corner by the entrance to the kitchen. As Murphy carefully dialed Leah Goldblatt's number, he noticed that the telephone was caught in the cross fire of noise between the kitchen and the counter.

He could barely hear the phone ring on the other end of the line, and when at last a man answered, Murphy thought he could hear the distinct roar of a party in the background. He shouted, and he was sure the man was shouting back, but the two could barely hear each other.

"I'm a friend of Elisa Linder!"

"Elisa? I don't know if she's here. Hey! Quiet back there! A friend of Elisa is on the line!" The background din seemed to get louder. *"You'll have to speak up!"*

"I'm looking for Elisa!"

"She's as likely to be here as anyone else! Come on over!"

"Is she in town?"

"Everybody is in town! Can't you hear?"

"But Elisa—"

"Come on over. But leave your instrument home . . . no room! Standing room only!" The telephone clattered down onto the receiver, leaving Murphy shouting at a dial tone.

Unwilling to wait in line, Murphy stopped a rosy-cheeked grandmother, her arms laden with boxes. "I'm in a bit of a hurry," he said politely. "Would you sell me some of that?"

"An hour I have waited in line, young man!" She seemed indignant.

"One box of anything. I'll pay you double what you paid."

The woman's eyebrows rose with interest and the bargaining began in earnest. In the end, Murphy paid what the entire load of food had cost, and emerged from Demel's with only one small package of roasted ham. The aged Frau seemed content and chuckled happily as Murphy skated off down the slick sidewalk with his prize.

Murphy had crashed a few parties in his day, but never one so unusual as the party at Leah Goldblatt's little flat. From the street outside the tall, ancient apartment building, Murphy could hear the clarinet of a Benny Goodman recording. He checked the address once again, hoping that this was indeed the home of the cello player. Satisfied, he followed two black-coated Hasidic Jews up the narrow flight of stairs to where people spilled out the door of an apartment, clustering in groups of four and five on the stair landing and sitting on the steps, leaning on banisters and against the walls. The music was Benny Goodman all right, but the strange mixture of guests and gate crashers at this party made Murphy wish that he had bought a chocolate torte from the woman at the pastry shop. A wide white banner stretched over the front door and proclaimed: WELCOME, ZIONISTS, FRIENDS OF ERETZ ISRAEL, SHALOM!

Murphy had passed three synagogues in the neighborhood on his way to Leah's flat, but now it seemed that everyone had congregated here. He held tightly to his package of ham. No. It would not be wise to put a ham on a table crowded with gefilte fish and herring and a dozen different homemade strudels.

He had unknowingly entered the Jewish district of Vienna, and a gathering on behalf of Zionism, at that. Perhaps such a meeting was safe in this part of the city, but Murphy could not help but wonder about the wisdom of being so open in these times. After all, it was only two years since Dollfuss had fallen to the Nazis. And wasn't Hitler screaming about the dirty socialist Jews just across the border? In Vienna Hitler had first made his link with the anti-Semites while he struggled to survive as an artist in a city overflowing with artists. And Vienna had also given birth to men like Theodore Hertzl, the father of Zionism. Such were the paradoxes of this city.

Murphy squeezed past a small group of girls who blocked the doorway. He scanned the faces, searching for Elisa. Conversation drifted up from every corner of the room. The topic of each little company was not the weather or the season, but *Palestine*! Who had gone or hoped to go. Who had chosen the United States instead, and why.

"The riots are terrible in Jerusalem now, she said . . ."

"The Mufti stirs them up."

"There is talk that the British will restrict immigration even more."

"Like everywhere."

"Samuel has gone to a kibbutz in the Negev."

"Negev? Where's that?"

"The desert. Like Moses in Sinai."

"This is all well and good, but I'm going to New York."

"America! The place is drowning in the Depression. Nobody gets visas to New York America anymore!"

"I have an uncle. He lives there and will write a letter for me. He will vouch for me."

"Yes. Yes. To get into America it is only possible with connections."

Murphy could not see Elisa anywhere among the bobbing heads in the little flat. A tall handsome man with fists full of crackers and a full mouth walked by. He seemed more interested in food than in politics. Murphy grabbed him by the arm.

"I'm looking for Elisa Linder."

"Who isn't? She's got my violin." He swallowed and smiled. "My name is Rudy Dorbransky. You are American, aren't you?"

A hush fell over a small circle of men and women around them. *To get into America you must have connections!* Murphy felt the eyes penetrating his back.

"No, Russian," he said, and the hum started up again. No one wanted to go to Russia. "So, you know Elisa?"

"Yes." Rudy seemed disappointed. "So, how do you know her?"

"We are old friends."

"Well, you won't find her here. Haven't you noticed?" He seemed bored. "Every year Leah puts on this party for the Zionists in Palestine. To raise a few shillings. A Jewish version of a Christmas party, yes? We finish playing *La Traviata* at the *Staatsoper,* and then everyone comes here. Every year. It is a tradition if you're Jewish. Which Elisa is not, and neither are you." He cocked his head and smiled curiously at the box of ham that was slightly open. "Pink and rosy stuff there." He seemed to enjoy Murphy's embarrassment. "Not exactly kosher."

"Is Leah anywhere around, then?" Murphy pretended to look around the room as though he would recognize Leah.

"Of course." Rudy raised his eyebrows in amusement. "You are standing right beside her." He jerked his thumb toward the petite, animated young woman who stood in the center of a group of teenaged girls and told them in glowing terms about life on a kibbutz.

Murphy turned away from Rudy with a nod of thanks and waited for Leah to take a breath.

"Young, strong hands, that is what they are calling for. It is no difference—boys or girls. They are treated alike. Work with the same enjoyment—"

Murphy cleared his throat and plunged in. "Fraülein Goldblatt? I have heard a lot about you. From Elisa Linder."

"Oh?" She was not happy with the interruption. "And you are?"

"John Murphy."

"The Russian?"

"American," he whispered, but again the conversations fell silent and attentive. "A friend of Elisa."

"So what are you doing here, Herr Murphy?" The question was not unfriendly, but to the point.

"I was hoping she would be here."

"She is not. Everyone here is Jewish. Except for you. And possibly a Nazi agent or two prowling about to find out what we are up to. Fortunately it is not against the law for us to meet as Zionists in Austria. Not yet, at any rate, so they may prowl all they like." She blinked pleasant, warm brown eyes up at him. "Are you a Nazi, Herr Murphy? Or a Zionist?" She smiled.

"Neither," he nodded and smiled back. "Just a friend of Elisa."

"Well, you can see." She gestured around the room and Murphy noticed the contrasts of the men and women gathered there. Men in stiff white shirt fronts and white ties and black dinner jackets rubbed shoulders with Hassids who argued religious questions rather than political issues. Elisa would have seemed very much out of place indeed, even though she was Jewish—at least, half-Jewish. Of course, that was one bit of information that only Murphy seemed to know.

He lowered his voice. "I need to speak with you privately." He leveled his eyes to lock with hers, and the smug expression on her face faded away.

"Come on." She led him away from the clamor, through the back door, and onto a small iron balcony. "Elisa has not spoken of you," she said, somehow in tune with the seriousness of his errand. "Is something wrong?"

"I need to get in touch with her." He bit his lip, uncertain of how much he should say. Elisa had her reasons for maintaining anonymity. He must not betray the confidence she had placed in him on the train to Salzburg. "It is urgent. A family matter."

"Family? You know her family?"

Murphy nodded. "Her father and I are . . . friends. These are difficult times. You know that. It is most urgent that I speak with her."

Leah searched his face. She was well enough acquainted with secrets to know that Murphy carried something important with him. "She is not in the city. Not expected back until day after tomorrow. We start rehearsals for the New Year's concert then, and—where are you staying?"

"Sacher Hotel. She gave me her address as the Musikverein. I went there and . . . got your name. You are in the book. I didn't mean to—"

"That's all right. Half the people here have only come to eat." She shrugged. "You brought your own, I see."

Murphy liked this woman. There was a depth to her eyes not unlike that which he had seen in Elisa. It was not surprising that they were friends. "For later. I plan on staying in Vienna until I see her. Will you tell her I'm here? At Sacher Hotel."

"It is close enough to the Konzerthaus. Yes. I will tell her to meet you day after tomorrow. After rehearsal. Say, four o'clock?"

"Will she be in tomorrow night?" he asked, and the urgency in his voice caused Leah to rethink her suggestion.

"It is that important, then?"

He nodded curtly and frowned. "Yes. And I'm certain she will think so too."

"Then I will meet her at the station. If the train is on time, we will come at eight."

19

Vienna Rendezvous

Vienna was easily as cold as downtown Manhattan on December 26. In spite of the biting sting of the wind on his cheeks, Murphy found it almost impossible to stay indoors. He wandered in a desultory manner through the snow-covered garden at Schönbrunn Palace. The huge Neptune Fountain was frozen over, and the swans had long since gone south for the winter. *Probably to Palestine*, Murphy thought. *Smart birds. Smarter than Viennese Jews*. He decided he would talk to Elisa about those swans, and about where she must go for safety. For a long time he stood in front of the tall statue of Johann Strauss, who played his cold bronze violin in the Stadtpark. An inch of snow had piled on young Johann's head and clogged the strings of his instrument.

Murphy stared at the statue. He had heard that Strauss was Jewish and that Hitler had forged a new birth certificate for the long-dead composer, purging him of the Jewish stain in his heritage. If the Nazis did indeed gain control of Austria, Hitler's kind gesture guaranteed that Johann Strauss would continue his silent recital in Stadtpark.

Yet it was not the dead who caused Murphy concern now, but one living violinist who touched bow to strings and gave mere wood a voice that echoed back from heaven. It was not the continuing privilege of a bronze Jew to stand in the park that worried him, but the memory of a young woman nearly arrested for sitting on a public bench.

Of course Elisa had changed her papers, like Johann Strauss, but would that be enough to keep her safe if the tramp of German jackboots thundered down the Ringstrasse and drowned out the gentle playing of hungry street musicians in the park? There was only one way to be sure of safety when the Nazis came to town—that was to be elsewhere.

Murphy's breath rose in steamy mist as he tramped back toward the Sacher cafe for a hot cup of espresso—and maybe another piece of strudel. Old men still sat hunched over the morning papers as they had been when Murphy had left three hours before. Had they frozen, too, like Johann Strauss in the park? Maybe nothing in Vienna ever moved very far. Even the trolleys went around and around the Ringstrasse while passengers remained inside and stared out the frosted windows onto the city.

There was no news worth reading, yet Murphy read his paper like the others. Hitler had retired for the holidays at Berchtesgaden. Spain had stopped its civil war to celebrate mass. Afterward the Catholics on both sides of that conflict would no doubt return to kill one another with new dedication, but Christmas was supposed to mean peace, even in the midst of war. In America, the soup kitchens had provided an extra supply of chicken for the season, and lines of unemployed stretched around the block in every city from New York to Dallas—even frigid Minneapolis. Nothing much was happening, nothing much to read about. Lesser men than Johann Strauss were reduced to sleeping in parks, freezing in public places, using newspapers for blankets. Things were mostly rotten all over, even though it was the season of peace and goodwill. In Jerusalem and Bethlehem, Arabs were killing Jewish settlers, and—

Suddenly Murphy did not care if he ever looked at another newspaper. He folded his copy and put his hat on top of it as he sipped his coffee and stared back at the portrait of Emperor Franz Josef. *So where are you going to recommend that Elisa go?* He remembered the way yesterday's conversation had grown hushed when America had been mentioned. *To the soup kitchens in New York? Riots in Palestine? War in Spain? You think anyplace is safer than here? At least people still buy cream puffs in Vienna.* It was true. The Austrians faced their fiery trials with a cup of coffee in one hand and puff pastry in the other. There was something dignified and genteel about the way they denied what was terrible and somehow inevitable in their future. Elisa denied it all, too. Even in Berlin she had denied it. Even though she knew the S.S. agents were watching, she had sat down on the forbidden bench, played the forbidden song, and loved the forbidden man.

Now Murphy must take it upon himself to bring reality crashing down on her. Theo was almost certainly dead. The British ambassador was busy in Berlin giving Austria away like a captive bride to Hitler. While the Austrians denied the reality of the threat, the threat was hardening into an iron fist to crush them. And Murphy would have to warn this beautiful young woman: *Anyplace but Vienna! Anywhere in the world but Austria!*

———

Elisa could not bear to have her mother accompany her to the Kitz-bühel train station to say goodbye. Instead, they embraced and Elisa played the strong and confident role one last time for Anna. All the assurances she had gleaned as a child in her mother's care, she now played back. *"Don't worry. Everything will turn out, you'll see. We will all be together again. Don't worry. Don't worry."*

Franz took her to the Bahnhof alone, holding her hand tightly in his. He did not speak for a long time and she was grateful for his silence. When at last he spoke to her, she dreaded his words.

"Elisa . . ." he faltered, looking away over the ears of the little mare, "I told you about Katrine."

She did not reply or return his gaze when he looked back at her.

He cleared his throat, obviously unnerved by her silence. "I want you to know," he began again, and the words tumbled out in a rush. "Since that night when I saw you in the barn, I have not thought of her. I can think of no one but you at all—"

"Please!" She tucked her chin and stared at her mittens. "So much is happening. Please, Franz, I can't think about anything but my father right now."

He became instantly apologetic. "Yes. I'm sorry. I don't mean that I expect anything from you, Elisa, but . . . I wanted you to know how I feel about you. I—" He stopped and swallowed hard. She knew the choked, unspoken words at the end of his sentence and put her hand gently on his arm to stop him.

"Franz, it is not the time to speak of such things. I cannot . . . could not . . . find a way to answer you."

There was so much he wanted to say! So much he wanted to hear! As the sleigh entered the village, he heard the distant whistle of the train as it rounded Kitzbüheler Horn. What had happened to his heart since the first night he had come to this very place to pick up a holiday Feriengäste? He could not let her go so easily. "I am coming to Vienna." His voice was firm.

"Oh?"

"To see you." He pulled up the horse outside the depot.

"No, Franz." She closed her eyes, feeling embarrassed for him and ashamed of herself. "You must not. It won't work for us."

"I don't believe you mean that, Elisa." He gripped her arm and pulled her close. "You were *there* when I kissed you. You let me touch you, and I felt you wanting me."

She pulled free. "Not you. No. I shouldn't have . . . I'm sorry, Franz."

He sat back and stared at her. The hurt was deep in his eyes. "So still you love this . . . Thomas. The man you told me about." The disappointment was tinged with anger. "You let me believe—"

"I am sorry," she said again quietly.

"And what about me? I am just a peasant from the Tyrol, is that it? Just someone to mark time with. Kiss your hurt, and then you run off again to play." He grabbed her arm again and held her tightly. Seeking her lips, he kissed her hard, almost cruelly; then he pushed her away and stepped out of the sleigh.

He did not look at her again. He did not offer his hand to help her out when she sat in stunned silence. Like a porter, he unloaded her baggage onto the platform and he stood there until she made her way slowly up the steps.

"You must have many more in Vienna just like me," he said bitterly. Then he reached deep into his pocket and pulled out a small package wrapped in red tissue paper. He balanced it on top of her violin case and then turned away from her.

"Franz!" she called after him as he descended the stone steps and hopped into the sleigh. He did not look at her again and with a single crack of the buggy whip, he was gone. The crisp clip-clop of the horse's hooves was drowned out by the chugging engine of the train.

It was hours before Elisa found the courage to open Franz's final gift. As the towering Alps of the Tyrol receded in the distance behind the train, she tore the red tissue paper away and bit her lip in anguish. Gently she caressed the delicate wood carving as hot tears stung her eyelids. In her hands she held a perfect rendering of the holy family. Mary held the tiny infant Jesus as Joseph looked at her with such adoration . . . such *love!* Elisa held the figures up to the last light of day and gasped. Clear and unmistakable in the wood was the reflection of Franz, and the Madonna he had carved with such infinite love and care was undeniably Elisa!

She squeezed her eyes shut and resisted the tears. Pressing the gift to her heart, she whispered a wish, a longing, a prayer: *"Why can't I love a man like him? Oh, why? Why can't I love?"* She was sorry—sorry and ashamed that she had hurt him. But she could not find in her heart the answer he so longed to hear.

No, there was no one for her in Vienna—no strong arms waiting to hold her, no gentle smile or kiss good night. But she would be grateful to be back, grateful for the solitude of the practice rooms and the remoteness of the concert stage. In Vienna her embrace was the waves of applause that washed over her each night; her passion was expressed in the climax of the symphony, music echoing in her head like soft, loving whispers in the dark! In Vienna she could forget that they had been together and bury the hope that someone else might awaken her heart again.

"His name is Murphy," Leah said brightly as Elisa followed her out into the crisp night air of Vienna.

The smell of exhaust and the blaring of horns still seemed very far away as Elisa heard Murphy's name. "He is here?" she asked.

"I didn't give him your address." Leah was alarmed by the intensity in Elisa's voice. "I told you you would meet him. You don't have to go, you know. From the first I thought he was nothing but a stage door *Jäger* looking for a little . . . oh, you know how they are. Even though he is quite good-looking, in an American sort of way."

Elisa could not respond. A thousand thoughts assaulted her at once. *He would not have come here if he didn't know something. Maybe Papa is free. Maybe he knows where he is right now!* She grabbed Leah's arm and spun her around with such force that Leah's smile vanished. "Where is he? Where is Herr Murphy, Leah?"

"At the Sacher Hotel. Eating a torte and drinking a *kleinen Braunen* most likely. What else do Americans do in Vienna?" She seemed irritated by the demanding tone of Elisa's question, then puzzled as she took Elisa's hand. "What's wrong, Elisa? You are shaking all over!"

"Sacher Hotel. Will he be there? You are certain?"

"He seemed to want to see you as much as you seem to want to see him." She frowned. "What is this?"

"Did he say anything else?"

"He said he is a friend of your father's. He was a silly man—no, not silly, but clumsy. Came to our Zionist party with ham to eat."

Elisa was no longer listening as Leah recited the entire episode. Already she was scanning the road for an empty taxi. "Take my things." She shoved the violin case into Leah's arms.

"Where are you going?"

"Sacher Hotel, of course."

"Not without me." There was more disappointment in Leah's voice than concern. She knew that Elisa could handle whatever might come up with this American.

"Yes. Without you. Go home. Or better yet, take my things to my apartment." A taxi slowed as she raised her hand. "I'll see you there."

"You can't . . . can't go there alone!" Leah stamped her foot angrily as Elisa slid into the taxi and slammed the door.

Elisa glanced back as the taxi pulled away. Leah's brows were knit together in one dark, angry line across her forehead. Elisa would make up some story for her tonight—something interesting, passionate, and totally untrue. Leah enjoyed believing such stories about her tall blond friend. Anything would be better than having to recount the agony of the last two weeks!

———

The ride to the Sacher Hotel seemed unbearably long. Traffic snaked slowly along the Ring, yet Elisa could see nothing of the city she had so wanted to see. All her thoughts were filled with the memory of Murphy. His promise to help, his concern, his words of hope. *What if Papa is there with him now? Maybe Herr Murphy brought him out of Germany himself.*

She could barely count out the change for the driver, and finally over-tipped to avoid the waste of even one more precious moment. Excited beyond reason, she had somehow convinced herself that Theo was waiting with John Murphy at the Sacher Hotel. She ran across the plush floral carpet of the lobby without seeing. She had lost all sense of time and place. *Herr Murphy promised. God has heard. Frau Marta was right. Papa is here! Here! I can feel it!*

She banged the desk bell hard and leaned forward eagerly as the porter appeared. "Herr John Murphy, please. Please. What is his room? I am expected."

She did not wait for the slow, groaning lift to descend, but instead ran breathlessly up three flights of stairs to Murphy's room.

Whatever Murphy had expected from this rendezvous, this was not it. The eager, searching face of Elisa Linder told him everything he needed to know at a glance.

She did not seem to notice him as she brushed past and scanned the room. "Papa?" she asked. She was panting, barely able to speak, but she called for Theo again. "Papa?" And then a third time, more urgently, as the hope wavered.

Murphy stood back, helpless as she spun around and clutched his jacket. "Where is he? Do you know? Leah said—"

He sputtered. "He isn't here . . . I . . . he isn't here." He felt confused, almost frightened by the strength of her belief that Theo was *here!* All gentle images of Elisa falling into his arms had vanished.

"You told Leah . . . that you are a friend. *Are.* Is he alive? Is he still in Germany? Where is he? *Please!*"

"Sit down . . ." He tried to guide her to a chair, but she shook herself free from his hands.

"I don't want to sit down. I have been sitting . . . waiting . . ." Tears came now, and Murphy felt even more helpless and confused. He was sorry he had come, sorry to be even partly involved in this mess.

"Please. Calm down."

But she did not calm down. "Where *is* my father? Mama is sick with worry. We can't tell the boys for fear they'll—please tell me!"

"I don't know where. Exactly."

She glared at him. Her eyes cursed him for coming here to offer even a moment of false hope. He wished he hadn't come. Boy, did he wish he were back in Berlin! To face her heartache and disappointment unprepared was almost more than he could stand.

Murphy cleared his throat and became very businesslike. "You have to sit down," he demanded. "Sit. There." He pointed to a chair and was surprised when she bowed her head slightly and obeyed.

She inhaled deeply and did not attempt to fight off her tears. "I was so hoping. I thought that maybe . . ."

Across from her, he sat on the edge of his chair with his hands braced stiffly on his knees. He wanted a drink. Badly. "You need to calm down," he instructed, trying to sound like his father had sounded when he talked to Murphy's mother.

Tears fell like heavy rain. Her face became red. Her nose ran. "Yes, you're right. I'm sorry." She gasped in choppy sentences. "Have you got a handkerchief?"

He did not have a clean one, so he brought her a towel from the bathroom and sat very quietly as she blew her nose and then looked at him with sad and swollen eyes. "Take a deep breath," he repeated in an even more authoritative voice. "Calm down."

She wiped her eyes. "I am calm." She assured him, but tears still flowed, and she did not look at all calm.

He wished now that he had left a letter at the Musikverein—a note of explanation, Theo's final goodbye. No, he had to *say* all the terrible things to her. And she would not fall into his arms. She was more likely to simply fall onto the floor, and then what would Murphy do with her? For days he had dreamed that he was desperately in love with this strange young woman he had met on the train. Now he felt foolish and clumsy and uncomfortable. Where could he begin? What could he say? She was already what his father would have called a *basket case*. Maybe *he* was the basket case. He had combed his hair a dozen times in the last hour, splashed himself with after shave, and changed his tie three times. Now she was here. Within reach. The big moment.

"I don't think you should stay in Vienna," he said.

She stared back at him dumbly as though she had not heard what he said. "Herr Murphy, have you seen my father? That is why I have come here tonight. If you knew what we have lived with—" She lowered her chin and more tears fell.

"Wipe your nose." Murphy took the towel from her hands and wiped her nose for her. "Look. I'm a reporter."

"Then report!"

He plunged in. "Okay, then. I saw your father."

She clutched his hands. "Where?"

"In Berlin. At the Adlon. He came to my room to give me this." He took Theo's letter from his pocket and handed it to Elisa. "He asked me to bring it to you."

She stared at the letter. "Papa!" she whispered, fear filling her voice. "Papa!" she said again.

"We tried to help him." Murphy's words seemed inadequate. He explained the whole scenario to her. "Gestapo . . . S.S. guys, even. You should have seen the fellas. Everybody limped—"

"What went—" She swallowed hard. Her eyes became clear with the resignation that all had not gone as they hoped. "What went wrong?"

"The storm. My God!" He threw his hands up, not knowing what to say or how to explain the terror of that night. "Lightning everywhere. Every plane at Tempelhof was grounded, but your father said the storm was for him. God had given him the storm, see?"

"God." Her voice was hollow. "Yes. God."

"So," he frowned and shrugged. "I tried to talk him into taking the train."

"They would have captured him. Tortured him."

Murphy nodded. She was right. Theo had been right. Maybe he was dead somewhere up in the Alps, but he chose his death rather than letting the Nazis have their pleasure. "Yes. He wanted to fly out. I . . . helped him crank the propeller."

"And then?"

"The last time I saw your father, he was in the air. He said he was heading toward Prague." He would not say what he really thought had happened that night. Let her figure it out herself. "He asked me to tell you—you and your mother—he wanted you to stay out of Germany. Don't go back no matter what. You understand?"

She nodded, holding Theo's unopened letter in her open hands. "Yes, Papa, we won't go back. There's nothing to go back for."

"And he wanted me to tell you that Austria isn't safe, either." He was lying. Theo had not said that, but Murphy knew she would not listen if the words came from John Murphy alone. "Things are happening here . . . rotten things . . . just beneath the surface. Your father wouldn't want you to stay here. He wouldn't."

A slight smile curved one side of Elisa's mouth. She appraised him with bitter amusement. "Did my father say that?" She knew he hadn't.

"Yes." Murphy insisted on the lie. "He wants you out of Vienna. And your mother and brothers someplace safe, too."

"Yes. My mother and brothers." She looked away. "They will leave. I will get word to them, and they will leave Austria."

"You need to leave, too." He pushed the issue harder.

"And go where, Herr Murphy?"

"Anyplace. England. New York. Paris, maybe."

She contemplated his words, then looked toward the window. The lights of Vienna at Weinachten glowed brightly. "This is where my work is . . . my life." Murphy could not begin to understand what she was talking about. "Everything *I am* is here. In my . . . music."

"You can play your violin anyplace, can't you? Why Vienna? Why here?"

She did not answer his question. Instead, she looked at him knowingly. "My father did not ask you to tell me to leave."

"How do you know that?"

"He said Vienna is safe from the Nazis. They can't come here. He told me. Our last night on the train. Rome and Britain and France are sworn to protect Austria from Hitler. Why do you tell me my father said these things to you?"

"You need to get out." Murphy drew himself up. "If I could get every

Jew in Vienna out of Austria by wishing it, I would! You don't know how serious this thing is! They have plans for this place! Hitler hates Austria—hates Vienna, and hates you because you're Jewish! Don't you understand?"

"But here I am not Jewish. You forget. I have papers!"

"That's not good enough!"

"But Austria has a treaty. Papa told me, and—"

"You've got to get out of here! While there's time. I know what I'm talking about, Elisa and . . ."

She pressed her hands to her ears to shut out his words. Tears of anger came again. "They can't have everything! They can't!" she was shouting. "Our home! My father! All of Germany! They cannot have me, too! And never Vienna! Never! You do not understand! This is my life, my work! My father did not say it—*you* said it!"

"Yes! I said it!" Murphy matched her anger. He took her by the arms and gave her a little shake. "Wake up, Elisa! You can't stay here. And if you have any Jewish friends in that orchestra of yours, you'd better tell them to get out while they can!" He pulled her against his chest. Her heart was beating wildly, and he felt as though he held a frightened little bird in his arms. "Austria is at the top of the list," he whispered sadly. "Listen to me. Please. Vienna is already marked for the sacrifice, and the Jews who live here are marked, too."

She pushed him away, unwilling to hear what he was trying to tell her. A defiance came over her, strong and hard, like a woman who denies that the love of her life is dying. "When there is no Vienna, I will leave."

Murphy stared down at her, uncertain what he could say. "You must believe me. Hitler will come to the Ringstrasse."

"When that happens and there is no Austria, I will leave." She raised her chin and all the strength and beauty returned to her so strongly that it made Murphy's heart ache to see her there. He reached out for her, but she stepped back from him, avoiding his touch.

She stopped him with a look. "Thank you for your . . . concern." There was no warmth in her voice. He had told her what she did not want to hear, and now she was finished.

Nobody loves the messenger who brings bad news, Murphy boy. Look at the way she is looking at you. You told her that her father is being held somewhere . . . You don't know where. You told her to leave Vienna. Stupid. Stupid move. At least you should have taken her out for coffee before you told her Hitler was coming and her life is in the trash can . . .

"All right," he said quietly, defeated by his own bluntness. "I'll hold you to it. When Hitler comes, you'll go somewhere else. Agreed?" He extended his hand but she did not take it.

"You are wrong." She bit her lip and glanced out the window at her beloved Vienna. "It will not happen here what happened in Berlin. Austria is not Germany, Herr Murphy. However, I thank you for your concern. For trying to help my father, and now for coming here." She turned to go.

He laughed nervously. "Wait a minute! Uh . . . can . . . I see you again sometime? A concert maybe?"

"The season tickets are sold." Her tone was matter-of-fact. "Perhaps *next year.*"

At the rate things are going, there won't be a next year. He did not say what he believed as he walked her to the door. "I would like to see you sooner than that," he laughed again. "More often than that . . ."

She clutched her father's letter to her and smiled sadly at him. Yes, he was handsome, in an American sort of way. And he was brave and foolish, but . . . "No." She looked down. "I think not, Herr Murphy. My music . . . keeps me very busy, you see."

He nodded in resignation and opened the door for her. "Yes, well—good luck, then."

"Yes . . . luck." She turned then and was gone, taking with her all the images that Murphy had dreamed up over the last days in Vienna and Berlin.

––––––––––

Murphy stood at the window and watched her go, straining his eyes to catch one last glimpse of her as she melted into the crowd of bustling pedestrdans. He saw the slender arm raised up as she hailed a cab; then he shrugged as she slid into the backseat. The first time he had seen her had been just like this moment. Only she had been a beautiful stranger on Wilhelmstrasse in Berlin. He wished now that he had never seen her after that one moment of appreciation.

But he had seen her, again and again; every day in his mind he had seen her: slender, beautiful, and alone . . .

Within an hour, he had cabled New York with a request for transfer. Berlin was too depressing. It would simply emphasize his helplessness. The slide of Austria and Vienna into the German abyss seemed inevitable, and Murphy did not want to hang around and watch it happen.

Two days later in Berlin, while a soft snowfall dusted the city, Murphy received his assignment. The International News Service needed a seasoned correspondent to cover the civil war in Spain. Murphy was ready for a little action. Waiting for German propaganda releases at the Adlon was the kind of thing to make a man start to get soft. It gave him time to think about things he didn't want to think about. It gave him hours to dream about what it would be like to love one woman. Yes, the Spanish Civil War was infinitely preferable to living on dreams of Elisa!

Murphy had no regrets when he packed his bags and boarded a plane for Lisbon. Johnson and Timmons inherited the room at the Adlon—the one with the view, where he had first seen Elisa, then later Theo. As the aircraft circled Berlin for the last time, Murphy glanced downward. He could easily make out Lindheim's Department Store; from the roof to the sidewalk it was covered in the red swastika banners of the Reich. Lindheim's was no longer a Jewish store. From Murphy's vantage point, he could not help but think how very much the building looked like a flag-draped coffin.

20

Words Aflame

Elisa carried two violins to the practice hall: her own Steiner and Rudy Dorbransky's Guarnerius. She resented the bustling, cheerful sameness of the orchestra members after the holidays. What did they know about the things she had been through? What did they care about her father?

Rudy tapped her playfully on the shoulder. "Well, my ever faithful pawn broker is back!" He grinned. "And did you have a good holiday?"

She avoided the question. "I have your violin."

"I certainly hope so," he said with mock indignation. "Ah yes. My little gem is intact, I hope, after passing beneath the noses of the Gestapo? You didn't mention that a Jewish boy owned the case, did you?" He was teasing, but she could not smile at the joke.

"You shouldn't have sent it with me. Next time I'll just lend you the money, Rudy. I was terrified for your violin the whole time."

"Come, now. The Germans enjoy the sound of a fine instrument as long as the composer is German and so is the musician. Let's be fair—" He lowered his chin and gazed solemnly at her. "I would imagine that you were not too terrified to play it once or twice. I know how you covet my treasure, Elisa. Maybe one day when I am married to an extremely wealthy American woman—or a woman of means of *any* nationality—I will leave the Guarnerius to you. In my will. As payment of debt for all the times you have loaned me money." He winked and opened the case, pretending to inspect the instrument before he handed her a wad of bills. "That would make your very wealthy father happy. Have you told him the way he has financed the entire gambling operation of Rudy Dorbransky?"

Elisa looked quickly away. Rudy's words were striking too close to home. "He would not approve."

"He might. Wealthy men like your father understand the risks of gambling. I should like to meet your father someday. I am always interested in meeting men of substance. Does he play cards? Maybe he would like me enough to insist that you marry me. Then you could use the violin whenever you wanted, and I would be rich. Two dreams come true." Rudy had not noticed that Elisa was close to tears. He babbled happily along, tuning his instrument and swinging the bow around like a sword.

"Hello, Rudy." Leah swept past. "Got your violin back, I see." She was still angry at Elisa for sending her off with the luggage.

"A bit heavier than it was before," he whispered playfully. "Elisa has obviously smuggled Herr Hitler's stolen jewels out in it." He plucked the notes of *Deutschland Über Alles* and clicked his heels.

Elisa turned from both of them and carried her violin out onto the stage. Flipping through the music on her stand, she felt uncertain she could get through the morning rehearsal. She studied the score of Mendelssohn's *Elijah*. The opening words of the oratio cried out the question of her own heart: *"Help, Lord, Help, Lord; are you trying to destroy us?"* Somehow the thought that the composer had been Jewish was comforting to her. Yes, in Vienna, music by Jewish composers could still be played. Men like Rudy Dorbransky were still free to joke about the Gestapo. She was safe here. Her mother and brothers were safe, and perhaps, by some miracle, her father had made it across the border of the Reich. That hope and prayer would sing in her music this morning and carry her past the silence and the fears.

It was weeks before the icy waters of the Moldau River yielded up the body of Stephan Günther. It was remarkably well-preserved, considering the time elapsed since Sporer's gun had sent him tumbling from Charles Bridge. Officials in Prague guessed that he had been only recently murdered, and this information found its way into a brief article in the Prague *Zeitung*. No mention was made of his connection with the underground Nazi party in Czechoslovakia. His work as a clerk in the passport office before his mysterious disappearance was somehow not associated with his untimely demise. His identification papers were still legible. He had no money on his person . . .

"*Robbery*. . . ," Sporer smiled at the conclusion of the Prague police.

Karl Hermann Frank, second-in-command of the Sudeten Nazi Party, slammed his fist against the table. "We could have used this. Propaganda Minister Goebbels is not pleased! The Führer will not be pleased. If you had handled this correctly . . ."

"The man was a traitor, smuggling passports out of Prague to Jews in Germany. There was little else to do but kill him. . . ."

"But he was *German*, you fool!" Frank had been reprimanded by party members close enough to Hitler and Himmler to know that the news of a German murdered in Czech territory could be used effectively. Even the death of one member of the NDSP was reason enough for Hitler to rouse the nation with cries of *"persecution!"* and demands for liberation of the three million Sudeten Germans who lived within the borders of Czechoslovakia.

"You have wasted a perfectly good opportunity," Frank tossed the newspaper onto the floor. "There is no mention that he was a Nazi party member; no assumption that he was murdered by Jews." Frank spun around to face the unsmiling Sporer. "And you killed him before we found out who was paying him . . . where the passports were picked up . . ."

"He did not know anything!" Sporer defended.

"If you had not been so eager to shoot him, we would know that for certain! There has been a flood of Czech passports across the border, Sporer! There is a chain here that can be broken, if we can snap only one link! You did not snap the link! You simply silenced it!"

Sporer stared moodily at the floor. Perhaps Hermann Frank was right, but he was not the only one who silenced witnesses. "Yes! Like the Gestapo in Weimar, eh? How long had the border customs inspector lasted when they got their hands on him? Found with eight passports! Eight! An entire family of eight Jews . . ."

"They have all been detained . . ."

"Interned, you mean. And what do they know? They simply paid him money for the passports. *He* knew where they had come from, and Himmler tortured him to death without learning anything at all! Don't talk to me about silencing witnesses!"

The point was well taken. Frank sat down slowly and drummed his fingers on the table. "All the passports bear the official stamp of the government in Prague. The Reich cannot refuse to recognize them or the Gestapo would be arresting citizens of Czechoslovakia by the hundreds. Then the news would be to the advantage of Prague instead of Berlin." He cleared his throat and ran his hand through his hair in frustration. "Along with the passsports on the customs inspector, there were also some documents . . . information about a ship illegally bound for Palestine. Of course that information was relayed to the British and the ship was intercepted before it left Trieste." He looked curiously at Sporer. "It was chartered by an anonymous sponsor in Vienna."

Sporer was scarcely listening. "Another propaganda blunder in favor of the Jews. *Poor Jews*," he sneered. *"We only want to go to Palestine . . .* Yes. On a leaky Turkish freighter with a hull made more of rust than iron."

"You miss the point, Sporer," Frank was smiling. "Two hundred and ten passengers on that little boat. All obviously non-Aryan Germans carrying Czech passports."

"Proof that we do not have a trickle, or even a leak, but that the dam has burst."

"The Führer does not care how many Jews leave Germany. But these are the wealthy Jews! The ones who take German capital with them. They do not pay their taxes to the Reich." He shrugged with the simplicity of the thought. The Gestapo had thus far failed to stop the flood. Perhaps it would be advantageous to their personal careers if they could indeed break the one link in the chain. "Our comrades in Austria are in need of assistance, Sporer," Frank said. "And we are also in need of assistance. This little ship was chartered by someone in Vienna. Czech passports are appearing in the hand of every Jew who manages to slip out of the Reich without paying taxes. Perhaps we can put a stop to this ring, Sporer. Then think how we might be rewarded by the Reich for service to our Fatherland, ja?" He seemed suddenly very pleased with himself. He could spare Sporer for as long as it took. Where the Gestapo failed, they would not—and for now, at least they could still work with some independence. "It would be good, Sporer, if you would travel to help our brothers in Austria." he slapped him solidly on the back. "This chain is not so very strong. One link is all we need. Only one. Snap it!"

———

Nazi propaganda pamphlets, a copy of *Mein Kampf*, and a typed memorandum signed by Captain Leopold, the head of Austria's illegal Nazi party, were all laid out in a neat line on the table in the Herrgottseck of the Wattenbarger farmhouse. All the family was there.

Franz looked at his mother. Marta's lips were tight, her eyes downcast as Karl paced back and forth before a sullen and defiant Otto.

"What right do you have to go through my things?" Otto demanded. He flashed an angry look at Marta, who did not answer.

Karl stopped before him and raised a hand as though he would strike his son. His hand trembled with anger and the disappointment of discovering the truth about Otto. "You will not speak with such disrespect to your mother!" he said in a voice so quiet, yet so full of rage, that they all held their breath with the expectation of something terrible.

Otto did not acknowledge his own disrespect, any more than he would acknowledge that what he had done, and was doing, was wrong. "Those papers are mine. Soon such words will be for all Austrians!" His jaw was set in a firm, hard line. "Chancellor Schuschnigg is not the savior of Austria. An independent Austria is nothing! They carved us up after the war. Made us a fragment. Cut us off from Hungary and destroyed the empire of the Hapsburgs. They have made us nothing!"

"And you . . . you and your Nazi friends think we will be something if we are joined to Germany?" Scorn filled Karl's voice. "Your grandfather fought the Prussians of Germany to keep Austria free! And now you wish to join these—" Karl picked up the well-read copy of *Mein Kampf* and in one motion threw open the door to the stove. He scanned a page and the color on his cheeks deepened. "Yes. Herr Hitler would give the German people more living space by taking that which belongs to others. And what will happen to the people who live in these lands after Hitler sends his troops in?" He did not need an answer. Hitler had written the answer in his book.

"We are Germans," Otto said in a voice that asserted his sense of racial superiority. "What does it matter what happens to the vanquished?"

"We are Austrians," Karl said through clenched teeth. He began to tear pages from *Mein Kampf* and toss them onto the flames of the stove. "And we are *Christians!*" His eyes seemed to blaze as the flames devoured the evil words of the madman across the border.

"First we must be Germans!" Otto shouted back. "You cannot destroy his words! He is the heart of Germany! Of the Greater Reich!"

"Then the heart of Germany is black and vile," Marta replied quietly in a trembling voice. "It has no place at the Herrgottseck of this home." Her eyes were filled with tears, but she was even more resolute in her declaration than Karl had been. It was plain what she was saying. Otto could not stay there. His beliefs were a betrayal of everything she had raised her sons to be. Gretchen burst into tears at the words of her mother. Young Friedrich stared at her and then back to his brother as they faced each other. This was no simple discussion of politics or the Anschluss of Austria with Germany. No, it was much, much, more.

"Before Hitler came to power, there were many of us," Marta said calmly, "who believed it might be better if Austria became a part of Germany. Yes. Maybe better for our farms and families to be part of a greater state." She paused and watched as Karl tossed the last of *Mein Kampf* into the flames. It hissed, and the corners blackened and shriveled. "But now—" She shook her head. "They mock God. They mock our Lord Jesus, the Christ, and they mock the nation to which He was born."

"The Jews!" Otto scoffed. "They killed Christ!"

"No!" Karl whirled to face his son. "*You* killed Christ! And I killed Him! And the words of your madman crucify him daily!" His voice boomed. "When law and justice are distorted and the innocent are condemned, the crucifixion begins anew! Listen, Otto! Listen, my son!" Karl threw open the door and the cold winds of March blew into the Stube. "Listen to the voice of your Jesus as you help destroy His children!" He cupped his hands around his mouth and called words of Jesus on the cross: "Father . . ."

The mountains echoed back, *"Father . . . Father . . . Father . . ."*

"Forgive them . . ."

"Forgive . . . Forgive . . . Forgive them . . ."

"They don't know . . ."

"Don't know . . . don't know . . . know . . . know . . ."

"What they do!"

"What they do . . . they do . . . they do . . ."

When the last of a thousand voices died away, only the sound of the wind was left. Karl kicked the door shut. He looked at Otto as if he had never seen him before. The young man before him was not the beloved son, but a total stranger who had come to dwell in a familiar body. "You *do* know what you are doing!" he said. "You will lay the innocent out on the cross. You will take up the hammer and press the spike onto His loving hand and you will *strike*! And *strike*! And *strike again*!"

"The Jews are the Christ killers!" Otto defended. "And they would exploit every good German worker!" His eyes became transfixed as he repeated the words he had come to believe. "We will not be free until—"

"*Take the hammer, Otto!*" Karl shouted. "*Crucify Him!* Crucify the innocent children and the women who bore them. Murder their husbands and take their homes and shops for the Greater Reich! You *know* what you are doing! *You know!* Sell your nation and your soul and *crucify them* as your evil master orders. But you will find you crucify me as well, and your mother, and your brothers, and your sister!"

Gretchen wept loudly at her father's words. "Oh, *Otto!*" she moaned. "Please *don't!* Mama, tell him to stay! Tell him to still be our Otto!"

Helmut and Friedrich lowered their heads then, and Franz saw tears also in the eyes of his younger brothers. But there was no softening on the face of Otto. His eyes narrowed in determination. He had chosen his way as the way of Nazi Germany, and the time for discussion was past.

Marta fought against emotion, but she could not speak. The family sat in heavy silence for what seemed like a long time.

At last, Karl stepped forward and reached his large calloused hand to touch Otto. Otto moved slightly, avoiding his father's touch. "You are my son," Karl said with a sadness that betrayed the depth of his pain.

Otto smiled a disdainful smile. "I have no father but the Fatherland," he said cruelly.

Karl flinched as though he had been struck. He stepped back as little Gretchen wailed and ran to embrace her mother. Marta held her and stroked her head, not ever taking her eyes from Otto. "If that is so, Otto," she cried, "then you have no mother!"

Only then did Otto show some twinge of regret. He winced and said to Marta, "Someday you will see that I am right, Mother. Then I will come home."

She shook her head in solemn disagreement. "No, Otto. Do not come home until you see that you are wrong. Then we will be waiting for you. Your loving family . . . waiting . . ." She broke down and buried her face in Gretchen's shoulder. "Don't cry," she tried to comfort the young girl. "Don't cry, Gretchen." But her own tears flowed freely.

Otto stared at them all for a moment as the sound of sobs filled the house. He glanced briefly at the crucifix above the table, and then he pushed past Franz and went quickly up the stairs to pack his belongings.

———

It was to be a year before Murphy returned to Vienna. In all that time, he hardly thought about Elisa Linder at all—at least not more than once an hour. The groaning world had turned its attention to the bloody civil war in Spain where the Spanish rebels of the Fascist General Franco fought against the coalition of leftist Republican and Loyalist government groups for control of the nation.

As Britain and the powers of the League of Nations declared their policy of nonintervention, the union of Hitler and Mussolini supplied men and equipment to Franco's Fascist forces. For ten months, Murphy shuttled back and forth between the Italian and German troops of Franco's army, then back again to the Republican forces who fought them. A million Spaniards died that year, and Murphy wondered if he hadn't seen each one.

Men with hands tied behind their backs fell riddled with bullets in the streets of Madrid and Toledo. Women and children perished on the open roads, strafed by German fighter planes.

The entire war seemed to be a showcase for Mussolini's Blackshirts and the mighty mechanized forces of Hitler's Reich. The Spanish themselves died unadorned by medals or protected by armor plate and tank tracks. Dark-eyed children cried hungry in the streets of besieged Madrid, and Murphy wrote what he saw:

"Insurgent airplanes dumped more than 100 bombs into the suburbs of Bilbao today but did not fulfill General Emilio Mola's threat to blast the Basque capital to bits. Terror-stricken inhabitants, mindful of the Insurgent commander's warning he would bombard the city without mercy if it did not surrender by today, ducked for cover as nine bombers and seven pursuit planes roared over Bilbao."

Murphy had counted the planes himself, and noted without amusement that the aircraft were German-made. On two of the planes he could distinctly make out the swastika beneath a fresh coat of paint. He mentioned this in the New York dispatch, but for some reason that information had been cut. Later he heard that his story had gone page four in *The New York Times*, lost amid the hoopla of the British coronation of King George VI. There it was again. The world cared more about what Princess Elizabeth and Margaret Rose did during the ceremony than about the real world:

"No-man's land was covered with dead and wounded after a terrific battle yesterday. Squads from both armies roamed the area in the night looking for wounded. . . ."

Two weeks later, Murphy read the article that had beat him out for the front page: *"Princess Margaret Rose, 6½, tried her best to act as a princess should at a coronation, but once she yawned right at the venerable Archbishop of Canterbury. . . ."*

With a sigh of resignation, Murphy had left the newspaper beside the open ditch that served as a latrine for Loyalist troops. He was certain they would know how best to put it to use.

It was five long, hot summer months before London and Paris found the courage to present an ultimatum to Italy and Germany to withdraw their "volunteer" forces from Franco's Fascist troops. By then, Murphy had seen the inside of every stinking prison and field hospital on both sides of the line. The hospitals, he noted grimly, smelled as foul as the prisons. Both were filled to overflowing with rotting men, women, and children. Blood had fertilized the hard, rocky soil of Spain. A million dead. For what? For the proving of Fascist strength; for the forging of Germany and Italy in a deadly war game that was staged to show what they were capable of. The ultimatum given to Germany and Italy by France and Britain was answered with yet another Insurgent attack. This time 270 German-made planes took to the skies above Toledo, Brunete, and Teruel. France and Britain had been slapped in the face, and they did nothing to respond.

In his last dispatch, Murphy shouted the words over a shortwave radio just before he boarded a small plane back to England.

"The Republican government troops were unable to resist the attacks!" he shouted.

"Repeat that, Murphy!" a faraway voice crackled in reply.

For the third time, Murphy repeated the information, ending with the terrible news of resounding defeat. "An Insurgent communique announced that government lines had collapsed under the offensive which hit *'Like a bolt of lightning'!"*

"Like what?"

". . . A bolt of lightning! Put that in quotes, will you? I heard it from a German 'volunteer' Luftwaffe pilot! So much for ultimatums!" Now Murphy was simply yelling into the radio without the slightest concern whether he was being heard or not. None of this stuff could go into his story, even though every word of it was the truth. "What makes that screwball British Prime Minister think Hitler is going to give a hoot about these ridiculous British-French ultimatums now? Huh? They're nuts!"

"What?"

"I said *they're nuts!* And you can print that, too!"

"We can't . . . print that, Murphy!"

Angry at everyone, Murphy shouted louder. "Right! Yeah! Not enough human interest, right? A million dead women and kids . . . not enough. Well, how about this for the front page?" Bitterly he began to recite a lead to the copyman on the other end of the shortwave. "Try this: *Many dinners were spoiled in Madrid tonight when the rebels chose from 7:40 to 8:50 to bombard the city with considerable intensity. We had a perfectly good dish of succotash ruined in our hotel by one of three shells that hit nearby.* How's that?"

"Great! Really good human interest. People understand having supper interrupted."

For a long moment, Murphy simply stood staring at the radio. Then, in one last gesture of disgust, he flicked the switch to the "off" position and stalked out onto the airfield to board his plane.

21

The Call of the Homeland

It was Christmas again in Vienna. The silent night of 1936 had stretched into the long, silent year of 1937 for Elisa. No word had ever come from her father, and after a few months they had even given up hope of hearing anything at all. Broken and aching, Anna had left the little mountain village of Kitzbühel for the anonymity of a little house in Prague that Theo had purchased two years earlier. Elisa had visited twice, but the undisguised loneliness of her mother's expression made her want to hurry back to Vienna to her work and her life of busy solitude.

She had not heard from Franz again. John Murphy, she had heard, was somewhere in Spain. Thomas served his masters in Paris. As the months crept by without news of her father, Elisa somehow came to blame Thomas for Theo's disappearance. The love she carried for him once again turned to hate and a consuming rage against what her friend had come to believe. But sometimes in the dark of night the anger dissolved into a heavy ache of longing and desire. When the morning came, as it always did, she would look into the mirror and chide herself for being so foolish. Then she would immerse herself in the frantic schedule of rehearsal and performance and a social life that revolved around the other members of the orchestra.

An uneasiness had settled gradually over her dear Vienna in the last few months. Signs had begun to appear in the shop windows along the Ring like those she had seen on Unter den Linden in Berlin in 1933. *"Juden verboten!"* Even though her papers said she was a Czech of German heritage, Elisa did not go to those places. Months before when the great airship *Hindenburg* had crashed in flames in Lakehurst, New Jersey, she and Leah had gone to watch the newsreel at the cinema. Leah had been stopped at the door and refused entry because she was a Jew. Elisa had nearly slapped the arrogant little doorman, but instead, she had told him to go back to Germany in no uncertain terms. Then, she had taken Leah and Shimon out for a lovely meal at Sacher's and they had drowned their sorrows with a bottle of delightful white wine from the Wachau, a place just beyond the Vienna Woods.

"Remember Johann Strauss." Elisa had raised her glass to toast the Jewish composer.

"Right now I am thinking about Theodore Hertzl and his dream of Zionism and a Jewish state, if you don't mind," Leah remarked dryly. Then she confided that she and big Shimon had plans to move to Palestine as soon as they had enough money.

At those words, Elisa felt such a sense of emptiness, such loneliness, that the rest of her conversation had been difficult and forced that night.

Other members of the orchestra were drifting off—some to America, some to France, and a few to Palestine and the hard life it offered. Leah dreamed that one day she would be there, and now she shared that hope with Shimon Feldstein. They would be married two weeks after the New Year, and had plans to spend their next Passover in Jerusalem as husband and wife.

Elisa tried not to resent this crazy plan of her friend. She tried not to envy the fact that Leah had fallen helplessly in love with the brawny, stoic tympani player. *Do they have tympanies in Jerusalem? Or even an orchestra? What will you do to make a living? You are a cellist, Leah, not a farmer! Are you crazy? Is there life anywhere but here in Vienna?* Elisa wanted to say all these things, but she did not. After all, her own life was such an empty mess—what right did she have to shoot down Leah's bright dreams in flames, just as the Hindenburg had burned? *Be silent. Smile and listen politely.* Only once did she run trembling with fear to Leah.

On the front page of the *Berliner Zeitung* was a photograph of the Grand Mufti of Jerusalem standing beside Hitler. The British had demanded he leave Palestine because of his leading role in instigating the riots there. The caption read: *Haj Amin el Husseini vows with Führer's help to banish Jews from the Holy City forever.* When Elisa insisted that Leah and Shimon must not go to such a place, they had simply stared at her as though she spoke in a foreign tongue.

"You cannot understand, dear Elisa. We are Jews, and that is our homeland."

Elisa, although she was half-Jewish, could not understand. Leah was right about that. But she did know what it was to be a target of Hitler. She had seen it destroy her family, the very life of her own father.

"Austria is safe," she insisted. "Chancellor Schuschnigg has pacts with Italy and England and France. Hitler cannot come here! It is not possible! The whole world would rise up against the Nazis."

Taking her hand gently in his own, Shimon pointed to a shop across the street with an ugly sign in the window. *Juden verboten!* "They are here already, Elisa," he said gently, even sadly. "Hitler sends more Nazis across the border each day. They come in leather pants and thick brown shoes like peasants, but they fool no one. Even Chancellor Schuschnigg is frightened. And have you not seen that the palace of Baron von Rothschild is empty? The baron is a Jew. He now lives in Prague, not Vienna."

Elisa stared at the floor. "My mother is in Prague," she whispered. "My family." She had never told them about her father, and for this moment, she was relieved that Anna and the boys had taken refuge in Prague. Shimon's words sent a cold blade of fear through her heart. "My father says that Czechoslovakia is like Switzerland," Elisa volunteered cautiously. "The constitution is like in America. Why don't you go there to live? There are orchestras there. The German Theatre and the Czech National Theatre—much more cultured than the wilderness of Palestine!"

Shimon and Leah laughed at her suggestion, and Elisa had pretended she was not serious. But she was serious. The thought of losing Leah's friendship made her reel. Quietly, in the secrecy of her heart, she prayed that their immigration visas would not be granted. But Leah taught Elisa the words *Aliya Bet*—illegal immigration. And only yesterday Leah told her that it didn't really matter if she and Shimon were granted permission. They were going to Jerusalem, and the matter was settled.

Lately, a steady stream of German refugee children had passed through Leah's apartment. All were bound for Palestine, whether they had been granted the necessary papers of permission or not.

Children who came from Germany with nothing suddenly had passports and visas to France where they would board ships in Marseilles bound for Palestine. Elisa had seen a passport once when a child had shown it to her proudly. Leah scolded the little girl, then looked at Elisa almost apologetically. "Dangerous, but something that must be done. I trust that you will not mention it."

Elisa nodded. She knew all about forged papers. They were expensive and hard to come by. German-Jewish children came with nothing; they left with identities. Purchased how? By whom? With what money? Elisa did not really want to know. She knew too much already. If it was indeed true that Nazis were infiltrating Austria's police and government as Shimon insisted, then this sort of activity could be life-threatening. Elisa remembered quite well the unexplained disappearances of people in Germany who were involved in such operations. Couldn't Leah and Shimon be content with their own safety? Why did they involve themselves so deeply?

The thought made her frown. For the first time in months she thought of Murphy. She, too, might be rotting away in some German camp right now if it hadn't been for his willingness to get involved. Of course, the fact that he was an American newsman almost guaranteed that no one would slap him in irons. He had not risked his own safety, as Leah and Shimon were now doing.

There was a reason Murphy had been called to London. There was business here. A visit at the International News Service offices, a stop at the BBC. He had a few interviews set up with members of Parliament who were diametrically opposed to one another on matters of what must be done about the Germans, what must be done about the Italians, what must be done about Spain and Austria. Actually, only a handful believed anything must be done at all. The rest, along with the citizens who now walked along the London sidewalks, were numb and uninterested. After all, the issues at hand did not affect the price of curtains, or a new tea tray, or the comfort of one's shoes.

London was cold and gray. Frumpy matrons and governesses with perfectly groomed children in tow joined the line of clerks and shopkeepers at the bus stop. Murphy was the only person in the group without an umbrella, and that immediately marked him as a foreigner. Snugly buttoned bank officers stared at him as if to warn him that if it rained—and it most certainly would—he should not expect to share their shelter. *Only a fool goes out without an umbrella! After all, take a look at the front pages of the newspapers. Every photo shows Prime Minister Chamberlain with an umbrella in hand! A sensible chap, the PM!*

Yes. Sensible. Murphy made his way through the groups of standing men who held tightly to the leather straps inside the big red bus. The eyes of the ladies glanced quickly away from him as he climbed the curving steps up to the open top deck. This was proof that he was not sensible in the least. After all, anyone could leave an umbrella somewhere in a moment of forgetfulness, but to sit on the top deck of a London omnibus in the dead of winter was madness!

Grateful to be alone, Murphy stretched out on the wooden bench and squinted as the cold wind stung his eyes. He had a day to kill—eight hours to loll around. It had been a long time since he had been so privileged, a long time since he had ridden in something other than an ambulance packed with dying men, or on the deck of a German-made tank through nameless towns that all looked the same in their heaps of rubble. Today, Murphy had determined that he would see it all: *The Strand, Pall Mall, Abbey Road, Baker Street.* And all for only fivepence, courtesy of the London General Omnibus Company.

Wide streets and stark brick houses seemed to be reaching for whatever glimpses of sun the London December would offer. It seemed little different than Baltimore, or some snug district in New York where blameless citizens talked about the weather or the boss or . . . maybe politics? Not likely nowadays.

In Spain the cities and towns had all blended into one endless, bloody shell of dying embers and dying people. Humans, not unlike these, who had once bustled down the lanes with some singular purpose—something to buy: *"But I won't pay a shilling more than one and ten!"*; someone to meet: *"He's always late!"* Yes, Madrid had been like London once.

Murphy had seen it before the bombs, before Franco's Fascists and the Nazi planes.

The bus careened solidly around a corner. A scruffy-looking newspaper boy waved a placard at the passing pedestrians to entice them to buy his paper.

MADRID SHELLED AGAIN!
3 DRIVES STARTED BY FRANCO'S TROOPS

Murphy watched as a well-fed woman in a fur collar walked her well-fed dog past the newsboy. He had a sudden urge to scramble down the steps and ask her what she knew about Madrid, and if she knew anything at all about the Spanish Civil War. He watched dozens of cautious, umbrella-toting citizens march past the screaming headline.

"Madrid? In Spain, isn't it?" They would likely answer if he asked. *"Very, very far away from here, you know. And the Spanish rebels. Quite to be expected what with that hot-tempered Latin blood! Never touch us here, though. Madrid is quite far from London."*

Murphy closed his eyes. Images of burning buildings and the red lines of tracer bullets against the night sky filled his mind, and he was in Madrid again—in Toledo, Teruel, and Brunete! Screams of women and the cries of orphaned children came to him in waves of sickening reality.

The careful people of London could not see it now in their anxiety over what Christmas gifts to buy, but Madrid was *here*! It was on Baker Street and Covent Gardens, on Oxford Street in the myriad of shops. It was *here*, amid correct behavior, and in Regents Park, where a python swallowed a live chicken whole before crowds of gawking spectators who gathered at the Serpent House to watch.

"Now, that was interesting!" Enough of this doomsday stuff about Hitler and Spain and Italy! Enough nonsense about the Nazis infiltrating Austria! Like Madrid, Vienna is very far away, and quite foreign. Never mind that Churchill believes Hitler is *The Serpent*. Does it matter if the Nazis and Italians aid Franco, or if little Austria is swallowed whole? Why should that concern London?

"Just don't go out without your umbrella, Chamberlain!" Murphy shouted out loud. No one heard him, of course. He was the only passenger on the top deck, and the wind carried away his voice until it was lost in the blaring din of Christmas traffic.

––––––

Winston Churchill, during his long months of enforced political retirement, had laid many of the bricks of Chartwell himself. Now, spidery trails of ivy clung to the face of the main house. It was rather cold inside, and many of the rooms were closed. Murphy had heard that the venerable statesman had been reduced to supporting himself through the free-lance writing of political essays. Perhaps business was slow for him these days.

He was dressed comfortably in a smoking jacket and loose trousers. Everything about him reminded Murphy of a bulldog—the jowls and furrowed brow, the pale complexion of his balding head, his manner of moving, the thoughtful growl of his voice. He did not seem either angry or defeated, though Murphy had heard of deep, black moods of depression that haunted Churchill in recent days.

The room was clouded with cigar smoke, and Churchill glowered at Murphy through the haze as a butler poked the blazing fire in the fireplace, then slipped quietly out.

"You are a correspondent. In Sshpain."

"Almost a year."

"Umm. Yesh." He seemed to chew his words. "I began in Africa. The Boer War." He dismissed the point of common ground as quickly as he had brought it up. "You see how far that has taken me." A slight smile and a raised eyebrow spoke of the irony in his statement. Now he was indeed regarded as a public doom-crier. "And how did you find Madrid?"

"Hungry. Bleeding."

"The worst quarrels arise when both sides are equally in the right and in the wrong." He studied Murphy for a response, then thought for a moment before he continued. "Both sides desperate. One side backed by Communists; the other, Fascists. The cruelties and ruthless executions, the appalling hatreds unleashed make it only too probable that victory will be followed by the merciless exterminations of the vanquished."

"That policy is already being carried out."

"Of course. Both sides have, no doubt, read *Mein Kampf*. Hitler has said quite plainly that there will be no prisoners of war. He has also written that the total purpose for humanity and society is to prepare for war. Which he has done and continues to do, while we sit here on our hands." The bulldog eyes flashed as he spoke and he raised his voice as he might have addressed the Commons. "Thank God for Anthony Eden. At least there is one sensible man in His Majesty's government. It was his ultimatum that stopped the piracy of foreign ships in the Mediterranean, his good sense that established French and British anti-submarine patrols at Nyon. There is no doubt that the spectacle of eighty Anglo-French destroyers patrolling the Mediterranean made a profound impression on Europe."

"And yet the latest ultimatum to the Germans and the Italians to withdraw from Spain has failed." Murphy was scribbling notes furiously as Churchill cleared his throat and glared at him.

"The Prime Minister—" He paused and looked off as though he could see his words in print. "Mr. Chamberlain is determined to play suitor to the two dictators: Hitler, Mussolini. In July of this year he invited the Italian ambassador to Downing Street. Mr. Eden was not invited to the meeting." The brow furrowed in disapproval. "Mr. Chamberlain spoke of his desire for Anglo-Italian relations. Count Grandi suggested he write a personal appeal to Mussolini. The letter produced no apparent results, and the relationship with Italy got steadily worse because of Spain."

Now Murphy came to the heart of the question. "What does this mean to Austria? After all, in the Rome protocols, Italy is sworn to protect Austria's sovereignty, along with Britain and France, should Hitler make good his threat to annex Austria."

Churchill almost smiled—a smile filled with some bitterness. "I have heard that here, in government circles, there are those in power who have determined that Austria is a small sacrifice to pay for peace. In the last year Mussolini has cast his lot with Hitler; that is quite evident. Only the Austrians—and a few others—seem to care about Austrian independence." He leaned forward in his chair and leveled a steely gaze at Murphy. "Henderson, the British ambassador to Berlin, has seen a map of the Greater Reich in Herr Göring's home." He narrowed his eyes and sat back heavily. "Yes. Henderson is a friend of Herr Göring, and he has seen the map. There is no boundary on it between Germany and Austria."

Murphy stopped writing the ominous words. He felt sick. He thought of Vienna. Of Elisa Linder. "If Italy refuses to help, certainly Britain and France would not allow such a violation." He thought of the python and the live chicken in Regents Park.

"As foreign minister, Anthony Eden still gives our policies some backbone," Churchill conceded. "But he and Chamberlain are on opposite sides on a number of issues. Mr. Chamberlain is quite prepared, it seems, to kiss the hand that slaps us. Single-handedly, he wishes to bring us peace. At what price? And is it not the peace of the dead? I do not know the answer. Anthony Eden is hated by the Italians and the Germans both for his courage and for his determination that there is a line that must not be crossed." He drew deeply on the stub of his cigar. "Mr. Eden is much like me in his attitudes. With the exception, of course, that he is still in harness." He cleared his throat and growled, "And you can see where my convictions have gotten me. Political exile. Still I proclaim that we *must* arm ourselves even as the Germans are doing. No, no. There are those who say the Nazis are already invincible." He shook his head slowly. "Have you heard that your own American Colonel Charles Lindbergh has been to visit the German Luftwaffe?"

Murphy nodded. A sense of anger and embarrassment simmered in him at the mention of the great hero who had crossed the Atlantic solo in 1927. He had returned home in victory. Now, he had recrossed the Atlantic as a guest of the Reich. His tour included an exhibition of Luftwaffe fighter plane capability that had filled him with admiring words for his Nazi hosts. After proclaiming that the Germans had an air force that was unbeatable by any nation of the world, he had come to London to dine with the American ambassador to Britain, Joseph P. Kennedy. "Better to appease the Germans" had been the verdict of these two representatives of America. "We can't possibly hold them back by any force of arms. Better negotiate with them and give them what they want."

American pacifist sentiments rippled through the League of Nations. Statesmen mumbled among themselves and reacted with a defeatism that served Hitler's purpose perfectly. He had presented his philosophy plainly in *Mein Kampf*: *"The skillful and unremitting use of propaganda can persuade people to believe that Heaven is Hell.... For the broad mass of the people in the primitive simplicity of its heart more readily falls victim to a big lie than a small one...."*

"Yes. I'm afraid Colonel Lindbergh has been an unknowing tool for Herr Hitler's propaganda. Unbeatable? Unstoppable? Terrible words. Evil words when one is eye to eye with the Serpent." There it was again— Churchill's view that all of Europe faced the Serpent. The statesman had a look of disbelief on his face. "And our Prime Minister has chosen to believe a man like Hitler. A man who has written such words!"

"Has the Prime Minister read *Mein Kampf*?"

"Recently, Mr. Eden quoted the passage to him...." He thought for a long moment, making certain he had it right. "Hitler declared simply, *'In political life there are no principles of foreign policy. Foreign policy is only a means to an end. In matters of foreign policy, I shall not permit myself to be bound....'*" He seemed satisfied that he had spoken correctly.

"And what did the Prime Minister say when Eden told him?"

"He told him to go home and take an aspirin. Yes. The PM's advice to the foreign minister. But Hitler is more dangerous than a head cold . . . more virulent, more contagious. And fatal."

Churchill rose slowly and crossed to a cluttered desk. Shuffling through a stack of papers, he skimmed their contents, finally choosing one. "Unless we are strong, and sensible—" He did not finish his sentence. He handed the paper to Murphy. It was a transcript of Hitler's writings: *"Every Jew is proof of the enfeeblement of our national life and of the worthlessness of what we call the Christian religion. One would need a heart as hard as crocodile hide not to feel sorry for the poor exploited Germans and—which is identical—not to hate the Jews and despise those who defend these Jews or are too cowardly to trample this vermin to death. With bacilli one does not negotiate.... They are to be exterminated as quickly and thoroughly as possible."*

Murphy looked up from the page that continued for many paragraphs of the same madness. "Yes. I saw the practice of this in Germany." He thought of Elisa and Theo. Had Theo survived? Had he been found? Was he now in some prison in Hitler's Reich?

Churchill nodded and continued staring out at the winter-brown trees of Chartwell. Again and again he had spoken in Parliament, and finally, he had been sent home to *"take an aspirin."*

"It all is written down. His every plan. For Germany. For the world. I am no prophet. No Jeremiah. He has written the future himself." The great man sounded helpless, alone in his terrible knowledge of the future. Was he now seeing the bombs and tracer bullets above the London skies, as

Murphy had seen them in Spain? His majestic voice dropped to a whisper. "Death stands at attention—obedient, expectant, ready to serve, ready to shear away the peoples *en masse*; ready, if called upon, to pulverize, without hope of repair, what is left of civilization. He awaits only the word of command."

22

Biedermeier

On Elisa's music stand was the score of Respigi's *Pini di Roma*. The program of tonight's concert had been changed only two days before when someone from Chancellor Schuschnigg's office had passed the word along that some "great man" from Italy would be visiting Vienna. They had not mentioned who the guest would be, but everyone buzzed among themselves that it would have to be someone very high up indeed to request such a change. *Mussolini himself? Count Grandi? Perhaps the King?*

Whoever it was, the Austrian Chancellor would be accompanying him. A concert in Vienna was almost standard fare in Austrian politics. Across the border in Germany, Göring invited foreign dignitaries on hunting trips. Such adventure appealed to those with a thirst for blood. But here, it was said that Schuschnigg hoped to calm the wild beasts of international politics with music. Tonight the musicians would play with that goal in mind: *Rome, Austria's ally. Pledged to stand with us if we are threatened. Friends and protectors . . .*

Beyond the glare of the footlights, the buzz of the audience seemed particularly animated tonight. Elisa tried not to look up into the boxes where dignitaries always sat. Instead, she scanned the score and looked up across the empty conductor's stand to see Leah looking back at her. *Dear Leah. Her warm brown eyes so full, so sad tonight.* In the soft light of her music stand, Leah looked almost like the Madonna figure in the living nativity at the Schottenkirche. Elisa remembered Franz, laboring for hours over wood until at last it seemed to breathe. *Leah, you would make a better model for the mother of the Christ Child than I. Why do you look so sad, Leah? What do you see tonight that causes you to look at me that way?* Elisa looked away, unable to bear the intensity of Leah's eyes any longer. Was she saying goodbye? *Not yet. Not so soon. Not until the spring.*

She told me they would not leave until spring. Suddenly she wondered who would take Leah's chair after she had gone. No one would ever take her place . . .

Elisa placed the clean white cloth on the chin rest of her instrument and joined the dissonant clamor of tuning instruments. A minute passed before the house lights dimmed and silence fell over the audience. There was one moment of suspenseful pause as concertmaster Rudy Dorbransky emerged from the wings bearing his treasured Guarnerius violin in his hand. Thunderous applause rose up and he nodded his thanks, the perfect model of decorum.

Elisa was always amused at the way he managed to carry off the image of dignity and authority even when his head was splitting from a hangover. Handsome and talented, he had been the logical choice for concertmaster after Max Helmann had left for New York last July. The position had somehow given Rudy a sense of responsibility. Although he was still rumored to be seeing the wife of the Nazi and he still managed to lose his concert shirts in card games from Paris to Amsterdam, he had not once hocked his precious instrument since he had accepted the concertmaster's chair.

Elisa felt a surge of pride for him now as he bowed to the audience and then to his comrades. He raised the Guarnerius and gave the long, clear note by which all others found their pitch. Even in that one solitary note, the voice of the Guarnerius sang clear and strong to the highest galleries.

And then, as if in reply, came a noise from the upper balcony. A voice, distorted with rage shouted:

"No Jews on our Vienna stage! Heil! Heil Hitler! Germany for Germans!"

Elisa gasped, and as a thousand heads pivoted to see the madman, a shot rang out! Screams filled the hall; women in silks and satins scrambled for cover behind the seats. Musicians and instruments clattered to the stage as music stands toppled and swayed. A bullet, clearly meant for Rudy, gouged the stage beside his foot as he ducked behind the conductor's stand. Elisa clutched her violin to herself. Strangely, in the tumult, she noticed small things: tears and handkerchiefs, men and women making the sign of the cross. And then there was Rudy, cowering behind the little platform as wild bullets splintered the stage. He protected his instrument, shielding it with his body as though it were a child.

"Get him!" a strong voice shouted in the balcony.

The gunman tossed his weapon at a dozen men who scrambled over the backs of chairs to wrestle him to the ground. There were more wails at the discovery that a man had been wounded.

"Call a doctor! Please! A doctor!"

The whistles of the security guards echoed in the auditorium as they clambered up the broad stairs to handcuff the madman.

"Heil, Germany! The Greater Reich is coming!" he shouted as he was

led away handcuffed. "You will see then, Schuschnigg! Germany and Austria are one! Germany for Germans! Death to the Jews!" At that, someone
had the good sense to crack him on the head with a club, and he was
carried out of the building as the bleeding concertgoer was taken away
by ambulance.

Musicians and audience milled around in tight, stunned little groups.
*How could this happen here? How in Vienna? No one was killed, thank
God. Has the Chancellor gone?*

Musicians checked their instruments for damage and tried to repair
clothing torn in the headlong scramble to safety. Leah, weeping openly,
embraced Rudy, then clung tightly to Elisa.

"You see—" She could barely speak. Her strong, sure fingers trembled.
"It is only a matter of time. You see now why we must go. Oh, Elisa! Did
you hear it in his voice?"

"He is a madman!" Elisa snapped angrily. "One crazy person."

Leah wiped her eyes and gazed at her friend, fear simmering just
beneath the surface. "After Dollfuss was murdered, Chancellor Schuschnigg expelled forty thousand such madmen. They are Austrians. Just
across the border in Germany. Elisa, do not be a child. If Hitler comes—"

"He will not come!" She was adamant.

"If he comes, those forty thousand angry Austrian Nazis will come
back with him. One man we may throw to the ground. It will not be so
easy if the Nazis come home. . . ."

Elisa had no reply. The hall was still packed with shocked men and
women, disheveled, but still glittering in the lights of the concert hall.
There, among them, Elisa saw the pale face of John Murphy. He sat ten
rows back on the aisle; his eyes were riveted on her. His hat was on his
lap. He was dressed in a navy blue double-breasted suit that looked
strangely out of place among the white ties and black, formal coats of the
men around him. He did not smile, but raised his hand to her in brief
greeting.

Elisa felt herself blush. "Herr Murphy," she mouthed, and a flood of
terrible memories came back to her. What was he doing here? Why had
he come tonight? Such a terrible night. He always seemed to be around
on the most terrible nights of her life.

"Who is that?" Leah was suddenly suspicious. She had been talking,
but Elisa had not heard her words.

"Someone I knew . . . once." Elisa turned away from Murphy's open
stare.

At that moment Rudy Dorbransky, his thick black hair tumbling down
across his forehead, stepped up onto the platform with raised bow in one
hand and violin in the other as a signal for silence. One group at a time,
the knots of people turned their hushed attention to the concertmaster.
"We have heard from the hospital!" he called. "Herr Wertheim has received a flesh wound only! He will recover!" Wild, exultant cheers rang

out from the stage and the galleries in the auditorium. "The criminal is safely behind bars! We pray he may not recover!"

Relieved laughter and more applause broke the terrible tension. Men clapped one another on the back and women wiped away tears of joy. Once again Rudy raised the Guarnerius and a hush of expectancy fell on the crowd. "Our instruments are undamaged!" He flashed a smile as laughter rippled. "Nor are we hurt permanently! Pray, let us continue our concert—it is the *Biedermeier* thing to do!" The crowd roared their approval. Yes. The *Biedermeier* thing to do—the Austrian way to face near disaster. "Take your seats, please. It will take us a few moments to sort out our music!"

Elisa had never been so proud of Rudy. Indeed, he played his role of concertmaster well. Vienna would always be Vienna, no matter who came or went. As Elisa played, her heart sang that night. Yes. These people could face anything and then sit down to a concert as though the worst had not almost happened. And the madmen of Hitler's Reich *were* behind bars or across the border in exile. Leah was wrong. Hitler would never dare to march here.

The crowd sprang to its feet in one, continuous roll of thunder. Six curtain calls, a standing ovation. The audience applauded until their arms, less strong than those of the performers, ached.

The musicians finally left their stands on the empty stage; their instruments were packed away by the time the applause died. And then the wings were filled with gushing matrons holding tightly to the arms of their elegant escorts. Everyone seemed to want to gather around Rudy. He accepted their praise with an untypical and probably insincere modesty.

Elisa and Leah grinned at him from the sidelines, then inched against the flow of traffic toward the stage door.

"A cup of Kapuziner?" Leah asked, calmed by the evening's smashing success. The opening moments of their performance had now receded like a bad dream.

"Kapuziner?" Elisa made a thoughtful face. "No. No. Tonight something special, ja? In honor of Rudy's escape and sudden fame, I will take you to Cafe Sacher for a cup of *Rüdesheimer!*"

"Black coffee, Asbach-Uralt brandy, and cream." She looked at Elisa in mock disapproval. "Yes. That sounds like something suitable to honor our darling Rudy." She laughed as Elisa pushed open the heavy stage door. "Did you see the way he cradled the Guarnerius? Better death than injury to his sweet fiddle!"

Elisa joined her laughter; then her smile faded as she looked down and noticed the tall handsome man leaning on the banister at the bottom of the stairs. He tipped his hat and pulled the collar of his dark wool overcoat closer around his chin.

"I thought you would never come out, Fraülein Linder," Murphy said in very clear German—tinged, however, with an easily recognizable American accent.

Leah drew herself up and mumbled. "Stay by me. Another stage door *Jäger*." She marched arrogantly down the stairs, but Elisa did not follow.

Murphy stepped aside for Leah, then stuck his hand deep into his pocket. He gazed at Elisa as he had throughout the entire performance. She had seen him out of the corner of her eye. His suit and necktie stood out from all the others, and she could not help but notice that he was there, and looking at her only. "For a few minutes I was afraid you had given me the slip," he said in English.

She understood him, although Leah did not. "Herr Murphy. Yes, now I remember—" She pretended to have difficulty remembering. "The American reporter. Are you still . . . reporting?"

He ignored her question. "You see," he said, also ignoring Leah's indignant glare, "last year you told me I would have to wait a year to hear you play a Christmas concert—you remember that?"

She nodded, suddenly embarrassed that she had been so cold to him. "So you are back in Vienna after a year," she replied brightly. Too brightly, she thought, hearing her own voice.

Suddenly Leah gasped, "Now I remember! The American! Yes. You came to the party with ham!"

Murphy lowered his chin slightly as though he was addressing an accusation. "Ham, yes. But my heart was in the right place."

"Yes! Yes! And then Elisa met you at the Sacher Hotel and wouldn't tell me a word, but she moped for weeks and—" She drew herself up and put her hand over her mouth. She had said too much.

"Leah imagines things . . . she imagines that she remembers things," Elisa said with a hard, silencing stare at Leah. "That is why I am Leah's only friend in all the world."

Leah's eyes grew wide. Her lips were tight as though she were trying very hard not to speak. Then, she opened her mouth. "Is *that* why you wanted to take me to the Cafe Sacher tonight, Elisa? And buy me *Rüdesheimer*?"

Elisa felt her cheeks grow very red. Murphy was looking hopeful, so she denied it, even though Leah was probably partly right. "No. The Sacher is the only place left that still serves decent brandy and unspoiled cream in their coffee." She was defensive as she reluctantly descended the steps.

"Well, I just happen to be staying there again. Would you ladies permit me to buy?"

Leah accepted for both of them. Elisa would have accepted, but she would have at least made him wonder first. "So what are you in Vienna for, Herr Murphy?" She did not want to give him the impression that she was really interested.

"To hear you play; I told you." He looked straight into her eyes, then let his gaze drift down to her mouth and her throat and the top button of her coat.

Elisa felt herself flush under his gaze, and silently cursed her tendency to blush.

"Yes. Well, you have heard us play. Now what?"

Murphy pulled out a fist full of tickets and held them up as they walked under the light of a street lamp. "I said I wanted to hear you play."

Leah thumped her chest. "Now *here* is a music lover!"

Elisa stared at the tickets in wonder. "How many?" she choked.

"How many will you play between now and January sixth?" he smiled confidently. He was making an impression. That was clear.

"Sixteen," Elisa answered weakly. She was flattered, but somehow uneasy by a man so dedicated after a year of silence.

"That's right. Sixteen. Row ten on the aisle. Almost directly in line with your chair."

Did he have no shame? Elisa blushed more deeply. Leah was grinning deliciously by now. Elisa could almost hear the wheels of her mind whirring.

"Well, you two," Leah said in a very sensible voice, "Shimon is in bed with the bronchitis. I must see to him. Shimon would be quite worried if I didn't go tuck him in. Good night; enjoy your coffee." She shook Murphy's hand and winked. "I'm sure I will see you again soon, Herr Murphy." Then she turned off toward a waiting trolley car, and they watched as she wrestled her cello case up the steps.

Elisa fumed inwardly. Leah had deserted her to this American. No doubt he would ask her unpleasant things like, *Have you heard from your father?*

"Have you heard from your father?" Murphy asked as the trolley clanged away.

"No." *Next he will ask me about Mother.*

They walked a few silent paces. "How is your mother?"

"How would you expect her to be in such a case?" Elisa let the irritation creep into her voice.

Murphy frowned. "Yes. You're right. Silly question."

"And don't ask me why I am still in Vienna!" she snapped, suddenly peevish. Maybe she would strangle Leah tomorrow and first chair cello would be empty before spring, after all.

"After tonight I might think you would give it some thought." Murphy was still frowning.

"Is that why you have come here, after a year?" She whirled around and stood facing him just outside the ring of light from a street lamp.

He stared at her again. Lovely face, slender throat—he seemed to touch her with his eyes; then his gaze caught hers and held her. She did not like the way he looked at her—as though he had some claim on her, as though he knew her . . . *intimately.* She backed up a step, trying to escape the rush of warmth his eyes brought to her. "I have felt"—he did not take his eyes from hers— "responsible. Like I need to . . . look after you in some way."

Is he really saying this after a year? "We barely met. I hardly know you, Herr Murphy." His eyes held a smile as if they were sharing a joke. She did not appreciate his expression. "And you do not know me at all!" Her voice was loud—defensive, even angry now. "And why do you smile at me that way?" she demanded.

"I know you better than most," he teased. "I've helped you pack your underwear—twice!"

Elisa's head drew back as if he had struck her. *Is that why he seems so—so familiar with me?* She drew back her hand and slapped him across the face. "I am sure the clerks at any lingerie shop in Vienna will be happy to show you whatever you wish! You cannot expect the same from me, Herr Murphy!"

He put a hand to his cheek and winced. "I—I'm sorry," he stammered. "I didn't intend any insult." She stared at him coldly. "Good night," he finally added in English.

She replied in very distinct English as well, "No, Mister John Murphy; the words are *goodbye!*" At that, she spun around and strode away from him. She almost hoped he would follow her, but he did not.

23

The Coming Fire

On this cold Sunday in December, the French Tri-color waved proudly from atop the Eiffel Tower. The bells of the great cathedrals of Paris rang out as though to announce the coming of Christmas. More Frenchmen seemed called to stroll along the waters of the placid Seine than summoned to attend the services, however. Young and old, Parisians lifted their faces to the sunlight like the trees that reached out with barren branches in hope of finding warmth.

Dressed in a brown double-breasted suit, Thomas von Kleistmann walked slowly along the beautiful Champs Elysees. Somehow the gray-green of his military uniform would have seemed out of place in this peaceful setting. As the military attache of the German Embassy, he knew that his transfer from Berlin last year had been intended to remove him from the hot political climate in the capital of Hitler's Reich. His banishment hardly seemed like a punishment.

Behind him, a young woman was singing quietly, *"Paris sera toujours Paris...."* "Paris will always be Paris." For Thomas, the words were a comforting reminder that all the world had not dressed in the gray uniforms so common now in Berlin. The colors of bright print dresses, loose cable-knit sweaters, and berets blended like blooming flowers in the crowded cafes. Occasionally a *gendarme's* blue uniform could be spotted among the Paris pedestrians, but these officials lacked the arrogance of their German counterparts. *No,* thought Thomas, *this assignment is anything but an unpleasant exile.* At every opportunity, he laid his uniform aside and mingled with the ordinary people of the city. When he spoke, of course, his accent carried a trace of German inflection, but the city was filled with thousands of Germans who had come to Paris to escape. Many were Jewish, but many others were political dissidents who had crossed the border when the first roundups of anti-Nazis had begun in

1933. All of them had some other ultimate destination in mind—America, or perhaps Palestine, or even South America. In the meantime, the French had been patient with the hordes that filled the city. After all, there was plenty of room along the banks of the Seine.

French waiters hardly bothered anymore to ask Thomas's nationality when he ordered coffee or a glass of strong red wine at a cafe. They might have turned him out had he worn his uniform, however. The political creed of Paris was *"Live and let live"*—except in the case of their sinister German neighbors. They could see the results of Nazi policies in the faces of the refugees, and a German uniform was more likely to evoke a sullen comment than the customary greeting of *"Bon jour!"*

The city was, of course, filled with agents of the Gestapo as well, each in search of some particularly important criminal. Thomas himself had seen the lists—the endless Nazi lists, photographs and files passed his desk daily. He had little doubt that his own name was in a file on someone else's desk, but somehow, it did not seem to matter anymore. If worse came to worst, he would simply melt into the masses and disappear among the thousands who had come here.

He made his way toward *George V* subway station, his hand deep in his pocket, fingers nervously touching a letter. Although he had written Elisa a dozen letters addressed to the Musikverein since he had arrived in Paris, he had not mailed any of them.

But the German censors had no access to mail posted in France and received in Austria. When he had written her from Berlin, he had assumed she had not gotten his letters. Now, he was certain that this was one letter he must mail, and for the sake of her life, he prayed that she would read it and hear his warning.

Instinctively, he looked over his shoulder as he dropped the envelope into the letter box at the station. Even if he was being watched, even if the Gestapo in Paris wanted to know the contents of his letter, they would have to go through the French postal service to do so. Considering French attitudes toward the Nazis, it did not seem probable.

With a sense of satisfaction, Thomas boarded the subway train that would take him near the German Embassy. He stood as others crowded on board. A young couple stood just in front of him. The man clutched the leather strap with one hand and slipped his arm around the slim waist of his dark-eyed lady. Throughout the ride, they faced one another. She smiled up into his eyes, hardly noticing the discomfort of the cramped car. Thomas watched them, suddenly filled with longing for Elisa more intense than any he had felt since he had watched her leave Berlin so long ago. She had looked at him with the same soft glow he saw in the girl's eyes now. How foolish he had been to turn away from all that!

But then, that had been Berlin, where a man's heart belonged to the state. This, on the other hand, was Paris. Men were still free here—free to love whomever they chose. The girl on the train caressed her young man with a look. He pulled her tighter, unaware that anyone was watching. She smiled, and Thomas looked away as the memories of Elisa's touch and smile became too painful.

At the next stop he inched past the couple and stepped off the train. He stood for a moment until the knot in his stomach eased. *To be here in this place without Elisa!* The thought of her made him angry all over again that he hadn't insisted on seeing her that night in Theo Lindheim's office! After all, he had ended up leaving Berlin anyway. The Gestapo had accused him of being with her, even though he had not. What difference would it have made?

He exhaled slowly as he walked from the station and raised his eyes to the glaring red of the swastika flag that waved over the embassy building. In Berlin, the sight of that flag had frightened him away from the one woman he had ever loved. Here in Paris, it seemed small and insignificant. Its crooked cross only mocked him. "If she will answer me," he whispered in French, as though her native language was now unworthy of his emotion, "God, if only she will answer my letter..." He did not finish the thought aloud. His stirrings were too deep for words.

Thomas had seen the secret memorandum that had passed over the desk of Ernst vom Rath. As third secretary of the German Embassy, Ernst was capable in his post, but he was not a Nazi. Very quietly one night over drinks, he had confessed his doubts about Hitler's regime to Thomas. And Thomas had in turn told him that he loved a girl . . . a girl in Austria who was half-Jewish. Somehow the mutual confessions had given the two men a solid base of friendship. Thomas knew that the Gestapo was watching Ernst vom Rath, and he had warned him.

In return for the favor, Ernst showed Thomas the memo . . . the one concerning increased Nazi activities in Vienna and Prague.

"If your girl is still in Austria," Ernst had said in a whisper, "you should warn her. Tell her to get out. The Anschluss is coming. The Führer demands it, and it will be so—unless he should suddenly not be the Führer any longer." There had been a trace of hope in Ernst's last words.

Thomas read over the orders: Austria's Nazi underground would step up acts of terrorism while at the same time creating an incident to give Hitler's armies an excuse to march to Austria to "restore order." A chill ran through him. He did not know how much time there was left for the little nation. If he could, he knew that he must do all he could to bring Elisa to Paris . . . and into his life again. He had no plans beyond that, but he was certain that she *must* leave Vienna, and then they would find someplace in the world where they could be safe together.

"Well?" Leah asked pointedly as she unwound her long scarf and hung up her coat at rehearsal the next morning.

"Well what?" Elisa did not attempt to hide her irritation.

"What do you *mean*, well what? You know perfectly well *what*."

Elisa looked blankly at her little friend. "Well, nothing. Besides, I'm not talking to you."

"For how long?" Leah did not seem unduly alarmed.

"Maybe forever." Elisa opened her violin case as Rudy swept into the theater like a conquering hero.

"That will be the day." Leah lugged her cello case over to a long wooden bench beside Shimon, who still did not look well. "Tell her to talk to me, Shimon," Leah instructed.

"Why?" He did not smile. "You talk enough for both of you. For me too. For all of us."

"Bravo, Shimon!" Elisa applauded him. "You should have heard her talk last night!"

Shimon looked very tired. "I *did* hear her," he sniffed. "She told me all about the American journalist. How he has bought tickets until January—"

"Sixth," Leah finished.

"Right," Shimon nodded. "And how he took you out for coffee at the Sacher Hotel." He smiled at Elisa's deep blush.

"Now you see why I won't tell her anything!" Elisa snapped.

Shimon nodded and blew his nose. "Yes. Of course. But you will still talk to me, won't you?"

"If you won't tell her."

"Agreed." The big man stuck out his hand to shake in agreement. "So . . ." He paused. *"Well?"*

Elisa plopped down on the other side of him and whispered in his ear as Leah looked on sullenly. "I slapped his face."

"That sounds promising!" Shimon said loudly. "Before or after coffee?"

"We didn't have coffee." Elisa spoke in an almost inaudible voice.

"Very promising indeed!" Shimon replied. "I *like* this fellow!"

"Well, you will have plenty of chance to meet him," Leah said dryly, even though she could not hear Elisa's end of the conversation. "He is not only coming to performances, he is here now."

Shimon raised his eyebrows. *"Such* a music lover!"

"Where is he?" Elisa demanded.

"Outside. On the landing. I just saw him peering in when Karin came in."

Elisa glanced toward the stage door. It was freezing cold outside and the wind howled through the alley. "Well, don't let him in!"

"What did you slap him for?" Shimon did not bother to whisper, and Leah smiled as though she had won a victory.

"She slapped him? Very promising!" Leah leaned around Shimon and winked at Elisa. "Shimon and I dated for months before I had occasion to slap him."

Shimon winced at the memory. "Oy! Can she hit!"

"Now everyone will know, Shimon." Elisa drew herself up. "You said you wouldn't tell."

He spread his big hands innocently. "Did I tell? I thought I only asked a simple question: *Why did you slap the American?*"

Rudy stopped and grinned handsomely down at Elisa. "You slapped an American? Why would you do that? The only way you can get a visa to America is if you know a nice American."

"He is not nice," Elisa retorted.

"I like him," Leah volunteered. "He's out there freezing on the steps and she won't let us let him in."

"Why did you hit the poor fellow?" Rudy seemed overly interested.

"That is nobody's business." Elisa picked up her violin and began to play a scale.

"She won't tell us." Shimon and Leah spoke at the same moment.

Rudy shrugged and sauntered past them, directly to the stage door. He opened it slightly and a blast of cold air swept backstage. "Are you the American that Elisa slapped? Come in. You will certainly freeze to death out there."

Elisa closed her eyes as a new, deeper redness climbed to her cheeks. "I will never forgive you all," she mumbled as Rudy continued the loud conversation with John Murphy.

"You're the fellow that lunatic was shooting at last night," Murphy said clearly. "Just the man I wanted to see. I'm a journalist, and I thought I might have an interview."

Rudy bowed majestically. "Of course. I am flattered. But first, you must answer the question we have all been waiting to hear."

"Sure."

"Why did Elisa Linder, our lovely violinist with the red face, slap you? Especially when we all know how valuable Americans are in these uncertain times."

Murphy grinned a sideways grin and glanced toward the object of their interest. Elisa sat rigid, waiting in horror for him to reveal that he had said something about her underclothes. "Well, I . . . I said something ungallant, I'm afraid."

Silence descended over the orchestra as everyone paused to hear his explanation. "Well?" Rudy demanded. "You can't have an interview for something as brief as that. I am always being slapped, and I know the implications."

"I can't say more," Murphy said. Elisa glanced at him almost gratefully. "Unless she refuses to go out with me after tonight's performance. If she refuses, of course, I will tell."

Her eyes flashed a furious response. "Blackmail!" she hissed.

"I knew I liked him!" Shimon laughed.

"Bravo, John Murphy!" Leah clapped her hands in approval.

"You are all traitors," Elisa pouted.

"Not really, Elisa," Rudy said in a patronizing voice. "We all simply do not want to see you spend your nights stagnating in your little flat. This slap is encouraging!"

By now a dozen more members of the orchestra had joined in the game.

"So?" Shimon asked Elisa. "Do you accept his offer and go out with him tonight? Or does he tell us all what happened and get the interview with Rudy?"

"*Blackmail!* I accept under duress. And he won't enjoy it, either!"

Rudy shook his head thoughtfully at her angry reply. "You are not getting a bargain here, Herr . . . Murphy, is it? She must go out with you for at least three nights, or you can tell us why she hit you. Our orchestra is like a little family here, you see." He inhaled deeply. "You see? Smell the coffee brewing? We even have breakfast together, and we *love* gossip. Elisa should be nice to you."

"It's too late," Elisa stood up. "I will never be nice to him."

"In that case"—Murphy was still smiling—"three nights after performance. Coffee at Hotel Sacher . . . or I tell."

"Then . . . *yes!* You are a cad. A stage-door *Jäger!* The love of decency does not abide in you!" Elisa stormed off.

Rudy extended his hand to Murphy. "Very good, Herr Murphy. I have never seen Elisa so . . . roused up, you might say. If you are all those terrible things, as I suppose most American journalists are, then I congratulate you! And you may have the interview *gratis*. You are a man after my own heart. As a matter of fact—"Rudy patted Murphy on the head—"we even look to be about the same size. You should wear proper attire tonight, I think. I have a fencing mask at home. Shall I bring it?"

Laughter rippled through the group. Elisa was the only one not backstage. She had taken refuge in the bathroom until the moment rehearsal was scheduled to begin, and then she slipped out to her chair, not daring to look up at any of her smirking friends.

Murphy had rented a tuxedo for the night's occasion. As he took his place on the aisle of row ten, he felt confident that he matched the splendor of those in the audience around him. As the members of the orchestra filed in, Murphy noted with amusement that with only one exception, they all glanced toward him and indicated their approval of his presence with a brief, barely perceptible nod or smile. He nodded back, raising his hand with a slight wave until those seated around him whispered their conjecture about who the handsome young man in the audience must be.

"*Certainly someone important.*"

"*Then, why isn't he in a private box?*"

"*Probably royalty.*"

"*Yes. The aristocracy are all impoverished. That explains it.*"

So, Murphy had become a duke or a prince for the duration of the performance. People bowed in deference to him during intermission. He did not speak to anyone for fear of blowing his cover. Throughout the night, only one person ignored his presence completely. Even though he knew he was in the clear line of Elisa's vision, she did not acknowledge him once. As a matter of fact, she looked *everywhere* but at him. Occasionally Leah glanced his way, however, approval radiating from her eyes. He liked her a lot. She might prove to be a valuable ally as the season progressed, and he was quite sure that Leah liked him, too.

The evening's program was the Mozart violin concertos. The full orchestra was not performing, and Murphy noticed that there was no need at all for Shimon's drums. He assumed that the big man was probably back home in bed. Rudy Dorbransky, however, soloed with a mastery of his violin that defied his claims to be little more than Vienna's greatest cad.

Rudy had granted the interview that afternoon, and began the conversation by claiming that nothing was more important to him than wine, women—and his violin. Then Murphy asked questions, and he had discovered that there was much more to the virtuoso performer than temperament. He was, off the record, deeply committed to an independent Austrian state.

" . . . Without it," Rudy said solemnly, "you will see us no more in Vienna. You will no longer hear our music. Vienna is a melting pot. Tonight you will hear the sweet melodies of Wolfgang Mozart. The Nazis will claim his music is only theirs. But he was not a German. He was Austrian—a part of the great nation of Austro-Hungary ruled by Franz Josef. Listen, Herr Murphy, there is beauty and love and acceptance in the music. Austria gives birth to Mozart, and the Germans compose the Horst Wessel song, ja? And 'Deutschland Über Alles—Germany Over All.' "

Rudy stretched out his strong hands. "That is one tune my fiddle does not know. If such terrible songs come to Austria, then I will leave. Like the rest, I will run! In the meantime I will not step down from the stage because some madman shoots his pistol from the gallery. You ask me if I am afraid? I play the music of my Austria; he plays something else. As long as there is Austria, I am not afraid."

Murphy had wanted to tell him to get his passport in order, that the end of Austria seemed to be approaching, but he did not. He only listened with admiration to the words of Rudy Dorbransky, as now, he listened with awe to the music he played so beautifully. In the end, Rudy had asked him not to print his brave words. "They are for my heart alone to know, and certainly there are those in Vienna who would kill me more readily for what I have told you. There is no use stirring the kettle to boil. Let them think I am a mindless, harmless Jewish violinist. It is much safer that way for me."

As Murphy listened to the depth of emotion expressed in Rudy's playing, he wondered how anyone could think the man was mindless. And with that realization, Murphy shuddered at the thought that there was indeed a mindlessness that would silence such great talent because the definition of beauty had somehow become linked with race, and blood, and *Aryan* culture. Rudy's self-made image of "man-about-town" may have protected him on some levels, but it could not protect him from what was coming. Not even the profundity of his talent would protect him from the brutality of those who defined beauty as *German-Aryan.*

Murphy had never actually intended to write an interview with Rudy Dorbransky for publication. He had only used that as an excuse for his presence at the hall that morning. He had come to see Elisa. Now, as he watched the young man in the spotlight, then turned his eyes on Elisa, he was struck again by the madness of German rhetoric. Rudy was openly Jewish in a culture threatened by the insanity of *Mein Kampf.* Elisa carried her mixed race with the confusion and secrecy of one who had already seen the vision of fire, and yet could not believe that the flames were even now licking at her heels. Rudy had already decided when he would leave. Elisa refused to acknowledge that she would ever leave. This made Rudy more sensible than Elisa in a thousand ways.

This morning's barter had been a game; but the truth was, even as Murphy sat through the performance, he was calculating how he might best persuade Elisa that Hitler's fire was about to leap over the Alps and consume the varied beauty of Austria, whose citizens, for the most part, believed that *differences* made life more interesting. It certainly kept after-dinner conversation lively and coffeehouses open and flourishing until all hours. Unhappily, these very differences threatened to destroy Austria. The radical left and the violent right had, in their fanaticism, caught the vast, reasonable center in a terrible cross fire. Chancellor Schuschnigg shuttled back and forth between the two extremes, trying to bring reconciliation to them all, even as Hitler's secret vassals, the wolves of the Reich, gnawed away the foundations of reason.

Reason! yes. That is the word. And how can I make her listen to reason? If Theo Lindheim had survived, she would be out of here by now. She adored her father. She would have listened to him. What can I say to her? What?

In the soft light, Elisa's skin took on an almost ethereal glow. She drew her bow across the strings in counterpoint to the strong melody that Rudy played. The beauty of the woman and the music seemed to be united, and Murphy held his breath in awe at the sight of her. An ache, so profound that he had to shut his eyes for a moment, filled him nearly to overflowing with tears. He caught himself, controlling his emotions. It had been so long since he had experienced anyone or anything so beautiful. For a year he had been witness to Nazi disregard for innocence and beauty in Spain. Spain was only a practice bombing run for Hitler and Mussolini. Vienna was certainly their next target. *How can I tell her so that she will believe me?* It was their goal to crush anything that varied from their stunted perspective of the Aryan ideal. *How can I convince her? Rudy, Leah, Shimon—her friends . . . family, really. The fire is coming. The fire is already here. It consumes everything that is not forged in its own furnace of hatred. It feeds on people like you, Elisa. And talent like yours, Rudy Dorbransky. Your lives will be sacrificed to feed its flames. This moment is only a memory even as it happens; the only reality left to us is the coming fire.*

He had seen it in Madrid. He had glimpsed a frightening vision in London. Now, he looked upward as redolent melody swirled into the highest reaches of the hall. In one horrible instant, he saw the stars winking down through charred and gaping holes in the roof. *Yes. The molten rain will fall here, too. Terrible, terrible, scorching rain.*

24

Elisa Awakens

Elisa and Murphy were seated at the same table where Murphy had spent his loneliest Christmas a year before. It was ten-thirty, but the busy waiters of the Sacher Cafe were still serving late dinners. Elisa smiled and waved at the omnipresent string quartet in the corner. They recognized her, of course, and Murphy wondered if there was anywhere in Vienna where a cup of coffee could be served without being accompanied by music. They began to play as Murphy ordered *Tafelspitz,* the boiled beef and dumplings that had been a favorite of Emperor Franz Josef. It seemed the only logical choice with the portrait of the emperor watching over them.

Elisa continued to look at the musicians; then, for the first time since they had left the concert hall, she spoke to Murphy. "Do you like the music?" she asked in English.

He was startled, both by her use of his own language and by the question. "Beautiful," he answered, feeling like the musical ignoramus he was.

"Do they play this often in America?"

"Well . . . I don't know. Probably." He wished she knew something about the jazz of Scatman Caruthers.

"But you like Dvorak, personally?"

"Personally . . ." He hedged. He had never heard of the guy.

"And this?"

"This?" He had the feeling that he was being set up. Was she trying to pinpoint just how much he lacked in the way of musical education—that they really had nothing in common beyond one terrible night on the train from Berlin? Maybe she was right. "I'll be honest, Elisa," he confessed, hoping his honesty would stop her subtle attack. "I don't know anything about music. Nothing. Except that I find it beautiful. As beautiful and stirring to listen to as you are to be with." He reached across the table to touch her hand, but she pulled it away.

She quickly looked back toward the quartet as though she had not heard him. "This is the *Amerikanisches* . . . the *American* composition of Dvorak. I thought perhaps you listened to it often in America since he wrote it there."

"He is an American?"

She laughed nervously. "No. Czech. From Prague. But the happiest time of his life was in America. A place called Spillville, I-Owa."

Murphy brightened. "Iowa!" he exclaimed. "Spillville, huh?"

"You have been there?" Elisa seemed interested in his response.

"Lots of farms in Iowa."

"Yes." She looked dreamy. "I can hear that in his music. Do you hear it, Herr Murphy?"

"Just Murphy," he corrected gently. And yes, he did seem to hear the sound of horses and buggy wheels on dusty roads—and maybe the sound of crickets on a summer night when a fella sat in the porch swing with his girl. "Yes, it sounds a lot like home. In the summertime."

"He wrote it in the summer. 1893. The only happy time in his life. He wrote it in only three days, and when he finished, he said, *'Thanks to the Lord God. I am satisfied. It went quickly.'* " She turned her eyes on Murphy as though she were no longer angry—in fact, never had been. "America must be a beautiful place if it sounds like this."

Murphy took her hand and did not let go, even though she tried to pull away for an instant. Then she let her fingers rest in his palm—warm and soft like a little bird. How he *loved* her hands! "Would you like to go there, Elisa? Would you like to see America? I'll take you to Iowa if you want to go; I can take you there!"

She lowered her eyes. "I would someday love to go there. But I do not really know you, *Murphy*. I cannot go with you."

"Then I'll send you there. I'll stay here, and you go to America." His heart was beating fast. He was grateful for the music of this Dvorak guy in the background. If she wouldn't listen to words, maybe she would hear *freedom* and *safety* in the music.

"A generous offer. But I must work."

"You can work there . . . like this Dvor . . . whatever-his-name is."

"He came back. Back here to his home. My family . . . what is left of our hearts without Papa . . . live in Prague. A democracy. Like in America."

"But too close, Elisa. *Hear* me! *Too close to Hitler!* The *eclipse* has begun! The shadow is already touching the face of the sun! In America you would be safe. Rudy was right; I can write a letter to sponsor you—"

She looked at him calmly, without response. "My family is in Prague," she repeated.

"I can get them to America, too. My parents have a farm in Pennsylvania."

"We cannot leave my father, Murphy. My mother will never leave until we know for sure—"

"If you knew . . . if you knew for sure he didn't make it, then would you leave Europe?" He leaned close to her, his eyes pleading with her.

"I . . . how could I leave Vienna?"

"You could come back. When this thing blows over, you can come back—"

"I do not know the term . . . *blows over.*"

"When the danger is past. When the storm is over." He frowned and licked his lips nervously. Was she listening? Was she hearing the *reason* in his argument?

"There is no storm in Vienna. Only some . . . disagreement. America has no disagreements? I have read about the Great Depression. There are many Communists marching there. Beggars on the streets, and talk of revolt. People are hungry there, and the land is—" She chose her words carefully as she recalled the magazine articles and photographs about vast tracts of farmland that had dried up and blown away. "There is a *bowl of dust* where I-Owa used to be, ja?"

"Things are tough at home, yes." He felt his arguments being blown away like the dust. "But we aren't neighbors with Nazi Germany."

The waiter brought out big helpings of *Tafelspitz*, then bowed and backed away without interrupting their conversation. "We have beggars here in Vienna, to be sure," Elisa replied defensively. "But there is nothing so terrible as we read about America. It is not like it was when Dvorak was there. Besides, the President Roosevelt and your Parliament has said very clearly they do not want refugees from Europe taking American jobs."

"I can get you in!" he insisted. "Our farm—in Pennsylvania. I wrote my parents. You would be most welcome, and there isn't a drought there."

"Why would they take in total strangers?"

Murphy squeezed her hand. "Not strangers, Elisa. Elisa, I want you to *marry me!*" He was almost as startled by the words as she was. She took her hand from his and looked quickly away. The music played louder behind him, and Murphy could tell that his proposal had been a terrible mistake. Not a mistake, really—it was an *accident*. He hadn't *meant* to say it. The truth was there, in his heart, but he regretted the words the instant they popped out of his mouth. "You may divorce me later, but let me at least get you out of this mess," he said, trying to redeem his hasty words.

Elisa did not reply. She seemed embarrassed by the question. Most certainly she could not go to America under such circumstances. His offer no longer depended on news of Theo Lindheim or convincing her that America was a safer place to be at this moment in history. She dismissed all of that and looked at him with gentle pity. "Herr Murphy . . ." She again lapsed into her own language.

"Murphy," he corrected again; then he passed a hand over his face. "I did not mean to say that," he said. "I . . . I don't know how that came up. I'm sorry."

She smiled sadly and leveled her penetrating blue eyes at him. "I thank you for the offer," she said with dignity. "It is, of course—"

"No." He raised his hand to stop her. "You don't have to say more. It was a . . . shock to me too." He laughed nervously.

"Tonight I won't slap you." She laughed too, and the tension dissolved. "*Unless* you tell my friends why I slapped you *last* night! Then you had better duck."

He raised his hands in surrender, feeling defeated in more ways than one. "We started our relationship as allies. No civil war is impending, I hope. *Friends?*"

She nodded and lifted her first spoonful of *Tafelspitz* in a toast. "To friendship, then, Murphy."

"To friendship," he responded in kind, feeling somehow comforted by her words. "Now, I want you to promise me something."

She looked doubtful. "Perhaps."

"If you find things getting rough around here, remember my offer. And I don't mean the marriage offer—"

"So fickle, Murphy? Well, it was the best offer I have had all day." She was trying to lighten the conversation.

Murphy would not let the subject pass. "What I mean is, if I am right—and I hope I'm not, but just in case things go badly for Austria, I want you to think about America, will you?"

The quartet played the third movement of Dvorak's composition. "As often as I hear *Amerikanisches Streichquartett*, I will think about America . . . and you. But I must remember that Dvorak chose to end his life in Prague, ja?"

She was politely patting him on the head and telling him thanks, but no thanks. She would not offer him even one small word of encouragement. Throughout their meal she talked of Leah and Shimon; Rudy and the tone of the Guarnerius violin compared to the voice of a Stradivarius. She asked questions about Pennsylvania and Murphy's career in New York, but America was not a place she looked to for any answer to life's difficulties.

Their first evening ended on a hopeless note for Murphy. Somehow he had hoped that she would invite him to her flat for coffee, but she did not. With a firm handshake, she thanked him for the *Tafelspitz* and refrained mercifully from mentioning his proposal again, then got into a taxi and went home alone.

———

Leah was waiting for Elisa when she arrived home. She had let herself into Elisa's flat and had brewed her own cup of tea, entirely without an invitation. Elisa almost rolled her eyes at the sight of Leah sitting at the small kitchen table.

"Have you lost your lease on your apartment?"

"No." Leah sipped her tea matter-of-factly. She gazed thoughtfully at the row of houseplants perched on the windowsill.

"You have come to water my plants?"

"At least they are the one thing alive in this apartment." Leah made no effort to soften what she had come to say.

The comment cut deep into Elisa. Was her solitude that obvious? Was it that terrible? "Don't patronize me!" she snapped angrily. "If you have something to say—"

"All right. If you think you can hear it."

"There is nothing I need to hear. I am fine. My life is exactly what I want it to be. It is my own choice to be alone! My desire!"

"Don't tell me about desire!" Leah raised her voice. Her usually warm brown eyes flashed angrily. "Stop *denying*! You can play that self-sufficient game with everyone in town but me, Elisa. I have known you too long! I remember those long nights in school in Salzburg when you dreamed of your Thomas! It's been over a year since you mentioned him, a year since you came back from Berlin and he was no longer the one you dreamed about or spoke about! What happened, Elisa? You are dead inside! We joke. We laugh. But that is as far as our friendship goes now. What has happened to you?"

"That is none of your business!" Elisa was shouting. She had never before shouted at Leah.

"You have turned to wood. A dozen fellows ask you out each month, and you will have nothing to do with them. Tell me, for your own sake, what happened to Thomas von Kleistmann?"

"I can't tell you. But I can tell you that you have no right—"

Leah stood suddenly. "All right. Your best friend has no right. Does anyone have a right? You have become a stranger to me. To yourself. The most encouraging thing I have heard in months was that someone made you angry enough that you struck him."

"Leave me alone, or I will strike you as well!" Elisa stood trembling with anger.

"Well, at least that is proof you are still alive," Leah said flatly. "I know you love me. Do you love this Murphy fellow as well?"

Tears began to flow from Elisa. "No. I love Thomas. I want him. And I hate him because I cannot have him! Oh, Leah!" Instead of striking her friend, she wept against Leah's shoulders in a desperate embrace. "Oh, Leah, I have loved Thomas so long. All of my life, I think. And now—" She wanted to tell Leah *everything*! About Berlin, her father, Murphy on the train, Thomas . . .

"You are wrong, Elisa, not to tell me. You bear it all alone. And there is much I think I know already."

Elisa hesitated, trembling inside. How much did Leah know? And how did she know anything at all? "What?"

"Does the name Lindheim mean anything to you?" Leah said gently.

Elisa felt suddenly faint. She groped for a chair. Leah sat down beside her. "How?" Elisa said pitifully. "How can you know this?"

"Last spring," Leah said solemnly. "When you were in Prague with your mother. After that terrible Christmas you had when you would not tell me what happened . . ." She pressed her fingers to her forehead. "A letter from Paris."

"Paris?" Elisa had heard from her mother that Thomas had been transferred to Paris.

"From a person named Herschel Grynspan. It came to the Musikverein. Addressed to someone named *Elisa Lindheim.*" She paused, carefully watching the expression on Elisa's face. "Lindheim. The watchman asked if that could be you. I told him it was impossible, and he sent the letter back unopened. Dangerous. Dangerous thing, Elisa. Especially in these times. Elisa Lindheim. That's you, isn't it?"

Elisa nodded bleakly. She felt the color drain from her face. "Yes."

"Your father?"

"Theo Lindheim."

"Oy!" Leah frowned. They sat together in silence for a full minute as the implications of such a revelation made impact. "So," Leah sighed, "you are not Aryan." Her eyes were full of pity for Elisa. "This is not a good time to be Jewish."

"My father is Jewish. My mother is Austrian."

"So to the Nazis you are mixed race. *Mischling.* First degree." Leah spread her hands in helpless frustration as she questioned God in the silent gesture. "And you would not even tell me."

"I just told you."

"I knew anyway. We will hope no one else knows. Hope that no more letters come addressed to Elisa Lindheim. The name is too close. Couldn't you have chosen something further removed from your German-Jewish name?" It was not a question that needed answering, really; it simply expressed Leah's fear for Elisa.

"I suppose you can guess what happened to Thomas."

"Yes. Of course." Bitterness thickened Leah's voice. "The Nuremburg racial laws."

"Yes. He said—" Elisa choked back a sob again.

"If he said anything at all . . ." Leah wrapped a protective arm around Elisa. "If he did not take you away that instant and leave a place where such laws can dictate love, then he is *unworthy* of you! For *him* you have shut your heart away, Elisa? For a coward like this man? How could anyone not love you?" She was indignant, and Elisa was comforted by the rage of her friend.

"My father was arrested, and I told myself I could never love Thomas.

As long as he was part of such a pack of—"

"Unkosher swine!"

"Yes. But still I dream of him at night. I still remember . . ."

Leah frowned and studied Elisa's face. "The two of you were lovers then?"

Elisa flushed and she murmured, "I thought we would marry one day."

"Enter Hitler and the Nazis." The anger in Leah's voice was real. "Exit Thomas."

Elisa sobbed against her again as if all the hurt and anger inside her needed to be released. "Why? Why has this happened?"

"I have another question for you, Elisa. Why do you still hold on so tightly to someone who would cast you off so terribly? What possible worth can you see in such a man? What respect for one who would deny your family?"

"It was the *law*; he could not—"

"Nonsense. There is right, and there is wrong. The Nazis have turned those two absolutes upside down. You are not a racial half-breed, a sub-human. You are *Elisa*, beautiful and talented and . . . so very alone," she finished heavily.

"What can I do?" Tears brimmed in Elisa's eyes.

"Do you enjoy playing the martyr in love?"

"No."

"You must. Otherwise, why do you act it out so completely? You are not made of wood or stone. Look at you!" She brushed away Elisa's tears with her thumb. "You look terrible! Your eyes are all swollen and puffy! Oy! Such a mess you are. I have never seen stone weep, although wooden trees can sometimes become sticky with sap." She pulled a handkerchief from her pocket. "So blow your nose before you drip on me."

Elisa laughed through her tears and obediently blew her nose. "Leah, you have seen me in the most terrible states!"

"What are friends for? You threaten to hit me, kick me out of your apartment, and now you almost drip on me!"

Elisa laughed again and sat up, feeling better than she had felt in almost a year. "Well, now I can tell you that we are almost blood relations."

"Does that mean you're going to come to the Zionist meetings?"

"No."

"Smart girl. Hold on to those Aryan identification papers. You are worlds ahead of us if the world caves in."

"The world will not cave in."

"We can hope," Leah said with a wave of her hand. "Vienna may not notice as long as the coffee does not run out. Speaking of which, how did it go tonight with John Murphy?"

"He proposed."

"Americans work fast," she smiled. "Did you slap him again?"

"No. But I told him no." She looked down at her hands, feeling suddenly shy. "But I *like* him, Leah. A lot. I . . . wanted to kiss him before I got into the taxi. I wanted him to kiss me. It has been a long time since I felt that way about anyone. A year ago in the Tyrol I met a boy; I let him kiss me, but nothing was *awake*. You know?"

"And this Murphy? He wakes you up?"

"Yes. I . . . kept hoping he would kiss me. But he is so—"

"American. They believe you when you play coy games. The French never believe that every woman alive isn't ready to make love. The Italians have the same mentality. Germans—I am sure they have a manual of proper rules of order for such things. The English—well, I always wonder how there got to be so many little Englishmen running around!"

Elisa was laughing out loud by now. "And what do we do with the Americans?"

"They are sweet puppy dogs, I think. Be kind. Be kind to Americans. Be kind to John Murphy, Elisa. He bought tickets to sixteen concerts, and I think he probably loves something besides the music!"

Elisa became suddenly silent. Tears filled her eyes again as she remembered an old family story. "My father did the same after he heard my mother play here in Vienna for the first time. He was on leave from his squadron, and while the rest of his friends spent their nights in the Seventh District with those . . . women, Papa came every night to hear her play." She looked up at Leah. Her eyes were shining. "Every night he came to hear her. They got married. She loves him still, and if he still lives, I am sure his every thought is for her. Always I have wondered—even with Thomas—if any man could ever love me the way my father loved my mother."

"Then tomorrow, at rehearsal, play your violin for *him*, Elisa. Play for John Murphy and listen to the song your heart sings." Leah closed her eyes for a moment. "That is how I knew I loved Shimon. Big, silly Shimon. I played for him. Felt my music reaching out only to him. Like a prayer, yes? Like a hymn to God. And love came back to me in the music." She looked at Elisa who seemed transfixed. "Well?"

"Tonight at the concert, I did not look at him. But I felt him there looking at me, Leah. And I did not want to give my music to him; but somehow . . . I felt him taking each note like a kiss, drawing the bow across my strings as though he were the musician, not I." She raised her eyebrows, slightly surprised that she could express so precisely what she had felt.

"Yes." Leah nodded with approval. "Perhaps you should take another long look at John Murphy. And play for him, Elisa. For *him*!"

25

"God Alone Should Have My Heart"

On this cold and snowy afternoon, Elisa had agreed to meet Murphy after rehearsal. *Friends, yes. Just friends.* And yet, when she emerged laughing from the theater, he thought his heart would break with the ache he felt for her. She waved goodbye to Leah and a half dozen other young women from the orchestra, then greeted him with a wave and *Guten Tag, Murphy!* She skipped down the stairs, and he saw the flash of her red skirt beneath her heavy blue woolen coat. Her golden hair was covered by a bright red scarf, and he could not help but think that she would make an ideal model for some craftsman carving angels in a tiny stall in front of the Rathaus.

"Are you ready for shopping?" Her cheeks were already rosy with the bitter, bracing cold. "Something for your mama, ja? For her Christmas in Pennsylvania." She stood before him, her chin slightly upturned as though she was waiting for a kiss. But she wasn't, so he didn't.

He took her violin from her and then felt warm and pleased when she linked her arm in his for the walk to the Ringstrasse and the teeming Christmas shops. He knew that she held his arm as a hedge against the slippery ice, but all the same, her touch added a magic to the spell of the street musicians and the decorated shop windows.

"Something small for her," Murphy instructed. "Something beautiful and delicate." He was looking at Elisa. "Maybe an angel I can send air-mail."

"A woodcarving, perhaps!" Thankfully, she did not notice the wistful look on his face, and when she glanced up at him he tried to conceal the emotions that were tumbling out.

"Perfect," he agreed as she tugged his hand toward the makeshift stalls of village artisans who had gathered from all over Austria to sell their wares to Vienna.

Drums filled with scraps of wood burned in the midst of the artisans' market. Men and woman gathered around to warm their hands before they strolled on through displays of wooden toys, hand-crocheted lace and linens, jewelry, carpets, and carved creches.

Above the cheerful voices of the shoppers, the sweet violin music of "Good King Wenceslas" rose up from behind a semicircle of polite listeners. A scuffed violin case lay on the ground beside the old peasant musician, a few coins were tossed into it, and Elisa stopped to hear him play the entire melody.

Murphy drew a deep breath at the sight of her tender, transfixed expression while she listened to the beggar musician. She applauded louder than the others who drifted away after tossing the most meager of offerings into his case.

"Lovely," she said. "*Sehr* schön . . ."

He doffed his ragged cap and bowed deeply to her, then smiled a toothless smile, "And you also are sehr schön, Fraülein!"

Murphy tossed two shillings into the case. The old man had said what Murphy was afraid to say. He ached to tell her, but he could not. Not after last night's accidental proposal, at any rate. *Friends, Murphy. Just friends.*

"We are looking for a booth of fine woodcarvings," Elisa said to the musician. "Where is the finest at the fair?"

The old man looked at her strangely, then squinted as if trying to bring up some memory. "The finest, Fraülein, are from the Tyrol co-operative, of course. The booth—" He pointed down the row to where men and women crowded before a wooden stall. "The finest of Tyrol."

Elisa and Murphy made their way through the throngs, stopping for a moment before the open fire of an oil drum. Rich and poor were gathered here. Murphy remembered the farmers' market of his boyhood in Philadelphia. Perhaps the world was not so very different, after all.

The Tyrol woodcarvers' booth was a display of work from all the Alpine villages. Tiny angels and wise men hung on golden threads from the top of the booth to the bottom. Mary and Joseph knelt beside oxen and sheep overlooking a dozen variations of the newborn Christ Child. Behind them now, the old musician played "Stille Nacht" as the carver in the booth explained the origin of each of the delicate pieces.

Murphy could see better than Elisa, who was standing on tiptoe behind a very tall man and a rather large woman as they chose their creche.

"Do you see anything you like?" Elisa called up to him.

Murphy scanned the multitude of carvings. "There are almost too many, too beautiful to choose one." Then he stopped at the sight of an intricately carved Madonna holding a tiny, lifelike baby Jesus. Joseph looked on with *such love*, not at the infant, but at the woman. Murphy almost gasped in astonishment. As if someone had heard his thought, the image of the young woman was that of Elisa. Clearly *Elisa*! And in a line, above the carving, a row of angels played intricately carved violins as they floated on their golden threads. *Elisa! All Elisa!* Murphy looked down at her living, breathing beauty. How could this be?

"How may I help you, mein Herr?" The merchant directed his gaze at Murphy. He noticed that Murphy's eyes were riveted to the carvings. "Beautiful, ja? Hand carved in the Tyrol. The finest."

"Yes. I want them all. The angels—"

"All the same? The whole dozen? You do not wish some variety?"

"All twelve of them—and just below that, Mary and Joseph, please."

Elisa could not see his purchase and tugged his sleeve impatiently. "Not all the same, Murphy. It is better if some are different. Each from a different village."

"No," Murphy insisted, in spite of the fact that these particular angels seemed to be a bit higher in price than the others. "All the same." He passed a handful of bills to the startled but pleased merchant.

"Our finest. Most lovely. They seem to breathe their praise and one can almost hear their song, ja? 'Glory to God in the Highest!' " He took them down and wrapped them carefully in newspaper one at a time.

"May I not see?" Elisa asked impatiently.

Murphy grinned down at her, feeling foolish, and yet, somehow, like he had captured part of her to take back to his room with him. "No." He was firm. "Not until I get a little tree first." He took his package and tucked it under his arm, holding both the violin and the angels with the same arm so he could clutch Elisa's hand with the other.

Her face was still raised as she tried to see the rest of the booth over the heads of the crowd, and impulsively, Murphy bent down and kissed her lightly.

Again, he had shocked himself. He started to apologize, but she put a finger to his lips and smiled up into his eyes. "A friendly kiss, Murphy," she said softly. "Froeliche Weinachten. Happy Christmas." Her voice was gentle, like a song. She took her hand away and lifted her chin expectantly. This time it was no accident. Murphy pulled her near to him, and in the midst of the crowd, he kissed her. He felt her lips part slightly as she leaned against him. For a moment, the rush of warmth was so strong through him that he imagined she might have to hold him up. The world spun. She pulled away, then stood oblivious to the clamor around them.

"You have made me feel alive again." She laid her head against his chest.

Murphy had trouble finding his breath, let alone speaking. "Yeah," he replied.

"Angry. Embarrassed. Pursued," she laughed. "Desired—" Her voice was still wistful.

"Elisa," Murphy gulped. "Elisa." The name itself was magic to him.

"Yes, Murphy?"

"I think I want to sit down," he breathed. "And then can we do that again?" He was confused. "Friendly—uh . . ."

Throwing back her head, she laughed and pulled him stumbling away from the crowd. "Come on, Murphy. What you need is a good strong cup of Turkish coffee!"

———

Elisa led Murphy down an uncrowded side street and down steep stone steps into a small, dimly lit coffeehouse. He heard the music before they entered the room.

She looked over her shoulder and smiled at him, and for that moment, all the terrible visions he had seen for Vienna vanished. It was easy to understand on such a day and in such a moment how people could pretend that there was nothing else in life but this glorious city and the music . . . Elisa's music.

A small man in a black turtleneck sweater and wire-rimmed glasses played a guitar at a table near the front of the room. He looked to be about twenty-five. His eyes were closed as his fingers moved over the frets and strings creating a sound as complex as an orchestra.

"I wanted you to hear something different today," Elisa whispered as they moved quietly through the crowded tables, finally finding an empty table in the back of the room. "He studied under Segovia," she explained. "From Spain, where you have been. He is here for further training. Starving, like all musicians—but at least no one is blowing up his guitar."

This afternoon, Elisa ordered for them. They drank strong, black Turkish coffee while the young guitarist played work by Bach that was originally written for solo violin. Elisa explained that the gifted, hungry Spanish guitarist was one musician she could listen to without mentally dissecting his work. "Other violinists," she said as the candlelight flickered on her face—"I listen to them play and think about technique or interpretation. You see?"

"Yes. Like reading another writer's work."

She nodded, grateful for the simple comparison. "Exactly. But I cannot compare this man's guitar techniques with mine on the violin. So, this is my secret place, Murphy. This is where I come to worship."

His smile faltered. She had lost him there. Faith was only a distant memory in his own disillusionment and search for meaning in life. "Worship—like in a church? I don't understand—"

She took his hand and closed her eyes. "Just listen, Murphy," she whispered.

He listened with her, closing his eyes to shut out the coffee cups and the brick walls of the cellar. He recognized "Jesu, Joy of Man's Desiring." He had not known that Bach had written the melody. Wasn't this a song played at Christmas by bent old ladies in lace collars at little pump organs? The hands of the young Spaniard somehow created a cathedral in this dark meeting place. And Murphy felt his heart lifted with Elisa's as he listened. He squeezed her hand. "Beautiful," he said when she opened her eyes. Indeed, it was the most beautiful music he had ever heard. Was it because he was hearing it with her?

She softly sang the chorus:

> "Jesu, joy of man's desiring,
> Holy wisdom, love most bright;
> Drawn by Thee, our souls aspiring
> Soar to uncreated light. . . ."

The melody written by Bach had words, too? And it spoke of God, the source of joy, wisdom, and love. He hadn't known. He had not imagined all the things she must hear in the music that was as familiar to her as the craft of words was to him. More than sound, it was a prayer and a hope—a reaching out to the Creator. "Drawn by Thee, our souls aspiring soar to uncreated light. . . ." He leaned closer toward her, afraid that if he let go of her hand, she would vanish. "What does it mean?" he asked. "Explain it to me."

She smiled. "Explain it?" She had never been asked to explain the music and words of Bach before. "Can't you hear it, Murphy? Can you not feel your soul drawn upward until you almost touch His face? I come here often, alone. I do not tell my name to anyone. But here I close my eyes and lift my heart to God. Someday perhaps Segovia or this student of his will play in St. Stephan's Cathedral, but until then I come here—"

"Why have you brought me to your secret place?" He could barely speak in the hope of her answer. He had only glimpsed her heart as she played. Now she was opening up so much for him. *Why?*

"Because . . . I . . . for so many months now I have prayed for joy, for wisdom, for love—someone who could soar with my soul . . ."

Murphy felt almost overwhelmed. Suddenly he wanted to know everything there was to know about her. He longed to discover her and the music of her life. What words were hidden in every melody? What had he heard but never known the meaning of? The music was different now. Slower, but still intricate. "What is he playing now?"

"The *Arioso*." She sensed his eagerness. *"I stand at the threshold. . . ."* She seemed curious. How could anyone not know this? "You have not heard the verse before?"

Murphy nodded. "Not in music. I stand at the door and knock . . ." He remembered the words from his childhood, the picture of Christ standing at the door.

" 'If anyone hears my voice and answers, I will come in.' Yes. Jesu, Creator, knocking and hoping we will hear. And I want to hear Him, Murphy. It has been so long—" She did not finish. The music spoke to her and for her.

There was so much more to this woman than he had bargained for. More than a willing kiss or a bright smile; she was at this moment showing him a part of her soul that he sensed she had never shown to anyone before. He carried a dozen little angels in the box. The image of her physical beauty could be duplicated . . . but *this*! He looked into her eyes, and in their depth he saw her very soul. He saw himself as one she trusted enough to share herself with. And he wondered if he could find the depth in his own heart that she had found in hers. What had she learned in her loneliness this year that she offered so freely to him?

"Was Gott tut, das ist wohligetan," she said as if in answer to his silent question.

"What God has done is rightly done," he translated. Then he frowned. "I don't think I can agree with you on that one, Elisa."

"Nor can I. It is the song. Cantata 99. But maybe someday we will be able to believe that God knows what He is doing . . . not now, Murphy. But maybe someday—when we see holy wisdom, and find love and hope that is greater than our darkness. Is God evil? I ask myself sometimes when I think of my father and the others who suffer now, maybe even more than Christ on the cross. But I do not come here to question, Murphy. I come here only to worship and remember, *Gott soll allein mein Herze haben. . . ."*

"God alone should have my heart," he translated again.

"Yes. A child's bedtime prayer my mother taught me. And no doubt Bach's mother taught him. That is his Cantata 169." She laughed at the expression on his face.

"Is there any thought at all that you cannot find in music?" He was teasing, but she answered him with a steady, serious gaze.

"In answer to your question, Murphy, listen to me play tonight. You in your rented suit and your fistful of tickets. Tonight you must *listen* as I play, and tell me what you hear."

"If I see, or hear, or feel any more, Elisa—" His heart was evident in his voice. Desperate. In love as he had never dreamed possible.

She touched his cheek. "Thank you." Were those tears in her eyes?

"Why are you thanking me?"

"For not thinking I'm . . . silly."

"Never. You just whet my appetite. I may become a music lover, after all."

She inclined her head slightly, amused at the thought. "No doubt. Something very important for a musician to have. One plays, the other . . . loves."

Again, he felt the room spinning around him. What was she saying? Was there more in her words? Like the music—level upon level of meaning beyond the notes themselves. *Don't play with my heart*, he wanted to beg her. But he simply accepted her touch; then he kissed the palm of her hand. *God alone should have her heart, she says. Does that exclude the love of all else? Is there room for her to love me?*

"Sitting here like this with you," Murphy said haltingly, "makes me almost afraid. What happened between last night and this moment? Why have you decided to share so much of yourself with me?"

She smiled a careful, thoughtful smile. "Last night, for the first time in a long time, I was reminded of something my father did." She did not tell Murphy what it was. "Something reminded me of my father—" She looked away and frowned. "And . . . it has been a very long time since I have even tried to reveal my thoughts with another person. A very long time." This brief, unsatisfactory explanation ended her moment of sharing.

This one hour together had left him even more hopelessly in love with her—desperate for her safety, eager to be her protector, and hungry to know her. Had it meant anything beyond the breaking of a long spiritual silence? He wanted her to feel what he felt, but he was afraid to push, and more frightened that she would walk away from him forever than he had been while facing Nazi bombs over Madrid.

She glanced at her watch as the music ended and the young Spaniard put his guitar away. "I have to go to the Musikverein before the doors are locked. My mail will be there. Maybe a letter from my mother."

"Will you come back to the hotel when you are finished?" He tried to sound light and matter-of-fact. "I have a surprise for you."

"How much time do you need?"

"An hour?"

She nodded and slipped into her coat. "An hour then," she agreed, kissing him lightly.

The memory of her lips beneath his burned fresh in his memory. He did not want to let go, even for an hour. He grabbed her hand the moment before she turned to leave. "Only an hour. Promise."

She did not speak, but raised her face to his and let him kiss her once again—an electrifying, all-consuming kiss that drove every thought from his mind. Then she pushed him away and skipped lightly up the steps of the cellar while he stood grasping the railing and staring after the bright flash of her red skirt.

"God, what is happening to me?" he said aloud as she disappeared. Then he ran up the steps and searched the teeming crowds of Christmas shoppers for one last glimpse of her. But she had already melted into the throngs.

26

Decision

How long has it been, Elisa asked herself, *since I felt this way?* Months of memory ticked off into a year and a half. *Thomas and I that evening we picnicked by the Spree River. He took me in his arms and stroked my hair*—She stopped herself mid-thought, not wanting to mix her image of Thomas with this fresh, new feeling for John Murphy. Had she ever before admitted that she could possibly love any man but Thomas? Now, as she strolled along the sidewalk, she turned the images of the day like pages in a photo album. Yes, she could love him; given time, sweet days and hours like today could melt into love. She touched her fingers to her lips. His kiss was still with her—just as Thomas's kisses had haunted her for so long in the night, Murphy's lips seemed only a thought away. It was cold out. She could see her own breath rising up like the breath of the shoppers who trudged past her. But she was not cold.

Everything about Murphy seemed diametrically opposed to the things she had loved about Thomas. Thomas carried himself straight and correctly, like the aristocrat he was. Murphy was tall and slim, easygoing and relaxed. Athletic and confident, Murphy moved with a loose stride, while Thomas had always seemed to march. Murphy carried his heart and convictions quite openly. She had heard his anger as he described the senseless killing of the war in Spain. His affection had been evident in his eyes last night and again this afternoon.

With Thomas, she had never been quite certain of his love until the sun slipped away; then he became filled with a passion and fire that had stolen her breath in its fierceness. He had left her silently, bewildered that he could desire her so strongly and yet never say the words *I love you.* Always she had assumed that men did not say such words, or show themselves vulnerable to a woman. How she had longed to hear Thomas say all those things!

She sighed and quickly climbed the steps of the Musikverein. Of course none of that mattered now, except by way of comparison. Murphy was so very different—tender. Perhaps she could learn to love him as she had once loved Thomas. Murphy was no soldier, nor was he a saint, but words were his gift, his craft. He would not be afraid to tell her . . .

———

The mail slot bearing her name contained two letters. The one on top was postmarked from Prague and was from her mother. That had been the only mail Elisa expected. She flipped the other envelope over and stared hard at the postmark. *Paris*. With a gasp, she recognized the handwriting. She closed her eyes, feeling suddenly faint. Groping for a chair, she sat down carefully on a piano bench and stared at the white envelope. There was no return address. Only her name, in the distinct Germanic script of Thomas von Kleistmann.

"Why now? Why today?" she asked aloud as the caretaker walked past.

"Are you ill, Fräulein?" he asked.

She was trembling, but she managed a smile and shook her head no in reply.

He was unconvinced. "Do you need me to call someone?"

Leah? No. Not Leah. After our talk last night, she would call me a fool for not tearing the envelope in half before I even read it. Murphy? How can I explain this? Perhaps it is word of my father. Perhaps it is the words I waited for Thomas to say . . . She closed her eyes, afraid of what waited for her inside the crisp envelope.

"Yes. Please. I need a taxi."

———

It was the smallest of all Christmas trees, but Murphy had carried it happily upstairs without waiting for the elevator. In his room he had unwrapped the angels and the rolls of red and gold ribbon and a dozen brass candle holders and long white tapered candles.

Now the candles illuminated the room in a soft light. The branches of the little tree were covered with bows, red and gold, of all different sizes. And the angels—Elisa's angels played their violins from the branches. "Bach, no doubt," Murphy said as he placed the carving of the Holy Family beneath his little tree.

Now, as the minutes crawled by, he paced back and forth in the room, stopping to peer out the window at every passerby. It was growing dark, but the city seemed to glow, and he was sure he could single her out among the shoppers below. He was certain he could spot her anywhere.

He was so full, so hopeful and expectant as he considered the words that had passed between them this afternoon. Always in the back of his mind was the warning that he must not move too fast. She was like a beautiful white-tailed doe in the forests back home. He must approach quietly, slowly, so she would not bolt and run.

As for himself, he knew it was too late for a warning. His heart was shot through. He was smitten, finished. The ladies of the cabarets would hold no temptation for him now. He had an angel on the string. An angel with a violin.

He sat down and stared at the tree. He got up and moved an angel from one branch, carefully securing it to another. He moved the angels around a dozen times, admiring the effect of the candlelight on the gold ribbon.

He sat down again, then got up and stood at the window. *Not more than an hour.* She had promised. Where was she, then? Maybe she had been hurt, slipped on the ice and gotten hit by a bus, or . . .

Murphy ran his hand across his face. She would come. She had promised. And this would be the best Christmas he had ever had. He prayed that she was not hurt. *Maybe bad news from home?* The thought made him exhale loudly. If she did not come soon, he determined, he would go look for her! But if he went looking for her, she might come, and he would miss her. *Better stay put.*

After an hour and a half, his nervousness melted with the candles into pools of disappointment. He switched on the light and blew out the dozen flames. *She has some reason why she couldn't come. I'll bring her here after the performance.* He comforted himself with the thought, then went in to shower and shave and dress for the evening at the symphony. He would listen to her play; listen to the melody as though he had never heard a note of music before. Tonight, Elisa had promised to play for him. And when she was done, he would bring her back and show her his small surprise. Then maybe he would talk to her again about the farm in Pennsylvania, and she would listen to him.

The two letters lay opened before her on the table. She had drawn the shades hurriedly, sending the pot of geraniums crashing to the floor. Her hands trembled uncontrollably as she skimmed each letter again one at a time.

Dear Elisa,

Wilhelm is in the hospital . . . emergency surgery for appendicitis. He will fully recover, but we cannot come to Vienna for the holidays. . . . My darling, we know that you are committed to a full schedule of work this season and we'll simply all have to muddle through this Christmas, I'm afraid. . . .

Normally such a disappointment would have shattered Elisa. But now she could barely comprehend the words. She held the letter from Thomas up to the lamplight. The page shook so in her hand that she laid it down again to read it.

My only Elisa,
There can be no doubt in my mind after these many terrible, lonely months. I love you. . . .

The letter went on, page after wrenching page. The silence was broken. He wanted her to come to Paris. Join him there, and there they would marry and disappear somewhere to live together forever. Did Elisa dare believe him? Hadn't she loved him to the exclusion of all else in her life? Hadn't she begged God to bring him back into her arms? And now, the night after she had given him up, tried to shut him out of her heart and turn her hope toward another, he was back, passionate and yearning in his desire to see her. He would marry her to the exclusion of his country and his duty to the Fatherland! It was all there. In Germany, Thomas would have been arrested and sent to Dachau as a traitor! He *loved* her! He had told her he could not love a non-Aryan and retain his hope of serving Germany! He had cut her heart in pieces, he had deserted her and her father when they were both in the most need!

"I hate you, Thomas!" she shouted to the empty room. Then she bowed her head and wept—wrenching, aching sobs that left her weak and exhausted. "And I love you," she said with a terrible finality.

At the bottom of the letter, Thomas had left a cautious way for her to reply. Not an address, but the telephone number of a little Paris cafe.

Every evening between seven and midnight, my darling, I will wait at the cafe for your call. Ask only for Thomas. The owner is a friend of mine, and he will know it is you. You must not mention your name or mine. I cannot be certain even here that the Gestapo is not having telephone lines tapped. Use a public phone, dearest. Please do not delay. You alone hold my heart.

Forever,
Thomas.

Elisa looked at her watch, calculating the time difference between Vienna and Paris. She would call Thomas at the stroke of seven that evening. For the first time since she had been chosen as a member of the Vienna Symphony, she would miss a performance. She looked at her trembling hands. It would not be a lie to say she was too ill to play tonight. A phone call to Leah would relay the message. There was a roster of capable substitutes who could take her place for one night. The music was not difficult.

Suddenly, the awareness of dear Murphy crowded into all her plans. She thought of him for the first time since she had seen the Paris postmark on the envelope. His eyes, the warmth, the gentleness of his kiss all came back to her. *One hour*, he had said. She was already two hours late!

Had she not promised to play for him tonight? He would be waiting there for her in his rented tuxedo, his pocket full of tickets.

"Why did you write to me, Thomas?" She slammed her fist on the table. "I could have been happy!" She wept again—for herself and for Murphy. She would not play for him tonight. Not tonight. Not ever.

The voice of the orchestra manager on the other end of the line sounded entirely unsympathetic, even angry. "We will be short in the first violins tonight. Rudy Dorbransky had an appointment with the maestro this afternoon, which he did not keep! Probably drunk! And now you call in!"

"It is unavoidable," Elisa insisted, staring down at her shaking hands. "Call a relief musician."

"At this late hour?" He clucked his tongue and turned to someone passing by on his end of the phone. "Elisa Linder is calling in sick, and Rudy has still not shown up."

Elisa could not hear the mumbled reply, but not one at the concert hall was happy. She felt sick to her stomach. Never had she missed a performance. Never. How could they treat her so callously? "I will be back tomorrow."

"Are you sure?" The voice became suddenly sympathetic. "The maestro reminds me that you have played even when you have been ill before. He says you should take care, and . . ."

Tears of relief welled up in her eyes. At least *someone* realized she would not call in unless it was a dire emergency. "Tell the maestro thank you. I will be back tomorrow."

She wished them luck with the evening's performance and hung up. Now, what was she to do about Murphy? Should she call him? No. She could not bear to hear his voice. And if she contacted him at the hotel, he might come to the apartment. She rested her aching head in her hands and stared down at the broken geranium on the kitchen floor. Hadn't life been almost perfect today? *Almost!*

With a sigh, she put a kettle on to boil and took her stationery from the inlaid mahogany writing case her father had given her for Christmas four years before. They had all been so happy then, even in Berlin. Worried, yes. But happy. Thomas had stood at her shoulder and watched through the window with her as the brass band marched past their house to serenade President Hindenburg in front of the Presidential mansion. He had been a good man, old Hindenburg—tower of the Weimar Republic. And he remembered Theo kindly each year with a card. *In gratitude for your service to the Fatherland. . . .*

A lifetime ago. It must have been someone else standing at the window of the house in Berlin. "Was that really me?" she murmured as she began to write.

"Dearest Murphy. . . ." She determined that she would tell him everything. She could not lie to him, even though she could not face him either.

Today, if someone told me that I would not live to see another day,

I would say, 'Was Gott tut, das ist wohligetan! Then God has rightly created this day as perfect for me!' And I could not be sad because I have spent one perfect day with a wonderful man.

She paused, lifting her pen. She felt so inadequate with words. Words were Murphy's craft, not hers. She could lift her violin and play *goodbye* a hundred different ways. But how could she *write* it?

She tried again. In her soul she could hear the sad, clear music of *Peer Gynt*, the Prelude of Act Two. Was there music playing somewhere in the building? No, it was her soul remembering the song of Ingrid's lament. She took a deep breath, trying to keep her hand steady as she wrote.

> As perfect as our time has been together, I must not see you again. I have loved a man for many years. I told you about him on the train from Berlin that terrible night. I thought I would never see him again, but now he has written and asked me to marry him. Please do not come to find me. I will leave Vienna with him, I suppose; you hoped I would leave Vienna. We have had one perfect, perfect day, and I find myself suddenly wishing that I had met you when I was a child, that my first kiss had been from you, my first embrace. But that cannot be altered. I have belonged to him since the summer of my eighteenth year. It is right then that I be with him. . . .

The whistle of the kettle shrieked, and Elisa wearily brewed herself a cup of tea. The lament of the Prelude still echoed in her mind. *Why this song?* she asked herself, *the song of a woman abducted from the one she loves?* But Elisa could not love Murphy. She hardly knew him. What was it, then, that pulled the bow with such dissonance across her heart?

She read the letter again, satisfied that she had explained clearly and gently. He was a compassionate man. He would not force himself past such a plea. *I must not see you again!* She signed it, then folded it and slipped it into an envelope. The hot tea burned her lips, as if to scorch away the memory of Murphy's kiss. "He will be easy to forget," she said aloud to herself. "One day. Only one day, only a smile and a kiss. I will not think of him again."

Resolutely she took her handbag and the letter downstairs to the small flat of the concierge. He was an old man, Jewish, and wore a crocheted kippa on his head. He peered at her through thick spectacles. Behind him on a tiny two-burner stove something simmered in a pot. He smiled broadly and bowed.

"You have come for dinner, Eleeeza?" Then he slapped his forehead with his hand. "Why aren't you at the hall? You are sick?"

Her hands were no longer trembling. "Not as well as I would like. I . . . need to ask a favor." She eyed the kettle on the burner. "But it is your mealtime."

"Nonsense! What is it?"

"There is a young man—"

He looked pleased. "A young man! Gut! Sehr gut, Eleeeza!"

"I was supposed to meet him tonight after the performance, Herr Haupt, but I cannot go."

"You are not playing tonight! Oy! You should sit down, maybe? You are soooo ill!"

"No. It's not that . . . I—" She extended the note. "Could you take this for me to the concert hall?"

He took the envelope from her and read the instructions aloud. "Deliver to Herr John Murphy. Row 10, right aisle." He studied her for a moment. "Yes, of course, Eleeeza. I will take it."

"Thank you. I'll call a taxi. If you will give it to the doorman and ask him to take it to Herr Murphy just before the performance begins." She handed him enough cash to pay for the taxi and to tip the doorman at the concert hall, as well as a handsome tip for himself.

He bowed again, sensing that it would be inappropriate to ask any more. This was more than a favor; it was an assignment, and she was paying him a week's wages.

"Anything else?" In affairs of the heart, he was always discreet with his tenants. Elisa Linder had simply never shown any indication that her heart was vulnerable to such involvement. No doubt this was a farewell note; Herr Haupt had not even been aware that she had even said *hello* to any man since she had lived in the building. At least this was something!

"No, danke." She looked embarrassed. "Just make sure you tell the doorman not to give it to him until just before performance. And"—she frowned—"I will not be here tonight."

He pursed his lips and nodded vigorously. "Ja, Eleeeza." Slipping the note into the pocket of his coat, he took on a very official air. She was certain that Murphy would get the note.

Elisa watched from the window of her flat as Herr Haupt got into the taxi. He had dressed for the occasion in his finest three-piece suit, and had replaced the kippa on his head with a dignified Hamburg hat. He looked the part of an ambassador. Thus ended her perfect day; the decision had been made. She would go now and call Thomas, hear his voice for the first time in eighteen months. Why, then, did she feel so terribly unhappy?

27

Change of Plans

Murphy clutched the red velvet arms of his seat as if the concert hall were an airplane about to take off. All around him the audience buzzed with anticipation. Musicians wandered onto the stage to mingle the noise of their instruments with the trumpeting, hooting clamor that emanated from the stage before the concert.

Elisa's seat was still empty. Murphy searched the wings as each musician emerged. Where was she? Didn't she know that just her presence was symphony enough for him? Leah had not yet come onstage either, but tonight she was to solo; and Elisa had informed him that as soloist, Leah would come out after the others. Probably the two of them were back stage chatting.

He shifted nervously in his chair and glanced down at the evening's program. *A watched pot never boils,* he reminded himself. If he would calm down and read, Elisa would be there when he looked up. Tonight she would smile at him. She would play for him. He would nudge the matron in satin and furs beside him and say, *"That's my girl . . ."*

Tonight they would play a cello concert by *Dvorak*. Murphy recognized the name—the guy who spent his summer in Spillville, Iowa. He loved America; maybe that was what Elisa would tell him tonight in her music— that she wanted to go to America with him after all. Just like Dvorak. The thought did not calm Murphy. He looked up again, scanning the rows of string players. Still no Elisa!

Clearing his throat loudly, he looked back to the program and began to read. Tonight he would be able to talk to her a little bit about what he had heard. *Dvorak learned of the death of Josephina of whom he had been extremely fond. His song "Leave Me Alone" was a favorite of hers.* Murphy frowned. *"Leave Me Alone"?* Was that the message he was supposed to listen for?

He rolled up the program and thumped it against his thigh. Still no Elisa. A few more musicians straggled in. Maybe she had a solo, too. Maybe she would come in after everybody else. After Leah. After the conductor. *Where is she?*

A short, balding man with a gray goatee came out to sound the note of the concertmaster. *Where is Rudy Dorbransky?* Elisa's chair remained vacant even as applause rose up around him and the houselights drifted down into darkness.

A soft tap on his shoulder caused him to turn. A uniformed usher said his name. "John Murphy?" The whisper was barely heard; the conductor emerged, and the hall was filled with thunderous applause.

Murphy nodded and the usher handed him a white, square envelope. Murphy could not read what was lettered across the front. He strained to see in the dimness of the auditorium. His eyes darted from the envelope to the empty seat, then back again. More applause sounded as Leah Goldblatt came onto the stage. *Applause, and applause, and applause,* but the petite cellist looked strained in her acceptance of the ovation. *Where is Elisa?*

In an unmistakable gesture, Leah looked toward the vacant chair in the first violin section. Then she turned her gaze full on row ten, right aisle!

Murphy swallowed hard. Leah was worried, too. In that one terrible instant he knew that Elisa was not coming. He looked at the white square in his perspiring hands. Then he stood and dashed out of the hall, even as the applause around him faded away.

———

"Lasst mich allein! Leave me alone!" The message of Elisa's note was much clearer than any music could be. Murphy stared grimly at the little Christmas tree in his room. The whole day had been some grotesque and cruel joke.

"Yeah, Murphy!" He threw his jacket angrily onto the bed. "Get the message, buddy? Sure, she'll play for you! Just like Dvor . . . whatever! *Leave me alone!* Sure—just listen real good tonight; you bet she'll play for you. She wasn't even there." He picked up her letter again, able only to see the words: *I have loved a man for many years. . . . I will leave Vienna with him. . . . I have belonged to him.* There was no doubt about her meaning.

With a cry, Murphy wadded up the paper and threw it at the tree. It stuck in the branches, and suddenly all the tiny wooden angels began the melody *"Leave Me alone!"* "You had it coming, Murphy!" he yelled at himself as he glimpsed his own agonized reflection in the mirror. "She tried to tell you that first night and you didn't listen! Taught you a lesson, didn't she? Huh?"

And what a lesson! Couldn't she have chosen an easier way? Yes, the day had been perfect. She had made it perfect, and then pulled the rug out from under him.

He opened the closet door and stood staring blankly at his own clothes for a moment; then, with a shake of his head, he pulled out his suitcase and began to toss his clothes into it. He *would* leave her alone! She was leaving Vienna—that was all he had been worried about for the last year. Now some other guy had taken care of his worries. He wouldn't have to think about her anymore, wouldn't worry if Austria did fall to Nazi Germany! Austria and Vienna could roast, for all Murphy cared!

He picked up his telephone and called the front desk.

"This is John Murphy. What time does the last plane leave Vienna? For where? I don't care. For anywhere. I just want to be on the plane—" He stared at the angels. At Joseph looking so longingly at Mary. At least Joseph had not made a fool out of himself. Murphy had won the Fool of the Year Contest.

"Paris? *Paris has a branch of the International News Service. Sure, anyplace is home to me where there's an INS office.* Sure, book me on that flight, will you? Great. An hour? Sure. *That gives me lots of time. I'll need somebody to take back this monkey suit for me tomorrow.* Right. Thanks."

Murphy finished packing in record time. He even had a few minutes to pull the angels off the tree branches and pitch them back into their box. "Ten . . . eleven . . ." He would leave eleven angels. Didn't every man need at least one souvenir of his broken heart? Almost with reverence, Murphy plucked the last angel from the tree and slipped her into his pocket. The others he would leave for Elisa and her boyfriend—a wedding present.

Carrying his small suitcase and the box of carvings, he hailed a taxi and gave the address of the airport, with one stop in between.

———

It took an hour before the call was put through to the Paris telephone number Thomas had given her. Now, waiting in the public telephone office, Elisa stared blankly at the wall where government posters urging support of Chancellor Schuschnigg and an independent Austria hung.

She felt strangely emotionless, as though she were a spectator, watching herself pay the operator, watching herself sit down to wait, watching herself watching herself. Had she ever been so numb?

Of course, she was doing the right thing. Could there be any doubt? She had committed herself to Thomas six years before. She had committed her heart to loving him even if he never loved her with the tenderness that she had longed for. She loved Thomas, didn't she? Wasn't this the moment she had prayed for and waited for? *Then, why am I so numb?* Even the whispered song of lament had died within her after she had watched Herr Haupt take the letter.

The voice of the operator interrupted her. "Fraülein, your call to Paris has been put through. Fraülein?"

Elisa turned her head to look at the woman behind the tall switchboard. "Paris?"

"Yes, Fraülein," she urged. "You can take it in that booth. I will transfer the call there."

So the moment had arrived. Thomas waited on the other end of the line. Elisa moved toward the walnut phone booth unhurriedly. She closed the glass door behind her and the light came on, illuminating yet another poster proclaiming Austrian independence against a foreign aggression. She stared at the phone for an instant, unsure that she would pick it up. Then she watched her hand grasp the receiver and heard her own voice say the name, "Thomas."

A faraway voice crackled into her ear. "Elisa? Elisa, darling?" He had forgotten his own warning about not using names. "Is that you?" Thomas—familiar, yet strange to her. Eager, hopeful, breathless. The way she had once felt about him.

"Yes, Thomas, it's me."

"Darling!" The voice was almost tearful in its relief. "I was so afraid! So afraid you wouldn't get my letter; then so afraid that once you had it you would throw it away."

"No, Thomas. I would never throw your letter away." Her heart finished the line silently: *Like you threw me away.*

Then he said the words. "I love you, darling! I have always loved you! Can you hear me, Elisa? Do you hear what I am saying?"

"Yes. I can hear you." She listened to her own words. Could she not find some slight intonation of excitement? *Forte, Elisa!*

"Are you all right?" He sounded worried.

"I . . . I don't know. Not about anything anymore." She startled herself, not intending to express the slightest doubt to him now that he had come back to her.

"Yes." He sounded understanding. "I knew you might feel that way. But when we are together, you will see! You will see that you are the most important thing in my life!"

Maybe that didn't matter. Maybe she didn't really care anymore what was important in his life. "If only you could have said these things last year!" Now the emotion came—questioning, accusing. Why had he stood by while Theo Lindheim was arrested? What did it matter what Thomas felt? Her father was gone. Their family shattered, run out of Germany. And Thomas, and men like him, had let it happen.

"Last year I thought I could make a difference if I stayed. I have been in Paris since last Christmas. And Elisa—about your father—I know how hurt you all are. He was like a father to me as well."

Then you are the worst kind of Judas. The thought stunned Elisa with its clarity. "Thomas," she suddenly decided, "I cannot come to Paris."

"Then I will come to Vienna. I know there is much we have to heal."

"No. My life is good here. I have found a life of my own."

"Another man?"

She did not answer. Thoughts of Murphy, his eyes full and warm, came to her in a rush. And then she remembered the letter. "No. I mean, I don't know. Thomas, I . . . I think I may be falling in love with another man—"

The line crackled so badly that for a moment she thought they might have been disconnected. Then his voice faded in again. "Don't worry. We will be better than we were before. I'm coming to Vienna, darling. After the first of the year I have some time. I am coming to Vienna!" He did not wait for her reply. "You are mine. You have always been mine." The voice faded out again.

Elisa felt suddenly desperate to see Murphy. "I have to go now."

"I love you, darling! Goodbye."

"Goodbye." She hung up and stepped from the booth, feeling suddenly awake, and icy cold with a new fear inside. *Murphy! Have I let him go? Have I chased him away? He loves me. I see it in his eyes. Maybe he never got the letter. Oh, God, please, make him not get the letter!*

———

Her skin was ashen as she jumped from the taxi and ran up the steps of the hall. She could hear the deep, mellow sound of Leah's cello, but she did not think about music now; she only thought about him. *Row ten, aisle seat.*

"Fraülein Linder!" the orchestra manager whispered hoarsely as she came backstage. "Are you not home in bed?"

"No."

"You look *terrible*! Go home!" he insisted.

Elisa tiptoed to the wings of the stage and stared out past the orchestra, past Leah, past the maestro and the footlights. The aisle seat, row ten, was vacant! She stood shaking her head in dismay. The hand of the orchestra manager tapped her lightly on the shoulder, then pulled her back.

"Go home! You are delirious to be here. Rudy has not come either, but they are managing."

She staggered past him, then stumbled down the steps and back to where her taxi waited.

"Where to, Fraülein?"

"Sacher Hotel. Please hurry."

It was only a short distance, but Elisa was unsure that her legs could carry her now. *Please, God, let him be there . . .*

———

Murphy took the steps of Elisa's apartment two at a time. His taxi waited down below in the street. He would not stay, even if she asked him. He had already decided that. She had said it all in the letter, and he would not force himself on her again. But the least he could do is leave her the angels—say goodbye and good luck, maybe give her a piece of his mind for stringing him along like a ten-pound catfish on a line.

He knocked on the door, softly at first. Then he waited and knocked again harder. A door opened on the floor below and Murphy heard a voice call up. "You are looking for Eleeeza?"

"I have a package for her." He called down the stairwell.

"Well, Eleeeza is not at home."

"When will she be back?"

"I cannot say. She had to meet a young man, I think."

Murphy did not answer. All the things he wanted to say to her suddenly made no difference. A stiff jolt of sick disappointment told him the truth about himself. He had not really come here to bring her a box of angels. He stood at the door and knocked, hoping she would let him in, into her heart like the music of Bach in her secret place. He wanted to tell her, wanted to ask her, wanted . . . her.

"It's just as well," Murphy said with a terrible resignation. "Just as well she isn't here." He placed the box carefully at her threshold like an offering.

"You want me to tell Elisa you were here?"

"No. No. It doesn't matter. I'm just a messenger. Tell her a messenger came. Danke."

Murphy did not look to the right or the left as he marched down the stairs. He did not touch the banister. Her hands had caressed the smooth wood a thousand times and he feared some magic in her touch might remain there and would somehow root him at the foot of her steps to wait until she came back again. *With him*, whoever *he* was. Murphy had made enough of a fool out of himself.

The cold air felt good on his face as he emerged from the building. He stood in the street and inhaled a moment to clear his head of the sense of her nearness. Then he squared his shoulders and got back into the cab.

"The airport," he said quietly. "I'm going to Paris for Christmas."

———

Breathlessly, Elisa ran to the front desk of the Sacher Hotel. An indolent, dignified clerk looked at her from over the top of his reading glasses.

"Please," she said urgently. "Can you tell me the room number for John Murphy?"

"It is against policy. We call up to rooms, you see, before we give out the room number. Suppose he didn't want to see you?"

"Call him. Tell him Elisa is here, and there has been a terrible mistake. Please call him up. I was supposed to meet him here this afternoon, but I was delayed . . ."

The clerk's face registered amusement at her eagerness. He smirked unpleasantly. "Well, I am sure I cannot call him up, Fraülein."

"Please. If you tell him it is Elisa—"

"I am very sorry, Fraülein. Herr John Murphy has checked out, you see. He left here"—he glanced at his watch, making certain he was precise—"a half an hour ago. I'm sure his plane has left by now."

"Plane?"

"Yes, Fraülein. He had a plane to catch."

"To where?" Her voice was too eager, too pleading. The clerk had seen such cases before. A young female trying to track down a man . . .

"I am sure I can't tell you where he has gone, Fraülein." He answered as his duty demanded. "But Herr Murphy is most certainly gone."

When Herr Haupt called up to Elisa on the stairway, reporting the successful completion of his mission, she had simply thanked him, picked up the box on the threshold, and inserted the key into her lock as quickly as she could. She had no strength left for more than that.

Sinking down onto the bed, she opened the package. "Murphy," she said dully, staring without seeing at the jumble of tiny wings and golden strings. Without bothering to undress, she laid back and pulled the blanket over herself before she slipped into a deep and dreamless sleep.

Elisa had lost all track of time and place when the urgent voice of Leah pulled her reluctantly from her sleep.

"Elisa! Wake up!" Leah shook her roughly. "Please! Elisa!"

Groggy and confused, Elisa opened her eyes and pulled herself up to sit on the edge of the bed. "Leah, how did you. . . . What time is it?"

Leah scraped a chair across the floor to sit down directly across from Elisa. "I let myself in. It is almost two."

"In the morning? Why aren't you home in bed?"

Leah looked at her disheveled friend. "You're still dressed. You went to bed in your shoes."

"I . . . I don't feel well."

Suddenly Leah embraced her and said in a tearful voice, "I'm so glad you're all right. So glad. They said you had shown up during the concert, and then left. I thought maybe you had heard about Rudy!" She broke down. Her shoulders shook with uncontrollable sobs.

"Rudy? Rudy?" Her own troubles seemed to take on less significance. "What? What happened, Leah? Is he hurt? Dead? What has happened?" She remembered the clear anger in the voice of the manager. Rudy had not shown up for his meeting with the maestro. He had not made it to the performance.

Leah's chin trembled. She shook her head in disbelief at the horror of the night. "After the performance, the police came—dozens of shupos backstage. They would not let any of us go home. They asked questions and questions about Rudy!" She started to break down again, but caught herself. "They wanted to know if we had seen him. What had been his state of mind. They even detained the maestro, Elisa, as though we were criminals! And then they told us—" She covered her face with her hands. "Oh, Elisa! So terrible! The man who shot at Rudy that night at the concert—he was the brother of Irmgard Schüler!"

Elisa recognized the name. Irmgard Schüler was the woman Rudy had been seeing for over a year. Her husband, a leader in the Austrian Nazi Party, had been imprisoned for his activities against the Schuschnigg Catholic government and Austria. He had been released, but even then, Rudy had continued to see this woman. So. Her brother tried to kill Rudy. "So much for his motive." Elisa said quietly placing a hand on Leah's arm.

"The man killed himself. In prison, Elisa! Only this morning. He left a terrible note about the decadence of the Jews. How Rudy had destroyed the life of his sister and the honor of his family!"

"Rudy is not a good representative of morality, is he?"

Leah's eyes blazed in fierce defense of Rudy. "You don't know! You don't know anything about him at all! He and Irmgard Schüler were never lovers. They were friends, and . . . she helped!"

"Helped? Helped what?"

"It doesn't matter," Leah moaned miserably. "She is dead now. They found her murdered tonight in her flat. Terrible. Horrible . . . *horrible*! And they are saying Rudy did it! Elisa, they say *Rudy murdered* her!" She sobbed again, harder now, making no effort to control her tears.

Elisa could not speak. She simply stared at Leah in disbelief. *Gentle, silly Rudy? How could he murder someone? He could barely stand to step on a spider. He grew faint if he nicked himself shaving.* "Surely they have made a mistake."

Leah looked at her with tear-filled eyes. "No mistake. They say he left proof all over the apartment. Oh, Elisa! They say he cut her throat! It cannot be! This is too terrible! They said she tried to break off with him after her brother killed himself, but Rudy wouldn't let her! And now they are looking for him! All over the city! He has simply vanished. Could this be happening? *Our* Rudy?"

Elisa got up stiffly and put the kettle on to boil. Her head ached, and she could not think. "Do you think he could have done it?"

"Never!" Leah cried, following her into the kitchen. "Another Nazi trick. Rudy says the government is full of them. He told me that Irmgard had given him the list of names. Secret party members! She was no Nazi, no adulteress—not any more than Rudy Dorbransky is capable of . . . *this*! It will be in the morning papers. The guards warned us that there might be anti-Jewish demonstrations, that we should stay home. The concert has been canceled for tomorrow night. When we left, there was already an angry mob outside shouting against Jewish musicians."

"Half the orchestra!" Elisa was angry at the news. "Yesterday Rudy was a brave hero. Tonight they would lynch him."

"If they believe half of what is being said—no, not said—*shouted* from the rooftops of Vienna! Elisa"—she shook her head sadly—"it is not only bad for Rudy, but for the rest of us as well. Maestro warned us that there would probably be police watching our flats to see if Rudy attempts to make contact." Her gentle face contorted with grief. "I don't want to go home." Her words were no louder than a whisper. She could barely speak.

"But you must." Elisa was surprised at the force of her words. She took Leah by the shoulders. "They must not think you have been anywhere but at your flat. If they can do such a thing to Rudy, they can also arrange something for the rest of us. By the end of the week the entire orchestra could be implicated." She was being sarcastic. "Pretty soon they'll write in the papers that we are all involved in the scandal!"

Leah nodded. Elisa was right. "Yes. Yes, of course. I should go home. I . . . I should go." She seemed confused, searching for her coat, even though it was right in front of her.

"Wait, Leah." Elisa put a hand on her arm. "Shimon is ten minutes away. Let me call him. You mustn't walk home alone."

Fear flashed in Leah's eyes. "No. Not alone."

"Sit down, then. I'll fix you a cup of tea, and we'll call Shimon."

Shimon arrived fifteen minutes later. Leah and Elisa had barely uttered a word in all that time. The big man helped Leah put on her coat. He seemed unable to find words to express what he was feeling. A fresh and terrible nightmare had come to awaken all of Vienna in a wave of anti-Semitism. As certainly as the sun would rise over the shining, cultured city, there would be a new melody played in the streets by morning. At last the lyrics of the Reich's Horst Wessel song had found a way to breach the fortress of the Alps and take root in Austria.

Raise high the flags! Stand rank on rank together.
Storm troopers march with steady, quiet tread. . . .

28

Rudy's Secret

It was still dark when the phone rang in Elisa's flat. She had not slept since Leah and Shimon had left two hours before. She had simply sat in the gloom and replayed the events of the last week over and over again in her mind. Suddenly, her personal problems seemed insignificant. Maybe Murphy was right about Vienna and his warning about Austria's future, after all. She reached for the phone, hoping that it would be Murphy on the other end of the line; then she would tell him—

"Hello, Murphy?" she asked eagerly, surprised that his name had come so easily to her lips.

"Not Murphy," a man's voice replied haltingly, as if his teeth were clenched in pain.

For a moment Elisa did not recognize the voice and then she gasped, "Where are you?"

"Don't . . ." Rudy groaned. "Don't say . . . anything. . . . Come. Please hurry." He gave an address in the Seventh District, the area of Vienna filled with brothels and cheap cabarets.

"Are you all right?"

"Just . . ." The voice faltered. His breathing was labored. "Hurry." He hung up, leaving her stunned and frightened on the other end of the receiver.

She bit her lip and stood blinking at the telephone. *What? What am I to do? God, help me. Tell me. Help us.* Might she not be arrested too if she was caught with Rudy? She closed her eyes and tried to think. She did not believe Rudy had hurt anyone. The desperation in his voice had reinforced that belief. He was in trouble, accused of a crime he could not have committed. Every Jew in Vienna would stand accused by morning.

She slipped on her coat and stuffed all her spare cash into her handbag. He might need it. Rudy always needed money . . .

Prostitutes stood in the doorways of the seedy hotels along the Lanterngasse. A few drunks staggered past her as she hurried down the sidewalk, scanning the shabby facades of the buildings for an address. *Number Six. Flat D.* The building seemed to lean against its neighbor. Even the bricks of the red-light district looked hung over. Ragged shades were drawn. No light came from behind the torn curtains. From somewhere, deep in the darkness of the street, Elisa could hear the music of an accordion playing a sad melody she did not recognize.

Green paint on the door was chipped and flaking. The number 6 was stenciled on the glass, but was barely legible. For an instant Elisa nearly turned around to run back down the street—back to the Ring, to the great Burgtheatre and the familiar halls of the Musikverein. This was no part of Vienna that she recognized, and she was afraid.

The door opened slightly and a young woman with rouged cheeks and bleached blond hair whispered, "Come on! He is waiting!"

Elisa's heart thumped wildly in her ears. What was she doing here? Why had she come? She should have called Leah. But why hadn't Rudy called Leah first? Why Elisa? She followed the young woman up stairs that seemed to be only propped against the bare brick wall. The woman seemed frightened as well. She stopped in front of the door marked with a rusted metal *D*. Then she jerked her head and stepped aside, waiting for Elisa to open the door.

The doorknob was rusted and stiff. Elisa gripped hard and shoved the thin wooden door as the young prostitute hurried away, back down the creaking steps.

The room was dark and cold—almost as cold as outside. It smelled of urine and vomit, and she felt her throat tighten with fear and revulsion.

"Elisa," Rudy's voice rasped. A match hissed and sputtered as he lit the stub of a candle.

"Rudy?" She asked. The man before her was barely recognizable. Crouched miserable on the bare mattress of a small cot, the candlelight flickered on a face swollen and disfigured. As he spoke, she saw that the once straight and glistening teeth were broken. His right eye was almost swollen shut. "My God! Rudy!" she cried. "What have they done to you?" She rushed to his side and knelt on the filthy floor.

"I am a dead man, Elisa," he said hollowly. "But I must tell you . . . everything."

"Let me call a doctor," she gasped, noting the blood on his shirt.

"No. It doesn't matter." He lifted his left hand toward the light. The hand was smashed and mangled. His first and second fingers were severed at the first knuckle and blood oozed out of the stubs, soaking the torn sleeve of his shirt. "I am dead," he said again as she cried out.

"Let me call a doctor!" she pleaded.

"What difference?" His words came with difficulty. "They will not let me leave this room alive when they find me. They cannot. They cannot, because I am innocent."

"Of course you are, Rudy, darling." Elisa was weeping openly. "We all know that. All of us in the orchestra." She could not take her eyes away from the mangled hand that had played with such power and beauty.

"Listen to me," he rasped. "I could not call Leah. Shimon. The others. They will be watched. But you—" His face contorted with pain. "Listen. You must take my violin."

"No. No, Rudy—"

"Listen!" he demanded. This was not time for her to argue or offer sentimental words of reassurance. "The violin case . . . I hid it . . . at the Musikverein. Behind the cupboard with Haydn's skull . . ."

She knew it well. "Yes, Rudy. You want me to sell it?" She could not think what he must be telling her.

"Take it to Leah. She will know. Tell her . . . *they* came. Four of them, and knocked me out. When I awoke, Irmgard was dead. Dead. Terrible . . ."

Now he wept, but she was afraid to touch him. "Oh, Rudy. Poor dear Rudy."

"And they had done *this*." He held up his hand again. "But I crawled away in the night. Back streets. Shadows. Irmgard gave me the papers before. They are in the case—" He shuddered. "With the passports."

"Passports?" Elisa gasped. Suddenly all the months and years of Rudy's behavior played back to her like a familiar melody with a new interpretation. He had been smuggling passports in his violin case! Long absences from the rest of the orchestra, disappearances and days in hiding when she had thought he had simply lost at cards and couldn't pay his debts.

Rudy almost smiled as he saw understanding flash across her face. "Yes. Passports, Elisa. Last year. In the station at Prague. When I gave you the Guarnerius . . . what happened when the train was stopped for customs check in Weimar?"

The memory of the vulture-like inspector came back to her. He had waved her through. The violin case and her suitcase had been taken behind a screen, and . . . and what? "The Nazi inspector—"

"One of us. Dead now. Gestapo got him. Shot his assistant in the station when he tried to run. The inspector was not so lucky . . . like me. Eight passports you carried to him, and the rest—including your own father's passport—you brought them to your house. To your father."

Elisa shook her head in disbelief. How could any of this be true? "My father?" she asked with a cry.

"Theo Lindheim." Rudy said the name slowly. "*Lindheim*. A good man. Good."

"You *knew*, then? About me? About Papa?"

Rudy could only nod. He struggled for breath as he spoke. "Irmgard."

He said the name of the dead woman. "She got it all for us . . . his file. They knew, the Gestapo knew, he was helping us."

Of course. She remembered the night they arrested him. Hadn't they said they had questions about his donations to Zionism? But her mother had assumed it was something she had done.

"They will never let him go." Rudy's voice was barely audible. "Like me." He let his broken hand rise and fall like a torn flag.

"He is *alive*?" She begged as the life seemed to ebb from Rudy, "Please! Please, Rudy! Rudy! Is my father alive?"

He turned his eyes on her in one final effort. "*Dachau!*" He whispered; then he closed his eyes and lapsed into unconsciousness.

There was no need to call a doctor—no need for the money she had stuffed into her handbag. Rudy Dorbransky would be dead before she could reach her home, before she could dial a number on the telephone— possibly before she reached the bottom of the stairs in this grim and stinking place. She had never seen a man die before. But Elisa knew that this morning, Rudy would be mourned only by the anxious young prostitute who rushed in after Elisa left the room. Privately Elisa would grieve; members of the orchestra secretly would lament, but Vienna would celebrate the death of this race defiler. No doubt the papers would say he had held off police in a desperate battle that lasted for several hours in the heart of the Seventh District. Someone would think of some reasonable excuse for the condition of the body. Bullet holes would be conveniently provided, and there would be a celebration.

It had begun. Just as she had seen it begin in Berlin in 1933. . . . Murphy had been right all along. Yes. Vienna too.

Elisa's eyes were dry as she rounded the corner of her own street. *Dachau!* echoed in her mind, driving out the sight of the dawn's first pink banners in the eastern sky. *My father is alive.* If being in such a place was living. Her father had taken part in all those activities Elisa had feared in Leah's little Zionist meetings. He had not sold his soul like Faust, and yet the flames of Satan scorched him even now. *Dachau!*

She did not know what to do. There was much that would happen in Vienna the next few days. Mourning. Celebration. The triumph of evil men over good. When it had settled down, Elisa would go to the Musikverein to the case where Haydn's skull grinned out at the music students. The Guarnerius was safe there until then.

———

Murphy watched the news from Vienna clatter over the teletype of the INS offices in Paris. Timmons had flown in two days before from Berlin, and Johnson was coming Christmas Eve. Berlin was a gloomy place of long food lines and glum people pressed into participation in the torchlight processions with the mobs of Hitler youth and S.S. hordes. Nobody in the news service wanted to spend Christmas in Berlin this year.

Holding a steaming mug of coffee in both hands, Murphy stared into the cup as Timmons read the terrible story of Rudy Dorbransky, the Jew who had fallen in love with the Nazi's wife.

Timmons sounded almost amused. "Boy, this one has it all! Attempted murder, by the female's enraged brother, of course. Then suicide—the enraged brother again. Then the girl friend gets enraged and tries to break it off, and the boyfriend bumps *her* off! The civilian vigilante committee cornered this guy in some seedy brothel in the Seventh District this morning. Bumped *him* off and caught a prostitute in the cross fire. Killed her, too. Everybody dead. Like something out of—" Timmons thought, trying to make a comparison that seemed appropriate. *"Phantom of the Opera!"*

Murphy sipped his coffee as though the news was only news, but inside he was churning. "I interviewed Rudy Dorbransky." He glanced at his briefcase. He still carried the notes. "That guy was no killer."

"Ah, come on, Murph," Timmons blew his nose loudly. "You never know what a guy'll do for a dame. I mean, I've seen the most seemingly calm joe go absolutely nuts. You don't know . . . this guy might've gone crazy when she said he wasn't the one for her."

Murphy frowned. He was certainly not going to go nuts over a dame. Not even Elisa Linder. He had already made up his mind about that. "I'm telling you, the guy was not the type."

"Says here he was a real ladies' man. Drunk. Gambler. Sounds like the type to me."

"Don't believe everything you read in the news." Murphy took another sip of coffee, scalding his mouth. "Reminds me of the day after Hitler took over in 1933. Remember?"

"Nope," Timmons answered truthfully. "I wasn't paying attention."

"The Nazis burned down the Reichstag. That's like burning down the Senate building."

"Why'd they do that? The guy won."

"They wanted to make a point." He smiled at the irony. "You see, the Nazis only won with one third of the vote. So they wanted to emphasize that they were right about the rotten Bolsheviks and Jews."

Timmons was interested now. "How'd they do that?"

"They burned the place down themselves and arrested a Jew. The guy was innocent. But he got convicted all the same."

Timmons squinted into the light fixture as though something profound were written there. "Reminds me of the time I wanted to get my big brother in trouble. Gave myself a bloody nose and screamed that he did it."

Murphy nodded. The comparison was apt. "Well, I don't believe Rudy Dorbransky did it."

"Too bad you didn't stick around to find out, Murphy. You missed a great scoop."

"I don't care." He leaned back and put his feet up. He was lying. He did care. The news made him sick. Just like German bombs had made him sick in Madrid. But he wasn't going to show Timmons. He didn't even want to admit it to himself. "I'm on vacation, anyway. Besides, until I get assigned and paid, I'm not interested. Right?"

The door to the editorial office slammed behind him. "You gotta have an assignment, huh, Murphy?" The voice of Eddie Griffith boomed louder than the rattle of the wires. "Well, we just got a call from Winston Churchill!" He swore, a long line of unrelated words that somehow conveyed his excitement.

Murphy turned to glare at the cigar-chewing INS editor who looked as if he might have spent the first half of his fifty years in the boxing ring. "So what?"

"So you're not on vacation, Murphy. Churchill is with some high-and-mighty in the British government, and they want to talk to you." He swore again. "Only *you*, John Murphy!" He imitated a curtsy, pulling out the sides of his baggy trousers. "So get off your duff, your Lordship. I got a call in for your ticket to Cannes tomorrow."

Thomas already had his ticket to Vienna tucked away in his pocket when he entered the vast hall of the Notre Dame Cathedral. The vaulted ceiling seemed to reach toward heaven. Light streamed through the colors of the leaded windows, only to be diffused and lost as it reached upward. The huge auditorium seemed strangely empty this January morning, although voices echoed from one of the many alcoves where saints gazed down on flickering votive candles.

Thomas had no trouble finding Ernst vom Rath. He knelt, as if in prayer, before the statue of Our Lady. Thomas knelt beside him and was uncertain for a moment if Ernst had noticed him. And then, the pale, fine-boned embassy secretary spoke in an almost holy whisper.

"Canaris sends word that the moment has come." Ernst did not look at Thomas, but raised his eyes briefly to Mary. "I am to remind you that you have promised to answer when called."

A cold wave of excitement passed through Thomas. Every word that Admiral Canaris had spoken to him a year ago in Berlin came back with a clarity that made him tremble.

"This may be your death warrant," Canaris had said.

"You have not yet said what is required of me."

"I am not yet certain what is required of you. But I know you must swear by your duty . . . "

"Duty to what? To whom?"

"Your conscience. Only that."

For a year, Thomas had hoped and prayed that Admiral Canaris's promise to call him to duty would become a reality. Now, as he knelt beside Ernst vom Rath in this quiet place, he wanted to shout with the joy of what he heard.

"The generals—Bomburg, Von Fritch and the others—" Ernst's voice was barely audible. "They say the madman must be stopped."

So someone in the German High Command has drawn the line! How can Hitler be stopped? What must I do? A thousand questions flooded Thomas's mind, but he did not dare speak for fear of breaking the spell of Ernst's words.

"Hitler, Himmler, the S.S. have sent orders to the Nazis of Austria," Ernst continued as he fingered the beads of his rosary. "They have a plan. They have chosen a Jew who will kill German Ambassador von Papen."

"Kill their own ambassador?"

"He is unpopular with the S.S. They want him out of the way in Vienna. And Hitler wants an excuse to blame the Jews for disorder in Austria. Then he will march."

"Mein Gott!" Thomas raised his eyes toward a crucifix just beyond the alcove. *So von Papen was to be the sacrifice!*

"There is but one hope." Ernst looked at Thomas for the first time. "We must reach the British with word of this or Austria will be gone. Hitler will be firmly entrenched in his power."

Yes! To stop Hitler—this appealed to Thomas's conscience. "What must I do?"

"The British foreign secretary, Anthony Eden, is in Cannes on holiday. Winston Churchill will join him there. You must go to them. Warn them that the German High Command is ready to act if only they can have the promise of the British to back them. They will take control of the Chancellery, and *arrest Hitler*! But they must know that Britain and France will stand firm. No appeasement to Hitler! When they capitulate, it only serves to strengthen his image! The British Foreign Secretary Eden is a man in favor of strength. God has brought him here to France at this moment! You must reach him, and tell him to warn the Austrians about the plot against von Papen." He handed a folded slip of paper to Thomas, who put the note into his pocket.

"When will this happen?"

"Soon. There is not a moment to waste. Tell them the German High Command is ready to act. On the paper is the address of the Nazi headquarters in Vienna. They will find the dispatches from Germany there. They will find *proof!*"

Thomas felt drunk from the rush of adrenalin that surged through him. Perhaps Germany's headlong dash into war could be stopped, after all. Admiral Canaris had *not* forgotten his duty to conscience either. "Who in the High Command . . . ?"

Ernst smiled slightly and gazed upward, pressing his hands together in a prayer of thanks. "You would be surprised, I think, to know how many—and how influential—are the German leaders who support our cause." His voice dropped to a whisper. "But it is better for everyone,"

Ernst said, "if the names are not known. You cannot tell what you do not know."

Thomas nodded. He knew that vom Rath's words were true. The S.S. had eyes and ears everywhere.

"Plans have been made to bring Hitler to trial," Ernst concluded. "You must tell them all of this. We must have their promise that Britain will stand by their pledge to Austria in spite of what Italy might do. *Tell them,* Thomas. They must stand by their pledge!"

Beads of sweat formed on Thomas's forehead as Ernst vom Rath crossed himself and rose from his knees. "I will leave tonight," Thomas said, mentally calculating how he could cash in his ticket to Vienna in exchange for a ticket to Cannes. Perhaps, if all went as planned, Thomas could go to Vienna and explain how he had been a part of the final overthrow of Nazi tyranny. *Then she will know!*

"Stay here," Ernst whispered. "Fifteen minutes. We must not ride back together." He turned on his heel and walked briskly from the great cathedral.

Thomas stayed longer than fifteen minutes. He stayed on his knees, his heart raised in hope of guidance and success. Surely God would hear. Surely he would answer such a prayer!

Murphy stepped out of the elevator of the plush resort in Cannes, France, at the same moment a tall, proud-looking man about his own age emerged from the room occupied by Winston Churchill.

"God direct you, gentlemen," he said in a voice tinged with a German accent and full of deep emotion. He bowed slightly, an aristocratic bow, then shut the door behind himself as Murphy pretended to look for another room number on the doors that lined the hallway.

The German, darkly handsome with clear blue eyes, looked at him, and Murphy saw both fear and suspicion cross the rugged face. The question *Gestapo?* flashed in the blue eyes, and then anger caused his lips to press together tightly.

Something is up, thought Murphy, and he was pleased that he had chosen this day and this moment for his interview with Anthony Eden and Winston Churchill. The German put his hat on and waited impatiently for the elevator. *Definitely German. Military bearing. Puts his hat on indoors, even if he is dressed as a civilian. Yes, German. Aristocratic. Military.*

As the German stepped onto the elevator and the doors clanked shut, Murphy walked back toward Churchill's suite. He did not knock until the groaning motor of the lift carried the German away.

Churchill answered the door himself with a suddenness that almost startled Murphy. He was dressed in a suit with a bow tie, and his face seemed flushed with excitement. Behind him, Anthony Eden, tall and handsome, stood gazing out to sea, his hands clenched behind his back.

"Oh." Churchill's voice sounded disappointed. "Of course. Yes, Murphy. I nearly forgot our appointment." His words seemed unusually clipped, and he did not ask Murphy in. "Mind if we make it another time? Something has come up. Perhaps tomorrow."

"Sure. I'll be here." Now it was Murphy's turn to be disappointed.

Anthony Eden did not turn around, but he called over his shoulder, "No, Winston. Let's proceed with the interview, shall we? Perhaps we have more to say now, eh?"

Churchill moved his bulk to one side, holding the door open for Murphy. "Yes, well, we already know you can write, Murphy. You've done a fairly decent job of reporting where Great Britain's appeasement policies have led." He drew in his breath sharply as though he was trying to calm himself. "John Murphy, I would like to introduce you to Foreign Secretary Anthony Eden." He smiled as Eden turned around. "Unfortunately, for the purpose of your story, I can only call him a *high British government official.* And in your story he must be referred to as your *source.* You do understand?"

Murphy nodded and extended his hand to Eden. The handshake was firm, the expression intense, almost brooding. "I am sorry I was unable to meet with you in London," Eden said, indicating that Murphy should sit down. "My position makes it nearly impossible to meet with newsmen and discuss policies with any openness at all. Here, perhaps we can talk more frankly." He paused and looked at Churchill and the two exchanged an unspoken understanding. "We can perhaps better explain the need for Britain and France to stand firm against Hitler's aggression. In London, of course, where Neville Chamberlain hopes that international issues may be settled by a nice chat over tea and crumpets, I could not tell you what I believe will save us from yet another devastating war. If you do not use my name, Mr. Murphy, the world will be better off."

Murphy nodded and took out his notebook. "I gave my word to Mr. Churchill. I am good to my promise."

"Yes. Yes, I believe you are." Eden and Churchill took chairs opposite Murphy. "The bully on the block will not be stopped by tea and crumpets, Mr. Murphy. He has an appetite that would never be satisfied if he devoured the whole world. With that in mind, let me say that the Foreign Office is painfully aware that great explosions occur by the lighting of one spark when there are piles of explosives stacked everywhere. And there are, indeed, heaps and mountains of explosives in Europe. The trick is, to take the fire out of the hand of Hitler without igniting the bomb ourselves."

Throughout the interview, Murphy could not shake the feeling that the young German he had met in the hallway had something to do with stealing Hitler's fire. But he did not ask. He simply took notes, allowing Eden to say what was safe and circumspect. Perhaps there would be a more appropriate moment to ask about the German. Murphy hoped the man would be close at hand when the final story broke.

29

The Concertmaster's Legacy

The issue of Rudy Dorbransky's guilt or innocence had been settled in the cafes of Vienna long before the police finished asking questions.

Vienna society could certainly forgive a man for murdering his mistress in a moment of passion. After all, hadn't a certain Hapsburg Crown Prince done the same thing to his mistress and then killed himself at Maerling Palace outside of Vienna? Austria had forgiven Prince Rudolf, although that page of Hapsburg history was still discussed over glasses of Grinzing wine. But Vienna would not, and could not, forgive the handsome concertmaster. No. Rudy Dorbransky was guilty past forgiveness—not of an affair with a married woman but of mixing affairs of the heart with dangerous affairs of state. After all, Dorbransky was not a prince; he was a Jew. Jews had no business falling in love with Aryan women—most of Vienna agreed with Herr Hitler on that point.

And so, the city simmered on an open flame. Rudy Dorbransky had gotten what he deserved, and now the Jews of Vienna would get a warning. They must remember *Biedermeier*! They must remember where they belonged in society! All of this was discussed and agreed upon as correct even in the most genteel of the Viennese cafes over strong cups of Turkish coffee.

It took the members of the secret Nazi party to turn the issue into action, however. As polite society raised their eyebrows and whispered the latest gossip about the sordid affair, Captain Leopold's men drained their steins of beer and grabbed their clubs and rubber truncheons on the way out the door.

A five-minute walk from St. Stephan's great cathedral lay the Judengasse district, a part of Vienna since the sixteenth century. There Leah and Shimon lived near the synagogues; here the civilian gangs of Captain Leopold chose to make their point.

The newspaper accounts were very matter-of-fact in their stories:

Two young Jewish men, scholars at the Yeshiva school in the Ju-dengasse, were attacked after they left the synagogue last night. Shouting slogans against the Jews, a group of Nazi sympathizers beat Shaul Neiman and Philip Thrupstein, then broke windows and scrawled warnings on the walls of the synagogue and several apartment buildings in the area. Shaul Neiman was dead at the scene by the time the ambulance arrived, and Philip Thrupstein is in critical condition at Rothschild Hospital. Thrupstein and other witnesses at the scene reported that the gang numbered between seventy-five and a hundred men. The State Police are still investigating. It is advised that citizens not having urgent business in the Judengasse district should avoid traveling there at this time.

Other than this one paragraph, there was no other mention of the incident. After all, hadn't the Jew Dorbransky gotten what he deserved? And shouldn't other Jews be made aware that they would also get what they deserved unless they remembered their place?

Overnight, posters appeared on the streetlamps along the Ring: *Avenge the blood of Irmgard Schüler! Jews out of Vienna now!* Such signs, decorated with swastikas, were torn down by the Shupos, the Austrian police, by noon. But Vienna had gotten the message. So had the Jews of Vienna.

Elisa tucked her head against the cold wind and hurried across Karlsplatz toward the Musikverein. Wisely, she had waited a day before going to the building, as Rudy had instructed her. She had waited alone in her apartment, expecting a knock and an interrogation from the Shupos. Somehow she had been overlooked; no police had come to her door.

Today, as Rudy's body was cremated for shipment back to Poland, the curious citizens of the city crammed into St. Stephan's Cathedral for a final tribute to Irmgard Schüler. The bells tolled out the years of her short and tragic life. Elisa counted the haunting, ominous clang as she quickened her pace—now, almost jogging toward the portals of the Musikverein. The bell tolled for the last time as she reached the steps. *Twenty-seven! Irmgard was only twenty-seven!* Elisa shuddered, but not from the cold. The words of Rudy echoed in her mind. *They* had killed the beautiful young woman, not Rudy. And then *they* had made certain that Rudy would be blamed, and all the Jews of Judengasse with him. *They* had done it all, just as *they* in Germany now held her father!

The back door of the building, the student's entrance, was open. Elisa slipped inside and stood for a moment as she listened to the echo of a piano from the practice rooms downstairs. The usual hooting, thrumming clamor of practicing students was silenced; they had probably all gone to the spectacle of the funeral. They would go out afterward for lunch and beer and make the occasion a sort of holiday, no doubt.

Panicked, Elisa stood rooted for a moment. She looked down at her own violin case. It was empty. *It will not do,* she reasoned, *if I am being watched, to enter the Musikverein without a violin case and leave with one in hand.* If she was being watched, certainly *they* would notice such a thing and stop her to discover that she carried the violin of the murderer Dorbransky. The thought made her heart drum a warning in her ears. She wavered, considering going home and forgetting it all. Rudy's words— frightening words—could not free her father. She could call Thomas and tell him that she had heard that "someone" had seen her father in *Dachau.*

Dachau! How could one terrible word from the lips of a dying man change her life so entirely? Before that word, when there had been no hope, she had drifted in an aimless, unfocused yearning that someday there might be word from her father. The thought had become an unreal dream that she had linked somehow with Thomas von Kleistmann. *"Maybe he will rescue him. If Papa is alive, maybe Thomas . . ."* This unreal dream had ebbed and flowed with the passing of every holiday and anniversary of the last year.

Now, just when she had let go of hope and yearning, there came a word of such hopelessness, murmured in such despair, that Elisa wondered why it had awakened hope in her again. *Dachau! Papa is there. Alive! Yes, that is hope!*

From the first days of Hitler's reign, that name had become a symbol of all that embodied hell. It *was* hell, torment encased in charged barbed wire and block houses and machine guns. And it was here on earth. In the terror of his last moments on earth, perhaps Faust had glimpsed *Dachau!* Perhaps in his vision of the *Inferno,* Dante had glimpsed the demons in the guard towers and those who walked with whips among the prisoners. And yet this inescapable inferno of Nazi brutality and terror had suddenly given Elisa hope! Theo Lindheim was alive; he was there, in Dachau! In the deepest abyss in Germany, her father breathed and hoped and prayed for his family. Elisa could feel his thoughts, even now, as she walked down the narrow hallway. The practice rooms she passed were empty and silent. The sound of her heels followed her toward the glass case where the skull of the composer Haydn grinned out at students and musicians. Elisa could see the skull in the dim light at the far end of the corridor. Hollow cavities stared at her as she approached the case. Long, yellowed teeth were clenched tightly as Haydn stood guard over the secret of Rudy Dorbransky. *Dachau!* There was life and hope in this apparition of death.

She halted a few feet in front of the skull of the great composer. For a hundred years the head of Haydn had watched as the young musicians of the Musikverein had grown old in these halls until they became like him, like Rudy. Elisa was perspiring. She stared back at the blackness of the eye sockets, the hollow, unseeing darkness that seemed to see everything . . . *everyone!* And in the eyes of death, everyone looked the same. Somehow, Elisa saw herself grinning out of the glass box. Had Rudy hidden the violin here as a warning? Had he known? Had he stood here and looked at death and seen himself, too?

She looked back over her shoulder, feeling eyes peering at her from behind. But there was no one, only the faint melody of a piano playing somewhere in the maze. Perhaps it was Haydn playing. A cold chill swept through her, and she drew her breath in and stepped forward as though asking permission to take the precious violin of Rudy Dorbransky. Dear Rudy, now in ashes in a baggage car on the way back to his mother in Warsaw. *What is to become of me?* She asked the question although she saw the answer in the glass box before her. *Sooner or later, Elisa.... And so, you see, if you take the violin and find the secret papers, you are in no more danger than if you simply grow old. This is your future, Elisa. Sooner or later.* The sound of the piano stopped. She shuddered and reached behind the wooden base of the skull's little glass casket. She almost hoped that the violin would not be there, but the familiar leather beneath her fingers caused her to gasp as she pulled it free. Then, as though leaving a counterfeit offering to the silent composer, she slid her empty case back where Rudy's had been.

Haydn watched as she retreated hurriedly down the hall. His sightless eyes had watched for a hundred years. By now it was certain that even the very young and beautiful walked the same dark corridor, *sooner or later.*

Herr Haupt peered around the corner of his door as Elisa entered the building. He looked grim, almost frightened as he called to her. "Eleeeza! P-s-s-s-st!"

The violin case felt hot and dangerously alive in her hand. She tried to look nonchalant on her way home from the Musikverein, but she felt as though the case would jump out of her hands and fall open on the sidewalk, spilling Rudy's precious papers out for everyone to see. The walk had been a nightmare, and now Elisa dreaded having to talk to the old concierge of the building. "Good morning, Herr Haupt." She attempted to sound cheerful, but somehow the words fell flat.

"Not such a good morning, I think, Eleeeza! Have you heard the news this morning?"

She shook her head. She waited with one foot on the step and her free hand on the banister as he told her. She did not want to hear the news, but Herr Haupt would follow her up to her doorstep if she didn't listen now, so she stood ready to make her break when he was finished.

"Oy Vay!" he exclaimed. "She has not heard the news!"

"No. Please, Herr Haupt, I am tired."

"The authorities are expecting more trouble in the Judengasse. Everyone is warned. The Nazis are planning something after the funeral today. This Dorbransky fellow has brought trouble on his own people."

Elisa did not reply as he continued.

"The authorities have just got the wires back into the Judengasse—"

"Good. Then I can call my friend and check—"

He held up a hand for silence. "Wait! They have just got the wires up when along comes more fellows and cuts them down again. They have also cut off the electric. I lived there for my first twenty years, you know. Before they had electric, we managed. Life is not so terrible without electric. Your friends will be fine unless they maybe go out into the street. The Shupos expect more trouble."

So that was the news. She nodded, feeling cut off herself. There was no one but Leah that she could talk to about all this. And Rudy had instructed her to take the case to Leah alone. "Danke, Herr Haupt." She did not give him a chance to say more. Instead, she ran up the steps and into her own apartment.

"Fraülein!" The little man called desperately after her. She pretended not to hear him. "Eleeeza! Wait . . . !"

She had already inserted her key in the lock, but to her horror, the door was unlocked. Suddenly it opened and before her a tall policeman in uniform was staring down at her. "What . . . ?" She was at once frightened and indignant. How dare this man come into the privacy of her apartment! Then she saw that he was not alone. Two others were with him. Both of them were dressed in civilian clothes—dark blue suits and scuffed black shoes run down at the heels.

"Fraülein Linder," the tall policeman began apologetically, "I am afraid we shock you by our presence." He smiled and seemed embarrassed. The two men in civilian dress simply stared back at her as though *she* were the intruder.

"Who let you in?" she demanded, angry at their impudence.

"Herr Haupt."

"Then Herr Haupt should be discharged. It is his duty to oversee our apartments, not let strangers in."

"I'm afraid he had no choice." The smile was cold now. "You see, we have interviewed everyone in the orchestra but you." He stepped aside to let her into her own apartment.

"Yes. I was ill the night this all happened."

"Ill?" asked one of the civilians.

She had said it now, and must not change her story. The violin inside the case seemed to shout at her. *Be calm! Stay calm! If not calm, then angry* . . . "Yes. I got a letter from my mother in Prague. My brother is in the hospital there, and they will not be coming to Vienna for the holidays. I am committed to stay here through the season. The news made me ill."

"But"—the second civilian checked his notebook—"we have been told that you left here for a period of hours."

"To make a phone call." Elisa wondered if they could hear her heart beat.

All three men looked at the telephone sitting on the kitchen table. "A phone call?" asked the man in uniform.

"International. You can check if you like. I was at the telephone office. My call was placed shortly after seven in the evening and put through after eight." Her matter-of-fact tone seemed to convince them. They looked at one another.

"Did you see Rudy Dorbransky at any time that evening?"

Elisa stared at the three of them, suddenly reminded of three crows perched on a wire. "No, but I wish I had seen him. I would have told him to give up his silly infatuation. He was the most talented and sensitive of all the musicians I have known—"

"You knew him well, then?"

Careful, Elisa. She set the violin case down beside the small floral sofa. "Nobody knew Rudy Dorbransky well, Officer," she said, letting her sorrow overflow in her voice.

"And did you know Frau Schüler?"

"Only by sight. Ridiculous woman!" The scorn sounded authentic. If she didn't know the truth about Irmgard Schüler, Elisa might have continued to feel the scorn. "Now she's ruined a lot of lives, hasn't she? Yes. If I had seen Rudy that night, I would have told him—"

The first civilian-dressed policeman studied his notes. "You came to the concert hall that night. But you were not well?"

"My friend Leah had a solo. I wanted to hear. . . ."

"But you were ill? And still you were out traipsing about?"

"I am a violinist," she said arrogantly, acting the part of a prima donna. "I had bad news from home, as I told you. My hands were shaking. I was shaking all over. I couldn't have played. I couldn't have held my violin, but I didn't want to stay home alone, either. The manager insisted I go back home, so I did."

Again they exchanged glances. She shoved her hands into her pockets, hoping that the three men would not see them trembling now. The violin case seemed to scream for attention, yet none of the men seemed to notice it. Rudy's violin. The case filled with secret papers. Its very presence in her apartment would somehow tie her into the intrigue. She already knew what *they* were capable of doing. Against her will now, the vision of Rudy's hand came back to her. She flexed her fingers, then clenched her fist. Of course his body had to be cremated. There was too much to explain otherwise.

She glared back at them. Were these men Nazis, too? She had heard there were secret members of the Nazi party within the Austrian police force. It was impossible to tell by looking. How could she know such a thing? Had these men, perhaps, been part of his murder?

The shorter of the two civilian-dressed men cleared his throat. "Fraülein Linder," he began. "We heard from certain sources that you were on occasion a financial resource for Rudy Dorbransky."

"He always needed money," she nodded. The violin case almost rocked with the news it carried. Elisa did not look at it. "If you . . . gentlemen are going to stay a while, would you like a cup of tea? It is very cold out, and I need a cup." She did not wait for their answer. She opened the door, concealing the violin case behind it; then she tossed her coat and gloves onto the bed. Calmly she walked past them into the kitchen to put the kettle on as though they had just dropped in for tea.

The short man followed her to the kitchen. "There is no delicate way to ask this, Fraülein—"

She knew in advance what he would ask. The question amused her. "Then simply ask."

"Were you and Dorbransky ever . . . were you . . . lovers?"

"No." She smiled patronizingly. "And no again. We all knew about Rudy's outside interests. Gambling and women. My interest in Rudy was as a musician. Such talent! Wasted over a woman!" Suddenly she felt tears sting her eyes. *"Wasted!"* She let the tears flow. She covered her face with her hands and sank down into a small wooden chair beside the table. "Now this! Horrible! Horrible! What next? And what do you want with me? If you don't leave me alone, give me some rest. I may never play again!"

"We have interviewed everyone in the orchestra, Fraülein Linder." The voice of the uniformed officer was gentle. "We simply overlooked you. The incident is really cut and dried except for a few small details. Dorbransky had a reputation in this city. This is not much of a surprise to us, although I am certain it is a shock to you. We expected Rudy Dorbransky to end up in some such way. If that is any comfort to you," he finished awkwardly.

"No, it isn't!" Elisa's tears were real. "No comfort at all. The orchestra has lost a fine violinist. Possibly one of the finest of our century!" She did not dare mention what she was really weeping about. *His hands! How could they do that to such hands?*

"Thank you. Yes." One of the civilian-dressed officers cleared his throat nervously. "We simply had no choice but to come here since you were not with the others. Simply routine."

"Then go away and leave me alone!" She demanded through her sobs. "First my brother, and now this!" She stretched out a trembling hand; she did not have to pretend to shake. "How am I supposed to play when I come home and find police in my apartment? I will tell the maestro! He will have a word to say to your superiors!"

The three men had begun backing away from her presence. Now the shortest man threw open the door and tipped his hat in farewell. "Perhaps this was not the best time to come," he said by way of apology. "Goodbye, Fraülein! I hope your brother recovers!"

Elisa stared at them as they backed out of the room. She hated them for their questions and for their intrusion. Surely they had seen Rudy's hands! They had viewed his torn body and broken teeth. And yet the Austrian Shupos had come *here* to interview her instead of finding the Nazi butchers who had mangled him and murdered a woman besides!

And what about that Jewish boy in critical condition at Rothschild Hospital, and his friend who lay cold and still at the morgue right now? *Why aren't the Shupos making arrests of the real criminals in Austria? Why have they come here?*

She wanted to shout at them, but she did not. The door clicked shut behind them, but she could not even find the strength to get up and slip the bolt into place. She sat, still sobbing, for what seemed like a long time. She had gotten herself into something much deeper and more frightening than she could have dreamed of. Hadn't she left all that in Berlin? No, Berlin had followed her here. It had followed them all. She felt no sense of relief that the Shupos had left. She was still seeing the grinning skull before her, and Rudy's strong, capable fingers dancing on the strings of the Guarnerius.

The tea in Elisa's cup sat cold and untouched on the table before her. It had been nearly an hour since the Shupos had left her apartment. She still had not opened Rudy's violin case. She would wait, she decided, to see if they came back.

Minutes ticked slowly by and Elisa realized that she could not remember the faces of the officers who had been in her flat. She could visualize shining buttons of the uniform, scuffed black shoes and bulging vests; but try as she might, she could not remember even the vaguest detail of their faces. The thought frightened her even more as the hour passed and they did not return. She must not have ever looked at the faces. Her eyes must have darted to buttons and vests and shoes and the violin, then back along the same route. She had looked above their heads, around them, at the floor and the ceiling and the door, but never at their faces. What if one of them followed her now? How would she know who it was? The two in civilian clothes—one tall, the other shorter. But how would she recognize them? By their shoes? And had they noticed how unsettled her eyes were? Did they suspect?

She sat motionless as these thoughts assailed her. She was so alone. She was even uncertain now if she should contact Leah. What if they were watching her apartment right now? Rudy had been so smooth and confident in his deception, and yet look what had happened to him! Even with his violin case stuffed with secret documents, he had looked every man straight in the eye and splashed his famous smile around among the women. No one had ever suspected him, and yet, look at his finish!

Elisa rose slowly from the table and pulled the door back. The violin case, scuffed and innocuous, was still there. It did not shout a warning or burst apart as she stared down at it. And yet, inside, Rudy had said there were passports and secret files from the Gestapo. *Dachau!* That word again. *Dachau! He is alive! My father is alive!*

She picked up the case. It felt no heavier than it had ever felt. Always when Rudy had left it with her, she had guarded it because of the priceless Guarnerius violin it contained. Now, she knew it held something far more precious.

Laying it on the table beside her untouched teacup, she drew a deep breath, then popped the locks open. The sound of the snap startled her. Rudy had opened this case last. *While he still had his fingers and his smile. Why? Why, God?* She closed her eyes briefly at the thought. How many times had she seen him swing the case around and strum it playfully like a ukulele as he sang some ridiculous American song he had learned from one of his lady friends. He had played his role so well that no one could have known. She certainly had never suspected him of being anything more than a talented, unscrupulous playboy. But *they* had known!

She tried not to think of the baggage car on its way to Warsaw. She tried not to imagine the handful of ashes that was all that was left of Rudy. She drew herself up and found courage in the word *Dachau!* "Papa!" she said, opening the lid of the case.

The Guarnerius was still draped in its blue silk scarf. Two bows were attached to the top of the case. Beautiful bows . . . Rudy had been so proud of them. *"From Paris. Ebony and gold. Here, Elisa. You want to try a real bow, this is it."* Then he had pretended to fence with her, jumping onto the conductor's stand and waving the bow like a pirate with a sword. *"And look,"* he laughed. *"The bow maker put a picture of himself in the frog. He looks a bit like a frog. You think that's why they call it a frog?"* Everyone had laughed at the show. It was so easy to laugh at Rudy.

There were good memories inside the case. Elisa found herself laughing and crying at the same time as she pulled back the silk scarf revealing the glowing wood of the Guarnerius. No papers tumbled out onto the table. The violin rested quietly in its green velvet nest. *Where are the papers?* She lifted the instrument and looked beneath it. There was nothing there. She checked the small compartments on either side of the case. Still no papers. No hint of Dachau or illegal passports. She pulled open the larger compartment at the top of the case. The registration papers were there. Nothing else. *Nothing!*

Elisa stared down into the empty case. Green velvet. Blue scarf. A violin case was certainly not like a magician's hat, and yet, somehow she kept expecting the promised treasure to materialize. She checked the inside again, opening and closing each little compartment, then running her fingers across the velvet lining to see if she felt anything at all beneath it. There was nothing there but the soft plush velvet beneath her fingers. She placed the instrument back in its nest and tried to peek in through the F-holes. There was nothing inside the violin. She sat down heavily and rested her chin against her hand. For the first time, the thought entered her mind that this had been Rudy Dorbransky's last, terrible joke. Perhaps there had never been any papers at all. No passports. No secret file. But how had Rudy known her real name and that of her father? Could Leah have told him? Would Leah break such a confidence?

Her head throbbed with the disappointment and then tension of the last few days. The violin case held only its precious cargo. She glanced over the registration papers of the Guarnerius. The measurements and the exact description of the scroll and patterns in the wood were listed. Then, at the bottom was a tiny scrawled note in Rudy's handwriting. *"In payment of debt, this instrument is transferred to ownership of Elisa Linder on this date. Dec. 19, 1937. Signed Rudolf Dorbransky."*

Elisa read the words again and again. *"In payment of debt..."* The date was three days before. The date of Rudy's death. Had he known what was about to transpire?

Suddenly exhausted, Elisa closed the case, picked up the instrument, and stumbled off toward her bedroom. It was all too much. The disappointment of the contents and the tension had made her numb and sick.

Perhaps that is why the skull of Haydn had grinned so hideously at her. Perhaps he knew, like Rudy, that this was all a horrible joke.

A dull ache throbbed in the back of Elisa's head. Rudy had once joked with her that he would leave the Guarnerius to her in his will. Now it was hers, through circumstances so haunting and horrible that she wanted only to rid herself of the priceless instrument.

How she longed for the reassuring presence of Murphy! He would know just what to do. He could tell her. But he was gone, now, probably forever. After all, how many times could a man be turned away and called back again in the same week?

She put the violin out of sight in the closet, then sat forlornly on the edge of the bed. She picked up the small box that Murphy had left for her. It was the only reminder that it was Christmas. She lifted one angel from the jumble and held it up to the light from the window, turning it around. There seemed to be something familiar about the features of the carving. She picked up another one and held it beside the first; then, with a gasp, she tore through the top drawer of her bureau until she found the figure of Mary and Joseph that Franz had given to her the year before.

She had almost forgotten the love with which he had carved the figures. Side by side, there was no mistaking the similarity of the angels and the face of Mary. How touched she had been by the light in Joseph's eyes as he looked at Mary! And Franz had looked at Elisa with the same tender light. He had held her with the same hope. She had left him so easily, so cruelly. Elisa could still remember his anger at the station. No doubt Murphy now felt the same anger. It seemed strange to her that Murphy's last message to her had been a box of angels carved by another man who had once loved her.

First Franz. Now Murphy. Good men, both of them, and they hated her now. She did not blame them, really, and she was sure that there would be no calling back what she had so carelessly tossed away.

There was no use wishing that Murphy would come and tell her what she must do. He wouldn't come. He couldn't help her. He didn't care anymore.

She frowned and lay back on the bed. There was no one to help her now. Rudy was dead. Leah was in the Judengasse, Murphy gone. Thomas . . .

Her thoughts whirled in a fog of exhaustion and despair. She closed her eyes then, and with the name of Murphy on her lips, she drifted off into a restless sleep.

30

Bloodbath

It was almost four o'clock in the afternoon before Elisa awoke with a start and sat up to look around the room in confusion. A thousand thoughts seemed to tumble in on her at once. Murphy. Thomas. Leah . . . something about Leah! And Rudy! She struggled to free herself from the tangle she had made of her sheets and blankets; then she ran to the closet door and jerked it open to be sure that she hadn't dreamed the whole dreadful thing. No. It was not a dream. The Guarnerius was still locked inside the case, safely, in the closet. No papers. No hope for her father after all.

Still, she could not shake the thought that she might have missed something. She retrieved the instrument and checked the case and the violin again, then slammed the lid in frustration. Even in his pain and suffering, Rudy had told her to take the violin to Leah. Was he capable of misleading her at such a moment, or had his mind simply slipped into the delirium of his battle with death?

Almost mechanically, Elisa obeyed him. She brushed her hair and slipped on her warmest coat, then grabbed the violin case on her way out. There was certainly no reason for her to feel nervous now. There was nothing ominous or secret about the case. It was just like a thousand others in the city of Vienna. As she locked her door behind her, she was reminded with a surge of anger how the old concierge had let the Shupos into her apartment. What good did it do for her to lock the door?

Herr Haupt stuck his head out of his apartment as she passed.

"Have a good Christmas, Fraülein Linder." He did not call her Eleeeza tonight. His greeting reminded her that it was Christmas Eve. She had forgotten that as well in the last few days.

"I will pray there are no surprises waiting for me when I get home tonight," she replied, allowing her indignation to creep into her voice.

"They *made* me open the door, Eleeeza!" he called after her.

She left the glass entry door slightly ajar as she left the building. A blast of cold air answered the old man in her wake.

The great, gleaming city seemed all but shut down. Already families had begun to pull into themselves and the privacy of their own hearths. She had seen Christmas Eve in Vienna before, but never alone. This afternoon, she *felt* alone. She remembered last year, the way Franz Wattenbarger had looked at her with such love and longing. How far away that all seemed now. How they had hoped for some miracle together! With one heart they had imagined Theo sweeping into the little church at Kitzbühel like the shepherd in the story, just in time to worship the Christ Child. But it had not happened, and no amount of wishing could make it so.

She tried to walk quickly across the icy sidewalk. The shoppers were gone. Shops had closed early. Only the cold, cruel wind cut through the streets of the city now. If the mobs had rioted after Irmgard's funeral, there was no evidence of it. Bits of paper littered the streets.

Elisa boarded a nearly empty streetcar. Karlsplatz was also empty. It seemed as though the cold wind had blown all of life from Vienna. The makeshift booths and stalls of the flea market had been emptied, and the merchants had all gone back to their little villages. Elisa thought of the warmth of the Kitzbühel farmhouse, the gentle sound of carols, and the crackling of the fire. So far away.

The trolley rumbled past the State Opera House on Kärtnerstrasse, then on toward the stately spires of St. Stephan's Cathedral in the heart of the Old District. For an instant the clouds broke and afternoon sun streamed down like a spotlight on the roof of St. Stephan's. When she was a child, the colorful zigzag pattern of the shingles had reminded Elisa of a giant gingerbread house decorated with neat rows of icing. *God's gingerbread house,* she had called it.

When her father had disappeared down the narrow lanes of the Tuchlauben to talk business in Yiddish with the Jewish cloth merchants of the district, she and her mother and brothers had wandered for hours within the majestic building. They had listened to the tolling of the enormous Pummerin bell as it had boomed out the hours. Cast from a Turkish cannon, the bell had rattled the stained-glass windows like artillery fire. "So loud God can hear it in heaven and the devil in hell," her mother had said. *But from this place,* Elisa thought, *God can hear even the quietest whisper.*

Just a short walk from *der Steffl,* as the Viennese called St. Stephan's, Leah Goldblatt had grown up listening to the same bell. Perhaps as children, the two little girls had passed in the street and never known that they would eventually find such friendship and love for each other. As a child Leah had attended the synagogue nestling beneath the shadow of St. Stephan's. Elisa had been raised feeling the strangeness of the Jewish culture in which her own father had grown up. The men in their yarmulkes who spoke in such a strange language as they bargained had made her uncomfortable. Little boys with bobbing sidelocks running through the narrow Judengasse had caused her to giggle behind her hand while her mother whispered that she must not stare.

Elisa had not liked the Jewish district of Vienna with its memories of massacres and persecutions. And now she wanted to forget that her father was somehow linked to these people and their tragic history. Did that not also link her in some way?

As the trolley rumbled toward Stephansplatz, she kept her eyes on the roof of the gingerbread cathedral. *Der Steffl* was where she belonged. She tried not to think about the other—her father as a young boy, dressed in black coat and sidelocks; her grandfather like the old men in white beards and black hats on their way to morning prayers. No, she still did not like it. The shadow of the Judengasse had chased her family from Germany. Even though the Lindheims talked and dressed like everyone else; even though her mother was not a Jew and her father had only memories of his life before, this shadow—*non-Aryan; mixed race*—had hounded them with slogans and hatred. In the end, her father's sympathies and Nazi hatred had landed him in Dachau . . . that is, if Rudy had been telling her the truth.

The sky was growing darker as Elisa stepped from the trolley in front of Stephansplatz. Narrow lanes ran off from the cathedral in every direction like a rabbit warren. *Judengasse, Hoher Markt,* the cloth district of *Tuchlauben*, and Leah's little apartment overlooking the *Judenplatz*; Elisa knew the narrow lanes and baroque buildings well. Why, then, did she shudder now at the thought of walking there alone?

She held the violin case tightly and wavered a moment, wanting to run up the broad steps of St. Stephan's, away from the medieval city that sloped away from the hill and wandered down the narrow lanes of crooked houses into the Jewish district of the city.

There were no cars on *Jasomirgott,* the street called "So help me God." Everyone was tucked inside safe and warm. A sudden blast of wind howled around the corner as the street narrowed into a dark lane and tall houses shut out what remained of the afternoon light. The Milchgasse broadened again into the cloth district of Tuchlauben, and Elisa stepped into a doorway to button her coat tightly around her. For a moment, she closed her eyes and thought of her father holding her hand as they had walked from arcade to arcade. The memory was almost too painfully distant to give her pleasure. The attempt to capture the past instead reminded her of the terrible present, and the fact that Berlin, too, had been full of such happy memories for her. Would the pleasant thoughts of Vienna also be swept away by the Nazis? She shook her head to clear her mind, then stepped back out into the biting wind.

Elisa looked up into the windows along the lane. Lights burned, but not Christmas lights. Eight bright candles on the window ledges flickered as she entered the Jewish district. It was Hanukkah here near the Judenplatz—a strange Jewish holiday that she did not know and could not understand. She felt sorry now that she had not at least put up a Christmas tree. Maybe when she got home tonight she would get out the little box of Murphy's angels. She had so hoped that her mother would be with her to decorate.

God, what has happened to me? The world is upside down! The heaviness of her loneliness and the horror of Rudy's death seemed almost crushing as she made her way toward Leah's little flat. Here and there was a boarded window, but other than that, there was little evidence of the rioting that had swept through the area around the Judenplatz. In the dim light of evening, Elisa could see patches of fresh paint on the outside of a few buildings. She could imagine the terrible, obscene words that had been painted there. Germany was decorated for Christmas with such words. No Jewish family in Berlin would dare light a menorah for their holidays.

The lane opened suddenly onto the square of the Judenplatz, and Elisa gasped at what she saw. The synagogue was just ahead. Walls were still splattered with red paint. Or was it the blood of the two young Jewish men attacked here? The sound of strong male voices emanated from within the building as the men of the district chanted their evening prayers and psalms commemorating the festival of lights. In a broad brush stroke, the words *CHRIST KILLERS!* were splashed across the side of the building along with a dozen terrible threats and slogans. Tonight the Jews inside the old synagogue of Vienna were praying for more than some ancient miracle. No doubt they had raised their voices to ask for a new deliverance from persecution.

Here and there around the square, windows were shattered, and an unbroken line of red paint touched every building like a ring of blood. On the facade of the house on Judenplatz 2, there was a relief showing the baptism of Christ. Just beneath that, a plaque told of the terrible events of 1421: two hundred Jews were burned at the stake while rabbis took their own lives by slitting their throats with kosher butcher knives rather than be burned by the Viennese. Elisa shook her head in disbelief. On either side of the lettering a large red swastika was scrawled. *Juden! The day is coming again when your blood will run in these streets!* The words were distinct against the white wall of the house. The hands of the carving of Christ were smeared with red, and above His head was written: *"You will be baptized in blood as you baptized him in blood! Jews leave Vienna!"*

The voices from inside the synagogue did not betray the emotion that must have been felt at such a warning. Was the sound of the great bell of St. Stephan's a sound they dreaded? Elisa glanced up toward Leah's apartment. The dark windows looked down on the statue of Jewish playwright Ephraim Lessing in the center of the square. Then Elisa saw that even the statue had not gone undesecrated. A wide swath of red was splashed across the groin of the statue: *RACE DEFILERS WILL BE CASTRATED.* Her eyes turned to the hand of the statue: the first two fingers of the left hand had been hacked off and red paint smeared on the hand and arm! "Oh, God!" she cried, feeling suddenly ill. "Rudy! Oh, Rudy!" She leaned heavily against the side of the building, uncertain that she could walk past the statue to Leah's apartment. She drew her breath in slowly, trying to control the nausea.

Behind her, she heard a stirring, and turned. Across the plaza she saw the flickering lights of torches as a slow tide of men emerged from the dark lanes and oozed into the Judenplatz. They did not speak or shout, but Elisa heard their feet against the cobblestones. She stood, unable to move forward or run back, as yet another group approached from behind her. Then came the first shout, "Austria for Austrians! Jews out of Vienna! Austria for Aryans! Christ killers! Christ killers!" The cries rolled toward her in a hideous wave of rage and hatred. The words echoed back like the voices of ten thousand in the narrow lane of Judengasse. Elisa ran forward into the Judenplatz as the sound of smashing windows crashed like cymbals amid the tympani of angry voices.

Elisa cried out as a group of men spotted her flight and ran toward her. They had waited, waited until Vienna had slipped inside for Christmas Eve. They had waited until there was no one left at St. Stephan's to see what they would do to the Judenplatz.

"Hund!" a young man shouted at her. *"Idiotic whore!"*

Elisa forced herself to keep going past the mutilated statue of Lessing, on toward Leah's building. Then, as she watched, a rock was thrown and the glass from Leah's window fell to the street. She cried out, but now the noise of boots and shouts, stones and clubs was too great.

Two hundred men converged into one foaming mass before Elisa's eyes. Suddenly they were upon her, and she was caught in the vortex of the whirlpool.

"Hey! Come on!" A young man grabbed her by the arm, grinning. "I've caught a Jewish whore! Come on! Let's teach these Jewish swine what it feels like to have their women violated!"

"Let's teach them a lesson!" Other hands grabbed her as she screamed, knocking the violin case out of her hands.

She could not hear her own screams as she was shoved and pulled onto the cobblestones. Two young men pinned her to the cold ground as someone tore at her coat, sending the buttons flying. She forced herself to look at their faces. *Faces! Remember their faces!* Grinning, leering, crowding over her, the men held their torches high. It was another time, a distant century filled with horrors in the Judenplatz. She was sobbing, screaming her name, but they did not hear her.

"Let's teach them a lesson!" A thin-lipped man with pale skin stretched over prominent cheekbones stooped over her. She could see her own terrified face reflected in the glass of his wire-rimmed spectacles.

Hands tore at her dress, then pulled the cap from her head. Long blond curls tumbled out onto the wet, icy street.

"Sporer!" an angry voice called and the smile faded. "Sporer! Stop!" The crowd parted.

"She's Aryan!" someone said in disgust. "She's not Jewish! Look at her hair!"

She looked up as the attackers released their grip on her arms. Suddenly she recognized the man who had made them stop. He was angry, pushing away the ones who had intended to rape her there in the Judenplatz.

"Elisa!" Otto Wattenbarger shouted.

She could not say his name. She could not say anything. Fear and humiliation had driven words from her. She put out her arms to him and he lifted her up; then he cursed the men around them until they backed away and ran off to find some other prey.

"What is she doing here?" the one called Sporer asked defensively. "In the Jewish district on Christmas?"

"Shut up!" Otto threatened in reply. He pulled her torn coat around her as she leaned heavily against him. "Get out of here, Sporer, or I swear I'll kill you now!"

"We thought she was just another Jewish whore," Sporer shrugged and stalked off.

Otto watched him melt into the violent crowd, now roused to a fever pitch, then turned to Elisa. "I'll get you out of here."

"My violin!" she cried, looking for the instrument. "My violin!"

"Elisa!" He could barely make himself heard as he shouted above the din. "You must not be here! Come, I will take you back. Back to St. Stephan's." He reached down to retrieve her violin case. Brushing it off, he held it tightly as he took her arm in his strong grip. Then she saw the swastika armband tied to his coat.

"No!" she shouted, wrenching herself free. The memory of Rudy came fresh to her mind.

"Elisa!" He grabbed her again. "It's me! *Otto Wattenbarger!* Elisa, I will get you to safety. Out of here! You *must* stay with me!" he said through clenched teeth as he gave her a little shake.

"Otto!" she cried, feeling herself go limp. "God, oh, *God!* Help me!" The tinkle of glass was met by the shouts of young strong men dashing from the synagogue. They, too, had clubs. They had been ready when the Nazis came this time.

Otto propelled her away from the screams and shouts of the street battle. The spires of St. Stephan's loomed ahead in the dusk. He shook her again when they reached the bottom step; then he placed the violin case beside her. "Don't go back in there, Elisa!" he warned. The shouts echoed from the narrow lanes. "Don't go there again, not *ever!*"

The sirens of Austrian police cars shrieked and whirled as they passed Stephansplatz on their way to the riot. Otto left her there, and at the sight of the police, he ripped the armband from his sleeve and walked calmly toward a waiting streetcar on the other side of the platz.

Elisa watched him go, staring after him as he boarded the streetcar, paid his fare, and took a seat near the front with his back to the window. Although it was the same streetcar that would have taken her home, she did not want to share the same space with him. It did not matter that he had saved her from the mob. He had been part of that mob. He had called her attackers by name. They had looked at him with fear and respect.

The discarded swastika armband fluttered across the platz. The streetcar lurched into motion as two more police cars wailed toward the Jewish district. Elisa pulled her torn coat closely around her and climbed the steps of St. Stephan's to take shelter beneath the massive portals until another streetcar arrived at Stephansplatz. *I will remember their faces,* she promised herself. She felt no gratitude toward Otto. He had simply rescued what he thought was an "Aryan" woman. Had he known her father was Jewish, no doubt he would have let Sporer do what he wanted with her, just as they had done what they wanted with Rudy. Poor, dear Rudy. Had Otto been a part of that as well? Had he destroyed the hands and then the man in the name of *Aryan purity?* Was it possible that the son of Karl and Marta Wattenbarger had come to this? Could he be the brother of gentle Franz?

Elisa had not noticed that she was crying. The cold wind stung her cheeks, and she wiped tears away with the back of her hand. Staring after the lights of the streetcar, she remembered the words of Franz as he had told her of the snowflakes on the peaks of the Alps. *There are places I can show you ... two snowflakes so close together ... yet when they melt one runs north, to Germany, and the other runs south.* Two brothers. The same parents. The same house. The same church. And yet, Otto had come to this. No, Elisa was not grateful to Otto. She hated him for the path he had taken, for the power his voice had held among such evil men, for the torn swastika armband, and for the warning he had given to her. There had been a vision of the future in his words: *Don't go there again, not ever.* Somehow his unspoken prophecy of evil yet to come to the Juden-platz frightened her more than all the pleas of Murphy and Thomas that she must leave Austria. She feared for Leah now, even though the Austrian police were at this moment battling against the Nazis. What if the police had not come? And would there be a time when they joined the men of Otto and Sporer?

It was fifteen minutes before another streetcar appeared at Stephansplatz. Elisa climbed the steps, ignoring the curious look of the driver as he stared at her torn coat and disheveled appearance.

"Are you all right, Fraülein?" he asked as her hands trembled and fumbled with the coins.

"I slipped," she muttered, "on the ice."

"You are bleeding, Fraülein. There is blood on your coat collar."

She raised her hand to touch a sticky place on the back of her head. She hadn't felt the pain; there had been too much else. "It's nothing," she said dully, taking a seat in the back. Indeed, compared to the realization that Austria was filled with men like Otto from decent families and homes, the blood on her coat was nothing. On this Christmas Eve, peace on earth was far away. Austria was bleeding internally from a mortal wound that divided families even as they shared their Christmas meal together tonight. The heat had come to melt and separate even those who shared the same womb. The division had begun. Brother against brother, son against father. Tiny streams and tributaries had carried the snowflakes far apart into two great rivers that flowed inexorably toward different destinies. Some would be swept away against their will, lost in the churning, boiling current. *Don't go there again, not ever!* Lost, like Rudy. Trapped, like her father.

Elisa held no delusions of some safe, middle ground after tonight. Her denial vanished as she stared out at the familiar streets of a deserted Vienna. Every door in the Judenplatz had been marked with blood. Her own blood stained the cobblestones at the foot of Lessing's statue.

31

The Violin's Treasure

"Eleeeza!" called the old concierge as Elisa climbed the stairs to her apartment. "You have company!"

She stopped and scowled down at him. The memory of her unwanted visitors earlier that day was fresh in her mind. "Who, Herr Haupt?" She was grateful that her appearance was hidden in the shadows.

"Leah, your friend and—"

Elisa did not hear the rest of his sentence. She ran up the steps and threw the door open, calling Leah's name with such relief that she forgot everything else. She wrapped her arms around the little cellist, holding her tightly. "Oh, Leah! You're safe! *Safe!*" She was crying again.

Leah gasped as she saw the blood on Elisa's collar. "You're hurt, Elisa! What happened?"

Suddenly Elisa noticed that they were not alone. Three young children watched with wide eyes from the sofa. Elisa gaped back at them. She would not say what had happened to her in front of two small boys and a little girl. "It's nothing."

"Nothing! You're still bleeding!" Leah exclaimed with alarm.

"I slipped."

"Beneath a streetcar?" Leah helped her off with her coat. "Look at you!"

Elisa was certain that Leah was unaware of what was happening in the Judenplatz right now. "How long have you been here?" she asked, still looking at the children. *So these are Leah's little refugees . . .*

"About an hour." Leah was still fussing about the cut on Elisa's head. "I knew your mother would not be coming and that you would be alone. Everyone in the Judengasse is waiting for something." She added in a whisper, "I thought it best to bring the children here."

Elisa nodded. Her face was grim and serious. "I have just come from your apartment. Stay here tonight, Leah."

The shock of understanding passed over Leah's face. She did not reply but simply looked back at Elisa. The presence of the children was a painful muzzle. No doubt these little ones had known too much of violence and hatred in their brief lives. Both women restrained themselves, but the horror of what had happened was evident in Elisa's face. Leah simply shook her head slowly in disbelief as if to ask, *What next? What can happen next?* The first riot had been bad enough—two Jews attacked and beaten within view of her apartment window. Hadn't *they* found satisfaction in the murder of one Jew and the terrible slogans painted on the walls? Suddenly Leah noticed the violin case on the floor beside Elisa. She looked at it in disbelief, then back to Elisa again.

"Rudy?" she asked.

Elisa nodded curtly. She would not say anything right now—not with three pairs of frightened young eyes staring at her. She managed to smile at the children, walking past Leah, who seemed stunned at the sight of the case.

"Guten Abend," she nodded. "I am Elisa." Her voice was gentle and controlled as though she were coaxing a lost cat from a widow ledge. "I look terrible, I know. But I slipped on the icy stones. Leah, you must fix them hot chocolate while I clean up and change," she instructed, not certain that Leah heard her. "Would you like hot chocolate, children?"

Three heads nodded in unison. Elisa guessed that the two boys were about seven and eight years old. The little girl was no more than five. She had thick blond braids and wide blue eyes. Elisa tried not to think what it would be like to be five years old and torn from family and home, forced to flee as an enemy of the Reich.

"Leah"—Elisa's words were soothing to all of them—"you know where everything is?"

Leah nodded, tearing her eyes from Rudy's violin case. "Of course." She stared hard at Elisa. "I know." She was speaking of more than cups and saucers and chocolate.

"Good." Elisa was suddenly relieved. Somewhere in the violin case were the papers Rudy had spoken of. Leah knew where. *Thank God!*

As the three children quietly sipped their chocolate around the kitchen table, Leah slipped into the bedroom with Rudy's violin and closed the door behind her.

How? When? Where? Her questions rushed out as Elisa washed and changed. Leah's expression shifted from exultation to grief and horror as Elisa related the whole story.

"He told me to take it to you," she finished. "I could not find anything in it. Nothing at all."

Leah nodded. "That is the idea," she said quietly as the impact of

Elisa's story settled heavily on her. "No one else could find anything either. Unless they knew—"

The violin case lay unopened on the bed. Leah reached out to touch it. "Show me," Elisa said. "Show me, Leah." There was a determination in her voice that caused Leah to start. "I have carried this case into Germany. My father knew its secret. Show me, Leah." Her tone left no room for refusal.

Leah stroked the case. "It has held so many lives. They never guessed. It has been under the noses of the Gestapo a hundred times. Irmgard passed documents to us, names of those about to be arrested. That's how your father knew for sure. We were just too late for him. The Nazis had planned his arrest weeks before. We sent your own passports and the names on the lists. Yes, your father knew what was inside the case. Last Christmas when you came back with the case and your father did not return, we opened it after Rudy redeemed it from you." Leah smiled sadly. "Your father had sent enough to us in gems and bills to purchase seven hundred passports. Illegal passports for German Jewish children. Do you know what a great man your father was?" She turned her eyes on Elisa. "So many saved, but not himself. And he wanted you protected from all of it."

"Rudy said he's not dead!" Elisa picked up the case. "Irmgard got his file! Put it in here! Show me, Leah! I have to be part of this now. My father can't protect me from it any longer! I have to know!"

Leah pressed her fingertips to her forehead. "There is a reason Rudy called you," she said after a long time. Then she took the case gently from Elisa's lap and placed it back on the bed. With deft and confident fingers, she opened the case and pulled back the scarf to reveal the violin.

Elisa frowned as she scanned the inside of the case, trying once again to guess where the priceless documents were hidden. "Show me," she whispered hoarsely.

With a strange smile, Leah took the Guarnerius from the case. The plush velvet lining looked unremarkable: just like any other violin case. As if to demonstrate, Leah lifted the lid of each little storage compartment. "Nothing there but resin, a spare tuning peg, strings—right?"

"I have gone through it all," Elisa said impatiently.

At that, Leah placed her thumbs against the locks again and, with the lid open, pushed the locks downward three times. She threw a sideways glance at Elisa, who was watching with rapt attention. Then she grasped the interior of the case and pulled upward. The entire inside of the case lifted loose from the outer shell, revealing a space half an inch deep on the bottom in which five passports and a thin file were stored. Elisa reached forward to touch the documents; then she looked at Leah who was grinning smugly.

"And now—" Leah lifted the Guarnerius and began to twist the two bottom tuning pegs. Strings slackened and fell off. She slipped the pegs from their slots and placed them in Elisa's palm. "Go ahead. Pull them apart. Ebony wood with a gold tail piece and a tail button to match." She nudged Elisa. "Go ahead. Pull!"

With her fingernail, Elisa pried off the little tail button, then pulled out a wad of cotton. A shimmering row of diamonds spilled out. "From my father?" Elisa asked.

"Right under the noses of the Gestapo. Into our hands in Austria, transformed into passports and ransom for children across the border in Germany. You see, eventually, the Reich does get its cash, but we get lives in return." Leah picked up the file containing information about Theo Lindheim.

"And what about my father?" Elisa asked, staring down at the gems.

"That's what *this* is all about." Leah slapped the folder. "When he didn't get out, we saved enough—fifty thousand dollars' worth, we figured." She tapped the bow, the one that Rudy had pretended to fence with. "There's more in there, as well."

"You saved money?"

"Gems. Irmgard had been trying to discover your father's whereabouts for a year." Leah frowned at the thought of Irmgard Schüler. "You see why I was so angry when you spoke badly of her?"

"Rudy said they would never let him out." Elisa felt suddenly fearful. *"Never!"*

Leah did not seem to hear her. She was already checking the five passports in the bottom of the case. "Yes, yes"—she opened each folder and shut it again—"these will do for the boys with Shimon and Albert. But still nothing for my little ones."

Elisa did not care about passports for the children. All she wanted was some reassurance that her father would somehow also find his freedom. She flipped through the file. There was a photograph of Theo. Description, age, some reference of the crime of assisting underground Jewish organizations. *Captured near Munich December 18, 1936. Interrogated in Brown House at Munich. Solitary Confinement. Transferred Dachau under name Jacob Stern. May 23, 1937. Jew. Political enemy of the Reich, known for anti-Nazi sentiments and activities.*

"Can he still be alive?" Elisa asked, alarmed when she saw the date of Theo's transfer to Dachau.

"He's alive." Leah spoke with certainty. "Otherwise it would be listed in the file when he died." She was still frowning down thoughtfully at the stack of passports. "If you can call Dachau being alive," she added. She was instantly sorry she said it. Elisa looked wounded by the words, stricken at the thought of her father in such a place for so long.

"Look," Elisa said weakly. "They have copies of all our letters here. From Innsbruck. They know everything about how he escaped from the Adlon. John Murphy's name is here, and . . ." She felt ill. "And they say that Thomas came to the store the night we left Germany. *Thomas* was there! Did he . . . is Thomas von Kleistmann any part of this organization?"

"No," Leah said. "If he went to warn your father, he acted on his own. If he tried to help you, it was apart from us. By then Theo knew already. He had seen the list. We have heard that Theo warned fifteen others to leave Berlin. They were on the list as well."

"*Thomas,*" Elisa said with amazement. "Yes. He must have come to the office that night. My father said it was a messenger, but—" She turned her gaze full on Leah. "He will help us," she whispered. "I have to talk to him. He can help us."

Leah looked doubtful. "Be careful, Elisa. You must not tell him anything." She touched the case. "*Nothing* at all about all this. You must act on your own if you choose to ask Thomas von Kleistmann for help."

A soft knock sounded on the door and a small voice called, "Fraülein Leah? We are finished."

"There is a more immediate problem now," Leah said, staring at the five passports. "What can we do with these little ones until we can get them passports and proper papers? They can't stay in Vienna. Not now."

"Fraülein Leah? Fraülein Elisa?"

Elisa looked at the box of angels beside the bed. With her toe, she absently nudged the lid from the box until the jumble of violin-playing angels smiled up at her. Elisa was suddenly involved, just as her father had been, in the lives and the lists of the Jews of Germany. "There was a reason Rudy called me," she said. "I am Aryan . . . on paper, anyway. I am a violinist. And I carry a violin case . . ."

"What are you saying?"

"I'm saying I will carry the case. You must tell me everything—*everything*. Where I must go. Who I must see." Then she looked toward the bedroom door. "And I will tell you a place where we must take the children. A family in the Tyrol who have lost their son. I will talk to them." She put her hand on Leah's arm. "The children must not come through Vienna any longer. We'll find another place for them while we get their passports."

32

Dachau Night

Cold, silent night had come without darkness or peace to Dachau. A huge stone wall topped by electric wires ringed the massive prison compound. From the towers, machine guns bristled and stern, black-shirted sentinels kept watch. Harsh floodlights glared down upon the stark white walls of the barracks, bleaching color and life from the scene.

From the door of Barracks 11, a thin skeleton of a man emerged dressed in a black-and-white striped uniform. He stood blinking up into the lights and turrets, then stumbled from the step. His face colorless, he walked with a jerking motion as he moved toward the forbidden area where the lights beat down unrelentingly and signs declared that those who stepped across the low wire would be shot. The figure did not seem human. His thin clothes flapped in the chill wind like the rags on a scarecrow.

Scharf Geschossen! The black lettering warned.

The scarecrow trudged on toward the forbidden line. He did not look at the guards who shouted to him, or halt at their command. Like an image on a black-and-white celluloid film, he lurched across a bleak cold screen. The guard dogs barked, straining on their leashes. One guard, then another, then still another clicked rifle bolts into place; the sound echoed hollowly across the silent night, a grim counterpoint to the crunch of ragged shoes against the snow.

"Judenhund! Halt!" cried a guard as he took aim on the stripes. A bony knee lifted a foot over the wire.

The figure seemed not to hear the words, the threats, the shouts. His hollow eyes stared past the harsh lights as though searching for something—some color, perhaps a single star.

Then, in a rattle of machine-gun fire, the black-and-white stripes jumped forward in a strange jerking dance that tore and stained the fabric—red, perhaps, if there had been color. But there was no color—only the white glare of the lights, and a body tumbling forward as a spirit broke free and sailed over the walls of Dachau toward colors and stars.

The entire incident had taken only moments. Shouting sentries fell silent once again. They would let the body lie where it had fallen as a warning for other inmates.

Inside the long, unheated buildings, Jews and Social Democrats, Catholics and Protestants huddled in close packed rows, trying to sleep, trying to keep warm, trying to forget the sound of the gunshots. Thousands of them were crammed into barracks that had been built for only a few hundred at best. In the morning there would be numbers missing from the roll call. They would die tonight and be cremated, along with the one who had committed suicide by crossing the forbidden line. Then they would be shipped home in little boxes like Christmas packages. A slip of paper would offer the explanation: *Died of natural causes*.

These were Hitler's gifts to the German people and the Greater German Reich. He had swept the cities clean of beggars. He had pulled dissenters from their pulpits and public offices. Day by day more Jews were defrauded of their property; their belongings were scooped into the coffers of the public building funds or the armament industry. The humans themselves had been swept into grim, black closets like Dachau. The Aryan cities of the Reich were becoming pure for German culture once again. Those who were missing were those who had somehow disturbed the conscience and peace of mind of the German people. What difference did it make if a few thousand, more or less, came back in ashes? A handful of dust to spread in the rose garden? What difference would it make if eventually a few million died, more or less—as long as there were no beggars, no gypsies, no Christian dissenters, no Bolsheviks, no Jews. The Aryan race of the great Thousand-Year Reich must be pure! Society must be pure! Sweep the dust into Dachau and forty other camps in Germany. Had not the Führer proclaimed his purpose in the Christmas broadcast? *"I am doing the work of the Lord!"*

After four months in solitary confinement, Theo Lindheim had come into Dachau. Like Pastor Niemöller and Pastor Jacobi, he had been given a false name and a new identity with the prison identification number. He was too well known among the people of Germany for the S.S. to risk some news of his fate being leaked. Those men who had been prominent or popular before Hitler came to power were all called by other names within the walls of the camps.

But somehow, it made no difference. Theo was listed on the records as Jacob Stern, but still prisoners quietly saluted this unnamed war hero when he passed by in the exercise yard. To speak his name and be heard would mean a beating with a rubber truncheon, or worse. And so, faceless men, cold and ragged, saluted Theo with their eyes when he passed. They spoke without speaking, and between them was a covenant to remember what Germany had been before all this—a covenant to remember that although they were imprisoned, those who lived outside the walls were also captives of Hitler's brutal rule.

No one was free in Germany now. *No one!* The streets were clean. Great buildings of white stone were being erected everywhere to the glory of the Reich. There was no disagreement and no freedom. Germany was a nation of prisoners, ruled by a government of jailers. Göring himself had said, *"I would like to see all of Germany in uniform, marching in column."*

Tonight, outside the walls of Dachau, neat rows of field-gray uniforms marched through the streets of Berlin and Munich and Hamburg in eerie torchlight procession. Perhaps they were warmer than those inside the walls of Dachau; perhaps they had more to eat; but they, too, had lost their names. They had no faces. Their breath sucked color and life from the very air as they raised their arms as one mob to shout, *"Sieg Heil! Heil!"*

Like Faust, the mob had sold its soul to the devil for the sake of . . . what? Clean streets? New buildings? Jobs and possessions stolen from another human being in the name of "Aryan racial purity"? In the name of this purity, Hitler had robbed even the Christ Child in the manger of His identity, declaring: *Jesus was not Jewish; it could not be! His young mother was not Jewish! We must eliminate these slanders from the German Christian religion! We must expunge all traces of Judaism from our churches! The very thought that Christ was Jewish is unthinkable!*

Tonight the Nazi storm troopers and Hitler Youth marched row on row. *"Gott mit uns*—God with us" was inscribed on every belt buckle. The sound of their boots on the pavement was like the echo of the Roman Legions on the stones of Jerusalem's streets when a young Jewish woman gave birth to a son in a cave above Bethlehem. That son had grown to manhood with the sound of marching legions in His ears. The crash of soldiers' boots had followed Him to his execution; the ring of their hammers had crashed against the spikes in His hands and feet, and a soldier in field gray with a swastika on His arm had driven the lance into His side. Soldiers had killed the Jewish child called by the Hebrew name *Emmanuel . . . God with us.* Like the S.S., they had come by torchlight to arrest Him in the night. They had thrown Him into prison, pulled out His beard by the roots, and beaten Him. *"Hail King of the Jews!"* they had jeered.

Yes, there were echoes of that time and place tonight in Dachau. In the endless rows of skeletons dressed in rags lived the poor and the homeless, the shepherds and wise men alike who looked for a Messiah to deliver them. In the arrogant cruelty of Hitler's army, once again the generals of Rome sought to crush even the barest ember of hope from men's lives. But even here there was forbidden light—even in the hell of Dachau.

In the corner of Barrack 8 men huddled together for warmth tonight.

They jokingly called their corner the *"Herrgottseck—The Corner of the Lord."* As Theo Lindheim crouched on a wooden pallet between a Catholic priest and a Jewish cantor from the synagogue in Strassburg, he thought that perhaps the only free men left in Germany shivered within these thin walls. Here, with all else stripped from them, these men could be only what they were, for good or for evil. It was almost Christmas. It was just past Hanukkah. Tonight a priest without vestments, a cantor without tallith remembered the Festival of Lights and the One who was proclaimed to be The Light.

For the holiday, the prisoners had been given an extra ration beside their five ounces of bread to eat. Guards had distributed a raw potato for each man in the barracks. The eight in the Herrgottseck had carefully hoarded their treasures for the feast tonight. Now, eight potato halves were placed in a circle before each man. They had been hollowed out, and a wick made from an oil-soaked rag had been placed in each one to form a candle. At great risk, the priest had stolen a match from the kitchen.

A cold draft sifted up through the boards of the barrack's floor. Theo shivered and pulled his thin blanket around his chin. He prayed that the draft would not snuff out their match. Somehow the lighting of these candles tonight had become the focus of his existence, the reason he continued to breathe and think and hope when so many had given up.

Outside their circle of eight, someone mocked them in a hoarse, bitter whisper. "So, Priest. Here is Christmas. Peace on earth. Of course this is not earth, ja? But purgatory. Almost hell, only not warm enough. Hell would be better. Warmer."

"Shut up!" another voice hissed from the darkness. "Let them alone."

"You think your little candles will warm you?" mocked the voice again.

Yes! Theo wanted to shout. *Yes! This one defiant act of worship will warm me. Please, dear Lord, do not let the flame die. Please let our candles burn!*

"Come closer," said the cantor, and the eight pressed in shoulder to bony shoulder, ribs and spines and skulls forming a wall against the threat of a hostile wisp of air. The potato candles were moved forward into a tight circle, their wicks placed together at the center. The cantor held a small bundle of straw and the priest held the match. The only match.

"Tonight," the priest said quietly, "God has provided only one match. And so we who are both Jews and Christians worship as one in this place."

Theo could not see the priest's face. They all looked the same in the darkness, but there was a smile in the voice of the priest. So it had taken Dachau to bring priest and cantor together. Dachau, 1937. Christmas. Hanukkah. A moment of covenant among men who suffered together.

The cantor's voice was like a song as he spoke. "Tonight we remember the great miracle that happened in the temple. After the enemy had desecrated our place of worship and we drove him out from Jerusalem, there was oil enough to light the lamps for only one day. And God caused the flames to burn for eight days until more oil was sanctified. On this darkest night of our souls, when we find no light within ourselves, we ask God for a miracle—"

"What miracle can you expect here?" taunted the voice outside the circle.

"Only that the light will burn. That we will remember God is with us," replied the cantor.

"Gott mit uns! God is with the Nazis! Can't you read it on their buckles? I was beaten by one of those buckles," he scoffed.

The priest began to sing softly:

"O come, O come, Emmanuel,
And ransom captive Israel,
That mourns in lonely exile here
Until the Son of God appear—"

Other voices joined him softly in the song.

"O come, Thou Rod of Jesse, free
Thine own from Satan's tyranny;
From depths of hell Thy people save
And give them victory o'er the grave."

From the far corners of the barracks, weak voices added their strength to the song. Theo closed his eyes and sang loudly. Never mind that the *Kapos* would come and beat them—*never mind!* And if they were shot for singing, what did it matter?

"O come, Thou Dayspring, come and cheer
Our spirits by Thine advent here;
And drive away the shades of night,
And pierce the clouds and bring us light!"

Theo opened his eyes as the one match sputtered into flame. The tiny, fragile flame touched the bundle of straw, and the cantor, his voice clear and bell-like as he sang, touched the fire to the wicks of the eight Hanukkah candles.

"Rejoice! Rejoice! Emmanuel
Shall come to thee, O Israel!"

For an hour the candles burned as the cantor and the priest led the men in songs of hope and deliverance. And indeed, a great miracle happened there that night: no guards came near the barracks; no clubs smashed the heads of the thousand who joined the songs. For one hour that barrack in Dachau became synagogue and cathedral where men lifted their hearts with one voice to the One God.

———

Leah and the three children stayed with Elisa, while Shimon waited out the storm of the Judenplatz with another orchestra player on the other side of the city. The Austrian police arrested fifty-four Nazi demonstrators as Hitler began enraged broadcasts against the government of Chancellor Schuschnigg. The Austrian Secret Police, armed with new information about Nazi activities in Vienna, raided the Austrian Nazi headquarters.

How the government had gotten access to secret orders issued from Germany to Captain Leopold's thugs was a matter for discussion in every cafe in the city. Obviously the Austrian Nazis had a very bad leak. Orders issued by Himmler in Germany had been discovered: an *incident* was to be provided as the excuse for Hitler's armies to march into Austria. The planned incident was the murder of Germany's ambassador to Austria, Herr Franz von Papen. The instructions from Germany indicated that the assassination of von Papen must be blamed on a Jew—a Bolshevik, if at all possible. When Germany's ambassador was cooling in the city morgue, it would be expected that the Austrian Nazis would riot, at which time the German army would march in and restore order.

The secret agenda of Adolf Hitler was no longer a secret. Of course, no word of the plan was printed in Germany, where Hitler raved about the Nazis of Austria being denied their rights. But everywhere else, the documents were passed from hand to hand, and a shudder coursed down the spine of every professional diplomat from every nation. *"You mean Hitler was actually going to have his own ambassador bumped off for the sake of the cause? I dare say!"*

Mention of a scurrilous forgery was made in Hitler's tirades. Such broadcasts were listened to without amusement in Austria. His demand that the Nazi party members be set free at once was also no laughing matter. Perhaps the man doing the hardest thinking in the entire situation was von Papen himself. He was not ready to become the sacrificial lamb on the altar of Hitler's plans to take over Austria. Needless to say, the German Embassy in Vienna was a quiet and unhappy place.

No one argued that Vienna was no place for German-Jewish children without proper papers. "Grüss Gott," Leah said quietly as Elisa left the apartment. "God bless . . ." It was a prayer as much as a way of saying goodbye these days.

———

Elisa made her way quickly to the telegraph office. She paid and passed the simple message across the counter:

TO: HERR KARL WATTENBARGER KITZBÜHEL TYROL STOP WISH LODGING FOR SPINSTER AUNT AND THREE SMALL CHILDREN ON HOLIDAY DECEMBER 27 STOP PLEASE REPLY TO ELSA FAMBICH MAIN TELEGRAPH OFFICE KÄRTNERSTRASSE VIENNA IMMEDIATELY STOP

She instructed the telegrapher that she would return tomorrow afternoon to see if a reply had arrived; then, with a nod of the head she left and returned home by way of the bakery for a load of cream puffs and strudel for the restless children. Elisa bought a newspaper from a shivering boy outside the Konditorei. She stood staring silently at the front page for a moment, astonished at the photograph of the man Otto had called Sporer.

"He's a very bad man, Fraülein," offered the newsboy. "Albert Sporer is his name. A German Nazi."

She glanced at the boy. "Yes. Very bad. An evil man." She wished now that she had not burned the memory of Sporer's face into her memory.

"You can see—" The boy stepped forward to share her paper with her even though he had dozens of his own. "They say he is wanted even in Czechoslovakia for murder. The Czechs want him back to hang him, but Chancellor Schuschnigg will throw him into the darkest prison in Austria." He seemed satisfied with the pronouncement.

Elisa scanned the page, reading with alarm that the Nazi party in Germany had already protested the arrest of Sporer as "interference with the right of Austrians to self-determination."

"I hope there is a hole deep enough for him," Elisa muttered, and the newsboy laughed in agreement. She looked at the child then. He was dressed in rags and wore a yarmulke on his head. His eyes were bright at the thought of such a wicked man as the Nazi Sporer being tossed into a dungeon. "Where do you live?" she asked gently.

"On Judengasse," he replied.

"Then you saw them?" He was no more than nine years old—too young, she thought, to see such things as the riot in the Judenplatz.

His bright smile left as easily as it had come. "Yes." His deep brown eyes seemed old beyond their years. "We saw them. But Mother says they will not be back. You see in the newspaper, Chancellor Schuschnigg will not let the Nazis come to Austria. We will be safe in Vienna."

Elisa recognized her own hope in his words. Only a few days before, she had said what the Jewish boy said now. She had believed the hope then.

She looked again at the face of Sporer. Thin lips and high cheekbones. Wire-rimmed glasses on a sensitive face. He could have been an artist or a poet, but the words of the Führer had become an evil cancer that had twisted this man into a form so frightening—she shuddered at the thought and tried to see the image of Sporer as though she had not felt his grip on her in the street, as though his breath had not been hot and violent against her cheek. *Do men and women looking at his face in the newspaper see what I have seen?* she wondered. *Has he always been this, a contagion of hatred, capable of infecting other men with his disease?*

She thought of Otto then. It could just as easily have been his photograph on the front page. Perhaps one day it would be his face that would be condemned. Yet his mother had told her that Otto had once thought of becoming a priest.

From far away, the distant memory of her father's voice came to her.

In the soft glow of his library he had read aloud to his children, and a shudder had coursed through her as she heard the words of Faust's evil spirit: *Wrath grips you. The great trumpet sounds. The graves are quaking. And your heart, resurrected from ashen calm to flaming tortures, flares up....*

Without another word, she tipped the boy a shilling and walked slowly home. There was nothing more to explain. Sporer, Otto, the men in the Judenplatz, the mobs of Germany—all had given their hearts to wrath and fire. There was no room for goodness in such a bargain with the devil. All else was crowded out and forgotten. In a sickening flood of realization, Elisa knew they were capable of anything. Of *everything*! Even the unthinkable. Had she not seen it in Rudy's hands, and then again when she lay beneath Sporer in the Judenplatz? Yes. She had seen the look of disappointment on his face when Otto had shouted that she was Aryan. He had *wanted* to hurt her! He had *hoped* that she was the enemy! Her cries had given him pleasure!

Like the newsboy, she prayed that there was a hole deep enough to contain such all-consuming evil. But the dull ache in the pit of her stomach warned that the evil growth had already spread far and sent a taproot deep into the heart of Austria.

In Paris, banner headlines screamed the plot of Austrian Nazis against von Papen. There was no mistaking the intention of Hitler in spite of his enraged denials.

Thomas scanned the newspaper and leaned back in his chair, propping his feet up on the desk. He had done the right thing, going to Churchill and Eden. Admiral Canaris and the others had done the right thing to send him. The British had gotten the word to Schuschnigg in time; surely, the world would put a collective foot down to stop the madman at the helm of Germany. Perhaps there would be no need for the generals to revolt. Now, certainly Britain would demand a halt! Prime Minister Chamberlain would hold up the military might of Britain. The French would trumpet their denunciation of such tactics as Hitler's diabolical scheme.

Thomas rubbed a hand over his face in relief. It had been worth the risk. Now if the world would come to its senses, it might be unnecessary for Thomas to leave Germany. The life of his nation could return to some sanity again, and he and Elisa—

"Thomas." Ernst vom Rath poked his head into the office. His cheeks were pale, and beads of sweat stood out on his forehead.

"What is it?" The sense of elation left Thomas as suddenly as it had come.

Meet me, vom Rath mouthed silently as he held up two fingers. Then he shut the door. Thomas listened to the clack of his heels across the marble floor of the embassy.

Thomas arrived at Notre Dame a full five minutes before vom Rath. As he knelt before the statue of Mary, his heart thumped wildly. Was Ernst coming to warn him that he had been discovered? Had he been trailed by the Gestapo in spite of his elaborate route to Churchill's hotel suite in Cannes? The memory of the man who had seen him in the hallway came back to him. He must have been Gestapo. Plain clothes. An agent sent to sniff him out.

He jumped in spite of himself when Ernst knelt beside him. Thomas glanced at the shaking young diplomat whose eyes looked beseechingly upward as he spoke.

"At a dinner here in Paris last night," Ernst began, "your Anthony Eden tried to talk to the Italian ambassador, Grandi." The words were half choked, a horrified whisper. "Eden wanted to find out how Mussolini was reacting to Nazi pressures on Austria."

Thomas looked at vom Rath. He was blanched, white as death. His clenched hands trembled. "And?"

Tears swam in vom Rath's eyes. "Prime Minister Chamberlain was there, too. He kept changing the subject. Said how he and Mussolini were friends. Talked about Anglo-Italian reapproachment." He swallowed hard. "About friendship between Britain and Germany. Britain and Italy . . ." Vom Rath buried his face in his hands. "Chamberlain didn't let Eden say a word! Count Grandi was on the phone to Hitler this morning. They're all laughing!" He turned tortured eyes on Thomas. "It doesn't matter that Hitler planned to have his own ambassador killed. The British Prime Minister is still talking small talk over tea and cakes! Are they mad, Thomas? Are they mad? We risk our lives to ask for some show of strength, and this is what they reply with! The Führer mocks Chamberlain; Mussolini imitates him to the amusement of his friends. If the English are still talking friendship, what hope have we got of stopping Hitler? What hope?"

"How did Anthony Eden react?"

"He asked Grandi again if Italy intended to support Austrian independence. After all, Italy has always stood by the Rome Protocols to protect the integrity of Austria." He looked back toward the statue. The votive candles reflected against his skin in a blood-red light. "Eden asked if Mussolini and Hitler had some sort of agreement about Austria." He frowned as though he could not believe what he was about to say. "Then Chamberlain interrupted again. Insisted that they have a bit more tea. That the only business that should concern them was England's relationship with Italy!" Vom Rath sat, motionless. He was drained, frightened for the future and for himself.

"The Italians hate Eden because he's one of the few in the British government to demand the Italians pull out of Spain."

"Then they celebrate a great victory tonight. Prime Minister Chamberlain had emasculated his own foreign secretary in front of Grandi. Tonight both Mussolini and Hitler will no doubt drink a toast to silly Chamberlain and his umbrella. And the rest of us—what do we do now?"

Thomas rose from his knees. He had no reply. There was nothing left to say in the face of Chamberlain's actions. The British Prime Minister had already decided that peace meant appeasement. What did it matter to him if there was an incident in Vienna? What did it matter if German troops marched into Austria? Vienna was not London, after all. Thomas looked around the massive cathedral. It was empty with the exception of a few tourists and Ernst vom Rath and himself. He felt suddenly sober and clear-headed, as though everything he had hoped and thought and done in the last few days had been the dream of a drunkard. So, this was the reality. Berlin was coming to Vienna—then, probably, to Prague. He leaned his head back and stared up into the huge rib cage of the vaulted ceiling of the cathedral. Would the Nazis also come to Paris one day? To London? Where could he take Elisa that they would be safe?

He looked down at his own hands. The glow of the candles also caught him in the bloody reflection. Ernst vom Rath remained trembling on his knees. He closed his eyes in prayer as Thomas walked away from him. Ernst felt it, too. Was there any place left that would be safe?

33

Sanctuary in Kitzbühel

The answer from the Wattenbargers in Kitzbühel came promptly the next morning.

THREE ROOMS ARE AVAILABLE FOR THE SPINSTER AUNT AND HER YOUNG CHARGES STOP PLEASE NOTIFY OF TIME OF ARRIVAL STOP TRANSPORTATION WILL BE WAITING STOP

Elisa folded the message and put it in her pocket. She could imagine the shock on the face of Franz when the spinster aunt turned out to be Elisa Linder. Would he still be angry at her, she wondered? Or would the anger of his love be softened into pleasant unconcern by the passage of a year? She had been cruel to him, she knew that now. She had been even more convinced of it when she had looked into the faces of Murphy's little wooden angels and recognized the touch of their creator.

If she had known any other place in Austria where the children would be safe, she would not have taken them to Kitzbühel. But at least within the walls of the Wattenbarger household, the lines between good and evil were defined. Otto was in Vienna, far from the soft, gentle voice of Frau Marta and the warm, playful teasing of Herr Karl. Elisa had seen the way her own brothers had been transformed in the midst of these good, simple people. Their frowns had turned to raucous laughter, and their pale skin had taken on a glow from the mountain air. Those days had made the terrible grief of Theo's arrest somehow bearable. Frau Marta had comforted her mother then, and she would comfort three children now. With Otto in Vienna among the thousands like him, Kitzbühel would be a safe place for the children until Elisa could get their papers to them. From there, they would travel to the south of France, where Baron von Rothschild was establishing homes for refugee children.

Elisa found courage in the knowledge that her father had been part of the chain since the beginning. Theo Lindheim had helped smuggle to safety something far more valuable than the artwork that Hitler and Göring stole from Jewish homes—seven hundred children, Leah had told her. There was something holy in the number. Even behind the walls and wire of Dachau, Theo Lindheim's life had counted for something. But it had cost him the freedom to leave Germany before leaving became impossible. Seven hundred children had passed through to France or Prague and then on to Palestine while Theo had remained behind.

Elisa's heart nearly burst with the pride she felt for her father. She should have known, but she had not been able to see past her own worry and the safety of her family. Rudy Dorbransky had never met Theo, and yet, in a way, he had known him better than Elisa.

"Men like your father understand the risks of gambling," Rudy had said.

Now Elisa understood the risks of this desperate gamble as well. She had seen Rudy's hands. She heard of the horror of the German prison camps. The memories—cold cobblestones on her back, hands holding her down—were still fresh in her mind. Yes, she understood clearly.

Strangely, in the terrible *knowing*, she had lost her fear. For a year she had hoped in impotent misery for a miracle. Suddenly she discovered that there was a miracle in the works, and her father had been a part of it! She could be a part of it, too!

She ate her supper alone, then walked to the main telephone office where she placed her call to the cafe in Paris at seven o'clock. Somehow she was certain that Thomas would be there. She was not surprised when the operator called the name she had given, *Elsa*, to announce that her party was on the line.

She closed the door of the booth behind her and sat down, exhilarated at the sound of Thomas's voice.

"Hello . . . Hello? Is that Elisa?"

"Yes, Thomas. Elisa." She spoke without hint of sentimentality, as though this were a business call and they were discussing the price of violin strings.

"Elisa, darling! I have been hoping—"

"Just listen to me, Thomas!" she instructed firmly.

"You need to leave Vienna soon, darling."

"*Listen!* I need to see you."

"Yes. Yes. When will you come?" His voice was eager. "I have been thinking that we might get passage to Argentina. Then on to the United States, if you like."

"No! You must not do anything like that. I need you to stay where you are, Thomas! Listen to me. My father is alive! He's *alive*! You can't help him if we're on a boat to Argentina."

A long silence answered her. "Theo is alive?" he asked in disbelief. "We were told he died in a plane crash. Just beyond Munich. They've only just said so. Canaris heard it from the Gestapo, and—"

Impatient, Elisa interrupted him. "Can you leave Paris for a few days?"

"Right away? No. Maybe in a few days."

"When?"

"The day after tomorrow I could—"

"All right." She was surprised by her control. He would do what she told him, of that she was certain. "Go to St. Johann in the Tyrol. Stay at the inn near the train station. On Sunday take your skis to the Kitzbüheler mountain. There is a marked trail to a small chalet at the Ruppen-Alp. It's about three hours from St. Johann. If you leave early enough, no one will be on the trail. I'll meet you at the Ruppen-Alp at nine o'clock in the morning."

Thomas seemed surprised by her determination and impressed by her insistence that their meeting not be observed by anyone who might take note of it. Obviously, in his position, he could not show up in a city like Vienna without being trailed. Nor could she meet him in Paris with the assurance that they were not being watched. Thomas would have preferred to purchase tickets on the next steamer from Marseilles, but he agreed to the meeting. This new, self-determined Elisa intrigued him. He agreed without hesitation to the plan. He did not ask her where she would be staying or what she had in mind after they met on the slopes of the Kitzbüheler Horn. He only wanted to see her again.

———

Elisa left the telephone office. It was already late, but she walked alone through the park where she and Murphy had gone to buy the little wooden angels. The place was deserted now; the open-air market of the joyous Christmas season had disappeared as though it had never been there at all.

She tried to find the spot where she had kissed him and he had looked at her with such breathless longing. But all the landmarks were gone, swept clean by wind and covered by fresh snow.

The stars were out now, bright ice and fire shimmering in the night skies. She thought of her father and wondered if he watched the same stars and thought of her, imagining her free and safe in Vienna. The last few terrible days had cleared her life of every landmark but the one irrevocable hope that Theo was alive, that by some miracle he might come home again to his family. She tried to find some words to offer up that hope as a prayer, but there were none, so she walked to the small cellar coffeehouse where the young Spanish prodigy played his guitar.

She sat at the same table where she had sat with Murphy and there, far away from the great booming bells of St. Stephan's Cathedral, she let her heart rise on the music once again. When she had prayed for Theo and for her own strength through melodies that soared beyond the dank walls of the little meeting place, she listened. And the answers came back to her strong and clear in the cantatas of the man who began each work with the inscription: *"Jesu, juva—Jesus, help!"* Had that not been Elisa's own prayer?

"Wachtet auf, ruft uns die stimme—Sleeper awake, a voice is calling..." the music sang to her.

"I am awake, Lord," her heart sang back. *"Never before so awake. But, Jesu, juva! What am I to do? I am a musician. I have never done any more than play a violin. I am not brave or strong like my father. Jesu, juva! Show me what I must do."*

"Weiderstehe, doch der Sunde—Withstand firmly all sin, lest its poison infect you. Withstand firmly all sin, lest Satan bind you..." The music played the warning, and as Elisa listened, she knew that there was a bondage more terrible than her father suffered now within the walls of Dachau.

"Gott soll allein mein Herze haben." She sang the words so softly that no one in the crowded room could hear her. "God alone shall have my heart...." Her sweet voice whispered a reply to God, and in that answer she could see the men whom she had loved and who had loved her in return: Thomas, Franz, dear Murphy who had touched her so gently with his eyes as they had listened to these songs only a week ago. It seemed like a lifetime before, yet her heart stirred again at the memory of Murphy's face. She frowned and closed her eyes, trying to shut out the intrusion of his memory. If God alone was to have her heart, then why did she think of this man at the moment of her vow? Was the love of a man one of the things that God demanded she stand firm against?

The answer whispered back to her, joyfully and without a doubt: *"Was Gott tut, das ist wohligetan! What God has done is rightly done!"*

Together, she and Murphy had questioned the words to this song, yet now they played back to her, not as some vague philosophy, but as the answer to her own question about John Murphy. Again and again, he had appeared in her life. Suddenly she knew she loved him, and that it was good to love him. But he was gone now. He had left her, or, rather, she had forced him away. How would she find him again? He had vanished, like all the traces of their day together.

Again the reply echoed: *"What God has done is rightly done!"* That alone was to be her answer. The young virtuoso played the last notes on his guitar and then, to a smattering of applause, he laid his instrument back in its case.

Somehow it was those last lyrics that came back as a challenge to Elisa. What she had questioned before must now be accepted and believed. If her heart was to belong to God alone, then she must have faith that He did not make mistakes. Men might fail miserably—that was in evidence all around. But that which was done by God would not fail.

Murphy was gone, her father in prison. Rudy Dorbransky was dead. For a moment, Elisa wavered at the challenge *to believe*!

The music faded away, and Elisa's soul quietly sang one last prayer:

"Lord, I believe; help my unbelief! Jesu, juva!"

The three children slept like tumbled dominos leaning against one another as the train chugged steadily into the Alps of the Tyrol. The vast, majestic beauty of the mountains somehow soothed Elisa. She had lived so long beneath the oppressive tension of the city that she had almost forgotten the peace that seemed to emanate from snow-capped crags and pastel mists that clung to mountain slopes as the tops of the peaks soared and then disappeared into the clouds. She could see her own reflection in the glass of the window as though her face were superimposed on the panorama that slid past as the train wound higher toward its destination. A soft voice spoke within her: *"God who has created this has also created you."*

"I have been away too long," she murmured. She hummed the melody, *"Jesu, joy of man's desiring; holy wisdom, love most bright. Drawn by thee, our souls aspiring soar to uncreated light. . . ."*

Elisa looked at the sleeping children. They were only three of millions now in danger. *One soul,* she thought, *so much more beautiful than all the mountains God has created, and yet men like Otto, like Sporer, would admire the unfeeling mountains and destroy little ones like these.*

Her father had seen the irony in that. He had chosen to help children rather than run to the safety of these mountains. The thought again brought tears to Elisa's eyes. She had not known her father, not really. She had not seen into his heart a year ago when they said farewell to Berlin together. Theo had not been grieving for the loss of his freedom or the loss of his business, or even for Germany—he had grieved for the children of his nation: for those who were being molded to hate in the Hitler Youth, and for those who were being pursued by that hatred. He had grieved because there was nothing more for him to do—no way to stop it, no way to change what was happening. Had he sensed that his presence in Germany would somehow jeopardize the operation that quietly moved Jewish children from beyond the borders of the Reich to safety?

Elisa knew her father now. She saw him clearly, as she had never seen him in all the years he had simply been her father. He was, indeed, a hero of the Fatherland. Perhaps one day those children who now marched in endless columns of the Hitler Youth would stumble on some fragment of truth left behind by men like Theo Lindheim, and they would know their souls were created to soar toward light, wisdom, and love. Then they would know they had been robbed of their childhood, lied to by men who had sold their souls. Hitler had proclaimed that his reign would last a thousand years. A thousand years of hatred and destruction. Would these mountains still stand as testimony to God's creative love? Would there still, in the face of such evil, be hearts and souls that aspired to soar to that perfect love?

With her eyes embracing the beauty of the Kitzbüheler Horn, Elisa prayed for all the children as she knew her father prayed. She prayed for those who marched with upraised hands and for those who ran from the tramp of the endless columns. At last her heart had found room to pity even those who could not see God's hand in the beauty of His living creations. She prayed the darkness would not last a thousand years, and that she might live to see it end. . . . But still, she could not pray for a man like Otto. He had forsaken all that he knew was right. He had offered himself up voluntarily. He had chosen to align himself with men like Sporer as they attacked the Judenplatz. And if he had known her heritage, no doubt he would have cheered Sporer and watched her raped without a twinge of conscience. He and others like him had turned away from light, and the shadow of their evil eclipsed the sun.

As the train stopped momentarily in St. Johann, Elisa found herself scanning the platform for some glimpse of Thomas. She was glad she had instructed him to stay in the little village on the other side of the mountain from Kitzbühel. If he was followed, he would not be traced to her, and the haven for the children would be secure. She frowned and pulled the shade, suddenly aware that she did not want to see him until it was time, until they met one another at the chalet in the isolation of the mountain slope.

The children slept all the way to Kitzbühel. Elisa nudged them awake and helped them to sit up one at a time.

From their first hour in the apartment, Leah had taught them to call Elisa "Aunt Elsa." And so that name came naturally to them. There was no effort in the title.

"Are we there, Aunt Elsa?"

"Almost to the mountains, Aunt Elsa?"

"How much longer, Aunt Elsa?"

"Just a few minutes longer, children." Elisa smoothed rumpled hair and clothes. "And then a nice gentleman will take us on a sleigh ride to a chalet in the mountains."

The little girl blinked at her and frowned. "And then will Mommy and Daddy come?"

Elisa looked at her for a moment, and then pulled her close in a warm hug. She stroked the long blond braids and remembered how she herself was still waiting for her father to come home. She closed her eyes, and for a moment she felt strong, invisible arms embrace them both. "You see those mountains, Gretchen?" Elisa asked gently.

"Of course!" The little girl sounded indignant. "I am not blind."

Elisa laughed and hugged her again. "Your mommy and daddy can see them, too. And every day they talk to God, who is bigger than the mountains, and they ask Him to whisper happy things to you. When you feel lonely, you must close your eyes tightly and listen to what they ask God to tell you."

All three of the children closed their eyes at once, and words once whispered with a good-night kiss or a song sung heartily at a picnic by the river came to each of them.

"Can you hear what your mommy is saying?" Elisa asked. Three heads nodded in unison. "Good. Those are your words alone, children. You may whisper back to God and He will tell Mommy and Daddy what you say, ja?" Heads nodded again and the lips moved silently. "But you must not say those words to anyone else. Remember what we said? Like a game of hide-and-seek; we must not tell where we are going or where we have been."

"Can we ask God to tell Mommy where we are?" the oldest boy asked seriously.

"Yes. And be sure and tell Him how beautiful it is. And that you are very happy." Elisa mussed his hair. He did not smile.

"But I am not happy. Not very happy. I miss Mommy," he answered. "I miss her hugs. I don't know why I was sent away."

A pain like a knife stabbed Elisa's heart. She extended her arms and pulled all three of the children close to her. "Yes. And I miss my mommy and daddy, too. Will you hug me? I need a hug to make me feel better." Chubby little arms embraced her fiercely around her neck and waist and shoulders. Clean, shiny hair and sweet-smelling skin brushed her cheeks, and as the three tried to comfort their new Aunt Elsa, they were themselves comforted. They stayed close for a long time and then drew back one at a time.

"Do you feel better, Aunt Elsa?" asked Gretchen.

Elisa nodded seriously, thoughtfully; then she smiled. "Yes. Yes, I do."

All three children smiled at once; they were relieved that they had helped this kind and very beautiful woman.

"Me too."

"So do I."

"I feel better too."

The train slowed to a stop, and outside in the corridor, the conductor called, *"All off for Kitzbühel!"*

Elisa smiled more broadly. "Then here is one more secret I will tell you. When you feel badly, find someone who feels worse than you, and do something nice for that person."

"What if no one feels worse than me?" asked the second boy.

"There will never be a lack of people who need hugs, and never enough people to hug them, Stefen. And when you hold someone who is sad, then that person will also embrace you, and you will feel better too."

"All off for Kitzbühel!"

Elisa gathered their meager belongings and guided them off the train. She drew the sweet, clear air of Kitzbühel into her lungs and glanced quickly around the station. They were the only ones who had disembarked, and there, staring at them in wonder, stood Franz Wattenbarger.

His golden-red beard was a little fuller, his leather knickers were a bit more worn; but other than that, he looked exactly as he had when she had seen him last. Happily, he only seemed surprised at her appearance with the three children. There was not a trace of anger on his handsome face.

He pointed at her and then looked at a slip of paper. *You?* he mouthed.

She smiled sheepishly and nodded. "Hello, Franz."

He strode toward her with his hand extended. "Elisa!" he cried. "I thought I would not see you again after the way I behaved. I thought I had driven the most perfect and beautiful guest forever from the Tyrol."

"Oh, Franz!" She was so *glad*, so *relieved*, to see him. He pumped her hand, then stared happily at the children.

"You are the spinster aunt? And these are your—" He frowned slightly. The realization flooded him that she could not possibly be aunt to these children. Elisa was the oldest child of her own family and her brothers were certainly not wed! "Your nephews. And very pretty niece." He did not ask questions. Instantly he knew there was some reason for the deception and he played the charade expertly. It had become necessary to play such games even in the Tyrol. Without missing a beat, he chatted amiably as he loaded their things onto the sleigh.

Elisa asked him questions about his family, but he did not ask her about Anna and the boys or her father. She was grateful for his immediate grasp of the situation.

He teased the boys and jollied little Gretchen and talked about new calves and colts and a litter of kittens that would all become excellent mousers. Perhaps the children would each like a kitten to play with while they were here? Soon he had them all giggling shyly, and Gretchen cuddled up beside him and laid her head against his arm with the declaration:

"I want to marry you when I grow up."

Franz threw his head back in laughter. "Well, I am already taken, Liebchen! You are six months too late!"

Gretchen seemed momentarily disappointed. Elisa laughed with him. It seems she had wasted all her worry. Franz had recovered nicely.

"I knew someone wonderful would grab you up," Elisa said.

"Mama said, the best cure for a broken heart! She is beautiful. And she can cook!"

"I never could cook. I would have disappointed you."

"I consoled myself with that for a while after you left." He looked at her sideways to judge her reaction. "Also, she can milk a cow and help deliver a calf."

"Never!" Elisa laughed.

"*And*," Franz added proudly, "she is going to have a baby. Mama will have grandchildren! She is delirious with joy! You know Mama and children . . ." He looked at the three sitting wide-eyed in the sleigh.

"Just perfect." Elisa felt all the old guilt soar away from her. Franz had no regrets, no simmering flame. She was embarrassed that she had imagined him pining away up here in the mountains. He had been ready to marry when she had happened into his life last year, and she had been the closest available female. Now he talked to her as though she were an old schoolmate, a friend. She had always liked him before, always believed that he would make someone a wonderful husband. It simply could not have ever been she. "Congratulations, Franz. Yes. Frau Marta and grandchildren. And Herr Karl—your father will look just right with children on his knee."

Of course, she had the hope that these three children would be accepted and loved and comforted as well. But she said nothing until after they had been fed and washed and tucked into the enormous feather bed with the carved vines that wound up the bedposts.

That night, Frau Marta, Herr Karl, Franz, and his shy young wife Helene sat together around the table in the Herrgottseck. The time had come for all pretenses to drop.

"So now we have two Gretchens in the house," Frau Marta said quietly. "Elisa, can you tell us please what this is all about?"

Franz's arm was around Helene's shoulders. "We know already, Mama, don't we? We knew last year when Elisa's father did not come."

"These children—" Karl smoothed his long, drooping moustache thoughtfully. "They are not Austrian?"

"No." Elisa leveled her gaze at the old couple. "They are Jews. From Germany."

Nods of understanding passed around the table. "Ja," Marta said sadly. "But you have taken a risk bringing them here. You knew that our Otto was—" Tears filled her eyes. "Certainly, last Christmas you noticed that he had pulled away from his family, from his God, and from Austria."

"It was no secret," Elisa acknowledged. "Two snowflakes—" She glanced at Franz, who knew instantly what she was talking about. "But I knew I could bring the children here, Frau Marta . . . because . . . because I knew Otto was not here. I saw him in Vienna."

Frau Marta covered her mouth with her hand. "You saw him? We have not heard even a word since—"

Herr Karl continued for her. "He left us. Left home, you see. It was not right that he stay among us. And so he left."

"Was he well?" Marta leaned across the table. "Did he speak to you? Anything?"

Franz looked gloomy at the mention of his brother. "Where did you see him?"

Their faces were so eager and concerned that Elisa knew she must not tell them *everything*. "I saw him on the street. Just for a moment. I had . . . fallen. He helped me up." She swallowed hard. "But he was with men who are known for their politics. Men who support the Anschluss with Germany, and who openly hate the Jews."

A look of resignation crossed their faces. "So," Karl said. "Since he is there, you knew you could bring the little ones here."

"Yes. Just for a while. You see, things are so very dangerous in Vienna now. There are gangs of men—" Elisa started to explain.

"We read it in the paper," Franz said. "What was done in the Judenplatz. Terrible . . . terrible."

"We can pay you, of course."

The family looked embarrassed. She did not need to mention money. That was not a question. "We have food enough to feed a dozen children," Karl replied quietly. "What more does a child require? A little love. Happy times. A warm, clean place to sleep. Mama has been tucking children into bed for nearly thirty years. My mother and grandmother and hers before her have rocked babes to sleep in this old house. By the grace of God, we can provide all that is needed for these three little souls, and a dozen more if you choose to bring them here."

"Money is not required," Frau Marta added. "We have lost a son. There is much love in our hearts for many more." She raised her eyes to the crucifix above the Herrgottseck. "He says that if we offer a cup of cold water in His name to a child, we have done it to Him. Dear Elisa, bring the children! For Jesus' sake I will feed them fresh bread and butter and milk and dumplings and strudel . . . Oh! That I may feed the Lord through the lives of these little souls whom He loves!"

And so, that night it was settled. The Wattenbarger family would feed and house the refugee children until they could be sent along the line to the homes in Palestine or the schools that Baron von Rothschild had set up in France. They considered it a privilege, as though Christ himself had come to share their home and their food.

Throughout the night, they talked about the best way to bring the children to the farm. No one doubted that there would be many more to come.

"It is best not to bring them here to Kitzbühel . . . perhaps to St. Johann, and then over the mountain. There is a place—"

"Yes, I know the place. I must meet someone there tomorrow," Elisa said. Suddenly she was filled with the awareness that up to this moment, every footstep had been guided by a stronger hand than her own—even the footsteps that had taken her to the terrible encounter in the Judenplatz. *What God has done is rightly done!* God had seen the desperate children and the terrible darkness that would cover the earth. And He had provided some hope, a few small shimmering candles that illuminated a narrow path to safety. In that instant, she felt like weeping with relief. None of this was up to her. She had only to make herself available, and God would do what must be rightly done.

She looked up at them, her eyes brimmed with tears. "I was afraid to come here. I knew it was right, and yet I was afraid—for foolish reasons." She did not confess that she had been ashamed to see Franz again. "Now I am so grateful for you all."

Frau Marta grasped her hand; then Karl and Franz and Helene clasped hands together in the center of the table. A sorrowing Christ gazed down on them from the crucifix as He alone bore the weight of the world's approaching darkness. And there, in that sheltered valley, they made a covenant with light. They would shine when all else was black as pitch. They would shine until the eclipse of evil slid away.

34

Return to Germany

The sun was not up when Elisa climbed onto the sleigh with Franz and Helene. No one had asked her the purpose of her trip to the Ruppen-Alp, but Helene had offered the use of a fine pair of skis as well as her own fur-lined boots for the journey.

A petite redhead, Helene seemed the perfect counterpoint to her handsome, well-muscled husband. She looked at him with adoring eyes and he returned the adoration. Elisa was confident that by next Christmas Franz would have fashioned his angels from another model. If Helene knew that Franz had once loved Elisa, it did not seem to bother her now. When they reached the end of the snowy road at dawn, Helene helped her strap on her skis and then hugged her briefly and sent her off with a cheerful "Grüss Gott!"

A full two hours of hard cross-country skiing lay ahead of Elisa. She had loved the sport as a child and as a teenager, but it had been two years since she had skied so far. She hoped to arrive before Thomas, but as she topped a little rise above the chalet, she spotted him standing outside the door beside his skis. It was not yet eight o'clock in the morning. She was hot and sweaty beneath her warm ski clothes. Thomas looked refreshed and rested—and overjoyed to see her. He stepped out from under the eves, and the morning sunlight shone against his thick black hair. She had always loved his dark hair and swarthy skin—perhaps because it was so different from her own. He looked no different than he had eighteen months before when she had last seen him at the Bahnstadt in Berlin. How she had loved him then! And how torn she had been by him. Love and hate, fury and regret, had tormented her.

But this morning, she felt none of that. There was no spark at seeing his eager smile. She smiled back as she slid toward him, and she waved a ski pole in greeting, but her heart did not race as she had once dreamed it would. She did not fall into his waiting arms or kiss him and let one kiss soothe away the hurt of his betrayal. She was free of Thomas von Kleistmann as she had not been since they were children playing together, as she had not been since they had been intimate beside the Spree River one summer night long ago.

He walked toward her with his arms out and embraced her as she stopped. She returned his embrace dispassionately, and when he continued to hold her tightly and whisper her name, she let her arms drop.

"Hello, Thomas," she said matter-of-factly. The smell of bay rum on his skin did not make her head spin.

"Elisa, darling—" Thomas rushed on, oblivious to her restrained tone. "I reserved a room for us."

She pushed him away firmly. "I did not come here to sleep."

He looked confused, hurt by her manner. "Neither did I." He moved toward her again.

She gave him an icy glare, then knelt to unstrap her skis. "I did not come here to make love, either!"

He knelt beside her. "You have every right to be angry with me . . . I know. I've been terrible. Life has been terrible. But now we can be married, and—"

She kicked her feet free of the skis, and snow hit Thomas in the face. "You're wrong about that," she said, surprised at the cold determination in her voice. None of his tricks, none of the sweet words would work anymore. "I'm here because I need something from you. Not your love, not physical intimacy—although there was a time when I would have done anything for that."

"You don't have to do anything. I've realized—"

"So have I. It's taken me a long time, Thomas, but I've realized a lot of things, too." She propped her skis next to his. "You say you have a room."

"Yes. I . . . I thought . . ."

"You were mistaken, Thomas," she said curtly. "I am here because I have heard that my father is alive. I need your help—your influence. I don't want anything else. But on the honor you have prized above all else, you owe me something—and my father. . . ."

———

The chalet was permeated with the aroma of frying sausages and eggs. The clerk at the desk looked knowingly at them as they walked up the stairs to the room Thomas had rented.

"This is a safe place." Thomas locked the door behind them. A roaring fire crackled in the fireplace. Elisa stood in front of it to dry out her damp clothes. She did not look at the massive bed or at Thomas, who still gazed at her longingly. "I should not be so eager, Elisa. I know. I have abused your love badly."

Elisa's eyes flashed angrily. "I tell you, I didn't come here to talk about our relationship or what you could have done differently. Nothing can change that, and the truth is, I simply don't care anymore. I am past it, Thomas. All I care about is my father." She pulled out the crumpled file from beneath her sweater and tossed it onto the bed.

"I know how difficult it must be for you to respect me after—"

"You want to earn my respect?" she snapped, wishing that she could maintain a cool reserve, but suddenly finding that it had vanished. "Read that!" She jerked her head toward the file. "Then do something about it."

He looked as though she had slapped him across the face. In a way, her challenge *was* a slap that startled him into the realization that winning her back was not simply a matter of a promise of marriage, a bed, and a fire in the fireplace. He hesitated a moment, then picked up the file. Opening it, he sank slowly to the edge of the bed as he read all the details of Theo's escape and saw his own name mentioned in the report as well. And Theo was *alive*! In Dachau, but as of ten days ago, he was still alive.

"Where did you get this?" His voice was ominous; he recognized that such a file could be obtained only under great risk.

"None of your business."

"What are you involved in, Elisa?" he demanded.

"I want my father home."

"Elisa, do you know what it means to have such a file?"

"Do you know what it means to know my father is rotting away in Dachau?"

"I let him escape," he said defensively.

"And they caught him when his plane was forced down. You did nothing."

"I didn't know. Canaris said he had been killed. I thought—"

"If I can find out the truth, why can't you?"

He stared helplessly at the pages of the document. "I . . . I just don't know what the truth is anymore." He shook his head and looked at her pleadingly. "I thought, hoped, that what we once had was true."

"If it had been anything more than lust, Thomas, you could not have let me go."

He gazed at her. There was truth in her words. But he hadn't really known what love was then. "I had to live without you before I knew how empty my life was."

"And I had to live without you before I found how full life could be." Her answer cut him, and he winced with the sting of it.

"What do you want me to do?" he asked, suddenly embarrassed by the bed and the flickering firelight. "How can I prove to you—make you love me again?"

"I won't love you again." Her words were firm.

He stood and walked toward her, pulling her to him and kissing her as she struggled against him. Again and again he kissed her until she simply accepted his kisses without response. When her coldness finally penetrated his consciousness, he pushed her aside. "What has happened to you?"

"I gave my heart to someone else. It isn't yours to command anymore."

"And now *you* command *my* heart," he said miserably. "Tell me what you want. You loved me once. I can make you love me again." For an instant she could read his thoughts.

"Not that way," she warned. "I will never love you if you force me— never."

The thought left as quickly as it had appeared, and he was a contrite little boy again. He sat down and put his head in his hands. "Forgive me," he whispered. "I have thought of nothing but you since—since I let you go away. Nothing but you."

She did not answer him for a long time. "My father loved you like a son, Thomas. I—" She thought of all the good times they had shared together. He had been her friend before they had fallen in love. She had always loved him in one way or another, and now she softened in the face of his abject misery.

"Theo Lindheim is the only father I ever knew. Elisa, believe me, if I had known any of this. . . . You can see that I am implicated in the escape. Of course I saw him go. I couldn't help *except* by letting him go, but surely you see that I love him too." He began to weep softly. He had lost everything. "I thought if I stayed, I could make a difference."

She did not dare move to touch him or comfort him. But she softened her voice. "If you can contact the right people in Germany, we can pay to ransom him."

"I simply didn't know that he was still alive—in that hole! Do you believe me, Elisa? I didn't want any of this. I never wanted to give you up! I thought it would all blow over. But every day it gets worse. If only you knew! If only I could tell you what I've been doing." He wondered if telling her of his secret missions as liaison between the German High Command and the English Foreign Minister would change her mind about him.

"My father is alive," she replied. "If you love him, if you love me as you say you do, then give me some hope! Tell me you'll talk to them about him."

"Yes. Of course." He wiped his eyes with the back of his hand. "Even if you give me no hope of ever—" He could not finish. "Just tell me you can forgive me." He held out his arms to her and almost automatically, she moved toward him to embrace him.

She stroked his hair. *Poor Thomas.* "Yes. We were always friends before. I almost forgot that. I loved you from the time we were children playing on the swings; you bailed out and broke your ankle. Remember?"

He gave a short laugh. "And you were my nurse. A little tyrant! Always warning me, telling me what to do." His words were muffled as he buried his face in the nape of her neck. "Tell me what to do now, Elisa. I will do it. Anything—just tell me."

She was suddenly sad that everything had gone so wrong between them. Of course, it would have been so easy to simply blame the world and Hitler and the darkness. But there was no use in looking for blame. Neither of them had been able to see beyond their passion. They had forgotten the simple things, the everyday things, that had once made them fast friends. Now they were different people. Elisa was someone else, at any rate, and she felt that her future would lead her far away from this man who longed to hold her forever.

She looked up into his face and smiled gently. "I haven't had breakfast yet. Shall we bring it upstairs? Then we can talk together like when we were children making secret plans. And we'll decide what to do."

Leah tossed the small packet onto Elisa's table as the kettle shrieked on the stove. "I'm glad it went so easily for you," Leah said cautiously, testing Elisa's willingness to participate in yet another venture.

"You're glad—" Elisa caught the question in her friend's voice and stood poised with the teakettle in her hand. "And what else?"

"And—" Leah sat down and shoved the packet toward Elisa. "This."

"I am too tired to play guessing games." Elisa did not even pour the water into her cup. Her legs still ached from the journey to the Ruppen-Alp. Her mind was swimming with thoughts about her father and Thomas and the children—faceless children with nowhere to go. "So tell me what you want, Leah? Why have you stayed up waiting for me half the night? I can barely see straight. Just tell me what you want to tell me; then let me go to bed, will you?"

Leah looked tired, too. She smiled a half-smile and unwrapped the packet. Two passports spilled out onto the table—fresh, clean, official passports with the seal of Czechoslovakia embossed on the front.

Elisa's first thought was that these were the papers for the children she had just carted off to the Tyrol. She groaned. The three could have gone directly to Prague and saved her a trip.

Leah flipped open the front cover and revealed photos of two very young children. One, Elisa guessed, was about two. The other was an infant. Residence was noted as Prague, and their names were Maxmillian Linder and Celeste Linder. Elisa was listed as their mother and Pietr Linder as their father.

Elisa gasped and stared at the writing on the document. *"Me?"* she cried. "What is this, Leah?" She laughed and pitched the passports back at her unsmiling friend.

"It was a decision we had to make while you were gone."

"What decision?" Elisa wished that Leah would have waited until morning to spring this on her.

"Their real parents"—Leah opened the passports so that the cherubic faces of the children looked in on the conversation— "are Zionist activists."

"Like you."

"No." Leah looked at her to measure the effect of her words. "They are in Germany. Munich, to be precise. Their days may be numbered. If they are arrested, the sort of confinement Germany offers would be fatal to the children."

Elisa rested her cheek on her hand. "I'm so tired," she whispered. "I am dead on my feet and you approach me like I am a cat about to spring and run away. Just talk plainly to me, Leah, or I may throw you out of the apartment."

Leah drew herself up. "All right. We need you to go to Munich to get the children. And then to take them to a safe house in Prague."

"Go back to Germany again?" Swastikas and barking S.S. men swam before her eyes.

"Yes. For the sake of two children."

Elisa studied the faces and names of the children. "Linder. Little Linder-kinder. My mother will be so proud to have grandchildren. I am happy to see they are not born out of wedlock. My husband's name is Pietr? Is he handsome, Leah?"

"You're telling me you'll go?" Leah looked confused by the punchy banter.

"Yes. Anything. Only let me sleep a while first."

"Tomorrow afternoon, then? You are cleared for five days from the orchestra. We're only doing small chamber pieces. We don't need you right now, anyway."

"That makes me feel even better," Elisa remarked dryly as she stood and stumbled out of the kitchen, kicked off her shoes, and fell into bed with her clothes still on.

———

The risk of returning to Germany under a false passport and carrying illegal documents did not fully occur to Elisa until the train passed from Austrian soil onto Germany's frontier. She relived the horror of her escape from Germany the year before as men and women in uniforms and trench coats swarmed onto the cars. But Elisa raised her chin and looked as though she were above the fear that seemed to course through the other passengers.

Throughout the trip, she sat next to a young woman whose Aryan pedigree was impeccable. Her papers were in order, and yet she was ordered off the train and strip-searched simply because she had dark hair and eyes and looks defined by the Nazi investigators as "Jewish." The young woman did not return to her seat.

If the searches going into Germany are so thorough, she wondered, *what will it be like coming out of the country?*

"You are Czech?" asked the officer.

Elisa was suddenly intimidated by the question. Would he not recognize that her accent was that of a Berliner? She had spent a good deal of time in Prague. The best she could do was imitate the high German accent of the Germans who lived in isolation in Prague. "German," she answered. "But born in Czechoslovakia. As so many of our people."

"Aha!" He smiled at her answer. She was *racially* Aryan, and he accepted her reply. "Yes. You speak very well. We see quite a few Germans from Czechoslovakia . . . the Sudetenland, who speak a Slavic tongue as well." He rocked on his heels in a self-satisfied way. "Natural, I suppose. Do you? Do you speak a Slavic language?"

Elisa could speak a halting form of the Czech dialect. She did not know how to answer. "My parents were both from Berlin. They would not permit me to speak Czech, except to the housekeeper."

Yes, this was an appropriate answer. A good Aryan answer. Keep even the language pure. "Then you can help me, Fraülein," he said with a smirk. "There is an elderly gentleman from Prague. A Slav. He speaks no German, and I cannot make myself understood. Would you—?"

Elisa's smile froze on her face. If she refused to help, the officer would sense that something was wrong. If she accepted, then the elderly Czech would undoubtedly know that she was not from Prague. He would instantly take her for the foreigner she was. It was a dangerous game to play. *"Ja, Herr Oberleutnant."* She addressed him in a title far above the rank indicated by the insignia on his uniform. This seemingly unintentional flattery pleased him.

"Good! Come with me."

The smile still fixed on her face, she followed him down the corridor to where a little man sat surrounded by three other Reich officials who questioned him in broken Czech.

"Stand aside," barked the officer who had questioned Elisa. "The Fraülein is from Prague. She can help us."

The little man looked at Elisa. The officer showed him her passport. *Czechoslovakian. The emblem of his nation on the front.* The man looked from the passport photo of Elisa, back into her eyes again. She silently prayed that he would not give her away.

"From Praha," said the officer, laying his hand on Elisa's shoulder.

The man looked at the passport again and nodded grimly. Elisa managed a smile. She sat down beside him. Could he see her eyes pleading with him? *Of course you will know. You will know I am not a native of your country. But please! Understand what this means.*

The Czech adjusted his pince-nez and greeted her cautiously.

She replied in broken Czech. The corner of his mouth twitched. He did not let his eyes look at her passport again. From the instant she opened her mouth, he knew it was false. The knowledge flickered in his eyes for the barest instant; then he broke into a wide grin and greeted her in enthusiastic Czech, as though she were indeed from Prague.

"I am so glad to have a fellow countryman to talk to!" he exclaimed.

She felt the eyes of the German officers on her. "Thank you. And how can I now help?" The word order was mixed up. The little man paid no attention to her fractured use of his native tongue. He had grasped the situation and took firm control.

"Tell the Germans I have come to visit my brother in Munich who is ill." He repeated the message twice, slowly and in different intonations so that Elisa would understand.

Dutifully, she repeated his words in German, which she hoped contained a trace of a Prague accent.

"You sound almost like a native Berliner," said one of the officers.

"Her parents were from Berlin," explained the officer who had brought her. "They had the good sense to shelter her from such a harsh and low-born language as these Czechs speak."

The officers nodded in unison. It was easy to see that this lovely young woman was of the highest Aryan heritage. They watched her admiringly and their attention was suddenly turned from the old man to the beautiful translator. A few more questions were directed toward him; then they began to question her.

The old Czech looked at her quizzically. "Thank you, madam. We help each other in these times."

She left the compartment, still feeling cornered as the officer escorted her back to her own seat. "Now tell me why you have come to Germany at this time?" He smiled and rocked up on his toes again.

"My family is from Germany," she replied. "So much is happening here for the sake of the German people. I simply wanted to see—"

"You are alone in Munich?" He tugged his earlobe thoughtfully.

Jesu, juva! she silently prayed. She could see the spark of interest in the officer's eyes. "Yes. Just sightseeing."

"I know Munich well. I am free tonight when we arrive in the Bahnhof. Would you allow an officer of the Reich to show you some of the sights?" He moved nearer to her.

"Herr Oberleutnant," she said demurely. "I am quite weary."

"Just an hour or two," he insisted. "Have you had your evening meal?"

Could he see the stab of fear that coursed through her? "I am . . . I . . ." She stumbled over the words as though she had forgotten how to speak German as well.

"A favor . . ." He raised an eyebrow. "For the good relations between the Fatherland and the displaced Germans of the Sudeten, ja?"

He was Gestapo. His very nearness made Elisa feel ill. And yet, there was no way to escape him, it seemed. As the train lurched onward toward Munich, he sat down beside her in the empty place where the dark-skinned German girl had sat. *What became of her?* Elisa wondered. These men could do as they liked . . .

She cleared her throat. "I do not know you," she said firmly.

"I am an officer in the Reich. That is sufficient introduction," he retorted.

"Is that a guarantee that you are a gentleman?" she asked haughtily. She did not like the look in his eyes.

"The Reich would not have it any other way."

Elisa knew that these new German supermen were paid a bonus for marriages to a woman of pure Aryan lineage. Blond-haired women with fair skin and light eyes were pursued and adored. Love was not a question in Germany. Only purity of race. "What can you show me of Munich in an hour?" she asked doubtfully.

"Whatever you would like to see," he answered, slapping his hand against his knee. "It is the New Year tonight! Heil 1938! There are dances, costume balls—" His eyes danced with excitement. "Would you like to see the beer hall where the Führer was arrested as a young man? I can show you where it all began, if you like, and then you may go back to Czechoslovakia and tell the Germans there that it will not be long before they can truly call themselves Germans again! Would you like that, Elisa?" He put his hand on hers. "I insist; as an officer of the Reich, I insist that you be my guest." His voice was pleasant as he spoke, but there was no missing the fact that he had made a decision, and she would have to obey.

"How can I refuse?" She played the role of a flattered woman.

"You cannot," he said with satisfaction. "You must be my guest for this evening in Munich, but I will be your slave, ja? I have an automobile at my disposal, wherever you wish to go. And if you decide you would like to stay out longer than an hour or two, I am off duty until four o'clock tomorrow morning, when my train leaves for Berlin."

Elisa could not believe what was happening to her. As she stepped into the official staff car of the Gestapo agent outside the Munich train depot, she wondered if she might meet her father sooner than she had expected—in Dachau! She held tightly to the violin case and prayed that the officer would not see her hands shaking.

"Herr Oberleutnant," she began as the car pulled away from the curb.

"Please, Elisa!" he insisted, slipping his arm around her shoulders. "You must call me Alfred! Beneath this uniform I am only a man."

Elisa could not help but wonder if this same man had not been one of those who had interrogated her father with the aid of rubber truncheons. "Yes. All right. Alfred, then. I would love to see the beer hall where the Hitler movement began." She would flatter his insane pride, let him glory in all the things he had helped to create in Germany. Red banners draped every building. Uniforms were everywhere. Munich was an armed military encampment. When they arrived at the beer hall, a costume ball was going on. Steins of beer overflowed. Tables and long benches were packed with noisy revelers. A polka band played loudly as young soldiers and women dressed in native costume whirled about the dance floor beneath the swastika flags.

In the noise and dim light of the vast hall where the Nazis had tried and failed in their first attempt to overthrow the Weimar Republic, Elisa felt like a cat locked into a cage with a pack of hounds. Songs of Germany's victorious future were sung again and again. Lusty voices boomed out the Nazi hymns with fervent passion while she listened and tried to look entertained.

Alfred gulped his third beer and leaned across the table to shout above the din, "You will have to learn our songs, Elisa! Soon you will be singing them in Prague also! Glorious! We will soon all be one people! One Reich! One Führer!"

She had heard the slogan before as Hitler had screamed his speeches over the radio. The masses had become infected with the disease, and now the slogans and chants tumbled from their mouths with the ease of breathing!

"And where are those who opposed Hitler?" she shouted back. "Where are they, Alfred?" She could not help asking the question. Was there anyone still free in Germany who did not sing the songs and shout *Sieg Heil* on command?

He thumped his chest proudly, somewhat drunkenly. "That is my job!" He grabbed her by the arm and pulled her up. "You want to see? Ja? You want to see what we have done with them?" He was grinning wildly as he shoved his way out of the celebrating mass into the narrow Munich street again. "Come on, then! You can tell them how we clean the streets in Germany! You can tell the Germans back in Prague that we won't stand for the Bolsheviks or the Jews when we get there."

He raced the engine of the car and careened through the streets of the city. He had drunk too much; he smelled of stale beer, and his eyes were red-rimmed in the soft light of the dashboard.

"Where are we going?" Elisa asked. "It is longer than two hours now." Her fear was close to the surface. "You promised you would be a gentleman," she said as he drove out of the lights of the city and headed into the dark countryside.

He simply laughed in reply, then turned sharply onto an unmarked dirt road. "You're afraid of me?" he asked.

"Please!" Her breath came faster. Where was he taking her? "You promised me if I would only escort you—Herr Oberleutnant! You promised me . . ."

"And I am a man of my word. A German and a gentleman." His words were slurred. The road was muddy and deeply rutted; the wheels spun as he drove up a small slope. "You see!" he shouted triumphantly. He stopped the car, and there before them was a brightly lit compound. White floodlights. Barbed wire. Huge stone walls. Guard towers and machine guns.

Elisa did not have to ask the name of the place. She suppressed a groan, controlling the desire to scream the name of her father. *Dachau!*

She swallowed hard and asked softly, "Why are we here?"

Alfred laughed and pounded the steering wheel. "You asked the question!" he exclaimed. "I told you I was your slave tonight! Am I a man of honor? You asked me where all the people had gone that had opposed the Führer!" He gestured out the windshield at the colorless compound. "And here they are!" He frowned. "You are not pleased?"

Elisa simply stared. She wondered if he could see that the color had also left her face at the sight of the impenetrable fortress. *Papa!* her heart cried out. "It is . . . big," she managed to say.

"Yes. And we are constructing others just as big. It needs to be big. Jews. Bolsheviks. Gypsies—we need a place to put them. Clean up Germany." His words had taken on an almost holy awe of the wonder of such efficiency. "And I am part of it all. I do my duty. . . ." He droned on, but Elisa could not hear him any longer.

Row upon row of buildings sizzled beneath the light. She could make out the silhouettes of the sentinels in the towers. *Papa lives beneath their gaze. And yet they do not see him. They see only bodies.*

"This is our answer to the human debris. . . ."

Papa, I am here. Look up. Past the walls. Can you hear me call you? Please live for us!

"They die quite easily here. The process of natural selection. Survival of the fittest. The Aryan will survive. We were meant to rule and the others. . . ."

The savage barking of dogs echoed through the night. A shot rang out, then a cluster of popping sounds as a machine gun flashed fire in the distance. "What was that?" she jumped.

He laughed again. "Nothing. Sometimes they kill themselves. There is a forbidden zone, and those who are weak-willed go there. It is an invitation to be killed. At night, if you watch, there are always several. It is like watching for falling stars, ja?" He held up his wrist and grimaced at the time. "Alas, fair Elisa, I must get back. It is a thirty-minute drive back to Munich, and I have a train to catch." He leaned close to her. His breath reeked of beer, and she felt sick at the smell of it. "Haven't I been a good boy?"

"Yes," she answered hollowly, still unable to take her eyes from the tower where the fire had burst from the gun.

"Then will you give me one kiss?" He was smiling.

She turned her head to stare at him. What kind of man could ask for a kiss within view of such a horrible place? "Not here," she said, feeling her stomach turn. "I am not used to thinking about people dying so easily."

He shrugged and started the car. "You will get used to it. You will see. We will make the world safe for those of German blood. You will not have to worry about your children. One day we will all live in a great state. The Thousand-Year Reich."

She sat silent and rigid as he talked on and drove back toward Munich. "Take me back to the beer hall," she said at last as they entered the city. She was sure she would be able to disappear into the crowd there.

He hurried around to open the car door for her, then pulled her up and kissed her hard on the mouth. The violin case was between them. Elisa gripped it tightly as though it were a shield.

"Perhaps I will see you in Prague?" Alfred stepped back, then took her hand and kissed it.

She felt her throat constrict. "Perhaps. Thank you for showing me what we might expect."

He waved his hand toward the beer hall, where the polka music boomed and the thump of feet kept time to the melody. "We are all good-natured people! We will bring such enthusiasm with us when we come." He bowed, kissed her hand again, and then with a final wave, he drove away.

Elisa felt the world spin around her. She groped toward a parked car and dropped to her knees on the cobblestones. She was violently sick; her head throbbed as she pulled herself up and then walked carefully toward a waiting cab.

The driver assumed she was one of the musicians. He smiled over his shoulder; then his smile faded at the vision of the pale, pained young woman behind him.

"Where to, Fraülein?"

"Bavaria Hotel," she said with difficulty.

"Too much beer, Fraülein?" he asked sympathetically.

Too much. Too much everything ... She stared silently out the window and prayed for her father ... and for Thomas as he traveled through this sick, unhappy land to help her father.

35

Vision of the Apocalypse

Since the night of the eight candles in Dachau, the scourge of typhus had raced through the weakened prisoners, and men died by the hundreds in the barracks of the camp. The eight of the Herrgottseck were spared for a short time. The priest and the cantor joined the man they called Jacob Stern, breaking rocks for road work in the day and comforting the dying men of the barracks through the night.

There was no medicine to heal, nothing even to ease the pain of those racked by fever. The worn-out blankets did little to keep them warm. They died with the names of wives and children and sweethearts on their lips. They died calling out to God for mercy. They died cursing God for their fate.

At five-thirty each morning, those who could walk staggered out to wait in ragged lines for roll call. The guards delighted in making them stand for hours in the cold until dozens more dropped to the ground to be kicked and beaten.

On the bitter morning of December 31, 1937, Theo answered to his number as he had done for a year. He had almost forgotten his own name. His number and new identity had been crudely pressed onto a base metal tag, then locked onto his wrist on a thick bracelet made of chain like the collars of the guard dogs. But the dogs were treated more humanely then the men.

Six rows ahead of him, he could see the swaying figure of the priest. Theo knew that the priest had also contracted typhus. The skin on his face and bald head glowed with fever. His eyes were red, and he could barely stand this morning. To the left of the priest, the cantor stood. His head was bowed and his breathing labored. So soon the candles flickered and dimmed before Theo's eyes. Where was the light they had sung about? Where was the hope they had affirmed: *"And Thy word broke their sword when our own strength failed us!"*

The priest was the first in his line to fall. The shouts of the guards filled the prison yard. Blows to his back and head failed to bring him to his feet. As prisoners watched and wept silently, the priest lay still and lifeless beneath the furious blows of the guard's boots.

The cantor turned to look at Jacob Stern. Tears of anguished helplessness streamed down his face. The two men locked eyes. *Remember the covenant! Remember what is done here!*

The body of the priest was left where he had fallen. Inmates marched around him, stumbled over him, grieving numbly for the loss of such a light.

By nightfall, the cantor, too, lay delirious on the wooden pallet. His soaring fever kept the men around him warm. Jacob Stern shared his ration of watery soup with him, holding his head and forcing some liquid down his throat.

Brown eyes, pleading, looked up. "Tonight I call you Theo, Jacob Stern." There was a hint of a smile on his cracked lips. "There is no need for me to fear what they do to me. Theo Lindheim. We know. We all know you." The eyes were glazed with fever. Theo stroked the man's head. "You must not talk, Nathan," Theo said softly. "Save your strength."

"Why? I will not need it by morning." He knew. He licked his lips and closed his eyes. "Promise me—"

"What is it?" Theo asked, bending his ear close to the mouth of the dying man. "What, Nathan?" There was pain in his voice. Could the cantor leave them so soon? After such a night of hope, could they lose the light of two such men in one day?

"Say Kaddish for me." The words were soft. "Remember my Jahrzeit."

"You must get well," Theo insisted.

"No. Too tired. No oil in the lamp . . ."

"You *must* not die."

The cantor's eyes suddenly became clear. "Remember the covenant. Live, Jacob Stern . . . *Theo*. And tell them. My wife and children are in Strassburg . . ."

"I will tell them how you sang for Hanukkah. I will tell them about the lights."

"Yes, the lights. My wife's name is Reba . . . tell her." He closed his eyes and slept.

Theo sat clutching his knees and watching the cantor through the long night. He dozed, then jerked his head up to watch and wait again. Some time before daybreak, the rasping breath of the cantor fell silent, and in a broken voice Theo began to sing as the spirit of the cantor soared above the walls of Dachau.

By ten-thirty that morning, Elisa was already in the Marienplatz of Munich, waiting as Leah had instructed her. At precisely 10:45, she entered the public restroom and placed the water-tight package containing seven passports into the tank of the toilet in the last stall.

The old woman who worked as the restroom attendant simply smiled at her and handed her a towel after she washed her hands. That much of the assignment had gone easily.

Elisa emerged onto the Platz again just before eleven o'clock and searched the teeming crowds of market-day shoppers. She was to meet the young couple Leah had described to her and the two tiny children she was to take from them.

Her own grief for her father was still sharp and intense. The thought of taking two children from their parents, possibly forever, simply piled grief on top of grief.

At eleven, in the tower above the huge square, the Glockenspiel clanged out the hour as figures of knights and ladies danced in front of it. All eyes in the Platz were turned upward for the show—all, that is, except for Elisa's. As her eyes scanned the square, she prayed that she would find them, and prayed again that the parents would have changed their minds. How could anyone give up children?

Behind her, she heard the cooing of a baby. She turned suddenly to face a young man whose features were so filled with anguish that there was no mistaking who he was or why he had come. Two young children were in a covered pram. Elisa's gaze fixed on the father. Her eyes brimmed with tears of sympathy for him. He bit his lip, looked one last time at his little ones and then at Elisa. They did not speak.

As the clock above them finished chiming, he turned on his heel and disappeared into the market crowds. For a moment, Elisa stood beside the pram, then put her hands on it and pushed it through the throngs of people. The children did not even notice that their father had gone. They did not protest or complain or cry. Wide-eyed, they stared at the bustle around them. The baby was soon rocked to sleep by the bump of the wheels against the cobblestones.

Soon little Max was also asleep. It was a small miracle for Elisa. She had spent the night imagining that they would gape at her and scream hysterically for Mommy and Daddy.

Even as they boarded the streetcar for their ride to the Bahnhof and the train to Prague, the children slept without noticing that the hands that guided the pram were not those of their father. They slept on and on.

Amid the clamor of the public address system in the station and the whistle of the trains, they still slept. As Elisa struggled with violin case and small suitcase and the pram, a porter assisted her onto the train. She was worried about the little ones when they lay so still beneath their blankets. Still, she was afraid that she might wake them and begin a wail that would not go unnoticed. She left them in the pram and rolled it between the seats in front of her. She could see the faces of the children, their cheeks pink and healthy. They breathed deeply and peacefully as the train chugged back across the German countryside toward the border of Czechoslovakia. Beautiful children. How could their parents bear such a parting? She wondered now what the mother must be feeling. And how would the children react when they finally woke up and saw the worried face of a stranger staring down at them?

Elisa pulled the small suitcase from beneath the pram. She opened it, relieved to see an ample supply of diapers, bottles of milk, and a tin of biscuits for the two-year-old. On top of it all was a large bottle of cough syrup with instructions scrawled on the outside. *For restlessness when traveling. Baby 1 tsp. Max 2 tsp.* The children were not ill. Suddenly it became clear to Elisa why they slept so deeply. They had been given the medicine to make them sleep. For their own safety as well as Elisa's, the possibility of fearful tears within the grim borders of the Reich had been eliminated.

Elisa closed the case and pulled out the passports. "Thank you," she sighed, uncertain that she could have handled screaming children and Gestapo agents, too.

Her relief was so great that she found herself actually able to chat pleasantly when the Gestapo prowled through the cars checking papers at the border.

The train slid into Czechoslovakia without one question. And the children did not awaken until the whistle blew for Prague.

———

For three days, Elisa stayed in Prague with her mother. She did not tell her about the two children who had gone from Germany to safety without ever once seeing who had delivered them. She did not tell her mother that she had watched from a hill above Dachau or that Theo might be alive inside the living hell of that place. She waited to hear how her mother was bearing up.

Anna shared her hopes with Elisa as they washed the dishes one night in the little house Theo had bought for their safety.

"Every night your father comes to me in my dreams," Anna told her wistfully.

Elisa could see that the strain of the last year had taken its toll on her mother. For the first time, Anna looked older. Her eyes seemed hauntingly sad, as though they had seen a thousand years of suffering in only one.

"Then you are together sometimes," Elisa said gently.

"It is a strange and wonderful thing to dream." Anna passed her a plate. "Every night God restores what I have lost during the day. Such sweet dreams! Every night we are at home in Berlin—your father in his library, and I at the piano. Just like it used to be. Or we are together in Paris. Or once again you are all small and we walk through St. Stephan's while your father shops for the store. And sometimes we sit together and talk."

"What does he say?" The thought of the machine-gun fire at Dachau clouded Elisa's face.

Anna looked into Elisa's eyes. "He tells me I should not worry. That we will be together again one day." Tears brimmed in Anna's eyes, and she quickly looked back into the dishwater. "And I believe that. Yes. In heaven we will see one another again if not in this life."

Elisa put down the dish towel and hugged her mother. How she wanted to tell her about the file! About Thomas! But she did not dare. Wasn't there enough for Anna to worry about? Theo had saved his wife from knowing what he was doing in Germany. Elisa would not tell her mother that she had been back to Germany for any reason.

"Oh, Mother! I do hope it is in *this* lifetime that we are all together again! The house in Berlin, all the things that were our life then—none of that matters if only we can be together!"

Anna seemed not to hear Elisa's hope. "Of course, in the daytime, when I wake up and he isn't here," she sighed, "I feel empty and gray inside. Like an empty box. But I have my dreams. Yes. Each night a merciful hand reaches out to soothe all the wounds that man has inflicted on us during the day . . ."

"Do you believe he'll come back to us, Mother?" She did not want to give Anna false hope. Until she heard from Thomas again, the information would be more cruel than kind.

"Believe?" Anna considered the word. "I can't believe anymore, Elisa. But I hope. And I pray for him with every breath and heartbeat." She tossed her head and looked out the window to where the hundred towers of Prague blended into the soft light of dusk. "I look at the stars and the sky and I wonder if he can see them too. And if he is . . . *gone*, then I imagine that he is looking back at me. And I whisper happy things to him. About you, and the boys. Maybe he can hear and is happy too. But no, I cannot believe that he will come through that door and take me in his arms again. I had to give that up, or I would have died from longing. Sometimes it's better to give up." She frowned and shook her head. "I'm not making sense, am I?"

"Yes, Mother. I think I understand. *God alone must have my heart. . . .*" Elisa sang the melody of the song to her.

Anna smiled. "Always music, Elisa," she teased. "Yes. I have given up and given my hopes and beliefs to God. He knows. There is no other answer that I can find."

————

On the way back to Vienna, Elisa could not help but think how her mother hoped without *knowing* any of what Elisa knew. Anna had been able to trust that the fate of the one man she had ever loved was not in her hands, but in hands far more wise and capable than her own.

Elisa was glad she had not given her any more to hold on to. And as the weeks passed with no word from Thomas, she became more convinced that her silence had been merciful for Anna.

————

The waiting room outside the office of Admiral Canaris was crowded with young men in uniform who had come to offer some information or beg some favor from the great man. Thomas sat among them as they smoked or chatted quietly about innocuous subjects like the weather or the fight scheduled for June between the Nazi pugilist Max Schmeling and the black American Joe Louis.

"The Führer is confident that Schmeling will defeat the Negro. Aryan blood will tell."

The Americans would delight in a victory for this Joe Louis fellow. Imagine! They support a Negro instead of a white man . . . an Aryan! They say he can't even talk properly. Poor Max will be fighting a gorilla. A strange place, America!"

Thomas listened absently to their conversation. *It's a shame,* he thought, *that Hitler's grand schemes cannot be settled between nations in man-to-man combat. One champion to each state. A duel to the death. Then the bout between Joe Louis and Max Schmeling would settle the issues about which Hitler harangues day in and day out.*

He drummed his fingers nervously on his knee and tried not to think about the file in his briefcase. *Jacob Stern. Inmate Dachau.* Why had Canaris told him Theo's plane had crashed in the mountains beyond Munich? Why had he told him Theo was dead? Was the word *Dachau* synonymous with *Death* inside the Reich now? Of course not. He had heard stories of men who had been ransomed out every day. And some minor offenders had been released. Priests and pastors who had recanted their blasphemies against the Nazi regime had been set free on occasion. Jews were only freed on the condition that great amounts of money passed into the proper channels, however. Theo Lindheim was now definitely in that category. Under the name Jacob Stern, his freedom would come with payment. Now Thomas would act as broker with the powerful.

"Von Kleistmann." The secretary's voice was matter-of-fact. "Admiral Canaris will see you now."

Canaris did not look up from his sheaf of papers as Thomas entered the room and raised his hand in salute. Neither man uttered the words "Heil Hitler." Under the circumstances, such a salute would have been preposterous. They were alone, without witnesses, and there was no need to pretend.

"Sit down, Thomas." The silver-haired officer sounded weary. The burden of events had aged him. The certainty of the future had robbed him of hope. "What do you want?" He was curt, but it did not alter Thomas's determination.

"Theo Lindheim is alive," he answered without ceremony. He opened his case and tossed the folder onto the desk of Canaris. "Read that."

Canaris looked at the folder with scorn. "I have one just like it," he said, shoving it back toward Thomas.

"No, sir." Thomas tried to correct him. "It says that Theo Lindheim is not dead. He is an inmate in Dachau. Under the name Jacob Stern. It's all there. He didn't die in a plane crash."

Canaris leaned back and pressed his fingers together. "It would have been better if he had."

"You mean you know this?"

Canaris nodded. "For some time."

"But you said—"

"I said he was dead. To silence you. You ask questions which are none of your business about men who are declared criminals to the Reich."

"But he isn't—"

"He *is* dead, Thomas. Forget the issue."

"How can I forget? He was like my own father. A great hero of the Fatherland."

"You think there aren't a thousand others just like him rotting in the concentration camps right now? We have no power. Himmler and the Gestapo have all the power with Hitler. All we have to do is involve ourselves in one escape and we will find ourselves in Dachau, or in some dark cellar with our backs flayed open. Himmler has the ear of Hitler in matters of arrest. Within the borders of Germany, Himmler is the one who decides who will live and who is an enemy of the state." He tossed his pen onto the stack. "Here in the Abwehr, we deal with the military intelligence, as you well know."

Thomas was not expecting a lecture. "But Lindheim was your friend!"

Canaris leaned forward in an angry whisper. "You little fool! Don't you realize what's at stake here? One by one Himmler is eliminating the old guard of Germany! I am most certainly on his list! And so we watch in silence as a man like Lindheim disappears, because if we help him, then we too, are the enemy." He sat up straight. His clear blue eyes were rimmed with red as he stared fiercely at Thomas. "Forget it! Hope that if we endure long enough, this evil will pass, and perhaps Theo and the other thousands will still be alive to appreciate what we try to do."

"You are doing nothing!" Thomas was unafraid as he challenged Canaris. "You let innocent men die and do nothing!"

"You are wrong," Canaris sighed. "I am hanging on with my teeth. There are others. You know them. We watch as the Führer foams at the mouth and slams his fists against the wall and orders the arrest and death of anyone Himmler accuses of being anti-Nazi. And we hope we will not be accused."

Thomas stared at the file. "Then where can I go? How can I help him?"

"Go back to Paris." Canaris picked up his pen and began to write again. "Forget about him."

"I can't."

"You must. For the sake of Germany, we must not also die in Dachau. You have a job to do." He pointed the pen at Thomas. "I order you back to your post. There you will receive your orders. The jails are full of good men, von Kleistmann. Full. Your job is to remain free in this hell. Some will have to be sacrificed. Theo Lindheim is dead, and the matter is closed."

He did not return the file. Nor would he, Thomas knew. The matter was closed, locked away in the impenetrable vaults labeled *Sacrifice for the Fatherland*. At best it was a trade-off. Canaris had chosen to ignore the fate of guiltless men in the hope of regaining some position of power among the madmen who now conducted the policies of the Reich.

Thomas rose slowly and looked down at the Chief of Military Intelligence. "Didn't you see this coming?" he asked quietly. "Why did we wait so long? How did it come this far?"

Canaris hung his head, passing a hand over his eyes. "How? Why? A thousand times a day I ask myself. Did we see? Perhaps. Yes. We could have stopped it. We could have." He looked up toward Thomas. His face was haunted by the vision of Apocalypse. "But now we see so *much* more clearly! So much more horribly what will be unless . . ." His words sounded hopeless. "And now there may be no stopping, no turning back. A Jew like Theo Lindheim. Ten thousand other great men—my God, Thomas, it is only the beginning. Only the beginning. The tide is so strong the current carries us away. *Hitler has surrounded himself with sycophants and lackeys who think and speak as he does!*" He sighed and shook his head sadly. "Yes, we could have stopped it. Perhaps there is still hope that a few of us may still. But the machine feeds on human life. Germany is filled with men whose only duty is to arrest and interrogate. The watchers and the watched. I am watched by Himmler's Gestapo. So are you. Do not be mistaken. We must move carefully, Thomas. And if there is even one shining fragment of hope left that we might stop him, then nothing else—no single life—matters."

Canaris stood and walked to the window to stare at the Chancellery building. "Put the innocent to death in your heart so that you may live to see evil kick and twist slowly on the end of a rope." He looked at Thomas over his shoulder. "Stay alive, von Kleistmann. There are so few of us left."

Thomas shook his head and left Canaris's office in silence. Perhaps the admiral was right, after all. Perhaps one man's life did not matter so much if they had a chance of stopping Hitler's madness. Theo Lindheim would consider it a fair trade—of that Thomas was certain.

Lindheim will never come out of Dachau alive, Thomas thought grimly, *and I still have a chance to help put a stop to this insanity.*

Elisa would be better off believing that her father was dead. Her false hope and her insistent probing could only cause more trouble for everyone. *A small lie,* Thomas reasoned. *And one that could soon become truth. A gentle, compassionate lie to make life easier for everyone.*

36

Behind the Wall

Letters of protest against Murphy's editorials flooded *The New York Times.*

"We in America have enough to deal with...."

"Why entangle ourselves in the arguments of Europe...?"

"Thousands of our own are out of work! Doesn't Mr. Murphy think there is enough to do right here in our own country without..."

"America is safe behind the Atlantic Wall. The quarrels between the Nazis and the King of England are none of our business...."

The citizens of the nation had made themselves heard! No one wanted any part in Europe's quarrels. Let the Nazis have Austria! Let Franco have Spain! Let Italy take Abyssinia. Where was Abyssinia, anyway? What did that have to do with finding work for unemployed millions in the soup lines of America?

Murphy read his orders from the editorial department while he finished his coffee at a small cafe across the street from the INS office in Paris. Eddie Griffith delivered the telegram himself, shrugged and said, "Sorry, kid," and walked off.

Murphy scanned the message like a man reading his own death sentence:

AMERICA SICK TO DEATH ABOUT WAR AND APPEASEMENT STOP WILL NOT BE RUNNING ANY MORE OF YOUR EDITORIALS STOP STICK TO STRAIGHT REPORTING STOP IF YOU NEED TO PREACH FIND ANOTHER JOB STOP TAKE THE ISOLATIONIST VIEW STOP TAYLOR

Murphy would have laughed if he hadn't felt so disgusted. A year ago in the Adlon Hotel, Timmons had told him, *"Nobody likes a Jeremiah."* That was why people avoided Winston Churchill like the black plague. Suddenly, Murphy had the plague, too! So here it was in black and white:

the American people didn't want their indigestion acting up when they read the morning papers. Murphy had touched a raw nerve. He had suggested that England and France might appreciate a little help from their big cousin across the waters. He had mentioned that together the democracies of the world might put an end to trouble before it went any further. The trouble was, Murphy had not been home in three years. He didn't know his country anymore. America had turned inward to its own devastating problems.

"Safe behind the Atlantic Wall," Murphy muttered to no one as he wadded up the telegram and tossed it onto his empty plate. He stared at it for a long time until the waiter carried it away and presented the bill. *So they aren't impressed that the Nazis would kill their own ambassador to take over Austria. Plot to kill him, pardon me. I need to keep this accurate. To the point. Nobody cares. So why should I? Why not just pack up and head back to New York?*

The only answer he could come up with this morning had something to do with a certain violinist in Vienna. He was disgusted with himself, convinced that he must subconsciously enjoy his own pain and suffering. After all, she was "just a dame," as Johnson would say. Nothing unique about dames. They were all pretty much alike.

Murphy rubbed his head and wondered if Elisa was still in Vienna or if her shining knight had carried her off to safety. He pulled the little wooden angel out of his pocket and gazed at it for a moment, then looked at his watch. He could still make the morning train if he hurried. There was nothing much to keep him in Paris now. Vienna seemed to be the place where the blade of the guillotine was slowly sliding downward.

Murphy could not even find the emotional energy to care anymore. The American readership had already shown him what they thought of his writing. *John Murphy, man least likely to win the Pulitzer Prize.* Maybe somebody would take pity and send him and Winston Churchill off to an asylum for unwanted Jeremiahs. Murphy paid his bill and walked between the crowded tables toward the exit.

Near the door, he stopped and stood gawking. *The German!* The man from Cannes who had walked out of Eden's suite and looked at Murphy like he wanted to choke him. The German stared hard at Murphy; then he got up suddenly and stalked back toward the kitchen. When he turned to look once more, Murphy gave him a jaunty "Heil" sign. The German simply turned away and walked through the swinging doors of the kitchen area.

"Hey!" Murphy muttered aloud. "I'm nobody, fella!" He was laughing at the irony of the fear that he had seen cross the German's face. "I'm practically unemployed." No one even looked up or noticed his little performance. He shrugged and left the cafe, determined to ask Churchill about this grim young man next time they met.

Not everyone in America lacked appreciation for prophets. There were a few dark souls who gazed eastward from the shores of the Atlantic and caught some glimpse of the gathering storm over Europe.

President Franklin Roosevelt sighed deeply as he let the copy of *The New York Times* fall to the floor beside his wheelchair. He believed the prophecy even before he had read John Murphy's editorials and articles. On his desk was a stack of the latest intelligence reports from Europe. Publicly he had called the nonintervention policy of the League of Nations in Spain tantamount to offering support to Hitler and Mussolini. And yet, the regular *Fireside Chats* broadcast to his hungry, suffering nation proclaimed the neutrality of the United States in all matters concerning Europe. Now Colonel Lindbergh had come home from his visit with Göring, declaring the invincibility of the German Air Force and the German war machine! America believed Lindbergh. *"There is no use quarreling with Hitler!"* they cried. *"If war came, so what? At least American lives would not be lost! Not like the last war!"*

The President understood the mood of the nation. It took twenty years to raise a son and only one hour of war to kill him. Roosevelt had sons of his own. Hadn't he told the people that? Hadn't his voice crackled over radios in West Virginia and Maine and in farmhouses in Iowa and Minnesota? He had promised them. There would be no war to claim their sons. America was *neutral*!

He placed his palms on the wheels of his chair and turned from his desk to face the window. It was dusk. Darkness had already come to Europe. Last night he and Eleanor had watched the latest films in the basement theater. Just as though they had gone to a movie in the Roxie, the President had watched newsreels showing Lindbergh walking with German generals. The Germans had provided the film, he heard later. And then he had seen the arrest of the Nazi terrorists in Austria and watched as Hitler raged before thousands in the Sportpalast. Later, in the movie, Cary Grant had declared, "Put Hitler on the funny page!"

This morning, Roosevelt had read a transcript of Hitler's speech. It was nothing to laugh about. A plea had come from British Foreign Secretary Anthony Eden, asking for an indication from the United States that the great democracy behind the Atlantic Wall might aid in finding some solution. Throughout the day, Roosevelt had read and reread Eden's secret dispatch. He had pored over the articles and assessed public opinion once again. There were only a few men brave enough to say what they knew to be true. Everyone else hoped that if they hid their heads, the storm would pass quickly by.

Roosevelt frowned. He knew better. Hitler was hungry. More hungry than the millions who lined up right now in soup kitchens across America. Men would steal and kill and lie when they were hungry. Maybe not all, but some. And there were a few among them who would do all those things even when they were satisfied.

He wheeled himself back around to his desk and picked up the telephone. "Ring British Ambassador Lindsay for me, Sec'try Welles!" he drawled. Then he hung up and began to write his reply to Anthony Eden:

> *Perhaps it is time that the great democracies of the world join together in a conference in which the political aims and claims of certain European states—primarily Germany and Italy—would be examined. It might be to the advantage of peace if we might see if these "hungry states" would be satisfied with an equal access to the world's raw materials....*

———

President Roosevelt's message was passed on to Sir Ronald Lindsay with the warning that it must be treated as top secret until the British communicated their opinion on the possibility of such a conference. After all, a president with a Congress so rooted in neutrality dared not openly involve himself in an attempt to stop Europe's quarrels.

Within hours the letter was placed inside a diplomatic pouch bound for England. But this thin thread of hope could not have reached London at a worse time. Anthony Eden, who would have understood the significance of Roosevelt's offer, was still in France. The envelope, marked *Top Secret*, was instead placed on the desk of British Prime Minister Chamberlain.

It was discussed politely over tea with the PM's chief advisor, Sir Horace Wilson, and undersecretary of state for foreign affairs, Sir Alexander Cadogan.

"Eden, of course"—Wilson's tone was disdainful—"would accept the President's invitation joyfully, I have no doubt."

"Well, he's off on the Riviera with Winston now, isn't he?" added Chamberlain. "I think it's best if we say nothing to Eden about the matter, don't you agree?" He leveled his gaze on Cadogan, who had already, in fact, attempted to reach Eden by phone and then had dispatched the message by special courier, who had missed Eden's train in Marseilles by five minutes.

Cadogan did not attempt to conceal his disapproval. "I think it most unwise to make the decision without at least consulting the foreign secretary! The message is addressed to Eden."

"Such a conference is impossible," Chamberlain explained like a schoolmaster instructing a stupid pupil. "It will only interfere with our own plans. You see, we plan to work for a reestablishment of friendship with Fascist Italy. Their conflict in Spain is . . . well, it really has nothing to do with England, has it? And Anthony Eden has been so disapproving . . . the Italians don't like Anthony, I'm afraid."

Cadogan sat in stunned disbelief. Chamberlain was personally making his own foreign policy without consulting either the Cabinet or the foreign minister! "But what about the President of the United States? This is the first indication that the United States might even put a toe in the water; are we going to turn him down?"

Chamberlain shrugged. "We don't need them." He was smiling benignly. "The Germans are people. The Italians are people. Why, my brother Austen and Mussolini's brother were great chums in the twenties! Practically family. We can reason this out. We are practical men."

Cadogan sat glumly silent for a moment. At last he spoke. "Yes. And in the last war, the German Kaiser and the King of England were cousins as well. Didn't stop ten million deaths in the trenches though, did it?"

Chamberlain's patience fled. He sniffed and raised his chin in indignation at Cadogan's remark. "Quite enough. Cable the President!" he snapped. "Tell Roosevelt that we cannot accept his offer because we have much more fruitful prospects of our own." He sipped his tea again. "And really, Cadogan, Eden need not hear of this. No need at all. It will simply upset him, don't you agree, Horace?"

Sir Horace, who had been enjoying a biscuit, nodded. "One can't expect to take such a message seriously. What good would it do for us to sit around and chat about Germany and Italy? Wooly nonsense, you know, just wooly nonsense!"

"You have your orders, Cadogan. Send the wire, will you?" Chamberlain looked down his nose at Cadogan—a defense against the anger and disapproval that must have been evident on the undersecretary's face as he stalked out of the room.

President Roosevelt, the wire began, *in the absence of Foreign Secretary Anthony Eden, I regret to inform you that Prime Minister Chamberlain. . . .*

———

New inmates crowded into Dachau faster than the bodies of the dead could be carried away. Every day brought frightened, bewildered men into the roll call. Neat lines of living dead were taught, by the sting of a lash, to stand for hours on end in the freezing cold; to eat thin, watery soup made from a few rotten vegetables; to suffer without argument at the hands of the master Aryans chosen as their keepers.

Theo envied the priest and the cantor now. Daily rations grew shorter, and the cruelty of the guards toward men too sick to work became more intense. At night the moans of the dying created a scene from Dante's *Inferno.* Each morning, those who were dead and those who were dying were taken out of the barracks.

This morning, a pale dawn broke over the distant mountains. Perhaps a Bavarian farmer watched it out the window as he ate his breakfast, Theo thought. Such shimmering pastels would be beautiful if a man could simply sit and watch the colors change. But in the brutal cold of the lines, guards with jackboots and whips were beating those who had trouble standing. Kicks and screams drowned out the sound of the birds. Blood was brighter than the sky. Theo stared straight ahead and thought how lucky were the men who had died.

Two guards shoved an old man into line next to Theo. *Julius Stern* was his name; the shining new prisoner identification band read: *J. Stern.* The guard shoved the butt of his whip under Theo's chin.

"A new prisoner," he growled to Theo. "Another Stern. Two Sterns we have in this line now. Are you dogs born of the same litter?"

Theo did not reply.

The guard continued. "You will teach this old man the rules, Stern," he warned Theo. "If he breaks them, *you* will be punished!" With a hard blow to the side of Theo's face, the guard walked on.

Theo did not raise his hand to touch the trickle of blood that flowed down his cheek. He did not acknowledge his pain.

"Your name is Stern also?" asked the old man.

"Shut up!" Theo hissed. The first rule must be silence on the line! The old man understood and obeyed instantly. Out of the corner of his eye, Theo could see that the hands of Julius Stern were soft and plump. His chin was pink where the S.S. had shaved off his goatee. Weak eyes squinted into the harsh morning light. He was short—at least a head shorter than Theo—and he filled out the striped prisoner's uniform. *It is good that he has extra weight,* Theo thought. *Soon enough he will burn away every extra ounce on his body.* Theo pitied his new charge. The soft hands trembled with confusion and fear at what had befallen him.

Throughout the long, cold hours of that first day, the old man worked in front of Theo. The rocks cut his hands as he labored with the other men to build an embankment for a road. He tried to sit, gasping for air.

"Don't sit," Theo whispered through clenched teeth. "I will pass the stones around you. Only don't sit. They will shoot us."

The old man put a hand to his heart and wheezed words that Theo could not understand. Theo knew that his new companion would not survive long if the guards drove him as ruthlessly as they did the younger men. But then, that was the idea, after all. It was the policy. Those who could work for the sake of the Reich deserved to live.

That night the old man lay on the hard wooden pallet of the Herrgottseck where the priest had died. He clutched his chest and breathed with difficulty as he tried to talk to Theo. "They have broken my eyeglasses," he moaned. "I cannot see my own hand."

"Stay by me." Theo's voice was urgent. "You must do what I do or they will beat us both, Herr Stern."

"Why have they done this?" The old man began to weep softly. "I am not even a German. I am Austrian, from Vienna!" His voice was pleading, but there was no one there who could help him.

"An Austrian!" A voice called from another pallet. "There are this week a hundred Austrians here. New men. Since Schuschnigg arrested those Nazis in Vienna."

"But I have committed no crime!" the old man protested. "I am a professor of literature at the university! Not a German! My colleagues tried to convince me to fly back from Brussels, but I was afraid! I was terrified of the airplane, you see, and so I took the train and—" He shook his head in confusion. "I had a copy of the book by Kafka—*The Trial*. How was I to know that the Germans arrested men for having such a book? I could have sent that back on the plane, but I brought it to read—just to read on the trip across Germany, and they arrested me! I have been days in a prison in Munich! They cut off my beard and took my glasses, and now I am here without knowing how. Or why! Like the man in *The Trial!* Imprisoned and condemned and executed without ever knowing why."

Theo let him run down; then he leaned over him. "You must not say more about your arrest, Professor Stern," he whispered. "There are informers even here. In this place we are like the man in Kafka's book. That is why the book is forbidden." He put his hand gently on the old man's arm. "You must stay with me, Professor. Are you hungry?"

The old man turned his head away miserably. "Too tired to eat."

"If you don't eat you will die." Theo helped him up. "There is a rule that you must come to get your own ration. Five ounces of bread a day. Eat half tonight. Save the rest for morning." He spoke to Stern as if he were a small child. "Come, Professor. I will help you."

The old man squinted at Theo. "Have I stepped into Kafka's book, Jacob? Have I lost my mind and lost my way and now am condemned to live out the fate of a character in a book?"

Theo could see the cataracts on the old scholar's eyes. He was almost blind, yet they had taken his glasses, his books, and his life from him. Theo tried to think what would bring the old man to some reality other than this present horror. "So you are a professor of literature?" he asked. "I met my wife in Vienna." He would not mention Elisa, but the thought of her music and the symphony made him suddenly eager to ask a thousand questions of the old man. "Do you go to the symphony? To the Musikverein?"

"Yes. I always have season tickets." His voice sounded choked. That world seemed so far away now.

"You will be back in no time," Theo tried to comfort him. "A small infraction. You will be released." He chose to ignore the mocking laughter of those who overheard his comment. "Tell me, please. What did the orchestra play this year at the Musikverein? Can you remember the programs? The music? And the musicians? Do you . . . can you describe it all to me? It has been so very long since I have heard music. Violins. Please, Professor Stern, tell me about Vienna? How was it when you saw it last?" Somehow Theo's simple, eager questions returned dignity and composure to the old man. He sighed, and as thin, green water was poured into filth-encrusted bowls, he began to speak about Vienna as it had been. Theo was suddenly relieved that the professor was nearly blind. The old man could not see what he was eating. Perhaps his sense of taste was not so keen anymore, either. He only grimaced slightly as he sipped the stinking brew and talked about the music and the city to Theo and the others who joined them in the Herrgottseck. For a time, the professor was lecturing again to a captive audience. For an hour his role was a comfort to inmates and to himself.

They had almost forgotten the world outside these walls, and tonight it came back to them.

"The first program at the Musikverein last year was *Elijah*! Oh the *power* of it! The chorus was superb!"

"And the strings?" Theo asked, picturing Elisa by the light of her music stand. "The violins, Herr Professor?"

"The violins? Ah, what can one say about the violins of the Vienna Symphony, Jacob? They are the finest, ja? The finest in the world. . . ."

37

A Hell More Fierce Than Dachau

Murphy sat in the highest balcony of the State Opera House where the night's performance was about to be played. He was sure that Elisa would not see him from this distance—if indeed she was still with the orchestra and hadn't disappeared with her long-lost love.

He was angry at himself for coming tonight. It seemed to be a particularly cruel form of self-torture to sit in the farthest gallery and stare at the empty chair in the first violin section and wonder if she would appear. *Hope* she would appear; then hope again that she was somewhere else, far away from Vienna. The guys in the press room had talked about men who had gone nuts before over some dame—like King Edward, giving up his crown. Now here he was sitting in an auditorium, like a peeping Tom climbing a tree to look in a window at a girl. He couldn't remember ever before having the feeling that he was looking into someone's *heart.* But that was the way Elisa had made him feel.

"Why am I doing this to myself?" He said aloud. Then he slammed the rolled-up program against the empty seat beside him and stood up to leave.

Just then, the musicians began to filter out onto the stage. Shimon at the tympani. Leah, wrestling her cello, checking the score. Members of the first and second violins and violas. He stood rooted in front of his seat. And then Elisa came from the wings. Her long golden hair fell over her shoulders, and she brushed it back and tossed her head. Her skin was smooth ivory in contrast to the long black gown. Someone spoke to her and she leaned down to whisper a word in reply. She nodded and smiled at Leah as she passed and then, as she reached her chair, Murphy sat down in perfect unison with her.

He ran his hand over his face. He was perspiring. *Why is she still here?* He squinted, trying to catch some glimpse of a ring on her hand. He was too far away. If there was a wedding band, an engagement ring or something, he couldn't see it. *Why didn't I bring opera glasses?*

The balcony had begun to fill with concertgoers. A fat man who looked like a bank clerk sat down in front of Murphy. The man had opera glasses, and Murphy tapped him on the shoulder.

"Bitte . . . may I borrow . . . ?"

"Mein Herr, there is nothing to see yet!" He laughed and passed the glasses to Murphy, who sighed with relief.

He focused the tiny glasses on Elisa and instantly felt his heart constrict. Her eyes were intense as she studied the music. Slender fingers held the violin. He thought of those fingers intertwined with his that day in the open-air market. And suddenly he rejoiced. There was no wedding band on her hand!

As quickly as his heart rose, it fell again. "So what?" he muttered as he handed the glasses back to the fat man. Then he stood to go again, saying, "Bitte, bitte, bitte," as he inched past patrons and tried not to tramp on their toes. At the end of the aisle, he turned for one last look at her. She raised the violin and tucked it beneath her chin. He wished he could be her violin. She drew the bow across the string, and Murphy turned around to go back to his empty seat once again. "Bitte, bitte schön! Bitte!"

He sat down with a sigh and tapped the fat man on the shoulder again. "Would you sell me your opera glasses?" he asked the startled man.

The man shook his head and stuck out his lower lip. "Nein! My wife bought them for me before she passed away last Christmas."

"How much do you want for them?"

"I will not sell them, Mein Herr!"

"What are they worth?"

"But they are not for sale!" The fat man was angry and indignant.

"Fifty dollars American." Murphy opened up his wallet.

"Why did you not simply buy a ticket in the orchestra seats? Or rent a box?"

Murphy counted out the bills. "This is all I could get."

"The only seat? On a Wednesday night?" The fat man eyed the bills.

"Yeah. Lucky for you." He held out the bills.

"Nein . . ." The fat man hesitated. "But I might rent them to you."

"How much?"

The fat man rubbed his chin thoughtfully. "Fifty? Ja?"

Murphy was about to agree when a soft, urgent tapping interrupted the transaction. He turned to face a smiling old woman who held out her opera glasses. "For fifty dollars, you may buy mine. And my umbrella as well."

"Done!" Murphy gave her the bills and she passed the opera glasses and the umbrella forward as the fat man grumbled unhappily and scowled at her.

Murphy focused on Elisa again and imagined himself opening the umbrella and jumping off the balcony to float down to her. At that moment, as though she sensed his gaze on her, she turned her eyes upward to the gallery.

Murphy wanted nothing more than to have her see him. He wanted to stand up and shout her name, to tell her that he was in love with her and to beg her from his lofty perch to marry him.

But he did none of that. He lowered the glasses when she looked away, then sat in silent misery as the concert began. When it was all over and the applause had died away, he blended into the rest of the crowd and wandered disconsolately back to his hotel room at the Sacher.

Elisa slowly climbed the stairs to her apartment. She reached into her pocket and pulled out the keys, then stopped and drew her breath in sharply.

In the darkness at the top of the stairs, the form of a man sat in the shadows.

"Who are you?" Elisa asked, feeling the same terrible sense of the foreboding that had followed her through tonight's concert.

The man stood. She clutched the banister and stared up at the familiar figure. "Thomas?"

"I have been waiting," The words of Thomas were a frightened whisper. "Quickly, please."

She wavered a moment, then hurried past him, unlocking the door and throwing it open. Thomas slipped in, but neither of them reached for the light. The window shades were up. She set the violin on the table as Thomas locked the door behind them, and she closed every shade before switching on the lights.

They faced one another across the room. Her face contained a thousand questions, and his replied with a furrowed brow and a hard-set jaw.

"My father?" she said at last, holding tightly to the back of a chair.

He shook his head slowly. "I'm sorry, Elisa." As if the pain of her own heart had struck him too, he grimaced. "I saw Canaris. He knew already. They all knew. It is over—there is no more to be done . . ." He did not have to speak the lie. She interpreted his words as he wanted her to believe.

Elisa pressed her lips together tightly and tried to hold back tears of disbelief and disappointment. "Thomas?" she asked bleakly. She wanted his answer to be different, somehow miraculously changed.

He moved toward her, his arms stretched out to comfort. He allowed her to think the worst, to believe that her father was dead. He had failed. Theo Lindheim. There was no appeal, no answer, no money that could buy Theo's freedom. It was best for her to believe he had died, to grieve, and then to go on with her life—far better than imagining his torture in that hellhole called Dachau.

"I'm sorry." Thomas began to weep with Elisa as her tears pushed past the barrier of control.

She fell into his arms and let him hold her as she cried for the death of all hope, for the haunting echo of the challenge: *"What God has done is rightly done."* How could *this* be right? How could she accept this? How could she carry news of such tragedy back to her mother? "Oh, Papa!" she sobbed. "Papa!" Now they would have to grieve again. They had given up hope before only to have it offered to them once again. *Cruel, cruel hope!* Pulled away, wrenched from their hearts in some terrible, cosmic, cat-and-mouse game! How could she keep her promise to *believe* in the face of such heartache?

"Poor Elisa." Thomas stroked her hair softly and kissed the cheeks that were wet with tears. "Poor, poor, darling . . ."

She leaned against his chest and let him hold her. Then he picked her up and carried her to the sofa where he cradled her in his arms as if she were a small girl with a broken toy.

She wept for a long time until finally she fell asleep with her head on his shoulder. She was glad he was there, glad she was not alone on such a dark and terrible night.

———

A soft rain had begun to fall by the time Murphy reached the hotel. He opened the umbrella he had purchased at the concert and stood dumbly in the middle of the sidewalk as people hurried by him seeking shelter in the building.

"Why was she still there tonight?" Murphy muttered to himself, turning back toward the Opera House. "And no wedding ring. Maybe she just told me all that . . . about some other guy . . . because she—" He could not finish the thought. There was, after all, no reason for Elisa to lie about something like that unless . . . unless she just wanted to get rid of Murphy. But if that was the case, then why did she kiss him like that? And why take him to the little cellar joint with the guitar-playing Spaniard?

He turned back toward the entrance of the Sacher Hotel. But he could not make himself move toward its warmth and comfort. He had to see her, had to talk to her. By now she would be home.

Automatically, Murphy raised his arm and hailed a passing taxi. Within ten minutes he stood outside the building where she lived and stared up at the drawn shades. A sliver of light escaped from them. Elisa was still awake!

He smiled and let the raindrops hit his face as he watched a shadow move across the shade . . . *her shadow*! And then, another shadow moved toward her! Their arms reached out. Murphy felt suddenly foolish as the two shadows melted into one long embrace.

Murphy had the sudden urge to hurl the closed umbrella at the window like a javelin. But he did not. He wanted to slam his fist against the hard, cold stone of her building and call her a thousand foul names, but he did not. He knew a man who had broken his hand just that way, and then the boyfriend had come outside and beaten him senseless for such language. No, Murphy was beaten badly enough already. At this moment, Joe Louis himself could not have punched him harder or knocked him down any more completely than the image of the shadow boxing going on upstairs.

He wiped the rain off his face as the large shadow scooped up Elisa and carried her away. "Oh, God," Murphy breathed at last as emptiness consumed him.

There were no taxis. He was drenched. Numb and cold, he walked through the puddled sidewalks and never thought to open the umbrella. He was sick before he reached his room at the Sacher Hotel; he flung himself onto the delicate petit point chair without changing his wet clothes. He just didn't care.

In one final gesture of despair, he took out the little wooden angel from his pocket, threw it on the floor, and slammed his heel down hard on it. It splintered into a thousand pieces.

"So much for love," he muttered, wishing he had a drink. "So much for you, John Murphy."

———

Soon Professor Julius Stern's rags hung on the old man's skeletal frame just like the stripes on all the other prisoners. He seemed tiny and fragile without his bulk. Theo had watched the old man's flesh melt away as they scrambled in the rocks each day. But the old man's mind grew sharper as the grief of his fate somehow dulled. The guard's command for Theo to watch over the old man had developed into an inseparable friendship that flourished and grew and kept the two men known as Stern alive. Each night they sat awake and whispered to one another snatches from books that they both loved. They would discuss a passage until exhaustion pulled them into a numb and dreamless sleep. For Theo, the arrival of Julius Stern had meant the saving of his sanity. It became more obvious, however, that for the old man, his time in Dachau would mean death unless something happened very soon.

The lights had been extinguished for an hour. An almost total silence had fallen over the packed barracks. Prisoners clung to their precious few hours of sleep. In these moments they could forget the horror that daylight would bring. Only Theo and the old man still lay awake.

"You took Goethe's *Faust* with you, Jacob?" the professor asked. "Why Goethe?"

"It is the finest . . . the best written of all the stories about Faust." Theo replied, hoping that his comment would stir up an argument between them. Such discussions kept their blood flowing and their minds awake.

Tomorrow on the rocks they would think of what they said tonight, and such thoughts would dim their awareness of the cruelty around them.

"Yes. Perhaps in the German language, Goethe's *Faust* is the best," the old man conceded, and Theo was disappointed at the ease with which he had won the argument. *"But,"* the professor added, "have you never read the Faust tragedy written by Marlowe?"

Theo could have cheered. The old man had not failed to find some comparison, some controversy. *Keep the mind sharp! Remember that we are men, not animals in a cage!* "It can hardly come up to Goethe's Faust!" Theo scoffed. "The comedy, the wit, the moral lesson—"

The professor was silent for a time, and Theo was afraid that he had drifted off to sleep. Then he spoke. "Perhaps before Hitler, I would have agreed with you. As Goethe writes the play, Faust is saved in the end and the demons are given a phantom to carry off to hell—a pretty picture that men may do as they like, that they may sell their souls to Satan, and still God will snatch them from the pit of hell." His words were more thoughtful and serious than they had been before with any of a hundred different topics.

"That is what our guards think, surely," Theo said. "That is why Goethe's *Faust* would be the best version for Germany now."

"They would be better off, these Nazis, to read what Marlowe had written, and tremble."

"Marlowe is English."

"The English have a better idea of right and wrong. They still believe in hell, I think, and perhaps that keeps them from brutality. Germany has ceased to believe in hell. And so they create hell for innocent men and have no fear that they themselves will ever face condemnation. I tell you, Jacob," the professor whispered to Theo, "Germany has sold its soul, and the fire it brings to the world will come back to itself. Hitler is Satan. *Mein Kampf* is his book of black magic. Germany is Faust. And the hour will come when . . ." His voice trailed off.

"When what, Professor?" Theo asked, hoping the old man was not falling to sleep.

"Like the Faust of Marlowe, Germany will watch the clock run out. And there will be no salvation." Nearly blind eyes stared up into the darkness of the barrack's rafters. And then the voice of the old man began to read from the pages of a book he couldn't see, from a script seared upon his brain:

> "Ah, Faustus, Now hast thou but one bare hour to live,
> And then thou must be damned perpetually!
> Stand still, you ever-moving spheres of heaven,
> That time may cease, and midnight never come. . . .
> Let this hour be but a year, a month, a week, a natural day,
> That Faustus may repent and save his soul!"

Theo listened to the words, and a chill of horror flooded over him.

Had midnight come for Germany? Was it too late for repentance? Too late to change the course that led irrevocably to damnation?

> "The stars move still, time runs, the clock will strike,
> The devil will come, and Faustus must be damned.
> Oh, I'll leap up to my God! Who pulls me down?
> See, see where Christ's blood streams in the firmament!
> One drop would save my soul—half a drop: ah, my Christ!"

Theo's heart beat in the rhythm of the terrible words. *Too late! Too late! Too late!* The first drop of innocent blood spilled; the first brutal laws of Nuremburg had marked the bloody path. And everyone who had been silent now was stained with guilt. Only the guiltless were within these walls. Inside the very churches of the nation, men prayed prayers that God could not, *would not* hear! They were prayers meant for Lucifer. *Gott mit uns* on the buckles of the soldiers should have read *Lucifer mit uns!*

The voice, the unearthly whisper of the old man, uttered the last words of one soul, a million souls, who had made a covenant with Evil for the sake of fleeting pleasure:

> "Oh, spare me, Lucifer!
> See where God
> Stretcheth out his arm, and bends his ireful brows!
> Mountains and hills, come, come, and fall on me.
> And hide me from the heavy wrath of God!
> No! No!
> Then I will run into the earth;
> Oh no, it will not harbor me!"

Before his eyes, Theo saw a vision of jackbooted S.S. guards begging the stones of the rock quarry to cover them. The earth and air alike glowed red, and hot hail fell on their backs, just as the lash of their whips had torn the flesh of innocent men.

> "O God,
> If thou wilt not have mercy on my soul,
> Yet for Christ's sake whose blood might have ransomed me,
> Impose some end to my incessant pain;
> Let Faustus live in hell a thousand years,
> A hundred thousand, and at last be saved!
> Oh, no end is limited to damned souls!"

The professor stopped the recitation suddenly and turned to Theo. Even in the darkness, eyes covered by cataracts could see clearly, and he said with such sadness that Theo thought they would weep together, "Pity them, Jacob. Pity them for the evil they worship and the end that will surely come to them. Weep for our tormentors who have forgotten that they are also eternal. There will be a moment when it is too late to beg forgiveness . . ." He sounded weary now. The evening's discussion was over. The professor was right.

> "Oh, it strikes, it strikes! Now body turn to air,
> Or Lucifer will bear thee quick to hell!
> O soul be changed into little water drops,
> And fall into the ocean—never to be found!
> Ugly hell, gape not! come not, Lucifer!
> I'll burn my books. . . ."

The professor fell silent. Soon, his breathing became deep and even in sleep. But Theo lay awake in the gloom as the cries of Marlowe's Faust echoed in his mind. For so many months Theo had believed that black had become white and wrong had become right. Wasn't the whole world upside down? Hadn't Hitler proclaimed that the masses could be made to believe that hell was really heaven? Yes, of course. That was plainly written in *Mein Kampf*, like the black magic of the books of Doctor Faustus. But one day Germany would cry out, *I'll burn my books!* And it would be too late. The Nazi murderers would cry for mercy, but they were judged already. *The stars still move, time runs, right is still right, and there will be an end to evil one day.*

In the cold, the filth, and the stink of Dachau, Theo Lindheim found a moment of consolation in the recitation of the old professor. He was suddenly glad that he was the man being beaten instead of the man who swung the lash. There was something holy and sacred in the foul swill and the crust of bread that they were fed each day. In the dust of the rock quarries, their lives became a cathedral dedicated to a righteous God. It was better, somehow, in Germany these days, to die behind these walls. Because all souls are eternal and the hell of Dachau would only last for a brief moment in time, it was better to suffer now than to cause suffering.

From that night on, Theo was no longer afraid. The fierce hatred he felt for the well-fed S.S. officers and guards settled into a quiet pity. *"Burn your book of Aryan magic!"* he wanted to shout. *"There is a hell more fierce than Dachau, and it lasts forever!"* But he did not speak to his tormentors. Instead, he spoke quietly of the end of suffering to those who were tormented and dying in this place. Every night, like the priest and the cantor, he moved among the moaning men, a shimmering light of hope. They died in his arms. They died with the names of wives and sweethearts on their lips. They died with kaleidoscopic visions of color and stars and hope dancing before their eyes. And unlike Faust, their tormentors could not reach them in the morning.

38

The Nightmare

That long and terrible night, Thomas shared the dark plans of the German High Command with Elisa as she sat next to him. Words that were only meant for the ears of British Foreign Minister Anthony Eden and Winston Churchill now tumbled out of him. Since he could not comfort her with hope for Theo, could he not offer some consolation in hope that the madness in Germany would end?

"I know why you think you cannot care for me," he said, staring at her hands. *Those same hands that caressed me so willingly.* "But you must know the truth. All of it, Elisa. I cannot carry such knowledge. I cannot go on unless you know the truth of who I am and can believe in me as you once did."

She did not reply. She seemed not to hear. Was she thinking of the walls of Dachau? Of her father and the flash of the machine gun?

Thomas continued. It did not matter if she heard him. He would at least *try* to explain! "In July of 1936—" He spoke as though to a judge and jury, his voice a monotone. "Just before I was ordered not to see you again, Hitler instructed the General Staff to draw up plans for the occupation of Austria. It is called *Plan Otto.*"

Now Elisa's eyes flashed angrily. "Since July? A year and a half ago?"

"I had only heard rumors of it. I could not say anything. I am under suspicion myself." He waved his hand as if to express the horror and frustration he felt at such a plan. "So many of us feel the same." He stared toward the window shade as though he sensed something . . . someone, outside in the rain. Then he looked back at her. "A year later, on June 24 of this last year, Hitler gave a special directive making the plans official. Three months ago he told the Chiefs of the Armed Forces that Germany must have more living space, and that this could best be found in eastern Europe."

Elisa simply stared at him when he paused to let the implications of his words sink in. "Poland?" she asked incredulously. "He has set his sights on more than just Austria?"

Thomas nodded. "Czechoslovakia. Poland. White Russia. The Ukraine. The Chiefs of Staff know that this would involve a major war, and as for the people already living in those countries—what does Hitler plan for them?" He looked genuinely frightened. "There are men"—he chose his words carefully—"in the General Staff who see the total folly of such a plan." He did not mention names, many of whom Elisa would have known. A few had served with her father twenty years before and were once men he called friends. "Hitler has said that Germany will have to reckon with her two hateful enemies, England and France. For them, a German Colossus in the center of Europe would not be tolerable. And yet"—he shrugged helplessly—"our army grows each month while the lack of willpower by the British government and France spurs Hitler on in his belief that now is the moment to begin."

"And Austria? What of Austria?"

"*Plan Otto* will be the first of the steps undertaken, unless—"

"Unless what, Thomas?" His words had driven grief for her father into the background temporarily.

"Hitler has broken every article in the Versailles Treaty, and he is wild with his success. First he rearmed Germany. Then he established the draft. Third, he reoccupied the Rhineland and has established the military barricade of the Siegfried Line along the border of France." He turned his eyes on Elisa. "Now he has established a strong friendship with Mussolini in Italy."

"And so"—she thought over his words and came to a conclusion—"the time is right for this *Plan Otto*? He will invade Austria soon?" She remembered the horror of the bloodbath in the Judenplatz, and she could almost hear the tramp of jackboots on the peaceful street below. What had come to Berlin would come here as well. "But, Thomas, you said *unless*. Unless *what*?"

He did not answer right away. "What Hitler has not been able to do with bombs and terror and money to support the Nazis in Vienna, he is quite ready to accomplish through diplomacy." He took her hands in his and held them. His eyes begged her to understand why he had stayed away so long, why he had been unable to run away from his duty. "I have been sent to certain high officials in the British government. I was instructed to share at least part of Hitler's plans with them. They are aware of Hitler's aims for Austria, at any rate."

"And?"

"The Chief of Staff, General Blomberg, is ready to take over the German government . . . if the British are prepared to *strongly* resist the takeover of Austria."

"You have told the British this?" She was amazed, ashamed that she had not even dreamed that Thomas would be part of a force within the German command to stop Nazi tyranny.

"I did not mention Blomberg by name, of course. But there are many others who stand with us. With every victory that Hitler wins because of the diplomatic appeasement of other nations, he becomes more wildly popular with the German people! Elisa, what he says is believed and acted upon as though he were a god. He has such power, such terrible power over the people! He needs to have a few defeats before they will see. He needs to be stopped cold in his tracks by the great nations standing up to him. The German nationalistic fervor is at such a high pitch that we must move carefully. Do you understand what I am saying?"

She nodded and squeezed his hands. Then she reached up and brushed back a tumbled lock of his hair. "I'm sorry I doubted you." She could barely speak. "I should have known there was a reason you stayed."

"I was ready to leave." He frowned, not quite able to accept her praise. "I am such a small cog. I did not know about all this until after I wrote you. I believed that the German High Command was simply letting it slide away. Himmler and his Gestapo have been undermining Canaris and the Abwehr for over a year. The maniacs work the hardest to drive the sane men out. And it is working . . ." He drew a deep breath. "But there is hope. Fritsch and Blomberg are holding Hitler back by their disapproval of the plan. They keep begging for a little more time."

"I remember them both as very strong men."

"They are not blameless, though." Thomas looked sad. "Some of the guilt must fall on every man in the High Command, every officer in the military." He bit his lip. "Even the very small cogs. I can remember cheering when he announced that we were going to reoccupy the Rhineland. It was, in a way, like saying my father had not died in vain in the last war . . . we would all be Germans and *proud* once again! And that is the poison which has infected our country, Elisa. Beyond that, there is a madness, an evil, which I cannot explain. It is that evil which has claimed men like your father as victims. I am more afraid of this than anything. If Austria is taken, Hitler will bring the madness with him. And Austria is the door to Czechoslovakia."

"My mother and brothers—"

"And Czechoslovakia is the door into Poland. If it begins, this terrible eclipse, it will not stop until the darkness is accomplished." He looked exhausted. He laid his head back on the sofa and closed his eyes for a moment as she simply looked at him. Like her father, Thomas had carried on a secret life that she had not suspected. Elisa touched his head softly and his mouth curved in a slight smile. He knew he was forgiven. Could he hope again that she might love him as she had before?

After a few minutes, he sighed deeply and fell asleep on the sofa. She got him a pillow and tugged off his shoes, then covered him with a blanket. How long had he gone without sleep, she wondered?

She was exhausted as well, but all that he had told her spun in her mind as she lay down and tried to sleep. She thought of her father. Theo would have told her that the life of one man must sometimes be sacrificed for the good of others. Theo had lived that belief to the letter. And now Thomas, too, had in a way sacrificed his life. For the sake of what he believed was right, he had turned away from her. She could forgive him easily for that, but tonight she could not find the love in her heart that she had once felt for him. The world was threatening to explode in an all-consuming flame. How could she think of herself? Of her own fate? There was so much more at stake. Thomas knew. Theo knew. Thank God someone in the German High Command knew. And there were people like Leah and Shimon and Rudy, people like the Wattenbargers, who *sensed* what was coming and chose to fight it on a personal level. They could do nothing to stop the massive international tidal wave that threatened now to engulf the world, but they would at least find high ground and provide a lifeline for all who were struggling.

As Elisa drifted off to sleep, the faces of the children came back to her. Three in Kitzbühel. Two from Munich. It had been so simple to help them! And how many thousands more were there? *Jesu, juva!* Her own problems were very slight indeed compared to those children. If *Plan Otto* were accomplished, not only Jewish children in Germany would be threatened, but those now living in Austria as well!

That night, Elisa dreamed of trainloads of little ones, all of whom had her last name. They slept like little tumbled dominos as the trains moved eastward and Hitler screamed, *"Living space for Germans!"* Elisa rode atop the first train and argued with an S.S. officer who carried a machine gun.

"Not to the east! Hitler will take the east for his Reich! Turn the trains around! These are my children! My children! My home is west. I have room for them, a place for them! Do not take them east!"

For hours as she pleaded, the black-shirted officer laughed at her. He hooked his thumbs in his belt. His belt buckle gleamed *"Gott mit uns."* On his arm was the insignia of a skull and crossbones. His laughter was louder than her pleas. She reached up to slap his face, and a mask suddenly dropped away, revealing the face of Lucifer. He laughed more uproariously as Elisa shouted that he could not take the children.

"I take them for the burning!" he shouted back through his laughter. "They are dead! Already dead! And so will you be!"

At the pronouncement, she turned to look at the rail cars, and all the sleeping children had become heaps of bones. Her own hand withered before her eyes and the flesh dropped away.

"Jesus, help!" she cried, and then the face of Lucifer changed to rage. He lifted a claw to strike, and once again she called, *"Jesu, Juva!"* And a wind came and blew the Evil One from the train where she stood.

Then Thomas called to her from far away, *"Elisa! Darling! Elisa!* Wake up. It is only a dream. Just a dream!"

She opened her eyes to see Thomas's worried face over her. It was still raining. She reached her arms up to him and he embraced her. "Terrible," she choked. "So real . . ."

"Just a dream." He rocked her. "Only a bad dream."

"All the children. Going east. I tried to tell him there was a place for them, but he laughed at me." She was drenched with perspiration and trembling all over.

"Whose children?" Thomas asked.

"Mine. A million children. And I loved them all." She wept now, unable to shake the images that had come to her. "God help me. God! They *are* mine! And Papa must have had the same dream."

Thomas patted her gently. "I'll make you tea, Elisa. It will help you wake up. We all have nightmares nowadays. A cup of tea will help."

He padded away and she listened to the sounds of the water filling the kettle and the clank of metal on the stove. Outside the rain was falling. Her own reflection looked pale in the mirror, but the horror of her dream receded after a few moments. She was grateful that Thomas was with her. She wiped her eyes and managed a weak smile when he came back into the room with a dainty flowered teacup in his big hand.

"It is almost morning," he said. She noticed that he was washed and his hair was combed. "I have to go before daybreak." He kissed her lightly on the forehead.

"You are leaving?" She was surprisingly disappointed.

"I need to get back to Paris. I shouldn't have come here, but I couldn't bear having you hate me without knowing—"

"I don't hate you," she whispered.

"But you don't love me, either." He shrugged and smiled sadly. "But then, maybe neither one of us has time for that now." Touching her cheek, he looked into her eyes as though he really saw her. "Those children, Elisa," he questioned. "Are they the same ones Theo was helping?"

"I suppose."

"And are they yours as well?"

"I hope so." She frowned and looked away. Had she ever felt such a burden? Ever such a responsibility?

"Then you must be very careful." He kissed her lightly. "And if you should ever decide you need a husband—" He shrugged again. "You know how to reach me."

"Café de Triumph." This was farewell. There was nothing more to say. There was no calling back what had once been for them. *Perhaps another time? When things were different?*

Thomas took the teacup from her and placed it on the floor beside the bed; then, he took her in his arms and kissed her once again, letting his mouth linger on hers. She did not push him away. This final gesture brought tears to her eyes. It was truly over between them.

"For old times' sake," he said hoarsely. Then he grinned. "I am glad I can remember you like this—your hair mussed and your eyes swollen and red. It might make my long nights more bearable."

She listened as the door to the apartment shut and his footsteps retreated down the stairs. Six weeks before, she would have begged him to stay. She would have run after him in the rain. Now she simply whispered, *"Grüss Gott, Thomas. God bless . . ."*

That same morning, there was reason for joy within the orchestra, and also reason for grief. Shimon and Leah had received their travel visas permitting them to travel and settle in Palestine. The visas demanded that they travel as a married couple, a provision that delighted Shimon. Not only would two travel cheaper than each singly, but the wedding night could be celebrated much earlier. At that suggestion, Leah consented to a civil ceremony only, with the "real" wedding to take place after they arrived in Jerusalem, just as they had planned.

The precious documents were passed from hand to hand among the orchestra members. The date of their exit was three months away in May, and yet still Elisa felt a pang of sorrow at the thought of Leah going away.

Tears clouded her eyes. "What will I do without you?" She could barely speak.

"You'll come to Palestine, too." Leah tapped her chin in a chin-up gesture.

Elisa frowned and studied Leah for a moment. Ever since they had known each other, Leah had talked of Palestine, dreamed of Palestine, raised funds for Palestine, and welcomed lecturers who had come from the desolate land to talk of new and wonderful beginnings. Lawyers and teachers and musicians had drifted off to become farmers and tree planters. This was not for Elisa. She was certain even now it never would be. Her only real interest in the place was as a refuge for German-Jewish children; and if the truth were known, she thought that America was probably a better place to send them. There were bread lines there, certainly, but no Arab mobs rioted and burned at the will of a religious fanatic like the Arab Mufti of Jerusalem. *America!*

As though Leah had read her thoughts, she laughed and said, "No, not you, Elisa. Never you for Palestine, I think. America better suits you. No doubt after your first day in the hot sun of Jerusalem you would be sunburned." She winked as the male members of the orchestra hooted and teased Elisa. "You should find yourself an American to marry! Like that Murphy fellow you sent off. Silly of you to chase him away, Elisa."

Elisa did not laugh. The subject of John Murphy was still too painful for her. "He did propose to me. That night at Sacher's."

"What?" Leah exclaimed. "And you let an American passport get away?"

"He is more than just a passport." Elisa mumbled, turning away.

"Then find him!"

"His proposal was . . . just to help. I couldn't do that to a man. Tie him up like that."

"Are you out of your mind?" Leah cried. "Do you know what an American passport could do to help us?" She was serious now, and spoke in an urgent whisper. "I was going to suggest that we simply pay some American to marry you. For your own safety. And now you're telling me that a man already proposed—just to help—and your conscience won't let you tie him up? Elisa, wake up! This may go on a long time. You need the protection an American passport can give you. If you're going to stay here, please, use your head so you don't lose it."

"I can't marry him. Not anyone. I . . . I care for him, Leah, and I won't use him."

Leah simply stood with her hands on her hips and stared at Elisa.

"If you won't think of yourself, think of the operation. Find him. Find out if his offer is still good. He is probably getting proposals from women every day—all of them offering good money to use his name and get a passport. One of these days he'll get an offer too good to pass up, and then we will have lost him. And since Hitler has begun screaming about how dreadful Czechoslovakia is, you can bet the Gestapo will start giving you trouble with your Czech passport."

Elisa still had not told her about the night in Munich with the Gestapo agent. The thought made her shudder. "Murphy is gone." She replied. "If you think it's that important—"

"That important! Shimon has already set the matchmaker to looking for a match for you. It doesn't matter if he's poor, ugly or stupid, dear, as long as he's American!"

———

Elisa did not share any of what Thomas had told her with Leah or Shimon or the others. Twice more she traveled to Kitzbühel with precious cargos of little ones, and always she remembered the terrible nightmare of trains full of children moving slowly, inexorably, eastward. The farmhouse haven of the Wattenbarger family was west from Vienna, but still, it was not far enough west. It was *still* in Austria, and if the plans of the German High Command and Thomas were stopped, if the British and the French failed to stand firm and continued to appease the madman Hitler, then Austria would be swallowed!

On the morning of February 5, 1938, while Elisa was returning to Vienna from the Tyrol, a newspaper boy passed through the train car with his papers held aloft as he announced the headlines:

"German Chancellor Hitler dismisses General Fritsch and Blomberg!"

With trembling hands, Elisa purchased a newspaper and read the latest news from Germany. Hitler himself had assumed the supreme command of the armed forces. In one stroke, he had removed power from the hands of the men who hoped for moderation. As if he had some supernatural second sight, he had smashed the men who had opposed his will. As much as it is possible for one man to make his will absolute over spheres so vast, Hitler had done so. Now he had assumed direct and complete control not only over the policies of the German state but also of the military machine. As she read, the nightmare images of the eastbound trains returned to her. Had the S.S. officer on top of the train been Hitler? She tried to remember his face.

In Vienna, the news of the sacking of two German generals in the High Command was received with shrugs of indifference. Of course, no one could be expected to understand the implications of such an event. What difference did that make to Vienna and Austria? Hitler was, after all, a dictator. Everyone had heard the stories about him, his mad rages against anyone who dared dispute him. Vienna was not surprised or even alarmed by the news. But Vienna did not know what Elisa was aware of.

She wanted desperately to talk to Thomas, and twice that week she called the little cafe in Paris. He was not there. And so she bore the burden of knowledge alone. Daily she prayed for the men in the British government who also knew of *Plan Otto*, and who understood what the loss of Blomberg and Fritsch meant. She hoped that those men cared enough to stop Hitler, who grew daily in his megalomania.

In the evenings, after concerts played without the old joy that had filled her once, Elisa sat in gloomy groups and listened to the tirades of Hitler against the English and the French and the government of Austria. Those first weeks in February, the shadows of darkness stretched longer until at last they crossed the border and touched the Austrian Chancellor Schuschnigg.

————

Thomas watched as Admiral Canaris paced back and forth in front of his desk. The dismissal of Generals Blomberg and Fritsch had sent shock waves throughout the few men in the German High Command who hoped to wrest the control of the nation from Hitler. Only a few weeks since Thomas had spoken with Anthony Eden about the secret plans of the conspirators, two key figures had been sacked, and now Adolf Hitler held absolute dominion over the military. He could, at a whim, strip a general of rank, discharge him from his duties in the army, or even have him shot for treason. The will of Hitler had now become the will of Germany. There was no separation of the two. In the military and in matters of state, now there was only one law . . . one *Führer*!

"Hitler has requested that young officers from every branch of the services be sent to Berchtesgaden." Canaris did not stop his pacing. "He wants to put on a demonstration to the young German elite of his expertise in military matters as well as matters of state. The illustration he will use with you is his domination of Austria."

"With me? You mean I am going?" Thomas felt stunned by the order.

"You are perfect for it. He will strut and posture and the young Wehrmacht officers will all applaud and stand in awe."

"But why send me? I am revolted by him."

"That is why I send you. You are a junior officer. Hitler intends that you fellow officers will go back to the ranks and tell the army what a magician he is, how none can stand before him." He stopped and stared at Thomas. "You and I both know that you will not be impressed, ja? Besides, I need a reliable source of information about the events at Berchtesgaden. I have the feeling that our dear *Führer*"—he said the word with sarcasm—"is simply singing the Requiem for Austria. This is all part of *Plan Otto*. Intimidation is his sharpest sword, and he uses it at will. You must tell me everything you see and hear."

"What will happen now, Herr Admiral?" Thomas pressed his hand against his aching temple.

"Hitler will summon the Austrian Chancellor Schuschnigg."

"And if Schuschnigg doesn't come to Berchtesgaden?"

"He is an honorable man. Young and foolish in many ways, but a man of honor. A man who hopes for peace without bloodshed. He will come." The eyes of Canaris seemed to see the scene before him. "Like a puppy who sidles up to a cruel master in hopes that there will not be a beating, Herr von Schuschnigg will come."

He sat down heavily in his chair, as though the certainty of the events had suddenly drained him of energy. "This performance with the leader of Austria is intended to show his power to the nations of the world, and also to those of us within the military who might seek to question his absolute control." He ran a hand though his hair. "Other generals have been invited to the farce, but only those Hitler is sure of. The rest are low-ranking officers who will be easily impressed by bravado and bullying."

Canaris sighed deeply. "If Schuschnigg is smart, he will not enter the Dragon's Lair, but I think he is not smart enough. He still hopes that Hitler will leave Austria alone with a few concessions here and there. He does not see that such concessions are simply an appetizer for our beloved Führer. The main course is Austria."

39

The Business
Arrangement

The International News Service office was relieved that John Murphy was already in Vienna when the first big story of 1938 began to break. Eddie Griffith wired Murphy from Paris and ordered him to stay in Vienna and keep his eyes and ears open.

He was soon joined at the Sacher Hotel by Timmons and Johnson and Amanda and a dozen other European correspondents who sensed that something big was on the way to Vienna.

Murphy was relieved to have the company; soon his room in the Sacher took on the old atmosphere of the Adlon Hotel in Berlin. Bored reporters played cards and joked while Murphy simply spent hours staring out the window, hoping in spite of himself that he might catch a glimpse of a beautiful violinist hailing a cab in the rainy street below. He did not torment himself by driving by the Musikverein or walking in the neighborhood where her apartment was. And he allowed himself the privilege of properly hating her for playing him for a chump when she was really in love with someone else. Still, he looked out the window and hoped.

It was eight days since Herr Hitler had taken over the complete control of the German armed forces.

"The guy is like Napoleon now," said Johnson, dealing the cards. "And what we need is another British victory at Waterloo, or pretty soon there'll be red flags flapping all over Vienna."

"We aren't waiting here for that," Timmons replied, drawing each card. "It ain't a question that it's gonna happen, it's a question of when and how."

The phone rang and Murphy reached to pick it up. He had connections at the new government offices. He had paid his informant well to pass along any news; now, the young man's breathless voice fairly crackled with excitement.

"Hitler has summoned Chancellor Schuschnigg to visit him in Berchtesgaden."

This was going to be Murphy's scoop. He wanted the story first, so he covered the importance of the conversation. "Yes. Four shirts to be laundered. Light starch . . ."

Johnson quipped, "I didn't know Murphy had four shirts."

The frantic voice on the other end of the telephone whispered. "The Chancellor has been *ordered* to Berchtesgaden! Ordered as though he is a servant, do you understand, Herr Murphy?"

"Yes. I understand." The news sickened Murphy. The move had begun. "And he is coming?" Murphy asked and his voice still sounded like he was discussing laundry.

"Yes. He and Guido Schmidt, his foreign minister. Gott! For months we have been building Austrian defenses along our German border. But nothing is complete! Nothing! Only foundations."

"When?" Murphy asked.

"They take the train to Salzburg tonight. Then they will be escorted up the mountain by sled and cross the German border to Berchtesgaden." He dropped his voice even lower. "I cannot say more."

"Right. Thank you." Murphy hung up the phone and looked at the little group of his card-playing cronies. "You guys going to be here all night?" He asked, picking up his coat and strolling toward the door.

"Prob'ly." Timmons seemed engrossed by his hand.

"Where you going, Murphy?" Johnson scowled at his cards. "You going to scoop us?"

"Just going out for a little air. You guys have stunk up this place. Empty the ashtrays in the toilet, will you? And if you order room service, don't put it on my bill." It was a normal kind of exit—full of insults and instruction. Murphy figured they would not even notice he was gone until the game broke up about four o'clock the next morning. By then he would have the story.

He grabbed a sausage sandwich at the train station and bought his ticket on the evening train to Salzburg. He had an hour still to wait when he spotted Elisa across the lobby. She carried a small suitcase and had two young boys in tow. He was sure that his mouth was hanging open when she looked his way and her eyes widened with surprise. She smiled and waved broadly. He shrugged as if to say, *Well, we meet again at last!* Then he sat down on the bench and began to pretend to read his newspaper. He hoped she would go away, but at any rate, he was determined not to let her see that she had any effect on him at all.

He heard the footsteps but did not look up. Her voice said with gentle amusement, "Can you read like that?"

He managed to focus his eyes on the newsprint. The paper was upside down. "Yes." He didn't miss a beat. "It comes from years of stealing other reporters' stories. You stand over their typewriter, see, and read upside down—" He tossed the paper onto the floor. "Fancy meeting you here."

The two boys eyed him suspiciously, but Elisa looked at him with relief, even *joy*. "I'm going to the Tyrol."

"Forever?" His voice contained a hint of bitterness. "You having the wedding there? Bringing along the groomsmen? Or is one of these the actual lucky fellow himself?"

She looked momentarily hurt by his flippant questions. "These are my nephews . . . Helmut and Kurt." They stuck out their hands; their brown eyes seemed serious and frightened, much too old for such youngsters.

"And I am John Murphy," Murphy said with equal seriousness. Then he looked again at Elisa. "It's been six weeks since you stood me up to get married. I thought you'd have kids of your own by now." He was still cutting.

She smiled sadly, then she looked away. "I tried to find you that night to explain."

"I'll bet you did." He lapsed into English, and she also answered in English, cutting off their conversation from the boys.

"You had checked out." She raised her chin in defiance to his challenge.

"You bet I did." He felt angry all over again. "Did you find your angels? Wooden angels. Looked just like you, I thought. So where's your husband?"

"I did not . . . it did not work out."

He remembered the scene that had been silhouetted on the window shade. He suddenly wanted to hurt her as he had been hurt. "Did you write him a note, too?" His eyes narrowed. "What have you got in your veins, Elisa? Not warm red blood. Ice water, maybe?"

The boys could not understand the words, but they recognized the anger in Murphy's voice. They looked to Elisa with alarm. She put her hands protectively on their shoulders. "I . . . deserve this, Herr Murphy," she said formally. "I know that." She fought to control tears that threatened to brim in her eyes. "Perhaps one day, another time, we can talk." She looked down at her two young charges apologetically. "I am sorry I bothered you."

At that, she turned and led the boys toward a bench at the far end of the terminal. Murphy stared bleakly after her, silently cursing himself for not showing her indifference instead of anger. *Next time*, he vowed, *I'll act totally unconcerned. As if she had not torn my heart to shreds and left me staring at blank walls and mentally drawing her picture there.*

Now, he sat gazing miserably at the back of her head as she regained her composure and joked with her nephews as they waited for the train. They would be on his train, he knew, and the thought made him hope that he would have ample opportunity to act indifferent and cool. He had managed to remain in total control while German planes had bombed

Madrid. Why was he trembling now? A return to Spain would be a welcome relief after this.

He stood and retrieved his newspaper, then wandered down toward the opposite end of the terminal, as far from Elisa as possible. He sat down facing away from her. He hoped she would look and see him *not* looking at her. For nearly an hour he remained rooted there, staring sightlessly at the same page of the newspaper. He had made certain that it was right side up this time. And as he stared, he asked her a thousand unspoken questions. And finally, in his mind, he came back to the reason he had come back to Vienna six weeks before. *Why are you still here? Don't you see what's coming? You still don't believe me? Get out of here, Elisa, or you might end up like your father.*

Of course he couldn't say any of that to her. She was already completely past the shock of seeing him, if it had been a shock. *He* had certainly felt shocked. The encounter had meant nothing to her obviously. He turned and looked over his shoulder. She was laughing at something one of the boys had whispered to her. Her hair was shining; her eyes sparkled. She had already forgotten that Murphy was in the terminal.

He turned back around just as the announcer called boarding for the train to Salzburg. He rose slowly and grabbed his little satchel without even glancing at her. Maybe he would manage to walk by her on the train. Unless she had a private compartment, and then he would not see her at all. He squashed his hat onto his head, fighting the urge to follow her as she boarded. And then, he hesitated and turned. He had lost the battle. He saw her look at her tickets and then start for the third car from the rear. Walking quickly toward her, he climbed onto the front of the car just as she helped the smallest of the boys onto the rear. He brushed aside the conductor who insisted he show his ticket number. Then he waited just inside the train as the first boy appeared at the opposite end of the corridor, followed by the second child, and finally Elisa. Her eyes caught Murphy's and held them for just an instant. Just as she had held his soul when the guitar music had played in the cellar cafe. He managed a nonchalant shrug, an unconcerned "who-cares" shrug. The light in her eyes flickered and he saw that he had hurt her. He was glad he had hurt her, and then he was sorry.

"You in this carriage?" he asked.

She nodded and then disappeared into compartment 3-E. He made a note, then waited until an elderly gentleman approached the same compartment and checked his ticket.

"Bitte, mein Herr." Murphy put his hand on the old man's arm. "Are you in 3-E?"

The man nodded and smiled, "Ja."

"I am in number 8-C. I have been separated from my family. Wife and two boys." His voice was a whisper. "Would you trade tickets and allow me to make it worth your while?" He pulled out five American dollars.

The old man nodded, snatched the bill away, handed Murphy his ticket while taking his, then tottered down the hall.

Murphy fixed a scowl on his face and opened the door to 3-E. Elisa looked up with surprise and then turned her eyes away uncomfortably. She seemed to be thinking, *How can this be?* Murphy was instantly sorry that he had traded tickets with the old man.

"Look," he said, "I know it's odd that we are thrown together like this. Maybe I can get another seat assignment once everybody is on board. Anyway, I'm only going to Salzburg." He did not sit down in the empty seat across from her.

"No." Her voice was a whisper. There really were tears in her eyes now. "I was hoping . . . please . . ." She smiled and moved a package out of the aisle. "Do sit down, Herr Murphy. That is, unless you *want* to change seats."

"Maybe later." He sat down with seeming reluctance. He would not show her how he felt. He would not let her see what she had done. But, he decided, he would ask her all the questions he had thought of in the last hour. "So, you're finally getting out of Vienna?"

"Only temporarily." She looked at the floor, at his shoes. He wished he had shined them.

"You don't mean you're coming back here?" He was alarmed.

"Yes. Tomorrow."

"And then when are you leaving again?"

"I'm not running away, if that's what you're asking." She again lapsed into English.

"Why not?"

"A million little reasons, Murphy." She looked at the children, then back to him.

He sat back and crossed his arms as he studied the boys and then looked into her eyes. "Your nephews?" he asked.

She shook her head in a solemn *no*, and suddenly he understood. "What are you involved with?" he said, scarcely able to believe that this was the same, unaware young woman he had fallen in love with. She had not believed him then; she had not seen the dangers in the back alleyways of Vienna.

"Rudy Dorbransky was a dear friend of mine," she said as though that offered every explanation.

"He's dead," Murphy replied in a clipped voice.

"Murdered."

"I thought as much."

"Nazis."

"And your little trip has something to do with that?"

She nodded. Her gaze cut a swath into his heart. "You are an American, Herr Murphy." She bit her lip and looked away, looking for the proper way to say what she needed to say. "Americans have connections that most of us do not have. Your country is neutral and you can move with more freedom than . . . others."

"Get to the point."

"I have been thinking about you."

He sensed that her thoughts had not been personal or romantic. Again, he drew his reserve up like a shield. He must not let her see what he was feeling. "I haven't given you another thought," he lied.

Again the hurt flashed in her eyes, but she controlled it quickly. "I did not expect that you would." She frowned. "But once you made me an offer. It was quite gallant. Not romantic, you said, but a matter of safety."

"You want to go to America?" he asked, feeling a sense of relief.

"No." The answer was absolute. "I want an American passport."

"An American passport!" he snorted.

"I realize how little you like me, and I am prepared to pay you for your assistance in this . . . business arrangement."

"You mean you want an American to marry you." There was not even a hint of affection or romance in the proposition.

"Yes. And you are the only one who has offered. No strings attached. You said I could divorce you. And now I make you the same agreement."

"That was then."

"And now I need your help more than ever. For the sake of Jewish children, Herr Murphy—"

He wanted to take her by the arms and shake her, but he did not. He wanted to shout at her for suggesting such a thing without even a hint that they had spent one incredible day together. Her voice held no emotion, no memory of their kiss. She was offering a cold and calculated business proposition. Marriage and a passport meant some extra element of safety for her and these children—wherever she was taking them. An American passport meant some access to the American embassies if the Gestapo turned the flame throwers in her direction. For Elisa, it was plain to see, the offer was simply a method of protection. Suddenly, her sweet attentions six weeks before became clear to him. He had made her that stupid, blundering proposal in Sacher's that night, and she had considered it carefully, strung him along until she found out that someone else was available. *Maybe a diplomat?* When that had fallen through, she had remembered Murphy again, and here they were.

His reserve became an icy glacier between them. He stared at her as though he held the utmost contempt for her words, and for her. "Yes," he said at last, "ice water does run through your veins, Elisa."

She bit her lip and stared him down. "You're probably right. But what runs though yours? You know what I'm doing." She tossed her head defiantly. "These two children are only two out of thousands. If Austria falls there will be thousands more. And then it will be Czechoslovakia, and then—" Her voice rose angrily.

"I'm the one who told you that!" he snapped. "That night in Sacher's."

"The night you proposed."

"I offered to get you and your family out of here. To America."

"Where I sit safely and wait to be divorced while these little ones—"

"I was hoping to help you."

"Very noble. You still can. And I'll pay you handsomely for your name, Herr Murphy." She glared at him now. "No strings. Like you said. You can get an annulment. All I want is the passport and the safety it affords me. Nothing more is expected."

"Been thinking about all this for quite a while, have you?"

"It was Leah's idea, actually. She has a good mind for such details. I simply want to avoid prison if the very worst comes, as we think it might. I am not looking for an emotional commitment."

"How much for my name?" A smile curled his lips. Murphy felt angry and mean. He hoped he could make this as difficult as possible for her after what she had done to him! The way she had used him! *What a chump I was!* he thought again. *To think she really was interested. I would have done handsprings on the railroad track . . .*

"Five thousand American. A year's wages for you, I imagine."

"Actually, I make seven thousand. And a year's wages might make it worth my while to get hooked up—even temporarily—with such a cold-hearted broad as you."

The whistle shrieked and Murphy looked out onto the platform as Chancellor Schuschnigg, escorted by several Austrian military officers, strode toward the back of the train. *The Anschluss with Germany was coming! Elisa would need that passport—that American stamp by her name . . .*

"I'll give you six thousand!" she snapped.

He turned his eyes back on her. "Seven," he said again. "Not a penny less."

"A thousand dollars will buy a visa for a child to get out of Germany. I won't give you seven! You can manage with six."

He wished now that she had mentioned the cost of the visas for the kids sooner. He wouldn't have bargained so hard. "All right, then. Six." He turned his gaze back on Schuschnigg and the government officials. Elisa followed his gaze.

"Isn't that . . . ?"

"Schuschnigg."

"Where is he going?"

"Berchtesgaden."

"Berchtes . . ." The word faded away and a shudder coursed through her. The realization that he was going to visit Hitler strengthened her resolve. "Then we cannot wait, Herr Murphy. You'll have to arrange the marriage immediately." Again the tone was businesslike.

He rubbed a hand wearily over his head. A fresh headache was moving rapidly up the back of his neck until even his hair hurt. "Yeah. I know a guy at the embassy in Vienna. I'll be back tomorrow night. We'll get it squared away. I'll bribe him, or something. Rush it through."

"We can pay for the bribe."

"Sure. Expense account. Huh?" He almost smiled. If he hadn't had such a headache, he might have laughed. "I'll tell him you're pregnant."

She did not find his comment funny. "I think you can manage without that. There is no use humiliating me, no matter how repulsive you find this. Bear in mind that it is not pleasant for me, either."

"Sure," he shrugged. "I'll meet you day after tomorrow. Noon, in front of the American Embassy. Bring the money."

"Six thousand. And the bribe?"

"A couple hundred should do it." The train lurched into motion and Murphy felt suddenly sick to his stomach. He stood abruptly and went to the door.

"Where are you going?"

"To another seat. Business is over, right?" He staggered out and spent the entire trip to Salzburg huddled miserably in the men's room. He remembered the words of his mother and muttered, "Be careful what you wish for, Murphy; you just might get her."

Hours later, when the train disgorged its passengers onto the cold platform of Salzburg Bahnhof, Elisa watched as Murphy sauntered easily after the Schuschnigg party.

Across from her, the two little boys slept peacefully, and only when the train chugged away from the station did she switch off the compartment light and draw the shade, and there, in the darkness, she wept silently and deeply for the wedding that would be no marriage, and the groom who would never be a husband. How he hated her! How clear that had been in his eyes!

She was almost sorry now that she had ever listened to Leah. She had been doing fine with her Czechoslovakian passport! Another trip to Germany. Two to Prague, and she had passed the customs checks without any of the difficulty she had experienced before!

She brushed the tears away as quickly as they brimmed over. It would not be good if the boys saw their new Aunt Elisa crying in the night. They had seen so many tears lately. She would spare them that if she could, and spare herself from the ridiculous thought that John Murphy had ever cared for her. *A business arrangement! Pay him and be done with it. That is probably what he had in mind when he offered his help six weeks before in Sacher's! Of course! That must have been his motive. He knew that Theo had left his family well cared for.* She came at last to the conclusion that Murphy had simply never gotten around to mentioning that he wanted money for his help when he had first offered it.

Somehow that thought managed to dry up her tears like a dam and strengthen her resolve to go through with the plan. An American passport! What doors that would open for her!

By mid-February, Theo was the only one left alive of the eight men who had lit their candles in the Herrgottseck. As typhus raged through the already decimated ranks of the prisoners, Theo gave of himself, his hope, his light. Like the oil in the Eternal Lamps on that first Hanukkah, he did not seem to lose the strength of his brightness. Although to look at him, the men and guards of Barrack 8 must have wondered how his fleshless frame bore the weight of his ragged uniform.

The final glimmer of eyesight left the professor, and the hand of Theo guided him through roll calls and days in the quarry. Theo saw for them both, worked for them both; he breathed for two men as though his blood flowed through the veins of the old man as well.

"What is it?" The professor asked one night. "What makes you will us both to live? I am an old man. God promises only three score and ten years. I have lived two years longer than my allotted time. It would not be so terrible, Jacob, if I—"

"I need your vision," Theo answered.

"But I am blind."

"You see better than most men."

"What I see is not my own. Other men have written my visions."

"Like Marlowe and his Faust? I had forgotten that we are all eternal. Good and evil men alike, we *are* immortal. This life is only a dream. Short, yet it decides the fate of our lives eternally. I had forgotten that until you reminded me."

"Did the words of Faust frighten you?" The old man's voice was gently probing, almost apologetic.

"No. It is not fear of hell that turns my heart from evil." Theo smiled to himself as though he had discovered a secret. "We have been privileged to see what becomes of men who give themselves over to darkness. They are no longer men. They are the creatures; we are still men." He reached out to touch the arm of the professor. "And yet, we all began exactly alike, like lumps of coal, maybe in different shapes and sizes. The fire and the pressure of hatred consumes some men until they consume others around them in a white-hot fire. And others, trapped in the same fierce pressure and terrible heat, become diamonds to glisten in the hand of God. To shine bright when the blackness is all around, to find love when others are burning in their hatred. Isn't that the essence of God?" He shook his head. "No. I do not fear hell. I am not afraid of evil. Black coal becomes ash."

"This you learned from Faustus?"

Theo thought for a long time. He was not certain where he had learned what he now believed, and so he was not sure that he could answer the question. "A long time ago I gave up hope of ever seeing my Anna again. Or the children. And in that moment, I suppose I died to what I was." He turned to the old man. "Yet when I let go even of life and put myself in the hands of God, I became free, Julius! And I said to God that in this darkness, I want to become a shining light. The men who have imprisoned me changed my name to *Stern*. Like your name. Stern means star. Do you think that the Gestapo knew how much I wanted to shine! There is nothing they can do to hurt me, Julius. Sooner or later every man faces death. They have not seen their own inevitable future yet. I *have* faced mine." His eyes were bright in the gloom. "I know I will not walk out of here a free man. And yet when I leave, I will be free."

The professor sighed with the contentment of a man who had eaten a delicious meal. "Meat and drink we have that they know not of, eh, Jacob? Two *Sterns*, together in our little corner. Lumps of coal squeezed until we think we cannot bear it." He chuckled. "Only I do find myself wishing that God would relax his grip a while and open His hand to find us shining and flawless." He sounded tired. "Yes. I do wish that it was accomplished, Jacob . . ." His voice trailed off into sleep.

Theo drifted off after him, wondering if philosophers and theologians might not envy their classroom of suffering.

40

For Love or Money

Tonight the northern lights cast an eerie red glow on the snows of Berchtesgaden. Austrian Chancellor Schuschnigg had been met at the frontier and forced to leave the men of his company behind in Austria. He was taken up to the hilltop fortress of the Führer by an escort of black-shirted S.S. officers. There, he was ushered into a room crowded with Wehrmacht officers who had gathered to hear their Führer conduct the business of the Reich.

Thomas stood at attention with two other junior officers as Adolf Hitler walked past with his entourage. The German Chancellor, now dressed in a brown military uniform, moved with an effeminate gait. Every few steps, his left leg jerked a bit with a nervous tic. His eyes burned with fierce anger, and his lower lip protruded slightly. He clasped his hands behind his back and stared out the picture window toward the Untersburg where Charlemagne was buried. Thomas had heard the legend that King Charlemagne had vowed to return one day to rule Europe. He had also heard that Hitler said it was no accident that he had chosen his mountain retreat overlooking the burial place of Charlemagne. Absolute control! That was Hitler's demand.

In the end, Hitler had determined that men might secretly question, but they would never again openly challenge as Blomberg and Fritsch had done. He would begin his demonstration of control tonight—here in the Alps overlooking Austria.

The room where Hitler sat with Schuschnigg was large. A fire roared in a fireplace. An oil painting of a nude woman hung above the mantel. She seemed to gaze down on Schuschnigg and Hitler with amusement. Thomas and a dozen others stood just out of sight of Schuschnigg, but they had full view of the Führer's face as he spoke to the frightened leader of the little country he threatened.

Hitler leaned back in his club chair and said scornfully, "Your pitiful defenses along the border are nothing more to us than an annoyance. I need only to give an order, and overnight all the ridiculous scarecrows on the frontier will vanish. You don't really believe you could hold me up even for half an hour?" He laughed a short, bitter laugh.

Schuschnigg sat rigid in his chair. Thomas wished that he could see the Austrian Chancellor's face. No doubt it was as pale as Thomas's own face. This was not diplomacy; it was threat and force. Thomas was ashamed to be part of such a meeting, and yet he knew his presence had somehow been ordained. Certainly, if he ever again had the chance to speak to Anthony Eden, he would tell what he had seen and heard.

"Who knows?" Hitler continued. "Perhaps I shall appear suddenly overnight in Vienna, like a spring storm. Then you will really experience something. *I would willingly spare the Austrians this; it would cost many victims. The troops will come first, then the S.A. and the Legion!* No one will be able to hinder the vengeance—not even I. Do you want to turn Austria into another Spain? All this I would like to avoid."

Schuschnigg cleared his throat and began to speak. The words were quiet, and Hitler leaned forward to hear them. Victory was already in the hands of the Nazi leader. "I will obtain the necessary information and put a stop to the building of any defenses on the German frontier. Naturally, I believe you can march into Austria; but Herr Chancellor, whether we wish it or not, that would lead to the shedding of blood. We are not alone in the world. This probably means war." Schuschnigg's words were only a hope that the other nations would help little Austria, and Hitler knew it. Thomas could think only of Anthony Eden and Churchill in England and hope that they had somehow conveyed his message to Chamberlain. Perhaps it would not be too late! If England would stand for Austria—

Hitler was amused by Schuschnigg's comment. "That is very easy to say as we sit here in armchairs. But behind it all there lies a sum of suffering and blood. Will you take responsibility for that, Herr Schuschnigg? Don't believe that anyone in the world will hinder me in my decisions! Italy? I am quite clear with Mussolini; with Italy I am on the closest possible terms. England?" There was a laugh in his voice. "England will not lift a finger for Austria. And France? Well, two years ago when we marched into the Rhineland with a handful of battalions, at that moment I risked a great deal. If France had marched then, we would have been forced to withdraw. But for France it is now too late!"

And in these comments, Hitler made clear that it was also too late for Austria. Moments later, Schuschnigg was presented with a written ultimatum. The terms that would prevent Germany's march into Austria included the appointment of the Austrian Nazi *Seyss-Inquart* as minister of security in the Austrian Cabinet. Next, a general amnesty would be granted for all Austrian Nazis under detention, including those who had assassinated Dollfuss two years before, and those like Sporer, who had rioted in the Judenplatz.

"And what of those citizens of Austria whom you have detained without cause in Germany?"

"Are there such cases? It would be a small thing to look into. Communists and spies, no doubt." He promised nothing.

The last item in the ultimatum demanded that the Austrian Nazi party be officially incorporated in the government-sponsored Fatherland Front.

"We will discuss this—" Schuschnigg began.

Hitler leaped to his feet and roared, "I repeat to you! This is your last chance! Your very last! Within three days I expect the execution of this agreement. Seyss-Inquart will be in your Cabinet! Our loyal Nazi party members will be freed from prison! Or you will find yourself waking to the sound of German boots marching up to the Hofburg!" He stomped from the room, leaving the startled Austrian alone and staring at the slip of paper in his hand.

For hours, Schuschnigg was subjected to the heaviest political and military pressure as the young officers looked on. *So this is the way Germany conducts business . . .*

At eleven that night, Schuschnigg signed the "agreement" and was promptly taken back to Salzburg in the sledge which had carried him up the snow-covered roads.

Thomas and the others were housed in barracks on the grounds where admiring soldiers spoke in awestruck tones about the strength and ability of Adolf Hitler.

But for Thomas, the experience was a nightmare. He carried his report back to Canaris, then buried his feeling deep within himself and returned to his post in Paris.

———

A jumble of clothes was piled on the bed behind Elisa. She had tried on nearly all of her best dresses, and nothing seemed right. What does a woman wear to her own wedding when it's not really a wedding? To wear white would be ridiculous; this was not exactly the wedding she had planned for herself when she was a little girl pretending to walk down the aisle. Her whole life seemed to be turning out differently than she had ever dreamed; even her "marriage" would be a charade.

Finally she settled on a royal blue wool suit that her mother had bought her in Paris last fall and sent along with a note that it looked "American." That was, after all, the purpose of this pretense, she told herself. She wanted to make herself look as American as possible, and she would start this afternoon at the American Embassy.

She dressed quickly, glad that she had never worn the outfit. At least wearing something new would help her pretend that this was a special occasion. The blue of the fabric made her eyes as blue as sapphires. The fitted skirt and jacket showed off her slim waist and hips in a way that drew men's stares. She looked modern. American. Like the film stars she had seen in the English-language movie theater.

She fixed her hair the way Katherine Hepburn had worn hers in the movie *Bill of Divorcement*. As much as Murphy disliked her now, Elisa felt sure he would have laughed at the irony of the film title and her desire to look as lovely as the star. She simply wouldn't mention it. She would be as beautiful and American as Katherine Hepburn, and act her part; then she would never see John Murphy again.

They were, after all, only two actors on a stage, saying words they didn't mean. Murphy would be paid well for his performance, and Elisa's payment would be the precious passport. Then, like the character in the Hepburn film, Elisa could pretend to be who she was not. She could go on living without Murphy as though they had never met, as though he had never kissed her in the park or bought sixteen tickets for the row ten aisle seat. And when it was all over he could have his bill of divorcement, or annulment, while she kept the American name and passport.

She straightened the seam in her stockings. They were silk, the last pair she had from Lindheim's Department Store. She had been saving them for some special occasion—her own wedding might qualify. Black heels and a black silk kerchief in the pocket of the suit finished the effect. She appraised herself in the mirror.

"Elisa Murphy," she said in English, "you look like American." She was pleased with the effect. Then, still looking at the tall, sad young woman who gazed back at her from the reflection, she wondered why she had worked so hard to be beautiful today. Had she done it for Murphy? He wouldn't care as long as he got paid. Did she want him to regret losing her love, to realize what a cad he had been? Maybe that was it. Even though she knew he had been acting from the beginning, she was sorry to have to wake up from the dream. What she had felt, what she *still* felt for him, was not an illusion. But the fact remained that he was not the knight in shining armor she had once imagined him to be. He was only a paid mercenary in her battle. What could not be accomplished for love was certainly welcomed for money.

———

Murphy's hands were shaking as he filled out the papers in the clerk's office of the American Embassy.

"Mother's maiden name?" He scratched his head. "I don't know her mother's maiden name. Harry, why do they ask such stuff?" He left the space blank.

The clerk was a rakish looking young man, with slicked-back hair and a vocabulary full of words he had picked up in the speakeasies around Los Angeles. His name was Harry Scotch, but he answered to his name by saying that he only drank bathtub gin. The truth was, here in Vienna he drank whatever was available whenever he had opportunity. This morning he had a bit of a hangover, but not enough to keep him from teasing Murphy unmercifully.

"Finally gettin' hitched, eh, Murph?"

"Not unless you can help me with these forms."

"She's kinda the cat's pajamas, huh?"

Murphy had not heard that phrase since 1933. "Yeah, Harry, she's nice looking."

"That's swell, just swell. If you gotta go"—he drew his finger across his throat—"it oughta be for a gorgeous dame."

Murphy grunted a surly agreement; then he scrawled something illegible in the space that asked for Elisa's place of birth.

Murphy was angry; he had been since the ride on the train to Salzburg. Everyone in the hotel and the INS office whispered about what a grouch Murphy had become, even though he had scooped them all on the Schuschnigg-Hitler story. Timmons supposed it had something to do with the fact that if the Nazis actually took root in Vienna, all the fun would float away down the Danube, just as it had in Berlin. Johnson speculated that Murphy was feeling the lack of female companionship and suggested that he ride down to the Seventh District before Hitler marched in and closed it down. At that, Murphy had kicked them all out of his hotel room and had thrown their stinking ashtrays out into the corridor after them. He was *definitely* not his usual good-natured self since he had come back from Salzburg!

"How long is this going to take?" he snapped at Harry, who was reading the form upside down and making helpful suggestions.

"In a hurry, huh, Murph?" He raised his eyebrows and winked. "She must be really somethin'."

"How long does it take?"

"Most ladies like the long-type ceremony."

"You got a short one?"

"Sure. We can do short. As short as you like."

"How's thirty seconds?"

"It'll cost you extra."

"You're charging me five hundred as it is, you little crook!" Murphy reached across the counter and pulled Harry up on his toes by his polka-dot tie.

"That's because you want the passport tomorrow!" Harry wailed. "Nobody gets a passport in one day."

"For five hundred? Bah!" Murphy's eyes were bleary from lack of sleep. "I want a quick passport and a quick wedding ceremony!" He shoved Harry back.

Harry looked at Murphy sideways. Love had definitely had a bad effect on him. "Sure, Murph." He sounded hurt. He smoothed his tie and thought for a minute. "And I'll even throw in a cigar."

"I'm not having a baby," Murphy scowled.

"Oh. I thought maybe—" Harry stopped short when Murphy looked daggers at him.

"And I don't smoke." He shoved the forms over to Harry. "And for five hundred smackers, *you* can fill these out."

"But I don't know any of the information!" His voice trailed off; he looked past Murphy as the door behind him opened and Elisa came in. "Well, helllooo!" He gave a low whistle, then whispered, "No wonder you're in such a hurry, pal."

Murphy did not hear him. He turned to look at Elisa and for an instant he thought his heart was going to stop. She looked like something off the cover of a magazine. A picture from Fifth Avenue in New York. He had seen the Garbo movie *Ecstasy* three times, but Garbo was never so beautiful as Elisa Linder in the royal blue suit.

He looked away quickly. He didn't want her to see him loving her. *Wanting* her. Strictly business. Business. *Business!* He told himself.

"Hello, Murphy," she said coolly. The slight accent was almost a whisper. He wanted to ask her to say hello like that again. He loved it.

"You're late," he answered curtly. "I've been trying to get these forms filled out. You do it."

Harry held the pen and smiled into her eyes. "Let me help, doll," he offered. Then he began to ask her questions and write the answers down slowly. Too slowly.

Murphy looked everywhere but at Elisa. The word *dazzle* kept ringing in his ears. His mouth got suddenly dry and he started to leave the room to search for a drinking fountain.

"Are you leaving, Murphy?" Elisa called after him. She sounded worried. She must not lose the passport!

"Thirsty," he replied in an angry tone. He really was angry, he decided as he stood out in the bustling hallway of the embassy. He had never seen her look so striking. Why had she gotten herself all dolled up for a phony wedding, anyway? Why hadn't she worn sackcloth and ashes and smeared goop on her face and put curlers in her hair? Did she have to do this to him?

Elisa stepped out into the hall, removed a long, fat, white envelope from her handbag, and handed it to Murphy. "Let's make this look real," she whispered. "I don't want anyone suspecting us."

He exhaled slowly, and they reentered the clerk's office.

"We're closed for the lunch hour," Harry said. "But anything for Murphy. He's a swell guy."

"Yeah, anything for me!" Murphy growled. "You mean five hundred bucks and me."

"For love or money," Harry shrugged.

She looked back at Harry. "How long will this take?" she asked.

"Murphy says he wants a short ceremony." Harry looked worried, as if he expected her to argue. Women always like long, gushy ceremonies, even here in the clerk's office of the embassy. Harry was no priest, but he had memorized all the *I-do* and *Do-you* stuff. "Since it is my lunch hour—" He started to explain.

"Fine. That is good for both of us." She looked nervously at her watch. "And how long for my documents?"

"Tomorrow?"

"Good." She smiled at Harry and turned to Murphy. "Are you ready, darling? Let's not wait any longer than necessary."

"Let's get this over with," Murphy muttered miserably. The envelope was burning in his pocket. He was burning. She had dressed this way just to torment him, but he wouldn't let it show. He would not give her the satisfaction of more than a glance.

"He's just nervous." Elisa patted Murphy's arm. "Now—the vows?" She flashed a smile at Harry.

"Sure." Harry shrugged and took out his little book. "Have you got rings?"

Murphy groaned. He had not even thought of it. "No. I . . . it . . ."

Elisa seemed unaffected. "We didn't have time. We can buy a band later."

Harry looked concerned. "We gotta have something." He thought for a moment, then reached into his pocket and pulled out a cigar. He removed the band. It said *White Owl—Havana.* "Just for now." He handed it to Murphy, who looked angry all over again.

"Get on with it!"

Harry nodded and tried to look like he imagined a justice of the peace should look at such a time. He smiled benignly into the set faces of Murphy and Elisa. "Do you, John Lee Murphy, take Elisa Marie Linder as your wedded wife?"

"Yes."

"You're supposed to say *I do*, Murphy," Harry coached.

Murphy rolled his eyes. "I do!"

Harry ran a hand over his cheek. He was sweating. Weren't these supposed to be happy times? The best part of his job? He decided that this must be some sort of a shotgun wedding without the angry father of the bride. "Okay. You do." Harry lost his place. He exhaled loudly. "And do you, Elisa Marie Linder, take John Lee Murphy as your wedded husband?"

"I do." Her voice sounded half choked. Yes. That was better. There was some emotion there.

"Good." Harry was pleased. "So, now, *John*, take the ring and take her hand and repeat after me."

Murphy took Elisa's hand. It was warm and soft, as he remembered it from that day in the park and later when they had sat across the table from each other. He would not look into her eyes. She would see his heart if he looked into her eyes, and then she would laugh at his misery. "With this ring I thee wed . . ." He slipped the White Owl cigar band onto her finger.

Harry rocked up on his toes. "I now pronounce you man and wife, according to the laws of the United States of America and in the name of the President of the United States!" It sounded official. "So! Murphy, you may now kiss your bride!" He clapped his hands together.

Murphy looked down at the floor. He supposed he should kiss her. It was part of the ceremony. Men were supposed to kiss their brides. And Elisa wanted to make it look good. He cleared his throat and turned to face her. He tried not to think as he bent down and ever so gently placed his lips against hers. It wasn't a kiss, really. They just touched lips and stood together.

Then the room disappeared. He reached out and put his arms around her, pulling her close against him. She was so soft. He pulled her tighter— like that day in the park; only this time his arms weren't full of packages, only of her. She let herself lean against him. Her lips, soft and sweet, trembled against his.

Why is she doing this? Could a woman kiss like this and not mean it? He couldn't breathe. He didn't want to breathe. He wanted to just die like this, with his arms full of this angel.

"Now that's more like it!" Harry's voice interrupted. "Okay, you two!" He was laughing. "Not *here*! You've got a lifetime to kiss like that! Remember my lunch hour!"

Elisa pushed Murphy away with gentle hands. Her eyes were misty and full of tears. He looked at her in spite of himself. He could not tear his eyes away from hers. "Elisa," he said in a hushed voice.

She smiled sadly and looked away as she stepped back.

"All right, bridegroom!" Harry was cheerful, as though his words had brought some magic to the subdued couple. "That's the short version. Now a few more papers to sign."

Reluctantly, Murphy turned back to the stack of forms on the counter. Elisa had already signed her name in all the right spaces. Murphy took the pen and tried to focus his eyes. He began to sign as she slipped out of the room.

"Wait! Elisa!" he called.

"You gotta sign or you're not hitched, Murphy!" Harry held on to his sleeve.

Murphy scrawled his signature a dozen times. His heart was pounding. Harry picked up the forms and scanned them slowly. "Hurry up!" Murphy shouted. He could not see the blue of her dress through the frosted glass of the door.

"One more!" Harry seemed to enjoy the fact that Murphy did not want to let his bride out of his sight. "Sign here."

Murphy signed blindly, then tossed down the pen and ran out of the clerk's office into the hallway. He bumped into the clerical workers and dashed out into the foyer and then onto the street.

The clang of the streetcar sounded at the corner, and then pulled away. Murphy stood on the curb and looked everywhere for some splash of the royal blue color she wore. For an instant, he thought he saw it on the streetcar. Then in a taxi. Then a sliver of blue disappeared into the crowded sidewalks and was gone.

"Elisa!" He crushed his hat between his hands and stood staring blankly at the busy street. She had vanished, and he was suddenly alone again. His eyes filled with tears. "Elisa!" he breathed. "I love you."

41

Farewells

"Where have you been all morning, Murphy?" Bill Skies yelled when Murphy walked into the INS office.

Murphy shrugged as if he weren't sure. All the fire had left him. He wouldn't yell back as long as the discussion did not come near to his raw personal feelings. "Nowhere much. What's up?" He sat down on the edge of Skies' desk and looked around the chaotic office.

"What's up? Everything's up! You know that! You started it!" Skies was almost hysterical.

"I didn't start it. I just wrote about it. Schuschnigg and Hitler had a powwow at the Cuckoo's Nest. I covered it."

"Well, Schuschnigg is letting all the Nazis out of jail. Including the guys who assassinated Dollfuss. Including this Sporer fellow, who is wanted in Czechoslovakia. They're just opening the gates and letting them out!" He looked flushed. His pop eyes bulged in his face. "Just opening the floodgates, and—" He waved his arms like a bird. "And Hitler is supposed to release the Austrians—some kind of prisoner exchange. Typical Nazi style. Innocent Austrian civilians for Nazi murderers," he said sarcastically.

"I'm not responsible, honest." Murphy was subdued. An invisible Elisa held his hand. Her breath was still on his cheek. He had already decided that he would personally pick up her passport and deliver it to her. And then he had changed his mind and then changed it back again. Now he just wasn't sure.

"How can you be so calm?" Bill Skies shook his head and swore under his breath. "We've got a new *Nazi* security minister in the Austrian government, by order of Hitler!"

Murphy knew that Skies had lived in Vienna for nineteen years. He could hardly remember New York anymore. This was his home. "Is that the good news or the bad news you've been wanting to tell me all morning? I knew all this. So what's up?"

Skies frowned, then picked up a memo. "London office has called for you three times this morning, that's what. There's trouble brewing there as well, Murphy. Foreign Minister Eden and Prime Minister Chamberlain are at each other's throats. Politely, of course. But Eden is still taking a hard line, demanding the withdrawal of the five divisions of Italian so-called volunteers from Spain. Chamberlain wants to be buddy-buddy with Mussolini no matter what." He handed Murphy the note. "You've been in Spain. You know Eden and Churchill."

"Yeah." Murphy scanned the message. It was urgent. He would have to leave for London immediately. And Elisa would have to pick up her own American passport. "It's a showdown then," he murmured.

"Yes. A showdown. Anthony Eden against Chamberlain. If Eden re-signs, Murph, the situation here will—"

Murphy nodded. Eden was the only man in the British Cabinet who stood against appeasement. The Italians and the Germans hated him be-cause they feared him. "Did you book my flight?" Murphy glanced at his watch.

"You've got an hour." Skies mopped his brow. "Timmons threw some stuff into a bag for you." He jerked his thumb toward a small valise in the corner. One of Murphy's good shirts was hanging out.

"Thanks, Timmons." He stared at the note again, and all that had happened receded in the face of this terrible news. He was grateful that he was being taken away from Vienna and Elisa right now. It would give him a chance to simmer down before he did anything foolish.

———

Who could say what motivated the keepers of Dachau to provide such a feast? And yet, there were the trucks, heaping with loaves of fresh bread. Not moldy crusts a week old, but real, golden brown loaves heaped in glossy mounds in the beds of two cargo trucks. Were the conquerors afraid that their slaves were dying off too fast from disease and starvation? There was an endless supply of slaves to be had. Why would they care about that? Bread, on the other hand, was a precious commodity. And yet this morning they brought bread to Dachau.

The trucks were parked a mere twenty yards from the forbidden zone. By the thousands the prisoners swarmed around them, pushing and shout-ing, hands upraised in a salute to *bread*! There was not enough for even a fourth of the men, and the competition for the loaves as they were tossed from the trucks became fierce and brutal. Men were shoved down and trampled as the complacent guards watched the entertainment from their gun turrets.

The professor held tightly to Theo's shirt as they waded into the throng. "There isn't enough!" Theo shouted above the din. "You'll have to wait back here!" He took the old man by the shoulders and positioned him behind the barrack's wall.

"Loaves and fishes!" called the professor cheerfully. "Fishes and loaves!"

Theo plunged in again, his eyes riveted on the brown-shirted soldier who tossed the loaves into the teeming mass of starving men. There was no mercy in this act by the Nazis; it was sport for them, and Theo knew that men would die fighting for one taste of freshly baked bread, bread without the particles of sand and straw, bread like they had eaten before they came to Dachau! The air was full of the scent of it, driving the inmates to a frenzy. Again and again Theo was struck and elbowed as he struggled against the tide.

Behind him, a new wave of prisoners was turned loose from their barracks. They swarmed toward the trucks and joined the weight of their hunger to the surge of the crowd.

Somehow, the professor was caught and spun around blindly in the human riptide.

"Jacob!" he called helplessly to Theo. "Jacob!"

But Theo did not hear him. Inch by inch he had worked his way to the tailgate where a thousand loaves remained to feed ten thousand screaming men. He reached upward as an elbow crashed down on his head, knocking him to his knees. Other feet and knees fell on him, cutting him, tearing his clothes and his flesh, crushing the air out of him. More men piled on top of him, pinning him to the ground, and he knew that he would die here, inches away from the tailgate of the truck and the bread that would allow him to live another week.

The weight of bodies became unbearable as men climbed on top of men to reach the feast. The world became dark and sounds grew more distant as his lungs yearned for oxygen that was not there. He tried to cry out, but he had no voice. Then suddenly, the weight shifted slightly and he moved his head and right arm. He drew a breath and crawled forward slightly, just enough. His legs were still pinned, but his head and torso were free beneath the tailgate of the truck. He gasped for air and lay heaving as his senses came back to him. He looked out between the tires of the truck. His eyes focused on the thin wire of the forbidden zone. The shadows of the guard towers and their machine guns fell across the strip just beyond the thin wire. And an old man with hands groping the darkness walked forward, shuffling toward the shadows and the wire.

"Jacob!" called the professor as he felt the blank air for some landmark to his fingertips. "Jacob!"

"Halt! Judenhund! Halt!"

"Jacob!" Old feet seemed drawn to the wire, pulled into the net.

Theo shouted in horror as the scene unfolded before him. "Professor Stern! Julius! Julius!" But the professor did not hear Theo's voice above the crowds behind him. Theo struggled to free his legs. He clawed the earth as he tried to pull himself forward. *"Stop! God! God! God!"* Theo sobbed as the shadows from the turrets raised rifles to their shoulders. "Julius! Go no farther!"

"Jacob?" The professor seemed to hear the voice of his companion. "Jacob?" Legs shuffled forward. A yard from the wire.

"Blöder Hund! Halt!" The clack of rifle bolts and magazine clips was louder than the voice of the professor.

Theo raised himself up on his elbows and stretched his arms out as if to catch the old man when he tripped on the thin cord and tumbled forward. "Julius!" The rattle of gunfire answered as bullets tore into the professor, holding him aloft for a moment before he crashed to the ground.

The mob of prisoners did not seem to notice the noise of the guns. They shouted above Theo's sobs as he watched the blood of the old man flow into the earth.

Feet still tangled in the wire, the professor lay blinking up into the sunlight as Theo called his name again and again. Theo beat his fist against the unyielding ground, watching as Julius reached one hand upward as though he would touch a face bent close over him. One more rifle bullet slammed into the body; the hand remained upright for an instant before it fell across the bloody chest and the professor lay still where he had fallen.

By the time Murphy reached London, the showdown was over. Eden had resigned. Chamberlain had won his battle for appeasement. He had circumvented his foreign secretary and begun negotiations with the Italians himself. Eden was effectively made to know that his opinion did not matter any longer. There was nothing left for him to do.

This afternoon, Murphy sat in the old room at Churchill's Chartwell Manor and simply listened as Churchill, growling like an old bulldog, explained the events of the last few weeks to him.

"And so Roosevelt's offer was turned down without even so much as a consultation with Anthony. Cadogan was waiting for us at the station when we returned from France. He told Anthony the bad news. I believe he might have resigned then, but Chamberlain smiled and told him that he could not resign over something which was supposed to be top secret." Churchill clasped his hands behind his back and stared out at the late afternoon sky. "It is a decision that leaves one breathless even now. How could he turn down such a significant offer from Roosevelt?"

Murphy was not taking notes. He sipped his tea and stared out the window past Churchill. "And now what?"

"The differences between Britain and Italy seem minor compared to the refusal of Roosevelt's overture. Have you seen the statement that accompanied Eden's resignation?" He shuffled through a stack of correspondence on the desk. "Here it is." He handed the message to Murphy.

Above Eden's signature were the words: "I have spoken of the immediate difference that has divided me from my colleagues, and I think I should not be frank if I were to pretend it is an isolated issue. It is not. *Within the last few weeks, upon one most important decision of foreign policy which did not concern Italy at all, the difference was fundamental.*" Murphy read aloud. "I do not believe that we can make progress in European appeasement if we allow the impression to gain currency abroad that we yield to constant pressure. . . ."

Murphy looked up. Churchill was scowling angrily. "The resignation of Eden is being proclaimed in Italy as another great victory for *Il Duce*. They are saying, 'You see how great is the power of our leader; the British foreign secretary is gone.' " Churchill shook his head sadly. "Eden was hoping to get some commitment from the Italians that they might stand by the Austrians if Germany invaded. It is hopeless to imagine now that Italy will stand by the Rome Protocols, or that Britain will lift a finger to help. All over the world, in every land, under every sky and every system of government, wherever they may be, the friends of England are dismayed and the foes of England are exultant."

"And what of the future?" Murphy asked, although he feared he knew what Churchill's answer would be.

"The resignation of the foreign secretary may well be a milestone in history. Great quarrels, it has been said, arise from small occasions but seldom from small causes. Eden adhered to the old policy that we have all forgotten for so long. Chamberlain has entered upon a new policy. The old was an effort to establish the rule of law in Europe, and build up through the League of Nations effective deterrents against the aggressor." Churchill considered his own words as though he was delivering a eulogy. Perhaps he was. "The new policy is to come to terms with the dictators by great and far-reaching acts of submission." He almost smiled. "The other day Lord Halifax said that Europe is confused. Perhaps *we* are confused, but I know of no confusion on the part of the dictators. They know what they want, and no one can deny that up to this moment they are getting anything they want." He sat down heavily in the battered leather armchair next to Murphy. "The future?" He shook his head slowly. "Seems to be whatever they have set their eyes on, whatever they reach out to grasp. Now that the one man with sense has been removed from the British Cabinet, what will stop them, Mr. Murphy?"

"Have all the Germans gone crazy?" Murphy thought of Austria and the tirades that Hitler blasted over the radio.

Churchill carried a knowledge in his eyes that he could not speak of openly. For an instant Murphy saw it there. "You may quote me exactly if you like, Mr. Murphy. What I tell you today, on February 22, 1938, is true now and will still be true fifty years from now or one hundred." He paused and Murphy took out his notebook.

"Then I'll write it as you say it, Mr. Churchill."

The gruff old man toyed with the stub of his cigar. He thought for a moment, then began to speak as though his audience was the whole world.

"Germany occupied the Rhineland only two years ago, the beginning of 1936. They broke the treaty. Now we know that a firm stand by France and Britain under the authority of the League of Nations would have resulted in the immediate withdrawal from the Rhineland without the shedding of a drop of blood. That might have enabled the more prudent elements in the German army to regain their proper position. It would not have given to Hitler that enormous ascendancy which has enabled him to move forward. Now we are at a moment when the next move is made. By bullying and threats, Austria has been laid in the thrall, and we do not know whether Czechoslovakia will not suffer a similar attack."

"But Austria still exists." Murphy tried to play the devil's advocate in the discussion.

"They have been forced to accept the political ultimatums of Adolf Hitler. How long will it be until the next ultimatum? And then what will come?"

Churchill got up and moved to the window once again. "Yes. This last week has been a good week for the dictators—one of the best they have ever had. The German dictator has laid his heavy hands upon a small but historic country, and the Italian dictator has carried his vendetta against Mr. Eden to a victorious conclusion." He turned to Murphy. "So, though we have not seen it yet, that is the end of this part of the story."

He looked out toward the last rays of the sun. "When I heard that Mr. Eden had stepped down, sleep deserted me. From midnight till dawn I lay in my bed, consumed by emotions of sorrow and fear. For a time there was one strong young figure standing up against long, dismal, drawling tides of drift and surrender, of wrong measurements and feeble impulses. Eden seemed to embody the life-hope of the British nation. Now he is gone."

He furrowed his brow. "I watched the daylight creep through the windows and saw before me the vision of death."

———

That night, Theo lay on the pallet of the Herrgottseck surrounded by men and yet alone. He had not gotten a ration of bread. It did not matter anymore. He wanted simply to be finished, just as the professor had wanted to be finished.

Like the man in *The Trial*, the old professor had been tried and executed without ever knowing why. But whom would Theo talk to about that now? If Julius had been there, they might have talked about his death. Perhaps they would do that one day . . .

But tonight the light in Theo flickered and the burning fever of typhus at last found its grip on his weary body. The guards had left the professor's body in the forbidden zone as a warning. They would leave it through the next day. Men would become hungry again after they finished their precious loaves of bread, and then they would notice the old man.

Theo would follow his friend soon enough. Like the priest and the cantor, the flame would waver and sigh and fade away. He could not keep the covenant to live and to remember. He must be content to be remembered by others.

The heat of his fever increased as he thought of Anna, her fingers dancing on the ivory keys of her piano. Elisa stood beside her, smiling softly as they played together . . . something . . . Schubert, maybe? Theo tried to think of the piece and the composer, but only the music floated around him. Melody by no one, owned by no one. Only music. Sweet sounds serenaded him until he fell asleep in his own bed once again, in his own house. Downstairs someone was baking bread and he could smell it. *"Rolls and butter for breakfast, Theo,"* Anna whispered to him.

"Anna!" He put out his hand to her and held her tightly until the sun streamed fiercely in through the window of Barrack 8 and an urgent voice called him back to Dachau.

"Jacob Stern!" cried the voice. "Get up! You must get up, Herr Stern! Roll call! Get up!"

Theo opened his eyes and looked up at the young, frightened face of a man not more than twenty. "I can't get up." Theo's voice was a choked whisper through the heat of his fever.

"Get up! You will die if you don't!" The man pulled out a piece of bread from beneath his shirt. "I saved some for you!" he said. "I saw them shoot the old man yesterday. I tried to get to him, but the crowd. . . . I missed hearing you talk last night." He shoved the bread into Theo's hand.

"Save it for yourself." Theo could not remember the name of the young man, although he had known it yesterday.

"Eat! Get up!" The man pulled him up. "Come on. I'll help you to the line."

Theo obeyed. The world swam in a yellow mist around him. He bit into the soft bread and chewed slowly, and the man guided him out to the prison yard as Theo had guided Julius the day before.

Cold air splashed against his burning cheeks and revived him slightly. The young man placed him in his slot on the line. Already someone new stood where the old man had been. Theo stood swaying and silent. He could hear birds far away. He hoped the birds would not perch on the electric wire on top of the wall.

A new officer emerged from the guardhouse. He wore an immaculately tailored overcoat. His boots shone in the sunlight. He held a clipboard and walked along the line. He shouted names, and men stepped forward to form another ragged line when he called them.

He walked slowly toward Theo, looking at the list and then at the faces of the men.

"Julius Stern!" he barked the name of the professor. No one stepped forward. Theo could not form words on his lips to say that Julius Stern had left the compound yesterday. The officer looked angry as he approached. *"Professor Julius Stern! Step forward!"* came the command. He stopped by Theo. *"Stern!"* He shouted again.

Theo swayed beneath his gaze. He raised his hand slightly as if to explain, but the air became a mass of humming black dots that closed in until Theo could not see or hear at all. He felt his knees buckle, and then there was no sight or sound for a time.

Distantly, the voices argued over his body. *"What's the use of this? He obviously has typhus. He'll die anyway. What's the use?"*

"Orders!"

Hands lifted him up. He was not free yet. He could not see Julius or the priest or the cantor or the others. The hands of his tormentors still touched him. From somewhere came the deep rumble of a diesel engine, and then Theo lapsed again into dreams of Anna and the children. The music came again sweetly to him and he slept, warmed by his fever and lulled by the melody.

Elisa's small apartment was crowded with friends of Leah and Shimon. They had all come to celebrate the wedding of the two. It had been a short civil ceremony, but Leah and Shimon were married, nonetheless. Shimon beamed happily; Leah blushed and spoke firmly about the next wedding they would have in Palestine, under a proper canopy and officiated by a real rabbi. But it was good, they all decided, that the *first* wedding be celebrated here among friends. They had been together for so long in Vienna, and who could know what the future held for any of them now? Only Leah and Shimon were certain for themselves. Palestine. In May. Only two months from this moment they would be in Palestine!

Elisa had not told anyone about her own wedding—not even Leah. She couldn't face their questions—her own. She had slipped away quietly from the American Embassy and pretended it had never happened. She and Murphy had only been parrots mimicking the words of the ridiculous little man in the embassy office, after all. It meant nothing—only that she was now the proud owner of an American passport. She was officially the spouse of an American—what a door her new name would open for her as she crossed the border into Germany!

This morning she had purchased a ring—a plain gold band, as she had planned. Afterward she had gone to the embassy and picked up her passport. It was all done and paid for. She would try not to think about Murphy anymore. He had kissed her hungrily, and she knew what that might lead to. She had learned enough from Thomas to know she should stay away from the brash and handsome American. Their arrangement was business. It would no doubt save her skin and make her adventures a bit less exciting. She welcomed the ability to hold out the documents that designated her as married. After that frightening night in Munich with the Gestapo agent, she would wear the wedding band like a shield.

The White Owl cigar band now adorned the head of a little wooden angel Elisa had hung from the lampshade in her bedroom. It looked like a crown, and made her think kind thoughts about Murphy. She would not allow herself any more sentiment than that, however. The times were too precarious for emotion. She had decided not to hate Murphy for being the money-hungry mercenary that he was, but every day she would practice *not* caring at all. She would remember that she now used his name at a cost of six thousand dollars. There was no sentiment in that. The kiss, she told herself, had been for the benefit of the embassy official who had married them. It was just a kiss—a dangerous kiss for her if she let it be, so she tried to think of other things when the memory of Murphy's arms around her surfaced.

There were plenty of things to think about tonight. It was not hard to put thoughts of Murphy on the back burner. Amid the good cheer of the group who laughed and joked and roasted Leah and Shimon, there was an air of foreboding. Anthony Eden, the one man who spoke openly for Austria, had fallen from power in England. Elisa guessed what such news might mean to the government in Vienna. Thomas had told her enough that there was no mistaking the darkness of such an event. She had tried every night to reach him and would try again until he could tell her what she needed to know to make a decision.

More terrifying than anything, for Elisa, was the sight of Sporer's face on the front page of the newspaper. She would not forget the way the Nazi had looked at her. Even though he was being released on the other side of the border in Germany, she felt ill at the thought that a man like Sporer was *free*!

This afternoon, while the members of the orchestra had gathered to witness the wedding, Chancellor Schuschnigg addressed the Austrian Parliament and said that Austria would abide by the terms of the agreement reached in Berchtesgaden . . . but that Austria would go no further! Later, when his remarks had been broadcast, the people of Vienna seemed to find comfort in what he said. Austria was *still* Austria! If Schuschnigg had hope for the nation, then so would the people who had voted for Schuschnigg and his Catholic party.

The new concertmaster tapped his spoon against his glass for attention. "Attention!"

The political discussions of the group died down and all turned their attention to Leah and Shimon at the front end of the room.

"Raise your glasses now! We should have a toast! A toast to the happiness of the bride and groom!"

There was a cheer and light applause as Leah blushed and everyone drank to their happiness.

"And may they produce many more musicians! We will import them from Palestine, ja?" Another cheer rose up.

"But God forbid any of them look like Shimon!" There was a roar of laughter and the big man bowed happily and waved cheerfully at the insult.

Elisa stepped forward. She put her arm around Leah and raised her glass. "May they all be jewels, like Leah. Shining bright and beautiful!"

Leah hugged her, and wine spilled along with a few tears as she whispered, "No, you are the jewel, Elisa. You are my *tikvah*. I will name our first child after you." The others could not hear the words that passed between the two women. Their eyes locked in a moment that said *goodbye*. Did they both somehow see the future? Elisa wondered if the feeling that filled her now was true, or simply the result of weeks of worry and the uncertainty that filled Vienna with every new political disclosure. As she searched the warm brown eyes of her dear friend, she felt that this might be among their last times together. She did not want to let Leah go. And Leah clung to her as well.

"Weddings do make people so silly, don't they?" Elisa said, laughing through her tears.

"Practical Leah!" Shimon called to someone. "She has already sent all our things off to Palestine! No plates! No silver!"

"As long as you have a bed!" returned a male voice.

"It was Bernard Filstein who said that. A horn player! What do you expect from the brass section!" Elisa found a genuine laugh then, and all the fears disappeared for a little while.

She was so happy for Shimon and Leah—happy about their visa, their love, and their hope. They had a future. Elisa must not content herself with simply living one day at a time as she carried the violin case of Rudy Dorbransky and brought the little jewels of Germany to safety.

As the party thinned out, Leah took her by the arm and said hoarsely, "If only you would . . . you could get a visa to Palestine. I am sure of it." There was such longing in her voice, but again, both of them knew it would not be.

"No. Remember? America for me. I'll stay here for a while and send you little bundles from here."

"Don't stay too long, Elisa." Leah was serious, frightened as she spoke. "It is only a matter of time. You cannot do what you are doing forever and remain safe."

"I have only just started," Elisa said. "And you want to fire me already?"

Leah did not laugh at the joke. "Promise me. Not too long." She took Elisa's hands. "Marry that American and go play your violin in New York."

Elisa hesitated, debating whether to tell Leah about her agreement with Murphy. "Must it be New York?"

"That is the only place I know besides Hollywood, America, where they make those movies. And I would not have you play your violin for the film stars. You are much too good for that." As she spoke, Leah held her hands tightly. Elisa could see that she was remembering Rudy's broken fingers. It was there, plainly on her face. *Get out before they get you, too! Get away, like Shimon and I!*

"I'll be careful," Elisa promised. Both knew she was not speaking of finding proper employment in America.

42

Losing Hope

Thomas had heard it all at Berchtesgaden, and now the words of Hitler to the Austrian Chancellor haunted him: *"I would willingly spare the Austrians this; it will cost many victims! First the troops will come, then the S.A. and the Legion! No one will be able to hinder the vengeance—not even I!"*

The Führer had made it sound as though the vengeance would not come to Austria *if only* ... But Thomas and a handful of others knew differently. He had seen the blueprint for *Plan Otto*. Hitler and the Nazis in Austria had failed to win the country by terror and coercion. Now was the moment to enact force. There was no *if only*.

Thomas stared at the newspaper that announced the resignation of Anthony Eden. On the same page was a speech Hitler had made to the Reichstag about Schuschnigg's visit to Berchtesgaden:

"I express my sincere thanks to the Austrian Chancellor for his great understanding and warm-hearted willingness with which he accepted my invitation and worked with me...."

Hope was finished for Austria. Thomas understood that. Everyone in the embassy understood that there would be no help from France or Britain if Hitler decided to invade. An air of expectancy permeated the place, almost suffocating Thomas. He thought about Elisa and wondered what she was involved with. How had she come by the secret documents about her father? What would happen to her when the inevitable end came to Austria?

The afternoon dragged slowly by. Thomas changed into civilian clothes and made his way to the crowded cafe where he picked at his dinner and prayed that Elisa would call him. Surely she remembered all he had told her. With the fall of Anthony Eden in England, she must sense that the end was fast approaching for her beloved Vienna.

Amid the smoke and the boisterous conversation of the Frenchmen who had come to argue the day's events at the cafe, Thomas could barely hear the jingle of the telephone when it rang. He stared toward the proprietor of the cafe expectantly, but the call was not for him.

Thomas did not drink wine tonight. He sipped cups of strong coffee until his frayed nerves felt tightly wound enough to break.

Eight o'clock:

"What is Austria to us?"

"And what was the Rhineland? The Germans will not dare to bother us, so what do we care?"

Nine o'clock:

"It is a small country, yes! But in the heart of Europe! If the Nazis take control, they cut off Czechoslovakia."

"Czechoslo . . . who cares? I cannot even say the name of it!"

"That is because you have too much wine in you, Emil!"

It was nearly ten before the phone rang and the well-fed proprietor wiped his hands on his apron, then answered it on the fifth ring. Thomas watched him. He nodded, spoke in a loud voice, then looked around the room in search of someone.

"Thomas!" he called. "Your lady!" He raised his eyebrows suggestively as Thomas sprang up and walked quickly to the phone.

"Hello, darling!" His voice was light with relief.

If anyone around could hear the conversation above the din, they would have heard the words of a man talking to the woman he loved.

"Yes, I know all about it. It is as it seems. . . . Yes, darling, please come at once. I can't bear to have you there, so far away from me. Please listen to me—I have never meant anything more in my life! You must come to me! I was there! I heard it all, and you must believe me. . . ."

His voice registered disappointment. His woman was obviously not ready to come to him. He continued to plead for a few moments longer. *"There is no more time. It is over, darling! Over!"*

The Frenchmen in the cafe assumed that some great *affaire du cour* had just ended for the German who spent his evenings among them. Love affairs always ended, and new ones began. Why then did the handsome German called Thomas look so pale when he hung up the phone? He seemed almost frightened as he took his hat and staggered out onto the blustery winter street.

"Too much coffee," one of the Frenchmen shrugged. "One should always have the good sense to drink wine before ending a love affair!"

————

Theo was uncertain how long he drifted in the white mists. There was a murmur of voices, the clang of metal, warm liquid soothing his skin and voices calling the name "Stern . . . Herr Stern" again and again.

Through his soaring fever, he was dimly aware of white sheets, white walls, sunlight streaming through a window. Someone lifted his head and placed a cup to his lips. He drank warm broth and the voices praised him from the mist. *"Sehr gut, Herr Stern . . . gut."* He awoke again to the sound of footsteps echoing briskly against a tiled floor. Gently hands stroked him, bathed him, dressed him. He wondered if he had died, but his aching body dissuaded him. No. He was not free yet.

"Herr Stern . . . where is your family?" German voices coaxed him.

He did not answer. He would not. This kindness—the food, the car—was simply a trick to make him tell where Elisa was and Anna and the boys. He would have none of it, and long after he was able to form words and speak, he remained silent.

"His mind is gone . . ."

"Herr Stern? Can you hear my voice?"

"Herr Stern, if you will tell us where your family is, we can get word. . . ."

Theo lay very still. He would not open his eyes until they were gone. He would not betray his family. He would not.

"Who is he?"

"Not Professor Julius Stern. No. They say the professor died. This one should have died as well."

"Will we send him back?"

There was no answer. The footsteps left his bedside, and Theo opened his eyes. Thoughts came with difficulty. He tried to piece the days and nights together, but time had vanished. He could grasp none of the events since the professor was shot. It was obvious that Theo had been taken to a hospital. The smell of disinfectant was strong. His own body was clean, even if it was unrecognizable. He still wore the wristband with the name *J. Stern* inscribed on it. Why had they mentioned the professor, he wondered? Why had they brought him here and pulled him from the brink of death? Was it truly to trick him into telling the whereabouts of his family?

Theo was certain that, indeed, they would send him back. Back to Dachau or some other dark place. But now he would rest silently. He would drink their broth. It was good, and he could feel strength returning to him. He would take what they offered without offering them the information they wanted in return. He would not say the name of Anna, who was by now safe in the little house in Prague.

"Herr Stern? Do you have a wife?"

He would not mention sweet Elisa, who still played her violin in Vienna.

"Where is your family, Herr Stern? We must know if we are to tell them you are ill . . . Herr Stern? Can you hear?"

"Perhaps the fever has made him deaf."

He would not tell them of the men and women he had worked with for the sake of the children. So many children in Germany . . .

"Have you any colleagues? Anyone at all we might get a message to?"

This was only a temporary reprieve from death. He had seen his own fate as he watched the men of Barrack 8 die. He knew that he must also die at the whim of his captors, but for now, he would not give them even a small satisfaction.

"Herr Stern? Herr Stern? Are you feeling better? Herr Stern? Can you hear me?"

"The fever destroyed his mind, I tell you. This one might as well have been left to die."

As though drawn by some invisible hand, Elisa stood overlooking Dachau once again. Behind her, the taxi driver sat behind the wheel with the engine still running. He was impatient with her curiosity about such a place as this. She was paying him handsomely for the side trip, but still he did not like it.

She stood on the hill and stared. Her skin was very pale and she did not move until at last he called to her out the window. "Fräulein!" She glanced briefly at him. "Are you planning on coming here on your next holiday?" He joked, but the machine guns and high walls were no joke. Being here in broad daylight was no joke, either. "Hurry up!" he yelled, "or I am leaving."

Elisa tossed her head and turned away from the sight of the grim place. She carried no hope in her heart now, but somehow it was like standing at a graveside. No, not at a graveside. There was peace in that, and there was no peace here!

"Fräulein!" the driver called again.

Elisa nodded and climbed back into the taxi. "It is so big," she said as though she had not seen it before.

"And they always have room for more," the driver returned. "Why do you want to come to such a place?" He wheeled around.

"I knew someone here," she answered.

"A guard or a prisoner?"

"Not a prisoner," she answered. Her father was free now. He had still been a free man inside the walls, of that she was certain.

"There are as many prisoners now as free men," the driver mumbled, and Elisa sensed he did not like the way things were moving in Germany.

She did not reply, and they rode back to the city in silence. Inside the hotel, her passport was checked again at the desk, and a tall corpulent man with a square face and broad shoulders questioned her purpose for being in Munich.

"I am a musician," she answered truthfully. "I am here perhaps to purchase another instrument. I understand that there are many available for sale here at reasonable prices." In fact, she had carried the violin to Munich to drop off nine concealed passports at the shop of an instrument repair man a few blocks from the Marienplatz. This was the most simple of all the operations so far. There were no unhappy children or brokenhearted parents to deal with. It was a simple matter of leaving the case and returning half an hour later. She had recognized the name of the repair shop the minute Leah mentioned it to her. Once before, Elisa had needed an adjustment on her bridge when she had played in Munich, and she had taken the Steiner into the shop of this very man.

"Yes," the man behind the tall desk answered. "Since we are getting rid of the Jews, you can find a thousand bargains. From diamonds to musical instruments, I suppose." He frowned and looked at the passport. "You are a Czech national? Married to an American. Ja. So that is why you speak such good German." He smiled and handed her back the document. "Danke, Frau Murphy. I hope you enjoy your stay and find what you are looking for."

The encounter had been uncomplicated. She was relieved as she settled into her room overlooking the old part of Munich. She hugged the violin case and looked down the Marienplatz. She felt somehow as if she were rescuing her father. He was dead, she knew, but to help others made her feel as though she were helping him.

How many thousands were there right now in Munich, she wondered, who looked for some miracle to save them from this madness? And how many more were there like the instrument mender, who worked discreetly in their little workshops to help the trickle of human life flow to freedom?

She wished that her father could have found someone to shelter him last year when his plane was forced down. Couldn't God have led him to an instrument maker? Or a tailor? Or a farmer with a heart that remembered freedom? "Why didn't you lead him, God?" she asked for the first time since Thomas had told her that there was nothing more to hope for.

She thought about her mother. When Anna accepted Theo's death, she let go. There was nothing left to be done, and too many questions could only lead to despair. Perhaps there was one thing to do: make certain that she would help as many as she could who might find themselves in the same terrible situation as Theo had.

Elisa took her evening meal in her room. She wore the gold band on her finger and kept the American passport within reach at all times. When she slept, the passport folder rested on the night table beside her bed. It was her one tenuous hold on courage. *Frau Murphy*, they had called her. The name sounded American. Beyond question of the Gestapo. The thought helped Elisa to sleep a deep and dreamless sleep. Tonight there were no nightmares of trains or boxcars full of bones; when she awoke, she was hungry and eager to accomplish what she had come for.

It was market day again. The organization picked the most crowded times for her to come to the city. Elisa ate well at the hotel, although she could tell the citizens of Munich were not able to get hot rolls and butter as easily as she could. There were long lines of scowling women waiting outside the bakery in the Marienplatz.

Elisa held tightly to the case and made her way through the throngs toward the instrument shop. There were no lines outside its door, and the glass windows revealed that there were no customers inside. She smiled confidently. It was all so well planned, so beautifully arranged. This was not a place where any illegal activities would be suspected.

A carved wood violin hung above the door. Elisa recognized it, and even remembered the old violin maker when he greeted her from behind the curtain of his workshop and shuffled out to help her. The place smelled like varnish and wood shavings. Like home. Of course a violin maker would help! He understood souls, music, prayers in the melodies. No one like that could stand by and watch lives destroyed. *Why didn't Papa remember this place and come here when he needed help?*

The thought pained her. For an instant, she tried to rewrite the story, tried to see her father here in his uniform asking the old Bavarian instrument maker for shelter. If Elisa had been God, she would have written it that way. And Elisa would be carrying Theo's passport to him right now. But it was not to be.

"Guten Morgen!" The old man adjusted his eyeglasses in appreciation of the lovely young woman before him. He did not remember her, or the fact that she had come to him with the Steiner years before. Or if he did recall, he did not mention it. As a matter of fact, there was not even a hint that anything unusual might be happening here. "How may I help you?" He looked at the band of her finger. "Frau—"

"Murphy." Elisa gave her new name. She felt proud of it, even if it was all pretense. "I need my bridge adjusted." She opened the case and pulled back the blue scarf.

The old man stared at the Guarnerius as if it was an old friend. "Ja." His voice grew distant, and Elisa imagined that at some time Rudy must have come into this very place. Or perhaps Irmgard Schüler, the woman murdered with him in Vienna, had carried it here?

His old eyes misted slightly. He touched the Guarnerius. "Of course. Frau Murphy. A beautiful instrument." He cleared his throat as if to rid himself of emotion. He lifted the Guarnerius, then plucked the strings to enact the little charade. A slight smile played on his lips. He seemed to be remembering.

"When should I come back, mein Herr?" she asked him, suddenly remembering that the name of the shop was *Guarnerius Violin Repairs*. "You are fond of Guarnerius violins?" Elisa smiled at him. He was almost cradling the instrument.

"Ja, this one especially." he whispered. There was no one to hear.

Elisa had guessed correctly. The old man had been part of the whole plan while Elisa was imagining that Rudy was an irresponsible playboy. The old man knew the Guarnerius. "It is magic," Elisa said, noticing the tears brimming in his faded blue eyes.

"Yes." His whisper was so quiet. "Once my father's. Once mine. Then my daughter's; then into the hands of a master. Now yours."

"Your daughter?" Elisa tried to make a connection. The old man's name was Töne. Rudy had gotten the violin from Irmgard Schüler.

"Her name was Irmgard," said the old man. "Töne, before she married. Yes. She was mine." His face became animated as Elisa pieced it all together. She would have embraced the old man, but just then the bell above the door jingled and another customer entered with a young boy in tow.

"A half hour then, Herr Töne?" Elisa said as though nothing had passed between them.

"No more. A quick walk through the marketplace is all, Frau Murphy." He quickly put away the Guarnerius and turned his eyes on the woman and her son as Elisa left the shop.

She felt suddenly as though she wanted to cry. There had been so much that Leah had not told her. Leah had defended Irmgard Schüler before Elisa had known anything at all. The old man had lost his daughter in the battle. How many children had he saved who were not his own? He could have turned his back and claimed that they were not his responsibility, but he had not. And the priceless violin, the Guarnerius that his father had named the shop for, had become his offering to the service of God's work. He had lost his daughter. Elisa had lost her father. In a way, they shared a fellowship of suffering that made them family.

She wished she could comfort the old man when she returned for the violin, but the shop was now occupied with two other customers. Herr Töne addressed her with correct distance, accepted payment, and she knew that nine passports had been left behind; and the old man had sent his heart back with her to get more of the same!

The crash of breaking dishes awakened Theo from a deep sleep. The voice of a man cursed, then retreated down the hall.

Theo propped himself up on his elbow and looked out the window at a patch of clean blue sky. He looked around the small, spotless hospital room, sensing that very soon he would be taken from this place. There had been something in the urgency of the voices that disturbed him. They knew his body had grown stronger, but they remained convinced that his mind had been damaged by the ordeal of imprisonment and his terrible illness. They would inevitably take him away. He had heard it in their voices.

Outside in the hallway he could hear two woman talking angrily, but he could not understand their words. There was a harshness that sent a chill down him. Perhaps they had come to take him back.

He had done his best to prepare himself if that was the case. In the night, when they only entered his room occasionally, Theo had lain awake and exercised, slowly and deliberately tightening, then releasing the muscles in his legs and arms. When the corridors were still and the night-duty nurse had passed by his room, he would sit up and place weight on his legs until he was certain that he could walk again. Not far, but at least from the barracks of Dachau to the morning roll call. Perhaps some prisoner younger and strong than Theo would help him through the work at the quarry just as he had helped the professor. Perhaps he could survive the ordeal a little longer. He still had hope to offer the others, after all.

"Has Herr Stern talked yet?"

"No. Nothing. Not a word. He eats like a well man. We leave the food, and when we come back the tray is empty. But he has not spoken even a word."

"If he has strength enough to eat, then . . ."

"The doctor thinks his mind is gone. Even dumb animals know enough to eat. There is no hope for this one. Better he should have died and been done with it."

"He is Jewish, there is no doubt. Circumcised. If worse comes to worst, the Gestapo will not mistake that. I have heard they shoot sick Jews in their beds."

They spoke loud enough for Theo to overhear, and he was certain that their words were meant for him. He lay blinking up at the white ceiling. When they came in he would look just the same as he had that morning. He would not even acknowledge their words of terror. They would not be able to frighten a response out of him.

He closed his eyes as a nurse entered the room and lifted his wrist to check his pulse. "Your pulse is rapid, Herr Stern," she remarked, tucking his hand back under the sheets. "Were you dreaming? A bad dream, perhaps? Yes, we are all having bad dreams now days."

She walked away from the bedside and he looked toward the patch of blue again. He was afraid to walk to the window. Afraid to see how high he was from the ground. If someone saw him standing there, he would be taken away immediately, and he did not want to lose even one bit of nourishment, one moment of precious rest. Still, he looked at the wrist bracelet and wished that it were off. Throughout the long day, he wondered how much it would take to escape from the hospital. There were no bars on the window. Perhaps he could slip out and disappear into the busy streets of . . . *of where?* He did not even know what city he was in. He had guessed Munich, since that was the nearest large city to the Dachau prison.

He knew Munich well. He had friends in the central part of the city. But he had no clothes, no money; and Munich was thick with Nazis. Here Hitler had established his first grassroots support. Theo thought of the possibilities of walking from the building and finding some haven in the midst of Germany's hell. But how? Most certainly there were Gestapo and S.S. guarding every exit and every floor. He would be picked up immediately. And that would mean an immediate return to the prison, the end of his temporary bed and decent food. It would simply mean the end.

43

The Time Has Come!

A breath of hope blew through Vienna on a warm wind. Word had come that Mussolini had sent a message of congratulations to Schuschnigg. He had done the right thing in being so agreeable with the Führer. Nothing more would happen now. Things would soon get better since Italy and England were talking again and Anthony Eden was out of the way.

Someone in the office of the Austrian government had let the contents of *Il Duce's* message leak out. It provided a day of optimism in the conversation of the cafes of the city. People shrugged and said, *"You see, things will be all right, after all. Austria will always be Austria."*

The people of the little nation were for the most part firmly behind Schuschnigg, and when, on March 9, he announced that a vote be held to demonstrate the political strength of the established government, the decision was greeted pragmatically. The plebiscite was intended as a vote of confidence in favor of a free and independent Austria. Who wouldn't vote for that? Only the Nazis. Only the Germans. Only Hitler himself.

It was raining in Vienna. Murphy walked down the Ringstrasse without an umbrella. The sidewalk was littered with hundreds of pamphlets announcing the plebiscite, which would be held in Austria on the following Sunday, March 13.

Murphy had heard that Mussolini had also sent along another message to Schuschnigg, this one dealing specifically with the vote.

"It is a mistake," Mussolini had warned. *"If the result is satisfactory, people will say it is not genuine. If it is bad, the situation of the government will be unbearable; and if it is indecisive, then it is worthless."*

Of course, no one in Austria doubted that the result of such a vote would be overwhelmingly in favor of the government. The simple question on the ballot was: *Are you for a free, independent, Christian Austria? Yes was the only option listed.*

At this moment in history, Murphy was certain that even the Jews of Austria would vote for the Christian government of Austria. This was a vote being held to show the world that the people of Austria wanted their independence! The plebiscite was for the benefit of Adolf Hitler, Mussolini, and Prime Minister Chamberlain, and anyone else who doubted the Austrian people's will to survive! A free, independent, Christian Austria? A resounding ja! would be heard the world over. But it would make little difference in the long run.

At the embassy, Harry Scotch warned Murphy that Americans in Vienna were being put on some sort of alert. Harry didn't know what that meant, and neither did Murphy. Harry suspected that it was a warning to lay in a good supply of booze and any luxury items that might suddenly disappear if the Germans decided to invade. He had acted on that suspicion, and now had an apartment full of things that were essential to his lifestyle.

When Murphy went to check on Elisa's passport, Harry asked about her with a sly wink that gave Murphy an urge to smash him right in the nose. Elisa already had her passport; Harry was surprised that Murphy didn't know about his own wife. "You know women . . ." Murphy shrugged.

"Did you get her a ring yet?" Harry asked. "I didn't notice if she's still wearing the cigar band."

Murphy pretended not to hear him and left in a hurry. Now he prowled along the Ringstrasse in the rain, searching for a wedding band. Something more than a plain gold band; he wanted it to be noticed on her hand by any Gestapo thugs that might corner her.

On the window of a small jewelry shop words were scrawled proclaiming that the owner was selling out and leaving Austria. Murphy stepped beneath the awning and looked in at the nearly empty case. There were still a few wedding bands on display, several with diamonds. Murphy didn't want to buy her anything that some goon might be tempted to steal. He walked into the shop. A little bell jingled over the door as he passed the threshold, and a small man with thick glasses and baggy clothes stepped out from behind a curtained workshop area.

"I saw your sign." Murphy stood dripping and awkward in the center of the small shop.

"Ja. You are looking for something special? We are almost empty."

"You're leaving Vienna?"

The man nodded and stepped up to a glass counter. "Here is what we have left. Only these. All handmade by me and my son." He plainly wanted to talk about jewelry, not leaving Vienna.

Murphy decided not to ask him where he was going or how he felt about it. *Mind your own business.* "I want a wedding ring. For . . . a woman."

"Ja. We have a few here." He pulled out a tray.

Murphy stepped forward and in an instant saw what he wanted. There, nestled on black velvet among a dozen others, was a band of blue lapis inset in gold with a gold vine entwined around the stone. It was simple. It was royal blue—the color he had searched for in the crowd outside the embassy. It made him smile and ache at the same time. He pointed. "The blue one."

Now the jeweler smiled. "Lapis lazuli. Blue, like the color of Gott's eyes, mein Herr. Ja. Beautiful."

Murphy thought about Elisa's eyes. They had such depth of color. He paid for the ring without ever questioning the price; then he tucked it into his pocket and left the little shop. He did not think about the rain anymore, and when he showed up on her doorstep like a soggy puppy, she smiled kindly at him and invited him in for tea or coffee.

"Are you lost?" She was amused at his appearance. She took his overcoat, but the rest of his clothes were just as wet.

"No. I've been gone from Vienna a while. The Eden thing." He was dripping on her rug. He looked at the petit point chairs and remembered the miserable night he had watched her shadow on the shade and seen two silhouettes kissing. The memory made him uncomfortable. He was suddenly imagining all that must have taken place in here that night. "Nice place," he said.

She was polite, but controlled. "Herr Murphy," she began, "why are you here on such a night?" She did not offer him a seat.

"Harry said you picked up the passport." He glanced toward the bedroom. A little lamp was beside the table. An angel—one of his—hung from the shade with a cigar band crown. Murphy was pleased. He looked away as her eyes followed his and suddenly she blushed.

"Yes. The passport. Thank you. I got it very quickly. Twice more I have been to Germany, and the document has made life much less complicated."

"You've been there since—" He frowned. "Even with all this going on? Don't you realize you might get yourself caught in the middle of a Nazi Panzer division heading this way?"

"I can take care of myself." She turned away, shutting the bedroom door. "But thank you."

He could not think of anything else to say. He was alone in the same room with her, and words just vanished. He reached into his pocket as the teakettle whistled. "I brought you this." He tossed her the small velvet box.

She held it as the kettle continued to shriek. She bit her lip and shrugged. "Why?" she asked above the noise.

"It reminded me of you." He wished she would turn off the kettle. But maybe she left it screaming on purpose. It's hard to get romantic with the noise of an angry teakettle in the background.

She shrugged and looked distracted, then laid the box on the table and went to fix the tea. "Herr Murphy," she said, "I know what you are thinking." Her voice was matter of fact. "This is a business arrangement. And it has been concluded, I think, when you were paid."

"Just open it. Then I'll leave," he said quietly. "I should have sent it by messenger, but I . . . I wanted to see that you are all right. Things are getting pretty heated on the other side of the border. I just . . ."

"I am fine." She carried out the cups and set them down beside the box.

She wore gray wool slacks and a blue sweater, and her hair was done up like some movie star Murphy couldn't remember. "No tea. I've got to get going. Just open it."

She didn't want to open it, he could tell. She picked up the box and held it. He couldn't see her face. She had turned away from him and soft strands of hair tumbled down on her neck. He wanted to touch her. But he didn't. She exhaled loudly and opened the box, then closed it quickly again and looked toward the kitchen and the steaming kettle. He was sorry he had come. She didn't like it. A blind man could tell that she didn't like it. He had been a sentimental idiot.

"I thought you could use it." His voice cracked like an adolescent teenager.

She still did not face him. She stood with her back to him in silence.

Murphy shifted uneasily. "Well, I should go now." He moved toward the door. She still did not speak or try to stop him. "Did you see that it was blue? Like your dress?" He asked with his hand on the knob.

She nodded once, but she did not turn to face him. She held the closed box in her hand and still stared at the kettle.

Murphy frowned. He wished she would look at him. He scratched his cheek and stepped away from the door, then sidled closer to her, moving around to the side, then stepping between her and the kettle. She was crying. Silent tears streamed down her cheeks. He looked at her for a moment as though she were a stranger. Just when he thought he had her figured as cold and heartless, she pulled this!

"You're crying."

She bit her lip and angrily wiped away tears. Murphy reached into his pocket for a handkerchief, but it was also dripping wet. "Just when I thought I had you all figured out—" she said, sniffing and taking the wet hankie from him. "Please go," she murmured. "Just take your coat and go!" She was still crying. She did not look at him. She stared at his shoes. They were muddy, and he had tracked mud in all over her rug.

"Elisa—" he said, reaching up to touch the red place along her jawline. This was the place where her violin rested. It made him wish that she would lay her cheek against his hand.

"Herr Murphy!" She stiffened and stepped back.

"Just Murphy . . . you know."

"No!" She was adamant. "*Mister* Murphy. I should not have let you in.
I thought you were someone else. I have guests coming tonight. To listen
to the broadcast. I thought you were . . ."

"Why are you crying?" he asked, reaching out to touch her cheek once
again.

"I cry easily. These are not happy times."

"You mean you would be crying, anyway? Even if I hadn't come?" He
laughed. "That's a relief."

"I am sorry," she apologized. "You should go now. I have guests coming."

"Right." He didn't move. His hand still touched her cheek, but she
would not lift her chin when he nudged it gently. She would not look into
his face, even though he was lost in looking at hers.

"Please," she said more brusquely. "My company is a man." She
stepped away from him. "He will not understand your being here."

Her confession stopped him short. He cleared his throat and fumbled
for his overcoat. "I thought you might need a ring," he said gruffly. "Something more than a cigar band." Then he remembered that she had said
she was expecting guests. "Who else is coming?" he asked. "You said
guests."

"A friend. With him." She went to the door. She would have him out
of the apartment and out of her life. She threw the front door open just
as the fist of Shimon was raised to knock.

"Guten Abend! It is Herr Murphy, isn't it?" Leah charged past Shimon
and pumped Murphy's hand vigorously. "How lovely to see you here!"
She looked toward Elisa, who slipped into the bedroom—to fix her
makeup or something, Murphy assumed.

"Are you staying for the broadcast?" Shimon patted him on the back.
"It will be good to have another man around while these woman gossip."
He scowled. "You are all wet, Herr Murphy!" He bawled to Elisa. "Get
Herr Murphy the clothes I left when I stayed here!"

Elisa emerged from the bedroom looking mildly unhappy. "Herr Murphy has an engagement."

"It's okay." Murphy was relieved. "I was just going to meet a few other
journalists to talk about tonight's broadcast by Schuschnigg. Just business. I can stay and hear it right here."

Since the first of January, seventeen Jewish children in all had passed
from Vienna to the farmhouse in Kitzbühel, then on to France or Switzerland. Now the house was filled with happy noises as an additional nine
waited for the papers that would open the way to some new homeland
far from the roaring of Hitler's Legions.

There was some amused satisfaction among the Wattenbargers this
week when they learned that the German ambassador was in the village

for a skiing trip while under his nose nine Jewish children learned to milk cows and played with kittens and helped with the baking.

"And that is as close as any Nazi will come to them," Franz said as he kissed his wife goodbye. The young bride held on to his arm for a moment.

"We will be praying that it goes well in Innsbruck," she whispered. "That the whole world will listen to the voice of Austria."

Franz nodded. Tonight he and his father traveled to Innsbruck to hear Chancellor Schuschnigg speak. He was, indeed, the voice of Austria; there seemed to be no one else to speak for the wishes of the little nation. Millions would listen to his broadcast, but Franz and Herr Karl would be among those twenty thousand in the square who raised their voices to cheer him on.

The verdict of the coming plebiscite was not in doubt. Although many of the youth of the nation were caught up in Nazi propaganda, they could not vote.

What remained was a million and a half workers who had just pledged their support after the outrage of Berchtesgaden. Another million and a half peasants would back Schuschnigg to a man without being asked, and the country's half million Jews and half Jews would mark their ballots *ja!* for Austria and Schuschnigg! Even without the monarchists and the Nazi stalwarts of the Fatherland Front, Chancellor Schuschnigg and Austria could be assured of at least seventy percent of the vote. Union with Germany was not wanted. All of Hitler's threats and desertion by the great powers could not change that.

Here, tonight, cheering thousands would give the world an answer to the question. Millions more would listen at home on their wireless sets. If this last rallying cry within Austria was only to be the dying scream of one alone and drowning in a sea rocked by apathy and tyranny, then at least the call would echo in the parliaments of every nation who did not reach out to help!

Kurt von Schuschnigg had come home to his native Tyrol to make his appeal. The streets and plazas of Innsbruck were crammed with men and woman who had come to add their voices to his.

Franz and Karl were near the front of the wooden scaffolding that was draped with the red-and-white flags of Austria. The Chancellor wore a loose gray jacket, and the green waistcoat of the Austrian Alps. He stood, and a roaring cheer erupted from the mass. Applause and shouts of "Long live Austria!" filled the air and all but drowned out Herr Karl's words as he leaned close to Franz.

"Mussolini can hear us now!" He was laughing. Even his drooping moustache seemed to smile.

"And the British and the French as well!" Franz replied.

Schuschnigg spoke for twenty minutes. This was his answer to Hitler's "gracious invitation" to Berchtesgaden! He ended his impassioned speech, "Tyroleans and Austrians, say *yes* to the Tyrol! Say *yes* to Austria!" Twenty thousand voices yelled themselves hoarse in the square, while the millions at home quietly cheered as well.

Finally, in the Tyrolean dialect, he shouted out the cry that had resounded in these same mountains one hundred and thirty years before when then men of the Tyrol faced death at the hand's of Napoleon's armies. *"Männer, es isch Zeit! Men, the time has come!"*

Long before the cheering died away in Innsbruck, Adolf Hitler turned off his radio and ordered the assembly of his General Staff. His face was livid with rage. He could not win politically in Austria; he had been certain of that for some time. He paced and frothed at the mouth. He called Schuschnigg a betrayer and a criminal, and he believed what he said.

He slammed his fists against the table and shouted the same ominous words that Schuschnigg had just uttered to the cheering crowds of Austria: *"The time has come!"*

44

Last Day of Joy

Elisa and Leah and Shimon were exultant after the speech of Schuschnigg. Things must work out all right for Austria! There could be no Nazi march to Vienna in the face of such overwhelming hope and support for an independent homeland. The vote had been taken by voice assent even before the ballot boxes were set up.

Only Murphy was silent and serious. He had determined that he would not dampen their spirits by his opinion of the whole matter, but he knew . . . he had seen. . . . There were other ears listening from the Dragon's Lair just across the border from Salzburg. Murphy heard that Hitler kept a telescope trained on Austria and looked through it often and with longing.

"Well, Murphy!" Shimon clapped him on the back. "What would the fellows at your hotel say to such a speech? What would the journalists think about such an event?"

Murphy did not want to answer. They were all smiling, looking at him. He knew his answer would wipe away their smiles even if it did not diminish their hopeless hope

"Murphy?" Elisa asked, sensing that he was not as optimistic as they all seemed to be.

"A good speech, as speeches go," he said with an attempt at a smile.

"And what?" Leah's tone was flat. "Tell us what you are really thinking," she insisted.

"I think—" He paused. He wanted to phrase this carefully. They were already looking puzzled by his lack of enthusiasm. He had not meant to bring business along with him. He had come to see Elisa, to give her the ring. Now she was looking at him as if he were a traitor, a doomsday prophet. Maybe he shouldn't say anything at all.

"Tell your thoughts." Shimon was frowning now.

"There are about four million Austrians who heard the speech tonight. A good speech it was, too." He bit his lip. "Of course, Hitler probably didn't like it much. It probably made him mad." He looked up into Elisa's angry eyes. He had been right. She didn't want to hear this. He continued anyway. It was too late to call back the gloom that had come from his mouth. "A vote can't stop tanks. It won't stop the S.A., the S.S., the Gestapo, or the Legion if they march into Vienna. You have all seen it. You know what is happening in Germany. I say to you, if you're Jewish, get out now." He looked fiercely at all three.

Elisa looked as though she might slap him. He had ruined their pleasant evening. "They wouldn't *dare* march after that!" she snapped.

"Maybe." Murphy would not argue. He shrugged, a gesture that let her know that she could think whatever she wanted but that she was foolish to think a few words would stop Hitler.

Shimon was more troubled by his words. "Our visas—" he began. "We cannot leave until May."

"I hope we all have until May," Murphy said quietly.

"Stop it!" Elisa snapped. She stood up and glared at him. "No one asked you here."

"I asked him, Elisa." Leah was startled by her friend's fierceness. She had never seen Elisa so angry before. "He has helped us."

"Helped us?" she scoffed. "He has helped himself, you mean!"

Murphy stood to leave. His presence was not a damper but a flame-thrower on the group. He shouldn't have come. "I'm sorry. I shouldn't have stayed." He searched for his hat. He was dressed in Shimon's baggy clothes, but he would deal with such things later. Now he only wanted out of the apartment and out of Elisa's way.

"This is our home!" Elisa shouted. "Can't we hope? Can't you at least give us one night of hope! Do you know how long it's been?" she started to cry, and Leah took her by the shoulders.

"Elisa! Elisa, please!" She shook her.

"I saw it! I saw Rudy and Dachau and the faces of the mothers when their children had to be taken away!" Elisa was sobbing, still shouting at Murphy. "Can't you leave us one night to be happy? One evening to believe that it can't happen here? It can't happen here! It *can't*! God, don't let it." She sank down onto the sofa and wept with her face in her hands as if she would break with the unhappiness of it all. "Only one night," she said again and again.

Leah patted her gently. She looked at Murphy. "I'm sorry," Leah said to him. "I . . ." Leah was embarrassed for Elisa and for Murphy.

"No." Murphy took his hat in his hand and stood staring at Elisa for a moment longer as she cried silently and held tightly to Leah. He had done this to her. She had been through so much already, and he had stolen away what might have been a short rest. There was nothing left to say.

He shook hands with Shimon and slipped out into the corridor of the apartment.

He was halfway down the stairs when the door behind him opened and Shimon called him. "Please, Murphy. Just a moment."

Murphy wished he could have gotten away. He was humiliated and somehow ashamed. "It's raining all over," he said, trying to shrug off the scene.

"She'll be all right." Shimon rolled his eyes. "You know these women when they are in love. Leah has had a few of these crying fits. These days, I think all women should live in Vienna and go see Dr. Freud, ja? No wonder he has such good business!"

Murphy had not heard a word Shimon had said after " . . . *when they are in love.*" So, Elisa really was in love with someone! "I shouldn't have come, I guess. I just wanted to see that she was all right."

Shimon waved his hand to dismiss the concern. "There is something else we must talk about now, out of hearing of the ladies. You think tonight . . . the speech . . . is meaningless?" he asked.

"It depends on Hitler. Hitler won't want the actual vote to take place, that is certain. I think we are in for a storm, Shimon. Be careful. That's what I was trying to say in there. The Nazis are out of jail now. Steer clear of the Judenplatz. Stay here tonight, maybe until after the vote."

"Yes, of course. And if you hear anything, will you come tell us? We will be here."

Murphy lowered his voice. "I hope I'm wrong."

"So do I. But it pays to be careful."

"They'll hit the railroads first if they come, you know. Have you got a car?"

"I can't drive." Shimon looked embarrassed.

"Are there still German children placed around Vienna?"

"Only four. Elisa was going to take them to Kitzbühel on Monday."

Murphy scratched his head. His mind was spinning. Four Jewish-German children would be a drop in the bucket if Hitler marched to Vienna. There would be half a million Jews looking for a way out, and Shimon and Leah would be among them. "I'll keep my ears open, Shimon. Maybe we'll get a happy ending out of this thing yet." He shook the big man's hand again and left him standing on the stairs. Murphy guessed that he would stay out of the apartment for a while until Elisa settled down. As for himself, he would be glad to get back to the smoke-filled hotel room and the griping, snarling, pessimistic pack of realists who could look at things with some clarity.

———

As Chancellor Schuschnigg returned from Innsbruck to Vienna, Leah and Shimon returned to their little home in the Judenplatz. Before the sun was up, Leah and Elisa had determined that Murphy was simply an incorrigible doubter.

Thursday, March 10, seemed to prove them right. The inner city was filled with joyful shouts of Austrian patriotism. "Heil Schuschnigg!"

"Heil liberty!"

And all voices joined together in the cry of "Heil Austria!"

Trucks of happy political demonstrators trundled around the Ringstrasse waving placards that proclaimed: *"Sunday is polling day! We vote YES!"* A rehearsal was called for the symphony to celebrate the victorious vote even before it had been cast, and Elisa made her way through the throngs on Kärntnerstrasse toward the State Opera House. The roar of Austrian planes thrummed above the city, and pamphlets fluttered down on the crowds like leaves on a fall day in the Vienna woods.

"Heil liberty!" Elisa shouted along with the rest. "Heil Austria!" She had forgotten her anger and found hope once again. She wished that she could see Murphy and tell him how wrong he had been! There had not been even a peep from Hitler in Germany, and the Austrian Nazis had all seemed to disappear from Vienna. There were a few scattered incidents around the country where Nazis had paraded and protested, but all in all, it seemed as though the Chancellor had made a correct decision. Even the new Nazi Cabinet member, Seyss-Inquart, seemed to be in agreement with the plebiscite.

That morning, the orchestra played patriotic songs of the Austrian homeland with a resounding joy. As they rehearsed, Leah and Elisa glanced at one another from opposite sides of the stage, grinning as they had in old times. Things would work out. Vienna will always be Vienna! Austrians had fought the Germans in 1866 when they were threatened; they would fight again if they had to. The Legions of Hitler would not march here!

Outside on every corner, music played. The little nation so torn between the right and the left was at last united to defy a greater threat.

The afternoon was spent over a long and happy meal. Elisa and Leah giggled like schoolgirls over everything and nothing. Murphy might have robbed Elisa of her one night of hope, but she would have this day. This last day of joy in Vienna.

The next dawn did not bring rejoicing with it, but the blackest of all Fridays in Vienna's long history.

Murphy was still lying in his red velvet canopy bed at the Sacher Hotel when fists slammed frantically against his door and the frightened voice of Timmons called out.

"Murphy! If you're in there, let me in! Murphy! Murphy!"

Murphy sat bolt upright. He had been dreaming about Elisa and he resented the intrusion. "What?" he shouted back, stumbling to the door as Timmons continued to pound.

Timmons fell into the room as if he had been pushing on the door. "They've closed the frontier!" he said without any explanation. He looked disheveled and was out of breath as if he had run all the way to the hotel. "We've been trying to get you." He glanced toward the phone. "Off the hook! At a time like this!"

Murphy scratched his head and straightened his rumpled pajamas, trying to figure out what. . . . Suddenly it came to him. "Tell me!" He was instantly awake.

"I was on the last train through from Germany!" Timmons was sweating. "There are troops! German troops! All along the border. *Thousands!* Tanks and trucks; they've closed off the frontier. Shut down the railroads. I just heard that Czechoslovakia and Yugoslavia have closed their borders to Austria as well. Every Jew in Vienna is going to be trying to get out!" He grabbed Murphy by the shirt front. "Do you hear me, Murph? Hitler is marching in!"

Murphy dressed quickly and left the room without bothering to shave. The International News Service office was in turmoil.

"Hitler has sent an ultimatum to Schuschnigg—" John read the latest dispatch. "Says if Schuschnigg will cancel the plebescite, the Germans stay put!"

The deadline for the Austrian decision was twelve noon—a half an hour away.

At noon, Schuschnigg was defiant in his determination to continue with his plans. He even ordered the police and the Vienna Front Militia to their posts. Security guards of the railway were issued arms. The oil company of Austria was asked to supply extra fuel for possible troop movements.

Hope rose briefly in the newsroom, and the ultimatum was extended until two P.M. Skies ran in with the news that an emergency meeting had been called, and the new Nazi Cabinet member had brought further word from the Führer: *"Cancel or else. Cancel immediately. No time left for discussion."*

A newspaper from Munich made the rounds. The front page declared that the Russian flag was flying in Vienna and that violent mobs were swarming the streets with shouts of "Heil Moscow! Heil Schuschnigg!" The Nazi propaganda machine was grinding out the stuff that wars are made of when reality is in short supply.

At two-thirty, it was publicly announced that the Chancellor had decided to call off the plebiscite and bow to the ultimatum of Hitler.

———

A new and terrible tension permeated the halls of the hospital. Doctors and nurses checked Theo's condition with barely a word of acknowledgement. Faces were grim and hard-set. Words were curt and almost angry, even between the workers.

Theo had eaten a meal of sausage and potatoes and two slices of fresh bread with butter. He lay back on his pillow and stared at the rainy sky. What was beyond the glass pane, he wondered? When they finally came for him, could he throw himself through the window and free himself?

At the approach of footsteps, he stared at the blank wall. It would not do to let them see that he was thinking. There could be no expression on his face.

A tall, dark-haired doctor entered the room and glanced at the clipboard on the foot of the bed.

"Except for undernourishment, he is well. Almost well, anyway. You would like to go home, Herr Stern?"

Theo did not respond. For days they had taken this approach, hoping to get him to talk. He would not. Anna and Elisa were safe. He would not offer them up as a sacrifice to his captors' terrible tricks.

"You have no one." The doctor let the clipboard fall. "No place to go. And now they are coming to take you again, Herr Stern. It is inevitable. We have nursed you back to life, and yet you will die. They will take you from here, and you will die." He turned on his heel and stalked out of the room.

Theo had heard the compassion in the doctor's voice. Or was it simply the sadness of a man who had fixed a broken machine only to know that it would be smashed again? It did not matter. The regrets of the doctor could not save Theo. *They* were coming. The doctor had said as much. Theo's reprieve was over.

For an instant, Theo wanted to scream, *"I'll tell you anything, only don't send me back!"* Was this not the worst kind of hell—to give a man some taste of cleanliness and life and then send him back to filth and starvation?

Theo squeezed his eyes tight and tried not to see the vision of brutality that reared up before him. He prayed, asking God to give him the strength to bear what must surely lie ahead for him. The thought of the wire across the forbidden zone and the body of his friend still and lifeless returned. This time it came as a temptation—how he had envied the professor his final freedom! How easy it would be now that Theo's mind was strong again and his body well nourished to simply step across the wire and be done. A quick end while he still was unbeaten and unhungry.

Then one word came to his lips—an answer he knew came from another voice deep within him. "No!" A thousand thoughts flooded his mind. If indeed, the Gestapo were coming for him now, why should he wait passively to be taken? If he was certain of his own death, why not die trying to escape? Here in the hospital he had more chance than behind the cruel barbed wire of Dachau!

Theo stared at the one patch of blue between the gray clouds. He sat up and swung his legs over the edge of the bed. Holding on to the bed rails for support, he stood. He felt weak, but he drew his shoulders back as he walked the six steps to the window. What did it matter if someone looked up and saw him standing there? They were coming anyway.

He leaned heavily against the window ledge and disappointment descended on him like a cloud that passed suddenly over the sun. His room was on the fifth floor and faced inward toward a small courtyard. There was no way down the face of the bricks, and the little garden area below was surrounded on all four sides by the building. Even if he could have gotten out through the window, the courtyard below was yet another prison to escape.

Back in his bed, Theo flexed the muscles of his hands and bony arms. These were hands that had swung a hammer to break rocks. His arms had found the strength to lift heavy stone up the quarry slopes for two men. These hands and arms were still strong enough to fight. But he must plan his attack. He must think. He closed his eyes and remembered the hammer in his hands and the crash of steel against stone.

45

Black Friday

Bill Jordan was an INS correspondent whom Murphy knew only slightly. He was based in Paris, yet somehow found himself in Vienna during the worst of all possible days.

Bill Jordan was Jewish. His wife, a young, pretty brunette from Germany, was also Jewish, and from long and terrible experience had learned what ultimatums from Hitler meant. Bill had already purchased plane tickets out of the Austrian capital for that very afternoon.

"But I've got to get my car out of here," he said with a shrug.

It seemed ordained. All day Murphy had been thinking about the children squirreled away around Vienna, the railroads at a dead stop, the borders slammed tight in the face of the crisis.

"How much do you want for it?" Murphy asked. "Nobody's going to drive it out of here if the Nazis march in."

Jordan looked disgusted. He liked his automobile. It was a practically new Packard coupe with a luggage compartment that opened through the backseat. But he knew Murphy was right.

"Three thousand." Bill looked grim.

Murphy laughed curtly. "Even at black-market prices, that's crazy, Jordan," he said. "I'll give you fifteen hundred."

"What? You've got to be joking! I had to pay that for the plane ride out of here."

"And you're lucky to get a seat on any plane at all," Murphy said. There was no sympathy in his voice. He was thinking about that untouched six thousand he had tucked away. He was thinking about the children that it would buy visas for.

"Twenty-five," Jordan bargained.

"Fifteen hundred. Take it or leave it. You aren't going to get that much from anybody else. Of course, the Austrians will buy it in a minute—with

Austrian money or Reichsmarks. But you know what that will be worth."

"Two thousand, then!" Jordan was angry. "Anybody in here want to buy a practically new Packard for two grand?"

There were no takers. Nobody in the newsroom had much more than two nickels, let alone two thousand dollars to spend on a car at the moment the Austrian nation was dissolving. Nobody even seemed to hear him.

"Don't be a dope," Murphy said. "Fifteen hundred American. Take it, and maybe I'll sell it back to you if I make it to Paris."

Jordan tossed him the keys. Murphy pulled the fat envelope from his pocket. He had taken it with him on the hunch that he would need it today.

"It's out there." Jordan looked like he had sold his sweetheart. "You want to see it?"

Murphy walked to the window. The car was a sweet, shining thing with green paint and a proud hood ornament. The tires were good. He had always wanted a Packard. "Has it got gas? They say there's no gas to be had anywhere."

"Some. Enough, maybe." Jordan was miserably counting his cash. "If you run out, it'll cost you another fifteen hundred smackers, and it'll serve you right." He sniffed and pocketed the cash. "Take me to the airport?" he asked.

Murphy solemnly shook his head. "Take a taxi. I need the fuel."

————

And so the rains came to Vienna—streaking panes of glass with tears, drumming out a march to war on every rooftop, crackling against the sidewalks and dissolving the little pamphlets like scorching, all-consuming fire.

With her fingertip, Elisa traced the frantic drops on her window and listened as they tore loose with a snap, exploding, on the wet cobblestones in the street below. The radio blared the terrible news at various intervals. First the plebiscite was canceled; then word had come that the Chancellor had been forced to resign and all the Cabinet with him except for the Nazi Seyss-Inquart. The final ultimatum had been issued from Germany. The frail and ailing Austrian President Miklas had been ordered to appoint Seyss-Inquart as acting Chancellor—*or else!*

So Murphy had been right, after all. The German troops would come. They were simply waiting for one person to refuse a demand from Hitler and he would order them across the border. Sooner or later it would happen, and they would come.

Elisa was frantic with worry for Leah and Shimon and the others who would be in the most immediate danger—known Zionists, Jews, anyone anti-Nazi would be signaled out first. Yet Leah and Shimon had not come here for shelter. Certainly they could not still be in the Judenplatz! The radio had said that the Nazis had made their presence known; now they ran wildly through the Judenplatz just as they had the night that she had seen Otto there. *Was Otto with them still?* Elisa wondered. *Had Sporer already crossed the border back into Austria?*

She shuddered at the thought. There was nothing for her to do now but stay indoors and pray. Bit by bit it was falling apart. And she could do nothing at all to stop it. No one to call. No place to go for help.

The certainty had risen with the first words of news. By tomorrow the troops would come, *and then the S.A., and the Legion! No one will be able to stop them.*

In that one brief instant of realization, a heart-stopping fear filled her. She stepped away from the window and turned around to stare at the room as though some evil, unseen presence had entered it. There was no one there. Nothing had changed. Her gloves and keys were still on the table. A newspaper lay open on the sofa. The clock still ticked. From where she stood, she could see the little angel hovering below the lamp-shade. Nothing was different—yet everything was different. Instead of Austrian Shupos in her sitting room, she could imagine the leering face of Sporer and the grim, chastising words of Otto: *"Don't come back here. Not ever!"*

"God, help me!" Elisa cried in despair. She fixed her gaze on Murphy's angel. Her fists were clenched and her breath came fast. She wanted to find a place to hide, to run down the stairs as she had the last night in Berlin with her father as they left the store. Only then Theo had been with her, holding her arms steadily and talking lightly with her as the eyes of evil had gaped at them from the darkness of the alley.

"Papa!" she shouted as the voice of Adolf Hitler blasted across the airways declaring the treachery of Schuschnigg and Germany's determination to yield to no man. *"Papa!"* she cried again. *"We have to get away! Help me. Show me what I must do!"*

The clock ticked. The voice roared on, drowning out her pleas. They were coming here. As they had taken over Germany, they would do the same here. Now it was no longer a matter of making quick trips to Munich and coming home to safety, returning to the warmth of friends and the pleasant, oblivious existence of the orchestra. All of that was being swept away in one day.

Elisa put her hand to her head and tried to shake off the fear and panic. She rushed into her bedroom and took the precious American passport from the top drawer of her bureau. Then she opened the small velvet case where the blue lapis wedding ring was nestled. Tiny golden leaves curled around the stone. Delicate flowers bloomed above the royal blue background. It was beautiful, the sort of ring presented by a man who loved his wife. The Gestapo would notice it. They would see that she was married—to an American. They would not touch her.

For the first time, Elisa turned the ring and looked at it carefully. Inside the band was the inscription: *Elisa—Song of Songs 5:16—Murphy*. She reached into the drawer of her bedside table and drew out the Bible she always kept there. Flipping the pages past Psalms and Proverbs, Elisa located the few chapters of Song of Songs and turned to chapter 5. Her heart caught in her throat and tears stung her eyes as she read the last sentence of verse 16:

This is my beloved, and this is my friend.

Beloved. Friend. Murphy. Elisa exhaled a deep, ragged breath. Maybe she had misjudged him, after all. Maybe there was a chance for something more than a business arrangement. Maybe . . .

She slipped the band onto her finger and closed her eyes. This would be her shield tonight. She needed something, someone. *Murphy?* She held the passport to her. The rain stopped, and the clouds over Vienna began to clear. She prayed for Leah and Shimon. For the children. For herself. For Austria. Everything was crashing to an end. *They* were coming. They had crossed the threshold even now, and there was no place for her to run. No place to hide. She could do nothing now but wait for the inevitable.

———

Murphy was one of a dozen newsmen picked to witness the closing act in the fall of the Republic of Austria.

"Schuschnigg and his Cabinet are going to broadcast at seven tonight!" shouted Skies over the increasing clamor. "That gives you mugs thirty minutes to get there. And they ain't waitin' for nobody! You can bet they've all got planes to catch before the Germans get here!"

Murphy glanced at his watch. He had promised that if he heard anything, he'd let them know. By now, Shimon knew as much as anybody. It was all over but the shouting and whatever blood was destined to be spilled in the aftermath.

He grabbed his hat and jogged out to the Packard. It started on the first crank, and Murphy slipped away from the curb, determined that he would make one stop before taking his place at the government Ballhausplatz among those privileged to witness the execution of a nation.

———

Elisa's street was deserted, just as Vienna now appeared deserted— waiting and watching from behind drawn curtains. Inside the dark foyer of the apartment building, the sound of German martial music seeped eerily from behind every door. Murphy took the stairs two at a time and tapped lightly on Elisa's door.

"Leah? Shimon?" she answered from behind the door.

Murphy's heart sank. Her frightened question answered his own dread. Leah and Shimon were not here.

"No. It's me. Murphy."

The clatter of locks told him that he was welcome. She threw the door open and then pulled him into the dark room. Her face was ashen and her hands were like ice. She clung to him. "Oh, Murphy! *Murphy!*" she cried.

He did not ask her why the lights were out. It was obvious. She was hiding in the dark like a frightened child. Lights were out all over the city tonight. Vienna was in mourning. "Where are your friends?" He took her by the arms.

"I don't know! Oh, I don't know! I have been here alone all day, hoping they would come."

"I told them to stay here," Murphy snarled angrily.

Suddenly Elisa was sobbing. "It's my fault. We—Leah and I thought it was nonsense—"

"No time for this now. Stop. *Stop,* Elisa!" He shook her lightly and kept his hands on her arms. "You're going to have to pull yourself together!"

She drew a deep breath. The tears stopped as suddenly as they had come. "Yes . . . yes, Papa."

"Elisa." Murphy was worried now. "It's me. John Murphy."

She did not reply. The clock ticked. Martial music oozed from the walls.

Murphy shook her again. "Elisa!" he cried. "Snap out of it!" he said in English.

"Murphy." She repeated his name. Her voice was controlled, *aware* again.

He pulled her to him in a brief embrace. He could feel her heart thumping like that of a frightened little bird. "You're going to be all right."

"Leah. Shimon. The children. I don't know where they are."

"The Nazis have closed off the Jewish district," he said. "I heard there were riots, but somebody in the newsroom checked it out. No violence. Not yet. Just a rumor. If they can make it here, they'll come. You stay here." He let her go and flipped on the light.

She seemed confused by the brightness of the lamp. She stood blinking like someone just awake from a long terrible dream. Her face was pained. "Don't leave me."

"I've got to."

"Please."

He saw the ring now on her finger and the passport in her hand. "Just for a while. If Shimon and Leah come, you must be here for them. I'll be back for you. I promise." One more quick embrace and he left her. He waited a moment on the stairs until he heard the rattle of the locks again. Even on the night the Gestapo had arrested Theo, Murphy had not seen Elisa so frightened. In a few minutes he would watch as the rug was pulled out from under a lot of other frightened people in Austria.

———

Equipment for the broad:ast had been set up in the corner room of the Ballhausplatz, which adjoined the grand staircase of the government building. Murphy remembered that it was only four years before within these same gold-and-cream walls that the Nazis had staged another terrible drama for all of Austria. The microphone was set up within a few feet of where Chancellor Dollfuss had been gunned down by a Nazi assassin's bullet. Now Hitler's assassination plan was to drain away the lifeblood of an entire nation.

Black Friday was coming to an end. Schuschnigg entered the room surrounded by a hushed group of Cabinet members. He looked strained, ten years older than he had looked the day before. *Men, the time has come.* Now Schuschnigg would announce to the entire world the truth about Hitler's peace.

As Seyss-Inquart looked on, the Chancellor told them of the terrible ultimatum issued under threats of invasion. He had been ordered to resign. Ordered to appoint a Nazi chancellor in his place. Ordered by the foreign government in Germany to create a new Austria under Nazi rule. All reports that workers were rioting throughout Austria and that the Austrian authorities had lost control were a fabrication of Nazi propaganda. Then, after a pause, he announced in the name of President Miklas that Austria was yielding to force. The Austrian army had been ordered not to resist. They had been told to withdraw in the face of overwhelming German forces: *"We are resolved that, on no account, and not even at this grave hour, shall German blood be spilled."*

Yes, that is what Hitler had said, Murphy thought. The blood on both sides of the border was German. *But what of those in Austria who do not share that distinction?* he wanted to shout at Schuschnigg. *Shouldn't some resistance be made for them? What of the bloodbath that is sure to come to Vienna's Jewish population? Can't Austria fight for them?*

But Schuschnigg was not made of the same hard stuff as his forebears who had fought against Prussian invasion. The very troops that he had called to alert that morning were now ordered to lay down their weapons in capitulation to evil. And then, in a choking voice, he cried his final words to his nation: *"God Protect Austria!"*

In the heavy silence that followed those words, Murphy knew that not even heaven would protect Austria now. If men would not stand for right, then no bolt of lightning would flash from the sky and stop what was about to happen.

An old man among the Cabinet members lurched forward on his crutches and shouted into the still-live microphone, "Long live Austria! Today I am ashamed to call myself German!" And then the technicians pulled the plug, and it was over. But at least one among the Austrian Cabinet had proclaimed that he was ashamed of that blood kinship so loudly touted by Hitler. *Yes,* thought Murphy, *it is a moment for shame.*

Murphy noted the tears streaming down the faces of Austrian soldiers and government sentries as he left the place. He watched as cocky young teenagers and swaggering men streamed out from their secret places wearing swastika armbands. Those who were ashamed stayed off the streets.

At last the Nazis had emerged. They had been sharpening their knives for this moment ever since the plebiscite had been announced.

Murphy did not go back to the INS office. He drove slowly past St. Stephan's, where the entrance to the Judenplatz was barricaded and held by Nazi youths. The arrests would begin soon. Murphy dared not enter the quarter now.

He returned to Elisa's apartment with the vague hope that Leah and Shimon would have somehow arrived there. He was wrong, and he was sorry—sorry for everyone in Austria.

46

Liberty and Captivity

Promptly at eight o'clock, the orderly brought in Theo's meal tray. He was a talkative young man, usually, and Theo would have spoken to him easily if he had not been wary of every Gestapo trick. In the barracks, sometimes the nicest inmates had been the informers.

"Well, Herr Stern! Another meal for the hungry monkey, eh? You eat, but you do not chatter. Ah, well. Good food tonight. Put a little more meat on your bones. You are looking much better. Much better." He set the tray down. Theo noticed the swastika armband on the youth.

Theo was glad the man had made the remark about the monkey; the insult eased the guilt of what Theo planned. Theo gulped down the mutton and the potatoes. There was no use leaving hungry. One way or another, Theo had determined that he *was* leaving. He stacked the dishes neatly on the bed table, then took the butter knife and the metal tray and stood waiting behind the door as the orderly clattered down the corridor.

"Well, Herr Stern—" The door flew open and the man entered cheerfully. Then he stopped and stood staring at the empty bed. "Herr Stern?" The question was barely off his lips when Theo slammed the metal tray across the orderly's skull. He did not make a sound as he crumpled to the ground.

Theo's heart was pumping wildly as he stripped off the man's clothes. He wondered what the nurse would say now if she checked his pulse. The orderly's clothes were baggy on him, but Theo notched the belt tightly and pulled the pajama-like green coveralls over the top of the stolen street clothes. The shoes were a problem. They were at least a size too small, but Theo crammed his feet into them and sat panting for a moment, trying to think what to do next.

The orderly moaned. He was coming around. Theo ripped a sheet into strips and gagged him, then tied his hands and feet tightly. With surprising strength, he hefted the orderly onto the bed. Then as the orderly gawked at the apparition of the mindless Herr Stern suddenly come to life, Theo threw a sheet over the man's head.

"When they find you, tell them Herr Stern says *Guten Abend* and *Auf Wiedersehen*, will you? I have enjoyed every morsel of food. Danke."

The orderly moaned. It sounded like the moan of a sick man, and Theo prayed that it would be hours before the staff discovered what had happened. He switched off the light, and with one backward glance over his shoulder, he looked out at the stars. *To be free! Colors and stars!*

The shoes squeezed Theo's toes, and he was conscious of his limp as he walked out of the room. He tried to assume the same matter-of-fact air as the orderly might have had, took the handle of the cart full of dirty dishes and trays, and began to wheel it quickly down the hall toward the marked stairway.

In an alcove, three nurses huddled together near a radio. Theo recognized the shrieking voice of Adolf Hitler and heard the thousands who cheered him and shouted: *"Sieg Heil! Sieg Heil! Heil Hitler!"*

The women did not look up or notice him as he passed by the nurses' station. This was the first time he had been grateful for the spellbinding voice of the tyrant.

Twenty paces from the stairs, he opened the door of a storage area and shoved the cart inside. Then he quickly stripped off the outer clothing of the hospital orderly and with a deep breath, he smoothed the wrinkled shirt and baggy wool trousers before he emerged again into the corridor.

Behind him he could hear voices, but the sense of what they said was lost amid the eerie chant of the thousands in the Sportpalast of Berlin. He lowered his eyes and strode deliberately toward the stairway. There was no guard there. No S.S. uniform. No plainclothes Gestapo agent. The stairway was empty. He could hear the groaning of the elevator as he clambered down the steps. He did not notice that the shoes were too tight. He could only think about the stars, the shining bits of ice and fire that beckoned him from beyond the walls and the wires.

God, he prayed silently as he felt excitement grow fierce and intense within him. *God, help me.* There was no more eloquent prayer to be found. *Freedom!* Hope swelled, and with that hope came the terrible fear that he might be caught before he walked out the doors of the hospital. What if he did not know where he was, what city they had taken him to? What if he was unable to discover a place to hide? He had not thought further ahead than the front door of the building that had held him prisoner. Perhaps it would be enough to draw one breath of free air. Perhaps it would be enough to die a free man, walking up the street. He would not die without a fight, of that he was certain. His hand slid down the cold banister as he reached the landing of the third floor. Below him, a door opened and footsteps clacked against the steps heading up.

Theo quickly opened the door and stepped into the hallway of the third floor ward. He heard the crying of children and, on this floor as well, the sound of Hitler's speech over the radio. *No wonder the children cry,* he thought grimly.

He waited by the door until the footsteps on the stairway ascended past him; then he slipped through the door and out onto the landing. Had the man on the steps above him been S.S.? Or Gestapo on evening rounds? *Certainly,* Theo thought, *there will be more.* In spite of his shaking legs, he quickened his limping pace until he was nearly running down the steps. *"Just one glimpse of the stars, God, and then you must show me where to go from there!"*

Tears streaked the face of Karl Wattenbarger as he gazed out on the stormy peaks of the Tyrol. "And so it is finished," he said to Franz quietly.

Their guns were propped in the corner by the door. All they had needed was one shout from Chancellor Schuschnigg, and they would have swarmed out to spill Nazi blood in the passes of the Alps.

"Not even a shot," Franz whispered as though he could not believe the day's events. Had they not all hoped and trusted?

Marta's voice was hoarse with exhaustion. "What else was there to do? Schuschnigg explained. The Italians refused to stand by us. The British wired to say they would not help. And the French would not even answer his calls."

"We would have died alone." Karl sounded angry. Not at his wife but at this terrible moment and those who had brought Austria to her knees.

Marta's eyes brimmed with tears as she gazed up toward the suffering Christ above the Herrgottseck. "My husband," she said in a hushed voice, choked with emotion. "My sons, you sons who are left to me—if we may not by the mercy of God die as free people, then we must, as our Lord Jesus, die helping others to become free." She raised her chin slightly as the tears began to flow. "Nine little souls have been entrusted into our care." She stubbornly refused to yield to the tears and brushed them away. "And with the merciful help of God we are put here to help them become free! So we cannot spill Nazi blood in the passes! We will fight them another way, and pray to God that He will send us little ones to save from their brutality!"

She had said it all. Karl nodded. "Yes, my dear wife. Brave Mama." He put out his arms to her. "Then the spilling of our blood will have some meaning in heaven, ja?" She embraced him. Only then did she let herself weep openly. A cross had come to them, and they must bear it for the sake of Jesus, for the sake of His little children. Sons and husband of her life as well must now be offered back to God in this service. Marta wept as though her heart would break. How she had hoped it would not come to this! Oh, how she had prayed the cup of suffering would pass Austria and her own little Herrgottseck beneath the crucifix!

———

Now Hitler was speaking over the radio. Elisa sat rigidly in the chair across from Murphy as the madman raved about the common racial bond between Austrians and Germans. The greater German Reich was about to be established!

The growling voice had brought Elisa back to herself. She smoldered silently, her blue eyes fixed fiercely on the radio as though she wanted to smash it.

She stood and switched it off, then whirled around. "What's the use of listening to such lies?" she snapped. "They will decimate the orchestra. Imprison doctors and professors and *anyone* who does not share that racial brotherhood! Then they will do the same to those they claim kinship with if there is a question asked!"

"Pack your things." Murphy's tone was low and urgent.

"Not until Leah and Shimon come!"

"If they haven't made it here by now—"

"They are family to me! I won't leave without them."

"The Judenplatz is sealed. I saw it myself."

"I'm not leaving Vienna without them."

"They have their visas—to Palestine!" Murphy argued.

"And you know just how much that means to the Nazis, don't you?" Her eyes were blazing. Murphy wished he had taken her away while she was frightened and meek. They could have had this argument across the border in Czechoslovakia or Switzerland. "Elisa, you can't do anything for them if they are caught, anyway."

"Like my father? No one lifted a finger for him. Not even God! And if I, who belong to God, do not help, then how can God help?" *She is talking nonsense again,* Murphy thought.

"Yes, like your father. Elisa, it is time to save your own neck. Do you hear me? Do you know what is happening this very minute on the frontier beyond Salzburg? In the mountains of the Tyrol? A dam has just burst. The flood is moving toward us. We can get out of Vienna now, *right now,* and no Nazi soldier will stop us to question. But if we wait—"

She wavered. "My passport. My American passport."

"They can arrest whoever they choose."

She shook her head slowly. The fear reared up again. "Murphy." She twisted the wedding band on her finger. "Please. An hour. We must wait one more hour." She seemed about to cry again.

Murphy looked at the clock. "Pack, then. It is eight-thirty. We are leaving at nine-thirty. With or without them."

She stared at him, her eyes wide. She could see the armies, hear the jackboots. After a moment, she nodded in agreement and turned to pack a few precious belongings.

Murphy gazed at the silent radio. He, too, could imagine the armies of tanks and troop lorries streaming into Austria at this very moment. He was worried. There was no guarantee, even with American passports, that they could cross into Czechoslovakia tonight. Tomorrow might be too late.

———

Theo was painfully aware of the prisoner identification band locked on to his wrist as he reached the lobby level of the hospital. He shoved it up under the sleeve of the wrinkled white shirt he wore, then stood breathlessly before the door that would lead him out into the main lobby of the hospital building.

He ran his hand over his chin. He was smooth shaven, thanks to the meticulous care of the nurses, but his short hair was no doubt disheveled. He passed his fingers through it in an attempt to straighten it; then, almost automatically, he patted the pocket of the orderly's trousers and discovered a wallet and comb. He held back a gasp, and with trembling hands, he combed his hair. There was no cash in the wallet, no change in the pockets; with a disappointed grimace, he tossed the wallet into the corner under the stairs.

He knew that beyond the door a legion of Hitler's henchmen would be patrolling the lobby, sitting in chairs and reading newspapers. There was no public place in Germany that was exempt from the watchers. *"One glimpse of the stars outside the walls. . . . All the rest does not matter."* He was seized with the sudden urge to hide beneath the stairs with the stolen wallet. But he raised his head. He was once again Theo Lindheim, fighter pilot, hero of the Fatherland. And he opened the door.

The lobby was indeed crowded. Young children strained against the grasp of their mothers. Old men waited, staring at nothing. And everywhere Theo looked, neatly dressed men in suits sat reading newspapers.

Theo stepped out from the stairwell. Across the lobby, a million miles from where he stood, was a wide set of double doors. They swung outward. Traffic roared by on the broad boulevard just beyond the sidewalk.

Like a man in a dream, Theo forced himself to place one foot in front of the other. He wanted to run and slam himself against the doors, but he did not. At a slow deliberate pace, he could control his limp somewhat. No one seemed to notice that he had no coat, no hat. He was simply one more bony old man in the lobby, walking toward the doors. To freedom. To the stars and colors. Blaring horns. Women with shopping bags. Men on bicycles. Shops and bakeries. Cars whizzing by and streetcars clattering over the rails. Thirty paces. Twenty. He counted his steps. So close. He reached out his arms to open the door.

A man in a pin-striped suit stepped in front of him, and Theo stopped. *Gestapo?* The man shoved the doors open ahead of Theo, then stepped aside and let him pass through ahead of him.

"Grüss Gott." The man tipped his hat. "And God help us all."

"Grüss Gott," Theo mumbled as he stared in wonder at the stranger who skipped away down the steps of the hospital. "Grüss Gott?" he asked as he let his eyes sweep upward toward the stars that sparkled above the city.

Theo staggered at what he saw: the great spires of St. Stephan's Cathedral were framed against the evening sky! Beyond that he could make out the top of the Vienna State Opera House and fragments of the Hofburg palace-fortress! Just then a streetcar trundled by. Two young men were unfurling a banner from the rear platform. Theo shook his head, unable to believe what he saw: the lettering on the car's destination sign read: *Musikverein,* but the flag on the streetcar was the bloody-red banner of a Nazi swastika!

All around him, the red-and-white banners of Austria were being torn away from the facades of buildings. It was cold, but Theo did not feel the chill.

He had stepped from one nightmare into another. Vienna, shrouded in swastikas! He wanted to rage against what he saw, to shout that it could never be! But he remained silent. He stopped and picked up a soggy pamphlet: *Yes for Austria! Yes for Schuschnigg!* He dropped the thing onto the sidewalk and gazed up past the red swastika banners to the star-framed spires of St. Stephan's. For this moment he was still a free man. Elisa might be somewhere in the city. *Elisa!* And he would find her; he *must* find her if she was!

Then he convulsed with coughing as the chill wind pierced him. He had no coat. No hat. His spindly legs could barely carry him. This was the first time since Dachau that he had walked more than a few shaky steps to the window of his hospital room. He scrabbled in his pocket in hopes of finding a shilling for tram fare; he would even ride on that car with the swastika flapping behind if it would only take him to the Musikverein. But there was not one coin in the pockets. The wind howled louder as he lowered his head and struggled against it. He would walk. He had survived Dachau, the quarries, typhus, and by God's grace he must have been mistaken for the Austrian Professor Stern and brought to Vienna. He knew he must force himself to move, or all that would be for nothing! *Tell my daughter I am here, God,* he prayed in numb confusion as the very ground seemed to slope upward against his progress, and the harsh freezing wind sucked his breath away. A hundred steps from the doors of the hospital, he had to stop and rest against a streetlamp. Carloads of hooting young Nazis raced by. Theo drew himself up, determined to place one foot in front of the other even though the pavement resisted him and the cobblestones threatened to hurl themselves into his face! "Elisa—she is—here," he panted. It was almost a mile to the Musikverein. He would begin his search there.

47

Night Vigil

The minutes dragged by like hours. There still were no footsteps on the stairs outside Elisa's apartment. She had barely spoken for the last fifty minutes as she packed a few of her most precious things into a small, scuffed suitcase. She took the angel from the lampshade and slipped it into her pocket. If Murphy had noticed, he did not comment. Instead, he paced back and forth in front of the sofa, paused every minute or so to look out the window onto the dark, deserted street.

Then he would glance at his watch and press his lips tightly together in concern. She knew that he would make her leave when the hour had passed. She prayed silently, desperately, for the safety of Shimon and Leah. Murphy was right. If they could have gotten away, they would be here now. She knew that, and yet she could not desert them. She would wait out this terrible vigil until the last second had ticked off.

In this moment she relived her last night in Berlin, the night she had left with her father. This apartment had been home. Full of happy thoughts and hopes—so many hopes. But all hopes died here tonight with the final words of Schuschnigg.

At last she broke the silence. "When we left home, my father and I—" She kept her eyes steady on the case of the Guarnerius. "I played for him. And for Berlin." She had not thought of playing now. She simply could not think of anything else to say to Murphy. "It is all over, isn't it?" she asked. "Like it was that night we left Berlin?"

He answered with a nod. There was pain in his eyes for her, hope that her friends would come. He grieved for her that the whole terrible night in Berlin had returned as a haunting echo, a counterpoint in her life.

"I'm so sorry," he said.

He was apologizing for stealing her hope away. He had been right, of course. Everything he had said was true, but he wished he were wrong.

She loved him for his grief. He had surprised her so often, and now he surprised her again.

He leaned down and took the Guarnerius case from the small stack of belongings by the door. "Will you—" he faltered. "You have never played for me . . . alone. And now . . . Vienna is . . ."

"Vanishing," she finished for him. She understood what he felt. Could they watch it go without one last, loving goodbye? She took the case from him and removed the instrument. She managed to smile at Murphy as she tucked it against her chin, and he stepped forward as if to ask one more favor. "What?" she asked him.

He answered by reaching out to touch her cheek and sliding his hand down to the gleaming wood of the violin. "It is part of you." He held her eyes. "I have always wanted to touch the two of you together." Was he embarrassed or just flushed with emotion? "You . . . your soul . . . the violin is your voice. So pray now, Elisa, and your prayers will be heard." He stepped back and stood with his arms crossed as he leaned against the door.

Elisa raised bow to strings, and for the last time, she prayed within these walls. She raised her heart for Vienna, for those who would remain behind and those who would leave and not return. It was over, over, *over*! And the melody cried out her anguish to God. Did He listen? Did He also weep for what was and what never would be again?

Outside the wind moaned through the streets of the great city, and all hope fled before it.

Theo stood outside the Musikverein. It was dark. Deserted. The wind tore at his thin, shabby clothing. Baggy trousers flapped around his legs. He was a ghost, a frail shadow of what he once had been. He was seeing the past and hearing the music of his youth as though he were an on-looker.

Here he had first heard his beloved Anna play the Schubert sonata. Here that he had fallen in love with her. A young, strong German man had waited for her each night just there, at the bottom of the stage door-steps.

Now that young man had grown old. A year in Dachau had laid twenty years on his back, and he could barely stand against the force of the wind. But he had come back. Somehow, miraculously, he was here again, and he would find the first child of their love. He would find Elisa if she was still here.

The old caretaker inside the Musikverein was drunk. He smelled of schnapps and his eyes were red as he swayed before Theo just inside the door.

"Elisa Linder? Ja. She was here only yesterday." He squinted as though he were trying to see Theo more clearly. "But that was yesterday and this is tonight. I don't know if she'll be back. Maybe nobody will come back. They'll bring in Germans to play. Aryans from Munich and Berlin. Everyone here will go into hiding, I suppose."

"Did she say anything yesterday?" Theo questioned. Even his voice had aged to a desperate whisper.

"Hello. Goodbye. How are you?" He shook his head drunkenly. "What is there to say?" He cocked his eye at Theo. "You better get out too, old man. You know what the Nazis do to beggars. You better leave Vienna, too."

Theo had already left the building. The caretaker's warning was lost in the howling wind that carried no snow or rain, only bitter cold.

As he looked at the quickly vanishing pedestrians, he felt confused, unsure where to go next. He was not even certain that he could remember any longer where Elisa's apartment was. That had been in another lifetime. *Before* . . .

His eyes returned to the spires of St. Stephan's. Once he had known Vienna like the back of his hand. The city was the same. It was his hand that was different now.

A five-minute walk from the Musikverein! Elisa had exclaimed that day. They had rented the place for a year and renewed it again the next year . . . but *where?*

The cold stung his eyes. He blinked up toward the bright crystal stars and prayed for help. He had come so far. Would he now die alone in Vienna?

His legs were shaking, but he set out once again. Pieces of torn Austrian flag blew past him. The shouts and laughter of the young Nazis echoed in the air. It was victorious, exultant laughter.

"Heil Hitler!" a young man perhaps eighteen years old shouted as though he was testing the sound of the words. The others shouted with him.

"Hey, old man!" They spotted Theo. "Are you drunk?"

Theo did not acknowledge the challenge. He continued to stagger forward, hoping that they would simply pass him by. Suddenly he found himself surrounded. They jeered at him, spit on him, reached out to push him from one side to the other of the tight pack. One final shove hurled him out of the circle and onto the sidewalk.

"Heil Hitler!" the voice rang out again like a gunshot—a proud and insolent voice, haughty, without wisdom or compassion.

Theo lay panting on the cold, wet cement for a moment. He reached out to grasp the stones of a building front to pull himself up. The wind resisted his effort, howling that he should give up, that he should lie still and quietly freeze to death. But Theo was a free man for now, and he would not be told where he should die!

"Elisa!" he shouted as loudly as he could, but his voice was a thin, bleating cry against the wind and the shouts of the Nazi thugs up the street.

His strength was gone. He struggled again and again to raise himself, but his legs were numb from the cold and feeble from the weeks of his illness.

From somewhere he thought he heard the sweet high melody of a violin. He closed his eyes and whispered the name of his daughter. *"Elisa."* He could do no more. The melody of Mozart played for him as it had that last night in Berlin. He had still been young then, and strong. *"Elisa. My little girl."* He smiled as a new blast of wind wailed around the corner. God could hear his voice, he knew. He prayed that somewhere Elisa might hear the whisper of her father. That Anna might hear him, and his sons with her. He tried once more in vain to stand, but his strength had disappeared. In one, final, heroic effort, he managed to pull himself to a sitting position. He looked up into the stars. Fire and ice in the heavens. Crystal windows. Doors through which a soul might soar. He coughed and chastised himself for thinking of death at this moment. There were doorways everywhere along the lane. He had only to rest a moment longer . . . just a moment . . . Then he could drag himself into the warmth and shelter of some building.

He leaned his head back against the stones and tried to catch his breath, tried to find some scrap of energy in his wasted body. Again the music faded in and out of the wind. It was no phantom, no dream—he could hear it! "Elisa," he tried to say again, but her name was a moan. *"Ahhhhh. . . ."* If he could only break free of his weakness, make his body obey him once again! The cold, the bitter cold, cloudless and cruel, was sapping his life from him. Like Austria, he was dying, and he knew it. He was dying, like all the dreams of the young, handsome officer who had waited for his love at the stage door.

Unless some hand reached to help him out of the wind, Theo knew that his soul, vital and strong again, would rise and soar to the stars. The shell of an old man would remain below to be taken away in the morning.

He did not try to speak their names any longer. But he sang them with the music of the violin. *Anna. Elisa. Wilhelm. Dieter.* They had been, and were even now at the last, his life. *Play for me, Elisa. I am here, just outside your window. Play for me . . .*

———

When the music stopped, Murphy pressed his fingers against his eyelids and breathed in what remained of the lingering melody. He did not speak for fear of breaking the spell of her prayer. Only when she moved to put away the violin did he say in a hushed voice, "There are no words left. But God heard. Somewhere, Elisa, He weeps with us . . ."

Elisa turned to stare at Murphy. *Here is a side of this man that I haven't seen before,* she thought. But she did not reply. There was nothing left to say. Time was finished. The hour had passed, and then some. She closed the lid of the case as though she had finished a book. She did not set the case down. She would carry it to the car.

Murphy went to the window one last time and looked down onto the empty street. Below, just outside the circle of a streetlamp, an old man sat looking up toward the window. He had no hat, no jacket. The clothes on his frail body seemed as though they would be torn away by the violence of the winds. The man raised his hand in the gesture of a drowning man reaching up from a stormy sea. He had seen the man before; he was sure of it. Frail and ragged a skeleton as he was, this was no beggar. He almost looked like—

"Stay here!" Murphy barked. "We can't go yet."

"Leah? Shimon?" Elisa asked hopefully.

"No." Murphy was out the door and down the stairs before she could ask another question. He saw her silhouette in the window above as he bent low over the old man.

There was something in the eyes that Murphy recognized instantly, however emaciated the body might be. He scooped up the frail figure, who could not have weighed much more than one hundred pounds. The old man was trying to speak, trying to form words on his lips as Murphy carried him up the stairs to where Elisa waited anxiously.

"What?" Murphy climbed the steps two at a time. The man was as cold as the stones he had been sitting on. Murphy kicked the apartment door open and stepped into the warmth of the room.

Elisa reached out toward the old man, as she had so often reached out to the children she had helped escape. She touched the icy, gnarled hand, and the old man turned his face toward her with a look that caused her heart to race.

He licked his cracked lips, smiled slightly, and breathed a single word: "Elisa . . ."

Elisa stared at him. "Papa?" she gasped. Then the room went black.

———

Theo had no strength for explanation. After reviving Elisa, Murphy undressed him, and they bathed his ravaged body first in cool water, gradually increasing the warmth of the water and raising his body temperature slowly.

Two hours had passed. Now Theo lay in bed, wrapped in warm blankets as Elisa sat beside him, quietly holding his hand and brushing away tears. He could only smile up at her and say her name in a hoarse whisper. Murphy stood like an impatient shadow framed in the doorway of the bedroom.

"We'll have to take him," Murphy said as Elisa helped Theo sip a cup of heavily sugared tea. "Tonight."

Elisa was frantic with worry and uncertainty. "Can't you see? He can't travel, Murphy. He is sick. Starved. Almost frozen to death. Not tonight."

"Then it won't be tomorrow either." Murphy sounded resigned. "They'll be here tomorrow. I just talked to Timmons at INS. Skies called ahead for me at the Czech border. They will let us through if we pay enough. Nothing has changed."

"*Everything* has changed!" Elisa turned on him. "He can't travel like this."

Theo could barely remember much of the story: how he came to Vienna, how long he had been in the hospital. But in the warmth of the bed, his mind had cleared enough to know that the boys who had pushed him to the street were only the forerunners of evil. He swallowed hard and groaned once in his effort to speak. Elisa turned to him. She was afraid for him. Afraid of losing him again forever. By some miracle he was here, and she could not bear the thought of anything happening to him. He must find a way to tell her: Murphy was *right!* They *must* leave tonight.

"Elisa," he said her name again. He had been unable to say anything else. "Home . . ."

She stroked his head. "Yes, Papa." Her voice was near to tears, "You're home."

He furrowed his brow and shook his head in disagreement. He opened his mouth. "Anna."

"Mama is fine! Oh, Papa, we will all be fine now!"

Murphy interrupted caustically. "Not if we don't leave now."

Elisa ignored him and stroked her father's hands. Murphy turned to leave, and Theo raised his voice to stop him.

"No!" he rasped as loudly as he could. "He . . . is . . . *right!*"

48

Hope for a Million Reasons

Murphy turned on the heater of the car full blast as Elisa made a bed like a nest in the luggage compartment of the Packard. If they were stopped along the way, their own passports might get them through. But Theo had no papers at all, and try as they might, they had not been able to get the prisoner's band off Theo's wrist.

Elisa was sick with worry, but the two-hour delay had convinced her of one thing, at least. Leah and Shimon were not coming at all. She had left her key in a hidden place beneath the worn carpet outside her door. Leah knew where it was. There was food enough for a week and a half, if they were careful. It was something—a small thing. A note was propped on the table, with a message that spoke only of hope and love and prayers, and told them they were taking Elisa's father home. Elisa had no explanation yet, either. How could she say more in a note?

Theo was dressed in layers of warm clothes and wool socks, then wrapped in every warm blanket in the apartment. He was asleep, and Murphy carried him easily down the stairs and put him into the luggage compartment, which opened into the backseat. Elisa whispered something to him, and he smiled as they put the backseat into place. Then they put her suitcase and two violin cases over the secret opening, and left without a word. It was well after midnight. The streets of Vienna were still wet from the rain of the afternoon, and lights reflected in puddles. It seemed that they were alone in all the city. Shades were drawn. The wind had died down after the last of the Schuschnigg pamphlets had been blown away.

As they passed the great Burgtheatre, Elisa tried not to think of what would take place there in the morning. For now, they were a solitary automobile, passing vacant sidewalks and darkened windows. Were the people sleeping or only lying sleepless in their rooms?

Elisa let her eyes linger for a moment on the Musikverein, and then on the spires of the great St. Stephan's. In the shadow of those spires, she sensed that Leah and Shimon were watching and waiting for the first terrible dawn of Nazi rule. Her heart grieved for them, even as she rejoiced that her father had come home to her in the eleventh hour, when all the marginal minutes and seconds had ticked away. If he had not come, would she have really gone with Murphy? Would she have left the key and the food and the note on the table and deserted them all?

Ahead, a great bonfire burned in the center of the road that led out of Vienna. A hundred young men stood around it blocking the way as they celebrated the coming of the conquerors and the fall of Austria.

Elisa drew her breath in sharply. She looked toward Murphy. His face was lined with strain. He tried to smile as the car slid up to the human barricade. Faces leered in every window. Bottles of vodka and schnapps were passed hand to hand, swilled until they were empty, then smashed on the road.

"Look pleasant." Murphy muttered under his breath. He unrolled the window slightly. Two inches. The fire illuminated everything and made the night an unholy backdrop to the long shadows of the young Nazis.

"No one gets through!" A brown-shirted young man said gruffly. He sported a stubby Hitler-style moustache, grown in the last few days in anticipation of Nazi victory.

Murphy looked at the bonfire, then back at the youth commander. "Heil Hitler," Murphy said coolly.

The young man had forgotten to say the words. He looked embarrassed, then clicked his heels and repeated the words. "Heil Hitler." He shrugged as if to explain that this was all new to him as well. "But still nobody gets through. You see." He pointed to the blazing heap.

"Looks like you're right. Here, at any rate. Where is there an open road?" Murphy spoke with authority, impatiently, and too loudly for the content of the question. Then he frowned at a schnapps bottle being upended by a boy next to the leader. "And is this the kind of discipline the Führer can expect from his followers in the Eastern Reich?"

The young man's eyes widened. "No! I mean, most of these are just boys who—"

Murphy interrupted with a wave of his hand. "Where might we find a road open to the east, so that we might prepare for the arrival of the Führer when he tours the Czech border?"

The audacity of the words startled even Elisa. Murphy's accent was decent, but still it was easy to tell that he was not German.

The young man seemed confused. "Well, I—" He frowned. "Who are you?" he asked.

"Count von Frank. Of the Sudetenland in Czechoslovakia. And my wife." Murphy turned to Elisa. She was pale, frightened by the gang of drunken young Nazis. "She is, of course, the stepsister of Field Marshal

Göring, who has arranged this entire event."

Elisa tried not to look confused. In the perfect accent of a Berliner, she said loudly, "My brother will not appreciate the roads being blocked by aimless hoodlums with nothing better to do."

The accent worked. The youth snapped to attention and said "Heil Hitler!" once again, then turned to his second in command, an apple-cheeked boy of about seventeen.

"Can you take Herr Field Marshal Göring's sister around this ridiculous bonfire, Hans? Take them through your farm, ja?"

Hans nodded fearfully, then turned around without offering the salute.

"You'll have to teach them better if you're ever going to amount to anything," Murphy said.

He backed away from the glaring light and followed the farmboy as he pumped on his bicycle toward the dirt road of his farm. No one had even asked to see their papers.

"And what if they had?" Elisa asked in a trembling voice.

"We are traveling incognito." Murphy smiled and winked, and then his smile faded.

A hundred yards from where they bumped over the rutted road on their way around the blockade, a caravan of vehicles topped a rise behind them and descended toward the bonfire.

"Murphy!" Elisa cried out. "It's them! Oh, Murphy!"

The main road ran parallel to them. The convoy was almost even with them, and in the glare of headlights and the huge bonfire, it was easy to see the outlines of the soldiers.

The lad on the bicycle struggled along in front of them, glancing nervously over his shoulder, first at Murphy and then at the German convoy on his right. Murphy gunned his vehicle and passed the boy just as the first of the troop lorries reached the flaming heap. The huge Nazi vehicle stopped twenty-five yards from the fire; then as the driver shouted out his window and the peasant boys scattered, the truck also gunned its engine and slammed through the blockade as though it were nothing.

The headlights of the Packard illuminated the narrow lane that veered sharply back toward the right, directly onto the main road. Murphy swerved and headed back to the highway, careening onto the asphalt road some three hundred yards ahead of the Nazi vehicles.

Elisa held tightly to the dashboard. Murphy pressed the accelerator to the floor and roared ahead of them. It was easy to see that the head vehicle had also sped up and was now in pursuit of them.

"How far?" Elisa cried over the noise of the engine.

"Twenty-five miles to the Czech border!" Murphy shouted. "If an American Packard can't outdistance a German troop lorry, something's wrong." He tried to sound cheerful, but the fact was that the massive pursuit vehicle was closing in on them. Murphy's worry reflected in his face if not in his words.

There were a dozen ways across the Czech border; naturally, Murphy had chosen to take the shortest one. But what was the shortest for them was also the first one the invading army had closed.

Probably a thousand cars had passed over this same road since morning. The Packard was the last before the swarm of swastika-marked tanks and trucks descended from the north and the west. Murphy and the precious cargo may have been the last of the civilian vehicles to slip out of Vienna that night without the Nazi order "Halt!" being shouted and a search being conducted. There would be no more after him.

The lights of the troop lorry loomed up behind them now. As Murphy's car neared the village, the truck's headlights flashed into the passenger compartment. A German troop carrier *was* capable of racing an American Packard!

For a moment, Elisa was certain that the truck would run over the top of their car and smash Theo where he lay hidden. But then the lorry backed off. As Murphy raced past the first few houses of the village, the lorry pulled off the road and simply let them go on. The race was over.

Murphy was sweating. He switched off the heater and wiped his brow nervously. "That was a game," he said. "Why? He could have had us."

The answer came soon enough. Every road had been blocked on the Austrian side of the border since word of the Anschluss had become official. Still nine miles from safety, a Nazi barricade had been set up. This one was not run by inept young boys, but by men—men with faces that Elisa remembered, and feared.

Piles of baggage and sleeping refugees lined the road. The checkpoint had been set up in a place where there was no way around. Grim, frightened Austrians stared at the passing vehicle, and ahead, in the glare of floodlights, Elisa recognized Sporer, with Otto Wattenbarger at his side. Together they commanded a force of about two dozen Brownshirts. Jackboots caught the light. They would not forget the salute, or their purpose in being on the frontier tonight.

"I'm sorry," Elisa whispered.

"Let me handle it." Murphy said. He did not smile now. He would not play games with these men. The pistols in their holsters were loaded and within reach.

A low moan issued from the baggage compartment. "Papa, the Nazis," Elisa warned as Sporer strode toward them. "Hush, Papa."

She could barely breath. Her heart was pounding as she watched the Nazis slam a man onto the hood of a car and brutally search him. Others knelt on the wet earth with their hands on their heads and machine guns trained on them. The nightmare had returned, this time with more force than before. The vengeance would come—it was here, just beginning.

Murphy and Elisa might get past with their documents, but what about Theo with the prisoner's bracelet? Had God brought him this far only to be taken again? Was this black night to be as it was when they tried to leave Germany together? Theo Lindheim would not survive a night enduring such cold brutality. *God?* Elisa managed a smile as Otto leaned down to address Murphy. He had not noticed her yet.

"Out, bitte," he ordered. "Everybody out." His eyes met Elisa's, and he paused mid-sentence. "Elisa Linder?" He seemed almost pleased to see her.

Murphy looked startled. "Murphy," he corrected. "She's married now."

Otto glanced at Murphy as though he had interrupted. "Married? Franz will be brokenhearted," he said, still addressing Elisa.

"Well, Franz is married too, Otto!" Elisa tried to sound as if this was a happy meeting of old friends. Murphy sat quietly as she bubbled on. "So? Are you married yet?"

"Only to my duty." He shrugged and pointed to his armband. He was surprised by the news that Franz had married. "And so I shall remain." His manner stiffened. "We need to have a look at your papers. A quick search only, Elisa." He grew even more distant. "You will have to step out."

Still smiling, Elisa obeyed. Murphy followed suit, praying that this man knew nothing about automobiles.

Otto looked over their passports. "Married to an American. You are John Murphy. And you now are Elisa Murphy." He handed back the documents. "Just a formality."

Murphy's eyes met Elisa's over the top of the car. They spoke silently of his hope that the events on the train so long ago would not be repeated. And yet the nightmare strode toward them. Sporer's peaked cap seemed as sharp as his face and his manner.

"What have you got here, Otto?" he demanded. Elisa had just watched him kick a man in the face.

"American passports. All in order." Otto replied, running his hand over the hood of the Packard.

"American? Tear it apart!" He slammed a fist on the Packard. Then he glanced at Elisa appreciatively. There was a hint of recognition in his pale eyes, and she looked quickly away from him, down at the wedding ring, and then at Murphy, who was fuming.

Sporer walked on to the next group of refugees who stood at a table pleading that they had family in Prague and must be let through. They were Jewish. Sporer knocked the yarmulke from the man and ordered instant silence. A small child clung to the skirts of her mother and looked up fearfully at the raging man who struck her father.

"A million little reasons..." Elisa remembered her words to Murphy when he asked her why she stayed in Austria. She had forgotten them. Forgotten the face of Sporer in her dream as the dreadful death train had taken away the children to the east. "Oh, God!" She muffled a cry as Sporer shook the Jewish woman and shouted.

"We know you Jewish whores carry away jewels from the Reich! Now

Austria is the Reich as well! You may not steal whatever you like from the German people! Strip her!" he shouted. "She's got something hidden, all right!" And then he began to tear at her clothes as the little girl cried and the husband wept and stared helplessly at the ground.

Otto seemed not to notice. Elisa turned to glare at him. "I saw your mother, Otto," she said in a low voice. She knew that Sporer would kill Theo if he was discovered. One blow would end his fragile, precious life.

"Well?" He was not interested. The raging continued in the background as the Jewish woman screamed and Sporer shouted again.

"You see what happens when you try to hide contraband from us?" The woman was half naked now. A small bag of coins dangled between her breasts. She tried to cover herself, but she was his demonstration of the vileness of Jews! "You see! She is stealing! And so!" His voice became almost playful. "Off you go!" He shoved her hard, and she fell to the ground weeping as her little girl gathered the torn clothes and tried to comfort her mother. Sporer booted the child and sent her sprawling as well.

Elisa wanted to shout, but she could not. Theo was a breath away from Sporer's hobnailed boots. And after a year of beatings, he had no stamina left to withstand such abuse.

Otto seemed embarrassed now. "She was stealing," he said.

"If ever I see Marta again"—Elisa leveled her gaze icily on the strong, handsome Tyrolean—"shall I tell her where I saw you on the night Austria became the Reich?"

He simply stared at her. His eyes seemed vague, as though he was seeing another place besides this depot of horror. He looked toward the stripped Jewess, then at the child and the humiliated husband. "Tell her what you like," he said bitterly. Then, he opened the door of the Packard. "There is no way to change it. No stopping it." He stepped aside for Elisa to get into the passenger seat. "There are those who will stay"—he looked at Sporer—"and those who will die." He let his eyes linger, not on the woman, but the little child. Then with a sad smile, he looked straight at Elisa. "And there are those who will run away."

"Are you finished?" Elisa asked, tears brimming in her eyes.

"With you? Yes." Otto drew himself up. "Heil Hitler," he said bitterly.

Murphy had watched it all; heard it all, and yet, he could not believe that somehow they had passed the checkpoint without being searched. He was relieved as they drove away. Elisa turned to meet the eyes of those ragged men and woman who knelt before the conquerors with their hands on their heads. She felt little joy; Otto's accusation stung her. She had not remembered those million little reasons. And yet, even as Otto had classified her with those who ran away, she remembered that there were some still who would stay: Marta and Karl, Franz and the other Wattenbarger sons. They had welcomed the little ones as if they were welcoming the Lord himself.

"Are you all right?" Murphy asked her as they approached the final barricade at the Czech border. It was manned by six stony-faced Czechs who looked like angels compared to men like Sporer.

"Yes," Elisa nodded. "But not everyone will run. He was wrong about that."

"What?" Murphy held out his hand for her passport.

She pressed the document to her heart for a moment and closed her eyes. In a moment they would pass to safety. It would all be over. In the village they would call Anna in Prague and tell her: *Papa is alive! He's coming home! Mother, a miracle! The hand of God has brought him back to us!*

"Passports, please." The Czech guard stretched out a white-gloved hand. Elisa gave her folder to Murphy, who was still staring at her strangely. The guard gave the documents a cursory glance, stamped them, and handed them back. "Pity the poor souls who remain behind," he said as he waved the Packard across the line and into Czechoslovakia.

It was over. A mile past the checkpoint, Murphy pulled the car to the shoulder of the road, and together they helped Theo out of the cramped space where he had hidden for the last two hours. Elisa sat with him and stroked his head as he slept while Murphy went to phone Anna.

Yes, it really was over. A year of agony and hope had ended for them on the very night that despair and brutality had begun for a half million others. Theo would be well again, and Elisa would tell him what she could never explain to Murphy, or Thomas, or her mother. They wanted her to be free and secure, out of the clutches of the evil that had taken over her homeland. They only cared about her safety. But there were others whose safety was important as well—a million others.

Marta Wattenbarger would understand. And Leah knew. Elisa would not run away to safety. She would continue to risk herself for Germany's priceless treasures.

Elisa bent down to kiss her father's forehead. It was warm, and his breath was even and unlabored. "You will live, Papa," Elisa whispered. "And when I tell you why I *must* go back, you will understand. *A million little reasons,* you will say. And you will understand. . . ."

Acknowledgements

First thanks belongs to Margaret Tait who has also brought Amy, David, Ernestine, Sharon, Basil and the joy of their creation of music into our lives. The heart of God must sing with them as they play. Also we express our thanks to those who are deeply involved in the creative process of publishing: Carol Johnson, Lance Wubbels, Jeanne Mikkelson come to mind first, but our gratitude extends to all the staff at Bethany House.

Thanks also to those who have helped in special ways. Bettie Turner, Tanya Turner, Kelli Thomas, Michelle Janis, Harrell and Paulette Knox, Naomi Samuels, Michelle Antonell, Debby Jameson and the wonderful neighbors in our little community.

As ever, our children and dear family sacrifice much for the sake of this work. For the blessing of their lives, we thank God.

Treasure In Jars Of Clay

by Nancy George with Jan Greenough

'Will inspire, encourage and challenge...a true story of
faith and trust plus courage and guts.'
　　　　　　　—Max Sinclair, author of *Halfway to Heaven*

Nancy George was a headstrong, rebellious girl, Vivacious
and energetic, who tried to be everywhere at once.

She met her husband, Ron, while serving with Operation
Mobilisation. During the drive back from Iran, three
months after their marriage, their van came off the road. 'I
lay there with my face in the earth. I could feel nothing: my
body had ceased to exist.'

During the months in hospital Nancy fought to recover.
Each new tiny movement gave cause to rejoice. Would she
ever be able to walk? To have children? To be anything
other than a burden to her husband and friends?

This profoundly moving account of Nancy's slow climb
back to life and Christian service is a vivid illustration of
the truth that God's power is made perfect in weakness.
Today she and Ron run People International, an agency
spearheading evangelism among Muslims in Central Asia.

MARC
Monarch Publications

14,000 Quips & Quotes

by E. C. McKenzie

* 14,000 entries organised into 528 alphabetically listed subjects.
* Offers quick reference to a wealth of useful, brief, to-the-point material.
* Quotes range from the frivolous and satirical to the reflective and timeless.

'Men with clenched fists cannot shake hands.'

'The more arguments you win, the fewer friends you'll have.'

'To grow tall spiritually, a man must first learn to kneel.'

'History does repeat itself. But not so often as old movies.'

'Obesity begins at home.'

'The two most beautiful words in the English language are: Cheque enclosed.'

E. C. McKENZIE was an internationally known collector of quips, quotes and fun facts.

Monarch
Publications

Love Is A Choice

by Dr Robert Hemfelt, Dr Frank Minirth & Dr Paul Meier

WHAT CAN YOU DO WHEN YOUR OWN LOVE HURTS YOU?

The dependent deals with the addiction. Around him or her stands a circle—parents, children, husband or wife—whose lives are profoundly affected by their relationship to the addict. They are the 'co-dependents'. *One in four people may suffer from co-dependency.*

The destructive relationships in co-dependency echo down the generations. The daughter of an alcoholic will frequently marry an alcoholic. The son of an autocrat may demand unquestioning obedience from his own children. The ghosts of the past are calling the shots.

Yet recovery is possible. As we begin to understand the hunger for acceptance—the 'love hunger'—that each of us carries, we can discover a love beyond human reason. God's unconditional acceptance, the authors insist, can provide the resources to break the cycle of addictive relationships.

It can set us free to choose how we love.

DR ROBERT HEMFELT is a psychologist specialising in the treatment of chemical dependency and co-dependency. DRS MEIER and MINIRTH have outstanding qualifications in the fields of physiology and psychiatry, and degrees in theology from Dallas Theological Seminary.

Monarch
Publications

Monarch Publications

Books of Substance

All Monarch books can be purchased from your local general or Christian bookshop. In case of difficulty they may be ordered from the publisher:

> Monarch Publications
> Owl Lodge
> Langton Road
> Speldhurst
> Kent
> TN3 0NP

Please enclose a cheque payable to Monarch Publications for the cover price plus: 60 pence for the first book plus 40 pence per copy for each additional book ordered to a maximum charge of £3.00 to cover postage and packing (UK and Republic of Ireland only).

Overseas customers please order from:

Christian Marketing PTY Ltd
PO Box 154
Victoria 3215
Australia

Omega Distributors Ltd
69 Great South Road
Remuera
Auckland
New Zealand

Struik Christian Books
PO Box 193
Maitland 7405
Cape Town
South Africa